Nobody LIKE US

KRISTA & BECCA
RITCHIE

CHARACTER LIST

Not all characters in this list will make an appearance in the book, but most will be mentioned. Ages represent the age of the character at the beginning of the book. Some characters will be older when they're introduced, depending on their birthday.

The Hales

Loren Hale & Lily Calloway

Maximoff – 25

Luna – 21

Xander – 17

Kinney – 16

Ripley (grandchild) – 1 year, 11 months

Cassidy (grandchild) – 1 week

The Cobalts

Richard Connor Cobalt & Rose Calloway

Jane – 25

Charlie – 23

Beckett – 23

Eliot – 21

Tom – 20

Ben – 18

Audrey – 15

The Meadows

Ryke Meadows & Daisy Calloway

Sullivan – 22

Winona – 16

The Abbeys

Garrison Abbey & Willow Hale

Vada – 16

The Security Team

These are the bodyguards that protect the Hales, Cobalts, and Meadows.

KITSUWON SECURITIES INC.

SECURITY FORCE OMEGA

Akara Kitsuwon (boss) – 29

Thatcher Moretti (lead) – 30

Banks Moretti – 30

Farrow Hale – 30

Oscar Highland-Oliveira – 33

Paul Donnelly – 29

Quinn Oliveira – 23

Gabe Montgomery – 23

Kannika "Frog" Kitsuwon – 19

PRICE KEPLER'S TRIPLE SHIELD SERVICES

SECURITY FORCE EPSILON

Jon Sinclair (lead) – 40s

O'Malley – 29

Ian Wreath – 34

Vance Wreath – 27

Chris Novak – 30s

Greer Bell – 30s

Ryan Cruz Jr. – 20s

…and more

SECURITY FORCE ALPHA

Price Kepler (lead) – 40s

Tony Ramella – 30

Bruno Bandoni – 50s

…and more

A NOTE FROM THE AUTHORS

Nobody Like Us is the thirteenth book in the Like Us Series. Even though the series changes POVs throughout, to understand events that take place in the previous novels, the series should be read in its order of publication.

Nobody Like Us should be read after *Unlucky Like Us*.

LIKE US SERIES READING ORDER

DECEMBER

"All of this has happened before.
All of this will happen again."

– *Battlestar Galactica*

1

PAUL DONNELLY

I've been avoiding funerals most of my life.
Didn't make it to my grandmom's when she croaked. Skipped out on mass for deceased aunts and uncles. Been to one wake for a cousin. But that was because I was thirteen and hungry and they had roast beef hoagies. I'm not big on death. It feels like the conclusion of something—and I'd just rather keep on running, keep on going, than celebrate any kind of ending.

On the grassy hill of a cemetery a little outside Philly, it hits me like a burst of cold December wind.

My first funeral is for a Calloway.

Not my mom.

Not my dad.

A fucking *Calloway.*

I'd laugh at the sheer shock of it—but can't laugh during a funeral. I have manners and all—even if everyone in the cemetery has been eyeballing me and Luna rather than the coffin that'll descend into the freshly dug earth.

Feels like we were the ones who died.

Like half the people here are lowering us into the ground.

At least I'm with her. In life, in death…at least I'm with Luna Hale.

I scrape a hand through my hair.

Yeah, I'm not dead yet. Luna leans into my shoulder, her warmth radiating against me, and my left arm is already around this girl.

I look down at her. Residual glitter is still stuck in her light brown hair, the strands sparkling, and her round cheeks are rosy from the biting winter air. Her black puffer jacket is too short to warm the length of her body, but I tuck her close to me.

She's mine. She's all mine, but from across the wooden casket, I spot a fortysomething woman with deep auburn hair yanked into a taut bun. Luna's therapist. If she could chuck stones, I'd be pelted to death by now. She would rather I let Luna go.

It's worse when I spot Luna's parents. Her mom practically turns her face into her husband's chest just to avoid me. Like I'm truly disease-ridden and toxic waste.

My stomach clenches.

It's not about me. She's just upset about who died. It's upsetting. This death. This whole thing. I try to convince myself, but it's also clear she's doing her best not to make eye contact with me.

Luna senses her mom's avoidance, and she shifts uneasily. I squeeze her in a side-hug.

A light layer of snow blankets the dewy morning grass. Everyone is standing, hundreds in attendance to pay their respects, and I only feel like a special invitee because I can see the gravesite. I'm not two or three rows behind friends-of-friends and other security.

I am on-duty though. Had to keep the press and paparazzi out of the cemetery, but I managed to sneak up to the front to be beside Luna. I'm Epsilon—been that way for three days—and my fellow SFE brethren are looking at me like I deserve to be shoved in the hole. O'Malley, most especially.

I meet the intensity of his glare with one of my own.

Fuck him.

My blood courses hatefully, and I despise this feeling. I want to release it, but after all that's happened, I can't figure out how. I'm afraid to live inside hatred, maybe more than I am to live inside the past.

I glance back down at Luna—she's worth everything. She's my everything. But I'm still partially in her world. One foot in, one foot out. Like with a big enough gust of wind, I could be blown away from her.

She springs on her tiptoes to whisper to me, "It kinda feels like we're being stared at."

I dip my head to whisper back, "Accurate assessment, I'd say. They're probably just jealous."

"Uh-huh," she says, her voice tense.

We both know they're not envious of the hell we've been going through. No one in their right mind would be.

They're also not envious of what happened to us three days ago—the same day we learned a Calloway died. Also known as the day another member of Luna's family walked in on me giving her head. History repeats itself in strange ways, and I don't know what it says about me that this happened yet again.

What didn't repeat: Keeping it under wraps.

Her entire family got wind of it today. Hence, being eyeballed during the funeral like we're the ones in the casket.

I'd say we already had some metaphorical or spiritual death of sorts, but it's not that easy to put me to rest.

THREE DAYS EARLIER

2

PAUL DONNELLY

"Let's go, my furry friends." **Arkham and** Orion lead the way into the Hale House. While Luna, Maximoff, and Farrow talk on the front lawn about the sudden death in the family, I give them a minute to themselves. Letting the Hales have this family moment. So I offered to bring the dogs inside.

Boxes of Christmas lights are on the front brick porch. I'd been stringing them on the roof before Maximoff dropped the bad news. I collect my phone and radio nearby, in a bit of a daze.

Life giveth and life taketh.

I've got experience with death of relatives, but not necessarily death of *loved ones*. I can't say how everyone will react, but I know it'll matter to a lot of people in the families.

I breathe out an odd heaviness on my chest and enter the Hale House. Nudging the door shut with my foot, I slip farther into the foyer.

It's still quiet.

I can't hear any creatures stirring except the big burly canines below me. They pull me into the living room, and I barely need to crouch to unleash the two towering Newfies.

Freed, they trot through a cracked door, on course for the kitchen. That's where their doggie bowls are, and I'm sure they've got food on the brain. Before I move, that same kitchen door opens wider, but Orion hasn't backtracked for extra pets.

Loren Hale graces the living room, winter coat gone from when he checked up on the progress of the Christmas lights outside. He's wearing a long-sleeved black tee, arrowhead necklace, and jeans. Cell phone to his ear, his brows are all knotted up, his lips drawn in a serious line.

He's staring right at me.

I freeze.

Should I go back outside? Feels like I'm in an old spaghetti Western with Luna's dad, and his sharp gaze is a warning that he'll pull a pistol if I so much as breathe wrong.

Except he's not verbally kicking me out. He's not waving me to go.

So for better or worse, I stay put.

"Yeah…yeah," Lo says to someone over the line. His voice is strained, almost somber. "I know that." He hasn't stopped looking at me.

I wind the leashes in a loop, gauging the temperature of the room. *Tense.* Prickly? Maybe that's just the hairs rising on the back of my neck.

Death.

Dead.

Someone has died, and it'd be easier for me if I enjoyed sitting in discomfort and morbidity—but I don't. Never have. Probably never will.

"I'm not putting out a statement, Daniel," Lo snaps. "*Seriously.* Okay, great…conversation over." He hangs up, then pockets his phone, still staring me down.

I bet he thinks I'm a bigger intruder hanging around during a family death. I nod to him. "I'm sorry for your loss," I say. "I know he must've meant something to you."

Lo's face contorts, perplexed. "What the hell are you talking about?"

What am *I* talking about?

His confusion mounts.

Fuck…

Me.

Shouldn't he know?

I'm more frozen. "You don't know?"

"Know *what*, Paul?" He shifts his weight.

I scrape a hand through my hair. Fuck, *fuck*. How could he not know? "Are you fucking with me?" I ask him. *Say yes.* I almost make the sign of the cross. I feel Catholic in my heart sometimes, even if the church didn't want me.

"No," Lo says, verging on anger. "I'm not fucking with you." His eyes are knives.

I assumed he'd been talking to his *publicists*. Wouldn't they want him to send out a press release about the deceased family member? I ask hurriedly, "What was that phone call then? The statement you're not putting out—"

"None of your business," he snaps. Then he expels a sharp breath, rethinking and glaring at the ceiling. "Daniel—a longtime board member of Hale Co.—wants me to say that my *daughter* didn't write any of her leaked stories." He emphasizes *daughter* as if I don't know he has one.

Pretty certain she's the girl I'm in love with.

I nod a couple times. "'Cause you sell strollers and diapers, not smut. Which doesn't make much sense since sex is what produces babies…" I trail off. He's glaring, and I'm trying my best not to crack a shadow of a smile.

"I'm not in the mood, Paul."

"I could get you in it."

"Or I could get you out of it."

Neither of us are smiling. "That, too," I mutter, not wanting him to revert to the original topic. I'm stalling. "Maybe this Daniel guy should read Luna's fics. He might like 'em."

Lo wheezes out a brittle laugh. "Yeah, the only thing Daniel Perth likes is when I say *yes*."

"Her fics are pro-baby," I defend. "The warrior princess on

Demos has like five of them." I cock my head in thought. "He may not like that they have horns though."

Lo's brows scrunch. "He couldn't give a shit what she's written. He just cares about numbers, and he's correlating the blowback from her stories with our profit margin—and it's a *dumb* correlation. There's about a thousand other fucking things that could point to the profit loss." He's heated, but he sighs out. "It's been an ongoing thing, not that you needed to know any of this." He claws his fingers through his light brown hair. "Don't tell Luna about it."

"Wasn't planning on it." It'd just hurt her to know there's discord at Hale Co. from the fallout of her writing. At least…I think it'd hurt her. But she's been handling the leaked fics a lot better than she did before her memory loss.

I'm about to make a quick exit, but as soon as I chuck the dog leashes in a wicker basket, Lo says, "You better not go."

I've wanted him to tell me that.

More than he'll ever know.

You better not go. But he's not pleading with me to stay because he's grown a liking to me—I have answers and he looks like he could butcher me for them.

Lo adds, "Not before you tell me what's going on. Why'd you say that? *Sorry for your loss?* Who were you talking about?"

"Maybe someone else should tell you…" I crane my neck over my shoulder, expecting Maximoff or Farrow to enter by now.

No one does.

It's just me. Alone. With Luna's dad.

"Why?" He's more pissed. "You and me. *Trust.*" He motions from his chest to my chest, as if the trust meter between us is teetering towards empty again.

"I'm just not the one who should tell you, I don't think."

His face screws up in several emotions. "You said *sorry for your loss.* You said *he meant something to me.* You know what I'm thinking? If it's that goddamn bad, then my phone would be blowing up. Ryke would be calling me. He would've already told me himself."

"I have no clue why your brother hasn't called you yet," I say. "Maybe he's taking a bubble bath."

Lo shoots me a look like I'm not helping.

I thought it was a funny image. I scratch the back of my head, turning to go.

"Did someone die?" Lo finally asks.

Slowly, I twist back.

I see on his face he doesn't fully believe it, but he's breathing harder like he might.

I stay quiet, a noiseless confirmation.

His shoulders arch, cheekbones sharpen. "Who?" Fear flickers in his eyes. He reaches in his pocket for his phone.

"Greg Calloway," I tell him. "Your father-in-law."

Patriarch of the Calloway sisters. Creator of Fizzle: the behemoth soda company that rivals Coca-Cola and Pepsi. Husband to the Crow. Grandfather to Luna.

Greg was old. I'm guessing it'd be expected at some point, but he'd been healthy for his age. It came suddenly.

"How?" Lo asks.

"Heart attack in his sleep."

"No, *how did you find out?*" His breathing heavies again.

If I answer this, am I throwing Luna's older brother under the bus? I take too long to respond.

Lo looks murderous. "I swear to God, Paul, if you don't tell me, you are going to rise up my shit list—and I've just bumped you down."

"So you do like me—"

"*Paul.*"

Maybe not by much.

No one said this was a secret. If it turns out it is one, I can ask for forgiveness later.

"Maximoff. He told me," I reveal, just as the front door opens and in walks Maximoff Hale.

3

PAUL DONNELLY

I can barely meet Maximoff's eyes.

Farrow with their two babies and Luna aren't far behind him. They shut out the cold winter, entering the warm living room where the wood-burning fireplace is lit. Flames crackle and spark, and I'm thinking I should skulk away from this family matter. Find a dark corner or something. It doesn't really involve me.

"Who told you about Greg?" Lo asks his son.

Maximoff hasn't even unzipped his Patagonia jacket yet. He casts a brief glance at me, tension thickening.

"You didn't know?" Luna asks her dad.

"No, I didn't know." He's staring down Maximoff now.

Luna sends me a wide-eyed look that says, *oh no.* She's on edge. Maybe for me. Maybe for her brother. Maybe even for her dad.

I want to tell her there's no hole too deep that I can't climb out of. That I'd do whatever it took to help her out too. That despite all the bad luck we've encountered and every misstep I've ever made, I know we'll still come out on top. Hope is the main thing keeping my head above water. I'm more terrified of ever losing it.

"Dad," Maximoff says slowly.

"How do you know, and I don't?" Lo asks.

"Grandpoppy Lo." Ripley cuts into the strained air. "Do you have-have a…" The little boy stares up at Farrow for the word.

"Popsicle," Farrow says. "He's been talking about them all the way here." To Luna, he explains, "Lily always gives him one."

It's a past that Luna can't remember. She seems appreciative of being kept in the loop.

Lo squats and makes a funny face at Ripley. "You want a popsicle? In the cold?"

Ripley nods his head vigorously. "Please?"

"Okay, Iceman." He stands. "We'll get you a popsicle. Only because you're my *favorite* grandson, but shhh." He puts a finger to his lips. "That's a secret between you and me."

Ripley nods, taking the secret-keeping business seriously. It's cute and all, and maybe Baby Ripley has softened Lo's sharp edges.

But Lo doesn't lead the little boy into the kitchen. Instead, he tells Farrow, "Popsicles are in the freezer. I need to talk to your husband."

"He's not at fault, Lo," Farrow says, defending Maximoff.

"And I'm not blaming him," Lo retorts. "I'm just trying to figure out what the hell happened."

"It's fine," Maximoff says to Farrow. "Take care of our kids. I'll just be a sec." He's unstrapping two backpacks from both his shoulders. They likely contain diapers and formula. Farrow takes one backpack. In the other hand, he's gripping the baby carrier where their newborn is fast asleep.

"I'll get that," I reach for the second backpack to help, looking forward to an exit. *Hopefully with Luna.*

"You. Stay," Lo says.

He's speaking to me.

It's not a hallucination or mirage.

"Why?" I glance around, trying to find the joke. Not even the couch has answers. Rug isn't funny either.

"Because this is what happens when you're the messenger." He gives me a half-smile. "And I don't believe in that old motto about them."

Don't shoot the messenger. Alright, yeah. He's prepared to shoot me down, right out of the sky.

Been there before. Experienced that.

Something tells me he's just keeping me on my toes. Not letting me get too comfortable in case he still needs to throw me outside like yesterday's trash.

Mission accomplished. I feel sprightly. Ready to be hurled in any direction.

"Dad," Luna says, more protectively but also uneasily. She glances from him to me. She has no memory of her dad *seriously* hating me. Like wishing the bubonic plague upon my firstborn sort of hate. Joke's on him though because I've never wanted kids.

"We're just talking," Lo assures her.

"He loves talking to me," I tell her with the cock of my head. I think she's smiling at my accent on the word *talk*.

Lo wasn't kidding when he said he's not in the mood. He has no rebuttal for me. No sharp-tongued quip back. Feels weird that I miss it.

Farrow hesitates to leave Maximoff in the crossfire of the unknown, but he's got his hands full. So he ushers Ripley into the kitchen. Luna takes Maximoff's second backpack and follows Farrow out. When they're gone, I just try to imagine Luna smiling.

It leaves me with a warm fuzzy feeling that's a whole lot better than the pained look on Lo's face.

"Does your mom know?" Lo asks his son the second the kitchen door shuts. They're squared off in front of the crackling fireplace, and I stand behind the sofa, furniture separating me from them.

"Aunt Rose is telling her," Maximoff says. Must be why Lily was at the Cobalt Estate early this morning. I stopped by the Hale House to help out since Lily is still on crutches. Only she wasn't here.

I lean against the back of the couch. Not saying a word.

Lo stares at the wall, unblinking. His cheekbones are razorblades. "So what—I'm the last to know?"

"Uncle Ryke said he'd tell you—"

"He'd tell me...but only after he told my own son." Lo raises his phone. "I haven't gotten a call from my brother or from Connor.

Wonder why." I hear the hurt in his voice. "Which one told you first?"

"I was on a three-way call with them—"

"Jesus," Lo winces.

"—they want to tell you *face-to-face*. Uncle Ryke said he'd be here soon, and I haven't known for that long either. I just found out on the drive over here." He motions at the foggy window. There is no Christmas tree around, no strand of garland over the fireplace mantel, no mistletoe hanging in the entryway, nothing to show we're five days out from the holiday. Other than the lights I was stringing on the roof outside, the Hales haven't had time for Christmas cheer.

My family stole that kind of joy from them the instant they assaulted Lily and kidnapped Luna, and if I could give back what they took, I would.

I'm trying.

I've been trying.

Lo stares off again. "They could've looped me in on that call. Christ, Rose could've told Lily *and* me together. Instead, I'm here." He slaps a hand to his side. "I'm *here*, and I learned from a *bodyguard*."

Wish he would've called me Luna's boyfriend, but I guess I'm not that yet. Luna and I are in a "no labels" pool. Looks murky here.

"I'm sorry, Dad," Maximoff says empathetically. "Ryke was supposed to be the one to tell you."

Lo cringes. "*Christ*, don't apologize for my brother. I love him more than anything, but he should've *never* told you before telling me."

"What does it really fucking matter?" Maximoff asks.

"Because you're my *son*, and pardon me for wanting to know the heavy shit in this family before my kids do."

Maximoff takes a tensed breath. "I'm not a child. I'm twenty-five—"

"I don't care if you've reached five-hundred-and-fifty. I'm still twice your age, and I'm *your father.*"

"He didn't want to tell you over the phone!" Maximoff shouts, then lets out a deeper breath, trying not to yell. "He *cares* about you. Everyone fucking *cares*, Dad, and after everything you've been through—everything you saw and heard with Mom and Luna—no, we didn't want to tell you over the phone. *We*." He points to his chest. "I was a part of that, so if you're going to be pissed at Ryke, at Connor, at whoever else for caring about you, you can add me to the damn list too."

Lo looks away, his eyes glassing. He seems to choose his words carefully as he says, "I'm not upset that you care, bud. But I'm your parent. That doesn't change because I...because life for me is harder some days. I'm *still* your father, and it's not your responsibility to look after this household like an interim parent. It never has been. It *never* will be."

"I don't think it will be," Maximoff says strongly. "I never thought it would."

The conviction in his voice is heard loudly, and they hold each other's gazes with weight and history I really can't make sense of.

This is a heavy moment that I probably shouldn't witness. I take a few steps backward. I glance at the kitchen door. Wonder if I could sneak out...?

Lo nods a couple times, then his eyes dart to me. *Shit.* I stay still as he says, "I'm mainly upset no one believed I could hear about Greg Calloway's death while I was alone." As if I can't read between the lines, Lo informs me, "They thought I'd go grab a bottle of Macallan that doesn't even exist in this *dry* house."

Looks like I'm stuck here.

"I can vouch that it didn't happen," I say lightly. "Been here the whole time." *Strangely.*

Lo waves to me like I'm greater evidence of his sobriety. He speaks to his son. "And just so you know—and what I'll be telling your uncles—this isn't close to anything that could knock me over. The fact that you all thought Greg 'I'm a shit grandparent' Calloway would put me on my ass is insulting."

My brows jump.

Lo is on a roll, barely pausing. "Sure, I loved him when he made amends with your mom and when I saw him only as her father. He was decent to Lil. He loved her more than her mother ever did. But I *hated* him when he started letting his wife treat my children like dog shit while favoring Rose and Connor's kids. You might as well have been invisible to him."

"He wasn't always visible to me," Maximoff says under his breath.

"It wasn't on you to make that effort. You're the *grandchild*. You're supposed to be doted on and loved, and he couldn't do either for you."

I blink a few times, remembering my grandmom. She's smoking in her recliner as I leave the apartment to find a bite to eat. It's eight p.m. She's not even looking at me. Not even as I unlock the door.

"As far as I'm concerned," Lo continues, "he's been dead to me for years. So has your grandmother. Any tears I shed will be ones of absolute joy."

My lips begin to rise.

"Jesus, Dad," Maximoff grimaces.

"What?"

"I can't celebrate Grandfather Calloway's *death*. He meant a lot to the Cobalts. Janie loved him, and Sulli always talks about the chocolates he'd sneak her as a kid."

Lo stares at him for a long moment. "God, you're such a Hufflepuff."

Maximoff groans.

"You have your mom's heart."

"Dad."

"That's a good thing. Keep it. You don't want mine. It's ugly."

"It's not," Maximoff refutes.

"That's exactly what she'd say." He smiles at him.

Maximoff starts smiling back, and it's good to see their relationship hasn't imploded. Seems like it'd take several dozen nuclear bombs to make a real dent. I try not to think about my dad. About the relationship I'm constructing from some desolate postwar wasteland.

I know I'll never have what Maximoff has with Lo.

I'm not wishing for what can't exist, but I'm hoping for something better than I had. My dad's clean. That's a start, I guess. I can tell myself it's a personal choice—to reconnect with Sean Donnelly—but it's still more out of necessity.

He's ensuring our family, the Donnellys, don't believe I ratted them out. They think I'm loyal to them because of my dad. Hell, my dad doesn't even know I'm the reason most are behind bars.

I think he'd kill me if he found out.

4

LUNA HALE

I've thought about eavesdropping a hundred and one times, and I've also wished for supersonic hearing. Alas, my ears are still of the average variety. I only pick up the anxious grumble of my stomach.

"You think my dad will kick Donnelly out?" I ask Farrow while digging through the freezer-burnt popsicle box. I try to find the best one for Ripley.

"He better not," Farrow says, slipping a protective look at the door. It's reassuring knowing that Farrow will throw himself in front of Donnelly if need be. I imagine Donnelly standing opposite my dad and maybe even my brother. It's a sad picture, and my heart pangs.

If he leaves, I'll leave with him. I try not to overthink the instinct.

I shut the fridge. Ripley is waiting patiently at his kiddie table, distracted by Arkham and Orion who lie close. He reaches for their fur.

"You like banana?" I ask, peeling off the plastic packaging.

Ripley inspects me with hesitance before nodding. *Can he see I'm not the same? I'm not her.*

Original Luna is still lost in my mind, but she's also in the pages of the diary. I found her in manuscript-form today. Hope glimmers brighter. I also try to hang on to Donnelly's words about Ripley just being timid around everyone.

The nearly two-year-old reaches up for the popsicle, and I place the stick in his hands. He holds tight.

Farrow asks him, "What do you say to your Auntie Luna?"

"Thank ew." Ripley licks the popsicle, beaming up at me like I'm the coolest, best aunt.

I smile back. Okay, maybe I'm not such a lame OG Luna replacement. I slide on a barstool at the kitchen island, the glittery hard-bound diary before me. While I might be able to learn a lot from myself in those pages, I also never want to stop building on the relationships that mean something to me.

So I ask Farrow, "Did the two of us talk a lot about Donnelly?"

He tilts his head back and forth, considering. "Not too much." His sleeves are rolled, revealing a cascade of tattoos, and little Cassidy is in his inked arms while he feeds her a bottle. "I have a feeling you kept the majority of your thoughts about him to yourself."

With the diary in my possession, it's not as frustrating hearing this.

Farrow adds, "It's not like I was an over-sharer." His face tenses while chewing on a piece of gum. "I could've told you or anyone else how much I love that shameless motherfucker—that he's been my family. But I never even came close to that."

"You just did," I say quietly.

Farrow takes a slow breath.

I lean forward. "I wonder if I was scared that you wouldn't like me with him."

His brows lift with a barbell piercing. "I wouldn't have been unhappy about it."

I start to smile. "Really?"

"You make sense together," Farrow says. "You've likely always made sense since you first met him, but I didn't really see it until later."

He knows Donnelly better than I do, maybe even better than I *did*. "You've seen him with other girls, right? Did they make sense with him too?"

Farrow arches his brows again. "No."

No is a good answer but not a completely satisfying one. I want a million words of explanation. "Why not?"

"Because most of the girls I saw him with—they just wanted to get *laid*. You've seen him." He jerks his head to the door. "He looks like a fun night. Not like someone you take home to Mom and Dad."

It's hard for me to see only the surface of Donnelly.

My first glimpse of him at the hospital—he was more than just the sexy scattered tattoos, the intriguing piercings, the sculpted muscle and lush chestnut hair. He was loving in the way he approached me. In the way he held me. He was daring. In the way he fought to stay at my side. And his magnetic, luminous smile always seemed to touch his blue eyes.

I could write a thesis on the Attractiveness of Paul Donnelly, but it suddenly hits me.

"I never took him home," I realize.

"You tried," Farrow refutes.

My dad didn't want him here. Not until it was safe, I've gathered. But it is now. "He's here now," I say, more to myself. *Please let him stay.* My mind reels over what Farrow is telling me. "Donnelly said he doesn't really go slow, but he wants to try to go slow with me."

"Yeah?" Farrow adjusts the bottle against Cassidy's little lips, but his eyes are mostly on mine. "You don't want that?"

I say nothing at first. Guilt washes over my face, burning my cheeks. But I let it out, "I want *fast*. Like super-sonic speed *fast*. And maybe I'm just like all the other girls he's hooked up with—because I, too, would love to get laid by Donnelly."

Farrow's lips stretch in a smile. "It'd be more disconcerting if you didn't want that from him."

"So...maybe you could tell him that it's okay to go fast? Step on the gas pedal? Don't locate the brake."

Farrow sucks in a breath between his teeth. "Luna—"

"Farrow," I plead.

"—he's eight years older than you. You can't remember having sex. I'm not telling him to do shit if he thinks it's too soon. The one thing Donnelly is careful with is *you*."

I groan, my forehead pounding the counter. "Idon'twanthimto-becareful," I slur together. "Not with this. I want him to destroy me. In the sexiest, hottest way." I say it to my lap but loud enough that Farrow hears. I lift my head.

Farrow chews slower on his gum. "Whatever your kinks are— you need to tell him, not me."

I don't even know if it's a kink. It's not like I have experience in the realm of sex or relationships, and I suppose that's the issue. I trace my fingers over the glittery diary cover. Did Original Luna document all her sexual exploits?

"What is that exactly?" Farrow asks.

"My diary."

His eyes narrow on the cover, no title or words. "No shit?"

"I just found it this morning." I'm tentative to open it, so I push it aside and watch Cassidy drink her milk. Farrow asks if I want to feed her, and my heart grows, excited for baby snuggles. Once the soft newborn is in my arms, I tilt the bottle so she can easily suck out the milk. "Hi there, little teeny tiny Cassidy," I whisper, her tufts of hair hidden under a purple cotton beanie. She's a brunette girl, but her hair color could have been inherited just as likely from Farrow as it could've from Jane.

Her eyes are a deep, deep blue, but those could also change color as she ages too. Maybe they'll morph into brown to match Farrow's.

A strange, ugly feeling twists inside of me. I realize how much I *don't* want her to resemble Jane. I hate that I'm wishing against the possibility.

"What's wrong?" Farrow asks me, his palms on the island.

I look over at him. He's in a casual lunge, not at all worried about me holding his baby, let alone feeding her. A pain sits on my heart. "Did I ever offer to donate my eggs?"

Farrow is taken aback.

"I didn't?" My pulse races.

"No—"

"Why didn't I?" I ask him fast, breathing harder. "I would've wanted to."

He combs his fingers through his ash-brown hair. "Shit." He glances at the door, like maybe he's hoping Maximoff will come assist him with this conversation.

I frown. "You would've said *no*," I realize—maybe that's why I never tried. I knew his answer. "You would've picked Jane—"

"No," he cuts in, his eyes glassing but he fights away the rise of emotion. "If you offered, it would've been harder not to pick you."

My ribs clench around my lungs. "I wonder if I thought you wouldn't choose me, so maybe that's why I never tried."

"Maybe," he breathes, "but Maximoff would've wanted to go with Jane."

I try to understand before the tidal wave of hurt crashes forth. "How come?"

"Probably because you're younger, and he'd have a point." Farrow pops a bubblegum bubble, then chews again. "And also the same reason why we might never use his sperm. Hale genetics." He lifts and lowers his brows. "Addiction."

Oh.

I blink a few times and cast a tiny glance back at Baby Ripley. He's still enjoying the banana popsicle and babbles to Arkham. I look back at Farrow. "He's a child of addicts too." They're already raising a son who has addiction in his lineage.

"Which is why I don't give a shit about your parents' history of addiction." He tips his head. "Your brother overthinks a fuck ton. I think he'll come around one day, but not right now."

I tilt the bottle of milk higher. I'm not vying to see myself in their baby. That's not where the jealousy stems. It has more to do with being the sister I wish I could be. The one who'd make this big grand gesture for two people I wholeheartedly, completely love.

Given the chance back then, I didn't take it. I hate that I didn't take it. "Maybe it's too late," I say quietly, "but if you're ever thinking of having more kids, I'd be willing to donate eggs. I want to help you both if I can."

Farrow nods a couple times, emotion returning to his eyes, but before he can speak, the door flies open. Donnelly saunters in, no one else, and he shuts the door gently behind him.

Just seeing him makes my whole being inflate with oxygen, with life. He makes my blood-cells sing.

"From my fresh newly-sprung experience," Donnelly tells Farrow, "if you're ever thinking it, don't drop bad news on Loren Hale's lap. He'll fling it back at you."

"Man, why the fuck did you tell him Greg died to begin with?"

My grandfather died. I haven't been thinking about it much, but now my stomach tosses.

"He cornered me," Donnelly refutes, standing beside his best friend. "I'm almost positive he loves putting me in positions where I can't escape. Probably because he knows I can worm my way out of a lot." He acknowledges me with an up-nod and a smile, one that softens when he sees the baby in my arms.

"You want to feed her?" I ask him. "She has a quarter of the bottle left."

"Nah, that's okay." His face is unreadable. "She looks comfy in your arms." He gives me another smile, and I send one back.

We professed our love to each other on the front lawn, his family is locked away in jail, and so today does feel like a renewal for Donnelly and me. A fresh start with the version of myself who only has a diary and a month of experiences with him. The newness is exhilarating and nerve-wracking because I can't figure out where we go from here.

But I feel that it's somewhere *up* and not down.

"You hungry?" Donnelly asks, opening the fridge. At first I think he's asking Farrow, but they both look to me for the answer.

"I could eat," I say, fighting a smile. Is this what a boyfriend would do? Butter and jelly my toast? Pop my Pop-Tart? Butterflies flap in my stomach until I think, *has a guy made me breakfast before? After a hookup?*

I stifle a wince, not loving the idea of being with anyone but Donnelly. It makes my body squirm even picturing a strange set of hands roaming over my thighs, over my hips and breasts. Like…a violation, but why would it feel *violating* when somewhere deep-down I chose those random guys? It was a choice.

Original Luna's choice, but she is me.

I know that.

Donnelly examines the fridge's contents, then glances at Farrow. "Think Lo will mind if I crack some eggs?"

"He'll definitely say something."

"And I'll definitely say something cuter back." Donnelly grins, and Farrow rolls his eyes, to which Donnelly just laughs. He pulls out a carton of eggs, a bag of shredded cheddar cheese, and a package of thick-cut bacon.

Cassidy has finished her bottle, and just as she fusses, Farrow takes her in his arms. She calms in his strong cradle, then he finds a burp rag from his bag and lies her against his shoulder, patting her back. He's a natural, but this is also his second, I remember.

I think someone told me Baby Ripley came into Farrow and Maximoff's life close to the newborn stage.

"What's with Dad and Moffy?" Xander suddenly strolls into the kitchen, his hair tousled from bed. Erebor, his Newfie pup, joins mine near the kiddie table, and I hear Baby Ripley giggle at the entrance of a third dog. "They're acting weird." He slides on the stool beside me. "Like they just completely stopped talking when I came downstairs."

Farrow and Donnelly exchange a quick glance, maybe not sure how to drop this news to my younger brother. I just go ahead and say it, "Grandfather Calloway passed away. We just heard."

Xander rubs his forehead, his face cinching, but like me, he's not all too moved. "Sucks for Mom."

"You weren't that close to him?" Donnelly asks, but I get the feeling he's also asking me. His eyes drift to mine.

"Not really." Xander hunches forward, elbows on the counter. "What's this?" He points to my diary, and I'm about to explain.

"Did you hear who died?" Kinney stomps into the kitchen, a phone in her hand. Unlike Xander who only has on plaid pajama bottoms, my sixteen-year-old sister wears a full face of goth makeup, turtleneck sweater, and black overall-dress.

"Did you?" I ask her.

"Audrey just told me." Kinney crosses her arms, zeroing in on the person at the stove. "What's he doing here?" She's eyeing Donnelly like he's an enemy encroaching on her territory. Her Newfie even lets out a low growl at her heels.

"Making breakfast," Donnelly says, chucking eggshells in the trash. "Want some?"

"Who invited you?" Kinney barks.

"I did," Farrow says before I can.

Kinney is disbelieving.

"He's cool, Kin," Xander says to her. "Chill."

Kinney throws up her hands. "Are we just going to act like his family didn't almost destroy ours? They *hurt* Mom and Luna. Am I the *only* one who cares?" Air vacuums out of the kitchen. I can hear the rapid *thump* of my heart.

Donnelly is frozen.

"I want him here," I tell my sister.

"Well, I don't," Kinney glares at him. "Not until you go back to your messed up family and make sure, with absolute certainty, that they will never, ever, *ever* hurt my sister again." Raw pain flares in her eyes, and I can almost see how distraught she must've been that night I was kidnapped.

Donnelly looks sick to his stomach, and I have this urge to pull him away from Kinney, from this situation entirely.

Farrow interjects, "Kinney, you don't know what you're talking about."

"I know exactly what happened," she retorts.

"He's done *enough*." That's not Farrow. It's my dad. He's standing in the doorway, Moffy beside him, and he tells Kinney, "Put down the pitchforks."

"*Dad.*"

"*He's done enough,*" Dad says so severely that Kinney blinks back a surge of sudden tears, then races out of the kitchen, pushing past our oldest brother.

"Kinney," Moffy calls after her. I hear her heavy footsteps up the staircase, and her dog Salem trots after her.

Guilt tightens my dad's eyes. "Can you go talk to her, bub?" He's asking Xander. And with a nod, Xander exits to go check on our little sister. I think about running after her too, but I want to show Donnelly I'm here for him. The pieces of my heart attached to him win out, and I swallow sisterly guilt like an oversized pill with no water.

A lump is in my throat, but some relief washes it down. I just witnessed my dad fiercely defending Donnelly, and I chart the evidence under *my dad likes him*.

"Raiding my pantry?" he asks Donnelly with a disapproving cock of his head. *Uh-oh.* "Go ahead. Help yourself to the eggs, the stale Froot Loops, the curdled milk. Don't forget the good stuff. Rat poison, top shelf." He flashes a half-smile. *Rat* poison? My mouth falls open.

Donnelly grins. "Appreciate you sharing your favorite food with me, Papa Hale."

"Luna's dad," he corrects, then shakes his head at me, like I've chosen to fall in love with the most grating specimen on planet Earth. On the contrary, Donnelly is the most mesmerizing earthling I've met thus far.

I doubt anyone could trump him.

"I'm making your daughter food," Donnelly tells him. "That alright?"

Dad wears another dry smile. "Only if you fear my every waking move while you do it."

"Dad," I say with widened eyes.

"What? He's in *my* house. I'm your father." He unspools a bag of bagels and slips one in a toaster. "No guy you're dating should feel at ease while they're here. They need to know with one wrong move, I will have them *sobbing* in their ugly little pickup trucks with their testicles rolling halfway down the street and into the sewer where they belong."

Donnelly glances back from the sizzling eggs. "I don't have a pickup truck, Luna's dad."

"I'll put you in one."

"Now you're buying me a car?"

Farrow bursts out laughing which makes me smile, especially as Baby Ripley giggles, and even my dad can't hide the rise of his lips.

Dad asks me, "Are you spending the night?"

I rushed to my childhood house to show Donnelly the diary, and I hadn't given much thought to plans afterward. My first thought: *Wherever Donnelly is, I want to be.* But I hesitate to even draw attention to him in relation to this question.

Too obsessed. Too attached, he'll think. Then he might pull us apart tonight.

"I..." I start to answer, but the door breezes open again.

This time, my mom appears, splotchy-cheeked and hobbling on crutches. Her reddened eyes instantly find Dad. "Lo, I—"

"It's okay, Lil." In a blink, they've collided, his arms woven around her gangly frame. He speaks quietly to her, and both Farrow and Donnelly say *sorry for your loss, Lily.*

She wipes at the corners of her eyes. "It was just unexpected... no one saw it coming..." Moffy abandons the bacon to hug Mom. I hop off the barstool to give her one too. She asks us how we're doing.

"Fine," Moffy answers.

"Okay," I nod.

"That's good." Her voice shakes a little but she intakes a breath. "Sorry, what were you saying, Luna? Before I walked in? I cut you off."

"Dad just asked if I was spending the night," I tell her.

Mom perks up like a reinflated helium balloon. "Yes, you should. Farrow, Moffy, and the babies are already staying. We'll all be together. Wouldn't that be nice?" She smiles at Dad like it's the warmest picture she could imagine. All her kids under one holiday-lit roof.

It's not so comforting for me, not if Donnelly isn't in the picture too. The urge to look at him is too strong to resist now. He's half-turned towards me while he babies the scrambled eggs in the skillet, pushing them around with a spatula.

Does he look as glum as I feel?

I turn back to my parents. "Can Donnelly stay?" I ask.

"No," Dad says the same time Mom says, "Yes." Their heads whip to each other. "Lily."

"Lo," she counters. "She's twenty-one."

The sharpest lines of his face seem to twitch. But he looks straight at Donnelly. "You stay, you'll be in the guest room. The lawn saw enough *kissing* to last a lifetime."

Mom makes a confused face.

"From *them*," Dad clarifies. "This house loves when we kiss, love." He nuzzles into her neck with playful kisses, and Mom flushes, clinging tighter to him.

While they're in their own world, my lungs have already expanded in a deeper breath. Especially seeing Donnelly's emerging grin. He slides a bowl of scrambled eggs to me. "How's the bed in the guest room?" he asks me quietly, leaning on the island.

My heart pitter-patters. He's accepting the invitation to spend the night. I take the fork from him. "I've never tested it out," I admit, and if my eyes say, *I want to, with you*, I sincerely hope he can read them.

5

PAUL DONNELLY

"My house rules. No sex under my roof. Do not break it," Lo warns with a cold glare. He shoves a bed pillow in my chest. He can't be any blunter.

"Dry house," I say. "Got it."

He's unamused. Not tickling his funny bone tonight, *also got it.* "You want your dick wet?" he asks. "Don't even *think* about my daughter. Think about the freezing pool I'm going to drown you in. It's right outside." He points to the window that faces the backyard and then flashes a half-smile. "Night, Paul." He pats my shoulder, leaving me alone in the guest room.

Now I'm lying on the queen-size bed, not even crawling underneath the fluffy white comforter, and I'm thinking about my swimming skills. Think I can stay above water alright.

That shouldn't be my initial thought. I should probably be thinking, *don't fuck Luna.* For more reasons than just her dad's house rules.

But I'm not planning on sneaking into her room. The temptation is down the hall, and I've got enough control not to slip in there. *Slipping in.* Yeah, that just makes me picture her pussy, and my mind is wrapped around her soft body, the intoxicating floral scent of her skin, her hair, and the fucking noises she makes when I rake my hands down her hips and clutch her thighs.

My breath goes shallow. "Fuck." I dig the heels of my palms in my eyes. "Someone just *died*, Paul." I cringe just hearing my own name from my own mouth, not even knowing why I'm using it. Other than the more Lo says it, the more I'm reassociating the name to myself. Feels fucking weird.

I drop my hands. Luna's pussy isn't even a bad thing to dream about. I could be stuck on a sick turntable of disturbing past events. Like the kidnapping, the row house. My family. My father. My *mother*. Fuck.

My face screws up. Yeah, I'd rather be descending into the gorgeous unearthly depths of Luna Hale. No contest.

I palm my dick against the black drawstring pants I'm wearing. Borrowed the bottoms from Farrow. With no underwear on, I easily feel the outline of my swollen head and my cock piercings. I imagine Luna up against the wall. My body pinning her there.

No one else is able to see her. No one else is able to touch her. Just me.

The visual is a hot stroke down my hardened length. My muscles flex, and I pump myself one more time.

The sudden death isn't shadowing a need for Luna, and it's probably because I didn't know Greg all too well. I'd feel more like an insensitive prick if the Hales were grieving, but only Lily seems to be truly affected.

I spent most of today on the roof, stringing up the rest of the multi-colored lights. Hale House looks merry and bright now, and I even helped Xander put up a flocked pre-lit Christmas tree.

But I didn't get a minute alone with Luna. Felt like Lo made sure of that. He stood behind me when I dug in the musty attic for a box of ornaments. He was around the corner when I attempted to steal her away into the laundry room.

I tried not to believe Luna's therapist put him up to it. Except, Lo took me aside and insinuated I needed to be careful with his daughter because of *trauma*. Not the first warning he's dished out to me. Doubt it'll be his last.

It's not like I've forgotten what she went through. What I went through. I'd rather just focus on what makes me feel good than what makes me want to punch a hole through the wall.

Misery isn't a bed I like sleeping in, and somewhere along the way, it's become miserable to be away from her. I know that too, which is why I keep glancing at the door.

She's right down the hall.

I'm best buds with the two-horned devil on my shoulder, and typically, I'd give in to these impulses (life's too short and all) but I'm not pressuring her like that. She's mentally a *virgin*.

I let out a tight breath. Without my sketchbook, I've been drawing on post-its I found in the guest room's mostly empty dresser. I outline a drawing of an abominable snow-alien, stopping midway through as the conversation with Lo hits my brain again.

I end up texting Farrow.

When you stayed here with Maximoff, did Lo tell you about the "no sex under my roof" house rule? I press send. They lived at the Hale House when the townhouse burned down, and they hadn't been married.

He replies after a minute or so.

No. I didn't get that talk. Did you? — Farrow

Pretty much. Got the third degree again. Guess he really hates my dick. I text back. My eyes ping around the many black-framed X-Men movie posters—a shrine to Lily and Lo's adoration of Cyclops, and maybe Rogue...and that shape-shifting chick who I would've said with absolute certainty was a blue alligator until I watched the films.

I send: You think he has cameras in here? Like a nanny cam?

I wouldn't put anything past him, man. Just sweep the room. — Farrow

I'm about to do just that, but before I can shift a muscle, the door creaks open. I prepare myself for another round of the Loren Hale Petty Special, which he seems to reserve solely for the guys looking to fuck his oldest daughter.

That's not all I want to be to her. Yeah, I want to fuck her, but shouldn't Lo be treating me different somehow? The way he's been talking, he's lumping me in with *all* the guys who could possibly date Luna, as if I'm just a mile marker on the road and not the destination.

You're not special, Paul.

I grind my teeth, but the ache in my jaw subsides the second Luna pops her head in the room. *It's her.* I feel my smile rising.

"Can I come in?" she asks.

"Only if you know the secret passcode," I tease.

"Have I forgotten it?" She speaks so quietly that I question whether I was supposed to hear.

I shake my head slowly. "No. You didn't forget." I'm not dredging up inside jokes that she can't remember. "I'll give you a hint." I bow forward, hanging my arms on my bent knees. "It's in the top five greatest places on my planet."

Luna hasn't emerged fully in the room. I only see her cute round face. Her amber eyes are sweeping me in slow, meticulous strokes. As though engraining the surface and depth of me for future memory.

"Your arms," she says.

Another smile edges across my mouth. "*My* top five," I clarify. "Not yours."

"Your arms are likely the greatest place to be for lots of humans," Luna says, resting her temple on the doorframe. I look into her, her gaze tunneling deeper into mine, and the intensity surges a powerful feeling in my body.

I've never had someone believe in my worth the way that Luna does, and she's staring at me with the same bottomless love she used to. *Keep your shit together.* I run my fingers through my hair. *Don't think about that night.*

I check her out. "I only care about my arms being the greatest place for you."

Her growing smile causes my lips to curve higher.

"Need another hint?" I ask.

"Uh-uh," Luna shakes her head. "A great place on earth for you...might be..." She thinks hard, her mind probably circulating through all the conversations we've had since she woke up in the hospital. "...Wawa?"

"Winner winner, ham hoagie dinner." I gesture her forward with two fingers. "Come on in, space babe."

As she peels her face off the doorframe and enters, I take in her attire. Black baggy sweatpants, the waistband rolled, and a lime-green tank top, but it's her sneakers and a sweatshirt bundled in her hands and a backpack on her shoulder that sound alarm bells in my brain.

'Cause she isn't dipping into my room looking to be eaten out. I know this is something else before she says it.

"Do you want to sneak out with me?" She searches my gaze, and I take too long to reply because she adds fast, "I don't even know if it can be called *sneaking out* since I'm an adult...and it's not like I live here, but it kinda feels like sneaking, I guess."

I spin the ballpoint pen between my fingers. "You planning on inviting your bodyguards?"

"No, I was...I was actually thinking of going alone. Without them and without..."

"Me?"

Flush ascends her neck, and I try not to stiffen but my joints aren't working right at all.

"Yeah, but then I realized that I'd rather go out with you. Hence, this pitstop." *She'd rather go out with me.* My head whirls a mile a minute, recalling a talk I had with Luna pre-amnesia. She told me about a past I wasn't a part of. Where she would sneak out. Where she would ditch her bodyguard. Where she would explore Center City late at night with no friend or family in tow.

This time, it's different.

This time, she wants to do everything with me. And she has no clue she's subconsciously replaying events of her life but including me in them. How do I even tell her? Am I supposed to? *Don't fuck up her recovery.*

She watches me slide the pen behind my ear and climb off the bed. "Is that a *yes?* You're coming?"

I slip her a smile. "Beats hanging out here alone." I snatch my jeans off the floor. "Plus, the blue alligator chick won't stop staring at me."

Luna sees the X-Men: Days of Future Past poster. "Mystique is an intense bean."

"Think her yellow eyes have been trying to penetrate my soul." I collect my Scorpions band tee off the armrest of a brown leather chair, then find my boxer-briefs on the cushion.

"In that case, she's the mutant enemy. No penetration of Donnelly is allowed on my watch." She crosses her arms in an X formation, the sweatshirt hanging over her shoulder.

"You gonna fight her on my behalf?" I grin.

"To the very death."

"No dying without me, Hale," I say seriously and grin wider as she observes, with this adorable pensive expression, how I'm moving across the room. Luna has always been insightful, perceptive, but the writer-brain in her has materialized tenfold since her memory loss.

All the tools she's used to create fiction, she's been wielding to solve the mysteries of her life. She's been hard on herself about finding answers, but I think she's coped better than most would. I'm glad she has the diary though. Seems like it'll remedy most of the things that've been frustrating her.

She sees me thumb the elastic band of my pants. "I can wait for you downstairs…"

"In a hurry?" I drop the drawstring bottoms. Buck-naked and unashamed as I step into boxer-briefs, I smile over at Luna. Her lips have parted, her cheeks rosy, and there is no other way to describe how she's staring other than she's soaking in my full existence. Not just my cock or tattoos, but the casualness in which I'm getting dressed.

"Not anymore," she mutters. "You're a peculiar person, you know."

"I don't know," I enunciate the words, sounding clearer, and I button my jeans. "Tell me about it."

That's when she pinches the green kyber crystal around her neck, the necklace I gifted her this morning. I'm still wearing a blue one, the chain colder against my skin. "I thought I'd come in here and need to convince you to sneak out with me," she admits. "Or in the very least, I'd have to convince you to let me go without my bodyguards. Wait—we aren't calling them, are we?"

I should most definitely text Frog and Quinn—maybe have them secretly tracking our whereabouts. But that'd entail lying to Luna, and I'm not doing that. I could be upfront about how she needs them, but in this moment, I just want her to need me.

I can take care of her.

It's just one night.

No one needs to know.

"Wasn't planning on it," I tell her, pulling the Scorpions tee over my head.

"Okay, good," she nods, more to herself, then releases her hold of the kyber crystal. "I guess I just appreciate how easy this was. So…thanks."

"No need to thank me." I shove my wallet in my pocket, coming closer to her. "I want it as much as you do."

Luna clings harder to my gaze, and I inhale a lungful of the pungent honeysuckle scent wafting off her. It whirls toxically around me, and we seriously need to go or else I'm gonna shove her against the wall, the mattress, some surface where I can feel her warmth against me.

"You driving?" I ask, my throat hoarse with pent-up arousal, but I clear it.

She tucks a piece of hair behind her ear, still flushed. "Um…

actually, I wasn't sure." She crinkles her nose. "I don't have a car here, and if I take my parents', they'll hear the garage. So that leaves us with a rideshare?"

Safety-wise, catching an Uber is a decent plan, but we wouldn't be able to talk much in the car. Sue me for wanting more alone-time with her. "I have an idea." I motion to the hall. "Go out the front door."

Quietly, we exit the guest room and tiptoe down the stairs and out the front entrance. As soon as the December cold hits us, Luna yanks the sweatshirt over her head. "You need a jacket?" she whispers.

It's chilly, but I'll survive. "The cold doesn't bother me. This way." I jerk my head to the driveway, and when we reach the curb, I let her know we're walking to the two mansions owned by Triple Shield, only one street away in the neighborhood. "I have keys to a security vehicle."

"Are you allowed to take it even if I'm not your client?" Luna wonders. It's not that she's not my client. It's that she pays Kitsuwon Securities for security, not Triple Shield, so my new boss won't like me using Epsilon resources for her. If I were still Omega, there'd be no issue.

"Not really, but I won't tell if you don't."

"Your secrets are always safe with me," she says softly. "But maybe too well since I've forgotten three years of them."

"Nah, that just makes you the best secret-keeper around." I slide my arm around her thin shoulders, hugging her closer, and Luna leans her weight into my side while we walk. Feels natural, being with her in the darkness and quiet of the night.

I've already signed my contract, so I'm officially Epsilon *today*, which is why I've been given this shiny set of car keys. But I've been a bodyguard long enough to know SFE is anal about the Range Rovers. And by SFE, I mean *O'Malley*.

A strange dark piece of me is delighting in this pea-sized payback. Where I'm taking his baby for a joyride with my...with Luna.

Anyway, fuck him.

The Range Rover is parked on the curb, and once we're inside the SUV, I crank up the heaters to warm Luna and the cold black leather interior, then I pop up the GPS on the nav screen. "Where we headed?" I ask.

She digs out her phone. "I was thinking this place. I've never been, but it looks interesting." She flashes me her screen—a Yelp review of a local dive bar.

Thirsty Goose.

I go still, unblinking for a stifling second.

"What?" She frowns, then rereads the reviews. "Is it a shitty place or something? There weren't that many pictures."

"Not shitty. It's a cool bar. They've always got free salted nuts and they usually play nineties rock." I grip the steering wheel loosely, then tighter as I drive out of the neighborhood. "But you've been there before."

She elevates in her seat like I plucked a shooting star out of the sky for her. "When did we go there?"

My muscles cramp. "We didn't go together."

Luna sinks back down. "We didn't?" Her brows pinch, as if she's trying to grapple with that lost memory. "I went alone?"

I nod. "You only told me about it."

She eases back against the seat, then after a minute of silence, she glances at me. "This is my favorite timeline—the one where you exist with me."

It surges through my chest, and I try to look at her, but I need to lean out the window and punch the security code on the gate. When I'm back inside and stepping on the gas, I reach out and hold her hand.

Despite the pain we had to crawl through, all she had to endure with my family, I'd say the timeline where I get to see her smile and blush and hear the brightness of her laugh—that is, and will always be, my favorite.

Just got to make sure I don't fuck it up.

6

LUNA HALE

A cosmic, unearthly happening. How else can I describe what's occurring between me and Donnelly? Original Luna frequented Thirsty Goose in secret, and I unknowingly tried to do the exact same but I rewrote the script and included her boyfri… well, he wasn't her boyfriend.

He's not exactly *mine* either, but he was bound to be hers. And doesn't that mean he's on the same path to becoming mine too? My temple throbs in the start of a shrill headache, the more I unravel these twisted strands of my life and his life.

I try not to concentrate too hard anymore. *Feeling* is better than thinking. Giddier sentiments flap in my stomach while the Range Rover bumps along the highway. To Thirsty Goose we go. Past midnight. On a voyage unknown to everyone but us.

I feel closer to twenty-one than to eighteen for the first time since the hospital. Like my life isn't defined by safety parameters and paparazzi and overprotective parents. Like I'm free to do what I want with who I want.

My smile softens on him, but he's too focused on driving to see.

He switches lanes. "How are you handling the whole dead grandfather thing?" he asks. "Were you close?"

"We never talked about my grandparents?" I ask.

"Not really." He casts a quick glance to me, then the road. "You wanna talk about them now?" He's hoping I do, I think, but he's being kind in giving me a lever to self-eject from serious topics.

I'm not aching to be a walled-off, guarded fortress anymore—and definitely not with him. I ball up the sleeves of my sweatshirt in my palms. "I wasn't close to them. My grandfather would say *hi* and ask the typical questions: *How's school going? What subject do you like?* It would end kinda around there." I shrug. "He always seemed uncertain of us."

Donnelly frowns. "What do you mean?"

I stare off at the road, illuminated by the headlights. "I saw how animated he became around Eliot and Tom and the other Cobalts. Like their futures were glowing embers, something to stoke, something that could burn bright." I blink, staring at my lap. "But with me and my brothers and sister—it felt like our paths were too dark to even touch." I look at him.

He's trying his best to hold my gaze.

"We had more chances to become addicts than they did. It just seemed like my grandparents knew we could all fall apart, so they didn't want to invest in us." I face the dashboard again. "I can't really be envious of Eliot and Tom. I think there's something catastrophic about nurturing a tiny fire into a raging inferno." I tilt my head to Donnelly. "It's the ways of the stars: burn too bright and a supernova will explode."

He tries to give me a small smile, but his lips flatline. "I get not wanting to bet on the losing horse and whatnot, but that seems premature. You were just kids."

"Do you think your life would've been different if you had people that bet on you?"

"It woulda been easier, for sure," he breathes. "Counting on yourself, always relying on *just* yourself...it's all you know after a while, and anything different feels strange." He's sitting more upright, his muscles flexing as he lowers the heat. "And I want to be upfront with you."

I sit more stiffy too, unable to really respond. I prepare for the worst, and my stomach already nosedives towards my toes.

He briefly seizes my gaze, but I inspect the kyber crystal around his neck. Then he says, "I didn't always bet on the Hales either. Most of the time in security, I was rooting for the Cobalts."

I can't be surprised, but that doesn't mean it doesn't hurt. "I saw your *Cobalts Never Die* tattoo on your knee," I whisper.

He nods slowly, gauging my reaction.

I lift my shoulder. "I'd be lying if I said I didn't look for one about my family—"

"Luna—"

"No, it's okay," I say quietly. "I would've bet on them too."

"That's just it," Donnelly professes, eyeing the road, then me. "I was afraid of the unsure thing because I didn't want to lose, but there's never been a moment where I haven't believed in you, Luna."

My lungs reinflate. His belief in me feels good to hear, and it's not so hard for me to understand why he'd distance himself from my family. Even though we're both children of addicts, he can't totally relate to my circumstances any more than I can relate to his. Not only is there an economic divide—I grew up in wealth, he grew up in poverty—but of what he's told me, his mom and dad were high most of the time.

If given the chance, wouldn't most choose to associate with the family that doesn't remind them of their own dark past?

It would've been difficult for him to be a part of the Hales. Yet, here he is. Trying to be a part of my family.

I study him again, realizing how much he loved her to do such a thing. *How much he loves me.*

Donnelly tries to decipher my expression, but again, he trains his gaze to the road. "I told you a little bit about this already," he says. "Maybe you'll read it in your diary."

"Maybe," I mutter. Before I crept into the guest room, I cracked open the diary and read half a page. My pulse skyrocketed, then I shut it fast. I don't bring it up now. "Were they worse when Moffy got with Farrow?"

"Your grandparents?"

"Yeah." I pause. "I had this feeling they wanted Moffy to end up with a girl. Like, they thought that him being bi was either a phase or just this weird period in his life that would pass. And it'd all be fine once he married a girl."

Donnelly looks me up-down for a split-second.

"What?" I ask him, eager for his innermost thoughts.

"I'd say your species is intuitive and all, but I think that's just you, Hale."

His quick compliments are some of the sweetest things anyone has ever said to me. "A great and terrible power," I sing-song. "Never to be used recklessly."

"Unless you're with me," he grins.

I grin back. "Unless I'm with you." My smile slowly fades in thought. "So my grandparents were awful to my brother?"

"Not your grandfather so much," Donnelly says, rotating the wheel. We're off the highway and meeting red lights in Center City. "Let's just say your mom kicked the Crow out of your brother's wedding."

I'm confused. "The who?"

It dawns on him: me not remembering. "Your Grandmother Calloway."

I laugh. "The Crow...who came up with that?"

"Yours truly." He lifts a couple fingers.

"I like it. It suits her." I cross my legs on the seat, and my smile widens picturing my mom ousting the pearl-clutching old lady from the biggest social event of likely that year. "My mom is awesome."

"Best mom around."

He says it proudly, but I can't help but think of his own mom. So many questions slam against me like a battering ram. *Do you like your mom? Do you visit her in prison? When's the last time you spoke to her? What's her full name?* I blink past the mental overload.

"You alright?" he asks, concern flaring his eyes.

I'm panting strangely. "Yeah." I catch my breath and lift my backpack to my lap, conflicted on whether I should dig out my diary

and read more about our past. I could even read it out loud to him…
but maybe that'd be weird. *He loves weird.* He loves me.

Why is my heart still skipping several beats? My brows crinkle.
Confusion begone! Mental powers are not working. I take out an
energy drink and rezip the backpack, diary stored away. "I know
you might've told me about your mom before, and maybe it's in the
diary"—*which is why I have a strange urge to look*—"but I guess a big part
of me would rather just hear from you than read about it. But I don't
want you to feel like you're on a hot seat."

"I don't feel like it," he assures fast. "I mean, I don't talk about
my mom much to anyone, but I'd much rather be talking to you than
to security about her. Which I had to do." He takes the energy drink
when I pass it to him. "I think I talked a little about her to you, but
not a lot. Strangely, I think your dad knows more."

"My dad?"

He swigs the pineapple-flavored liquid, then swallows. "He *pries.*
Hard-core. Mostly in the name of your safety, which I get. He's just
looking out for you."

How does prying about Donnelly's relationship with his mom
help *me?* Either Donnelly has the wrong read on my dad, or the
whole security situation to take down his family was more intense
than I realize. I wonder if both can be true.

"What's her name?" I ask the easiest thing.

"Bridget." He hands me the energy drink, just so he can parallel
park outside a grimy sidewalk. The rusting metal *Thirsty Goose* sign
hangs above a chipped black door, and a bearded bouncer scrolls on
his phone. He's seated on a stool. Bored and unbusy.

"I saw your birth certificate," I confess.

Donnelly unbuckles his seatbelt more slowly, but his smile catches
me off-guard. "Was this when you were snooping in my room?"

My lips rise. "Yeah. It was in a very tempting hiding spot."

"What about it?" He seems curious now too.

"I couldn't read your mom's last name. It was handwritten and
kinda illegible."

Realizations wash over him, and he nods a few times.

"You know her full name?" I ask, because for a minute there, I thought maybe he didn't.

"Yeah, I know it." Just as he opens his mouth, his phone rings over the car's speakers.

DAD

His father is calling.

7

Fuck, fuck, fuck.

"You don't have to answer it," Luna says, giving me an easy out. 'Cause I must look like I'm a second from tearing out the stereo system and chucking it out the window. It's how I feel. The desperate urge to remove my dad from the vicinity of Luna is violent within me, and it scares the shit outta me.

Pieces of me want him in my life after he stuck his neck out for me, after he acted more like a caring dad than a neglectful one. Yet, I'm still so cautious of him around her, and I can't turn it off.

It's all messed up, but dropping this call isn't an option. He's helping keep my cover with our family, and I need him, for better or worse.

"I'm gonna take it," I tell her. "Just don't say anything, alright?"

She nods vigorously.

In another world I could take the call outside the car or privately in a dirty piss-stained bathroom—but I can't leave Luna. If anyone recognizes her, it wouldn't be safe, and we've made it this far without a tail.

So I remove my phone from Bluetooth and answer the call against my ear. The best I've got at shielding Luna from his voice. "I can't talk long," I tell him.

"You around?" he asks casually.

"Around where?"

"The Rhino." He must be bartending tonight.

"Nah, I'm not near South Philly. You working?"

"Yup." I hear the ping of billiard balls in the background. "So Kieve and Shane stopped by earlier. Ollie's sons. They've been asking about your relationship to the Hales. I've been telling 'em you're just using that girl, that it'll come out in the public you're dating at some point, but it's fake for you, not for her."

It's the lie he's supposed to spread around our family. I try to relax my strained shoulders. "What'd they say?" I ask him.

"They thought you were a piece of shit. For leading the girl on."

I go blank-faced. "You serious?"

"Don't take it too personally. They act like they've got morals, but Kieve's cheated on his wife about a dozen times in a year. He'd fuck a trashcan if it had a pair of legs."

I try to untighten my death-grip on the phone while I listen.

"Really," he says, "they think you're in bed with the side of the family who've just been locked up, and they like to disassociate the *ties that bind* whenever it benefits themselves."

I stare harder at the air vents, heat still blowing into the car. "And you don't do the same thing?" I ask.

"I didn't say that." Glass bottles clink over the line.

I take a breath. "Where do you think I stand in all of this, Dad?" I ask him, not exactly sure how he sees me right now. He knows I only went to the rowhouse to protect Luna. I didn't go to warn my family about the cops, but he's not aware that I'm the reason they were tipped off.

"You're standing on an island alone, and I'm the only one who's gonna make sure you don't drown. That's where I think you're at." More clinking glasses. "So when are you gonna introduce me to your girlfriend?"

Never. "We just started dating," I say, trying to sound casual and not protective. Luna picks herself out of a slouch, and our eyes meet in a moment of clarity.

We're dating.

What else would I call this trip to a dive bar in the middle of the night? It's not a casual outing of two friends. I'm taking her to Thirsty Goose with the implication that I might kiss her, might buy her a drink, might even fuck her later...*slow down.*

Fuck me. Navigating the start of a relationship better be the hardest part of one.

"So what?" he shoots back.

"It's too soon."

"Alright..." He draws out the word, not happy about the rejection, but then he says, "What about Loren Hale?"

I go rigid again. "What about him?"

"You gonna introduce me since you two are so buddy-buddy?" I catch notes of bitterness in his voice.

"You think that's a good idea?"

"Why not? You like him, don't you?"

"Barely," I lie, avoiding Luna for a second.

"Well, you're always hanging around him every time I call. I wanna meet the man who's in my son's life. You can make it happen, can't you?" He sounds more impatient than threatening. "It's coffee, for Christ's sake. I'm not asking to attend his father-in-law's funeral."

He heard about Greg's death then. News must've broken online.

"I gotta talk to him. I'll let you know."

"K. If you want my advice before you go, poke a hole in it."

"In what?"

"The condom. Nothing says a free ride in life like getting a Hale pregnant." At this, Luna's eyes have grown five-sizes too big, and I realize it's so quiet in this car and my dad is talking so fucking loudly that she can hear *everything.*

Fuuuck. I scrape my fingers through my hair. "That's not happening."

"Think about it."

"Nah, I'm good. I gotta go."

"See ya soon."

I hang up and immediately twist towards Luna. "What you heard—I'd *never* fucking do to you. Ever. *Ever.*"

Luna closes her lips that've fallen open. "It'sokayit'sokay," she slurs together, speaking quickly. She edges closer to touch my arm, and I can't contain how much what he said is devastating me. My chest rises and falls with heavy aggression, and I smear my palm down my agonized face.

She splays a calm hand on my thigh. "With the strength of Thebula, I compel you!"

I choke out a sudden laugh. Smiling. I'm smiling. Almost instantly. "What are you compelling me to do?"

"To feel better." She shrugs. "It's all I have."

I blink back more emotion. "It's a lot," I choke out, then clear my throat. "What he suggested, that's not who I am. I need you to know that."

"I know that," she says unwaveringly.

I nod a couple times, aching to cup her cheek and kiss her. But knowing my luck, this date will come to an abrupt halt before it can start if we don't get out of this fucking car. So I slip my phone in my pocket. "You ready, space babe? Your universe awaits."

"Ours," she corrects, opening the door. *Our universe.* My ruptured heart feels full.

LUNA HALE

Original Luna has many fake IDs. I discovered this fun fact after a quick search of my childhood bedroom tonight. I am Chani Hawkins. Age 23. With the hood of my hoodie concealing my hair and shadowing my face, I feel unassuming, like a specter in the night. Not like the Luna Hale, daughter of notorious sex addict and alcoholic. Girl who writes tentacle smut. Girl who was kidnapped.

The bouncer appraises my ID, barely giving it a second glance. He doesn't even ask for Donnelly's. "You two have fun." Our breaths smoke the air, but Donnelly really does seem impervious to the Philly cold. He's not shivering. He reaches above my head to hold the door open for me.

On our way inside, I ask, "Why didn't he card you?"

"I have *over twenty-one* tattooed on my neck. Didn't you see?" He's teasing me. I've only seen three stars inked behind his ear. No tattoos crawl up his neck or decorate his throat.

"Really, though," I say, hearing the thump of an old rock song before I scan the completely dead bar. Pink neon lights swirl around the ceiling rafters, and the wooden stools and tables are empty of all patrons—sober and drunk. The lone bartender is texting behind a row of clean beer taps. I ask Donnelly, "Do you know him or something?"

I worry Donnelly called ahead and shut down the bar for us.

Normally, this would present itself like an epic grand gesture of princess proportions, but the façade is more depressing than exciting to me. I'd rather risk my dangerous reality than live inside that kind of fantasy.

He slides his arm around my shoulders. "Don't recognize him. I used to barhop over here with Farrow. But it's been a while. They probably hired a new bouncer." He slides a stool out of the way, so we can stand at the bar. "I don't always get carded anymore. Comes with looking closer to twenty-nine than twenty-one."

"Oh," I realize. "And I look…"

"Cute," he smirks.

"Cute and young," I sing-song.

He grins over at me, then up-nods to the bartender. "Hey, man, can we get two vodka Fizzes." The bartender mimes an *okay*, then begins pouring liquor and soda together.

"You want to do shots with me?" I ask him.

Donnelly leans sexily on the bar. "Watcha have in mind? Irish car bomb?"

I crinkle my nose. "I don't like stouts." A car bomb involves dropping a shot of whiskey and Irish cream into a dark-colored beer. Eliot would drink them more if they weren't so heavy, and he's the sole reason why I've tried them on occasion.

"Jager bomb?"

I think on it.

"Blowjob?" he asks.

"Never had one."

He grins.

I blush, my smile pulling so hard at my face. "You like blowjobs?"

"Love giving head." He says it so casually, and his grin expands even wider. "Or did you wanna know if I like the shot?"

"Both," I say, more unabashed.

"It's not my favorite shot." He pauses. "I heard the green ones are the best."

"We must investigate then. For science. Only green shots."

Donnelly's overwhelmed expression appears like a high-speeding train, whizzing on by so quickly that I wonder if my eyes were playing tricks on me. "You heard the alien?" he asks the bartender, who's already sliding the vodka Fizzes to us. "Two green shots. Whatever you can make."

Bartender says, "Cool. Keep the tab open?"

Before I can unzip my backpack, Donnelly has already slid his card across the damp, sticky surface. This is a date. It's not even a question now.

Warmth bathes my body, and my cheek muscles start to sting from smiling so much. If the bartender recognizes Donnelly's name on the credit card or his face from the news, he doesn't let on. "Sit wherever you like. I'll bring the shots to you."

That's how we find ourselves in the back corner booth, sitting side by side. Someone sloppily carved *Jordyn + Cole* with a heart in the wood. Most of the etchings are just names and dates.

I plop my backpack beside me and then pick up the drink, carbonation bubbling the surface. "It all started with Fizzle." I watch Donnelly clutch the glass, but he waits to sip too. "My family's legacy, the wealth. Without it, my mom's sex addiction wouldn't have even mattered to the public." The Calloways went from being faceless heiresses behind the soda conglomerate to internationally recognized, all because of one juicy scandal. "This was my grandfather's brainchild."

Donnelly raises his glass. "To Greg?"

"To Fizzle," I say. "It's the foundation of this reality. Without its existence, we'd be living in an alternate universe more shocking than Bizarro World. And…" I cling to his gaze that never shies from me. "I like my here and now."

Donnelly clinks my glass with his. "Me too." He grins into his swig of vodka soda.

I take a hearty sip, the liquor sharp down my throat. He could so easily be wishing and longing and *pleading* for OG Luna, for the past that was pulverized with her, but he's been nothing but happy to experience this new beginning with me.

My heart swells ten-times too big, and this pressure inside my ribcage is new. It's not anxiety or the weight of a burden. It's a rush of going from empty to being filled to the brim. I could gorge myself on love and be satiated for all-time just being in his presence.

Donnelly looks to me. "So you're fully enrolled in college now? Miss Ivy League." His bicep is lounging across the booth behind me, his muscle naturally cut without even flexing. His closeness pricks the hairs on my neck in a sensitive, yearning manner, and I somewhat control my breathing pattern.

"Uh-huh. I start after the holidays." He likely already knows these details, being security. It'll be different for me, since I don't even remember taking college courses like OG Luna. "You know I wouldn't have gotten into Penn if it wasn't for my last name."

"Use what you're given. Nothing wrong with that."

I gulp more alcohol and cup my hands around the cold glass. "Have you ever thought about going?"

"To college?" When I nod, he shakes his head. "I feel like I already went. Experienced everything at Yale that I'd want to, except I didn't earn the fancy degree."

I eye the beautiful ink along his other arm, a lion with a lush mane, a skeleton doing a jig, a tiny raven in the palm of a hand. "Would you ever tattoo full-time?"

He's quick to shake his head again. "I like security work." It's all he says before asking, "You know what you wanna do? After college?"

"Not really."

"What about your writing?"

I'm not good enough, I want to say, but the words sit like thick dried crackers in my mouth. "I don't know if it's worth it."

Donnelly puts a cigarette between his lips. "Worth what?" he asks, lighting the cig and blowing smoke away from me.

"The public condemnation," I mention. "It'll be a *thing*. Everyone will have something to say about what I write, how well I write. I apparently already went through it once, and it'd be on an even larger scale if I tried to put an actual *book* out there. Plus, everything I've written doesn't really have an end. It's the hardest part, to *close* something that I just want to live forever."

Donnelly skims my features, then nods. "I get it. I'd be sad if the Thebulan saga ever stopped."

I smile. "Like cry in your sleep sad?"

"Wet bed pillows, every night." He smiles back, this one brightening his blue eyes.

"You can wet my bed pillows," I offer.

He drinks me in. "Girl, I'll wet more than your bed pillows."

I grin, and not long after, the bartender delivers four lime-green shots. Donnelly sips it first, then nods to me like it's drinkable. Then we down one apiece.

Oh *wow*. My cheeks pucker. "Tastes like a lemon-lime Jolly Rancher."

"It's vodka though. Good news, the bartender isn't trying to kill us."

I laugh and then I throw back the second shot. Donnelly barely sips his second as we start chatting about the sci-fi genre and TV shows like Beneath a Strong Sentiment and Battlestar Galactica. Either my buzz begins to take hold or simply being with Donnelly makes me feel floaty, but I am a sprightly, happy being.

I barely notice more people slipping into Thirsty Goose and shedding winter jackets and scarves. Soon, more tables are occupied by thirtysomethings, and men are shoulder-to-shoulder at the bar. No one seems to pay attention to us any more than I acknowledge them, but I yank at the strings of my hoodie, wondering if that'll change.

"We may need a better disguise," I say.

He takes a long drag. "What've you got in your bag?" he asks, and smoke leaves his lips while he surveys the rowdier group near the frosty windows. They're arguing about football, yelling over one another just to shout, "fuck the Cowboys," and then slamming back beers. Donnelly smiles like it's a familiar scent in the nightlife air.

I'm digging through my backpack, pushing aside the diary. "Lots of highlighters." I put a handful on the table. "...and this." A jar of silver glitter, but the type found in craft stores, used for paintings and school projects, not makeup. "It must've been something she packed." I didn't really empty the contents of the backpack tonight, just added things I wanted.

I guess I never want to erase Original Luna. She's not only in the diary, but she's still within me. Somewhere.

Donnelly snuffs the cigarette in the empty shot glass. Then he squints to read the jar's label. "*Safe for skin unless it causes irritation.*" He's twisting off the lid, then sniffs it. "It'll do."

"Will you do me?" I ask while tugging off my hoodie. Only in a lime-green tank top, no bra.

Donnelly has turned to me, his foot on the booth's seat, elbow on his knee as he dips his fingers in the glitter. "I'll do you." His eyes lift to mine. "Carefully." His deep voice is more hushed, and his glittered fingers slide along my flushed cheek in a slow, sensual stroke. "Gently."

I can't look away from him. My breath shallows, and I nearly tremble as he thumbs glitter against my face. "What if I don't want it gently?" I whisper.

Donnelly stares into me, and I wish my mind-reading powers kicked in right *now.* Without much pause, he draws glitter lines across the tops of my breasts, then ascends to my collar, tracing the bone that juts out. And then higher, to the tender nape of my neck. I shudder, almost letting out a moan.

He breathes, "Seems like you love gentle."

"Then why do I fantasize about you grabbing me?" I ask and scoop out glitter from the jar. "Clutching me. Holding me. Hard." I skate my glittery fingertips slowly down one side of his face. His blue eyes sink so deep into me, I'd almost believe this is the definition of making love if someone told me. "Not unkindly," I say, and he shuts his eyes as I smear glitter over the lids, then down, closer to his lips. "But possessively. Like you're the only one who's ever supposed to touch me."

He opens his eyes onto mine.

I've never wanted *anyone* to kiss me as much as I want Donnelly to, as far as I can remember. My heart rate speeds out of control—excitement it'll happen and fear that it won't are rolled into one nervous pit in my stomach.

His thumb brushes my eyebrows, then the bridge of my nose, painting me with glitter, and for a second, my aching breath is the only sound I hear.

Until he whispers, "You ever feel like you're falling, it'll be in my arms." He speaks against the pit of my ear. "I belong *inside* you." His fingers claw up into my hair, and our gazes devour before he crushes his lips against mine. I bow into him, my mind bursting with light. My glittery palms streak down his neck.

He's kissing me. My body thrums. *He's making out with me.* Not gently, not carefully, but *passionately*, as if he's giving me his last breaths of oxygen so I'll survive the next minute, the next second with him.

Holy shit.

Our tongues wrestle, and my hips grind forward. I forget we're in a public bar. I forget everything except how much I love his lips on my lips and his aggressive clutch of my face. He's not letting go. He won't let go. I'm safe, protected, *loved.*

I don't know why these sentiments cocoon me with warmth and arousal the most, but they do. And a chant echoes in my head: *More, more, more.*

Give me more of Donnelly.

As my hands roam, I'm smearing glitter all over him. On his black shirt. Underneath his tee and on his abs, down his strong biceps. Likewise, he must be coating my cheeks, my hair, my black hoodie. We're a shimmery, scorching mess, and I couldn't care less who sees.

I just want to be wrapped up in him. He bears his weight on me, and my back naturally finds the booth's seat. He's kissing me into a supine position, and with his hands on my cheeks, with his body hovering on top of mine, I feel shielded by him. Protected from everyone and anything.

Donnelly interlaces my fingers with his and pins my hands above my head.

"Get a room!" a guy yells.

Donnelly breaks our hot and heavy kisses, then shouts back, "You offering yours?" It's a smooth wisecrack to a jeer. His grin even calms me, more so when he pulls me up against his chest. His hand on the small of my back, as though sheltering me from a possible storm. I'm facing his body and the wall, not the bar patrons, so no one else can see my face but Donnelly.

"Yeah, fuck no!" the guy shouts, not too hostile.

Donnelly laughs and tugs me on his lap. I'm straddling him. He's still hard, but he's doing his best to concentrate on our surroundings behind me. *Must be the bodyguard in him.*

He lifts my hood over my head. *Am I being recognized?* I don't ask. Instead, I pull the corner of his tee and peek at his ink. A bold butterfly is tattooed on his abs, but the black moth underneath is more stunning, more vibrant.

"The moth is more striking somehow," I tell him.

"It's the shading." He sips the last of his vodka soda and watches me trace the moth.

"It could be your true gift," I whisper. "You have a way of making the darkness emerge into light." I shrug. "It's *Star Wars* stuff."

He cups my cheek, and an overwhelmed look flickers in and out of his eyes again.

My temple throbs, like a prick at my brain. I stare into him, but I can't see... "Have I...have I said that before?" *I don't remember.* "Never mind." I'm scared because I really can't tell, but I glance at the kyber crystal around my neck. Likely, I did tell him. It makes the most sense.

"Love your *Star Wars* thoughts, space babe. You want my last shot?" He's good at lightening the air and making my cavernous brain waves feel more poignant rather than heavy. I think I love him for that.

I shake away remnants of a nagging feeling. "You don't want it?"

"Nah, too sour for me. Plus, I gotta drive." He hands me the shot glass.

I'm not ready to go, but he's also not rushing to leave either. I down the shot, the liquor burning my throat. He lights another cigarette. We pass it back and forth, taking drags and laughing as I attempt to make a smoke ring. He does a better job, and I stick my finger in the hole of his.

He grins. "Girl just desecrated my ring."

"Guy is thinking about desecrating mine," I throw out there, my cheeks heating.

Donnelly looks me over, clearly *considering,* clearly tempted. He hardens even more beneath me, and I instinctually grind forward. His low groan sticks to his throat. He clutches the side of my face, glitter shining across most of his skin. "*Luna.*"

"Donnelly." I ache.

"I can't hurt you."

"I'm not asking you to hurt me." I say it so quietly, I doubt he hears.

He plants a kiss against my temple, my cheek, my lips. I feel floaty again. Despite the unknown of where tonight will lead, trust feels inherent with him.

I yank at the hoodie strings, and the fabric swallows my face, only my nose poking out.

He kisses the tip.

I can't stop smiling, especially as he places his hands on the top of my head. "You recharging your galactic batteries or what?"

"Uh-huh," I mumble. "Powering up in the darkness. Being on Earth for so long drains me. Unless I have human contact."

"This isn't doing it for you?" He loosens the hoodie's strings, and the hood opens so I can see Donnelly's confused face.

I'm literally on his lap. He's hard beneath me. Those two facts should mean, *yes, human contact has been met.* But it feels like part way. I'm not where I used to be with him before the amnesia, and I want to go the full distance and then some.

"It's not enough," I whisper. "I'm a part of a greedy species."

"Think humans are right there with you. 'Cause I know what you mean." He caresses my cheek, and I could sink my whole face into his palm. I do actually lean into him, my buzz whirling my head. It loosens my muscles, and I curve my arms around his neck.

My smile explodes when he picks me up, his hands on my ass. I clutch him while he hops out of the booth, my legs wrapped around his waist. I don't want to let go, but we're in the middle of the bar—people might be watching. Maybe I should?

So I slide down him, my feet on the ground, and I swear his lips falter into a frown. Did he want me to stay attached to him?

Before I can make sense of this, he clasps my hand, leading me to the barstools. He wedges between two beer drinkers, but he's careful to pull me in front of him, his large hands resting on my hips. My pulse spikes at his touch, and I feel the return of my unrestrained smile.

Our drinks have run dry, so he orders more. Water for him, another vodka Fizz for me. And then Donnelly convinces the bartender to play Journey.

"Top-tier all-time American rock," he tells me as soon as "Lights" plays over the speakers.

The music entrances me, and I forget about the alcohol, abandoning it on the counter. Donnelly twirls me in a circle. My heart soars, and when he dips me, I latch solely to the sexiest gaze alive, one that consumes every ounce of me.

Once he releases his hold on me, he turns to grab our drinks. I take several steps backward, observing him like he truly is another species on a foreign planet.

He rakes a hand through his hair, the little hoop earring glinting in the pink neon light of the bar. And he speaks to the bartender, makes a gesture like *thank you*, then rotates to me with our drinks.

I've backed up into our table.

He's a man. A handsome, sexy, soulful, lighthearted *man*.

Have I ever been with a man like him before?

I don't know. *I don't know.* Does it even matter if I have? He's the only one I really want.

His stride towards me tilts my world on its axis, and I understand the phrase "weak at the knees" because of him, because my limbs want to turn to putty in his hands, because the mere thought of him touching me unbalances my physical hold on this universe.

I place my palms on the table, the only reason I don't wobble.

He faces me, then curves an arm around my frame—just to set the drinks behind me on the table. His musk is a heady fragrance swirling around my brain. The song he requested still blares over the drunken chatter, and he yells over the noise, "You like it?!"

I nod repeatedly. *I like you.* "It's a good one!" My heart pounds rapidly, and these urges slam at my body.

Be bold.

Be who you are.

Do what you want.

Who cares what anyone thinks?

No more wavering, I jump into his arms like one of the corny dance moves we did in the privacy of his bedroom. Donnelly catches me with the hottest grin, and my entire being *sings* as he whirls me in a circle. I raise my arms in the air, leaning back.

Then I fly forward, my hair sheltering us.

He laughs and sings against my lips, our foreheads nearly pressed together. I sing back, more off-key, and hold his neck. I rock my hips to the beat. He meets my rhythm with his own.

We're the only ones dancing in a crowded bar. People are staring. They might even be snapping pics of us, and he doesn't care about anyone. Except for me.

It is one of the most powerful sensations. To be set utterly and totally free.

He's kissing me. I could dance and kiss and love him for longer than a lifetime. I wonder if he already knows that.

We don't end when the music switches. We keep going. We're two glittery disco balls. Refracting light which pierces in every direction.

And as we grow sweaty, as I bounce on him, as he holds me—the songs change and the melody of one suddenly, sharply, grabs me. By the throat.

I can't breathe.

This song. "Baba O'Riley" by the Who. I know it. I've known it since I was a kid, but I *feel* it like a boiling wave rushing over me. But…it's cold. There are Christmas lights blinking in a rustic bar. It's dark except for Donnelly's face.

His hands.

He's holding me. *Literally.* He's holding me right now, but I think he was holding me then too. Is it…can it be…a memory? No, it can't be. It's almost Christmas now. It's too big of a coincidence. Isn't it?

"You alright?" Donnelly's voice sounds far away. "Talk to me. Babe."

It jolts me, hearing him call me *babe* without the *space* attached. "Huh?"

He's stopped dancing, stopped moving. He simply holds my ass so I'm clung to his chest. My hands are death-gripping his shoulders. Oh no. I remove my claws and see half-moon nail indents in his skin.

"Sorry," I choke out and try to capture my breath.

He shakes his head like *sorry* isn't necessary. "You alright? You blanked out." I think I scared him.

I'm sorry. I don't say it again. I just tell him, "I'm okay."

He wipes my forehead, and I realize I'm cold and clammy. "Let's get you some water—" he starts.

"Nice thong, slut!" a guy hollers. My green thong is riding high on my hips, and my black sweatpants are riding lower. Everything happens so fast. Before Donnelly can reply, I sense a stranger's hand reaching for me—to maybe grab and snap my thong.

Donnelly sets me on my feet and pushes me behind him, but one hand stays in mine. With his other, he shoves an athletic guy's chest and says, "Get *the fuck* outta here, man." He doesn't wait for the guy's response. He guides me to the bar, and his lips dip to my ear. "We're closing out. Gotta go."

I nod, understanding. It's not safe here anymore, and it has nothing to do with me being Luna Hale, American royalty.

One quick peek back, and yep, the guy is tracking us to the bar. He wears a dark green Eagles jersey, knit beanie, and a snide drunken smile, his brown eyes a little glazed.

"Hey!!" he yells at Donnelly. "She's asking for it, man!"

Donnelly is on an *ignore* setting. His hands are rooted to my shoulders, and he ensures my back is not to this asshole. Towering over me, Donnelly shouts to the bartender, "I need to close out!"

Bartender nods.

"Hey, I'm talking to you!" Drunk Guy sounds so close, and with another glance, I realize his shoulder has bumped into Donnelly's back.

"You don't say?" Donnelly feigns confusion. "Been thinking you were just speaking to the beer taps. Making enemies with the Yuengling." He grabs his credit card off the sticky surface. "Thanks," he says to the bartender, then rotates me towards the door. He's walking me out, but he whispers in my ear, "Go to the car. Lock yourself inside." He's slipping the keys in my palm.

I frown. "But—"

"I gotta grab your backpack."

Oh *fuck*. I didn't even realize I left it in our booth. *My diary*. What if someone steals my diary?! "I'll go with you—"

"Walk away, pussy!" Drunk Guy yells.

Someone else shouts, "Shut up, man!"

"You shut up!" Drunk Guy spits and continues trailing us.

I reach the door, but Drunk Guy is a few feet behind Donnelly. "Hey!!" he shouts more angrily. "I'm talking to you! Take control of your slut, man!"

Donnelly opens the door for me, and I see the tic of his jaw muscle, the narrowing of his usually calm blue eyes. He whispers, "Wait for me in the car."

I nod and inch out into the cold. The bouncer glances curiously between me and Donnelly but says nothing. Against better judgment,

I wedge my foot in the door right as Donnelly spins around on the asshole, and I watch.

"Shut *the fuck* up, man," Donnelly sneers and shoulder-bumps him on his route to our booth. I'm wishing more for Donnelly to return to me than I'm wishing for my backpack. As he rummages around the booth, Drunk Guy rears up behind him.

"Donnelly!" I warn.

His head swings to me, and his eyes flare in concern. I distract him—no, no, *no*. Drunk Guy pushes Donnelly. To where his stomach crashes into the table. Then Donnelly twists around and throws a fist at Drunk Guy's face. In one blow, the asshole is stumbling into barstools with a mouthful of blood.

A few other dudes start clapping near the window. Donnelly is quick to reach beneath the table, grab my backpack, and jog out into the cold. The door clangs shut behind him.

He's sweeping me for signs of breakage.

"I'mokayI'mokay," I slur fast, hooking a finger in his belt loops. "Are you?"

He exhales. "I will be once we get out." Concern still rests against his eyes. He curves an arm around my shoulders, buries a kiss in my hair while we walk, and my lungs reinflate. He brings me to security's parallel-parked SUV. Once inside, I lock the doors.

He cranks up the heat. "Check to make sure everything's in there before we go."

Backpack on my lap, I unzip and scrounge around, easing at the sight of the sparkly hardcase binding. "Diary is here." *Not stolen.* A fist raps my window. "Ahh!" I scream and flinch.

Donnelly's arm has instinctively shot out across my body to protect me, but I'm safely locked inside the SUV.

But there is a guy. Right outside the car window.

This isn't the drunken asshole from Thirsty Goose.

"Luna?" the stranger calls, squinting at the dark tint of the windows. I imagine he only sees the outline of me. I see all of him.

Mid-twenties, brown hair long enough to peek out of a beanie, a dangling cross earring in his earlobe, a leather jacket on a tall build, scuffed Vans—I have no earthly clue who he is.

My heart rate accelerates. "Who...who is that?" I whisper to Donnelly.

"I dunno," he says, unbuckling.

"No, wait, don't go." I'm terrified. Only the car door separates me from this random person, and if he's acting like we're acquaintances, then there's a high probability that Original Luna knows him.

He's part of her past, and I kinda, sorta, *really* want him to stay there.

Donnelly hesitates.

"Luna?! It's me!" He knocks on the window again. "Tell your bodyguard I just want to say hi!"

"Let me ID him," Donnelly says, making up his mind.

It's the smart thing to do. The protective thing. The safe thing. So I just nod, but I grip the armrests, sitting pin-straight against the seat like I'm about to explode forward in a rollercoaster. Donnelly has been afraid of his past hurting us, and now it's my turn to fear mine.

9

PAUL DONNELLY

This must be the night of the living assholes.
Dodged one in the bar only to be met with one outside, but this
one—this one—is worse. I've met my share of drunk fucks in dive
bars. Been one, probably. But I haven't met that many guys claiming
to be friendly with the girl I just started dating.

Friendly? I grimace. I hope he is *just* a friend of hers. Maybe he
goes to Penn. Maybe he's no one. Maybe he's a loser.

I try not to slam my door shut.

Maybe he's *lying.*

With a lengthy stride, I come around the hood of the Range
Rover, and the guy careens away from her window.

He raises his hands, which means I must look pissed. Can't feel
bad about it. He is fucking up my date. "Hey," he says, "Luna knows
me."

"Does she?" I ask.

"Yeah," he snaps back like I'm being unreasonable.

How?

It wouldn't be the first time someone claimed to be one degree
from the famous ones. When, really, the most they've done is browse
their Instagram feed and leave comments on WAC Fanaticon forums.

He could just be a fan with a warped sense of reality.

And I shouldn't wish for that threat. But why am I? Why is that easier to deal with than confronting a possible ex? She's allowed to have past hookups. I have 'em.

But she can't remember any one-night stands or casual sex, and it makes me want to hoist a drawbridge, fortify the walls of her fortress, load cannons, feed the alligators in the moat.

I can't ask if these guys are decent. If they hurt her. If I should shove him in a brick wall.

Just gotta Hardy Boy this myself.

"Who are you exactly?" I ask.

Right as he opens his mouth, a blond guy calls out, "Noah! You coming?!" He's among a larger group of guys, all flashing their IDs to the Thirsty Goose bouncer. Noah must've pulled away from his friends when he saw Luna getting in the car. Then he knocked on her window.

"Yeah, in a sec! I'll meet you inside!" he calls back, and to me, he says, "Noah Perch." He stuffs his hands in his leather jacket. "Look, if you just let me talk to her, I can clear this up."

"You're her friend or what?"

"We're not strangers." He outstretches his arms without removing his fists from the unzipped jacket. "I met her here. We've hung out a couple times at this bar. Then the back of my car, if you know what I mean."

It stabs my insides, and acid rises in my throat. Luna once confessed that she snuck out to Thirsty Goose and spoke to guys. She left out the part where she had sex with them, but that's not something she had to advertise. And again, he could be lying.

"You sign an NDA?" I ask him.

"A what?" He's eyeing my face weirdly, and I remember the glitter stuck to my skin.

"Non-disclosure agreement."

"No, man, there was no security with her. You're the first body-guard I've ever seen in person, let alone talked to."

And a good or bad impulse seizes me, and I ride it out as I say, "I'm not security."

His brows furrow. "What?" He scrutinizes my face and the ink on my arms. "No, you're *that* guy. The ass-whatever." *Ass-Kicker.* The nickname the fans bestowed upon me during the FanCon tour days.

"This ass-whatever isn't wearing a radio." My gun is also safely stored in the guest room of the Hale House. "I'm not her bodyguard."

Confusion hasn't left his face, but he starts to push past me.

I catch his arm, stopping him.

"If you aren't her bodyguard, then get the hell out of my way," he says, as though he's entitled to Luna just 'cause they've met and *maybe* fooled around.

"She's not interested," I retort.

His eyes flash hot. "Says who?"

"Says *me*."

He laughs like I'm a joke. "You? You're *nobody*."

"Nah, I am someone." I look him dead in the eye. "I'm Luna's *boyfriend*."

We have a silent, unblinking stare-off for a solid minute. Not gonna lie, if this were a dick measuring contest, I'd win. He seems small inside, outside, all the sides.

He blinks first. "No way."

Is it really that hard to believe?

He chokes out a laugh. "She's not the relationship type. But you'd know that, if you knew her at all."

I'm done with him. "Stay away from her." It's a simple threat that catches him off-guard. As I make my way to the driver's side, he gulps surprised air in his lungs.

And he shouts after me, "No way would she date the guy whose family kidnapped her! That's fucked up on so many levels, man! You shouldn't even be around her!"

It pierces my ears, scrapes against my brain, and I cage breath. *That's not true. We love each other.* I slam my door once I'm inside the Range Rover, and I start the car in near silence.

Only when I peel onto the road, do I look over at Luna, and her widened eyes scare the shit outta me. "Luna? You good?" *Please be good.*

She hugs her backpack. "Were you just marking your territory, or do you really want to be my boyfriend?"

She heard everything then.

I exhale a breath and fly through green lights. "I was definitely marking my territory, and I also wanna be your boyfriend." I try to hold her gaze, too eager for her response.

And ever so slowly, her lips hoist in the cutest smile. "I guess that makes me your girlfriend."

I grin back. "Looks like it." I've been hanging on to this goal post for dear life, and I just flew through it. Confetti cannons, stadiums of applause, champagne spewing in the air, I hear and see it all in my head, and my grin widens. I have the girl.

Relief follows the elation. *She's mine.* I take another big breath. One goal down. Gotta create more.

Goal: *keep your girlfriend happy.*

I glance at Luna. She's smiling, but it flickers in and out.

Tension still wraps around us. I just confronted a possible dickwad ex-hookup of hers. Noah Perch. The fact is a ticking bomb in the backseat, and by the way she fiddles with the AC and radio, I get the sense she's not ready to talk about it. The thing about starting a relationship when I've never been in one is trying to make it last.

10

PAUL DONNELLY

It's 4 a.m.—and after sneaking back inside her parents' house, we split to take showers in our separate bathrooms with the promise to meet for a late-night bite in the kitchen.

I beat her here first.

Not switching on the lights, I open the fridge, and the blue glow illuminates the warm, homey, lived-in space. Hardwoods are scratched from dogs and time. Cereal boxes are left out. Bruised apples slowly rot in a fruit bowl.

No glitz and glam like the Cobalt Estate.

I can't believe just how much I love it here, and I think it has more to do with her than anything else.

Remnants of her happy childhood exist all around me. The messy fingerpaint artwork of an alien abduction, hung above the breakfast table and signed *Queen of Thebula*. The Hale family pics stuck with superhero magnets to the freezer door. Luna makes goofy faces in most of the photos.

I smile and reach in the fridge, collecting a couple water bottles. I hear the squeak of floorboards and swing my head towards the door.

Luna flashes the Vulcan salute, her light brown hair wet on her shoulders. She's only wearing a black cotton dress with spaghetti straps, more like a slip. It teases my gaze to her exposed thighs.

Goddamn. Blood dives straight down to my cock, and I force my eyes up to hers.

She's blushing.

I return her greeting with the *I love you* hand sign. "Sparkle on, Hale." Glitter shimmers on her cheeks and in her damp hair. Scrubbing did nothing to remove the power of the craft supply for me either.

She smiles, a softer one, and her gaze travels over me. "I knew I'd find you in the light."

I'm standing in the blue glow of the open fridge. My chest rises. So much about our date tonight has spun me like a carnival ride to the past with her, and I'd jump on a whirling turntable a thousand times over.

Spin me till I die.

A grin edges across my mouth. "Girl, stop making me blush." I kick the fridge closed and see her smile grow.

After she gathers pretzels and peanut butter from the pantry, she hops on the counter beside the stove. She's struggling to open the jar.

I edge closer, and she naturally spreads her legs for me. *Fuck.* What's that cliché saying? A moth to a flame? Yeah, I'm the moth, and my hand slides against her soft thigh as I fit in the space between them. Her lips part in a breathy noise.

I flex to restrain a massive hard-on, and I thumb the fine lines of the galaxy tattoo on her inner thigh. My ears pick up her tiny moan caught in her throat. She looks down at my bulge. I'm only wearing Farrow's drawstring pants, the fabric thin enough to see the outline of my hardening cock.

Reddened flush crawls up her neck, and she tries to focus on opening the peanut butter.

"Switch," I say, my voice husky with arousal, but I exchange the water bottle for the jar of crunchy Peter Pan. "Is your fam not fans of Jif or are they just obsessed with the little guy in green tights?"

Luna has gathered water in her cheeks like a chipmunk storing nuts, and she almost spits it out in a laugh. After swallowing, she says, "Life's mysteries. What came first? My parents' love of Peter Pan or their love of the peanut butter brand? You know...this is the first time I've ever thought about it."

"Really? I'm shocked." I easily undo the lid with one twist. "I woulda thought peanut butter ideologies would rank pretty high for you."

"Jelly surpassed it." She caps her water, only to open the bag of pretzels.

"Smucker's or Welch's?"

"Smucker's," she sing-songs.

I cup her cheek. "I knew I loved you."

The heat of her flushed face warms my palm. She munches on a pretzel stick, then dips another in the peanut butter. "Can I ask you something?" Her voice is quieter.

"Anything." I promise without thinking it through.

"Have we done that before? What we did tonight?" Her amber eyes sparkle with anticipation, but they're also edged with darker confusion.

What we did tonight.

"We've never been alone together at a bar," I say, wanting to clear this haze for Luna if she's asking me to. "We've never kissed in public like that. I've never bought you shots when it was just you and me." I pause. "But we have talked about doing these things together. Going to bars. Drinking green shots."

"Only the green ones?" she asks.

My pulse skips, and I look into her, puzzled. "Do you remember?"

"No, but I could tell you were overwhelmed by it. I didn't know why."

Guess I didn't keep my shit totally intact back there. I almost couldn't believe we were doing the things we imagined doing together. Somehow, she led us to Thirsty Goose, to drinking green shots, to dancing in the middle of the bar (that might've been more *me*), but we're living the fiction that she would've written about us.

Our story is *real.*

Destiny. She's a beautiful bitch, and I'd love her more if she didn't try to fuck us at every corner.

I exhale slowly. "It's been an overwhelming, top-tier sort of night." I give her a slow once-over. "One I don't want to forget."

Her lips rise. "Me either. And hopefully I won't this time."

"You won't," I breathe. Nothing bad is happening to her again. I will throw myself in front of her before it does.

She stares past me, deeper in thought. "I...did have a strange feeling when we were dancing. Like we've done it before. It's when I stopped moving." Probably when she broke out in a cold sweat. She cracks a pretzel in half. "But it was probably nothing."

I frown. "We *have* danced like that before," I tell her.

"But just in our rooms?"

"No, one time we were at a pub. In Scotland. We weren't alone though. Your family and other bodyguards were around."

"Was it during Christmastime?"

"Pretty close to it, yeah."

Her brows hoist. "Was that band playing?"

"The Who?"

She nods.

I nod faster back. "Yeah. It was the same song we heard tonight."

Her eyes begin to well, but she shakes her head before I can fully embrace the moment as the return of a memory. "It's like it's *almost* there, Donnelly. Like I can catch glimpses of the picture through the fog, but it disappears before I can really understand it."

"It's a step forward," I say. "That's good news, Luna, no matter how small. And it's a *happy* memory."

She's recollecting more than just moments from the night she was kidnapped. I know she's been picturing the room where they handcuffed her, and I've been worried all she'd come to remember is that horrific fucking night.

It's the one thing I wish she'd always forget.

She seems more disturbed by the whole ordeal, her face

scrunching. "What if that's all I can ever see? Just these *cloudy* moments? What if they never feel real and they never look vivid? It's *taunting*. I wonder if it'd be better to see nothing at all." Tears prick her eyes, but she sniffs hard, keeping waterworks at bay, and she stabs the peanut butter with the pretzel stick. "A part of me still wants the full picture, the good and the bad and *not* the blurry."

"What about your diary?" I ask her. "You could've written about Scotland." I think about the confrontation with Noah Perch. "You could've written about your hookups…" I trail off at the sight of her wince. "It's alright if you did—"

"I don't want to read about it," Luna admits, her voice rising with short breaths. "I don't want to read about how I slept with that guy in the back of his car. I don't even want to read about how I first met you."

It punches me in the gut. "Why not?"

"Because *I* met you in a hospital, and reading about a moment I forgot might change how I see you now. I don't want it to shade my perception of you." Her voice falls hushed. "It's why I've been struggling to read past the first page. It starts with a moment where I *clearly* was attracted to you at my brother's townhouse, and I wrote it so…viscerally."

I strain my ears to catch that word. "Is that a bad thing?"

She shrugs. "I thought the diary would be more like a Q&A. I could ask it questions like, *Did I love you at first sight?* Answer: *Yes.* Or…*Have I ever had a threesome?* Answer: *No.* I should've realized I'd be waist-deep in emotions, insecurities, joys, and fears. But it's like experiencing these things *without* being the one to experience them. It makes me…"

"Sad?" I ask, 'cause she looks distraught.

Luna nods. "I love having my opinions about the past. I love having this *gigantic* piece of myself I never thought I'd find. It's comforting, in a way, knowing it exists. I just wish I could read the portions with the answers and not wade through all the parts I'd rather skip for now."

I rub her thighs, more consolingly. I can imagine it'd be tough to read emotional passages about the moments you've forgotten. It might even backtrack her to feelings she's already dealt with. Jealousy. Anger. Depression.

But I'm not a therapist or psychologist.

I should be offering Dr. Raven's services as a solution, but I can't mention the lady without feeling like she'll bury me.

"What about having someone else read it front-to-back?" I ask her. "You can ask them the questions you want answered without having to read the diary yourself. That way it won't shape your own experiences."

Luna brightens. "It'd be like…a guardian of my memories."

I smile as her hope resurges. "And it'd have to be someone you trust a hundred percent."

Luna stares right into me.

Breath snags in my lungs. "It can't be me." Every word is a weight in my body. *It can't be me.* I hate every fucking syllable, every letter, the mere sound of each one strung together.

Her frown hurts to see. She glances at the bag of pretzels. "That's okay…I just really trust you, so you were the first person I thought of."

"It's not that I don't wanna be that person for you," I express. "I'd volunteer to be your white knight…your human hero, any day of the week. Really, I feel homicidal knowing you'll write in another name for the job and it won't be mine. Maybe I should go stab a guy. What's his name? Phone number? Social security?"

Luna smiles a little. "Why can't it be you, Donnelly? You make the most sense. We're dating. You're my boyfriend—"

"I know," I interject, "but…" I almost yield and say *I'll do it*—it's harder to say I can't. But the truth is, it'd kill me to read her diary. A knot is in my throat, and I swallow hard before saying, "I don't know if I'd survive reading it."

Luna seems more understanding.

But I add, "I'd love to read about your happiness, but it's a *diary* and I know your pain is in there—and I can't read about it. It'll tear me up in ways I'm not sure I can handle right now." I feel like a dick even saying it—like I should be *more* for her.

Disappointing Luna feels inevitable, and I'm terrified this is the moment where she sees I'm not the Superman of her dreams. Though she's never asked me to be Clark Kent.

Still, I say, "You can scratch off the *hero* part if you want. I can just be your human."

She shakes her head vigorously. "You've done a lot for me this past month, and I don't even know everything you've done for me the past three years. This doesn't change that."

"I should be able to do this for you too." It's eating me up that I'm not even trying. Maybe I should *try*.

Before I offer, she says, "I get it. I think if our positions were reversed, I wouldn't be able to read your diary either. It'd hurt too much." She reaches up and slips a pretzel stick behind my ear. Her soft smile eases the tension in my ribs.

I let out a tight breath. "So which lucky duck are you choosing to be your memory guardian?" My best guess will be Maximoff, considering she calls him her *memory guide* already.

"I'm gonna think on it," she muses with a nod.

I grin. "I love a thinker."

Her smile returns. "My brain waves turn you on?"

"Straight to my cock."

Her eyes drop again, and her cheeks go rosy. Like the crank of a lever, the deep subject subsides into something much hotter.

Luna opens her legs even wider, the invitation too clear.

I have a hand on her hips, and with my other, I dip my fingers in the peanut butter and draw a heart against the nape of her neck.

Her body already starts trembling. A groan wrestles in my throat. Natural instincts are screaming to push into Luna. *Fuck her senseless.*

At the dive bar, she said she's not looking for gentle, but for fuck's sake, she's a *virgin* in her mind. She's more eighteen in her head than twenty-one, and how big of a bastard am I if I just forget about that and go at her like it's not her first time?

"Donnelly." Her aching plea quiets my mind.

"Open your mouth," I murmur.

She obeys, a smile twinkling in her eyes, and I make her suck peanut butter residue off my two fingers. The sensation fists me, squeezes me, strokes me. Her pink lips are suctioning around my index and middle fingers, and I have a handful of her hair.

I pop them out of her mouth, then put them in mine. Her breath shortens while she watches me slide my fingers between my lips. After my hands are clean, I clutch her cheek and dip my head towards her neck. Her breath hitches right as I lick and suck the peanut butter heart off her skin. I edge closer to Luna and feel the heat of her pussy up against my erection.

She shudders, and both of us naturally grind forward. I suck harder.

"*Donnelly*," she moans. The tiny whimpering noises she makes, her vibrating thighs—it's lighting me on fire. *Fuck me.*

Her neck isn't the only thing I'm dying to taste. God, give me her pussy. I need it.

I hold the back of her neck, and she's splatting a dollop of peanut butter on my chest. Her eyes stay pinned to mine while her tongue slowly, agonizingly, trails up my flesh.

This…this is killing me. Under *any* past circumstance, I probably would've already shoved my cock inside of her. The fact that I'm not is the biggest sign that miracles do exist, if I do say so. And the hesitation isn't even because we're in her parents' kitchen.

Though when she's done licking me, she whispers, "I could meet you back in the guest room."

"Or we could stay down here."

Disappointment sinks her shoulders.

I'm not trying to reject her. I squeeze her thighs. "I'm not convinced your dad doesn't have nanny cams set up to spy on me."

"Oh. That's a real possibility," she says quietly. "But you'd stay here?"

"I'm not rushing to leave," I breathe.

Her eyes flit around me, and she bites the corner of her lip. "What would you do to OG Luna right now?"

I'd already be fucking you. Our breaths sound in sync, timed, like we're already making love against the cupboards. I slip my hands back up her thighs, feeling her cotton panties. "I'll show you." I pull her off the counter, and her smile explodes as I carry her, as her legs wrap around me.

When I reach the breakfast table, I drop her feet to the floor and weld her back to my chest. I walk her closer to the table. She's breathing incredibly hard, and I whisper in her ear, "You can say stop."

"I don't want it to stop."

Yeah. "We have that in common." I take her hands in mine and outstretch her arms across the surface of the table. I'm bent over her thin body, her ass digging into my cock, and I keep hold of her hands for a stationary, sweltering moment. I'm burning the fuck up, especially as she breathes like we're already having sex.

Jesus.

My lips are against her ear again. "You feel how hard I am?"

"Uh-huh," she rasps.

"I'm only hard like this for you, *because* of you," I breathe. "You've been bad, you know why?"

She squirms, more so in pleasure. "Why?"

"You missed your daily fucking." I let go of one hand and lift her black dress, exposing her ass. I hook my finger through the side of her bright yellow thong and tug it upward. She writhes against the table, against my cock, and I rock forward, the fabric of my pants separating me from the bigger desire. Her wet, soaked pussy, that warmth, *fuck*.

"Wha-what happens," she stammers, out of breath, "if I miss it?"

I slide my leg between her thighs, breaking her apart, and my lips find her ear. "Then we make it up during your nightly fucking."

When she turns her head, I kiss her deeper, and my pulse runs so hot. In raw instinct, I arch into Luna. She pulls away from my lips to catch her breath.

Her body tries to skate forward on the table with my thrusts, but I hold her hands again. Her dress is bunched up around her waist, and her bare ass with the thong is teasing the fuck out of me. I want skin-on-skin. To feel her heat.

"Fuck me," she cries. "*Please.*"

I go as far as tugging down my pants, stepping out of 'em, freeing my erection. But I don't take off her thong. Instead, I reach down and push aside the cotton fabric, just to run my fingers between her wet folds.

Her breath hitches. "Oh my God." Her elbows slacken against the table. She becomes a puddle of pleasure as I circle her clit, as I slip my fingers inside her, and watching her quake is enough to unearth a groan from my chest.

My muscles pull taut, searing. When I take out my fingers, I flex forward, sliding my length against her pussy. Not going inside. The thong is still in the way.

"*Please*," Luna begs, her knees nearly buckling. "I need you. *I need you.*"

I need her, but I resist pushing inside. It's torturing me and her. I rub her ass, then clutch her hip, thrusting, teasing. Luna is shaking against the table, and I bow forward to reach her ear. "You ever forget this again—that you need to be fucked every single day by *me* just to stay alive—I'll remind you."

Her high-pitch noise is too loud, and I cover her mouth with my hand, not stopping the friction. My cock rubs against her clit, and she shudders into an actual climax. I drop my hand to her hip.

"*Donnelly.*" Her cry nearly does me in.

But Luna doesn't ease into relief. Her eyes say, *more*. And she starts yanking down her thong, but I catch her hand.

"Pleaseplease," she begs. "I want to."

It'd be so easy to slip inside her pussy from behind. Been at the perfect angle this whole time, but I told myself we'd go slow—and despite usually listening to my cock and not my big brain, I think I need to consider that she *has* had trauma.

Going slow is the only way I can make sense of not hurting Luna. There is no magical Band-Aid, no wand I can wave to ensure I don't ruin her. I'd never forgive myself if I caused more harm than good, and I'm sure a bunch of people already believe I've check-marked that box.

She's not one of them.

She's who matters most to me.

Luna breathes, "Don't you want to?"

Badly. I flex forward again, testing the idea. Her lips part in arousal. It's so fucking tempting to take her. I've never been in this metaphorical position before, where I need to be the one to slam on the brakes when we're literally a thong away from screwing.

But Luna is so vulnerable right now, and how she's giving herself to me is something that simultaneously turns me on but something I can't take lightly, not under these fucked-up circumstances.

I take her hands, rooting them to the table again. Her breath shallows, especially as I thrust against her ass, and I whisper, "I'd rather eat you out." And I scoop her in my hands and turn her, pushing her ass on the table.

"OhmyGod," she cries as I kneel between her spread legs. I'm buck-naked, hard as can be, and at the mercy of her beautiful, mouth-watering pussy.

I pull her thong aside. "Try to be quiet."

She nods repeatedly, falling back on her elbows. "I can be quiet."

I grin, and she watches me flick my tongue over her clit, then farther down. Her thighs tremble, but she cages a noise. Then I go to town, sucking, licking—the taste of her is soul-soothing. A breakfast-lunch-dinner-dessert craving that I can't find on this planet. Just hers.

Only hers.

I work my tongue in and around her, and her eyes try to roll.

She drops off her arms, unable to hold herself up, and I never stop trying to send her over. She's trying to hang on longer.

Fuck. I stroke my aching dick, all while I slide a finger in her wet pussy and lick her clit.

Then I catch the same *squeak* of the floorboards and the loudest gasp.

I turn my head to look behind me. *This again? When I'm going down on Luna?* It's not Jane walking in on us this time.

It's Luna's mom. She's shielding her eyes with one hand and already feeling for the door with the other. "I'm so sorry! OhmyGod. Why did I come down here?"

I worry more about Luna. She's beet-red, and I close her knees together and stand up. She's fully clothed. I never really took anything off her in that sense. Whereas, Lily has now seen my ass, and I'm trying to cup my dick and balls.

"Mom," Luna calls, scared. "Are you going to tell Dad?"

Lily hasn't peeked behind her fingers. "I don't know—"

My chest caves. Shit.

"Mom, please," Luna pleads. "We're together, me and Donnelly." She looks to me for backup.

I can't say how much this'll help. "We made it official tonight," I say while putting on pants.

Lily is a redder shade than her daughter. She keeps her back to us now. "Didn't Dr. Raven say to take things slow?"

I feel worse.

"We're going at our own pace," Luna says, quieter.

Lily seems conflicted and mortified. I can't put Luna in hot water with her parents. I think it might be better if I remove myself from the situation. Give it room to breathe and whatnot.

"I'm gonna go," I say.

"No." Luna catches my hand. "You're staying the night."

"Maybe it's good if he goes," Lily says, which I agree but hearing her say it is like watching a baby whale suffocate. Think I might be the baby whale.

"Mom—"

"Just for tonight," Lily says fast, not wanting to alarm Luna.

"I can go with you," Luna tells me.

"I want you to stay." I wrap my arms around her in a bear-hug. She holds tighter, and I whisper against her hair. "We're alright, but I need to go, Luna. Call me if you need me or if you can't sleep? I know a guy who loves droning on about Bass, and I promise he'll bore you to sleep."

"I don't think that's possible," she murmurs, stepping out of my arms. Her eyes are reddened, but she sniffs, then lifts a Vulcan salute. "Live long and prosper."

I kiss her cheek. "It's never goodbye, space babe." And then I walk away.

I hate this.

That's the truth. But I love her more, and it's better if I go. *It's better if I go.* I convince myself of this, and on my way out the kitchen door, I say, "Sorry, Lily."

Her palms are comically hiding her flushed face, but the way she ignores me isn't that funny. So I grab my shit from the guest room and leave the Hale House. Instead of hijacking Epsilon's car that I just returned, I consider asking Farrow if I can borrow his.

That entails waking him up. He has a newborn, and I'm not interrupting his few hours of good sleep tonight. So once I'm outside, I call another friend.

"You're so lucky I'm awake, bro," Oscar says, sounding alert like he's been up the past two hours.

"You in the great state of PA?" I stand on the curb, my nipples hardened peaks from the cold, and I tuck my arms closer to my body.

"We all are after the news."

Grandfather Calloway's death. Feels like an eon ago that I heard about it. "How soon can you be at the Hale House?"

"Ten minutes. Why?"

"I need a ride."

FANATICON FORUM

We Are Calloway

Posted by @lorensfavtaco616 #wac-mod

Luna x Donnelly Bar Photos Megathread
Discuss the bar photos of Luna Hale and bodyguard Paul Donnelly (formerly on SFO—word is he's been transferred to Epsilon?). Photos are posted exclusively on Celebrity Crush. (Article is linked.) Please be respectful of each other and the families, or you will be banned from the WAC forum.

@HolyHalesSpiderman: There are literally a dozen photos. Idk why anyone is questioning the legitimacy of the two of them. They're full-on MAKING OUT in that booth!

@Core6Supremecy: Not on the night Greg died.

@Charlie_Does_Me: Why are we not talking about that more? THEY WENT TO A BAR AND MADE OUT THE SAME DAY GREG CALLOWAY DIED?! Like seriously?! Do they have no shame?

@HTT_Lover32: Anyone have a video? Looks like they're dry humping in the middle of the bar.

@WWRCD_1989: Luna doesn't care about her mom at all. Lily just lost her father. You lost your grandfather. And you go and do this? Wtf is wrong with her and HIM?!?!

@WAC77Lover: I can confidently say I did not see this coming. Holy shit.

@XanderOnlyXander: ...how did we miss this? Luna and Donnelly? If they really are together, I wonder how long it's been. I bet it's new or else we'd have more evidence. This could just be a one-time hookup/fling situation. It's not like they've verified anything.

@hehecallowayxx: RIP LunaQuinn. Jk I'm still holding out hope. He's so hot. Luna deserves better.

@LorenIsKing1990: I CALLED IT! *this* has to be the reason Loren hates Donnelly. I'm telling you!! Everything makes sense now. They never fired him after the kidnapping bc he's with Luna. #facts

@WhateverWhoever: ~~She's so embarrassing. I can't believe anyone would even date her.~~ *Deleted by mod-bot for breaking forum rules.*

@HaveAGreatDay123: How'd Celebrity Crush even get those pics? You think they had a reporter who followed them? Or did one of the ppl at the bar just sell the photos to the tabloid?

@Love_Is_What: I bet they leaked the pics themselves to save face and make Donnelly appear less like a kidnapper.

@CobaltTwinsStanAccount: Pretty sure these pics make them both look 100% worse. ON GREG'S DEATH. Charlie Cobalt would never.

DONNELLY'S DAILY PLANNER
Sunday, Dec 23rd

Today's Focus: don't provoke any grim reapers or disturb the dead. Stay on the same sparkly page as your new girlfriend.

To Do:

- Funeral for Grandfather Crow.

- ~~Make nice with Epsilon.~~ (Gotta be realistic.

- That's not happening.)

- Smooth things over with gf's parents, please and thank yous.

- Leave for the lake house (with Hales or security???)

Notes: Been making myself scarce with the Hale household (minus Luna). Lily hasn't invited me back, but I'd fly there if I were welcome. Wish Xander needed a bodyguard 'cause it'd be a good excuse to stop by. Think I'm in exile. Will def fix that soon.

Got an earful from the new boss. Didn't think "PDA with Luna" would make his list of complaints. Price wanted me to inform security before I kissed her in public. I told him he should be thanking me for not disturbing his 3 a.m. beauty sleep. Note to self: The new boss man hates my jokes more than Papa Hale does. Forgot that about him.

Also! How do fans know I've been transferred to Epsilon? It's sus. That's not anything we advertise. Brought it up to Price. He thought it wasn't important. But idk, we *could* have a rat among us. Don't trust all of Epsilon tbh.

Good news: Been avoiding SFE like the plague. Haven't had to deal with them while I'm off-duty.

Bad news: Gonna see a lot of 'em at the funeral and lake house. Here's hoping I can continue the avoidance streak *prayer hands*

Lastly! Could barely sleep the last few nights. Missed Luna next to me. Woke up in a cold sweat when I realized she wasn't there.

Meals: Quick brekky in the penthouse. Meeting up with Luna at the funeral. Lunch on the way to the lake house? Dinner there??

Water. GF's Pussy: Better than Evian. It's all I need to survive.

Question of the Day: Do all crows go to heaven when they die?

11

PAUL DONNELLY

"Wait, wait, wait." Oscar shoots out a hand, but not to stop me from moving around my bedroom in the Philly penthouse. "That's not a rumor? You're shitting me?"

"You gotta get yourself some adult diapers, man, if you keep crapping yourself this much," I say lightly.

Farrow laughs while eating a red apple. He's leaning casually against my Van Halen poster and dressed head-to-toe in black. The past three days, he's been staying with the Hales for the holidays with his husband and kids, but he stopped by early this morning to drive me to the funeral.

"You don't have to do that," I said over the phone.

"Okay, but I want to," he told me, and I didn't protest. Luna wanted to join him and ride with us, but after a short talk, Luna and I agreed it's better if she uses this time to show her parents that she's not unhealthily attached to me and that we can be physically apart.

It's why I haven't seen her (outside of FaceTime) since the night her mom caught us.

Hearing Farrow's laugh, I grin and jump into black slacks for the funeral. Not even half-dressed yet. Whereas my two best friends look sharp and ready to say *bon voyage* to the penthouse and *hello there* to the cemetery. They came into my room about the same time I finished writing in the daily planner.

"It's not funny," Oscar snaps at Farrow.

"It's a little funny," Farrow says matter-of-factly and into another crunch of apple.

Oscar is the only one sitting. His ass is on the edge of my bed. I donated the floral grannie bedding to Goodwill and bought myself a nice white comforter and matching sheets.

Oscar is gripping his cell phone too hard, and it feels like he's actually pissed at Farrow. "Donnelly took Epsilon's *vehicle* when he wasn't on-duty, Redford. Your motherfucking maverick ass might find it hilarious, but this is *serious*."

"Hold on." Farrow swallows a bite. "I was laughing at his fucking *joke*, Oscar."

Oscar is still glaring at Farrow.

I glance cautiously between them, slowly fishing a button through my fly. "You two need a therapy sesh or what?"

"No," they say in unison.

Farrow rolls his eyes, then sighs. "Fine, okay, it's a little fucking funny to me that those fuckers are crying about their car's interior. It's *glitter*, not blood or semen."

"It's a *fireable* offense," Oscar retorts, then zeroes in on me. "Are you trying to get fired, bro?"

"No," I say with the shake of my head.

Oscar gapes. "Then *why* take the car? Why not clean up the glitter in the front seats at the very least? You're not dumb. You know Epsilon isn't Omega. Price isn't Akara—"

"I know," I cut in, taking my black button-down out of the closet.

"Then you know Price and his men were going to care if you took their Range Rover to go on a date with Luna. So what exactly was going through your head? And don't say you weren't thinking— because we all know you were."

Farrow's now looking me over like he's interested in this answer too.

I tell them honestly, "I was thinking about ruining O'Malley's week."

Farrow tips his head from side-to-side, then shares a look with Oscar.

"I wish you two wouldn't do that," I mutter, shoving my arms in my button-down.

"Do what?" Oscar asks.

"Act like you're my two overconcerned older brothers."

"We are older than you," Farrow says plainly.

"Barely." I try to find my nicest pair of black socks in my dresser. "And it's not the *older* or *brother* part I have a problem with."

"We're not *over*concerned," Oscar says. "We're just plain concerned, Donnelly."

"We all hate Epsilon." I stand up, abandoning the sock hunt. "So why is it that concerning that I wanted O'Malley to know I drove his car and put it away dirty?"

"Because it's not like you," Farrow tells me.

"It's a big risk for petty revenge," Oscar says. "And you work with SFE now. As much as we all hate them, you don't need to give those guys a reason to fuck with you."

"They'll always find a reason," I retort, heat coursing through me. "And what happened to Farrow finding their cry baby reactions funny?"

"Man, I wouldn't be laughing if you got fired because of it."

Oscar points at me with his phone. "You got lucky all Price did was dock your pay for a week." He pauses. "He really must want you on his team."

Yeah. He doesn't act like it, but then again, I haven't been the model bodyguard in my *very* short time on SFE. How long has it been? Hardly three days? I signed the paperwork the morning Greg died.

Really, though, I know Oscar and Farrow are right. I haven't ever sought retribution at the cost of something this important to me. This job. My career in security.

But my boiling blood won't lower to a simmer. "I'm never getting along with Epsilon, so what am I supposed to do?" I ask them.

"Be professional," Oscar says like it's so easy.

Farrow raises his brows. "Be professional? You know the shit they say to him, Oliveira?"

Oscar sighs. "Just ignore them. Rise above." He's clearly worried I'm gonna piss off SFE so much that they come at me like a freight train.

Farrow twists the apple in his hand. "Call me."

It's true that a lot of the Epsilon guys are afraid of Farrow. Especially O'Malley. I wish they viewed me as a fatal blow too, but I'd much rather enter any brawl with a friend than go at it alone.

Call him. I nod. "You asking me on a date? 'Cause I've got a girlfriend."

Farrow rolls his eyes again, and this time, Oscar laughs.

We're all smiling by the time the cracked bedroom door flies fully open. And in walks Kannika "Frog" Kitsuwon in a slim, long-sleeve black velvet dress. Her heeled boots clank on the floorboards and she's carrying an iced coffee.

Oscar eyes the beverage. "You do know it's thirty degrees outside?"

"And I'm inside." She swishes the ice. "Where it's seventy degrees."

Farrow grins at Oscar's constipated face, and I laugh.

She leans a hip on my dresser and turns to me. "I need some advice."

"You need more than *some* if your instinct is to look at Donnelly first," Oscar banters.

I blow him a middle-finger kiss. He's spouting truths though. I haven't been exuding upstanding role model behavior lately. What am I gonna do? Advise her on how to piss off O'Malley? On how to steal Triple Shield's vehicles to go for a joyride? That's where I'm at right now.

Still, I quip, "It's 'cause you're hard to look at, man. Been trying to tell you you're ugly."

"Only in your eyes, bro."

I smirk, and Frog chimes in, "It's the least Donnelly can do after he so very rudely did not call Luna's bodyguards—aka *me*—to Thirsty Goose."

"Sorry, Froggy," I say again. I've apologized already to her and Quinn. I expected the coldshoulder, but they've been anything but frosty.

"You get a pass because you're going through it. We're all going through it." She slurps her iced coffee, not elaborating. I wonder if she's still spilling all her emotions to Scooter, the tattooist I vaguely remember from Old City.

I end up asking, "You still talking to your main man Scoot about going through it?"

"Scooter," she corrects. "He's still as nice as when we first met, and I told you he gets me." So that's a *yes*.

"You check the age on his ID?" Oscar asks her.

"He told me he's thirty-four. So what?"

"He's old," Oscar counters, more protectively.

"You're *thirty-three*. Newsflash, Yale boys, you're all old by that definition."

Oscar raises his hands. "But I'm also not letting an eighteen-year-old cry on my shoulder."

"I'm nineteen—"

"Freshly," Farrow states.

"—and why not comfort a nineteen-year-old when she needs someone to talk to? Why is that so awful?"

Oscar frowns. "That's not what I meant—"

"What did you mean?"

Oscar eats air. I bet he has the words, just fears causing more destruction in his tender relationship with our youngest rookie. Farrow looks pained watching Oscar, and I chime in, "Think he means Scoot is trying to get in your pants by being a comfy shoulder for you."

She groans. "Not you guys too. He's *not* emotionally manipulating me. You don't know him! Quinn doesn't know him! Okay, so just stop throwing targets at a guy I know better than all of you." She huffs. Then in our collective silence, she asks me in a tinier voice, "Is it unprofessional to give your client a Christmas gift if she can't ever remember being friends with you?"

That's the advice she's seeking?

"Luna will like whatever you give her," I say.

"She won't be weirded out? Will the gift make her feel bad about losing her relationship with me? Should I ask her therapist first?"

I shut one eye at that last question. "No, no, I dunno."

Frog spins to Oscar and Farrow for input.

"Ah ah, that's his girlfriend." Oscar points at me. "He knows her the best."

"Oh, now my instincts to go to him first are correct," Frog deadpans.

I smile. "He'd give you a cookie, but Audrey stopped making them for him a year ago."

Oscar fake laughs, and I laugh for real. While putting on socks, Quinn is the next one barreling into my room.

"There you are." He sighs at Frog. "Is your radio off?"

"I wonder who used to do that," Oscar says under his breath, eyes darting between Farrow and Quinn.

Farrow gives him a middle finger with all the nonchalance in the world.

Frog checks her radio zipped in a fanny pack. "It's on now. Is Luna on the move?"

Already? I'm about to check my phone for a missed text, but Quinn is shaking his head. "Just making sure you didn't leave without me."

"That was *one* time."

"Seven times," Quinn refutes. "Just *slow down*. Why are you always in such a hurry?"

She mumbles while fiddling with the radio. "It beats hanging around you and Nessa."

Don't think he hears her, but I ask, "How are you and Nessa

doing?" It's a casual question. Hell, I'm sitting beside Oscar and putting on socks. I've got wool in my hands, not steel.

But his eyes flash hot on me. "Fine."

"She's *always* at our apartment," Frog tells Quinn. "You should be glad Nine's not charging her rent." She calls her cousin Akara by his nickname Nine.

Quinn says, "It's not like Gabe has slept there for the past week. There's room."

Oscar mouths to me, *Millie's*. So Gabe really is dating MK.

While Frog and Quinn bicker about apartment living, six-foot-seven Thatcher Moretti slips in the room more quietly. He goes straight for Farrow and speaks hushed to him. Farrow nods, then Thatcher puts a radio in his hand and more ammo.

Must be about security during the funeral, but Farrow catches his shoulder, says something quieter, and pats Thatcher's back. They're close. Bonded through marrying Maximoff and Jane, best friends. Shouldn't make me jealous. Never has before.

I sense the clench of my stomach. It's probably because I'm not on SFO anymore and Thatcher is—despite being suspended for failing his psych eval. I'm guessing that's why he's dishing out extra security info to Farrow. Thatcher has to give up the reins to someone.

"You meeting Jack at the funeral?" I ask Oscar about his husband while I pull on my second sock.

"My eyes will be on him, yeah, but I can't talk to him." Oscar's eyes darken. "Jack has to work *at* the funeral."

He's production. *Why...?* "They're filming the funeral?" As soon as I ask it, the room deadens, and I look up to see Akara and Banks in the room too.

Minus Gabe, all of Omega is here.

My pulse beats strangely, and I just turn to Oscar for an answer.

"They're filming it," Oscar confirms. "It's been a back-and-forth argument with the Calloway sisters and their mother. Production has been trying to stay out of it and just let them decide. Apparently, Samantha is adamant they show the funeral on the show. Jack said it was ugly. She threatened to get the lawyers involved, called them names, dug up the past."

"Shit," Farrow breathes.

Silence falls again, and I'd bet any unborn child of mine that we're all thinking we wish the Crow died instead of her husband.

I stand up, and the bed squeaks. Eyes veer to me like a lit neon *Welcome* sign. Only, I feel more like a *No Vacancy* budget motel at the moment. All booked. No room for personal one-on-ones, or in this case one-on-sevens.

"Hey, Donnelly," Akara says, his tone more uncertain than friendly. He doesn't know where we stand after terminating my contract with Kitsuwon Securities and trading me off to Triple Shield. He did it like I'm a stat on a page, a number that he needed to subtract.

But if not me, then it would've been the three rookies.

Better it was just me.

Just wish I meant more to him is all. I've been living at the penthouse. We're still roommates, but the place is so massive, it's easy not to bump into him on the daily.

I up-nod to him now, opening my closet. Am I hiding? No, I'm searching for a belt and hoping someone takes the attention off me.

"Price thinks you're trying to get fired," he says.

My chest constricts. "I'm not trying to get fired."

He snaps his finger to his palm. "Well, I'm supposed to tell you that if you do get fired, I'm not hiring you, so don't self-sabotage."

I ask, "Is that what you'll do?"

Akara looks pained. He pushes his black hair back. "Please don't make me have to make that choice."

Frog gawks. "Seriously, Nine? It should be an easy choice. He's your friend."

"We're a family," Akara says like it's obvious. *Is it?* They are all in my bedroom. How the hell did SFO end up here? "But this side is also a business."

My transition to Triple Shield—also *business.*

Akara has been trying to hammer that home. *It's not personal. It's the best move for the* entire *team.* On and on and on. But I don't see how this is a power play for Kitsuwon Securities. Farrow can't see it. Oscar can't see it.

He gives me to Price for what? He got *nothing* out of this transaction. I told him that.

He said, "Please trust me. This is the best move for the future of everyone."

Everyone but me, it feels like.

But I'd never hurt SFO. Even if I'm off the payroll. I've been trying to make this harder for *Epsilon*, not for them.

"I won't self-sabotage," I say quietly, not even cracking a joke about it. I just want to move on.

The air is thick. Akara tries to lighten it. "How come you've been staying here the past few days? I would've thought you'd be at the Hale's with Luna."

Banks asks, "Did her parents not like the PDA at the bar?" They know about the bar photos plastered in *Celebrity Crush.*

"Something like that," I say, slipping my belt through the loops. *Don't look at Farrow. Don't look at Oscar.* But I do.

The night Greg died and Oscar picked me up, I confessed the predicament I found myself in.

The kitchen.

Luna's pussy.

The table.

Lily.

The next morning, when Farrow called, asking where I went, I told him the truth too.

Oscar's reaction was like someone choking on a golf ball. So I'm not surprised he's struggling to stay composed now. His head whips from Farrow to me.

"The Yale boys know something," Frog says, perking up. "Wait, if this has to do with Luna, I should know too."

"Same," Quinn says, more aggressively towards me. Like I'm

sneaking around with his client, and granted, I am doing that. As her boyfriend.

Quinnie's a good bodyguard.

"I'm staying out of this," Farrow declares, eyeing me for a beat. He's letting me unleash whatever I want.

I could be vague and slither my way out of this conversation. Something compels me to go in another direction. It's odd to be cast out from SFO but also standing in a room with them. They're people I love, who I've relied on and who've relied on me, and maybe spilling this is like hanging on to the essence of a fact I want to be true: They'll always be here for me. Have they really left?

Will they really leave?

Whatever the case, I tell them, "Lily thought it'd be good if I left the Hale House."

"Why?" Thatcher asks.

"She might've caught me eating Luna out in the kitchen."

Frog gasps.

"Donnelly," Akara says like a disappointed parent.

Banks is laughing.

Thatcher is shaking his head.

And Quinn asks me, "Is Luna okay?"

"I didn't get to finish her, so in that sense *no.*"

Quinn glares.

Come on. "I didn't hurt her," I defend. Alright, maybe he's taking his bodyguard duties a little too seriously. "You know me Quinnie."

He eases. "I'm just looking out for her."

"You don't need to worry about her being with me. I'm always thinking about her," I tell him.

"Does Loren know?" Thatcher asks.

"Not that I know of." I look to Farrow.

Farrow chimes in, "Lily hasn't told him, of what I know." He makes a circle with his fingers. "All of us know, plus Luna, Lily, Maximoff."

That's it. Likely, it'll have the same trajectory as when Jane walked in on us. It'll disintegrate over time and be forgotten. SFO is good at keeping secrets. It's what we do.

I highly doubt anyone else will hear about it.

12

LUNA HALE

"Your mom what?" Tom is slack-jawed, open-mouthed stunned.

I considered sheltering this catastrophic life event, tucking it away in the dusty corners of my closet, but this is my new beginning, where I share—and maybe overshare—to the people who matter most to me.

This morning, Aunt Rose and Uncle Connor invited friends and family to a pre-funeral breakfast, and Eliot, Tom, and I snuck away to the library, carrying porcelain dishes of croissants, pain au chocolat, and fruit.

The library is one of Eliot's favorite spots in the whole Cobalt Estate. It could've been plucked out of a 19th century gothic novel, more macabre than modern. Heavy, velvet blue curtains frame a cold window, and a skeletal tree clinks against the glass. Dark wooden shelves seem endlessly tall as they reach the vaulted ceilings, and the only way to feel warmth is by sitting next to the crackling fireplace.

We've pulled three leather club chairs even closer to the hearth, and my two best friends are seated across from me. So I have a clear view of Eliot too.

I expected him to overflow with amusement. He is mirth and mischief.

Instead, his squared jawline has tensed, and he hasn't blinked for at least thirty seconds. "Your mom caught you in the act?"

"We didn't go all the way, but yeah."

"On your parents' kitchen table?"

"The breakfast table, but again, yep." I nod.

"Nudity?" Eliot asks.

"Not me. Just Donnelly. I'm ninety-nine percent positive my mom at least saw his ass."

"Shit," Tom says, wide-eyed. "I would've died. Just bury me if my mom ever catches me giving or receiving a blow job."

Eliot would survive any mortifying situation. Unless this has changed in the past three years, he's always been much harder to embarrass.

Maybe we're similar that way. "Honestly," I say quietly, "I've been more embarrassed getting an Illyana Rasputin question wrong during X-Men trivia." I pick at my fluffy croissant. "Donnelly looked more at me than my mom when she walked into the kitchen, and he just made it seem okay. Like what we did wasn't gross or a regret. So I never really felt ashamed by it. And I think my mom was plenty mortified for all of us."

Eliot hasn't produced a mega-watt grin. It unsettles my stomach.

"Are you...shocked too?" I ask him uncertainly.

"Only that you were caught in the act before me. I figured that'd be my crown." He pops a grape in his mouth, but trouble lines crease the spot between his brows. "What'd your mom do? Because we can't have her against you and Donnelly."

This is the source of his grim expression. I frown. "Has she ever disliked any of the bodyguard relationships?"

Tom shakes his head. "None that we know of. She's pretty much been the number one Marrow and Kitsulletti shipper online, and when the Thatcher cheating rumors wouldn't die down, she tweeted like every single day about how loyal he is to Jane. Shit, I think she even changed her profile picture to Highveira fan art back when Charlie stans dog-piled on Jack for dating Oscar."

That's a whole lot of history I don't remember.

It's devastating to think Donnelly and I could be the first *ship* my mom hopes won't sail into the Valinor sunset. My frown deepens. "She kicked him out of the house. That's what she did."

Tom's face falls. "I'm sorry, Luna."

Eliot washes down his food, then stands. "We can't have this." He slides an iron fireplace poker out of its ornate stand.

"What are we going to do?" Tom asks, slipping his fingers through his golden-brown hair. "We can't *stab* Aunt Lily into liking Donnelly with Luna."

"Violence is not the answer," Eliot says, staking the wooden floor with the iron tip. He leans on the poker like a cane. "I'm running through potential ideas."

He's plotting, and I'm not sure being tangled in an Eliot Alice Cobalt fix-it plot is a good thing. Eliot is fueled by chaos and revenge. Asking him to smooth over a situation is like enlisting a tornado to help restore a flattened city.

Still, having Eliot so passionately on Donnelly's side—on *our* side—breathes warmth into my heart. I don't want to accept this narrative with my mom either. I like the story where she has changed her license plate to our ship name—a ship name we don't even have! This relationship is as new for the public as it is for me.

I care less about what the world thinks of me and Donnelly, but by the strange roil of my stomach right now, I most definitely care about my mom's opinion.

"I'm not sure there's anything we can do," I mutter. "She's only said a few words to me after I apologized, and I think she's trying her best not to spill the beans to my dad."

Tom's brows spring. "He doesn't know?"

"No, *no*." I exhale a breath. "I think he'd hate Donnelly for eternity and there's no coming back from that if he finds out." I stare at the flames licking the fireplace logs and hear chatter of mingling guests throughout the house. It reminds me of why I'm even here.

Timing, Luna. I think I have the worst.

"Sorry, maybe I should've waited to tell you both." I tear apart another piece of croissant. "We're about to go to a funeral, and I wasn't thinking about…" *Our grandfather.*

Selfish. Disrespectful.

All the comments on Fanaticon rocket to the front of my brain, but Donnelly told me to block out those online voices. I try, even knowing they might be right about me.

"He's dead." Tom lifts his shoulders, his hand wrapped around a mug of coffee. "What's he going to do? Yell at us for talking about anything other than him?"

Eliot says, "No, that's just our dear, *lovely*, youthful grandmother." He arches and lowers his brows in a sarcastic wave. While we were downstairs, she brushed past us at the spread of breakfast pastries as Tom had been expressing his hatred of honeydew.

Eliot caught her side-eye before I did, and he quickly began reminiscing about a morning spent with our grandfather eating cantaloupe and tracking stocks on Bloomberg. His acting chops are scarily powerful because he convinced me that he had this past bonding experience with Greg.

It was totally fabricated on the spot.

"Are we bad people?" I ask them. "For not mourning him like we should?"

"I'm not going to cry about it," Tom mutters, staring at his coffee. "I mean, don't get me wrong, I loved him. He was always kind to me, and he took more interest in my prom date than anyone. He asked me all about him like I planned to marry the guy."

Prom? I claw for this memory, but it must've happened either during or after the FanCon tour. Days, weeks, months that remain fogged.

"Calvin Cross," Eliot informs me. "They went to prom as 'just' friends." He uses air quotes.

Tom rolls his eyes. "Dude, he's *boring*. I'd rather listen to Ben read the ingredients on a sour cream label than listen to Calvin discuss the fermentation of wine. He's going to knock the socks off some dude, but not me."

The Cross family aren't unfamiliar to me. They grew up in the same social circles and attended all the same charity functions, and Calvin went to elementary school with us. Our grandparents are closest to Olivia Barnes and her grandchildren, but I doubt they're as affluent as the Cross's, who own real estate around Philadelphia and New York.

"He wanted you to marry into the Cross family?" I theorize.

Tom mimes rubbing coins together. "It's all about wealth, Luna With No Middle. But, I don't know, there was a part of me that felt like he actually cared. He didn't have to ask if Calvin was a good guy, a gentleman towards me or whatever, but he did." He pauses. "I didn't, however, like that he chose to leave Moffy's wedding rather than stick around."

"No one did," Eliot says to his brother, but then to me, he explains, "He left with Grandmother Calloway. He said he couldn't let her fly back to Philly alone."

"Did he not trust her?" I ask. Their relationship has never made much sense to me. I imagine finding answers would be like trying to play a dusty Jumanji board game. You'd need to battle monkeys and killer vines to reach the bizarre end.

"Or did he love her?" Eliot muses. "He loved her so much that he'd rather be at her side in her distress than be apart."

"I've never even seen them *smile* at each other, dude," Tom says. "If love is that cold, then I don't want to be in it."

Eliot would drive a sword through his heart just for family, and I can't even imagine the lengths Eliot would go to for a woman he loved, especially if she were in distress. So I can see him sympathizing with this scenario, but it hinges on the idea that Greg and Samantha's love ran a million leagues deep.

"I think she had dirt on him," Tom says. "Something that'd hurt his reputation, and he chose money over being there for Moffy. That's all I'm saying."

Eliot nudges a log with the poker. "I can only hope at my funeral there's drama." He glances at me. "Grandfather Calloway is fortunate you've brought some."

"Just *some*," I note after a nibble of croissant. "I'm not bringing it all." *Please don't let that be me.* "But I am glad I told you two, even if it had to be today," I realize. "Because it's happened before—not that I can remember—but apparently I said nothing to you two last time."

Tom's jaw descends again. "You were caught with Donnelly or with someone else?"

I try not to cringe when I imagine someone other than Donnelly touching me. "I was with Donnelly."

Eliot is grinning now. "You sneaky sneak."

"The sneakiest," I sing-song, smiling back. "It wasn't my mom who caught us though. It was years ago, and Donnelly said when he went down on me, Jane walked in on us…" I trail off, eyes growing as two of their brothers stand in the doorway. "Uh-oh."

Charlie and Beckett heard everything I just said.

"Brothers. Cousin," Charlie deadpans, eyes on me for half a beat. "If you want private information to be kept secret, *lock the door.*"

Eliot waves the poker. "Who said we didn't want you to hear?"

"Yeah," Tom chimes in. "We masterfully constructed this plan."

My face is on fire, but I nod too. "Yep. All part of the tapestry." I shove my mouth with croissant, trying to avoid Beckett. He's not rotating on his heels and marching out of the door like a jealous ex.

He comes forward with Charlie.

The Cobalt twins couldn't look more different from each other right now, despite having similar lean builds. Charlie is dressed in all-white, and Beckett is in all-black. Charlie appears mostly apathetic, and Beckett seems *very* interested in what he just overheard. Even their hair is contrasting shades of brown.

Beckett settles on the vacant chair where Eliot had been sitting, and Charlie slides a footstool closer, taking a seat at the hearth.

My heart is pounding so hard, I can practically hear the nervous beat in my ears.

Beckett stares at me, and right as he opens his mouth, I blurt out, "I can't remember it. *Jane* walking in on me and Donnelly, I mean. I don't remember it happening, but it did."

Skin pleats between his brows, but his yellow-green eyes aren't narrowed or flaming with defensiveness like I've seen when I bring up Donnelly. "Did he tell you when it happened?" he asks.

"I think sometime in the fall. He said Thatcher had been fake-dating Jane because of a Cinderella ad?" I scrunch my face, hoping for this memory to plop magically inside my brain.

Nope, still gone.

Beckett hunches forward, and it's a weird sight, considering he has ballet-dancer posture. His hands fly to his face.

Eliot and Tom exchange a quick look, but I'm left out of that one. I glance at Charlie, but he's focused on his twin brother.

"I'm such an asshole," Beckett says, smearing his hands down his face. He rests his palms on his thighs, then shakes his head at me, apologies in his eyes. "I assumed—I shouldn't have *assumed*—that you didn't have history with Donnelly."

I'm startled. "It's not like I can remember it."

"Exactly," Beckett says. "It's not like you could defend yourself against the shit I said to you." Guilt impales his face, and his hand returns to his forehead. "I'm so sorry, Luna."

Charlie shuts a book loudly and eyes Beckett. "It's not like Donnelly told you he was eating out our cousin. And yet, how much did you tell him about your sex life?"

Eliot gasps. "Does he know more than me?"

"And me?" Tom adds.

Beckett blinks a few times, not denying. "He was my friend. And I didn't share my life with him expecting anything in return."

Charlie states, "I'd think *sharing* is a defining aspect of a friend-ship."

"Sharing." Eliot holds the poker over his broad shoulders like a barbell. "Like how often you share your life with us, Charlie? We live with you, and we don't even know where you go half the time."

"We're not friends. We're brothers."

"Cold."

Tom swigs the last of his coffee. "We should pull out a dictionary.

It'll help you learn the meaning of true friendship."

Is two-way sharing a defining aspect of friendship?

Charlie ignores Tom's quip like it's beneath him to respond. And then he turns to Beckett. "You cautioned *Moffy* against dating Farrow because you thought there was a power imbalance of knowledge—Farrow knew everything about the *famous* Maximoff Hale, and Moffy couldn't know that much about him. But when it comes to your own life, you don't care that someone held all your cards and gave you nothing?"

"We were just friends, and it's in the past, Charlie," Beckett says calmly. "What I did…was worse."

Silence spreads between the Cobalt brothers, and I remain entirely, utterly, *confused.* "What'd you do?" I ask.

Beckett struggles for the words, before he admits, "I chose drugs over him."

The bottom of my stomach falls. That…would've definitely hurt Donnelly. Even knowing Donnelly for only a short amount of time, I can see how deeply he loves his friends. To not receive the love back would be crushing for most, but for the source to be drugs is devastating. Because he has addicts as parents. How many times have they chosen drugs over him? To have that happen again…

Charlie looks shocked that Beckett spoke this out loud.

"Donnelly might not have told me about you," Beckett says to me, "but I doubt it's because you meant nothing to him. I think it's likely because you meant the most, and I know…the deeper things were always harder for him to share. It was like if he did, they were more at risk of being taken, and I can't fault him for keeping what he loved close. I'm really in no place to fault him for anything." He glances to Charlie. "And you shouldn't either."

Charlie nods a few times.

Tom winces as he places his empty mug on a cocktail stand. He massages his wrist.

I frown. "What's wrong with your wrist?"

Tom immediately stops the bone-massage. "Nothing."

All four brothers seem shady, and I look to Charlie, who tells me, "A fight with Ben."

Their brother Ben? "Ben hurt you?"

"No," Tom retorts. "It was an accident, and it was actually *Eliot*." By Eliot's grim expression, I know that's true. Tom glares at Charlie. "Like that is going to help get Ben to move to New York."

"He's better off in Philly. Stop trying to recruit him."

"He's our baby brother," Eliot retorts. "Does that mean nothing to you?"

Charlie can't respond. Noises escalate from downstairs. Chatter explodes, and a few shrieks. Eliot straightens off the fireplace, dropping the poker to his side. Hairs rise on my arms, and Tom's face scrunches in confusion.

"What the hell is that?" Tom asks, standing, but I think we're all realizing that neither Beckett nor Charlie move a muscle.

They know.

My heart hammers again, and I breathe unsteadily. "Is it...is it about me?" Why else did they come into the library? They have no pastries! They're not even *eating* with us. They came in here...for what? Clearly not to grieve with friends, when Charlie doesn't even consider Eliot and Tom worthy of friendship.

And as Beckett's calm eyes rest on me, and Charlie's more prickly ones meet mine, I suddenly feel as though they found me...to protect me.

"It only took..." Charlie glances at his watch. "Five minutes longer than I thought."

"What did?" I'm barely breathing.

"The night of our grandfather's death, your mom walked in on you and Donnelly. And the news just spread to the whole family."

Blood rushes out of my face. "H-how?" I stammer.

"Yeah, how?" Eliot snaps. "No one heard us talking about it."

"You mean outside that door?" Charlie motions to the library door. "The one we so casually walked through without all three of you noticing?" He cocks his head like we are very, very dumb.

I'm feeling particularly dunce-cap worthy.

Tom mumbles a curse in his hands.

Eliot narrows his blue eyes on the door, his hand tightening around the poker handle. "Who heard?"

Beckett more calmly says, "Our baby sister."

Tom groans.

Eliot loosens his grip on the weapon. "Hasn't she learned that loose lips sink the Cobalt ships?"

"She's sixteen," Beckett says.

"That's old enough," Charlie snaps, then tells me, "Audrey told Winona, Vada, and Kinney, and then they told me."

"They wanted to see his reaction," Beckett says to me, "but we knew it'd reach everyone in a matter of minutes."

Everyone. Chatter has muffled a little, so maybe it's all blown over. Maybe I still have a pulse. "Okayokay," I slur together. I'm sweating, and my mouth is dry.

"Luna?" Tom asks, concerned.

"Donnelly," I say, swallowing a lump. "He needs to know. He's at the penthouse getting ready. He should know, and..." I look up at Beckett, and I can't say I've ever been close to Beckett. I can't say in the past three years I ever grew closer. But the twenty-three-year-old Beckett Joyce Cobalt before me is likely the man that Donnelly knew and befriended—because his eyes are full of caring. "You should text him," I tell Beckett. "Let him know what happened."

His brows pinch. "Are you sure?"

This isn't just a new start for me. It can be a new start for Beckett. It's never too late to rebuild the relationships we hold close to our hearts, and I truly believe this one has never left Beckett's.

I nod. "Positive."

And then a knock sounds at the door, followed by the jiggle of the handle. Charlie must've locked it.

"Is Luna in there?!" my dad calls out. "I need to talk to her!"

Oh God.

Maybe I'm the one who should be buried.

13

LUNA HALE

Dad is trying to find you. Hes on his way up there.
Everyone found out about the mom thing. Let me know if
you need backup. Im here for you — Moffy

I missed my older brother's text, but I just
now check it, then I rest my phone on the windowsill. The library
is freezing over here, but once all the Cobalt boys disappeared, I
deserted the fireplace and pretended to be interested in a leather-
bound book left on the sill. I flip through The Canterbury Tales by
Geoffrey Chaucer while my dad has said zero words.

He's stared out the window more than he's stared at me, and this
moment feels catalytic. Like if I step foot in the wrong direction, the
timeline of my life will implode again and what I have with Donnelly
will try to unravel at the seams.

I take measured breaths and try to piece together the Middle
English text on each page. I saw Xander reading *The Canterbury Tales*
when he was twelve, not for school or anything, more so out of
curiosity. The media loves to portray the Hales as being intellectually
inferior, and that criticism can seep into us, even when our parents
tell us differently. Xander is smarter than he gives himself credit for.
Maybe I am too…

I lift my gaze off the book.

Dad catches my eyes, and my pulse skips.

"Can you sit down please?" he asks me first. His strict tone is gone, replaced with something foreign and soft.

I nod, then take a seat on the rungs of a ladder posted against the shelves. I keep the book on my lap, and my dad scrapes a stiff-looking wooden chair over to me.

He sits. He thinks. He looks up. "I want to give you the chance to speak first. Tell me…whatever you need to tell me."

"You heard what happened…didn't you?"

"I heard from your aunts and your mom and people I didn't want to hear from, but I'd like to hear your side of the story."

My side? "Um," I frown at the book. "Mom walked in on me and—"

"Your side of the *story*," Dad emphasizes. "I know the facts."

Stories aren't police reports where the series of events are listed in dry factual detail. Stories contain emotion, *feelings*, and it dawns on me that he's giving me a chance to share mine.

"I don't know where to start," I admit, brows scrunched.

"Start with him," Dad tells me like he's already found the culprit.

I take a deep breath. "*I* asked Donnelly out the night Grandfather died. Because when the world doesn't make sense, my feelings for him have. So I went to him." I stare at the book, gathering my thoughts. "We went out. We drank. We danced." I smile a little at the remembrance. "When I'm with Donnelly, I'm no longer scared. I'm not afraid of the world. I'm not afraid of the past. Of any darkness. All the fears I have about myself are gone because I'm my most beautiful self in his eyes, and he sees her before even I do." I wipe at an escaped tear. "He loves every version of me, and I love being with him, Dad. I love how he loves me completely. I love how uninhibited and mighty I feel when I'm with him. I could be a broken mess, and he'd still pick me up and try to love me back together. And he's already done it. He's already tried." I blink away more tears. "Do you understand what that feels like?" My chin quakes, and I brave a glance at him.

His eyes have reddened, and he nods slowly. "I've loved your mom at her weakest, at her strongest, at her most broken. And she's loved me at mine. There's never been a day where I haven't loved her."

It pools into my heart. "I could say I found that too, but I have a feeling I never searched. Love like this feels inevitable. Like it has always existed and will always exist." My temple thumps, but I push past the sensation and tell my dad, "That night, we talked about becoming official. Boyfriend. Girlfriend. We shared insecurities and thoughts of the future, and I felt normal. Like a twenty-one-year-old who wasn't just kidnapped and beaten down. I felt a million feet tall, and I wanted him…all of him, in every way." Heat swaths my cheeks as I refer to sex in front of my dad. "He's been more careful with me than you even know. He's always considering what happened and my health, even when I wish he would forget."

"But the kitchen," Dad says gently. "We *eat* there."

I wince and try not to visualize Donnelly *eating* me out there, but the clear connection seems to hit my dad because he grimaces.

"Jesus Christ," he mutters. "Never in a billion years…" He sighs heavily, then meets my gaze. We share the same amber eyes, the same light brown hair, but I have my mom's soft, round face and not the sharp edges of Loren Hale. "Were you expecting to be caught?" He's cringing as he asks.

"No." I shake my head over and over. "He thought you might've set up nanny cams in the guest room to spy on him, and I guess I could've offered my bedroom—but it must not have crossed our heads in the moment."

"Nanny cams?" He shakes his head now. "*Jesus.* Jesus." He expels a short breath, his brows cinching in deeper thought. "Sometimes…I think this is all my fault."

It hurts. "Why?"

"Because you're an adult, and I'm still so goddamn scared I'm not doing enough to protect you that sometimes I think I'm hurting you by trying." He pinches his eyes, then drops his hand. "I don't like how Lily—your mom—felt like she couldn't tell me about what happened. I don't like how you felt like you couldn't go back to your room because I was spying. I don't like the person I'm close to becoming…or maybe, I'm already him." He stares off at the bookshelf behind me.

I say what I feel again, and this time, I tell him, "I never want you to stop protecting me."

His eyes shoot up to mine.

"You're my dad, and I don't want that to change with time."

"It could *never*, Luna." His eyes bore into mine. "I'll always be your dad. I'll *always* try my best…" He gets choked up, and he has to look away. I wonder if he's thinking about the night I was taken. "…even when my best isn't nearly enough."

A pain wedges in my ribs. "That's all we can do, right?" I ask quietly. "We do what we can, the best we can, when we can. And we hope that's enough."

It's all the things he's told me when I was a kid.

"That's right," he breathes, nodding. "And I'm going to try to *ask* before I react." He sits up straighter and says, "I didn't like Donnelly at first, honestly. I thought he was disrespectful."

I wince. "Mom catching us in the kitchen probably hasn't helped."

His eyes tighten, and he blinks hard. "Yeah, well, nothing extra therapy won't fix." He flashes a half-smile that fades fast, and I can see he's doing his best to chuck the sarcasm in the garbage for this convo. "Joking." He swallows. "I've been getting to know him a lot better, and I can understand how someone who was raised with a father like his…" He works his jaw. "Let's just say *respect* probably isn't what would get him through a day."

It catapults me to the phone call I overheard, where his dad suggested poking a hole in the condom, and I cringe. "Yeah, his dad doesn't seem like a great person."

He stiffens, his eyes laser-beaming me. "Have you met him?"

"No." More heat swarms my face. "I kinda heard him on the phone talking to Donnelly." My stomach tosses, and guilt assaults me for even sharing this not so fun fact.

"What about?"

"I don't think Donnelly would want you to know." I thumb through the pages of the book. "He was so upset that I even heard his dad speak like that…"

Dad is on his feet, but he only rakes a hand across the back of his tensed neck. His nose flares. "I hate that he still needs to talk to that piece of…" He bites back the curse word, his cheekbones sharpening as he clenches his jaw.

I wonder if Donnelly's dad could carve a path to becoming a better person. "He is trying to help Donnelly in a way." I try to see the world from Sean Donnelly's eyes, and it's hard but maybe not impossible. "He seemed to be happy for him and me. But then there was that one thing he said…" I see Donnelly's sheer anguish, and I shake my head. "Never mind."

"What'd he say?" my dad questions.

"I, uh…"

"Luna." Now my dad is pained.

If I don't fill in the blanks, my dad will do that himself with more graphic, horrific answers rather than the tamer truth. "He was just curious about meeting you, and he gave some advice."

"What kind of advice?"

I'm burning up, despite the temperature drop. Window, help me!

"Fucked up advice?" Dad asks, as though he knows it would be.

My shoulders unbind, and I'm incredibly sad because I realize my dad has heard Sean give this type of advice to Donnelly before. This wasn't a one-off thing. "Can you just ask Donnelly?" I whisper. "I don't think I can tell you." It hurts too much to share, and I want to protect him. It should be his choice on how to let it spill.

After a long moment, he nods. "Okay. I'll ask your boyfriend."

My lips part in gut-punching shock. Did I just transport myself to an alternate universe? Is this real? "Did you just call him my…?"

"Is that not what he is to you?" he asks.

Tears invade my eyes, and I blink, the waterworks cascading down my face. I rub my cheeks fast and spring to my feet. In seconds, I'm hugging my dad, and his arms are wrapping around me. The beat of my heart begins to slow.

Pulling back, I ask, "You don't think I'm obsessed? That this is just a trauma bond?" I'm almost scared to hear the answer.

"If it is," he says, "then it's something your mom and I have, and we can't throw stones at glass houses, can we?" He produces another dry smile. "But he's landed himself in the middle of my very long shit list, so don't get too excited."

I think everyone is on that list. "What about Mom?" I ask, my smile descending into a frown. "Is she still upset...?" I trail off because his troubled eyes say, *it's complicated* and *yes*.

He seems more concerned about her. "She's *very* upset, as she should be. As I am. She's a sex addict who saw her daughter in a sexual position with a bodyguard in our kitchen."

Guilt invades, but I can't even imagine how this is affecting her. "I'll try to be more considerate," I whisper.

"Tell your boyfriend the same thing or I will. And if your mom sees him naked again—his funeral will be the next we attend."

14

PAUL DONNELLY

"I hate it here," Xander whispers at the funeral home, blood-red carpet beneath our feet while we're seated on a bench in a silent, dead-end hallway. No one shuffles through and bothers him or me. His leg jostles, and his head touches the wood-paneled wall behind us.

I twist a knob on the radio attached to my waistband. "You can't spell the word funeral without the word *fun.*"

He laughs, the sound fading fast. "I'd ditch if I could."

I might call him my *little* elf, but it's not like he's a little kid.

He's two days shy of being a legal adult and no longer a minor. Which also means I won't need to go through Lily and Loren for anything security-wise concerning Xander. I'm looking forward to it like a hot Wawa gobbler on Thanksgiving.

I ask him, "Why can't you just ditch?"

"Too many reasons. My mom. My aunts. My conscience. My sister."

I try not to tense. Maybe he's talking about his younger sister. "Why Kinney?"

"Luna," he corrects, eyeing the phone, then me like I'll be the first to surface what happened in his parents' kitchen. Everyone in the family knows about me eating Luna out. It's my unlucky day, but I've got a large stash of those.

"Luna?" I play dumb, scrunching my brows. "That's a cute name." I lean forward and scope out the end of the hallway where his family have been entering the viewing room.

"I'd hope you like her name," Xander says, "seeing as how you've been…" He cringes. "Don't make me say it, Donnelly. She's my sister."

"You don't have to say it." I'm not embarrassed, but I'm not trying to turn my elf a shade paler.

He taps his phone to his thigh. "I thought you wanted a relationship with Luna."

I give myself whiplash snapping my neck back to him. "I do want that."

"Yeah, but…" He shoves at the sleeves of his black button-down. "You two make out at the bar. You come home and hook up again. Then at the Fanaticon Convention, there was the late-night call into her bedroom. It sounds more like *sex*, man."

I knew he thought it was a booty call at the Con in San Francisco. He cautioned me then to play hard to get, and I have been trying to go at a slower pace. But not so Luna can chase after me. She's been through enough, and the last thing she needs are mind games.

It's the last thing *I'd* want in her position.

I glance over at him. "What I have with your sister, it's not…" *It is physical.* I can't deny that. "…it's more than sex."

"For her too?" Xander asks in a whisper. "She's only known you for what, a month?"

"Think so, yeah." I check the hall again, then whisper, "Why do you think she'd only want to sleep with me?"

"I'm cautious about it." His eyes flit to me, then away. "Look, most people in my life are more interested in having sex with me rather than getting to know me." His homecoming date comes to mind. "And I'm not saying my sister would do that to you, but before her amnesia, you had a friendship first, and now you have a…" He struggles to find the term. "Friends-with-benefits thing?"

"Nah, it's not like that." *I don't think.* No, I know it. "We're dating."

He nods repeatedly. "I think I'm just nervous you two won't last as long if she doesn't remember the past three years."

He's casting sparks of doubt my way, and I'm not loving this kind of Hale magic. I want to reverse this feeling. "We'll last," I tell him. "She's already fallen for me twice."

Xander nods again, glancing over at me and I glance back. We share a fleeting confident look.

He's been harboring guilt over his negative reaction towards Luna liking me, so I tell him, "There's no universe where you're at fault for us not dating sooner. Hope you know that."

"Yeah," he says under his breath, his voice strained. "Yeah, I'm trying." He lifts his phone. "Luna is supposed to text me when she's done looking at the open casket. We're riding together to the gravesite, and maybe you can sit next to her."

That's why he's at the funeral home for Luna. Xander is putting me in his sister's orbit. I love circling her—would do it all day—so I'm not complaining.

But I thought he'd give this up after the Con. I start to say, "You don't have to—"

"I want to," he interjects. "I'm still afraid there is a universe where you're not endgame anymore. And the Luna *before* the amnesia needs you around if she comes back."

She's all one Luna to me.

One girl to love over and over and over again.

"*...we gather here today to honor the life and* legacy of Greg Calloway..." Connor Cobalt addresses the mourning crowd at the cemetery—a sea of black dresses and black suits and morose eyes.

Not everyone is staring at the casket or the dewy grass.

I have my arm slung around Luna, and I suppress the urge to tug at my tie while people cast "looks" at me and her. Really, though, I think they're mainly looking at me. Like I'm the bad influence corrupting a young Hale. I desecrated this holy ground with my bad deeds.

Friends-of-friends-of-friends of the Calloway sisters think I have no shame or respect because I made out with Luna Hale the night Greg died.

Family of the Calloway sisters just learned Lily walked in on me performing award-winning oral on her daughter.

So any which way you turn it, I'm getting side-eyed.

The ceremony feels short. I keep thinking about Luna and our future, about everything *but* the grief surrounding me. I can't say how much time passes, but more than one person says a few words. From Daisy, to Lily, to Rose, and to Poppy—the Calloway sisters. Tears are shed. Tissues are handed around.

Then family members toss dirt on the casket.

Once it's all done, people begin to slowly, gradually, leave the gravesite. Luna and I aren't in a hurry to walk out with everyone. We face the polished headstone, and the air is somber and silent as family, friends, and bodyguards all depart for their cars.

Eyes veer back at me, then at Luna. As if we're a new stain on some royal bedsheets.

My brows knot, my arm snugger around her hips. More territorial than maybe I should be, but after all we've been through, I can't let her go because someone else thinks I should.

That's just where I'm at.

"You really don't like each other, do you?" Luna whispers, and I follow her gaze to fucking *O'Malley*. He's giving me the stink-eye, and I'm wondering if Luna is recollecting the fistfight between me and him at the bowling alley.

"He's never been a friend of mine, no," I mutter. She hasn't asked me too much about him, but I can see the confusion and interest all over her face now. All the shit he said to her at the bowling alley is fuel beneath my burning skin. How he said I'm lying to her, how I'm manipulating her to be with me. How he said he knows her better than I do.

Her frown deepens. "I wasn't friends with him?" She's questioned this before, but I have a feeling she just wants the answer from her past self. It'd be easier if she could consult her diary, but she still hasn't chosen her "memory guardian" to help with that.

"No," I say stiffly. "Not that I know of."

"I just don't understand why he's so protective of me."

It roils my stomach. "Probably 'cause he thinks I'm a piece of shit who's capable of..." I grit down on my molars, unable to even say *rape*. O'Malley accusing me of hurting Luna like that is a festering wound that'll never fully heal.

Luna wraps both arms around my waist, clinging to me. I hold her against my chest and look down at her. She looks up at me, no questions in her amber eyes this time. "He's wrong," she says.

I smile. "Now you're speaking dirty to me."

Her lips rise. "Dirty talk is well-taught on my planet."

"Mine too." I look her over while she openly checks me out, but her smile vanishes before our talk can edge into something more sexual.

"He should know he's wrong," she says quietly, but she sends O'Malley those very words through her pinpointed gaze. I love my space babe.

His eyes flame. I hate my co-worker.

I glare. "Pretty certain he believes I'm the Anti-Christ corrupting you."

"I think I'm more likely to corrupt you," she says even more hushed, and when our eyes catch, her cheeks redden. "Just a thought I've been having." It's the first time post-amnesia she's concluded that she's the bad influence. And she adds, "I'm the one who asked you to sneak out with me."

I warm her cheek with my hand. "You can't corrupt me, space babe."

Her lungs expand. "Are you sure?"

Am I sure that she's not toxic for me? That I'm not toxic for her? That we're not toxic together? *Yeah.* Because loving Luna has made me happier than I've ever been. On the outside looking in, we might appear like a weird mess, but inside looking out, we're the rulers of our own universe.

And I don't care what anyone has to say about us.

Except…maybe her mom.

"I wanted to go out with you," I assure her. "If you led me to do something I didn't wanna do…" *I would tell you.* I hesitate. I know I'm not that great at saying *no*, but I've set boundaries before and I've learned to redirect her instead of outright deny her. "…I'd guide us elsewhere."

"Elsewhere," she says softly, and her smile reignites. I fall into the brightness of it. "We balance each other out?" It's a question that I'd rather be a fact.

"Yeah. We do." I pinch the green kyber crystal around her neck. *The balance of the Force.* It's within all living things. "I've never feared being pulled to the dark side when I'm with you, Luna. If anyone was going to corrupt me, it would've never been you."

Her smile grows tenfold. "We are Jedi together."

"Are you my master or my apprentice?"

"Master."

I grin. "Knew you were teaching me the ways, all this time." I pull her closer and plant a kiss against her cheek, then I nip her earlobe.

She melts against my side, her smile unrestrained, but when she takes a second glance at O'Malley, I'd love nothing more than to chuck him into a black hole inside her galaxy, so he ceases to exist.

Luckily for me, his back is turned to us, but I watch him lead Beckett Cobalt to a vehicle.

Beckett.

I thought I dreamed up the text thread between us, but I double-checked and I'm not delusional. He did text me a heads-up before the funeral. So I wasn't shell-shocked that the *entire* family knew Lily walked in on Luna and me.

Been anticipating her dad burying me in a shallow ditch, but he hasn't said a word to me. This whole day has been strange, and it's not even noon yet.

I hang one arm over my girlfriend's shoulders and then put the cigarette between my lips, lighting it.

"Price to Donnelly." My new boss speaks over comms. "No smoking on-duty."

We're *outside.*

Who am I hurting other than my own lungs?

I try to grind away a blip of annoyance, and I comply, snuffing the cigarette beneath my foot. Luna frowns a little, but I don't tell her about the order.

She slides her hand in mine and leads me deeper into the cemetery. To smoke, I think. Xander is quick to follow. His hands are crossed over his black suit, wind whipping his shaggy hair. If he decides to leave, I gotta leave with him, but after our talk at the funeral home, he's more likely to stay attached to Luna's whereabouts.

Good for me. Bad for him? I dunno. I'm just hoping this isn't hurting his life in any way. That's the antithesis of what I'm supposed to be doing as his bodyguard.

Speaking of security, Quinnie and Froggy are strolling several paces behind us, and they're eerily quiet. Either they've pissed one another off into the silent treatment or they're just respecting the dead. Can't tell which until I glance back.

They're pissy.

Luna stops next to an old oak tree. She stuffs her hands in her jacket, pulling out a vape, and Xander squats to a black marble headstone. He inspects the old date and vintage name. He's a bit of a history buff, interested in lineages and ancestors and kingdoms. It's the fantasy brain in him, most likely.

My girlfriend (never gets old) passes me her vape.

I take a drag, and she checks her phone. Her nose crinkles with her brows. The start of a panicked face. One I'm more accustomed to seeing with her amnesia.

"You alright?" I ask, blowing smoke up at the sky. I hand the vape back. She takes a short drag, still glancing at her phone. I wave my hand. "Luna?"

"Huh?" Her collar is strict like she's caging some breath. Alarm fills her eyes, but she's not looking at me. She's super-glued to the phone.

Concern is injected in my bloodstream. "What's wrong?" I ask and draw her several feet from Xander. More out of earshot.

Her entire body is tensing, but she's still physically close to me.

"Is it the internet?" I throw out a guess.

She holds my gaze for a beat, her eyes big like she wants to tell me something. "I…" She looks scared, and really, it fucking terrifies me. I never want her to be afraid of anything *ever* again.

I bring her against me. She nestles her cheek into my chest and my warmth. Her body feels like a rigid board. I kiss her hair and slip my hand against her wrist. Her pulse is racing. I barely hear her murmured words, and I dip my head to her lips just to piece apart what she's telling me.

"I don't want this to hurt our relationship at all," she whispers. "Not when we just became something. But I think I need your help, Donnelly." One of her hands grips tighter to my beltloops.

"Whatever you need, I'm here. I'll always help you," I tell her.

Instead of fearing whatever has her freaked out, I hang on to the best part of her asking me for help. Luna sees me as reliable, the one she can depend on for anything. Why else would she be coming to me with her problems and not her older brother?

Makes me feel like her actual boyfriend.

Which I am, but damn, I'm really going to love the fuck out of this.

"Can this stay between us for right now?" Luna whispers.

"Yeah," I promise, hooking her pinky with mine. "It's safe with me."

Luna takes a readying breath and places her phone in my palm, trusting me with what's scaring her. An incoming text vibrates the cell.

I look at the new message and my stomach drops.

Come on baby. You know you miss me too. I'll give you the best time you've had all year. Promise 🖐 — Unknown.

What the fuck? Every muscle in my body is searing. *Who* the fuck?

Quickly, I type in her passcode. Unlocking the phone, I read through the most recent thread.

Unknown: I'm around if you can meet. Can't stop thinking about you.

Luna: Who is this?

Unknown: Cute. I know you saved my number. I was the one who put it in your phone.

Luna: Maybe I forgot about you.

Unknown: Tease. No way could you forget me. I made you come so hard, you said I was the greatest fuck you've ever had.

Unknown: Come on baby. You know you miss me too. I'll give you the best time you've had all year. Promise 🖐

The fear in Luna's eyes is worse than the sickness trying to burn my esophagus.

"How long has he been texting you?" I whisper, about to scroll up to see.

"Not long," she says, just as hushed. "That I know of. I guess Original Luna could've deleted old text threads. It seems like something I did."

"Probably in case anyone stole your phone."

"Yeah." Her voice is strained. "I don't know who he is, Donnelly, and I'm trying not to advertise that I lost my memories. It's all...so messed up."

"We'll figure it out." I tuck her closer again, and she relaxes more at the embrace. With one hand, I scroll through her contacts. First name I think of is *Noah Perch*. The prick outside of Thirsty Goose. Except, there are no Noahs saved in her phone.

Instead, I sift through an endless scroll of *Unknowns*. There must be about a hundred of them. My stomach cramps. "Luna..." I show her.

She pales. "I must've started saving numbers under *Unknown* after I turned eighteen—because I've never done that." Panic spikes her voice.

"It's okay—"

"No, it's not." She intakes a sharp breath.

I set my hands on her shoulders, then touch her cold cheek. "Luna. Breathe."

"Why would she—why would *I*...?" Her face falls. She's crushed, and it's killing me. "What if these are all the guys I've slept with? What if this is my body count?"

"So what if it is?"

She looks sick to her stomach. "I don't want it to be. I can't remember any of it. If it was good, if it was bad, if it hurt, if I liked it, if I hated it." Tears well in her eyes, and I hold her against my chest again, stroking my fingers through her glittery hair while she calms.

Frog asks over comms, "Is she okay?"

"Should we approach?" Quinn's voice follows.

I click my mic. "Just give us a few minutes."

"Sure. You are the boyfriend after all," Frog says, a smile to her voice.

Yeah, I've always liked Frog.

Quick glance at Xander, he's still at the headstone and he's scrolling on his phone now. Maybe looking something up, so I focus on my girlfriend. She lets go of me and slides down the oak tree. Sitting.

I join her. "Sad alien."

"This isn't a mystery I thought I'd have to solve," she says quietly. "The Who Did I Sleep With for Three Years and Tell No One unsolved case."

"You're not solving it by yourself." I tap back into her messages. "Have you tried calling this number?" I flash her the *Unknown* contact who just texted.

She shakes her head slowly. "I was scared to talk over the phone. I didn't want anyone thinking I forgot about them." Her panicked face returns. "What if...what if he's someone you know?"

I fight off a grimace. "I don't think it could be." *Unless this is O'Malley.* But it's not his number. And I suddenly realize, "This isn't a Philly area code."

"What is it then?"

I don't even have to consult Google. I already know the answer. 'Cause I lived there. "New York." I'm about to dial the number, but I hesitate. What's the chance they don't pick up and then I've opened a window for this guy to nonstop call Luna?

I send the contact to my phone. "I'm gonna call him later. Not on your phone though."

Her eyes are lost on her phone, which is still in my hand. "This might be worse than just those texts."

My muscles strain like I'm in a one-armed plank position. "What else is going on?"

"I get prank calls, sometimes. They're all Unknowns too. I can't figure out half of who anyone is."

So she's being harassed too. A pain wedges in my ribs. "Next time someone calls, let me answer it?" I ask.

She nods.

I hate that she's going through this on top of *everything* else. I want to take this off her plate, even if it should be something Quinn and Frog deal with. It falls more under bodyguard duties than boyfriend duties, but I promised I'd keep this between me and her for now.

"Can I go through your recent call history?" I ask her.

"Yeah. You can send all the *Unknown* caller contacts to yourself."

That's what I do. I'll have our IT team trace the numbers. Hopefully they won't ask too many questions.

I don't feel like I'm competing with guys that can crop up at any moment. Luna isn't interested in her past with them. She's just looking to me for protection *from* them, and I want to bubble-wrap her until she's waddling out of here like the blueberry girl from Willy Wonka.

Frustration knits her brows this time. "It might be too much to dig out from."

"Pile that dirt on me," I tell her, making a *rock on* gesture. "I'm already halfway buried. There's nothing I can't get out of."

"With a shovel?"

"Nah, I've got the best hands for digging myself out of shit, and I'll use them for us."

I let go of our phones when she grabs my hands. She inspects my callused palms with a sweet meticulousness. It double-thumps my heart.

"They are tough hands," she says, as if charting it down for history's sake. "Of the best digging caliber."

It reminds me of all the moments she's done something similar, of all the times she couldn't possibly remember. I have serious déjà vu again.

"See, I've got the hands," I breathe.

"What do I bring?"

"The heart." I eye her lips as she eyes mine. "You have two since I already gave you mine."

She presses a hand to her heart. "Feels mighty."

God, I want to wrap myself around her and hold her for the rest of eternity. Till death do we never part. "Your heart is mighty, Luna," I say.

Her smile appears, and it's a beautiful sight. I help her to her feet. Standing, I curve my arms around her shoulders, and she holds on to my waist with equal force.

I glance down at Luna Hale, at her soft pink lips and more

residual glitter near the creases of her amber eyes. "We're gonna dig ourselves out of every hole anyone tries to push us in, I know that."

"You're not exhausted yet?" she wonders.

"Not even close," I say. "Are you?"

"No," she says with more confidence. "I'd do anything to be with you." I believe her when she says it, but there are things I never want Luna to have to do.

She peers back at the freshly dug grave we wandered away from. Only a few cars remain, and beside a silver Rolls-Royce, an older woman shoots us a scathing look. Her wrinkly fingers clasp the strand of pearls around her neck.

The Crow.

"I think I screwed the chance at ever being her favorite," Luna says softly.

"Lucky you."

Her grandmother waits for her driver to open the door, but as soon as he does, she has to tear her glare off me. After slipping inside the car, she disappears.

HOLIDAY TASK LIST

Sent by Jane Moretti

This is an extensive list of your duties for when you arrive at the lake house. Please complete the decorating in a timely manner, as Christmas Eve is **tomorrow.** There is a separate list of who'll be cooking breakfast and lunch while our parents handle all dinners, you can see the meal plan for the week (page 3). Also, if you'd like to switch tasks with a cousin/sibling/spouse, that is acceptable, as long as **every task is completed.** Merci beaucoup! Joyeux noël!

Jane/Moffy: Unload and put away all food provisions.

Thatcher/Farrow: Chop firewood.

Charlie/Beckett: Shovel snow off front porch and back deck. (If no snow, help wherever needed.)

Sulli/Akara/Banks: Find and chop down Christmas tree.

Eliot/Tom: Outdoor lights – porch, bushes, etc.

Luna/*Donnelly: Reindeer duty (*unclear whether Donnelly is joining the family or security for the holidays. If security, disregard him from this list, and Eliot & Tom will help Luna.)

Xander/Ben: Tree lights. (Untangle first, then help wherever is needed until the tree is available.)

Winona/Vada: Garland and wreaths, inside and outside.

Kinney/Audrey: Trinkets around house, ornaments, and Cardboard Connor.

15

LUNA HALE

The lake house during Christmastime. As far as my memory stretches back, this place has been a sanctuary, even amid holiday mayhem and some fiery disputes. Like that one time Charlie made Ben cry and lock himself in his bedroom for five whole days. Ben was seven.

There have been sibling and cousin rifts. There've been burnt sugar cookies and smoky kitchens. Hundreds of unwrapped presents, many more smiles, home videos, and tears of joy and tears of sorrow. It is the recipe of every messy, lovable family, but ours just happens to be of the extremely wealthy variety. With security housing down the street and bodyguards posted round-the-clock a mile out so the public never discovers the cherry red lake house.

I love it here, and I'd like to believe all of this has never changed and will never change while we're alive. That even among the heartache and pain, this is the place where we get stitched back together.

None of us have taken off our funeral wardrobe. Even Tom and Eliot are in their designer suits while balancing on the roof and stringing lights against the gutter. I have a good view of them since I'm outside on the front yard.

It's already the evening in the Smoky Mountains, so we're trying to finish our tasks before sundown.

"You have a typo, Jane Eleanor!" Tom calls out when Jane carries tote bags of vegetable produce to the house. "It's not a task list. It's a *chore* list."

"You tell her, brother," Eliot grins.

"That is not the definition of a typo," Jane notes, struggling with the front door while her hands are full. I'm about to go help when Moffy exits and kicks out a doorstopper for her. She thanks him in French and says other words I can't translate as easily.

My older brother replies in the same language, but as she switches to English, I realize they're discussing the logistics of putting away groceries while Jane is also keeping an eye on her newborn. Maeve has been napping in a portable bassinet, currently located in the kitchen.

"I can get the rest from the cars," Moffy says, and she nods, vanishing from sight.

I have the most important task, and it has nothing to do with reindeer duties. A little bundled baby is warm and happy in a lavender sling against my chest, and I entertain my niece with side-shimmies and tickles. Cassidy coos and smiles.

I volunteered to babysit, and Donnelly was the first to look surprised.

"I like baby cuddles," I told him.

"I know," he said, unwrapping a decorative baby reindeer from a black garbage bag. "Just didn't think the dads would let someone babysit without a five-minute back-and-forth first."

Maximoff and Farrow are protective of their kids, I've deduced, and I wonder why they let me take care of Cassidy so quickly. Either they trust me enough or they think I need this. As therapy? Baby snuggling therapy? Is that a thing? I hope it's the former more than the latter.

Because the latter means they think I'm not doing so well, and I feel like I've just hopped on a brighter path. With Donnelly.

He's here as my boyfriend first. Weird.

The best kind of weird.

I smile.

"Daddy!" Ripley races after Moffy to a parked Ford truck. Uncle Ryke usually drives his truck to the lake house during the holidays. Otherwise, I don't see him use it much, except for the time he helped Moffy move into his college dorm at Harvard.

Most of the provisions for the week are in the truck bed.

Moffy turns around and tries to feign confusion at the giddy little boy. "Who is that?"

"Ripley!" He says his name so well for his age, and the pride on Moffy's face makes my smile mushroom. I still can't believe I thought Ripley was *my* baby when I woke up in the hospital, but times like this, where Ripley's blue eyes glint in the sun and his hair looks more like Donnelly's chestnut brown—I think it would've been stranger if I didn't consider it.

"You want to carry something, Rip?" he asks once he's at the bed of the truck.

"*Yes*," Ripley says clearly.

"Here you go." He snaps off a banana from a bundle. "Take that to Auntie Jane."

Ripley hoists the banana over his head, waiting for his dad to carry his own load of groceries, and Moffy packs himself down with a case of water, several totes, and the rest of the bananas. They go together to the house, but Ripley makes a detour to…Donnelly.

Moffy stops to wait for his son, and I watch Donnelly take a hesitant step away from the family of reindeer he's been uncovering from garbage bags. He wipes his hands on his black slacks, and as his eyes flit to me, I wonder if he thinks I'm staring.

I am staring.

I'm just interested in his relationship with my nephew, I guess. OG Luna knew. I only have small glimpses. Barely a peek.

"Here you go," Ripley repeats what his dad said and tries to hand Donnelly the banana.

Donnelly crouches down. "You brought this for me?"

"No."

"No?"

"Yes," he nods now.

Donnelly grins. "Gotta love a boy who knows what he wants." His eyes flash to me, the smile still in them, and my heart flip-flops. He takes the banana but acts like it weighs twenty pounds. "You carried this heavy thing all the way from over there?"

Ripley smiles. "It's a nana."

"I love a nana."

I laugh, and Moffy is smiling too. And then Ripley hops over to me. "Jump!" he tells me. "Jump!"

I blink, woozy as my head suddenly spins.

"Jump!"

He leap-frogs past me, aimed for Moffy.

I can almost feel the warmth of a living room.

"Jump!"

Donnelly is studying me with more concern, and I wonder if the blood has rushed out of my face. This feels less like an island of memory and more like the melting tip of an iceberg that disappears beneath my feet. I'm plunged into the ocean, struggling to find land, but I take a few deep breaths and try to push past the discomfort in my body.

"You okay?" Moffy asks first.

I nod. "Yeah."

He checks on Cassidy. "Thanks for watching her," he tells me for the umpteenth time.

"It's the best gig," I sing-song, but the melody sounds a little flat.

Still, Cassidy beams up at me. Moffy seems reluctant to peel away. I think more so because he loves her, less so because he's worried I'll fail. At least, that's what I want to believe. Once Moffy and Ripley are back inside, I head over to Donnelly before he comes to me.

"You remember something?" he asks. "You had that look."

"It just felt like a memory, but I couldn't see it." I shrug, trying not to be disappointed. It's easy when Donnelly stays more positive.

"No rush," he says. "You have forever."

With me, I wish he'd add.

I pretend he does, and I watch as he adjusts a mid-sized reindeer beside the baby. "You're really good with Ripley."

"That's all him. He's a sweet little kid." Donnelly stakes the mid-sized reindeer made of wire and lights into the front yard. A light layer of snow dusts the grass. He casts a quick glance back at the house, like he's worried Ripley will return, and when he notices that *I* notice him, he ends up saying, "The best place for Ripley is with his dads. Always will be."

"You don't like being around him?"

"It's not that..." He makes sure Tom and Eliot aren't eavesdropping, but they're not in view. I suspect they're working on the rear of the house. "He's the Donnelly that got out, Luna. I'm not fully out—"

"But—"

"I'm not," he breathes, then stands up. "There's a...*darkness* clung to me that I might never be able to fully detach from." His eyes fall to the baby in the sling, then he looks away at the rustling fir trees in the distance. "I love being here. With you. With your family." His gaze rests softly against mine. "But I'm always expecting the rug to be pulled out from under me, and it's bad enough you're standing on it now too."

"I think I've always been on the same rug," I say so quietly, I doubt he hears.

By the empathetic look in his blue eyes, I realize he caught the sound. "I hate that, you know. I want to pick you up and place you on Thebula's grass."

"Right beneath the Divothian Waterfall."

He grins. "You're soaking wet."

"Uh-huh," I smile back. "Drenched in the waters of immortality."

"With me."

My heart swells five sizes too big. "With you."

His grin edges farther across his face, and then he steps back to examine his work. "Prancer lookin' fine as hell."

"All the other reindeer are jealous."

"They'll just have to be." He straightens the mom reindeer, the entire family standing at perfect alignment. No one is even lopsided or crooked.

I bounce from side-to-side, and Cassidy begins falling asleep with the movement. "I have some good news," I tell him.

He glances my way. "Smother me with it, space babe."

"You don't have to crash at security's cabin this week. My dad said you could spend the night at the lake house."

His shock unsteadies him. He leans on Prancer, and the reindeer nearly tips over. Donnelly catches his balance and uprights the decoration. "Your dad? Loren Hale?"

I smile, glad I could deliver some happiness, considering he's always blanketing those warm sentiments over me. "My dad," I confirm. "We had a good conversation in the Cobalt's library this morning."

"Must've been some talk." He's still in shock. "What about your mom?"

"I...don't know." I think hard. "I just assumed they were a united front on this one. But...I guess I can't be sure. I haven't had a big talk with her yet. I figured she'd come to me when she's ready."

He lets this sink in. "I'm staying in your room?"

"Yeah, but I bunk with Eliot and Tom, so we're not totally alone."

It dawns on him. "Your dad knew that."

"Yep."

I've heard that ever since Moffy, Jane, and Sulli got married, the rooms at the lake house have been rearranged to accommodate the new spouses. It's begun to limit the remaining rooms, and there isn't an extra space for me and Donnelly unless we want to sleep in the storage closet.

"But it's a four-bunk bedroom," I add. "You'd just take the extra bunk underneath me."

"Bunk mates," Donnelly nods his head like he's digging this arrangement. "It definitely beats rooming with Epsilon. Massive upgrade."

I grin. "I'm happy to be your friendly neighborhood concierge."

"Let's just hope the friendly neighborhood concierge's dad is truly chill with me being her bunk mate."

"He's too preoccupied with my grandfather's death to worry about me," I say, and I'm not exactly sure it's true. But I hope it is.

Loud laughter cascades out of the house. "What the fuck, Kits, that's not true," Sulli says mid-laugh. "Stop laughing."

"You're laughing too," Akara points out while they descend the front porch stoop. "And it's a funny story."

She peeks back at Banks, who towers behind them. Her cheeks are flushed, and Akara teases her for being embarrassed in front of her husband. *They're both her husbands*, I remind myself.

Discovering the Kitsulletti triad has been like witnessing a shooting star in a far-off galaxy. While entirely mesmerizing, it feels like if I blink, it'll disappear. Like I'm imagining the event.

"You're saying you never slipped off the diving board?" Akara asks, coming down to the front yard. They've changed into winter gear and hiking boots, and Banks carries an axe over his shoulder.

"Never happened," Sulli says.

"And you weren't checking out the lifeguard?"

"No." She blushes. "Can we just drop it?" Her baby bump is more noticeable, but she's not due until next year.

Akara frowns, then glances back at Banks with a silent exchange. I don't know either of them well. I'm not even sure how much OG Luna did.

"We all had crushes when we were sixteen," Akara tells her. "Donnelly." He suddenly brings him into the conversation. "Who'd you crush on?"

His eyes dart to me, then the sky. "The moon. Round and sexy. Always out to play at night." He makes a crude gesture with his fingers, splitting them in a V, and sticks his tongue between them.

I grin.

Akara holds out a hand like it's strange evidence but evidence nonetheless. "There you go, Sul. It's not that big of a deal. The lifeguard wasn't that ugly—"

"It was you!" she snaps. "Okay, it was *you*. You were standing behind him, Kits. I was looking at *you* and I slipped—which I never do!"

Akara is stunned.

Banks buckles in laughter.

"It's not funny," Sulli groans.

"No, now it's fuckin' hilarious," Banks says, his laughter making Sulli's restart, but she tries to stop, then strides away from her husbands.

"Fucking *ugh*," she curses, then sees me. I expect her to ignore me since most family were told not to bombard me after the amnesia, but she approaches.

My stomach twists.

"Hey," she says. "You want to come with us? We're not going too far into the woods to find the tree."

"I, um…" I glance down at Cassidy. "I'm babysitting, so…"

"Oh fuck, yeah. Sorry." Sulli teeters on her feet, uncertain.

I want to visualize the friendship we had, but I can't picture it. Did we share inside jokes? Did we grow apart when she married Akara and Banks?

"Later?" Sulli tries again. "Maybe we can hang out with Jane. Or with our sisters?"

That sounds odd too, and my stomach overturns again. "Yeah, maybe."

I'm nervous about these social interactions that I built and can't make sense of. I want to *try*, but what if I just disappoint Kinney and Sulli and even Jane by being the Variant Luna?

They'd say there is no pressure, but I feel it more when I'm around the girls of the family. Partly, I want to preserve what I created, in hopes it'll exist and remain untarnished if I ever do remember, but here lies the trouble: I could never remember anything with them. And then what do I have left?

Sulli shuffles away, and Banks curves an arm around her shoulders, guiding her up the hill. Akara whispers to her, and I realize I fucked up that interaction.

We both lost a friendship, but it might be more painful for her. When we were young, we used to have a lake house tradition together. Ice skating on the lake in the early, *early* Christmas morning. Though, we ended that when we got older, and I wonder if maybe OG Luna reignited it during a time I can't remember.

My phone chimes in my pocket.

Donnelly places his gaze on me, and I already feel his protectiveness over me. Like he's bracing for another attack. Another stray text from a rando. Another catastrophe to shield me from. Another rug being pulled beneath our feet.

I check my phone and exhale. "It's just a Fanaticon notification for Bass. They're casting minor roles for season two."

He breathes out too.

I tuck my phone in my jacket, then bounce Cassidy a little. "Do you think we'll ever reach a place where we're not standing on our tiptoes, waiting to sprint?"

He starts to smile, which surprises me. "What do you have against sprinting?"

I shrug. "I'm not that fast."

"I'll carry you."

"I'll weigh you down."

"You're air in my arms."

I smile at the fantastical image. "You'll never stop, will you?"

"I don't know how," he admits. "That's the thing about the rug. You stop caring if it gets pulled when you figure out how to land on your feet when it does."

"Teach me how," I say.

Donnelly approaches with a grin. "And so the apprentice becomes the master."

"It was bound to happen," I whisper, my heart speeding out of my body as his hand slides against my cheek. He leaves some space between us to make room for Cassidy. And I suspect he'll shy away from doing anything more because of the baby.

But he's close enough.

And then…he dips his head, and he's kissing me. His lips meld against mine with a tingling heat, and his tongue breaks my lips apart, as if teaching me how to kiss for the first time.

My body sings and aches to bow against his tall frame. My mind ignites in neon shades. My pulse skyrockets through earth's atmosphere. All kisses should feel as world-altering as the ones with him.

Bang!

We flinch at the violent noise, but he keeps a protective hand on my neck. My pulse jumps into my throat, and Donnelly trains a vigilant eye on the front door.

"The wind must've blown it closed," he tells me. "You alright?"

"Yeah." I check Cassidy. She's calm and content. "Are you?" I ask him.

He nods, then flashes me the *rock on* gesture. He gathers the trash bags before a gust carries those away.

I help and pass him one. "I've thought more about my memory guardian." *I've made a choice.*

There's also a great, planet-sized chance that Donnelly won't love who I picked.

16

LUNA HALE

"I was just thinking about your memory guardian." Donnelly crumples the trash bags in his hands. "We must be riding the same wavelength."

"Uh-huh," I agree. "Different species. Same language."

"One of these days I'm going to morph into an alien and we'll be the same—then what are you going to do, space babe?"

"Marvel at the discovery of inter-species transmutation."

He's smiling so wide, but it falters when he asks, "So who'd you choose?"

"Just so we're speaking the same language still," I reiterate, "this is solely a guardian of my memories. Not the knower-of-all or someone who means more to me than you do."

Donnelly tightens his eyes at the sun. "Do I *like* this guardian of your memories? Are they a good person?"

I squint. "Uh...depends on who you ask. I would classify them as more of an anti-hero. A Loki."

"Eliot?"

"Good guess, but...no." My face burns because I can see the gears shifting at rapid speed in Donnelly's very intelligent brain. I had considered the possibility that he might not like who I selected, but I'm hopeful he'll warm up to the idea with context.

"It can't be Maximoff," he says like it's now a fact.

My oldest brother is not an anti-hero or mischief-maker. It is known.

"Maybe Loki isn't the exact right thing," I say. "He's like an archangel."

"Lucifer was an archangel," Donnelly reminds me, less humor in his tone. "Satan himself your memory guardian?" At this point, I'm positive he knows who I chose.

I squint even harder. "You're not far off, maybe."

He drops the trash bags, just to scrape his hands through his hair. Then he says, "I'll do it."

"What?"

"I'll read your diary. Front to back. I accept the position." He puts a hand to his heart, and my natural reaction is to shake my head. Pain crosses his face. "Why not pick me?"

"Because you were right when you said I shouldn't. It'd hurt you."

"Luna—"

"No," I say strongly, a fierceness surging forth that I don't quite understand—other than, I would do *anything* to protect him. Anything at all, and in a moment of vulnerability, he expressed his limit, and if this is my chance to barricade Donnelly from pain, then I'm going to take hold of it with all my might. "It can't be you."

His eyes redden, fighting emotion, and his gaze lands on me. "But Charlie?"

"He's already read all of my fics," I say quickly. "And he's a member of Mensa. If I need someone to judge when I should be told certain things, a literal genius kinda qualifies."

"I think you'd have a better shot asking an 8 Ball," Donnelly tells me, running both hands through his hair again and keeping them on the top of his head. "Got one in my bag if you change your mind."

"Why do you think it's a bad idea?"

"Not a bad idea." He drops his hands to his sides. "A risky one. Charlie...he's a loose cannon. I wanna trust him with you, I do, but I don't know what's going on in his head half the time, Luna. No one does. One day, he could protect your memories. Next minute, he might use them against you or someone else."

"I don't believe he would," I whisper.

"He has it in him though."

"I know," I say into a strong nod. "Which is why I'm choosing him while knowing the risks. I want to give him the chance. But I also know…I know he'd protect me over you, and it's one downside."

"Not a downside for me," Donnelly says.

"I don't want him to hurt you, *ever*." My breathing shortens. "Maybe he is the wrong choice." By choosing Charlie, am I putting Donnelly in the line of fire? Not long ago, Charlie did confess that he called Donnelly contaminated, disease-ridden, *horrible* things right in front of me, Moffy, and Farrow. He said it was his attempt at keeping me away from Donnelly until his family was dealt with. So to help me, he hurt him.

"This isn't about me," Donnelly says, rubbing the crease between his brows. "It's about you. You can't consider me in this—"

"You sound like Dr. Raven—"

"She's right in this instance. 'Cause I can't be a reason you backslide, Luna. If this is gonna help you move forward—if Charlie will help you—then pick Charlie."

My gut says *Charlie*, but it is like choosing a nuclear bomb. "There's another big thing I'm worried about." I drop my voice, careful so no one meandering around the house can overhear. "My brother."

Donnelly frowns. "Xander?"

"Moffy," I correct. "I'm a tad bit concerned he'll be hurt if I choose Charlie and not him. Given their past beef…" I shrug. "I don't want to choose Team Charlie over Team Moffy, but I'm not dumb. I know picking Charlie means I've chosen him in some small way, and maybe that won't be so small in my brother's head."

Donnelly thumbs his black paperclip earring, contemplating things. "He'll get over it."

"You think?"

"He's not at war with Charlie. Hasn't been for a while, and he's got a newborn." He looks at Cassidy again. "You can't worry about his reaction. You just gotta do what's best for you." Donnelly stares deeper into me. "Be selfish for yourself, Luna Hale. It's what I would do."

Donnelly understands survival better than I ever likely could.

Having his vote of confidence is all I really need. "Charlie might say *no*," I tell him. "I haven't asked him yet." I rock on my heels. "I kinda want to do it now and get it over with, but I have no clue where he is." There isn't enough snow to shovel off the front and back porch, so his holiday task could be anything right now.

"I got ya covered." Donnelly clicks the mic at the collar of his button-down. "Donnelly to Oscar, where's Charlie at?"

I'm smiling. Perks of dating a bodyguard. A bodyguard that is *technically* off-duty here at the lake house. It's what I overheard Price telling him. "If you're not with your client, you're not on the job. You need to learn how to keep work and personal life separate," the Alpha lead said. "There won't be mixing bodyguard duties with your dating life. Understood?"

Donnelly agreed, but it's not like he could say *no*. Now that he works for Price Kepler on Triple Shield, he has to abide by their rules.

Right now, Donnelly rolls his eyes at a response over comms. Must not be too nice.

I glare at his radio, kind of pissed they're treating him poorly. They should be happy he's a part of their team. He's a *spectacular* bodyguard. My brother loves him.

After another long moment, Donnelly sets his attention on me. "He's out back on the tree swing."

Weird.

But okay.

"Thanks," I tell him.

"Godspeed, space babe." He gives me a perfect Vulcan salute, and my heart soars out of my body. *This is my boyfriend.* Did I manifest him from one of my fics?

Feels like it.

I return the Vulcan salute, on cloud nine, right before Cassidy lets out a teeny-tiny piercing *wail*. Donnelly and I wince in unison, and I bounce the baby, trying to calm her. "Shhh, Cass," I whisper. "Shhh."

She sniffs and tries to settle.

"It might be the cold," I tell him. "Moffy said he just fed her, so I don't think she's hungry." I glance at the house, then think about Charlie outside on the tree swing. Will he still be there when I return?

"I'll take her," Donnelly suddenly says.

"You sure?"

He's already coming forward. "Yeah, I'm done here anyway. You go find Charlie." Quickly, he helps me detach the sling, and he's cradling Cassidy like a natural. No awkwardness as he tucks her against his chest. I'd think he's held a million babies over his lifetime, but I highly doubt the number is that high.

As we depart in two different directions, I cast a quick glance back. He climbs the front porch steps, his body language at ease but his eyes seem uncertain. I have a feeling he's not telling me everything, but I keep hope alive that we have time for these close encounters with one another. I want to discover all there is and all there ever could be about my boyfriend.

Leave no stone unturned.

 **LUNA HALE**

To reach the backyard, I navigate through a gravel pad where a plethora of vehicles are parked—from expensive, fully-loaded SUVs to the practical truck and more modest sedans. I take a couple steps and hear Audrey and Kinney somewhere nearby.

"Watch his head, Kinney," Audrey says in panic. "You're getting too close to the Subaru."

"They shouldn't have parked so close to us," Kinney grumbles. "Whose car is that anyway?"

"Uncle Stokes, I think."

Uncle Stokes is Sam Stokes, the husband to my oldest and least famous aunt. Aunt Poppy has dodged the spotlight, and I doubt that's changed much. From what my mom has told me, Aunt Poppy actively avoided the press and media attention. The big irony is that her daughter (my cousin Maria) became a movie star.

The Stokes don't spend *every* holiday with us, but it's not unusual for them to stop by the lake house for a few days. It's even less unusual since we're coming off the tail-end of a funeral. Though, I heard Maria missed it. Her flight from LAX to PHL was delayed and she's supposed to arrive tomorrow now.

"Why is he so heavy?" Kinney huffs like she's carrying a dead body.

I pass the blue Subaru, not seeing my sister yet. And then Kinney lets out a loud gasp.

"Oh...my..." Audrey is hyperventilating. "His head!"

I slip around a baby blue Land Rover and see Cardboard Connor's head on the gravel.

"I didn't do anything," Kinney snaps and points at the car. "It was the Subaru's sideview mirror."

"My dad..." Audrey is still holding the cardboard torso. "My dad is decapitated."

"Cardboard Dad," Kinney says. "And he's like seventy years older than this now." She gestures to the cardboard face of a young twentysomething Uncle Connor. "The young version of him is disturbing. This might be a Christmas miracle for my eyes."

"I'm never going to live this down," Audrey panics. "My brothers are going to tease me endlessly."

Kinney sighs. "I bet there's tape and superglue in the house. If we *have* to fix him, we can, but I still think we should throw him away."

"We can't be the ones to ruin a family tradition. Everyone already treats us like we're babies." Kinney's sixteen and Audrey turns sixteen next month, but for me, they've jumped from preteens to teenagers in the snap of a finger.

"I would rather hide and seek a new makeup palette than hide and seek a piece of dusty old cardboard," Kinney says. "Maybe that should be our next ritual."

Audrey catches my gaze from around the Land Rover. "Luna?"

Kinney rotates, seeing me. "Why are you creeping around here?"

Was I creeping? I was just passing on by! "I'm on my way... somewhere." Saying the full truth about Charlie will spark a million questions that I'm not exactly prepared to answer.

Kinney raises her brows. "Makes total sense." Got to hand it to her, she's perfected our dad's sarcasm, but the hostility in her green eyes is subdued. "You are okay though?"

"Yep." I nod and stuff my hands in my black puffer jacket.

"Okay." She looks me over, taking this as truth. It is one.

"Luna, *please* don't tell anyone," Audrey pleads with big glassy blue eyes.

"She won't spill," Kinney says confidently. "She's great at keeping secrets." It sounds like a frosty dig, like I haven't shared enough with her. I haven't been forthcoming and I'm not being extra wide-open now.

A pit lowers in my stomach. "Your secret is safe with me," I tell Audrey. "Lips zipped." I mime throwing the key behind my shoulder and I give her a double thumbs up.

Audrey blows out a breath of relief. "We owe you a million."

"We owe her *one*," Kinney amends. "Or we'll be indebted forever."

"One," Audrey says. "We owe you one *glorious* favor, the biggest ever."

"The tiniest favor," Kinney deadpans.

"You owe me none," I say. "It's on the house. A sisterly act of cardboard kindness."

"Thanks," Kinney says with a side-eye that I think is a smile. She heaves the cardboard torso with Audrey and reaches down, grabbing the head.

"Let's go through the side door," Audrey says. "Less people will see us."

I wish I could stay and watch them smuggle decapitated Cardboard Connor into the house, but I have a mission of my own.

Trekking down the side of the house, I slow my pace at the sound of voices, and I hug closer to the siding once I spot a metal ladder and plastic tub of garland. Winona is perched on a rung. Down below, Vada clutches a wreath with a velvet red ribbon.

"Without Ben around, it's *not* the same, Nona," Vada says quietly. "I don't know what he was doing, but at least the T-Bags didn't harass us this much at school."

The T-Bags?

I press my back to the siding of the house. Becoming one with the building. Now I am totally creeping, but in my defense, spying is just a tool. One I can use to catch up on history I might've missed.

Vada continues, "The bikini pics of us that they taped in our lockers—they got a slap on the wrist for it, even after both our dads complained. The teachers aren't going to do anything because Tate's grandfather donated so much money to Dalton, they named the gym after him."

Winona's eyes look puffy like she'd been crying. "I don't want to drag Xander into this."

I freeze at my brother's name.

"Tate literally followed you from Chem to Calc. If Xander even told him off *once*, Tate might leave you alone. The T-Bags suck up to him and basically kiss his ass, and Xander doesn't even realize how cunty they are because *everyone* wants to be Xander's best fucking friend, Nona."

"Or they could start harassing Xander," Winona says. "What if we open the floodgate to that?"

My pulse skips.

"His bodyguard walks the halls with him. Maybe yours should too."

"And what about you, Vada?" Winona asks softly. "You don't have a bodyguard."

"Tate also isn't stalking me from class to class. I think if they were as aggressive with me as they are with you, you'd already be tackling him during fourth period."

Winona digs at her cuticles. "Sometimes it's easier to pick a fight on behalf of someone else." She stands on the metal rung. "Let's just get through the rest of the school year without defaulting to Xander. He's graduating anyway. We'll have to figure out how to deal on our own." She reaches for a wreath.

Vada hands it up to her. "Yeah, you're probably right."

High school bullies, I know too well, but the T-Bags sound like a different breed from what I personally experienced. I want to help them and ensure they're safe at school, but I also wasn't supposed to hear anything.

First mode of action: Try to figure out how to pass them without being seen. Should I crawl? Moon walk? Pretend to wear an invisibility cloak?

I choose the latter. I stroll casually by as if I'm a collection of particles, invisible to the naked eye. Vada and Winona become suddenly more interested in hanging the wreath.

"Up higher," Vada calls out.

Winona rubs at her splotchy face and does a good job of rotating away from me.

I'm not the only one hiding.

Down the hill I go, the glittering lake in view. Ice thickens at the banks, but it hasn't totally frozen over this year. A good distance from the dock, a sturdy oak tips toward the water, and the swing attached to the wide branch sways from the wind. No one is sitting on the wooden board.

Charlie isn't there.

He must've left. I take out my phone. What are the chances he'll reply to a text? I shoot him a quick message: Where are you?

I press send and realize I sound too casual, not urgent enough. Then again, this isn't an emergency. But I could send an SOS...

My phone vibrates before I decide.

The Outpost — Charlie

How does he know about the Outpost?

It sounds more like a mountain town bar, but it's only about a half-mile hike. When I was eleven, Eliot, Tom, and I discovered an old wooden platform tucked between two oak trees. The ladder was rotted, but the bent and gnarled branches and thick trunk made climbing easy.

We theorized the structure was a long-ago hunting blind, but once we stood on it, we weren't staring at the forest where animals prowl. We had an unobstructed view of the calm lake and the landscaping mountains. Later on, we made a sign and called it the Outpost, and we'd sneak out there on warmer nights when we didn't need a fire.

That's where I find Charlie.

His legs hang off the platform. He's sitting and reading a massive paperback. When I scale the tree and touch the wooden planks, he doesn't raise his head to look in my direction.

I take a seat beside him and read the cover. *The Brothers Karamazov* by Fyodor Dostoevsky.

"Light reading?" I ask.

His gaze remains fixed on the book. "Shouldn't you be with the rest of the family, gathering together to mourn our dead grandfather?" He flips a page.

"I'm not sure how much gathering there is right now," I say quietly. "Everyone is busy getting the house ready for Christmas Eve tomorrow." I glance at the book. "I take it you're not going to gather."

"If I can help it, I will avoid it," he says and flips one more page.

"So...the Outpost." I stare out at the sparkling water, the evening sun casting rays of light across the rippling surface. "Did you follow us here one year? Or did I tell you about it?" *Maybe I forgot I told him.*

He licks his finger, turns another page. "Do you really think I would follow you?"

No.

I've never known Charlie to follow anyone, despite the world believing he's stepping in the same exact footprints his father left behind.

"I must've told you," I murmur, my brows crinkling as I scrounge for the memory.

"You didn't." Charlie reads a page silently for a moment, then says, "Did it ever occur to you that I'm older than your best friends?"

He means his brothers.

"It's occurred to me pretty frequently, actually," I say. "You have older brother tendencies."

Charlie side-eyes me with more interest than irritation. "I'm not like your older brother."

"I didn't say you were like Moffy." I try not to lean forward too much. Without a railing, the drop down makes me woozy. "That doesn't mean you don't land in the *older brother* category on the Venn

NOBODY LIKE US **151**

diagram." I zip up my puffer jacket as a gust blows through the Outpost. "You seem particularly irritated by your younger siblings."

"They are annoying." Another page flip.

"But I think deep-down, you would try to move mountains for them, if they really needed you. You just maybe don't feel all that needed, and sometimes, you like it that way. Because it's easier than watching people you love fail over and over again." I watch the light dance over the water, but I feel his gaze on me. "So…" Heat bathes my cheeks, feeling his stare, but I don't brave a glance at Charlie. "I have thought a lot about you being older than us." I whisper, "Maybe it's the writer in me."

Charlie shuts the book. "I found what you and my brothers call *the Outpost* when I was seven. Years later, Eliot tracked me here. I caught him, and next thing I know, there's a sign and cigarette butts and the lingering stench of weed." He eyes me like my decade of sin has never been a secret.

Guilty. "Eliot never told me you found it first."

"Clearly." He places the book behind him. "My brother loves a story where he's at the center."

Eliot might be a showman, but he's also thoughtful enough to put his ego into question. In high school, he bowed out of the lead role in Almost, Maine because he would've had to kiss Jeffra. He refused to kiss the girl who relentlessly bullied me.

"Reality is often colder than the stories we tell," Charlie says, lighting a cigarette. "But you know that." He blows smoke downward. "What do you want, Luna?" His eyes flit over to me.

I can't lie and say I came here for a casual chitchat. It's too obvious I didn't.

With a readying breath, I let it out. "I found a journal that Original Luna wrote—that *I* wrote. I'm not sure how detailed it is or what it says, but I'm nervous reading it from front-to-back will shade my perception of events and people. But if someone else reads it, they might be able to share helpful information, so I won't have to read the text myself. That way, I won't know *everything*, just some things, and this person would be a guardian of my memories. And that's my longwinded way of asking if you'd read my journal for me."

Wow that didn't go as smoothly as I hoped. No matter how ineloquent, I think I made enough sense. I cage breath, nerves assaulting my body.

Please say yes.

Charlie thinks for a half-a-second. "Sure."

"Sure?" My brows rise. "You can sleep on it. It's a big deal. It's my *diary*."

"You called it a journal," Charlie says.

"Same thing."

"A diary implies there are more personal pieces of information than just a journal. Scientists keep journals. They don't necessarily keep diaries."

Oookay.

"Well, I guess I'm not sure how personal it is. It's like a dournal."

Charlie smiles at the made-up word while taking a drag. I know his dad would have cringed at it. "Alright then," he says, smoke billowing out of his nose. "I'll read your dournal." He looks at my empty hands.

"It's in my duffel bag. I can bring it to you later. I didn't want to assume you'd say yes."

"Lack of confidence is noted," Charlie tells me, snuffing the cigarette against the bark of the tree. His youngest brother would not love the desecration of Mother Earth, but I'm not here to poke at the Charlie-Ben eternal feud.

Without another word, Charlie descends the platform, his book beneath his armpit. I follow him to the safety of the ground, and in silence, we hike back to the lake house. Reaching the clearing, I hear an engine cutting out.

His gaze swings to the graveled parking pad. Where a black Mustang just rolled to a stop. We wait as our youngest uncle exits the driver's seat. Uncle Garrison wears a black hoodie underneath a jean jacket—what he wore to Grandfather Calloway's funeral. Aunt

Willow has on a simple black dress, an old backpack hooked over her shoulder.

Hand-in-hand, they walk past the lake house and go straight to a little boathouse not far from the dock. It's where we store canoes, kayaks, lifejackets, and other lake toys.

I frown. "Strange."

"It is," Charlie agrees, and I figure he'll drop the matter. Until he sets course for the boathouse with the casual stride of a sightseer in Paris. Then he spins around, walking backwards, just to catch my gaze. "Are you coming or are you just going to stand there like a stupefied tree?"

Solving a mystery with Charlie wasn't on my bingo card today. But the invitation is all I need to accept the voyage. And the risk.

LUNA HALE

The boathouse is old. Like ancient. Rotted
wooden boards and peeled paint. Eliot, Tom, and I tried our first
joint in there behind a canoe, and we got caught because we screamed
when a rat crawled over Tom's foot.

It's a strange place for my parents, aunts, and uncles to congregate.
The only reason they'd choose it is because it's far enough from the
main house that they wouldn't be overheard or stumbled upon. I
don't think they imagined that two of us would currently be crouched
beneath the lone window, which has never properly closed.

So it's a good spot to eavesdrop, except for the fact that Charlie
and I are squatting near a pricker bush. One slight shift to the left
and I'm attacked by spiky foliage.

"Now that we're all here, can we please talk about this?" Uncle
Stokes asks.

"There's nothing to talk about, Sammy," my dad says, his voice
caustic. "The answer I gave over text still stands. *No.*"

"Come on, Lo," Uncle Stokes replies. "Things have changed now
that we've all seen Greg's will. You can't deny that."

The boathouse goes eerily silent for a beat.

Charlie is rigid.

I cage my breath. They're all dressed in funeral blacks. We just
came off resting my grandfather six-feet under the earth, and it
never really occurred to me there'd be greater consequences to his
death. Other than grief.

"Look," Uncle Ryke says, shifting forward, and his back now partially blocks our view of others. "Sulli has a fucking career. Winona's just a kid. So that leaves me and Daisy out of this whole *fucking* thing. If Greg wanted an heir, he should have brought it up when he was alive."

I glance at Charlie, but he hasn't taken his eyes off the window. An *heir*.

My first thought goes to Fizzle. Grandfather Calloway's brain-child. His long-lasting legacy.

"Your opinion on this still matters," Uncle Connor tells Ryke. "And you won't leave."

"Why is that, Cobalt?" he asks roughly. "Because Daisy has a vested interest in the company?"

"Because your niece or nephew may be the one to take it over, and you care too much about them to put your fingers in your ears."

Uncle Ryke doesn't counter or deny. He takes a heated step to the side, and I crouch a little more as my dad's sharp jawline comes into view. He's gripping a wooden workshop table on either side of him, and my mom wears his suit jacket. It hangs like a big potato sack over her thin frame.

"By all accounts, he was healthy, Ryke," Uncle Stokes says. "He didn't know he was going to have a heart attack."

"Wait, wait," my dad cuts in with cinched brows. "Are we just going to ignore the goddamn fact he was old? My brother is right. I don't care if Greg could run a 5k without huffing on an oxygen tank. Anything could've happened at his age—Christ, at *any* age. He should've had these conversations with us while he was still breathing. Like a decade ago."

"Agreed," Aunt Rose says frostily.

My dad cringes at being on the same page as her. They act like mortal enemies, but I like to imagine they're a ride-or-die pairing in disguise.

"Can we all just be calm about this?" Aunt Poppy asks, standing in the middle with her hands leveled. Her eyes seem puffy from crying. Aunt Daisy and my mom also wear morose expressions when I catch glimpses of them. On the other hand, Aunt Rose hasn't uncrossed her stiff arms.

She looks like a block of ice.

"We are calm," Aunt Rose snaps. "This is calm, Poppy."

Aunt Poppy sighs. "Okay, well, there's more." She eyes someone warily. The person is out of view, but I can only guess it's her husband Uncle Stokes.

"I have talked with Greg over the years," Uncle Stokes says, "about a successor."

"Wow," Uncle Garrison mutters before my dad, Uncle Ryke, and Aunt Rose go off.

"What the fuck, Sammy?"

"You've got to be fucking kidding me."

"And you never thought to tell us?"

Aunt Poppy tries to keep the peace. "Everyone—"

"No," Aunt Rose comes forward but directs her anger at Uncle Stokes. "You had no right to keep this from us."

"He didn't want his daughters to know," Uncle Stokes professes. "I just told *Poppy*. It wasn't easy keeping this from my wife, from my daughter. But Greg was absolutely *adamant*."

Uncle Ryke growls, "Because he fucking *knew* we wouldn't want that life for our kids."

"He didn't want the headache," Aunt Rose stews, pacing back and forth. I hear her heels click-click across the floorboards. "He's a coward."

"Rose," my mom and Aunt Daisy say together.

"It's the truth."

"He's *dead*," Aunt Daisy says tearfully. "He might not have been the perfect dad, but he was good and he cared. That should count for something."

I've come to realize more about my grandfather in these short seconds than maybe my entire lifetime. He feared conflict within his family so much that he took a bomb to his grave. He'd rather implode it when he couldn't feel its destruction.

Then again, maybe the bomb isn't a bomb.

It was just his dreams and desires.

I think Grandmother Calloway created enough friction with their daughters that he felt like any more from him would be fatal. So he was quiet and kind and nonconfrontational, and his true wishes could only be surfaced after he was gone.

It's kind of sad he lived his life without truly expressing himself and with fearing what would happen if he did.

"Can you really blame him?" Aunt Poppy tells the group. "You all go from zero to a thousand."

"Well, *Poppy*," Dad snaps. "It kind of comes with the territory when you have old men with cameras breathing down your kids' necks and your daughter is *kidnapped*." I freeze, avoiding Charlie's quick glance to me. "But sure, let's go from zero to two. We'll huddle around the campfire and roast s'mores while we discuss the dismantling of our kids' lives."

Aunt Poppy looks empathetic.

Uncle Stokes says, "That's exactly what she's talking about. Just take a breath."

"I'm taking many goddamn breaths, Sammy. Why don't you go suck on an inhaler?"

"Lo," Mom says with wide eyes. He calms down instantly for her, then whispers in her ear.

"Let's stay on track," Uncle Connor says, and the tense air seems to calm.

Uncle Stokes continues, "I've been having a few health issues—nothing that's too concerning at this exact moment, but Greg was clear that we needed a path forward. For the future."

"What kind of health issues?" Mom asks, frowning.

He's quiet.

"Jesus Christ," Dad mutters, but Mom pinches him, and he holds his tongue.

"For the sake of transparency," Uncle Connor says, "I think we should know. It'd give us a clearer timeline."

"He's not dying," Aunt Poppy clarifies.

"But I will eventually be stepping down as CEO," Uncle Stokes says. "I'm supposed to choose a successor...a protégé, before I do. Greg wants me to teach them everything I know, and his last wish was for that person to be family. So it's going to be family."

"No, see, we did this before." My dad releases his grip off the workbench and steps forward. "I had to compete with my brother, with Daisy, with Lily for the CEO position at Hale Co. And it was a hell that none of us wanted but we were fighting for—and I'm not doing that to my kids. Over my dead fucking body."

"But we were at least given the choice," Aunt Daisy says. "We all chose to compete for the CEO position."

Mom raises her hand like she's in a classroom. "Maybe we should at least tell the kids. They can decide for themselves. They're old enough to make those decisions."

Aunt Rose has stopped pacing. "They need to be informed that this choice will come with a gallon-sized tank of pressure. No sugar-coating shit. Taking over an entire company for some of them will be more like an ugly fifty-pound lesion growing on their back. Whatever future they want, it won't look like how they've imagined. It'll be fucking obliterated. Forever changed and spoken for, by a legacy they never wanted or asked for."

Uncle Garrison clears his throat. "Not that this isn't the wildest and weirdest thing I've been a part of all day—Willow and I have no stake in this. We're related to the Hale side, not the Calloways. *But* I figured you invited us here as the cool aunt and uncle, and seeing as how we're the youngest and understand what the geriatrics might not—"

Dad interjects, "I wish we all had glaucoma so we could unsee the ugly blob on your neck." It's a Batman tattoo.

Uncle Garrison lets out a dry laugh. "All I'm saying is that I remember being twentysomething-whatever and being faced with crossroads. I didn't always know exactly what I was going to do with my life, but having options opens doors. One of them could *want* it, and you just don't know it yet."

Aunt Willow nudges up her glasses. "They might've thought Sam would never step down."

My aunt is right. I've never imagined Fizzle as something to obtain. I always thought Uncle Stokes would be CEO forever, and then maybe a board member would ascend to the position. I didn't know how important it was to my grandfather for the company to be run by family.

The boathouse falls hushed again.

And as eyes shift, my dad looks to the window. I pop down below the sill. Charlie has pulled slightly back, hidden too. *Did they see us?*

Are they coming over here?

My heart pounds in the silence.

Uncle Connor says, "Who would even be in contention?" I exhale. "Half the children have careers. Some are too young."

"For fuck's sake, are we seriously going to do this again?" Uncle Ryke questions.

"They need to make this choice, not us."

"An *informed* choice," Aunt Rose snaps.

Uncle Connor replies in French, and mine is too rusty to understand anything except the word *darling*. It sounds like he agrees with her.

"What kind of choice is this?" Mom asks. "It's just pressure to be the one who sacrifices their life for the legacy."

"Maybe one of us should do it?" Daisy asks, and I imagine she's looking between her sisters. "We're the Calloway sisters. Dad wanted us to have it in the first place."

"You can't," Uncle Stokes says. "The board will want someone from the next generation. Someone I can train and mold."

"You're not playing with goddamn Play-Doh," Dad cuts in. "These are our kids."

"I'm aware, Lo. I get it," he breathes out, tired almost. "But I can't change Greg's will or the board or any of this fucking shit. It's just the way it is." He must look at Uncle Connor because he says, "And to answer your question, who would be considered? We'd obviously be looking at the ones who don't have current jobs and are at least eighteen—or about to turn eighteen." He's implying Xander, but he goes ahead and lists, "Charlie, Eliot, Ben, Xander, and Luna—"

"Keep Luna out of this," Dad interjects again. "She's had enough problems."

My heart catapults to my throat and rises to my ears. My pulse hammers so hard it's difficult to listen, and I feel a tug on my hand.

Charlie is pulling me away from the window. *What?* No! They're still talking.

I try to step back, but he yanks me harder and my knee scrapes one of the prickers. Ouch. To avoid a full leg of scratches, I slip to the side and follow his lead.

He's hiking up the hill towards the house. My breath is heavy, and Charlie is silent.

"You heard all that, right?" I ask him, wondering if I'm stuck in a dream-state. Any second now, I'll wake up in bed.

He's already pulling out his phone. Ignoring my question.

"What are you doing?" I ask.

Again, he says nothing.

But my phone pings, and I realize he sent a text. I'm a part of many different cousin group chats, so I can't be sure who he just messaged. Not until I read the name of the group chat.

A-SQUAD + LUNA

This...this chat must've been created in the time I'm missing. I scroll through the contacts listed beneath the chat name. Jane, Maximoff, Sullivan, Beckett, Charlie.

The A-Squad are the five oldest of our families.

Attic. Now. — Charlie

19

LUNA HALE

I'm not sure I've ever personally braced the musty depths of this attic. Holiday decor is located in the daylight basement's storage closet. A well-traveled location for all.

Whereas the attic looks like it was left behind in another era entirely. It's a spacious relic of discolored cardboard boxes, worn and yellowed furniture from the 2010s, old baby cribs, broken tricycles, and hidden junk.

Dust blankets every floorboard, except for the new footprints veering in multiple directions. The six of us are astronauts and we took our first steps on the moon.

I like to think I'm sitting on moondust and not just dirt and dust bunnies. I'm sprawled out on the hardwood, the only one choosing the floor as a seat.

Charlie rests his weight against an ornately carved wardrobe. He's not very alarmed considering the bomb we just dropped on Beckett, Sulli, Moffy, and Jane. I can't really point fingers since I've contemplated making moondust angels.

But this is serious.

I can see that in how my older brother hasn't taken a seat. He stands upright like an untouched, never-played-with Captain America action figure. "Were they ever planning on telling us about the will?" Moffy asks me and Charlie.

Charlie looks to me, waiting for me to respond to my brother.

He's been doing that. Shuffling the storytelling to me, even though *he* called this meeting. I kinda like just being the voyeur to the A-Squad. It's not like I remember being included in this group to this degree.

"Uh," I say. "That's a matter of perception, I guess. We didn't hear a definitive answer."

"And what is your perception?" Jane asks me from a rickety rocking chair. It creaks as she sits forward in curiosity, her fingers beneath her chin. She is somehow both feminine grace and clumsiness, a unique amalgamation.

"If we give it time, I think they'd tell us," I say.

"They were still debating it," Charlie says. "I didn't care to wait for them to decide either way."

Sulli sneezes into her palms.

"Bless you," Beckett tells her. They're sitting together on a squishy plaid couch.

"Thank you, *fuck*—" Another sneeze. Then a third.

Beckett takes out a deep blue pocket square from his tailored black suit jacket. I'm guessing he didn't cry at the funeral since he gives Sulli the unused silk cloth.

She wipes her nose. "There's no fucking way my dad would want me or my sister to take over Fizzle."

"It doesn't matter what they want," Charlie says.

Beckett asks, "And what if no one wants it?"

"It doesn't matter what we want either." He threads his arms loosely. "Our parents are going to sit in a room with lawyers and comb through our grandfather's will and see the cost of not obeying his final wish. They won't pressure us to be the lifeline, but there is pressure because this isn't just up to them. The board will see the consequences, and the people in those chairs will make sure a successor from the second generation is named."

Goose bumps pimple my arms, and I want to blame the draft as temperatures drop outside and the sun lowers.

Jane's eyes dart to Moffy. "History is repeating itself, old chap."

Moffy's brows knit together. "When my dad was forced to compete for CEO of Hale Co.—he said winning was losing. They all wanted it because it was the only way to ensure the people they loved wouldn't be stuck in that position. I bet they're worried we'll all do the same."

"Oui," Jane agrees.

"They didn't name any of you," I chime in.

Charlie cocks his head at me, possibly wondering why I would divulge this piece of information. But I'm wondering why he chose *these* four out of everyone to text. They're not even in contention!

"What do you mean?" Beckett asks, then looks to his twin brother.

Charlie speaks to me in a made-up language. That *I* made. It's the ancient language of the blood court on the planet Demos in the Thebulan saga. It shocks me at first, especially that he even knows how to pronounce the words like I intended.

He said, *Tell them.*

Moffy looks between us with furrowed brows, then his gaze settles on me. "You okay, sis?"

I must appear as startled as I feel. "Uh-huh." I take a breath. "Our parents talked about who'd be in the running, and they tossed out anyone who has a career."

"Who'd they name?" Beckett asks with more concern.

"Charlie, Eliot, Ben, Xander...and me."

Moffy rakes a hand against the back of his stiff neck when he hears our brother's name and mine, and Beckett's jaw tenses in a way I've never seen from him.

"What the fuck," Sulli mutters, then sneezes.

"Bless you," Beckett says smoothly again. "Why bring us here, Charlie? I can't protect them from this. You know I can't." His eyes redden, and it's not from allergies.

"I just wanted you here," Charlie says simply, then addresses Jane, Sulli, and Moffy. "I wanted to give you three the opportunity to take the helm. Because if any of you want it, now's the time to take it before we call up the younger ones."

"I don't want it." Sulli's voice sounds stuffed. "I'm having a fucking *baby* in April, and I just launched a fitness app with Kits and Banks." Her phone buzzes, and she adds after reading the text, "The two of which just chopped down a ten-foot tree without me and now they're asking what's going on." She left them in the woods to join this impromptu meeting. "I'm texting that I'll let them know in a sec."

"The ballet," Beckett says. "I can't." It's assumed that he can't take over Fizzle while also dedicating his life to dance.

Jane has her fingers steepled to her lips. "I can't either." Her apologetic eyes ping to us all, resting the longest on Maximoff. "I'd do this with you, but Thatcher is still suspended from security work, and I need to be with him and Maeve."

And then there was one.

Everyone now looks to Moffy—the brother I've always known would take a bullet for each of us. He would lose everything if it meant we had everything. That was also the brother who never fell in love.

He cracks his knuckles, barely breathing. His gaze is faraway.

"You don't have to," I whisper.

His forest-green eyes lift to mine, a struggle within them.

"He could," Charlie says, then tells Moffy, "What's it going to be, Superman? The cape is in reach. Take it."

Moffy casts a glance at the shut attic staircase, then digs in his pocket. "I need to call Farrow—"

"Can't make a decision on your own?"

"Don't be a fucking dick, Charlie," Sulli snaps. "He's allowed to call his husband. It's a big deal. If he took this on, it'd totally affect Farrow and their kids."

"He's the CEO of an award-winning philanthropy. He's sat in meetings at Hale Co., the only company of our families that rakes in close to what Fizzle earns. He has the most experience in the corporate world. That makes him the most qualified of us all." Charlie twists his head to Moffy. "So here's your chance, Maximoff. Fall on the proverbial sword. We all know you love doing it."

Moffy keeps a firm hand on the back of his own neck. His other fist is tightening around the phone, and his eyes narrow on Charlie in a much angrier way.

Charlie and my brother are now having a stare-off, each one glaring at the other, and my nerves spike. *Don't fight. Don't go back to what was.* My breathing shortens.

"You're scaring Luna—stop, Charlie," Beckett says quietly.

Charlie cuts his gaze to the side, then steps away from the wardrobe. He returns his attention to Moffy. "Is it hard for you? You can save everyone from years of being stuck in corporate hell," Charlie says, walking towards him. "Save your brother. Save my brothers. Save your little sister." His eyes flash to me, and in that one look, the world slows…and I sense that Charlie already knows how this will end before it does—that this is the fifth move in a chess match he's completed ten minutes ago. I wonder if he granted me passage into his mind, or if I have a tiny morsel of the power that only Beckett shares.

I can almost see through Charlie Keating Cobalt.

But it only conjures more questions. If he already knows what Moffy will choose, then is he toying with him because my brother is unbreakable? Or is he pushing Moffy for a greater reason? Can both be true?

Maximoff drops his gaze to me. He has a husband, a son, a newborn daughter, and a career he loves, and he'd only be taking over Fizzle so no one else would be imprisoned by it. The truth is, I don't want to be the CEO of Fizzle any more than they do.

It's a legion of work and responsibility and pressure. But my future is a lot less defined than his. He's already made a beautiful home on his favorite planet, while I'm orbiting the stars with Donnelly.

It's not fair for Moffy to always have to be there for everyone. And it makes me so happy to know that he has Farrow, who will always be there for him.

"I'll be okay," I whisper. "Believe in me."

Moffy slowly nods, and he finally says, "I don't want it." It's not that he can't take it, because he can. Maximoff Hale can do anything.

It is known.

I begin to smile.

The brother of the present continues to be even better than the brother of the past, and I wish he knew this as strongly as I do.

Moffy exhales, then turns on Charlie. "You're going to fight for CEO."

"Go ahead, say it like a statement and not a question," Charlie says in a bored tone.

"We're not begging you," Jane chimes in. "But if Ben and Eliot choose to go through this selection process, it'd be nice if one of us was there."

"They're adults. They don't need a babysitter."

"Please," Beckett says to him.

"One of us isn't past begging," Charlie says into a sigh, sounding like he's already folded his hand. "Call them up. Let's see if they even want in on this rat race." He swings his head to me. "What about you?"

I press my hand in the moondust. I can almost hear their thoughts. *She's been through enough already. She can't even remember three years ago. She's being dragged in the media. How is she fit to run a company?* I don't know if I am.

But I'm going to try.

"I can take it," I say. "I don't have much going on career-wise."

"And just like that, my name is in the ring," Charlie says dryly, then he looks right at Maximoff. "You're welcome."

"Thank you," he says deeply.

And I realize I've been anxious about their relationship for nothing. Moffy isn't jealous or hurt that Charlie is looking out for me—he wants him to.

We're waiting for Ben. He's the only no—
show, and everyone wants to explain this just one more time. But the clock is ticking, and it's so chilly that we've all put our jackets back on. Not all are as warm as others.

Jane has on a pink pastel faux-fur cardigan. Sulli, a turquoise parka. Moffy, a dark-green Patagonia all-seasons zip-up. Beckett, a black leather jacket. Charlie, a camel-colored peacoat. Eliot, a more expensive black peacoat. Xander, a hoodie. Me, a black puffer.

We're an eclectic bunch. No one was willing to touch the musty blankets that Eliot found behind a faded *Happy Birthday, Xander!* sign.

"Thatcher says there's going to be a deep freeze tonight," Jane says, typing rapidly on her phone. "Temperatures are dropping to the negatives."

Xander stuffs his hands in his black hoodie. He's popped a squat on a wooden stool next to me. "Ben's not coming up here."

"He'll come," Beckett says, his neck craned while watching Eliot rummage through the junk behind the couch.

Xander shakes his head fiercer. "You should've never tasked me to do the tree lights with him." He's speaking to Jane.

She frowns. "You do it every year with Ben."

"Yeah, because everyone treats it like our annual therapy session together," Xander says. "Clearly it's not working since it's *never* brought us closer, and I wish you'd all stop trying. We're two different people who have zero in common."

"Sounds familiar," Charlie deadpans. It's clear he's talking about himself and Ben.

My phone pings.

You good? Heard you're communing with attic dust bunnies — Donnelly

I should've texted him way earlier. Guilt knots, realizing I left him out while Moffy, Jane, and Sulli have been keeping their husbands in the loop. Granted, I'm not *married* to Donnelly. We're new. This is new.

I message fast. All good. Sorry I didn't text sooner. I'll give you the deets when I can.

I smile thinking about him downstairs in the lake house, spending the holidays with me, and I send a second text. Moon bunnies are good company but nothing like yours, space explorer.

I lie back on the floor and hoist my phone. Flipping the camera on myself, I stick out my tongue—the neon-green ball of my piercing in view, and I shut an eye, snap the photo, upload it in our message thread, and type: Me and the moon bunnies will see you soon 😄 🐰 🔴

I send that one too.

"What are you looking for?" Xander asks Eliot, who's rifling through more cardboard boxes.

"Something interesting. Something contraband. Maybe decades' old weed."

I ask, "Which one of our parents do you think stashed weed up here?"

"You can't tell me Uncle Garrison wasn't a pot head," Eliot says, hoisting a white tee that says *carpe that fucking diem*. He tosses it over his shoulder, then continues his search.

I glance at the phone, trying not to eagerly await Donnelly's response, but my heart pitter-patters and pitches and lowers.

"Look what we have here," Eliot decrees, his grin spreading. Everyone turns to see him holding costume headbands in each hand.

Red devil horns and a white angel halo.

"For you, dear brother." He tosses Beckett the angel. "And you." He throws Charlie the devil horns. While Beckett easily catches his, Charlie never reaches out, and the devil horns drop to the floor at his feet.

"They're backwards," I murmur to myself—very, very quietly, I might add. But Xander is close enough to hear, and he scrunches his face at me like I've lost sense of reality.

No one would call Beckett a devil and his twin the angel. No one but I guess myself.

He bends closer to whisper, "Did Charlie put a hex on you or something?"

"Not that I'm aware of." I check my phone.

Donnelly still hasn't texted back. *It's okay.* Why is my stomach descending to my butt? And did he feel like this when I left him hanging for too long, too?

"No one's feeding you bullshit, right?" Xander whispers. "Like no one's told you that Charlie saved you from a burning fire last year?"

"No." I pause, realizing I wouldn't exactly know if I were being fed bullshit, but I trust everyone around me—even Charlie. "Was I in a fire last year?"

Xander touches his stud earring. "No. Well, not last year."

"The townhouse fire," I say into a nod. I was already told about that mayhem. I glance at his earring, and a surge of heat suddenly burrows inside my body, the kind of warmth felt after embarrassment or the breaking of a fever. I've had these small glimpses of my eighteenth birthday before. Where I can *almost* see Xander getting his ear pierced that night.

It's still hazy.

It's still not clear enough.

Don't get frustrated.

"For Luna."

I blink out of the stupor, and I look up in enough time to catch the blue toy lightsaber Eliot hurls my way. Smiling, I twirl it a little, and then I click the button to power it on. The batteries are dead. Must be super old.

Beckett wears the halo with such cool nonchalance that he reminds me of Christian Slater from *Heathers.* Charlie leaves the horns on the floor.

While Eliot distributes more costume pieces, maybe from a past Halloween, my phone pings again, and my heart leaps.

He sent a photo!

I grin and bite my lip. Not just any photo. A sexy bathroom selfie. In the pic, Donnelly sticks his tongue between his fingers that are spread in a V. He's also lifting up his shirt, and his abs are worthy of being chiseled into marbled busts, revered outside galactic coliseums.

I type: You are a blistering hot human, space explorer. I'd do you. Without thinking, I send it.

Was that too much? Should I have said "I'd explore you" instead? I'm tuning out the chatter from my brothers and cousins. Thankfully, I don't have to wait with my thoughts for long.

I read the new message.

Which planet are we fucking on? — Donnelly

My grin explodes.

"Who are you texting?" Xander whispers, giving me a strange look.

"A human."

His amber eyes flash to the screen. The thread is very visible since I'm not actively tucking my phone to my chest. "Ew, fuck." He cringes. "Something I did not want to see," he mutters to himself. "My bodyguard and older sister sexting. Awesome."

My happiness can't be smushed, and maybe that's why Xander isn't really disgruntled. I quickly respond to Donnelly, *All of them.*

We're fucking on every planet in my mind. In his mind, we are withholding the *fucking* part. Donnelly is turning out to be a really big tease, and as much as I get wet just thinking about the never-ending foreplay, I must be a horny beast because I just want him *inside* of me.

It's not even the pleasure I'm seeking.

It's *him.* I want to know exactly how Donnelly treats me and handles me and caresses me during the most intimate minutes of my life. Does he look into my eyes while he pounds me? Does he hold me close? Does he take charge? Would he want me to? Having sex is a gateway into the depths of who he is—who we are together, and it's a journey I'm ready to take.

I'm edging closer to the answers. After the hottest moments I've *ever* experienced in my parents' kitchen, I can feel that.

But I'm not sure if he's fully ready to go all the way.

Patience, young Padawan, I tell myself. I am a novice at sex. He knows this. He's being careful. Even if careful is *frustrating.*

I'm trying not to push too hard, because I want to respect his desires too.

Jane gasps. "Mr. Lion!"

I lift my gaze off my phone.

Eliot has unearthed a toy lion, the stuffing oozing out of the torso. The material is faded to a muted yellow. "This is a cause for a formal apology." He rattles the toy at Jane. "I never dumped your precious Mr. Lion down the garbage disposal."

She apologizes in swift French. "Now can I have him, please?" She sparkles her fingers. Eliot chucks it in her direction, but Jane fumbles the catch. "Merde."

Charlie checks the time on his phone. "At what point are we calling it?"

"He said he's coming," Beckett says. "Just give him a second."

"It's been fifteen minutes. Send him an email."

"Charlie," Jane says, pausing her stuffing repair of Mr. Lion. "We're waiting for Ben."

Sulli says, "No one's stopping you from fucking leaving, Charlie."

He wears an irritated smile. "Tell me something that's not obvious."

"Whatever," Sulli mumbles, probably not wanting to engage in a long dialogue with our cousin.

"I've found something," Eliot says while I've been making moondust angels. The impulse was too strong to ignore.

I sit up, seeing him hold an old video camera. "There's an SD card in here."

"Let's play it." I spring to my feet, already spotting a thin-screen TV. Stored away and forgotten. "There might be cables around here."

"Should we watch whatever that is?" Xander asks. "What if it's porn?"

Charlie arches a brow. "We know what Xander is thinking about."

Moffy shoots him a warning look, then tells Xander, "I doubt our parents would make a porn tape, Summers."

"Not after what happened to our parents," Jane says in agreement. "Our mom and dad were filmed without consent, so it's unlikely any of them would take that risk."

"Here's an outlet." Eliot finds cable cords, then helps me drag out the TV where Moffy is standing. Within a few minutes, we've hooked the camera to the television. "Lights, cameras, *action*." Eliot presses *play* on the video camera, and the image is projected on the screen.

It worked!

20

 LUNA HALE

I rush back to my seat on the floor, and Eliot leans on the armrest of the couch. Moffy ends up standing between Charlie and Jane as we all watch the grainy picture become clearer.

Jane squints. "That looks like the Hale's living room."

"It is," Moffy breathes, and my lips part in surprise.

I recognize the staircase near the foyer. Garland is curled around the banister, and as the camera pans, I see velvet red stockings lining a fireplace mantel. Snow falls outside the window, and wrapped gifts lie beneath an eight-foot tree.

It's Christmastime at my parents' house.

I've never seen this particular home video. I don't think any of us have. Maybe it was misplaced years ago when our parents upgraded their camera to a newer model.

"That's Mom," I say as the video zooms in on the tree. On the cream-colored rug, my mom is festive in a gray snowflake onesie, and she has a little baby nestled between her legs, helping tear the paper off a present.

"And Dad," Xander breathes, and we all see Dad in red-and-green flannel pajama pants. He's sitting right beside Mom. "They're so young."

"He's my age," Moffy says in realization. "Dad. He's twenty-five there."

"How do you know?" Sulli asks.

"Because that's me." He's the baby trying to rip the present.

My heart swells and it just about bursts when we hear the person behind the camera narrate, "Moffy descends upon the box with a strong, baby grip and a devilish twinkle in his eye."

"That's my mom," Sulli says, her voice cracking with emotion.

Aunt Daisy is recording Christmas morning, and as the camera pans, Uncle Ryke comes into view. He's sprawled on the loveseat, his pajama bottoms matching my dad's, and his bedhead hair is thick and messy. A Santa hat lies lazily on his chest.

And Aunt Rose is on the couch in a classy black pajama set with red ornament earrings. Uncle Connor has his arm around her shoulders, and he's the only Scrooge, dressed in gray cotton pants.

Some things never change, since I've never seen Uncle Connor be festive. His cardboard variant is usually decorated with more Christmas cheer.

On Aunt Rose's lap is a wee little baby.

Jane.

"That's you, sis," Beckett says with a smile.

She smiles over at him, but her eyes are welling with tears. "Oui." She brushes a finger beneath her watery eye, then says, "Mom and Dad weren't just visiting the Hales for Christmas. This must've been when they all lived together in that house."

I've known that my childhood home used to belong to my aunts and uncles too, and then gradually, they moved out and raised their families in houses down the street.

Seeing them together at a time where they were so young…like us, it swells a sentiment so deep inside of me. It almost hurts to breathe.

Nostalgia is a strange force, and I know it can be one of good and one of bittersweet and one of bad. I'd like to believe this moment is one of pure good.

We watch.

"Devilish?" Mom's eyes widen. "He doesn't look devilish."

Dad aids baby Moffy in unwrapping his gift.

"Moffy looks adorable," Dad confirms. "The devilish baby is sitting on the devil's lap."

We all laugh, especially as the camera swings to Aunt Rose's pursed lips and fiery yellow-green eyes. Uncle Connor has a mega-watt, cocky grin.

"You do realize this is being recorded, Loren?" Aunt Rose grimaces into a smile. "So now your niece will see how much of a dick you are."

Jane raises the stuffed lion like a champagne glass. "We still love him."

"And now she'll hear her mom's foul-mouth," Dad retorts and then slow claps.

Eliot says something in French, and I imagine it's, *And we still love her.*

Uncle Ryke joins the slow-clap in the video. Aunt Daisy is good at capturing everyone's reactions, even Aunt Rose's ice-cold glare staking Ryke. He raises his hands in defense. "I'm in support of foul fucking language."

Sulli laughs, her eyes glittering and glassing seeing her dad. Young and still rough around the edges.

"I can edit it," Aunt Daisy offers, but trails off at Rose's glare.

"I don't want Jane's first Christmas *edited.*"

Aunt Daisy mock gasps. "Who suggested such a thing. They should be fined with a dozen chocolate chip cookies."

Uncle Ryke makes a gesture for Aunt Daisy to come to him. "I can give you something better, Calloway."

"Fast-forward," Charlie says.

"What? No," Sulli snaps. "Those are my parents."

"We've all seen them flirt a thousand times before. It's boring."

"You're fucking boring," Sulli retorts.

"Clever," he deadpans.

She flips him off.

After physical groping occurs between the Meadows on-screen

and the camera footage wobbles and shakes as a result, my dad shouts, "Alright. No Christmas flirting."

Eliot arches his brows at Charlie. "Like uncle, like nephew."

Charlie rolls his eyes.

No one fast-forwards the video, and Charlie doesn't reach for the camcorder to do it himself. We all fall hushed again and watch our parents on a peaceful morning. Uncle Connor and Aunt Rose are doing a crossword together while enjoying the company of loved ones. He tickles baby Jane's foot, and she giggles up at her dad.

Soon, they go into a disagreement about when to tell Moffy and Jane that Santa isn't real. Uncle Connor wants Jane to know the truth, but my parents are afraid she'll spoil Santa for Moffy and every other kid in kindergarten. They talk about the holidays when they were growing up, and how Uncle Ryke clung to Santa as a kid because it made him feel loved.

Even though I believed in Santa Claus as a child, I never needed to feel loved through a fairytale. I felt love in the smiles and laughter around the tree. In the way Aunt Daisy would gift T-shirts with holiday slogans to everyone. In the way we'd spend hours building gingerbread houses, only for most of them to fall apart in the end. In the way we'd stay up as late as we could, just to drink hot chocolate and fight over which holiday movie to watch. *The Grinch* and *Home Alone* and *Peter Pan* (the 2003 film, which my mom is adamant is a Christmas movie in disguise).

There was always a surplus of love. It was the best gift every single year.

"I never celebrated holidays with my mother," Uncle Connor says on-screen. "She found them pointless. I understand that fictional creatures can make you feel better, but we shouldn't have to construct a lie just for that emotion. Jane will be comforted with the knowledge that Santa *isn't* real and everyone else is living in fantasy."

Dad sighs. "Come on, man. Being a kid means getting to *believe* in the impossible. It means believing that fairies exist along with spells and magic, and that on your eleventh birthday you'll receive a letter from Hogwarts. It means thinking your presents arrived from a workshop in the North Pole and not the store down the street. And Connor…" His face twists at a thought. "I'm really sorry your mom took that shit from you. If you had even a semblance of it growing up, you would realize how special it is. Don't take that away from Jane."

Jane smiles fondly at the TV. "He didn't."

In the video, Aunt Rose says, "You know, we can see who figures out the truth first: Moffy or Jane."

Mom crinkles her nose. "That's evil."

"Well, it is coming from the devil," Dad says, then purposefully mugs the camera with a half-smile. "And Jane, if you're watching this when you're older, just know it comes from a place of love."

We all laugh, and Xander asks our brother, "Who figured it out first? You or Jane?"

"Jane," Moffy says with a laugh at the memory. "She told me like five seconds after she saw Uncle Ryke wrapping a present with a *From Santa Claus* tag."

"We were four," Jane explains. Of course the Queen of Curiosity would've solved that mystery at such a young age. She is a Cobalt, after all. "We agreed we'd keep up the ruse so none of you would know."

"Did you believe in Santa?" I ask Charlie.

"No."

That's all he says, but like Jane and Moffy, he also never ruined it for the rest of us.

As the video continues to play and our parents open presents from each other, we laugh and smile hearing their banter at the ages we are now. They've changed, but they are also so much the people we know and love who've raised us.

"You realize something," Jane says in deeper thought, her eyes filling again. She gives Moffy an overwhelmed look. "If this was our first Christmas, this was also the last Christmas they spent in that house together. My parents moved out the next year."

The fact lands more heavily in the attic.

Most of us are living in the penthouse together. I'm seeing my nieces and nephew grow up like Aunt Daisy and Uncle Ryke saw theirs. Sure we typically spend holidays at the lake house now, but this can't be the last winter where we're living together, is it? It comforts me knowing we haven't reached the split-apart point yet. And I can't foresee when it'll happen. Years from now?

I'm not sure I'm ready to end this, considering I don't even *remember* the years I roomed with them in the townhouse.

Right as the video footage goes fuzzy, the staircase creaks as its yanked down, and in climbs Ben Cobalt at six-foot-five. His cheeks are rosy like he'd been bracing the cold outside, and he keeps running a hand through his windswept brown hair.

He's not wearing a jacket though. Just a white Penn Hockey tee with the Ivy League's logo.

"Hey?" Ben says, but he's carried an awkward tension into the attic. His blue eyes flit to the grainy TV, which Eliot shuts off.

"Howdy ho," I give him the Vulcan salute.

Ben tries to force a smile, still uncomfortable, and his gaze veers to Charlie, then Xander. Yep, he's not too happy to share this musty attic with them.

"Eliot found a home video," Jane says quickly, trying to include her youngest brother into the fold.

Moffy does the same by going to him, "You need a jacket?" He's about to unzip his own Patagonia to give to Ben.

Charlie blinks into an eye roll. "Why don't you give him your pants too?"

"Why don't you give him your coat?" Moffy slings back.

"Because he's almost nineteen. He can clothe himself for inclement weather."

Ben lets out a dry, irritated noise.

Eliot freezes, worry crossing his face. "I'll give you my coat, brother." He starts shedding his black peacoat.

"I'm fine," Ben says, shifting his weight. "Thanks." He says to both Eliot and Moffy and avoids Charlie altogether.

It causes Charlie to push off from the wardrobe and move even farther away from Ben.

Beckett holds out his hands to calm the escalating tension. "We are all here for each other."

"Yes, we are," Jane says, eyeing each of her brothers.

Xander and I share a look, and I suppose for all the heartbreak among the Hales this year, the one thing it's done is bring me and him closer. There isn't a giant fracture in any relationship as big as the ones cratering the Cobalt brothers.

"What's this about anyway?" Ben asks us.

Sulli sneezes into the pocket square. "Fuuuck."

"I haven't been told yet," Eliot says, setting the video camera back in a box. "I'm as in the dark as you are."

"It's about our grandfather's will," Moffy explains.

Beckett hasn't moved off the couch, but I watch his eyes shift over every surface of the attic while Moffy begins rehashing Fizzle's need for a successor. Beckett even glances at me as I make one epic moondust angel.

Then he cranes his neck to catch Charlie's gaze, and he speaks in such hurried French—but I wouldn't say he's panicked. Panic reminds me of a knitted sweater unspooling into a snarled messy heap, and Beckett Cobalt is so put-together. There are no holes, no unwoven strands—the yarn is so tight, I wonder how there's room to breathe.

I sit up.

Beckett is motioning mainly to Sulli.

Huh.

Charlie replies in slower French, and whatever he says causes Jane to perk up. Moffy stops speaking in English about Fizzle. He listens to the French with toughened, concerned eyes.

Eliot's brows pull together—not because he doesn't understand what they're saying. He's as fluent in French as all the Cobalts and my older brother. So his confusion has to come from what they're discussing.

Ben asks something in French, and Charlie says something snarky.

I'm guessing since Ben grimaces and shakes his head in annoyance.

As the six converse in French, the tempo becomes heightened, like water simmering into a boil.

"What the hell...?" Sulli says, then glances at me with a *can you believe this?* look—like we've commiserated tons over being left out of French convos. I'm too late to reciprocate though, and her grief crashes against her face. She looks down at her lap.

I'm sorry. It hurts.

I try to focus on other things, like the body language of the French speakers. Beckett is now very alarmed, his body tenser but controlled, and he's touching Sulli's arm. "You need to go, Sul."

"What? Why?" Her eyes widen, especially as Jane is on her feet, gathering Mr. Lion and the shoes she kicked off.

"You're pregnant," Beckett says. "The attic hasn't been cleaned in years. We don't know what we're breathing in."

"Are you fucking kidding me?" Sulli groans, standing up. "Why did you choose the musty, gross attic?" She motions to Charlie.

"It's the only place I could be sure none of our parents would go. I'm sorry I didn't take into account that you're with child," Charlie snaps. "But maybe you should have."

"No," Jane says with more warmth than ice, but she holds a scolding finger up at him. "Do not, Charlie." She takes Sulli's hand quickly. "Let's go. I'm leaving as well since I'm breastfeeding."

Sulli is red in the face, like she might cry, and Beckett lets out a long, pained sound when both girls are gone. "She's sixth months pregnant. She's my best friend—"

"You could always find another," Charlie cuts in.

"I haven't since we were eight." Beckett sighs, taking the halo off his head and holding it between two hands.

Xander pulls off his hoodie, suddenly hot. "Can we go back to the Fizzle thing? We're supposed to be competing to be the successor?"

"If you want to," Moffy says, clearing his throat a little. He rubs at his arms. "You don't have to, Summers."

"You don't either," Beckett tells both Eliot and Ben.

"But you could," Charlie interjects, clearly wanting more than just me and him in contention. More people in the running means he's less likely to be chosen, but on paper, I think we all know Charlie is the best option.

"I will," Eliot says, rising off the armrest of the couch. "I'm conveniently between jobs—"

"You're unemployed," Charlie says.

"As are you, brother."

"Voluntarily."

Eliot motions to him. "If you're afraid I'm going to beat you in this race, all you have to do is drop out and give it to me."

Charlie grits out a smile and says nothing.

"Do you really want it?" I ask Eliot, because if he does—I might be willing to pull my name out of the hat so he can claim the title.

"Why not?" Eliot plants a foot on the armrest, propping his elbow on his kneecap. "I could do damage in the corporate world." A gleam touches his eyes.

Ben asks, "By lighting Fizzle on fire?"

"Chaos is good for the soul."

"For you, maybe," Ben mutters, his arms crossed as frost cakes the window. I can see his breath in the air.

"A nine-to-five in a high-rise," Beckett spells out for Eliot. "The board room isn't your stage."

"It can be," Eliot counters.

I wonder if the board would even accept someone like Eliot…or even someone like me.

"So Charlie and Eliot are up for CEO then?" Xander questions.

"And me." I raise a hand.

"You're doing this?" His jaw slowly unhinges. He's unblinking. "Really?"

I shrug. "Seems fun." I push myself to add more. "And I'd rather try than regret not attempting it at all. So, yeah, I'm going for CEO."

"Now I'm most definitely in the race," Eliot decrees, his concern touching me for a beat. He doesn't want me to be stuck among the pretentious corporate elite, and I don't want him there either.

Xander stares off at the rattling circular window. Wind roars outside, and then he says, "Me too. I'm in."

"You sure?" Moffy asks, his Adam's apple bobbing. He swallows incredibly hard, then coughs into his hand.

Oh no.

"Moffy?" Xander says, wide-eyed. "You okay, man?"

"Yeah." His voice is tight. He clears his throat again.

"Are there fire ants up here?" Xander wonders, shooting to his feet. "Did you get bit?" Our older brother is severely allergic, and he's also stubborn enough to wait until the last minute for an epi pen.

"It's not from an ant bite," Charlie says with zero urgency.

"Thank you, Charlie," Maximoff chokes out, clearing his throat *again*. "I'm fine."

"You're not fine," Beckett says, "your face is red."

"Is it? Feels the same." He scratches at his neck. "*Fuck.*" He coughs into his fist.

"I have some water," Ben says, since he'd been carrying a water bottle. "Here, Mof." He hands it to him.

He gratefully swigs, then tells Xander, "I'm okay. I'm *okay*. Really, Summers."

Xander eases back, but I don't think any of us believe he's totally fine.

I text Farrow. I think Moffy's having an allergic reaction to an ant bite. Help. I hit send.

"Ben?" Moffy asks, since he's the last to decide if he wants to compete.

Ben loosens his arms, shakes them out, and the confliction rests inside his gaze. He has more reasons to walk away than he does to accept the position. For one, he'd have to spend time hanging around Xander and Charlie just to battle for the win. Right as he opens his mouth, the stairs to the attic squeak.

"Wolf scout," Farrow calls up, carrying a trauma bag. He assesses his husband quickly.

"I can breathe. I'm standing," Moffy says fast.

"I see that." He chews on a piece of gum, then drops the bag at Moffy's feet, unzipping it. "Take off your jacket."

"Fornicating while we're in the room, the scandal," Eliot jokes with a grin.

"I'm leaving," Charlie decrees.

"Announcing your own exit is beneath you, brother!" Eliot calls after Charlie as he disappears down the stairs. Beckett is quick to follow him out of the attic.

Farrow ignores the audience, a hundred percent zoned in on Moffy.

My brother whispers under his breath to him, and Farrow nods, then rips a wet wipe out of the packet. "Take your shirt off too."

"Is he okay?" I ask Farrow, but as soon as Moffy sheds his button-down, the hives and bumps along his arms and chest are noticeable. Ohhh no.

Farrow surveys the attic with a long glance, then sees me on the floor. He eyes Moffy again. "Everyone out."

"Medical emergencies turn you on?" Eliot quips, but Farrow isn't in the mood.

"If he's having an allergic reaction to the shit up here, so can you. You all need to go."

I brush off the moondust, which has toxic properties most likely. But I'm not itchy or scratching as badly as Maximoff, so maybe the rest of us are immune.

Farrow is wiping Moffy's arms fast with the wet wipe. Moffy coughs out, "I'm okay."

"Sure. If you consider *hay fever* okay."

"I'm not running a fever, Farrow."

"You don't have to run one. Man, your eyes are bloodshot."

It's the last thing I hear before I descend the stairs after Ben, and Eliot and Xander are quick behind me. And as Ben cuts the corner in the hall, vanishing out of sight, I realize we never got his answer.

21

PAUL DONNELLY

Been at the lake house for less than twelve hours and the family drama hasn't disappointed. Think it's of a healthy caliber, all things considered. It's not like a verbal lashing has broken out in the kitchen, a plate thrown against the wall, and a face slammed into the fridge.

Her big family actually respects the mashed potatoes.

Anyway, only Moffy suffered from an allergic reaction. Dust can't bring my girlfriend down. She's sprightly, smiley, and strong.

The whole issue about Greg's will spread around the house, and it resulted in the parents basically saying, "It's your choice" and "Let's table Fizzle talk until after the holidays." Girl squad weren't too pleased to be left out of contention because of their ages. The parents were trying to reinvigorate the holiday cheer, not squash it any further, so I understood eliminating the talk altogether.

I still discussed it with Luna though.

And I'm pro-Luna. Whatever she wants to do in life, I'm here for. Within reason. I'm not gonna pass her a needle to shoot up.

She told me she's just chasing after the position to see what happens.

"Working at Fizzle might be soul-sucking," she said while we washed dishes after a grilled chicken and potato dinner. "It's why no one wants to do it."

Where I come from, people grind their whole lives for so much less. Most will never even see the outline of the C in CEO through the clouds. And here, the Hales and Cobalts are being catapulted into the sky. Difference is, they didn't ask to be launched.

Some are trying to stay rooted to the ground.

They're trust fund babies. If everyone had what they do, I think there'd be few people who'd choose an intense corporate job versus an artistic passion—or something full of leisure. So I can't blame 'em for wanting to step down from that responsibility.

Being CEO of something as enormous as Fizzle is like welcoming a beast in your bed. You don't know if it's the furry, cute kind or if it'll bite your head off in your sleep.

I don't want anything to hurt Luna or stress her out. Not a person or a fucking thing. But I don't know how this'll all go yet.

Luna dried a holly leaf serving platter I had handed her. "I can't really see myself being CEO of anything," she admitted. "But it sounds exciting to spend time with family since we kinda have to audition for the position. That's what Uncle Stokes said." She set the platter aside. "I have like a point-five percent chance of winning it anyway."

"Why do you say that?" I rinsed soap suds off my hands.

"They'll want Charlie. I think it's pretty much guaranteed. He's the most qualified after Moffy and Jane, and they bowed out."

I could see that. But I'd make Luna my CEO of just about anything. She's smarter than anyone gives her credit for, even herself.

Soon, the kitchen filled with more bodies and helping hands, so we ended our private chat.

It's been hard to come by—privacy. Don't get me wrong, I love her family—even if not all love me. Being included as her boyfriend (not a bodyguard) is what I've dreamed of. But there are so many people here—way more than just the Hales. Unless we go brace the freezing temps outside, the lake house is noisy in every direction, and it's impossible not to be walked in on or to run into someone else.

I thought I'd be able to have a one-on-one talk with Beckett this week too. Hash out some things. But I don't want to be under a microscope while I'm doing it. So I gotta save it for another date.

Same with me patching things up with Luna's mom.

Now it's late. First night at the lake house, and I've been relegated to the kiddie room with Tom, Eliot, and Luna. Heard the girl squad digs were better and bigger. These bunk beds are short, and in the corner, a finger-painted bookshelf looks like a summer craft project from years ago. Kindergarten stories about caterpillars blooming into butterflies are shelved. We're four grown adults coming home for Christmas to a childhood artifact.

Only it's not my childhood.

It's theirs, and I'm loving seeing what Luna's life probably looked like when she was younger and how happy it must've been. I'd want nothing less for her. It soothes the good ole soul to know.

The four of us haven't crashed yet.

Eliot and Tom sit on a top bunk, passing a bottle of red wine back and forth. Their legs dangle off the edge, and across from them, Luna and I are doing the same, only I have my arm around her shoulder and we aren't drinking wine.

Tom brought a stash of mini liquor bottles in a plastic bag and tossed them to us. I've unscrewed the whiskey while Luna has been sipping on vodka. They've been reminiscing about their middle school years, and I've been listening and drinking.

I'm forcing myself not to pull one of her legs over my lap. The urge is riding me hard, honestly. She's wearing knee-high candy cane socks, and a thin, silky black nightgown with spaghetti straps. Her nipples are perked against the fabric, and I want to run my hands up and down her body.

Typically, I'd just draw her leg over me. But those aren't just her best friends. They're her cousins. Don't know if it'd be uncomfortable for her.

"What's the weight capacity on that thing?" Tom asks me, and I snap my gaze off my girlfriend.

Earlier, I heaved Orion up on the top bunk. The dog wanted up, and granted, he could put his paws on the mattress just standing on his hind legs. Probably could've done a doggie pull-up, but I assisted.

Now the big furry Newfie is lying next to me, panting up a storm like he was the one who heaved his hundred-plus pounds up here.

I pat his side. He's a good boy. "Are you calling her son fat?" I joke.

Luna smiles into a sip of vodka.

Tom picks up his guitar, and his wrist is wrapped in an ACE bandage. "Nothing against Orion, but he is fucking *huge*, dude. And it wouldn't be the first time you two crashed down..." He cuts himself off, his eyes pinging to Luna in worry.

"What?" She frowns at me. "We crashed through something?"

"Yeah...an attic," I tell her. "Not the attic of anyone you know. It was on Halloween. Your dad's fiftieth birthday." If she wants more details, I'd tell her.

But all she says is, "Oh." Her brows scrunch. She can't remember it. With my arm hanging over her shoulders, I rub the skin near her bicep.

Tom smears a hand down his face, beating himself up over surfacing a memory she lost. "Sorry."

Eliot passes him the wine.

Luna collects herself alright, sitting more upright and shrugging. "It's okay. It's not like OG Luna had this moment. I have less, maybe, but I'm slowly getting more."

I smile down at her. "You gonna tattoo that on me?"

"Tomorrow," she nods.

"Oof, your dad is gonna love that," I grin and throw back another gulp. Whiskey slides smoothly down my throat. Tom bought the good stuff. And I'm not concerned about any weight limits for the bunk. If I thought we'd crack the bed, I wouldn't have lugged her dog up here. Eliot probably weighs the same as Luna and Orion put together.

"Did Luna tell you that I have dibs on naming her firstborn?" Eliot asks, and I'm grateful it wasn't during a swig of whiskey— 'cause I would've choked on it.

"Yeah?" I look to her.

She chugs the mini bottle of vodka, and my concern falls deeper on her. She wets her lips, then slowly screws the cap on the empty bottle.

"It was a bet," Eliot clarifies.

Tom strums his guitar, glancing between us, and I can sense his confusion to her reaction. But it's not all too jumbled for me.

Luna and I haven't had these big talks about the future. It's not something I really wanna do with an audience.

"A recent bet," Luna explains softly. "We both picked horses in the race for CEO. Eliot bet on himself."

"Toujours," Eliot says. Been around the Cobalts enough to know it means *always*.

"So if Eliot wins, then I agreed to let him name my firstborn. But if Charlie is chosen, then I get to name Eliot's child."

Charlie becoming CEO is most likely, we both know. It's a good bet. I could see her getting wrapped up in the moment with her friends and agree to one with those terms. I would've done it too.

I nod to Eliot. "What are your name options? Anything good?"

"I'm still brainstorming. Vegetables are on the table," Eliot says, leaning back on a hand. He's only in navy drawstring pants and a white tee. The heat is cranked up so high that I ditched my shirt a half hour ago.

"I kinda like it," Luna tells me, and I try not to glance at the hem of her nightgown, which teases at her thighs...her fine-line ink disappears up into the fabric. I want to trail her galaxy tattoo with my fucking tongue right now.

"Cabbage patch babies are dope," I say into a swig.

"Yep. And then there's pumpkin babies. Northern baby beans."

"Baby broccoli."

"Little baby bro," Luna sing-songs.

We all laugh.

She is my kind of girl. She always has been.

Eliot tips the bottle of wine to his lips, then leans forward, motioning to me. "Are you afraid I might be in charge of naming your firstborn?"

He's assuming Luna's babies will be my babies. Good assumption, considering we're together, and I like that he's projecting me into her future.

But my muscles contract, and Luna feels me tense. She's digging in the plastic bag for another mini bottle of vodka. I keep my arm around her.

"Nah," I say casually. "Not concerned about it." *Because I don't want kids.* I'd add it, but again, this is a talk I need to have with Luna before I tell the class, so to speak.

Tom plays a catchy melody on the guitar. "Do you plan for the future or do you not look that far ahead?"

I'm watching Luna twist off the new cap. "I've got goals."

She looks up at me, and I can see her asking, *I'm in them, right?*

I never want her to question what she means to me. "This girl's in the best ones." I grin down at her.

Her smile reemerges, and I could last all night looking at it. Looking at her.

Eliot mimes holding out a microphone. "Paul Donnelly, where do you see yourself in five to ten years?"

Tom mimes stealing the microphone. "And has Eliot Alice broken his three-date maximum? Because it's depressing."

Eliot leans into the fake mic. "I think Tom is referring to his own unrequited crushes."

"Oh my God, dude," he groans. "One day I'm going to turn what you think is impossible into my reality, and your jaw will hit the floor."

"And we'll celebrate in your name." He toasts his wine at the same time Luna raises her new vodka. They sip in unison. "But remember," Eliot says with a loving hand on the back of Tom's head. "'The best laid plans of mice and men often go awry.'"

Tom strums on his guitar just once, the corner of his mouth lifting. "Robert Burns."

Luna snaps her fingers like she's in a coffeehouse. And I realize the three of them have their own thing. A cadence. A rhythm to their friendship. It makes me think of Farrow and Oscar.

My friends.

My smile softens as I down the rest of my whiskey. It's cool being involved in her friend group. They start talking about when they'll sneak away from everyone and go into the woods.

"We should wait a few days. Let some heat die off this room," Eliot suggests.

"We're practically a smoke signal right now," Tom agrees. "Saying *look at us. Look at us.*"

"Sneaking should resume at a later date," Luna nods.

I scratch behind Orion's ears and ask, "Is that something we do?"

"Yeah, we have a spot in the woods where we do shrooms," Tom says so seriously I almost think he's joking.

He's not, so I just tell the room, "I'm strictly a cigarettes and weed guy."

"Huh," Tom says with a nod. "Interesting."

"Bad trip?" Eliot wonders.

Luna curls her ankle around my leg, and it distracts me in the best way, honestly.

"Seen more bad ones. Comes with the territory, you know," I say casually and make a *rock on* gesture. They know my family are meth addicts. I'm not about to paint a nasty picture. Not in these beautiful four-walls.

Luna looks more troubled, her face twisting.

"You alright?" I ask.

She tries to tuck closer to me, but she's stiff. Her eyes hoist to her friends. "Have I ever done anything more serious than shrooms and pot?"

Eliot and Tom share a quick glance, and I'm hurtled back to a conversation I had with her about drugs. *"Maybe another day I'll tell you,"* she said to me, not wanting to ruin the first time we had sex, and we were just lounging in bed, discussing drugs and the importance of November 1st.

How it'd been the day I lost Beckett over cocaine.

How it turned into a better day through her.

Tom pinches the guitar pick, hugging the instrument to his chest. "You sure you want to know this? You could just wait and see if your memories come back—"

"They might never."

Eliot slides his fingers through his wavy brown hair a few times. "We've taken Ecstasy and cocaine. That's all we've done together."

I'd rather guide her away from anything I wouldn't do. The list is short, but some drugs will always make me uneasy and those two are definitely on it.

She asks, "Was there anything I took without you two?"

"No. Not that you told us," Eliot says.

At this, Luna lifts her eyes to me, and a pit tries to burrow in my ribs. I slowly shake my head, just once. I have more to say, but the words are tar in my throat. Can't get 'em out fast enough. I'm resisting sharing anything too deep in front of her friends.

Luna thinks out loud, "Charlie might know."

Eliot straightens. "Why would our brother know?"

"Um, my diary." She takes about fifteen minutes to explain the Unearthly Reader and her new memory guardian. Eliot and Tom are supportive, genuinely good-hearted friends, and they're both smiling by the end. They see how this'll help Luna.

Plus, Eliot adds, "You know what this means? You now have the power to pester Charlie at all hours. I would abuse *the fuck* out of it."

Tom wraps his arm around his brother. "Which is why he'd never give it to you."

Luna smiles. "I'd call him now, but he likely hasn't read it all yet. I'll text him tomorrow."

They leave it at that, and I ask Tom about whether he likes listening to the same emo-punk music he plays. I learn he listens to a wider variety of rock, and we go down a music rabbit hole. My favorite kind. From grunge to indie rock to jazz to bluesy love songs, we drink and let the songs pour through the room.

I imagine scooping Luna up and setting her on my lap—my hands sliding up the back of her neck and into her glittery hair.

Must be a shared fantasy because as our eyes crash together, I see the same desires pool in her amber orbs.

I cup her cheek, and I kiss her slowly, tasting her against my lips, my pulse thumping with a soothing calmness. The whiskey buzz has nothing on kissing this girl. Feeling her soft lips, feeling her needy hands gripping my waist, feeling her body trying to draw closer to mine—it's heady. I skate my fingers into her hair and deepen the kiss.

Luna scoots nearer, and before I even touch her thigh, she moans.

Fuck.

22

PAUL DONNELLY

Her tiny frame goes rigid, her cheeks roasting against my palm, and I'm less embarrassed 'cause I just don't care who the fuck sees us and they're not my cousins. Truth be told, I could fuck in front of an audience. I have before, but it doesn't turn me on any extra. I'm just not bothered by voyeurs.

This isn't that though.

And Luna—what I've been through with her—it's changed some things in me. If I picture fucking her in front of other guys, like O'Malley, I want to slam the door in his face. He's not getting off on her.

No one is.

While Luna avoids her cousins, I take a glance.

Tom is oblivious, strumming on his guitar as he tries to match the chords of the song. Eliot was in a music daze, staring at the ceiling— and I'd bet he's pretending to still be in one, for Luna's sake.

"Maybe we should call it a night?" Luna whispers to me.

Yeah. This isn't gonna end well if we're up here together any longer, and I'm doing my best to kill a hard-on. Thinking about Orion drooling and the Birds losing in the fourth quarter and redheads.

I kiss her cheek. "See ya in the morning, space babe."

She reluctantly lets go of my waist. "May your dreams be of the wonderous kind, Donnelly."

"Yours too, Hale." I hold her gaze for another beat. Then I scale down the bunk without using the ladder. I pat Orion, glad she has this big, beautiful lug here. Even if I wish I could be the one pressed up against her.

After we say our goodnights to Eliot and Tom, we all hit the hay. I'm lying on the narrow bottom bunk beneath Luna, and Eliot switches off the lamp, plunging the room into darkness.

I can't see the rafters above my head.

I stare into the nothingness. Pitch-black. I wait for my eyes to adjust. They never do, so I shut them and hear the soft grunting breaths of the Newfie.

Time ticks.

Each creak of the bunk snaps my eyes open. My pulse spikes. I hear her flipping over on the mattress several times. I hear sounds of the Cobalt boys shifting and the hum of the heat flooding the room.

I smash a pillow against my ears, trying to drown out the microscopic noises. "Help a guy out, bunk bed," I mutter too quietly for anyone to hear. "Thought we had a friendship going."

I'm sinking into the foam mattress, probably too soft. Don't think that's the issue though. I start counting baby sheep hurdling a fence.

Come on.

Sleep.

Just go to fucking sleep.

I drift for a minute, and I'm entering a house. I'm searching through strange rooms where the drywall is rotted and ripped apart. My pulse quickens, and my boots crunch glass and syringes. I run harder, and I'm shouting out—but my voice is dead and muted. I'm pushing against shoulders as the rooms crowd with men, and as I scream these noiseless fucking screams, I feel myself calling out for her.

I'm screaming her name.

My pulse catapults—I throttle awake. Breathing heavy, I pat the bed in the darkness, the quilt twisted around my legs, and I roll over to check on the other bunk. No one else is awake. *I didn't wake them.* I swallow hard, my hands on my forehead.

I listen carefully and hear her breaths above me. I wish I could hold her. I wish I could feel the assurance of her pulse.

Reaching up, I touch the rafters. *You have her. She's safe.* My eyes burn. *You have her. She's safe.*

I pinch my searing eyes and turn onto my side. *We're not there. We're here. We're not there. We're here.* I repeat the chant until I slowly fall back to sleep.

"*Donnelly...Donnelly.*" *The voice echoes in* the distance, and a chill pricks my flesh. "Donnelly. *Donnelly.*" And then, "Paul."

My name slams against me, and I wake to a numbing cold—I'm standing. I'm outside in the freezing winter. And I'm staring right at Eliot Cobalt. Alarm shoots into my veins like pure adrenaline.

He speaks in French, not realizing he's not talking in English— or I've convinced him I am actually a part of the Cobalt brethren. Thinking the former is more likely, and I'm mentally stalling and skidding and slipping on what is an excruciating moment for me.

I was sleepwalking, and Luna's best friend, Beckett's younger brother, a Cobalt, followed me out. His thin blue pajama bottoms and the white tee, molded against his muscles, makes me think he *ran*. He ran after me and didn't even grab a fucking coat. Dark concern has washed away the bright mischief of Eliot. His uneasy breath smokes the air, cheeks pinker.

And is his hand reached out to calm me?

I'm calm.

Alright.

He's just not someone who should *ever* be in this place. I help him. I help his family. He doesn't need to help me.

"Just out taking a midnight stroll," I rasp, my voice raw from the dry cold, and I try to step forward.

"Do not move," Eliot warns, his palm flat against my bare chest, and a shiver snakes through my body. That's when I hear a tiny, nearly imperceptible *crack*.

I check the landscape behind him, and I realize I'm a football throw from the dock, from the boathouse. Glancing at my feet, I'm wearing navy blue *slippers*. Not mine. Don't know who these belong to. What's more concerning than stealing someone's footwear—we're not standing on the safety of the snowy earth.

Eliot surveys the length of the frosty ground as another louder splintering noise catches my ear. We're standing on ice. I walked out on the lake that just froze overnight.

"Go to the dock," I say. "This isn't gonna hold both of our weight." We might have less than a minute. All I hear is our heavier breaths and the foreboding creaking beneath our feet.

Eliot draws his gaze back to mine. "The ice is thin. It'll likely break behind me as I walk."

"Then run—"

"You don't understand—"

"I understand alright," I say fast, hearing the fissure, feeling the unstable surface underneath us. "You're worried you'll reach the dock and I won't—but I'm not following you. I'm going in another direction."

"The dock is the shortest distance."

"You gotta stop arguing with me," I say with the hard rise and fall of my chest, adrenaline trying to warm my shuddering frame and stop my teeth from chattering. "Just trust me, please."

He's conflicted. His muscles flex as he keeps his body still. "I'd never leave anyone—"

"You're not leaving me," I interject, hurried. "I can walk. I can move. And I'm not planning on taking a nighttime swim. You wanna be a sacrificial fish for me? Don't be. 'Cause I'm not gonna be one for you. I'm *running* as fast as I can in the opposite direction, and you should too."

Eliot gives me one quiet resolute look before he says, "Let's see if that's true." And instead of sprinting to the dock, he takes off for the longer route.

Fuck me. I have no time to think. As soon as our weight shifts, the ice breaks beneath my feet, and I'm not tiptoeing and taking my sweet fucking time. I just *go*.

And I don't chase after Eliot. Instinct isn't to fall behind and plunge into the water. Instinct shoves me toward certain safety, and I'm sliding toward the dock. Catching my balance, I'm inches away. Then my left foot dips into the bone-freezing cold water. I grip the wooden edge and pull my body onto the sturdy surface.

Eliot is still running and trying not to fall on the slippery surface. I sprint down the dock, my legs shrieking at the biting air, but I'm not slowing my aggressive stride. I watch him while I run.

He must've stepped on a pressure point in the ice—because the entire surface of the lake is collapsing behind him. The thunderous noise booms against my eardrums, and as my wet slippers touch the earth, I aim straight for the snowy bank where Eliot is trying to reach.

Fifteen feet from land, the ice gives out, and he drops into waist-deep water. "*Fuck*," Eliot curses, his teeth clanking. He walks forward in the slushy, melting mixture, and I carefully approach, the ice thicker near the bank.

Close enough, I clasp his hand and help him out of the lake. I have an arm around his back, and we're stumbling forward. Safely standing on the snow. No one is rushing out of the house. Seems like everyone is still fast asleep, but that relief is drowned beneath my concern for him.

Eliot tries to laugh through his chattering teeth. "There's a-a first time for everything." He casts a glance at the chunks of floating ice. Looks like dynamite exploded in our wake. "Never fe-fell through it before."

"Ditto," I shiver, wetness creeping up my pant leg from the soaked ankle. Eliot's bottoms are drenched, and he hasn't stopped trembling. "Let's get inside." There's a high chance I gave a Cobalt hypothermia.

Rose might try to kill me before Christmas.

But I don't give a shit about that, really. I'm worried about Eliot. Good thing there's a doctor in the house named Farrow. Bad thing I didn't think to sleepwalk with my phone. But hey, I grabbed slippers.

So at least I tried to protect my toes.

As we climb the wooden stairs to the back deck, Eliot is checking on me with several side-glances. Then he stops me midway.

"What...was that back there?" His body rattles, but he manages to gesture to the lake.

I don't follow his finger. "Testing out my penguin skills. Think I'm more of a dirt and grass mammal." I wish he wouldn't stall for *this*. "Come on, man. You're gonna freeze your nuts off. You need to protect your future progeny and whatnot." I ascend one step.

Eliot isn't following. He stays one stair below me.

Fuck. *Fuck.* I rotate back to him. "You don't want to procreate. I respect that. Luna might name your first kid Comet. Which is cute but probably not y—"

"You were sleepwalking," Eliot says with measured breath, keeping his teeth still. "You were...unresponsive for *four* minutes before you even made eye contact with me. I would say...you were acting, but then I'd be saying...you're a better actor than me. And I...I don't believe that's it."

The cold ices my lungs. Each breath is blistering, frigid hell. I scared him. I can tell I scared him, and who wouldn't be freaked out finding a sleepwalker in a hazardous spot? I never wanted to put Eliot in one too.

"I'm sorry," I say, throat closing. "Thanks for that." I motion to the lake, wanting to set it so far behind me. "Next time, you can just leave me. I'll find a way back."

"Ah, funny," he says with a weak grin, "we're just two court jesters...freezing to death on the stairs." He shivers. "The tragedies of us."

Yeah. Feel that. I tell him, "We could freeze inside—"

"This is a common occurrence then? The sleepwalking?"

I don't say *yes*. I'm rubbing my arms. "It won't hurt Luna—*I* won't hurt Luna."

"Never thought...you would." He fights through the agonizing cold to say, "Just concerned about you."

I don't want him to be. It's a sudden, slamming thought, and I can't halt its impact. It crushes me. "I'm good," I say, ribs constricting around my lungs. "Let's go." Another step up. He catches my arm this time. "Eliot—"

"There are backdoor cameras."

I didn't forget those. As security personnel, I have access to all the passcodes, but typically, the family will shut off the cameras linked to the back deck because of the amount of traffic in and out. This holiday season, every camera has been active. After the assault and kidnapping, they want to be extra safe, and I don't blame them.

But this also means... "The cameras caught me leaving the house." I didn't want to spend Christmas talking about my sleep problems with her family, and I sure as hell don't want my new boss to know I have them.

"Follow my lead," Eliot says, and this time, he sprints ahead of me. I'm fast and catch up to him as he reaches the backdoor. The red beady camera light is blinking as Eliot crouches to the lens.

"Bonsoir," he says in a shudder. "Do not be alarmed. I took a midnight dip. A dare of my own creation. You would be absolutely horrified, Mom. Which is...to my delight." He flashes a teeth-chattering grin. "Donnelly, here, went first, as prompted by yours truly. He withstood the ice better than I. Luna, you chose a strong one. Hugs and kisses." He mimes two cheek kisses. "Nighty night, heathens." He stands and grips my eyes, silently telling me to follow.

If this was just a dare, I'd stick my tongue out at the camera and say hi to Papa Cobalt, but this wasn't that. This whole thing is my fault. And now Eliot's covering for me.

I owe him.

I don't want to be indebted to anyone, let alone a guy *eight* years younger than me. What the fuck am I doing?

No control. I had no control.

23

PAUL DONNELLY

The warmth of the house suffocates me all at once, and we leave a wet trail into the living room, the ceiling vaulted. Balconies off the different floors overlook this homey but grand space. No one is hanging over the railings and eavesdropping. It's dark and cold and late.

I inhale a lungful of Christmas pine, the ten-foot spruce decorated in the corner. Gifts already hide the tree skirt. I find Eliot's phone on the leather couch cushion. While he sheds his sopping pants, I ask him if I can use it. He says, *yeah*.

I want to call Farrow for his medical opinion. 'Cause I have no clue if Eliot is hypothermic.

Eliot can speak, but he hasn't quit trembling. His lips are bluish.

I dial Farrow's number, knowing it by heart, and I fiddle with the switch on the gas for the fireplace. It roars to life.

"Eliot?" Farrow doesn't sound groggy.

"Donnelly," I answer. "What's the signs of hypothermia?" I could use the internet, but why do that when I have a better resource who's bound to say, "Where are you?" It takes Farrow about a minute to enter the living room. Even less time to assess the damage inflicted upon the middle Cobalt child.

"All wet clothes off," Farrow says. "Sit by the fire. I'll grab more blankets." But Eliot has already thrown his soaked pants and shirt over a rocking chair.

No shame about being naked, he walks a few feet to grab the only quilt. He flings it around his body and asks, "What about a hot shower?"

"It could shock your lower extremities. You'll want to gradually warm yourself."

"I love my doctor friend," I say into a smile, teasing him.

Farrow rolls his eyes, and I smile a little more. It's about the best I've felt since I woke up on the lake. He returns with a heap of wool blankets, then tells me, "You too." Like I'm also a patient.

"I'm not wet," I whisper as he comes closer.

His ash-brown hair is ruffled like he'd been in bed, and he runs his thumb over his lip piercing. He's looking me over, and now I'm shifting away from him.

"Donnelly." He catches my bicep, his voice as hushed as mine. *What happened?* is all over his face.

His concern is easier to cradle. Maybe because he's closer to my age. Maybe because we've known each other since we were teenagers. Maybe because we're both bodyguards and supposed to protect the same people. I can't say why exactly, but while Eliot is out of earshot, I tell Farrow, "It's my fault." My eyes burn. "I'll tell you another time."

Farrow nods, not pushing. "I'm serious, man. Your pants are wet, and you're shaking."

Right.

So I strip to nothing—already not wearing underwear. With a wooly green blanket tucked around my naked body, I face the fire and sit beside Eliot on the coffee table. Farrow brings us both steaming mugs of decaf before returning to bed.

I don't talk much. It doesn't feel like I need to.

Eliot watches the flames, hypnotized by them. And when he's toasty, he rises and nods in a silent goodnight. I nod back, my body unable to unwind. I can't unroot myself.

A lump ascends in my dry throat, and I try to swallow enough coffee to slide the ball back down. And then feet pad across the floorboards. I look to the left, and I see her.

Luna.

She's only in that thin black nightgown and knee-high socks, her hair messy on her shoulders, and her eyes rest easily on me. A sentiment more vital than air surges inside my lungs.

She collects one of the woolen blankets Farrow left behind. Quietly, she sits next to me on the table, then says, "Eliot told me what happened. He said you were out here alone."

Yeah.

I nod a few times, unblinking as I stare at the black ring inside my coffee.

He's Luna's best friend.

I'm eight years older.

I'm in security.

I never really wanted Eliot or Tom to see me as broken. Never wanted anyone to. I don't even view myself that way. How do I go back to just being the cool, down-for-whatever older guy in his eyes? Is that even possible? Was this inevitable by getting closer to Luna?

Her family and friends are going to get a good look at all my flaws, even the ones I've sprinted miles and miles away from.

And why—*why*-the-fuck am I sleepwalking so much?

I've got the girl.

My family is dealt with (sort of). I'm in the happiest place on earth. 'Cause the lake house does rival Disney World in my head. Most of my stressors are diminishing, aren't they? It makes no sense.

"You're shivering," Luna breathes, scooting closer. "You should use my heat. Your species still hasn't perfected temperature control."

A laugh rumbles from the depths of me. God, I am so in love with her—I don't think I'm ever gonna stop. It's the first overwhelming thought that warms me. I'm grinning, then I glance back at Luna. "My species is far inferior to yours, space babe."

Her gaze sinks into mine. "Only for some things."

"Only for some things," I murmur, lost inside her expression, of how she's looking at me, as though I'm the put-together, invincible one, when really I think it's her.

I think I'm sliding.

Slipping.

But I like this. Being with her. The comfort of Luna Hale is enough to thaw my blood.

I think about kissing her.

I think about holding her.

I think about loving her for all eternity and then some. Under her blanket, I curve my arm around her hips, feeling the silk of her nightgown and her warmth. She twists my blue kyber crystal between her fingers, inspecting the plastic casing. The chain is cold against my neck, and after she drops it, she claps her hands twice.

All around us, Christmas lights power to life.

The tree glitters with bright yellow bulbs. Dozens of multi-color strands illuminate the banisters of the balconies and frame every window. It's stuff of holiday movies. Stuff of pretend and make-believe, but it's real. It takes me a second to look away.

I grin at her. "The bringer of light. You gonna show me how?"

"I think you showed me, actually."

I understand the metaphor, and I shake my head repeatedly. "Nah. That was all you." I touch the top of her head. "Master." I touch my chest. "Apprentice. Remember?"

"That, I do remember," she mutters, sitting up a little off me.

It knots my chest, but I give her some space. Then I put my coffee down and adjust the blanket over her shoulders. Making sure it's not falling.

She knocks her knees into my legs, her cheeks flushing. Her eyes lift to mine. "Do you want to talk about it?" Her voice is nearly a whisper. "About what happened tonight?"

Not really.

I want to dive into her head and avoid reality. To slide down a figurative fantastical slope of alien abductions and planets so beautiful they could sear your eyes just by looking. But the longer I stare at Luna, the more at peace I feel, and reality doesn't seem so bad.

"I hate putting people out." I speak hushed. "Just as much as I dislike causing them any sort of grief. *This*. My sleep issues. I hate that it affected someone else. I wish I could control it."

"I have some experience with a body that does its own thing when it wants, and it sucks how much you just want it to work in your favor and how wishing for it feels empty, like dropping a coin in a well."

"Yeah, it does," I breathe. Her memories not being readily available to her—it's been tough on her. Someone else understanding what I'm going through, even tangentially, makes me feel less alone in a way. I slide my hand on her thigh.

She traces the veins that run from my wrist to my knuckles. "Are you going to come back to bed?"

With my other hand, I rub at the back of my neck. "I dunno. I feel like I owe Eliot, and I can't wrap my head around it."

"I don't think he's expecting anything in return. He's just the kinda guy who likes being there for his friends."

But he's not my friend. "He's your friend, Luna," I say. "For the past seven years, he's been someone I should protect, not someone who should need to protect me."

Luna considers this, then asks softly, "Is it so bad that other people care about you?"

My throat swells, and I blink a few times. "I'd rather he not, honestly." I look at her. "'Cause it means I'm not taking care of myself how I want to, and I've gotta figure it out." *I've gotta figure this shit out.* Without going through a sleep study or therapy—I'm gonna get through it. I have to throw a handful of coins in several hundred wells. One wish has to come true.

"What if you sleep with me?" she asks, then quickly clarifies, "*Just* sleep."

I tense at the offer.

"I can try to alert you if you're sleepwalking before you wander too far. Maybe you won't even do it if we sleep in the same bed."

"I could kick you or worse," I breathe. "I can't hurt you." *It'd kill me.*

She curls her pinky around mine. "I promise…that I'll wake you up if you kick or thrash at all. *I promise.*" She brings our pinky promise to her mouth, kissing her own thumb.

I inhale deeper.

It's hard to say *yes*. Even harder to say *no*. I want to hold her as I fall asleep. It sounds like the only comforting thing. Especially knowing I woke up earlier from the absence of her.

And it's not like we haven't "just slept" in the same bed before. The best night of sleep I had was in San Francisco. With Luna curled against my chest.

I raise our pinky promise to my mouth and kiss my thumb too.

Her smile grows.

"Sleep with me, space babe," I say.

Her lips keep rising. "I thought you'd never ask."

I laugh once, then lift her off the coffee table. I'm careful not to carry her. I set Luna on her feet before we go to the bunk room. Luna squeezing her legs around me will make me want to thrust inside her, and I am pumping those brakes like a motherfucker.

CHARLIE & LUNA'S TEXT THREAD

Dec 24th

6:03 a.m.

Luna: Hi, heidi ho ho ho. This is me. Luna. You know that, obv. No rush in finishing the dournal. But I do have a question when you do get close to the end.

7:05 a.m.

Charlie: I finished it last night.

Luna: Whoa...really? I just gave it to you yesterday evening.

Charlie: It was light reading.

Luna: Oh. Good reading?

Charlie: Do you want a critical review of your writing style or to help with your memories?

Luna: I mean...I wouldn't be opposed to hearing your review, but I would rather you help an amnesia girl out.

Charlie: I'll get back to you later. If not in person, then over text.

Luna: K! 👍 👍

9:47 p.m.

Charlie: Here again.

Luna: For a minute there, I thought you forgot about it.

Charlie: My brothers haven't left your side all day. I'm not doing this in front of them.

Luna: Prob wise.

Charlie: You don't date your entries, so I had to piece the timeline together contextually. You don't cover the entirety of the last three years that you've forgotten. Based on your use of present tense in certain areas, I've deduced that you started writing in the diary about three months ago. Which means you haven't written in it for very long.

Luna: That's bad then...?

Charlie: Not necessarily. It opens with you reminiscing about the past. And there are more spots where you reflect on past events. It'd be impossible for you to write down every moment of your life, but even with narrative blanks, this isn't nothing. These are your words and thoughts so you can take what's here as fact.

Luna: Okay. So my question is...do I mention any drug use???

Charlie: Cocaine, briefly. You don't list out any other drugs, but it's implied you've done more.

Luna: I don't say what *more* entails?

Charlie: No.

Luna: Any guesses?

Charlie: Why do you care about this?

Luna: Idk. It feels like I put foreign substances in my body without approving of said foreign substances. Even though I know it was me. Just a different me. Or the same me? It's confusing.

Charlie: Ask Donnelly about the FanCon tour.

Luna: Why?

Charlie: When you joined us, he saw you taking something before I did. So ask your boyfriend.

24

 LUNA HALE

Christmas Eve night.

It's 9:48 p.m.—and I'm cradling my phone in my hands, seated on a closed toilet lid, and staring wide-eyed at Charlie's response.

"What'd he say?" Donnelly asks, casually bent towards the cracked window. He hangs his arm outside, a cigarette burning between his fingers.

We snuck into the bathroom to smoke, and as much as I love the holidays for all the family-gathering and bonding, especially with my best friends, I miss having more alone-time with Donnelly. I've barely seen him today.

He volunteered to drive to the nearest town after my aunts realized no one bought coffee. And the coffee canister, left from the last trip here, quickly became empty.

I thought he'd be an hour max. But he didn't return until closer to dinner. He said it was foggy, and he was driving slowly. I thought maybe there was more to the story, but he whispered to me that he'd explain tomorrow.

Now it's late at night, and this is the time I'd usually spend with Tom and Eliot. Partaking in hedonistic engagements, sneaking off to the woods. That kinda thing. I knew they'd want to join my smoke break with Donnelly if I mentioned it. So I had to subtly imply that Donnelly and I were leaving to hookup.

I guess I could've just said, *we want to be alone*. But that also would've led them to the same assumption.

They think Donnelly is fucking me in here, when really he's still holding out.

But I thought he was only holding out *sexually*. I reread Charlie's last text. "He said I mentioned taking cocaine, which we already know, but I implied doing more. Then he said to ask you about the FanCon tour."

His eyes veer to the side, as if recollecting.

My heart picks up speed. "He said you saw me take something."

Donnelly straightens out of the bent position and reaches out for the phone. "Can I see? It's alright if you say no but—"

"You can see." I hand it to him, having nothing to hide. And I kinda understand needing to see the full context of the conversation. I'd want that too.

Reading, he blinks several times. I wonder if he's trying to drown the annoyed look crossing his face. Then he returns the phone and rests his forearm back outside. His body is ten-times more strained. Relaxed is not a word I'd anoint him with right now.

Nerves try to invade my stomach. "Were you going to tell me? Or were you scared to?"

"Not scared," he shakes his head several times, then takes a drag, blowing a wispy line of smoke out the window. "I wanted to talk about it last night, but I wasn't sure it's something you'd want Eliot or Tom to know." He shifts into a lunge position, both arms slanted against the windowsill. "If I brought it up then, you probably wouldn't have said much, and I would've rather actually had a conversation with you about it." He sucks on the cigarette for a beat longer.

Okay. He's been wanting to talk.

That's good.

I release a breath and stand from the toilet. I lean a hip on the other side of the window, facing Donnelly.

The Rudolph bath rug beneath our feet is soft and cozy, but I cross my arms at the colder draft. His gaze drops to my nipples, perked against my black silk nightgown. I've noticed he loves when I wear spaghetti strap tops, and I'm starting to believe this particular nightgown has magical properties of seduction.

I like wearing it. I like seeing how his blue eyes roam over my body with lust. How he looks as though he's seconds from pinning me to a bed and lifting the hem.

I reach out for the cigarette.

Donnelly passes it over, and I take a short drag, listening as he says, "I'm not trying to keep anything from you that you'd want to know. It wasn't intentional."

I nod. "Hearing that makes me feel better." I crouch to blow smoke outside.

He lets me hold on to the cigarette for a little longer. "There was a time when we were together where we talked about you doing drugs, but so briefly. I told you I knew you did 'em because I've heard some rumors, but I didn't know what was real because bodyguards talk. Some of it is bullshit. You said you'd tell me, eventually, but not that night."

"I never got around to telling you, did I?" Sadness sinks in my stomach, especially as he confirms my suspicions.

He nods and says, "I don't think you were doing anything as severe as meth or heroine. I think you probably wanted to tell me you'd taken Ecstasy."

I frown, and he slips the cigarette out of my fingers, just to tap the ash outside. The ashy butt was about to fall on the rug.

"Thanks," I murmur, then say, "I still don't understand. Charlie said you saw me take something during the FanCon tour, and the night we talked about drugs was way after that when we were kinda together?"

"Yeah."

"So why didn't you tell me about it that night you and I were discussing drugs?"

"'Cause we both already knew about it. It was sort of unspoken. I wasn't gonna bring it up then, for the same reason you didn't want to keep talking about it."

"Why?"

He sweeps me. "We'd just had sex."

Ohhh. Heat ascends my neck, and I wish I could picture exactly how he took me. "I'm feeling a wee bit jealous of her." I pinch my fingers and squint at the invisible jealous matter. "Just a wee bit."

Donnelly grins. "Just a wee bit." He shakes his head. "You shouldn't be. I'm gonna fuck you harder than I ever did."

It's a promise said so casually that I nearly buckle at the knees. Holy shit. His grin widens before he puts the cigarette between his lips.

"I'd hold you to it," I say, "but I can't remember us having sex, so I'd have to consult Charlie about how hard you took me."

Donnelly does not like that. When he isn't fond of something, irritation or anger doesn't radiate through his face. It's subtle. The tic of his jaw, the downcast of his eyes. "If you wrote about it," is all he says.

"Yeah," I say. "I'm not actually going to ask Charlie about that."

"If it's something you need to know—"

"I don't," I assure. "But I do still want to know about what you saw me take."

He nods. "It was the same night I tattooed you on the tour bus." He starts smiling, then laughs. "Christmas Eve, I'm pretty sure."

"Really?" I smile, and I'm surprised to feel a swell of joy rather than grief at hearing about this forgotten moment. "That must have been three…"

"Three years ago, yeah. I finished wrapping your tattoo on your forearm. We were in the middle of the bus at this booth-table thing. Oscar was driving, and Farrow had been with us for a second—but he left to go chat with him." Donnelly taps ash outside the window. "You went to the bathroom to look at the tattoo, but you brought out your toiletry bag. You were digging around for a sec, and I thought you were gonna take out your birth control or something. But you pulled out a baggy of pills."

Pills?

I'm about to ask what kind, but he's a good storyteller and I don't want him to jump around.

He continues, "It's not like you were showing me. Your back was slightly turned, but I could see. I was cleaning up my tattoo machine, putting away ink, moving around you. And Charlie—he went to use the bathroom around that time, so he must've seen you too."

"But we talked about the pills that same night?"

"Yeah," he nods, "but you gotta understand, we weren't friends. I barely knew you at the time. You'd *just* turned eighteen, and I was twenty-six. I had no business hanging around you before that as anything other than a bodyguard. And I didn't really wanna be alone with you then. I know what people think I'm willing to do, and it's just not who I am, you know? Not when you're that young."

I nod. "Yeah, I get it. You wanted to give it some time before befriending me, for the freshness of my eighteen to wear off a bit."

He shakes his head. "It's not like I was looking to ever befriend you, Luna. I was just kind of…drawn to you."

I squint in thought. "Like a pheromone?" I imagine Wallflower from *New Mutants* comics. "Maybe I had the superpower of pheromone control back then. I must have smelled like lust."

He smiles. "Didn't get close enough to smell you when you just turned eighteen. So I can't say."

"What does just turned twenty-one smell like?"

His gaze inches so slowly down me, I quiver, and he sucks the cigarette with casualness, blows more smoke outside, then says, "Lemme see." He steps forward, and one of his hands slips against the back of my neck, lifting into my hair. His head dips, and he breathes me in against my sensitive nape, his lips just barely skating across my goose-pimpled skin. I have to hold on to his waist to keep from trembling, pleasure trying to rattle my limbs.

"Your twenty-one," he whispers, "smells ripe." He pulls back just to caress my gaze with his. "Like you're ready to be eaten."

Please. "Yep. I'm ready," I rasp. "Eat me out."

Donnelly isn't taking the bait that easily tonight. He's not so ready to harvest me, maybe since we haven't finished the talk he wanted to have. I want to have it too. It's just distracting. How much I crave the sensualness and physicality of him.

He releases more ash outside, being careful about the cigarette in my family's bathroom. "Back to the tour bus?" he asks.

"Uh-huh," I nod, flush still bathing my face. I feel wet, so I cross my ankles, thighs gluing together.

"You alright?"

I nod a few more times. "How'd you ask her—I mean *me*"—I'm trying to think of us as *one* person more and more—"about the pills?"

"You cracked open an energy drink, and we caught eyes when you popped the pill in your mouth. I just asked you what it was. You shrugged and said, 'Adderall.'"

"Adderall?"

"Yeah. I think I said something like, 'You have a prescription?' and you shook your head. You seemed kind of tentative. I think you thought I'd rat you out to security. But I wasn't judging you for it, and you ended up asking me if I'd taken any before."

"Have you?"

"Yeah, once or twice at Yale. Hated how I couldn't sleep. I'd rather just have a nicotine high."

"Was I just trying to stay up late or something?"

He rubs at his face. "I, uh, dunno what you were trying to do, Luna. 'Cause most of us on the bus ate edibles that night, including you, so I got concerned seeing you take uppers after downers and washing Adderall down with more caffeine. I shoulda said something to you about it then, but I didn't. I just asked if I could have a swig of your energy drink. I drank a lot of it. Then over the next year, there were times where we were in group settings, and I'd see you do the same thing. I'd just say things like, 'That doesn't mix well.' You usually listened to me or let me drink whatever you were drinking."

I rest more against the windowsill. "What'd I seem like? Like mentally?"

He stares off for a beat. "It seemed like you were searching for a feeling. I can't say what it was, but maybe you figured doing drugs, having sex, drinking alcohol—anything, everything, that you felt like you couldn't do before you turned eighteen—was gonna help you find it."

I contemplate the past that I can recall. "I did feel trapped," I whisper. "Like I couldn't spread my arms high enough. Boxed in. Maybe I was searching for the feeling of being unraveled...it'd make sense why I'd be that careless with drugs."

"I think you learned that unraveled feeling is better felt without the drugs."

My lungs expand in a deeper breath, realizing I've already stretched my arms to the galaxy and come undone and felt so perfectly inside myself—like just being me is home. I haven't felt the urge to embark on some intense drug-fueled exploration this time around. Because I've already discovered the feeling I'd been searching for.

It was with him.

I lean my temple on the window frame. "You know how I read a little bit of the diary? Before I stopped?" I stare into the gentle blue pools of his shimmering eyes. "There was one line I wrote about you, and it's kinda stuck with me."

"What was it?" he asks in a near-whisper.

"I wrote about how comfortable you make everything." I try to remember the exact words. "You make it seem like 'living is just as easy as breathing, and sometimes I do wonder how it can feel that easy. Because in my head it's not easy at all.'"

Donnelly mulls over these words, his hand on his mouth, then jaw, then sliding along the back of his head.

"Do you just make it look that way?" I ask him.

"Nah, I'm not pretending." He slips me a slanted smile. "Living is as easy as breathing, Luna. It doesn't have to be hard, but I know it can be." He pauses. "When I was eighteen, I thought about it a lot too. I'd started getting out of the bad situation with my family. I was up at Yale with Farrow. I met Oscar. I made more friends who wanted good things for me. And it became easier and easier and easier…until I didn't notice it was hard at all."

It floods me, this luminous hope beyond the darkness. It's the effervescence of Donnelly. And he's telling me it's not just uniquely born to him. It's something to discover.

I wonder how long he's been guiding the way for me. How long I've understood his path is the brightest one to take.

"I know it hurts at times, what we've gone through together," I say quietly. "But…" I dive into his gaze. "This is easy. Being with you. It's not painful."

His chest rises in a stronger breath. He snuffs the cigarette out on the sill, then discards the butt, and he bridges the distance between us, his large palms sliding against my rosy cheeks.

I hold on to those affectionate hands. My heart catapulting to the cosmos.

He's staring into my entire being, his breath catching slightly in a near-groan. "I just want to be alone with you."

It's an ache. A shared yearning.

After he woke up sleepwalking last night, we squeezed together in the twin-sized lower bunk bed. Sexy, yeah, but we weren't trying to arouse each other. I wanted him to sleep through the night. He did. Now it's Christmas Eve, and all I can imagine is being pressed up against Donnelly again.

But the bunk bed has downsides. Mainly, we aren't alone. And he's dying to be alone with me. I'm craving to extend this alone-time past the bathroom and further into the night.

"I have an idea," I tell him.

25

 LUNA HALE

Most everyone is shut away in the privacy of their rooms, awarding us the perfect opportunity to rummage in the basement's storage closet for camping gear. Sleeping bags, a survival glow stick, pillows, foam pads.

Donnelly turns off the front doorbell security cameras for a blip, and once we're safely outside and out of sight of surveillance tech, he switches them back on. We're smiling and sprinting as we brace the cold in our thin layers—my silk nightgown, his black drawstring pants. We rush to the gravel parking pad.

In a matter of minutes, we've made a comfy, cozy bed in the back of the Ford truck.

Sharing the oversized dark purple sleeping bag, Donnelly zips up the sides towards our necks. I nuzzle farther under the bag, greedy for our collective body heat. My nose stays hidden, my eyes peeking out into the cold.

Donnelly grins down at me. The windchill isn't as hostile as last night, so I'm not shocked he's able to keep an arm out of the sleeping bag. "You care if I light another one?" he asks, maybe because we've been discussing drugs, and cigarettes are classified as one. It's just not a habit either of us are worried about, I guess.

Not now anyway.

"No. I'd smoke too if I could keep my hands outside." I only took a couple drags off his other cigarette. He didn't even finish it before he snuffed it out.

Cigarette between his lips, he lights it. The embers glow red in the dark. Then his other bicep curves around me, holding me closer to his chest. His head is propped on a pillow while I use his body as mine.

I smile, and my heart pitter-patters in a giddy way I love when I'm around him. Lying in the bed of the truck together, we gaze up at the clear night sky and the twinkling stars inside the immeasurable darkness.

It's peaceful, this moment with Donnelly.

We are on the very brink of Christmas. I'm sensing holiday magic swirling in the air. Then I wonder out loud, "What were your Christmases like growing up?"

He takes a long while to respond, unhurriedly expelling a line of smoke. Then he tugs on the sleeping bag, exposing my face to the elements. Cigarette between two of his fingers, he puts it to my lips so I can take a drag.

I try to inhale, but the gesture makes me smile more than anything. I blow out a little smoke, just as he says, "Empty."

My smile vanishes. "Empty?"

"Don't feel sorry for me," he says fast.

I nod once, my lips burrowed back beneath the sleeping bag. "No sorry feelings here."

The corner of his mouth pulls upward. "It wasn't even that I didn't have a tree. Or that most Christmas mornings, my parents would paper-bag a can of Fizz or some shit they found in their cupboards and call it a present. Like a used lighter that barely had any fluid left. A tube of toothpaste I bought myself a week earlier." He lounges back, eyes up above. "It was empty because they weren't there." He takes a drag, blowing out a quick cloudy stream. "Physically, they were there. On the couch. In the kitchen. Getting high. I'd call it a tradition, since it happened often enough to be one."

I press my cheek to his chest, hearing the slow *thud thud thud* of his heart. Calm. He is calm. With one arm, he still hugs me to his lean muscled build.

I realize that I've been the wealthiest girl on Christmas morning, and Donnelly might've been the poorest boy—and it had nothing to do with gifts under the tree.

"I'm glad you're here," I whisper, and I'm afraid I spoke too softly.

Until he says, "Me too." His smile sparkles in the night. "Whose planet are we on now? Yours or mine?"

"I think we're in outer space together, sharing a cryopod." I wriggle farther under the sleeping bag, my ankles sliding against his calves, and his hand skates across my belly. The spot between my legs thumps with greater need, a swelter beginning to brew in our pod.

"Destination unknown?" he asks, putting out the cigarette.

"Yep. To be determined," I say, watching him with rapt attention in the sliver of light outside the sleeping bag, my arousal rapidly and surely building. "Unless the destination is you inside me." I shoot my shot.

"Nah, that's not the final destination."

Air ball. "No?" I try not to be disappointed.

He grips the edge of the sleeping bag. He's hanging slightly over me, but he's on his side. "I can fuck you while we're in space."

Yes. Yes, I like this plan. Fuck me in space. Words don't release through my parted lips, an aching sound caught between them. My pussy already clenches as he tents the sleeping bag over our heads. Plunged into darkness and an escalating scorch, Donnelly hoists his body over me, his forearms rooted on either side of my head, and his lips effortlessly find mine in a sultry, slow-burning kiss.

My limbs quake. *Ohmy…*

I hear him snap the glowstick, and suddenly, we're bathed in a vibrant green light. He's by far the sexiest human I've ever rested my eyes against, and I sense him exploring me with the same carnal fascination. I brush my fingers against the carve of his shoulder muscles, down to the ink on his sculpted bicep, over to the ridges of his abs. All glowing in green.

He cups my face with two hands, bringing his forehead to mine, and I feel his entire body rock against mine. Whoa, *whoa*. A high-pitched sound tears through me. He's simulating pushing in me without literally slipping in. Fabric. Too much fabric.

I hook my fingers under his waistband, but he's stoking my pleasure, causing me to lose sight of my mission to unclothe.

He kisses me again, these seductive, breathtaking kisses that travel beyond my lips. He presses hot tracks along my collarbone, slipping the skinny straps of my nightgown off my shoulder. Then he draws the fabric down to my ribs, letting it pool at my hips.

My breath hitches as Donnelly kisses the lines of my flying saucer inked beneath my breast, and he rises to my nipple. Sucking.

"*Donnelly*," I cry, my legs vibrating, toes curling.

While teasing my nipple with his mouth, his hand sensually slides up against my cheek again, like he knows exactly where each piece of me exists without even looking. I am hot molten puddy underneath him.

His kisses return to my lips, only for a moment. Because he breaks away to rock against me again. *OhmyGodohmyGod*. His cock is so hard but trapped behind the thin jersey pants. His length bears against my heat. The pressure teasing and torturous.

His hand sheathes my cheek. "Think you should make reentry onto my planet." His husky voice caresses me.

I can't catch my breath, and I pant, "What are we returning for?"

"So I can show you what other things human men on Earth are good for."

Show me. Show me. "Show me," I ache, spreading my legs even wider. His hot hand slides against my thigh, up under my nightgown, but *not* under my panties. "Please. *Please*."

I'm an animal, clawing at him. His kisses are hungrier against my lips, then buried against my neck, but I feel feral in comparison. Despite how voracious my hands are along the valleys and planes of his hard muscles, his palms are controlled, measured, slow. Very, *very* slow in the way they descend and clasp and stroke. The strength of his clutch lights my core on fire, and the sensual, scalding *slowness* pains me in the worst-best way.

I shudder.

I squirm.

I writhe.

"Donnelly. *Donnelly.*"

"Luna." It's an aroused but warning *Luna*, as if I'm on the edge of certain danger.

"Please, please," I murmur against his lips. I want all the danger. Let's blast through the caution signs! To infinity and...*ohhh*, he's pulling my knee toward my chest while kissing me.

I cling to the way he handles me, as if he's well-versed in the art of sex, and we're pen and paper, about to sketch the hottest picture together.

But it's how he's holding my ankle with careful force as I jerk that does me in. I can't quite describe the noise I make, a cross between a whimper and a cry, and he mutters a husky, "Fuck." Arousal pummels us—me, more so, because I lose it.

I lose sense of where I am.

Black dots blur my vision, and I tighten and pulsate and come. *Ohhh my...fuck, fuck.* Sweat has bubbled up on my skin, and my back arches, my body bowing into Donnelly. I hit a climax so fast. My panties are still on. His drawstring pants are still on, and he didn't even finger me. Wow, wow, *wow.* I tremble into a shaky moan, and then search for breath.

"Donnelly?" I pant.

"I haven't gone anywhere," he breathes, releasing hold of my leg. He's more so leaning on his side now, studying my breathing, and the green glowstick is beginning to weaken, the color more muted. He presses a kiss to my temple, his eyes sinking into mine. "You alright?"

"Yeah," I whisper, my face roasting. *I came without him again.* It feels like if he were to touch my clit at all, I'd come in a heartbeat again. There is no post-climax lazy, oozy sensations for me. I'm still vibrating inside with the remnants of pleasure. "Can we still…? Are we going to…?"

"Have sex?"

I nod once.

He skims me for a half-beat. "I dunno, I think maybe we should hold off."

I think for a second. "Is it because I came without you?" I ask.

"No." He smiles a little. "I love making you come. Doesn't have to be at the same time as me."

Then…? "Was I too needy? Was I never this needy before?" I whisper. "Wait—don't tell me. I don't think I should know how I was in bed." I'll end up comparing my past self to my present self and getting insecure.

After combing a hand through his sweaty hair, he hangs his arm across my hips. My nightgown is still pooled at my waist, but Donnelly doesn't make me feel timid or bashful being this exposed.

"I know…" He feels for the words. "…that you don't wanna go this slow. But I need you…to go this pace. I thought we'd have sex tonight, I did, but I can't—I think I'd regret it if we did."

I'm listening closely. "How come?" I speak as hushed as him.

"You were in the hospital a month ago. I've got doctors telling me to slow down with you, Luna, and I could give a fuck about other consequences; I've bulldozed through most of 'em to get to you, but when it comes to your health, I just can't…I can't play around with that." He exhales a tight breath. "And I can give you a lot, I just can't fuck you yet. I feel good knowing I'm doing something to protect you…" He has to look away from me for a beat, but his arm stays on my body.

I start nodding, realizing this is as much about his needs as it is about mine. He doesn't want to rush too fast, too far, and I don't want him to regret any intimate moment with me.

"Okay," I breathe. "Okay."

"Yeah?" His chest rises, like maybe he'd been nervous to tell me how he felt.

He's not really rejecting me. The wait continues, and it's for good reasons. "Yeah, but should I be less...?" Wild? Aggressive? Needy?

He's shaking his head. "Be yourself, space babe. That's all I'll ever want."

I begin to smile, overwhelmed tears trying to prick my eyes, and I roll more on top of him. He clasps my hips while I straddle his waist, too far up his body to feel his erection against me. He said we can do a lot, just not have sex. I peer down at him. He doesn't desert my gaze, not as I say, "Would it be a bad idea if I blow you?"

His smile is almost there. Faint. On the edge. "You wanna blow me?"

The thought of exploring him closer and taking him in my mouth already flames my whole body. "Yeah, it's mission critical. Our future in space depends on it."

He's grinning with me and asks, "What happens if you don't?"

"We die, of course."

"Can't have that happen."

"No, we can't," I breathe, heat ramping up in our pod. "And it has to be me—I have to be the one to make you come, or else..." I near his lips, or maybe he's nearing mine. "...I'll faint."

He clutches the back of my head. "How you feeling now?" The husky rasp to his voice is so attractive, I could listen to him talk the whole time we're fooling around.

"Woozy." My thighs instinctively tighten around him.

He kisses me, another sensual, deep kiss that steals oxygen. I'm glad he pulls away or else I would've stayed glued to him, and I must proceed with the mission.

"You better suck my cock," Donnelly tells me, his grin too sexy.

"I'mgoingI'mgoing," I slur together in a hot rush, and I pretend I'm in zero gravity and drifting down our cryopod. He leans back on his elbows, but with one hand, he combs back my hair.

I draw his pants off his waist, past his ass, down his legs. He's kicking them off.

The green glow along his inked body is tantalizing, and I could lick every inch of him. *Focus on the cock, Luna.* He's so aroused, when I grip his shaft, his muscles flex in response, and a deep noise scrapes against his throat.

"Like this?" I ask, since I have very limited experience giving head. To be honest, I have *none* (that I remember), but the idea of the whole act is torching me with pleasure.

"Yeah, like that." His fingers slide into my hair, and he holds the back of my skull while I run my tongue along his shaft. "Fuck." His breathy, masculine *fucks* are electrodes shocking my clit.

I pull back from my own arousal, but I keep a hand around him. He's so big to me, and I love the veins traveling down his length. So I lick those too. His muscles contract again, and I wonder if he feels the ball of my tongue piercing. Speaking of *piercings*, he has two on his cock that I tease with the flick of my tongue.

His breath is heavier, hotter.

I kinda want a little guidance on what to do next, and as I look up at him, he must see it in my eyes. He sits up, bending forward. The sleeping bag is still tenting us. It feels bigger in here and less snug.

Donnelly touches my hand, which is wrapped around the base of his cock. "You don't have to be gentle about it."

I squeeze a little harder.

He grins like I'm endearing somehow. But it flickers in and out with arousal. "Harder than that."

I tighten my grip, and his hand is still sheathing mine. He's feeling my knuckles curve and fingers squeeze around him.

His abs flex. "Up and down." He moves my hand for me, and once I perfect the rhythm, he lets go, and the hot friction beneath my palm and the way his length twitches is trying to send *me*. His cock is so warm.

I squirm a little, pulsing. Aching.

His hand is back on my head. "Open your mouth." He instructs me on how not to scrape my teeth against him, and I feel more confident in my blow job pursuits.

I look at him as I grip the base of his shaft again and wrap my lips around his swollen head. His breath shortens and jaw clenches like pleasuring is slamming at him, especially when we lock eyes, and I try to go deeper. His hardness is sliding against my tongue.

"*Fuck,*" he grunts out, and he pushes my head down. *Oh my God.* I pulse, especially as he says, "You have to take way more of me than that."

I have to. It's a necessity. Our intimacy.

Our existence depends upon it.

I'd smile but I have a mouthful of him. I suck him up and down, but the sexiness of this moment, of how Donnelly is bowed forward and guiding me, truly overwhelms my body, and I try not to moan around his dick.

He flexes his hips upward, brings my head down, making me take more in my mouth, and I'm melting into the moment, into the *movement.* I realize I've stopped doing the work and let him completely take over. It's even better. I'm unthinking and just feeling.

He's practically fucking my mouth, and when my eyes flit up to his, his hand clenches in my hair, his muscles constricting.

Ohhhh. He starts to come, about to pull out, but I want to taste him. So I give him a look to *stay.* He does. When he's out of my mouth, he asks, "You need to spi...?" He trails off, seeing me swallow his load, and his smile turns into a light laugh. "Taste like top-tier man?"

"Uh-huh. Only the greatest kind."

He kisses my cheek, then nips my earlobe, and I laugh and crawl back on him, the pulsing between my legs screams for Donnelly, and he leans back, his head hitting the pillow. I straddle him, and his hands settle against my ass.

I touch the tip of my nose to the tip of his nose, staring directly in his eyes. "How was that?"

"I dunno, how's this?" He thumbs my clit, *underneath* my panties, and within three circles over the wet bundle of nerves, I jellify and cry into a mind-blowing orgasm.

Holy...*wow, wow, wow.* I fall on top of him, breathing hard, and he's laughing. I start laughing with him when oxygen returns to my lungs, and I roll onto my back beside Donnelly.

He perches on his forearm, looking down at me. "And to answer you, that was my favorite blow job I've ever had."

I smile. "It was out-of-this-world extraordinary," I sing-song. "For me too." I can see how much he loves me, just by looking, and it feels like the world is bestowing a gift upon me: To see love so fully expressed and to be its lucky recipient. In a quieter beat, I ask, "Why was it your favorite?"

He pushes a piece of sweaty hair off my forehead. "Besides it being with you, that was the most control I've ever had during a blow job." He grins over me. "Thanks for trusting me to face-fuck you, space babe."

I beam at how he says that. "Well," I say, trying to be very, *very* serious, "I wouldn't let you die."

His grin is my whole universe, it feels like. It contains every vibrant planet, every beautiful constellation, all the wishes made upon every shooting star. "No, you wouldn't," he breathes.

As our bodies slacken, as affection is shared in the silence, I ache for something different. Softly, I murmur, "Can you hold me?"

And so I find myself curled up against his warmth. He spoons me in the back of the truck, under the sleeping bag. Beneath the stars. I hold on to his forearms that wrap around my chest, and he buries one more kiss against my neck.

Somewhere deep-down, I know that I've never felt closer to Paul Donnelly than I have this night.

We wake to the early light. Squinting, I watch Donnelly stretch a shoulder and give me a sexy morning grin. My hair feels ratty and tangled, but I don't brush my fingers through the strands.

"Merry Christmas," I say, my lips rising as I sit up in the truck bed.

He slips me another smile while searching around for his phone. "Merry Christmas to you." The look he gives me is as dirty as it is romantic. Kinda like last night. He asks, "How'd you sleep?"

I shrug, the sleeping bag slipping off my shoulders. As soon as the chill hits, I tug it back up. "Not too bad. The foam pads were a good call—" I cut myself off as his phone rings.

"Fuck," he mutters, finding it much easier. He frowns at the random number, then answers it against his ear. Not even a half-second later, he pulls it down, then tells me fast, "I gotta take this." He hurdles the truck, landing bare-footed on gravel, until he jams his feet into boots.

I must be breathing oddly. He instantly rushes back to me, cups my cheek. "I love you." *He loves me.* "I'm not going far." *He'll be back.* He kisses me.

I'm worried for him. I can feel how much he doesn't really want to go. The kiss is reluctance to leave but also urgency.

As we break apart, I ask him, "Who's calling?"

His eyes crash into mine in a slo-mo collision. "My mom."

26

PAUL DONNELLY

Shoes on, I walk as far away from Luna as I can. Like the phone in my fist is a ticking bomb, and it shouldn't be within five-hundred feet of her. Didn't even have time to thank the truck for my favorite Christmas morning: Holding my girlfriend as dawn met the sky.

I'm walking *away* from the house.

Down the road.

Phone back to my ear, I hear the automated voice replay my options. "...this call may be monitored or recorded. To accept the charges for this call, press one or say *yes*. To refuse this call, hang up. To hear a rate quote, press two. This call is from an inmate telephone system..."

I can't think of anyone else who'd call me from prison right now, other than my mom. Uncle Scottie might, if he wants something bad enough.

It could be him.

It could be a cousin or uncle who just got locked up for assault, kidnapping, and possession of meth and couldn't post bail. They're all stuck in jail, waiting for the hearing.

Might be one of them.

I can't remember the last time my mom called. Somehow, though, she makes the most sense.

"Yeah," I tell the automated voice.

Put me through.

It rings and clicks, connecting.

"Hi, baby," my mom says, and I skid to a stop in the middle of the road. Snow-capped spruces border either side.

I stare at the rustling trees in the distance. My hair whips with the breeze, and I run my fingers through the strands. The cold barely touches me.

"Hey."

"...you've been good?" she asks tentatively, and I almost hear her adjusting the phone against her ear.

"Been good, yeah. You?"

"I'm doing really well here. Really well." Her voice sounds lighter than I remember. Less shaky. "Hey, your dad's been stopping by to visit, and he said you two are getting along better than ever."

I rub at the back of my head. "You've been seeing him a lot?"

"Two or three times a week."

I grimace. "You think that's such a good idea?" They're terrible together. I've always hoped they'd split apart, and not just one of those one-month arguments where my dad has to go crash on a cousin's lumpy sofa.

"Come on, baby." I hear the sharpness in her voice. "I know what you're thinking, but it's not like how it was. Okay? He's not using. He's been here for me. I'm clean. I've *been* clean. We love each other, and you know how much we love you?"

I fixate on one thing. "You've been clean?"

"Yeah." I hear her smile. "Yeah, it's been great. I feel like a whole new person. I can't wait to get out, and they're saying it might be earlier. I've been keeping my head down, staying out of trouble. You'd be proud of me."

I've clung to so much hope that my parents would turn a new leaf. That they would change.

Really, change.

Each time they took that hope, balled it up, and lit it on fire. What's left is a thick smoke-cloud of doubt.

So I've been here before.

Been down this road several times.

When I was sixteen and she first got thrown in. When I was twenty and she first got out.

When I was twenty-one and she got thrown back in. When I was twenty-two and she got back out.

When I was twenty-four and she got thrown back in. Same year, she got out.

And then when I was twenty-six and on a tour bus heading across the country, she got thrown back in again.

This familiar road leads to a jagged cliff. Or a dead-end. Or worse, a U-turn. 'Cause I'd rather run into a wall than face the same thing *over* and *over* and *over* again. At least with the wall, you hit it once and then the pain doesn't come back for more.

But something might be wrong with me, because in the back of my head, I'm still thinking, *What if it's different this time?* What if this really is it?

It worked out for Luna's parents. Didn't it? Why can't good things happen to mine?

Hope.

Luna has said I possess a good amount, much more than her, but I worry about having too much faith. Where hope feels more like a beautiful bastard, yanking me around.

But I can't lose it.

Hope.

I don't know how. Hope for a better life has been an underlying force in mine.

On the phone, I take too long to respond to my mom. She's already telling me, "I'd like to see you…I know you don't like coming around anymore—"

"It's not that—"

"I get it," she says quickly with more understanding than I'm used to hearing. "Really, you don't need to explain yourself. I haven't been the best mom, but that'll change when I get out of here. You know that?"

My eyes burn as I restrain emotion. "Dad said somethin' about you wanting to get into a recovery program."

"Yeah, yeah," she exhales. "I'm glad he told you about that. I, um…I gotta find the cash, but I'll figure it out."

I can help with that. The words rest on the edge of my tongue. For so many reasons, I shouldn't open that door. It took me forever to nail it shut.

I end up saying, "Scottie's getting my whole paycheck, so…" It's not true anymore. Loren Hale is paying him off, but my family still thinks the money is coming from me.

"Your dad's working on fixing that. His brother should've *never* taken that from you. God, it boils my blood. I can't believe him sometimes. The things he thinks he can get away with…" She sighs out a tight breath. "I'm so sorry you've been dealing with that."

I didn't know my dad's trying to resolve my *Scottie* problem. Strange feelings wrestle inside of me, and I tell her, "Yeah. You know how Scottie can be."

"He got another two years. Did you hear?"

"Yeah, I heard." He never got let out early like he thought he would, and my dad said Scottie had been so pissed, a screw came loose. Got in a fight with a guard. Did some other stupid, senseless shit. Think he might keep doing it until he's stuck there for a good decade.

The world's better with him behind bars. He'd cannibalize his own family for a hit. Sometimes, I think my mom would too.

Then sometimes, I think she's sweet enough to love.

Sometimes, I think I love her.

I can't even say why I do, other than the fact that she's my mom. And she had me when she was fourteen. Her life was rough. Her family kicked her out when she got pregnant with me, and she didn't have the type of money Lily and Lo did to dig herself out of the trenches she was drowning in.

I don't hate her. Not even a little bit.

I've never wanted to carry any hate in my heart. For anyone.

"You working?" she wonders.

"Nah, I'm off-duty."

There are things I'm going to avoid talking about.

But she doesn't ask me about my security job. She doesn't ask me about the rich Hale girl I was caught kissing in a dive bar. She has a TV in prison and magazines, so she knows—and I'm sure my dad told her about it.

What shocks me most is what she does say.

"You deserve time off," she says...lovingly. "It's Christmas after all." I hear her smile again. "Merry Christmas, baby. I hope next year is gonna be the best one for you."

My eyes burn so bad, I can't see in front of me. "Yeah." I hear my choked voice. "You too, Mom." When we hang up, I blink a few times, trying to remember a time where she's wished me a Merry Christmas. Trying to remember the last time I called her *Mom* over the phone.

Slowly, gradually, I spin back around toward the lake house. The road isn't empty anymore. Farrow is standing three car lengths away. Far enough that the gap should feel infinite and cold, but the space between us has never felt cavernous.

It's felt like he's always been right there, beside me.

I breathe easier. "Luna told you?" I ask.

"Yeah, she told me."

I almost smile, thinking of Luna going to Farrow. I like that she recognizes I'm not alone in this world either.

You are my family. That's never changing. I blink back more emotion, remembering what he said to me last month.

I love Farrow. It hits me—it hits me so hard that I look away from him. It's not the first time it's crashed against me this hard.

I was eighteen and he offered to answer my dad's phone calls. Like it was some simple thing. He never made a big deal out of it. Never even wanted a *thank you.*

Sometimes I wonder if he's the first person I truly loved. Because loving my parents never felt like this.

"Why'd your mom call?" Farrow asks, blowing on his bare hands. He didn't grab a jacket. He's only wearing a long-sleeve black Third Eye Blind shirt.

I walk forward. "To wish me a Merry Christmas."

His brows shoot up and pinch. "No shit?"

"Thought I hallucinated it for a minute too." I'm a foot away. "She hasn't said it in years. So…"

He's looking at me with caution tape over his eyeballs.

"What?"

"Man, that's the bare minimum."

"Didn't hear you say it," I tease.

He lets out a short laugh, then nods to me. "Merry Christmas, you blue-eyed shameless motherfucker."

I grin. "Merry Christmas, Dr. Kale."

"Hale."

"Right. Maximoff Hale's main man."

"*Only* man," Farrow corrects and flips me off.

I laugh, and as soon as he hears the noise, he's laughing too. On our trek to the lake house, the air is lighter, like oxygen is richer in this direction.

I contemplate my mom finally doing the bare minimum. It's a start, isn't it?

"She's got a long way to go," I tell Farrow. "Sky's the limit though. Maybe she can Peter Pan the clouds with the Hales."

He gives me a wary look.

"What?" I start grinning again. "Did Maximoff steal your Christmas funny bone? You deny him a blowie?"

He peels foil off a stick of gum. "Why the hell would I do that?"

"Resting your jaw."

Farrow throws up another casual middle finger, then pops gum in his mouth.

"It is the season of giving," I say lightly.

"And how's this season going for you?" Farrow asks me, referring to Luna.

"I think I'm giving all I've got, so I'd say pretty good." I smile at a thought. "Think all my girlfriend really wants for Christmas is for me to destroy her pussy."

"That visual, man," he shakes his head.

"Sexy, I know."

He blows a bubble, then pops it in his mouth. "It's not all she wants."

I nod. "Yeah, I know." My relationship with Luna isn't all about sex. It's a part of it, sure, but it's not all of it. We keep our leisure stride, the cherry red lake house in view. "I don't feel pressured by Luna. But I'm not used to holding out like this."

"If you're hesitating at all, you shouldn't have sex. Just let it happen when it happens. Don't force it or you'll keep thinking you did it too soon." He looks over at me. "You'll know when it feels right."

Yeah.

Trusting my instincts is easy when they haven't let me down. "How much I owe for the sex advice, Dr. Hale?"

He sucks in a breath. "This one's on the house, man, but I'll start charging both of you if you keep talking about ruining pussies."

I laugh hard. "*Luna* talked to *you* about wanting me to fuck her?"

His brows rise. "Yeah."

I can't stop laughing. I would've paid good money to see Farrow's reaction. "Fuck, I love that girl."

We're both smiling as we step inside.

It's loud already.

Bright chatter and laughter are a river flowing to the spacious living room, and we follow it. Luna's pajama-clad family are just gathering. Hales, Meadows, Cobalts, Abbeys, and Stokes. Some rub at their eyes and lounge with cups of coffee. Others mill around the furniture with more energy.

With Farrow next to me, I take it all in.

Tom tosses gifts underneath the overflowing tree. Like he just wrapped them this morning. Xander is half-asleep on the loveseat, and Kinney surrounds him with his birthday presents. Beckett chats with Charlie and their father by the sprawling windows, drinking out of holiday mugs.

Eliot collects names to be put in a Santa hat. "Merci, merci, merci," he says to the teenage girls as they drop a scrap of paper in. He goes around the room. "Merci, merci."

I smile as most of them start arguing about nominating Charlie to be the designated Santa. Sounds like he's never been randomly selected to pass out the gifts.

"We've never voted on it before," Audrey contends. "We *can't* break tradition. It's sacrilege."

The noise amplifies. People talk over each other.

I feel a bigger smile pull at my face.

It's the sort of radiant noise I find myself wanting to sit inside. Like those 3 a.m. nights in a club—standing too close to the amps, or blasting "Thunderstruck" on high volume with the car windows rolled up.

Farrow lifts his almost two-year-old son up against his waist. His eyes meet mine, an understanding in them. Really, he's the only person here who could understand what this feels like.

I've spent more holidays with Farrow than I have anyone else in my life. But they've never looked like this for me or even for him. There were some Christmases where we never left Yale. Where Oscar never left too. Where we'd all go eat a ham dinner at a local diner.

It was the happiest thing in the world to me back then.

But *this*…

This is what Farrow found. What I thought I'd never have.

I inhale the comforting scent of pine, coffee, and cinnamon. I listen to joyful noises.

And then the light of my fucking life slips effortlessly beside me. Luna wears a baggy sweatshirt over her nightgown, and immediately, I wrap my arms around her body and draw her back against my chest. She smiles up at me.

This is the new part. I've never had a girlfriend. I've never looked up and seen so much family. So much unconditional love.

On Christmas morning.

My eyes burn again, but with a feeling that's easy to welcome. I want this. I want this to last. I hope, and hope, and hope.

27

 **LUNA HALE**

"He got you a new phone?" **Xander asks,** cutting another slice of cinna-roll cake in the kitchen while I show him the latest Apple phone. Everyone has dispersed after the lazy morning unwrapping gifts and celebrating my brother's 18th.

He hates being the sole center of attention. Which has led him to always combine his birthday with the first bits of Christmas morning glee. It tends to shrink the spotlight on him. And he typically requests "group" gifts so he's opening less stuff.

The Abbeys bought him the newest VR headset. The Meadows got him a few Canyonlands tees and hoodies from their trip to Moab. Cobalts all chipped in for a vintage *Lord of the Rings* hardback collection. And my family gifted the wristwatch he'd been eyeing.

It's subtly pricey—not because it's plated in gold—but because it's one of the most complex timepieces in existence. It adjusts for leap years, displays the calendar, depicts the night sky including the location of stars and constellations, plus so much more. All while still being an old-timey analog clock.

Apparently, I'm the one who showed him the watch in the first place. *Do not remember that.*

It's ironic now, considering I'm the one who's lost time.

I show him the high-tech cameras on my phone. "Yeah, but Donnelly said the phone isn't my real present." I lower my voice to tell him, "He's going to tattoo me for free. Well, he said they're all free since I'm his girlfriend, but he plans to tattoo the same design on himself."

Xander splats the cinna-cake slice on a paper plate. "So a matching tattoo?"

"Uh-huh." I smile more. "He already has the design. I kinda hope it's something galactic. An otherworldly link from him to me."

"You pretty much already have that without the tattoo, you know?" Leaning against the counter, Xander picks up the cake like a cinnamon roll. Pinched between two fingers. "You fell for him *twice* after you couldn't remember him. Like, that's fucking insane and on par with the sci-fi greats."

"It's not as good as *Dune*. Or *Do Androids Dream of Electric Sheep?*"

"That book about androids?" He's referring to *Electric Sheep*. "It's overrated."

"It's a sci-fi classic."

Xander makes a face. "*Prometheus, Ex Machina,* fucking *iRobot*—all better android movies than *Blade Runner*." He knows *Do Androids Dream of Electric Sheep* by Philip K. Dick is the basis of the film *Blade Runner*.

I shrug. "I like the book better than the movie."

"Your story with Donnelly is way better, sis." He groans as the cake crumbles in his hand, dirtying the floor. "Fuuuck." He stares at it for a long time.

"I can clean—"

"I got it." He shoves the rest of the cake in his mouth, then throws a towel on the ground. Using his foot, he tries to collect the cake crumbs.

I snap a photo of Xander mid-chewing.

He almost smiles. "If it's not gross, delete it," he says with a mouthful.

"It's so gross. You look super ugly."

"Yayyy." His dry tone doesn't match the smile still cresting his face, but it fizzles out while he swigs a glass of OJ. "If it's not a Christmas present, why'd he get you a new phone?"

It's complicated.

At first, I wonder if I should lie or hop-skip over the full truth. It'd be easy to barricade Xander from this part of my life, but I'm a new Luna. The Luna who's tearing down walls and letting others see more of me.

"He just bought it for me," I explain. "Yesterday. It's why he was gone half the day."

"He didn't just go get coffee?"

"He said he went to the biggest nearby town to buy the phone."

Xander's brows pull together in more confusion. "Did yours break or something?"

"No," I say under my breath, careful that no one overhears. Footsteps pad along the floorboards, but no one enters the kitchen. "I've been getting a lot of messages from *unknown* numbers. Some calls too." I explain how they're mostly guys I can't remember from the past three years. "Anyway, Donnelly didn't want them to harass me anymore. I think he hated the idea of me panicking at every new text." My lips rise and my heart swells. "It was really kind of him, to even consider how I'd feel."

Xander nods a few times, just listening.

"He's planning to help me get a new number too, but he needed me there. We're stopping at the Verizon store on the way home."

"What about the *unknowns*?" Xander asks. "Have you figured out who they are?"

I shake my head. "Donnelly sent all the numbers to the tech team. I doubt I'll hear back this week." It's the holidays after all.

Xander scoops up the towel full of cake crumbs. "He's a world-class bodyguard."

"Yeah, he is," I nod resolutely, but strangely, I've been classifying this act as a protective *boyfriend*. Not so much a bodyguard.

A stampede on the deck causes us to look out the kitchen window. Several people head down the hill to throw around a football. Sulli, Banks, and Akara among them, as well as Thatcher. I spot Jane with Baby Maeve swaddled against her chest. I have a feeling she'll be more of a spectator.

I heard those five are leaving mid-week to spend some of the holidays with the Morettis in South Philly. Beckett is also cutting the trip short, but only to return to the ballet. He took time off for bereavement, but the Nutcracker is still in full swing.

Moffy soon joins with Farrow, shoving each other lightly down the sloped hill. I bet my mom fought for grammie cuddles and time with Cassidy and Ripley.

Sulli throws the ball to my brother, then Moffy tosses the ball in a perfect arch. It lands right into Ben's hands.

"I never thought I could be like Moffy," Xander suddenly says, and we watch our older brother laugh and wrestle against his husband before he slips past him and easily catches the whizzing football like he was once a collegiate star.

He's never played football, really.

He's just supremely talented at everything.

Xander and I are smiling because that's *our* brother. The rising star of the Hales. The one person who we can point to and say, *We're not all fuck ups. See.* Except the world will try to claim he's not one of us. He's a Meadows. That must be why he's so different. So much more athletic. So much more skilled.

Xander continues, "I figured he's a Hale outlier, you know? That it's not attainable for the rest of us, but I don't know, lately I've been thinking—why not? If it's in him, shouldn't it be in us too? I mean, look at you." He turns to me. "You're by far the strongest person I've ever known. Maybe stronger than Moffy. It makes me feel like I can be too."

I'm lost for words for a second. I didn't know Xander saw me as someone in leagues with our larger-than-life older brother. I thought, if anything, I'd be more like the inferior superhero with little to no screentime. You see her funky hair color in the background shot—but you aren't really even sure what powers she possesses.

"Is that why you want to compete for CEO?" I ask him.

"Yeah, I guess I want to prove that Hales aren't people that can be easily walked all over, and we're not that dumb. Plus, I get to spend more time with you. And a secondary perk, I'm pretty sure Charlie will take this home, so we don't have to be afraid we'll actually be imprisoned in that corporate hellhole for eternity, even if we go hard for it."

I smile. "Our motivations are similarly aligned, earth dweller. Though, I really don't want you to have it. I am your nemesis, watch out." I narrow my eyes into devilish pinpoints.

"I'm so afraid, ahhh," he says with the loose wave of his hands. "Kinney could help you with the intimidation factor. She told me I smelled like Cheetos this morning, which hurt me to my *core*." I can tell it didn't affect him at all. Xander is immune to most of Kinney's insults since he's grown up alongside her.

I should be spending more time with our little sister, but she's been glued to Audrey, Winona, and Vada this whole time. And I can't really say I'm any better. I've been attached to my best friends too.

I have an idea! *"Guardians of the Galaxy: Holiday Special,"* I throw out there. "Let's watch it now with Kinney."

Xander groans. "I hate that movie. Mantis still gives me nightmares crawling through Kevin Bacon's house like a demon."

"I bet Donnelly has never seen it," I say, instinctively thinking of including him. "Or maybe...maybe it should just be a sibling thing? Will Kinney ditch if I invite him?"

He shrugs. "I'd want him to come. Maybe his commentary will make it better."

Like we summoned him, Donnelly strolls into the kitchen, but instead of his usual casual, nonchalant stride, his muscles seem constricted. Rigid. *Something's wrong?* He up-nods to Xander. "Birthday boy. Can you give me a sec with your sister?"

"Yeah..." He draws out the word, confused. "Everything okay?"

"We're good." He motions from himself to me, and my heart rate eases. Okay, so this isn't about our new relationship.

Once Xander leaves the kitchen, Donnelly rests a hip against the stove. Facing me, he says, "I just heard back from IT."

My stomach drops. Certain impact is imminent. The asteroid is flying through space and too close to clipping our ship. "Already? It's Christmas."

"Yeah, but I told them to rush it, if they could." Donnelly takes good care of me, and I can only hope I'm doing the same for him. He explains how the calls and messages I've received lately were traced back to three guys in New York. "They're all friends."

What...? "You're sure?"

"Positive..." He rubs at his wrist, like he's not enjoying spilling these painful beans. "I've seen you with them before—not *seen* seen in person, but in tabloids, you were caught kissing 'em."

Oh. My stomach plunges straight to the floor. "Like at the same time? I kissed all three?"

"There wasn't a video, but I dunno, I guess."

Wow, okay, *okay*. Original Luna—*me*, I kissed-around town. I was single. There's nothing wrong with kissing whoever I want to, but the thought *now* makes me nauseous. Because I can't remember it.

I listen as Donnelly says, "There's been a rumor in security that your dad got them blacklisted from popular clubs in New York."

"Sounds like my dad," I mutter, staring beyond the floorboards.

"Which is why I wanted to ask you if I could go to him with this."

My bugged eyes snap up to Donnelly. "What?"

"Luna, your dad has information about 'em, and they all should be on security's watch-list. This one—the guy who texted you at the funeral—he's called you *seven* times in two weeks. And he's asking for a hookup, knowing you were kidnapped. He's a piece of shit."

"Maybe...maybe I remember him. What's his name?"

Donnelly expels a short breath, his hand slipping back through his hair. "Keagan Bell."

Keagan...Bell.

Bell, Keagan. I fight for an image, for a fact, for a sign—*anything* to help figure out my history with him. But...there's nothing.

Just tabloids of us kissing. Just these recent texts and calls that border on harassment.

"Okay," I murmur.

"Okay?" His brows spring.

I nod, knowing he just wants to keep me safe, and I want that too. Swiftly, his arms curve around my shoulders, and we're hugging so fiercely that I pretend our spacecraft is experiencing unexpected turbulence. And we're keeping each other stable with the mighty force of our love, with the enduringness of two cosmic entities.

If death occurs, it'll be in each other's arms.

JANUARY

"You have to be with other people...In order to live at all. I mean, before they came here I could stand it, being alone in the building. But now it's changed. You can't go back...You can't go from people to nonpeople."

– Do Androids Dream of Electric Sheep?
By Philip K. Dick

CHARLIE & LUNA'S TEXT THREAD

Jan 5th

10:12 p.m.
Luna: Do I ever mention a Keagan Bell??

10:45 p.m.
Charlie: No.

Charlie: Not by name.

Luna: Any mention of guys I met at a club?

10:57 p.m.
Charlie: Yes, but only in relation to your dad being protective. I can send you the excerpts if you want them.

Luna: No, that's okay. I just wanted to know my feelings on these guys.

11:44 p.m.
Charlie: Why?

Luna: Idk...I guess I want to believe I chose wisely and that I saw something in Keagan that I liked. But I doubt it'd make me feel any better to know.

Luna: Donnelly is the only one I really want.

Luna: If that wasn't clear.

Charlie: It's clear.

Luna: Phew. I was worried I'd need to spell it out in the sky.

Luna: I still might do that.

28

 **LUNA HALE**

January rings in the start of the year when New Year's resolutions have yet to be failed and the Orion and Taurus constellations brighten the winter sky. Fresh beginnings can practically be smelled in the crisp air. People light-footed with the hope of a good year.

I'd be prancing around too, if not for the new semester nerves. College.

Still can't believe OG Luna took a swing at it. She didn't quite hit it out of the park, which is why I'm at bat now, looking for my first homerun. And why—why am I thinking in *baseball* metaphors? Has to be because Donnelly was talking about the Phillies last week. He said he'd like to go to a game with me, Oscar, and Farrow in the spring.

I'm being included in his friendship circle, which might be as strange for me as he's felt being incorporated into mine. Sure, I'm friends with Farrow, but our interactions rarely involve both Donnelly and Oscar. To Farrow, I've mostly been "Maximoff's sister" rather than "Donnelly's girlfriend"—new titles, new feelings.

I'd like to think Donnelly and I would seamlessly fit in each other's worlds. I'd also like to think our two worlds can become *one.* But I wonder if that's more fanfic than reality.

I can't worry about infiltrating the deep bonds of friendship. Not when I'm…lost?

I glance down at my phone for the fourth time since I landed on campus. The digital map hasn't helped much.

I've been to the University of Pennsylvania a handful of times when I was an itty-bitty child. So the memories are fuzzy around the edges. Uncle Connor often gave speeches to business students, and I think my parents brought me along to hear him.

In the past three years, I'm sure I've ventured here twice as many times. But with those memories completely gone, I feel like an unprepared freshman who skipped out on orientation. Just feeling my way through.

I zoom in and out of the map with my fingers. It only makes me more confused, and I'm silently kicking myself for rejecting Ben's offer to be my campus tour guide. I thought I could do it myself.

It didn't seem so hard.

It's not, Luna.

These are just directions. Class hasn't even started yet! I blow out a long breath. I'm at a standstill next to a bubbling fountain. Water spurts out of a dome of cast iron ivy leaves.

Frog and Quinn stay ahead of me, waiting. Both sport Penn sweatshirts, appearing like regular ole college students. They're also young enough to blend in that *I* even forget they're here to watch over me and not attend lectures.

"Luna?" Frog approaches, toting a trendy leather backpack.

I think the most unbelievable thing would be her being friends with me. But Frog has said, "We were friends before you-know-what, but it's not a high priority—our friendship. Don't be that concerned about it or anything. I don't even think I should be telling you this." She let out a breath. "I'm your bodyguard first and foremost. Your Number One Protector. Quinn is Number Two, and ignore him when he tries to pull out the seniority card. He's still *two.*"

I liked her then, but she still seemed tentative, like I might shatter if she says the wrong thing.

Don't put too much emphasis on recreating lost relationships. Let things play out naturally. It's been a helpful tip from my therapist—even if she's implied that Donnelly forced the restoration of our love.

"Huh?" I mumble to Frog.

"Need help?"

"Isn't that cheating?" I ask her. "Normal students don't have security to help them find Stiteler Hall."

"Well, you're not normal," Frog says bluntly. "So you get to use all your tools in your arsenal. Like *me.*" She puts a hand to her heart. "Your sharpest tool."

Quinn snorts behind her.

She ignores him, her focus pinned to something past me. "Plus, lingering is not the best for someone who gets recognized."

Oh. I wonder if someone behind me did a doubletake. It sends a wave of urgency through me. "Lead the way," I tell her.

"On it." She practically hop-skips back to Quinn's side and they swerve to the right. Clearly, I was on the wrong path. As we walk towards Stiteler Hall, I peek at my phone. No new texts. No updates from Donnelly.

Not that there would be anything to update me on.

He's at work (well, technically at Dalton Academy protecting my brother).

I'm at college.

We're settling into our relationship routine, which should feel comfortable and easy but too many unknown variables hang in the air like ominous windchimes.

Like Fizzle.

Like his place within Epsilon.

Like my mom.

It's the first week of January. And I still haven't hashed out the "kitchen table" incident with her. I've had one-on-one chitchats about movies, her physical therapy, and my fics since I'm writing the Thebulan saga for myself. Just for fun. But she never surfaces Donnelly. Or the kitchen table.

That big elephant in the room has yet to be acknowledged.

Maybe it never will be. Maybe she just needs more time. Like months?

Or years?

I hope not that long.

I didn't want her perception of Donnelly to warp into a negative picture. To where she wouldn't root for us like she's rooted for Moffy and Farrow. I know things are just complicated and awkward because she caught us in the act, but I can't see how much damage really exists and what's just anxiety-fueled.

It hurts to think about.

I try and fling that guilt off my shoulders. Entering a brick building, my bodyguards locate the classroom in a snap, as if they've charted the classes on my schedule weeks ago and mapped out everything.

They likely did.

Prepared, they are.

As I broach the doorway, I come to an immediate halt. When I picked out my courses, I was sure to check the info about class size. Twenty students sounded big on paper. Twenty could fill a room in high school.

Standing here now, I can confidently say a twenty-person class is *tiny*.

There is no giant lecture hall.

No stadium of seats.

Just rolling office chairs pushed into a single U-shaped table. I'm early (thank you, Frog and Quinn) but the five students that are also punctual all rotate in unison to spot the newcomer.

Yes, it's me Luna Hale. Hi. Howdy.

They mutter to one another, eyes darting back to me. Heat crawls up my neck, but quickly, I sink into the nearest chair—the faster I'm off my feet the faster they'll stop staring.

Inaccurate.

And I don't love already starting off this class being wrong.

Across from my end of the U, two brunette girls stare straight at me, then whisper to one another with cupped hands to ears. It's such a comically eighties-movie mean girl move that I squint to ensure I'm seeing this right.

I feel someone sink down on my left. Then my right. My bodyguards, I realize. Quinn and Frog have taken their respective seats on either side of me. I've never had security walk the hallways of Dalton to protect me. They always stayed in the parking lot, and so the newness of having reinforcements at college is like sucking down pure oxygen too quickly.

I'm lightheaded.

Which is why I think I'm seeing things when the two girls start *hissing* at me. Hissing! Like lizards. I blink a couple times and they're still doing it. Is this a new insult that gained popularity sometime in the last three years?

The girls' hisses turn into a fit of laughter.

A dirty-blond preppy guy lets out a low groan. He's facing the whiteboard, and I'm shocked when he glares at the girls. "Shut up, Stassi. That's not even funny."

"It's hilarious," Stassi, I take it, replies, tucking a strand of glossy hair behind an ear, showing off a pearl earring. "And sticking up for her isn't going to get you laid, Carson. Luna Hale is taken."

My smile is traitorous. I shouldn't brighten at her words since she's obviously trying to make fun of me, but this is the first public acknowledgement of my relationship that I've heard in person.

"Is she though?" Stassi's friend pipes in, clicking the butt of her pen against the table. She's speaking loud enough that I can hear. "Her and that bodyguard just made out in a bar. It's not that serious."

It is serious.

I can feel them waiting on pins and needles for me to verify. It's why she's projecting her voice. So I can chime into the conversation and give them the juicy details.

They don't deserve them. I stay quiet, and I'm betting they think I'm small and meek. A little church mouse, but I'm not. I know I'm not.

Carson expels an aggravated sigh. "I'm not trying to get laid,

Stassi." He shakes his head at her burgeoning grin. "I can't believe we're related."

Stassi arches back. "Barely."

"Half-siblings," Carson says to me. "So you can blame her half of DNA for being a royal bitch."

Stassi tosses up a middle finger, then looks to Frog. "Love your tumbler."

Frog's Stanley water bottle is a pistachio green that Akara, her cousin, gifted her for her 19th birthday this December. Along with a year's subscription to his fitness app—to which Frog was the most delighted. "I'm going to tease Nine all year for this," she told me.

I don't catch Frog's facial reaction to Stassi. I busy myself with popping open my laptop, but I hear Frog say a quiet, "Thanks" to her.

"Do you know Luna?" Stassi digs for more dirt as students flood the classroom. With my back to the door, I only see them eyeing me as soon as they plop down in a chair.

It's okay.

This is normal. It's not like I've never been a spectacle before, but I wonder how many are thinking, *She was kidnapped. Do you think she's, like, mentally okay? I can't believe she made out with Donnelly in a gross bar. On the day her grandfather died!*

The horror!

I smile to myself.

Frog sips some water. "Yep, I know Luna. We're cool."

Stassi's friend snorts. "I don't think Luna Hale and *cool* have ever been in the same sentence."

"Beverly, you have to show her the lizard video."

I perk up. So there is context to the lizard hissing? I'm about to ask what, but Quinn coughs in his fist, and he scratches something on a notebook he brought as a "prop" to appear more like a student.

I read his handwriting: *you're in the video.*

Shit. And I almost asked about it. A heatwave assaults me, and my nerves suddenly descend like a swarm of locusts. Pretending I have my memories is harder than I thought it'd be.

"I've seen the video," Frog says. "And it's really cool that Luna memorized the dance from *The OA*."

Ohhhhhkay. Now I understand, and Frog truly is a godsend for providing that morsel of info so effortlessly. She's beauty. She's grace. She'll claw you in the face.

"Again," Stassi says, "we have to rework your definition of *cool*."

Carson rolls his eyes, then tells me, "Ignore Anastassia."

"Carson." A feminine voice from the doorway pricks my ears. "Being *nice* won't get you laid with the 'most famous girl at Penn'." Her mocking tone snakes down my spine. "Your Porsche might— but this whole white knight bullshit is bullshit."

I go numb.

That voice.

I know that voice.

I'd never forget it in a million years. Not even if the Earth was overtaken by Cylons and I was the last surviving member of the human race. That shrill, antagonizing voice would still be in my nightmares.

"Jeffra," Carson says. "Fuck off."

Yes, please. Fuck off to another class!

I'm rigid. Frozen. A statue of epic proportions.

Jeffra just laughs, then claims an open seat beside Stassi. Her eyes hit mine, and her lips purse and face tightens like a dried prune. I'm sensing she'd rather cross my name off her weekly agenda too. So this must be some bizarre coincidence that we're taking a class together.

She's not stalking me.

She grimaces at Quinn and Frog on either side of me. "You really have no friends that aren't either on your daddy's payroll or share the same DNA with you?"

Stassi frowns. "Wait..." She zeroes in on Frog. "You...?"

"Honey, those are her bodyguards," Jeffra says. Okay, maybe she is stalking me! No, that's silly. It's public knowledge who my bodyguards are, but it does say something that Jeffra recognized

Frog and Quinn whereas Stassi didn't. She's keeping tabs on me, for sure. I wonder if OG Luna did the same for Jeffra. Like making sure your mortal enemy is serving a life sentence of suck.

Stassi lets out a low whistle. "No way." She sizes Frog up. "No wonder you think Luna's cool. You're paid to think that."

Frog glares, clutching angrily to her Stanley. "That's not true. The only thing I'm being paid to do is not throw this water bottle at your face. So be lucky—*ugh*." Quinn kicks her under the table. She shoots him a fierce look.

Jeffra and Stassi ignore and start whispering between each other like their attention is too worthy of being on Frog any longer. It's rude.

I hate them.

I *almost* grab Frog's water bottle and chuck it myself.

But is that considered assault? Would I be expelled? These thoughts pile onto me as I take out my phone. Maybe I can look up the lizard video. If I performed the dance from The OA, it had to have been epic. My phone buzzes *in* my hand before I can even pop-up YouTube.

It's a text in a new group chat called *The Fizzle Five*.

You each need to come up with a new product or a marketing strategy for an existing product to present to the board as your final presentation. I've also emailed a list of events you'll need to attend beforehand.
– Uncle Stokes

I take a deep breath. Uncle Stokes referred to this as an "extracurricular" that won't conflict with any of our classes or schoolwork, but it's going to be more of a thorn than I thought. As several more students trickle into the class, I open my email and see the list that he was talking about.

Mock Q&A Panel

Mini Marketing Campaign Tour (will schedule this when Xander
has off a week)

MLB x Fizzle Collab

Fizz Gala

Final Presentations

I can just hear my dad seething with an "I told you so" ready to
launch off his tongue. Coming home from the lake house, Xander
and I had a longer discussion with our parents about auditioning for
future CEO, and Mom and Dad were not too enthused. That was to
be expected after what I overheard in the boathouse, but they were
mostly warning us about the workload.

"You're both young. Be young," our dad said. "Don't take this
shit on. No one is forcing you to."

I think Mom liked the idea when we pitched it as a bonding
experience with each other and our cousins. She even elbowed Dad
every time I mentioned *Ben*, like Ben and Xander will magically form
a friendship through soda bubbles and PowerPoints.

I can't say what will happen, but I didn't expect a full blown
campaign tour to be a part of the competition. The bright spot:
Donnelly will be there because Xander has to be.

I'm about to put my phone away when it buzzes. Speaking of my
boyfriend.

Dalton Academy is always out of paper towels. What up
with that? Paper towel thief here?? — Donnelly

I smooth my lips together, a smile hurting my face. I'm glad
Donnelly is watching over my brother at school. It's Xander's last
year. He's stressed about college applications. He's stressed about
this Fizzle competition. He's stressed about prom.

It's a high-stress time for him, and Donnelly's unconsciously
good at alleviating that kind of stress.

I **text back:** Boys' bathroom is definitely lacking the good stuff. Maybe the paper towel thief is giving them away to the birds.

He's quick to reply.

BRB going to investigate some baby bird nests — Donnelly

I smile so big that I jolt when I hear my name.

"Miss Hale," a man says sternly from behind me. "My class has a no texting policy."

Uhhhh…I'm a blazing ball of fire. Totally and utterly called out.

Swiveling in my chair, I peer back at the professor. Wow, he's not old. I have no clue why I thought he'd be a gray-haired, spectacle-wearing wise professor, but he is neither gray nor sporting glasses. He must be in his early-thirties, and his hair is dishwater-blond, the color of a tawny broom.

The narrow of his eyes is more intense without being behind lenses.

Still, I don't look away. He's dressed in a greenish-blue Boglioli plaid sport coat with a navy turtleneck underneath. I'm not Charlie though—I don't usually know the brand and price of men's fashion. But I happen to know *that* coat costs two grand since Eliot had been eyeing it all winter. He'd been asking Tom and me if he should splurge. Normally, I don't think Eliot would blink at the price, but being out of work these days has made him hesitate on some big purchases.

Inference Number One: Professor Wyatt Rochester has money—possibly more money than just a professor's salary.

Inference Number Two: By the way my professor is glaring at me, I suspect he hates my family.

Inference Number Three: He's one of those people who've seen the Hales in the tabloids and on entertainment news, and he's decided we all suck.

"Phone. Away," he snaps like I'm dense. He's giving Miss Trunchbull energy from *Matilda*, and I half expect him to send me to the Chokey or force me to eat chocolate cake until I puke. But he's already striding towards the whiteboard.

"Sorry," I mutter and quickly shove my cell phone in my bookbag.

Quinn's body radiates visceral heat beside me. I'm glad my negative feelings towards my professor aren't unwarranted.

The other students have sufficiently been terrified into silence. Even Jeffra doesn't give me a single glance. Her MacBook Pro is opened, and her hands hover over the keyboard in rapt attention. If this is Professor Rochester's first-day tactic to put the fear into his pupils, it's working. I'm just the ill-fated insect he had to step on in the process.

"Welcome to Television and New Media." He uncaps a dry-erase marker. "I'm Wyatt Rochester. Don't call me Professor. You can either call me Rochester or Wyatt. I don't care. What I do care about is that you arrive on time and you don't *waste* my time. Teaching is not my full-time job. It's a hobby, and I teach *one* class each semester biennially. You're the lucky ones the administration approved to be here. Which means you *want* to learn about the entertainment industry. And there's no one more qualified than me to teach you. I work for Rochester Industries, and *yes*, my family owns it. It's one of the largest entertainment and media conglomerates in the world. Now let's begin." He starts writing on the board. "As you all can see we have a celebrity in our class."

My stomach plummets to the core of the Earth. No. No. Please, *no.*

"Which is why I think it's a great time to cover a couple shows that have changed the course of television." He underlines what he wrote and backs away from the whiteboard.

I have to be pale white. A ghost. I feel floaty like I've ascended into a different plane of existence. One meant for unfortunate souls.

I read the two shows on the whiteboard:

PRINCESSES OF PHILLY

WE ARE CALLOWAY

Professor Rochester closes in on me. "And Luna, rest assured, you won't be getting special treatment with this one. You'll be graded fairly among your peers."

My grades are the furthest thing I'm worried about.

Right now, I'm just hoping I can survive. The drop/add period hasn't ended, and I told myself I wouldn't drop this class.

I wouldn't drop *any* class.

I would stick it out.

I would prove that I'm a Hale who *can* accomplish college and not just online. I would show that to my siblings. I would show that to the world.

The words on the whiteboard stare back at me. Taunting.

They practically say: *Fuck you for trying, Hale.*

29

PAUL DONNELLY

My professor already hates me. I think if he were to wish upon a star, it'd be so I'd explode into ash. — **Luna**

In one text, I can feel Luna's dejection. Like she bottled it up and sent it across electromagnetic waves from her cell to mine. It hits me hard.

I text back: If he hates you then he's not looking up at any stars. What's his name? Gonna find his address, hunt him down, egg his door.

Anyone who makes my girlfriend feel like shit is an enemy to me. Facts.

In this redo for Luna, I hoped college would be easier this time around. I wish I could plow through this shit-pile for her, but I'm not at Penn. I'm stuck in a prep school library.

Stuck.

I linger on the word. I don't mean for it to sound like I'm held hostage against my will.

I love my job—and I wouldn't ask to be on anyone else's detail other than Xander's. Being on Luna's (which the Powers That Be will never allow) isn't a road to success. I don't want any confusion in my head about what I am to her.

I'm her boyfriend. Doing *boyfriend* fucking things. Like texting her during some downtime at work.

Also, her therapist might actually be the one to explode like a raging supernova if she heard I was superglued to Luna 24/7.

I wait for Luna's response, but then catch movement in my peripheral. Slipping my phone in my back pocket, I stay sharp on the shifting bodies. They're trying to hide behind a towering bookshelf of alphabetized encyclopedias.

Two teenage girls, dressed like every other girl here—in Dalton's preppy plaid skirts and white blouses. Freshmen, most likely. They look fourteen, and I haven't paid much attention to any freshmen walking the halls. Xander doesn't interact with them, and they aren't in any of his classes.

Their attention is on a six-person oak table in the secluded back-corner. A stained-glass window streams blue and purple light onto the only person seated there.

My elf.

Eighteen and thriving.

He chose a spot in the dusty depths of the second floor of Dalton's library. In hopes he wouldn't be spotted during his study period.

I meander into the same row as the girls and pretend to be interested in the Discovery Science Encyclopedia on Earth. The planet on the cover makes me think of Luna—and as much as I'd love for her to occupy all my brain space, it's not a good thing in this moment.

"Ohmygosh," one of the girls whispers to her friend. "That's his bodyguard."

Spotted.

I pretend I can't hear them and peruse another book. This one on matter and energy.

"Let's go, let's go." The other girl grabs her friend's hand, and they dash out of the row like I'm about to arrest them.

Guess they realize loitering and ogling Xander wouldn't put them on my favorites list. I wouldn't influence his social life this much, but Xander has requested to be alone. So scaring them off it is.

I return to the table.

His tie is undone, and the silver chain of his necklace dangles over the book he's devouring. On the end of the chain is a silver pendant of a broken sword. It's the same weapon Isildur used to cut the One Ring from Sauron's hand in *Lord of the Rings*. I know this 'cause I did my research before I bought Xander the necklace.

A birthday present. Think he likes it. He hasn't taken it off since Christmas.

He's reading *Mistborn: The Final Empire* by Brandon Sanderson and munching on pretzel sticks. Which is contraband. I should know I got yelled at by the librarian for snacking in here last week.

His eyes lift, like he feels me staring. "You can sit, Donnelly."

"Nah, I like standing." My presence has deterred two girls already. I adjust the earpiece in my ear. "Can't wait to Boogeyman some more teenagers away. Gonna give your dad a run for his money on best Boogeyman status."

Xander lets out a laugh. "You have a long way to go, man." He thinks for a second, not diving back into the book. "Hey, what'd my sister get you?"

"For what?"

"For Christmas. I forgot to ask her, and you two exchanged presents in private."

Yeah, we did.

This isn't something I should be talking to Xander about. Not while on-duty. But Loren Hale's fears about me being a *buddy*guard are burnt toast. Just straight up crispy. I'd still eat it, granted, but Oscar would throw that shit right in the trash.

I'm not a buddyguard. It's not possible for me to be his friend like that when I'm dating his sister. I'm more so…his brother? I dunno. I've never had a little brother. I can't say if this is veering in that direction or not.

Xander cringes in my silence, then groans. "Shit, is it sexual? Because if it is—you can forget I asked."

"Luck in a jar," I say.

"What?" He stares blankly. "Is that a sex position?"

I hold back a laugh. "Could be, maybe, but I wouldn't know because your sister gave me glitter in a tiny glass bottle and labeled it *luck in a jar*. She's cute and crafty." And fucking hot, but I don't add that. He's still concerned this'll be a short-term fling with his sister— that she'll move on too fast from me, and I see him weighing pieces of our relationship that I'm not putting on any scale.

I can't live my life like that. I'd go nuts.

At least Xander is in our camp, rooting for us to last. Epsilon has several bets hinging on the timeline of my relationship. Most have money on a break-up in March.

Fuck them.

Xander nods slowly. "Sounds like a Luna gift."

"Right from her heart and hands," I say lightly and survey the row of bookshelves. Thought I heard a rustling. *False alarm.*

Xander buries his attention back in his novel.

Then comms go off in my ear. "Greer to Donnelly," the Epsilon bodyguard says. "Have you seen Winona today?"

I suppress an annoyed sigh.

This is the fourth time today I've been asked to check on other clients like I'm somehow the Teen Whisperer for all the famous ones at Dalton. It's really my own doing. I made this unfortunate bed by trying to be a team player with the enemy.

Coulda kept my mouth shut. But no—I told Epsilon what Luna overheard at the lake house. How Winona's having some issues with the T-Bags at school, specifically Tate. Luna didn't mind me going to security as long as she remained an "anonymous" tip, and so far, SFE hasn't demanded to know my source. And if they have suspicions it's Luna, they haven't ratted her out yet.

Greer had a short talk with Winona's parents. Don't know how that conversation went except for Winona *still* doesn't want her bodyguard in the halls.

Neither do Kinney or Audrey. And the girls convinced their moms and dads to give them another shot without a bodyguard shadow.

So that leaves me.

Paul Donnelly.

Sole survivor of the Dalton Academy Hunger Games. I haven't been ousted yet by my client. In fact, every morning, he asks, "You still okay with coming in?"

I always reply, "Would rather be in than out."

So while I'm here, Epsilon sits in the parking lot and has nothing better to do than radio me for updates. If this were a popularity contest, I'd chuck the sash into the garbage.

I click my mic and tell Greer, "Haven't seen her."

He's quick to reply. "She's in the science hall next period, if you could check."

"Negative," I say. "I'm in the history hall next period. It's on the opposite side."

"You'll be standing in the hallway all period. You can do a quick flyby."

And what? Stare at her classroom door? She's going to be *in* class. I'm about to say as much when I stop myself.

Team player.

That's me.

Or at least, I'm trying not to get fired. Trying not to put Akara in a position where I'm looking for a job and he can't hire me back. I take a breath before I click my mic again. "I'll see if I have time."

"Thanks," Greer says, a little relieved.

Now I feel bad. Because if I were him, stuck in the parking lot, not able to help a client, I'd be trying to use all my resources too. Turns out I'm like one of those raw materials on Planet Thebula. Highly valued. Limited supply.

The stairs creak, and I tip my head to the side. I spy with my keen eye…Easton Mulligan. Best friend to Xander. His chocolate-brown hair is cut shorter on the sides, and the dark navy Dalton blazer makes his skin look even paler.

Luna says he might secretly be part-vampire, and she told me to keep an eye on him to determine whether he glitters in the light.

No shimmery flesh from Easton yet, and he's largely a non-threat, considering he's the sole reason Xander has braced some crowded hallways before. I'd like to take credit, but Easton, as his peer and a fellow eighteen-year-old, is able to navigate these social circles in ways I can't.

He protects Xander from the school's piranhas—the ones who'd try to pretend to be Xander's best friend for clout and social media *likes*. Who'd chew him up and spit out the bones. Most seniors regard Easton as cool enough to try to know but he's too standoffish to actually befriend. So mostly, what people say about him is written in half-truths and lore.

He's the brilliant chess champion who won matches against rivals Faust and Maybelwood for four years straight.

He's the loner who skipped a month of school and backpacked around Auckland.

He's the suave knight who went LARPing with Xander Hale and made out with Paisley McWilliams in full armor.

High school gossip doesn't affect my opinions much. All that *really* matters to me is that he's a good friend to Xander. He's never put that into question.

Once Easton fixes his loose tie and lands on the second floor, I expect him to beeline for Xander. Instead, he stops a few feet from me.

"Hey," he says. "Can I talk to Xander?"

"Since when do you need my permission?"

"There's a rumor." He's digging in his pockets for something. *Cigarettes*, I think, but that'd make zero sense. I've seen him smoke in the bathroom, but he wouldn't be dumb enough to do it in the library. He pulls out a crumpled *hall pass*, tin of Altoids, a condom— he goes still, like I'm about to eviscerate him for carrying protection.

I know his parents are strict, but damn…

"Is the rumor in your pocket too?" I joke.

He eases. "No, that's just in the halls. *Fuck*, I can't find them." He sighs heavily. Before I ask, he says, "My car keys. I must've left them in the caf, and I'm supposed to drive my little sister to ballet in…" He checks his watch. "Thirty minutes."

"You have school though."

"Tell that to my father. I'm *never* to skip a single class, *unless* it's for the princess and the prince." He shoves the shit back in his pocket, and I watch his gaze fall to my waistband. "There's a rumor the administration is letting you carry a gun after everything that happened with Xander's sister. I thought maybe security is tight and I'd need to request access to him again."

Xander peers up from the book. "Wait, what? They think Donnelly is carrying a gun?"

I'm not allowed to be armed on Dalton's school grounds.

"Yeah," Easton says, "and..." His voice tapers off before he shakes his head. "Forget it." He joins Xander at the six-seater table. I walk closer.

"Forget what?" I rest an arm on the wall beneath the stained-glass window. "Continue that thought, Mulligan."

Easton slumps and rubs his temple with two fingers. "It's gossip, wise one. That's all." He's adopted the nickname Xander uses for me, as if I'm live action role playing as their sage protector. To be that for Xander and now someone else...it's like completing a goal I never thought to construct.

It's still strange. In the best way that *strange* can be.

I grin. "Been known to dabble in the gossip realms," I say. "Lay it on me."

"And me," Xander chimes in, wanting to know too.

Easton cringes and tells me, "People keep saying you're capable of literal *murder* and other heinous shit after what your family did. Add that in with the gun rumor, and you're basically a psycho to half the school."

Xander lets out a long groan, his hands flying to his head. "You can't be serious." He glares at the bookshelves like they've accosted me somehow.

Love the loyalty. Don't love that he thinks I need it right now.

Easton adds, "Everyone's just on edge."

"Rumor mill working overtime," I say.

"I'll set them straight," Xander tells me.

I shake my head. "Nah, it's good if they're all scared of me. Makes my job easier."

His gaze softens. "Yeah, but you're not a bad guy. They shouldn't think—"

"Don't care what they think, Hale."

His shoulders slacken, and his sigh is just as long as the groan.

"It'll blow over," Easton tells him, "and if it doesn't, we're out of here in May."

"Yeah..." Xander shuts his book.

For a split-second of silence, Luna pops back in my head. Her lack of text response pushes to the very front of my brain. *It's fine.* She's busy at college too. Nothing to worry about.

Except she's a prompt texter and will usually reply within ten minutes.

"Ughh, why are so many guys at this school absolute douchebags?" Vada Abbey has appeared, and my attention snaps into focus on the sixteen-year-old BMX rider with gap-teeth and a dirty-blonde French braid. She throws her messenger bag across the table but it thuds into Easton's lap.

"Degenerates," Easton says. "All of them." He slides her bag back across the table. "Including the girls."

Vada sits on the table near Easton. "I'd much rather be a degenerate than a cunty douchebag."

"Said no Ivy League hopeful ever."

Easton has made it clear he doesn't want to go to Penn or Princeton or Yale. He'd rather shoot for an easier college, but his parents are pushing. He's resisting, and Xander—I'm not sure of his plans yet.

'Cause he's not sure.

He's a teeter-totter. Vacillating between so many options. The world's his oyster though. He'll find his pearl.

I click my mic and whisper, "Donnelly to Epsilon, Vada has entered my AO."

Greer is fast as fuck to reply. "Is Winona with her?"

"Negative."

"Keep an eye on Vada," Greer tells me. "The T-Bags have been bothering her, too."

"Got it."

It's an understood agreement among all forces that Vada might not have a 24/7 bodyguard, but she belongs to all of us. We equally look out for her when she's around.

Vada leans back on her hands, her leg almost brushing up against Easton's knee. He doesn't move away, and my flirt-senses are tingling but I can't be certain something is going on between them. *Luna would know if she were here.* Her Spidey-senses are higher quality.

Girl rocks the Spider-Man suit better than Tom Holland.

I blink into focus again, just as Vada says, "You know Ben is at Penn, and he's not some Ivy League douchebag."

"Ben," Easton says like his name is acid on the tongue. Don't love the Cobalt slander, but I don't have enough evidence to say whether it's warranted.

Xander puts on red headphones, just at the mention of Ben.

Vada's face drops. "Xander."

"What? Ben is *Ben*. Why do you and Winona insist on bringing him up all the goddamn time?"

"Because he was our friend."

"He was *her* best friend and yours by fucking association, Vada." The instant Xander drives in the dagger, the instant guilt warps his face. "I didn't mean..." He swallows hard.

Just stand here. Do nothing. Study the walls. Picture Luna naked. Yeah, don't fucking do that.

Easton watches Xander's expression fall, then Vada's. "What is your obsession with Ben?" he asks her with genuine confusion.

Her face reddens. "It's not an *obsession*." She collects her messenger bag. "Did you two ever think that school might've been easier when he was here?"

"I didn't attend Dalton when Ben went," Xander reminds her.

Easton frowns at Vada. "Why was it easier for you?"

"Guys weren't..."

"Guys weren't what?"

"*Douchebags*, we've talked about this." She hops off the table, and his fingers slip across her leg.

"Vada," he calls after her, rising out of his chair. "Vada!" He casts a quick glance at Xander, who nods to him goodbye, and then Easton chases after the Abbey girl.

"Vada's out of my AO," I whisper in my mic. Cracking jokes on comms is ten times less fun when SFE is on the line and Omega are off it.

I wish my phone would buzz.

I force myself not to send Luna a nagging text. I'm on-duty. *Luna is fine. She's with Quinn and Frog.*

She's safe.

She's safe.

I'm uneasy, but that could be because, I dunno, my girlfriend was *kidnapped* by my own family not even two months ago. She's now bracing the world, and I believe in her—I will always believe in Luna Hale—but some things will *always* be out of our control.

Threats. Accidents. A busted toaster at Wawa on a Tuesday afternoon, no hot hoagies.

It's natural to be worried.

I'm not an overbearing boyfriend. I haven't even *done* any fucking thing to be overbearing. Fuck.

Fuck.

I need to stop thinking about her while I'm working, but I also hate telling myself to stop thinking about that girl. I'm in a pickle.

Or a catch-22.

Same thing, probably. Pickle sounds better.

Xander packs up his headphones, and I push myself off the wall and ask, "You going back to reading or what?"

"You mean procrastinating?" He slips the book in his backpack. "I should be working on the Fizzle product thing. Or college applications. *Or* AP European History homework. Aaaaand...I'm not." He slings the backpack on his shoulder. "It all sounds too daunting right now."

Thriving and stressed.

"Another time, another day," I say lightly. "You'll get it done."

He sighs out, "Yeah. I'm gonna head to my locker before the bell rings." He's quick-footed down the stairs, and I follow right behind, planning to lead the way upon exiting the library. For now, I trail him.

We land on the main floor, and my phone vibrates. On instinct, I glance at the message, weaving through the bookshelves with Xander.

Rochester. Wyatt. Professor. He works for Rochester Industries. I think he must live in a dark dungeon of hell, and I'd rather you not go there. Even if the egging might be satisfying — Luna

My stomach recoils. *Rochester*. How did this fucking happen—?

I look up right as Xander swerves around the corner. I can't catch his arm fast enough. His six-two build collides right into a girl carrying paint supplies on her binder. Said paint spills back on her white blouse in an oozy red river, staining her Dalton uniform.

I fight away a grimace. Blank-faced, just scenery. Just trying to *focus*. And not Luna. *Push Luna back for* one *second*. It contracts my muscles.

The girl is frozen, her mouth halfway open and unable to close. Too soon to tell if it's because Xander Hale made physical contact with her body or if she's distressed about her ruined blouse.

"Shit, shit," Xander curses in a wave of panic. "I'm so sorry—I didn't see you. Are you alright? Can I—can I help you with that?" He's reaching out toward her binder, the paint pooling on the surface.

"Can-can you repeat what you just said?" she asks with a blink. "But slower."

He exhales a breath. "I'm sorry. I didn't see you."

"It was an accident." She's juggling the canister of red paint and binder.

I try to place her, but I can't.

Heart-shaped face. Pin-straight auburn hair like she brushes each strand ten-times a day. Tiny pieces are braided and clipped in the back, and her white skin is still ashen from shock.

She's fumbling with the paint-splattered binder. "I just need to check my extra credit for AP Lit. I'm supposed to turn it in next period."

My *reads* are off today. She's not worried about her clothes. Or bumping into the famous teenager. She's concerned about her grades.

"Wait, wait," Xander says in a hurry, extending a hand for her to stop. "If you open your binder, the paint will slip in the pages."

"I *have* to turn this in," she panics.

"Okay, hold on." He unzips his backpack and digs out a black hoodie. He mops up the paint with the fabric. The girl is a statue, like one breath will detonate her extra credit work.

I scout the first floor with a glance.

Students have popped out of their study areas. They watch Xander helping the girl, some slyly snap photos, and the librarian is marching over. If snacking wrinkles the librarian's brows, then paint-splatters on the carpet is aging her about a thousand years.

Xander turns the hoodie inside-out, then balls it up. "It should be good."

She carefully peeks into the binder and exhales. "Thank God."

"Your clothes," Xander says. "Do you have any extra here?"

And for the first time, she registers how much paint soaks her blouse. "I, um, no." She winces.

The librarian clears her throat behind the girl. "Your name, please. And I'd like to know why you're carrying *paint* in the library."

The girl is oblivious to the librarian. After a couple tense beats, the girl sees Xander looking past her, and she spins around the same time the librarian snaps, "Are you ignoring me?"

"No, no. I…" She motions to her ear, and I see the hearing aid. The librarian doesn't give the girl the chance to say she's hard of hearing.

"You should *not* have paint in the library."

"I know, but I was finishing an essay during my study period and Mrs. Rodriquez needed help gathering extra art supplies—"

"That's no excuse."

"It was my fault," Xander cuts in, and the librarian goes quiet, as though she's just realizing Xander Hale is involved. "I ran into her. I'll try to clean it up after school."

"That's not necessary," she says, more calmly. Her decrepit face is hard to stare at, no lie. She zeroes in on the girl again. "This is your warning. If something like this happens again, Miss…"

"Spencer."

"Full name, please."

"Spencer Sadler."

"Miss Sadler, you won't be allowed in the library for the rest of the year. Understood?"

"Yes, ma'am."

Xander's face has twisted in confusion. "It's just *paint*. Jeez, you're acting like she murdered another student."

I almost smile. *That's my elf.*

The old bat bristles. "Dalton *expects* its students to take care of its property."

"It was an *accident*," Xander emphasizes.

"I'm not arguing with either of you about this."

"I'm not arguing," Spencer says quickly. "I understand. I won't make this mistake again."

Hell hath no fury like a librarian scorned—I've never said until now. I love librarians. I've met my fair share growing up and all of 'em let me eat *while* using the computer. They didn't care if I greased up the keyboards, as long as I wiped them down before I left.

Anyway, she should be protecting the books, not the carpet.

Xander is glaring at the librarian all the way back to her casket—I mean, *desk*. Then he asks Spencer if she's okay. She assures him, and he offers her his navy-blue blazer, shrugging it off.

She cautiously accepts. "You're sure?"

"I don't need it." Xander rolls up the sleeves of his button-down, his tie still loose and tangling with his necklace. "I have like ten more. So…if you want to sell it on eBay or cut it up and build a shrine to post on Reddit, have at it."

Rushing, Spencer slips her arms in the holes. "If I'm building any shrine, it's to my number one college, no offense."

"Yeah, zero taken," he smiles, and she slips a small one back.

Then the bell rings and his face plummets. Halls are going to crowd. Spencer sprints out the door like she's already late. I'm antsy to check on Luna and this Rochester shit. It shoots back to the front of my brain so fast, my head starts to pound.

"Ready?" I ask Xander.

"Yeah." He intakes a tight breath, and I lead him to the double doors.

He pauses at them. Literally solidifies to stone.

I'm not thinking about Luna in this moment.

Not worrying about the Rochesters, Epsilon, my dad, or my family.

My whole attention is on one guy.

Because this is my job.

Because he needs me.

Because as soon as he steps out of those doors, ten people rush up to him shouting about the European History exam, the theme for prom, and the girl who drove her car in the parking lot fire hydrant, and that TikTok Audrey posted on Beckett's account, and how could Superheroes & Scones discontinue the fan favorite white chocolate smash muffin. It's a cacophony of voices. Of people clamoring for his attention.

It's all I can do to walk ahead of him and clear a path to his next class. He's at the point where he doesn't even give a shit that people see him gripping the back of my shirt like a little kid fearing getting separated from their parent at a carnival.

He's just holding on.

And I can't get fucking distracted if I'm the person he's holding on to.

30

PAUL DONNELLY

The fucking Rochesters.

How did one of those demons become her professor? While Xander is safe and sound in class and I'm relegated to the hallway, I try to find more answers.

Luna didn't show me her schedule, and I didn't ask. I should've *asked*, but I figured her bodyguards would handle it. Frog and Quinn aced Bodyguard 101, and it's making no sense. There's no way they're in the dark on this.

So why wouldn't they clue Luna in? Why wouldn't they tell her that this professor might have an ugly vendetta against her family?

Twisting a knob on my radio, I switch the channel to Omega's frequency for a minute. Quietly, in my mic, I ask, "Donnelly to Frog, why didn't you tell Luna about the Rochesters if you knew one of those fuckers was her professor?"

Static crackles the line.

One breath later, I hear Frog. "We were advised not to."

"By who?"

"Her therapist. She thinks it's too much information all at once since the Rochesters are connected to a deeper past."

My nose flares, redirecting a simmering anger at Luna's therapist. *Don't hate her. Don't hate her. She's helping Luna.* This isn't the first time I've imagined the doc smoldering on hot coals. I have an urge to reach out to Luna's neuro-doctors. Get a second opinion, but maybe her therapist already conferred with them too.

I don't argue with Frog about her decision. She's just following orders.

I rest the back of my head against the blue lockers. As Luna's boyfriend, as the person who loves her down to the last molecule of her being, I want to give her the tools that'll protect all of her. How can she defend herself if she doesn't even know why someone is coming at her?

Frog and Quinn can physically shield her, but the cruelty of humans is an invisible cut they won't be able to stop. That's up to Luna.

"Wonder Bread, you still there?" Frog asks.

I lift my mic to my lips. "Yeah. Still alive and kicking."

"Her professor is an *ass*, and Luna is perceptive. She knows she's being picked on and probably for a bigger reason."

"Did she ask you about it?" I whisper.

"No. But I bet she'll ask you." Frog pauses. "You might not care about my opinion—but I think it's better to lead with the full story on this one."

Yeah. *I think so too.* I speak into my mic. "I do care, Froggy." I smile. "Donnelly out."

31

PAUL DONNELLY

Purple nebulas drift over Luna's face. Over my arms. Along the ceiling of her bedroom. Constellations and the Milky Way glow out of a galaxy projector, illuminating everything in lavender and fuchsia.

Sitting on the bed, we face one another. Close enough that we could be in a bathtub. Our knees are bent, legs split on either side of each other, and her fingers trace the ink on my shoulder blade. But she's looking into my eyes more than she's gazing at my tattoos.

After I got off work and came home, she immediately asked me about the Rochesters.

Her neuro-doctors have been guiding her through the delicate nature of recovering memories. She has an appointment tomorrow. So I made it clear that option existed, if she'd rather talk it out with them.

She said, "I just want to hear it from you, if that's okay."

I told her everything I know.

Now she's letting it sink in.

"They sound like Sith," Luna whispers, even though it's only us in her room. Plus, Orion. He's taking up half the bed, but I wouldn't push him off. I love the big furry lug. Love him even more close by us. "The Rochesters use the Dark Side of the Force, and the Dark Side uses them too."

Star Wars. I've read a bunch of the comics by now. Seen all the movies and watched *Andor* and *The Clone Wars* with Luna this week. Some of the lore feels open to interpretation. So I ask, "You believe all Sith are evil?"

"I didn't used to," Luna admits. "I liked to think Sith were just an alien species, and their traditions were passed on to others over time. To be Sith didn't mean you were born evil, but if you're taught the Dark Side, if you follow the Dark Side, then…" She shrugs, "that's what you are." Her eyes travel over mine, like she's feeling for the past she wants to see. "I didn't think *Rochester* was the same family that went to Dalton. I'd never heard of a Wyatt Rochester when I chose my schedule."

"He's the oldest. I don't think any of his siblings were in your grade either."

"I can't believe they moved into my parents' neighborhood in the past three years." She winces. "And then The Royal Leaks."

The Rochesters were the insidious hands behind those leaks. Where salacious, private pieces of information were posted online without the famous ones' consent. They denied the allegations. A lawsuit ensued, and they recently settled out of court.

Whatever undisclosed sum the Rochesters coughed up—it wasn't enough to me. Not when that asshole is singling out my girlfriend.

"Yeah," I breathe. I have my arms around her slender back. Her body is bowed towards mine.

"I wondered what The Royal Leaks were. People on Fanaticon mention it a ton. I thought, maybe, it was a promo or tagline for *We Are Calloway*."

"No, just somethin' those fucking roaches did."

"The Roaches," she smiles.

"Without the cock. 'Cause I am a cockroach, and we're not the same."

She crinkles her nose. "You're not a cockroach."

"Don't think I could survive a nuclear war? Three months without food? Forty-five minutes without air?"

Her smile brightens. "You are a cockroach-apedia."

"I know my species."

She shakes her head, then rests her chin on her kneecap. "I don't think you belong to that particular species. Cockroaches run when they're scared."

It crashes me into my childhood. "Yeah?" I open my mouth, but instead of saying shit, I look away from her for the first time.

Her body tenses against my palms, and I rub her back. Then I breathe, "I run."

My family.

I ran away from them when I was seventeen, but it's not what I've been doing lately. And anyway, I don't wanna bring them up.

Her fingers trail the ink along my collar, small typeface that reads: *Made in Philly.* But her eyes—her eyes are glued to mine. "I lost all my memories of you, and you never ran away from me."

"You're not what scares me, Luna."

Her body melts against my hands, easing. "What are you afraid of?"

"A world without cheesesteaks and tomato pie."

Her smile reemerges. It sends me to the moon. She asks, "What else?"

"You tell me yours."

"I'm afraid of…" She thinks. "Vultures."

"Figurative or literal?"

"Literal, but I guess both. I once saw a vulture picking at a deer carcass. It just seemed like a sad thing to happen after death." She stares into me. "Now you."

"Uh, great white sharks. Never seen one, but I'm swimming my hardest if I do."

Her turn. "Being a worse Luna than OG Luna." She says fast, "And I know it's all *me.* I am her. But I just want to do her proud. Myself proud. It's why…it's why I don't think I'm going to drop the class with the Roach."

My muscles flex in hot bands, and I lift my hand off her back, just to scrape my fingers through my hair.

"It's not what you would do," she realizes.

"*I run*," I emphasize.

I know who I am, but she sees me in a different light that I can't always make sense of. *That* scares me. I love how overwhelming it feels when she looks at me. But what if she only views me as this "human hero" because she doesn't have all the pieces of me? As soon as I give more of my past, as soon as she realizes I *am* a cockroach, will she even love me the same?

"You would run..." She's processing it.

"When people try to beat me down, I don't stick around for more."

Luna blinks, staring past me. "...sideways..." She's scrounging for words. "...people think they're kicking me down...but all they're really doing is kicking me sideways, away from them—you said that to me?"

My pulse skips. "Yeah, I did."

"I can't see it. I just hear you...I hear you saying that to me." Frustration knits her brows. "I wish I could see the *whole* memory."

"It might come in fragments," I say, feeling more hopeful if she's remembering words I've spoken.

"...you said something about..." Her concentration face looks like Eleven using her powers in *Stranger Things*.

"Don't burst a blood vessel trying to remember me."

She smiles, more focused on me. "It'd be worth the nosebleed."

"It's not worth that much."

"Small price to pay, I think."

"You bleeding?" I say. "Nah, that's not anything I'm paying. Sorry."

Her smile softens.

I hold the base of her neck and kiss her cheek. Her lips tease upward, and I kiss her lips more fully a few times. Her fingers dig into my shoulders with eagerness, and my cock twitches. I pull back slightly before I harden anymore.

We share a quiet, calm beat. Purple shadows swirl over her

beautiful face, and I breathe, "You know, you aren't a quitter if you drop that class. You don't have to put yourself in situations that are hard just to prove you can take it."

"Have you ever done that?"

"*No.*" It terrifies me that she's willing to. But I don't wanna hold her back either. "If it's something you really wanna do…"

She's nodding. "I think I'd be disappointed in myself if I didn't at least give it a shot." She adds, "If it gets bad, I can always withdraw from the course."

"Alright," I say.

Orion *woofs* at the door, then settles down. He must've heard footsteps. Luna scratches his furry belly and tells him, "I still can't believe you were an accomplice in a crime." The pet-sitter bugged his collar, which was how the Rochesters got info to leak. "I missed your unlawful activity."

"If he stands trial, I'll go down saying our boy's innocent." Fuck me. It just came out like that. *Our boy.*

Her eyes pop out, and a hot wave rushes over my body. I play it off with a *rock on* gesture and then rise off the bed. "You hungry? I can see if the roomies are planning anything." We'll do group dinners at the penthouse sometimes, and I could eat Thatch's chicken parm seven days a week.

"Yeah, but can we do take-out?"

"Works for me." We spend a few minutes deciding on which Italian restaurant. I've got chicken parm on the brain now, and after we place our orders through a delivery app, we're switching on the TV and waiting for the food. Leaning against the headboard, I scroll through new release movies, and Luna is on her phone next to me.

The air is tense.

Tenser than either of us enjoys sitting in. Because we keep glancing at each other, like we're wondering who'll be the first to break the dam.

"Watcha looking at?" I ask her.

She's on YouTube. "A video."

The vagueness cuts deep. Fuck…fuck. I glance back at her.

She's now frowning at her phone. I can't tell if the frown is associated with the video or with me.

I punch a button on the remote. I don't like this feeling at fucking all. *Fuck.* Another glance at Luna. Her frown is deeper.

I try to focus on the TV and read the description of *Solarbabies.* Another glance at her, and I ask, "What's wrong?"

She shrugs and tries to find the words. "Were you joking?" She lowers her phone. "Before…when you said he's our boy—did you mean it?"

I flip the remote in my hand. "Is it freaking you out?"

"No," she says fast. "I mean, I'd want him to be *ours.* Does that freak you out?"

"No," I admit. *But I don't want kids with you. With anyone.* It's just not something I'm ready to talk about, and I don't know if that makes me a bad boyfriend or what—but I keep that inside for now. Instead, I say, "I love him like he's mine."

Her lips rise. "He loves you like you're his too."

"You think?"

"I know," she says seriously. "I have seven senses. The seventh being pet-empathy. He only feels strong, strong love around you."

I laugh and reach over her body to pat Orion. "I love our fluffy boy." He licks my hand.

Luna is all smiles now, and I love making her feel good. Is that a crime? It's just easier to table the things that might make her sad or upset.

Tension eradicated, I slide my arm over her loosened shoulders, and she leans her body weight into me and shows me the video. It's from Penn. A recording of *The OA* dance Luna and I did in front of other students.

"I've watched it like five times," she says into a grin. "It always makes me smile."

"How come?" I ask, since that memory wasn't a pleasant one for Luna.

"You did it with me. I just like knowing my weird was reciprocated. And we weren't even really together then." She tilts her chin so she meets my eyes. "I can see how I would've fallen for you."

I feel like I'm falling for her a thousand times in the span of a minute, and it chokes me up for a second. "You have good taste," is all I manage to say.

She laughs, but the sound dies out when the video plays and zooms in on Luna rushing out of the dining hall. I chase after her.

Beside me, Luna murmurs, "That's the sad part."

"Can't have a sad alien with the sad parts."

She smiles and rests her cheek on my bicep. She's about to close out the video, but the footage fixes on Eliot as he confronts Jeffra.

I've never seen what happened when I ran after Luna.

Heat in his eyes, he shouts, "She did *nothing* to you! Are you stuck in high school?! Reliving your golden years?! Why do you insist on being such a—?!"

"Such a what?" Jeffra jeers with a laugh. "A bitch?"

"Crawl back to the hell you came from," Eliot sneers.

"Luna doesn't *own* Penn. I'm a student, just like her. If she has a problem with me, then she can quit. She's probably pulling Ds anyway. The grade and the male anatomy."

Acid drips in the back of my throat, and I cup my hand over the screen.

"I've already seen it." She peels my fingers off her phone.

"Yeah, I don't really want to see it," I admit to her, my chest tightening.

"Oh." She realizes I was trying to protect myself, not just her. "Okay." She pauses the video. "It's just there's this part at the end that doesn't make sense to me. I kinda wanted you to hear it."

Fuck.

"Can I describe it?" she asks. "You don't have to watch the video."

I scratch the back of my head, then glance at the TV, then her. "You can play it."

"You sure?"

"Yeah, go ahead." I blink a few times. She hesitates, but I encourage her enough that she plays the video.

Eliot nails a glare into Jeffra as he sneers, "What's it going to take for you to stop?"

"To stop what?" She crosses her arms.

"Bullying Luna."

"Oh my God, I'm *not* bullying her. Is that what she told you?"

"Call it whatever you want, Satan. You know what you're doing."

"Satan?" Jeffra smirks. "Clever."

"No, it's unimaginative and cliché. I can't even get inspired around you."

She uncrosses her arms. "There is something you can do." And then she curves her hands around his ears and whispers to him.

Beside me, Luna asks, "Can you hear her?" She increases the volume, and I take her phone, holding it close to my ear.

"It's too muffled." I'm not that concerned about what Jeffra said to Eliot. "She's trying to get a reaction out of him. It's what people like her do."

Luna nods and shuts off the video. "Yeah, you're right." She curves her arms around my waist, hugging on to me. "Are we watching Solarbabies? I love that one."

"Solarbabies, it is." Right as I start the movie, her phone buzzes. "Food here?"

"No…" Luna sits up off of me. "It's from my therapist. She's asking if you'd want to go to a therapy session with me—you can say *no*."

I think it over. Therapy hasn't ever worked for me, but I'm not opposed to joining Luna. Probably 'cause I've never done a joint session before, and what if it does help her? What if it could benefit me?

Then again, Dr. Raven isn't my biggest fan, and there's a chance I might unintentionally piss her off.

"Do you want me to go with you?" I ask Luna.

"Only if you want to," she says. "But I think it might be good if

Dr. Raven hears your opinions from you and not just through me. Maybe she'll understand you better."

I start nodding. "Let's do it."

"Really?" she smiles, and I know I've done the right thing by trying this out.

"Yeah, really." I watch her type out a response. "Tell her to set out snacks, not tissues."

Luna laughs, and I grin and tuck her closer, kissing her head, feeling like I can take on the Evil fucking Empire if I have to.

CHARLIE & LUNA'S TEXT THREAD

Jan 12th

8:12 a.m.

Luna: Do I call the Rochesters Sith Lords in my dournal?

Charlie: No.

Luna: Just Sith? Take out the Lord part.

Charlie: No.

9:08 a.m.

Charlie: You didn't want to take the New Media class the first time around because of the professor.

Luna: Oh.

10:11 a.m.

Charlie: Drop the class.

Luna: No can do, memory guardian. I'm sticking this one out ✋

DONNELLY'S DAILY PLANNER
Tuesday, Jan 29th

Today's Focus: think happy thoughts, soaring to the mf-ing moon.

To Do:

- No security work, took the day off.

- Joint therapy sesh with Luna + her therapist (survive and thrive)

- ~~Drop Luna off at Cobalt bros in Hell's~~ Kitchen.

- Stay with Luna in Hell's kitchen, see if Beckett wants to hit the gym? (it's his day off from the ballet)

Notes: The time has come, the walrus said. can't remember the whole poem, Think the walrus eats someone's babies? Idk, but I'm not being eaten today. The therapy sesh will come and go with me looking better than ever, Think it'll be chill, Luna said Dr. Raven won't prod me to overshare if I'm not ready.

Baby Ripley turned 2 on the 15th. Farrow & Maximoff got offered to sell the birthday party pics to Famous Now. For 1.5 mil! A lotta money for a 2-yr-old smashing a cupcake. No fancy party. Just family at the penthouse. Party was dope af, tho.

Filming for WAC has started back up. Got asked if I wanna be credited as "Luna's boyfriend" and do interviews, but Luna wants to pull out of the season. I also do *not* want to rehash the Night to Forget with production. So I'm out too.

About Luna: Spooning her at night is a masterclass in restraint. Cock wants in her. Brain says, not yet.

Other news! Quinnie is testy with me lately. Not sure why, other than he knows I have bad feelings about his gf. Maybe he's just angry Scooter spent the night in the Rookie Room.

~~Do not like that for Froggy.~~

Do not like *him* for Froggy.

Also!! Media is 100% obsessed with the Kitsulletti pregnancy and guessing the paternity b/w Banks & Akara. Sulli's been camping out in the penthouse to avoid the chaos. Another reason not to have kids? Think so.

Thatch made chicken parm yesterday for the penthouse fam. (Love him.) Can't believe he's still suspended tho. Gabe's been rocking Jane's detail mostly. I think? Not always walkin' the SFO streets these days.

Epsilon sucks.

That's all.

Meals: Chewing on my feelings in therapy.

Water: GF's Pussy: Tasted her last night *chef's kiss* will prob touch her again today. Gotta quench the gf's thirst. Doing the Lord's work.

Question of the Day: How many times can I make ~~tuna come in an hour?~~ Does a fairy die when you go on Lily Calloway's shit list? Am I that fairy?

32

PAUL DONNELLY

"Can you say something?" Luna asks in a near-whisper from the passenger seat. We're en route to New York to see the Cobalts. Done with therapy in Philly. I'm driving an SUV. Luna bought the Volvo: Black Edition earlier this month. It's a fucking beautiful car. Rides smooth, but she likes its safety rating the most. High marks.

The car isn't what's pressing me.

I can't even count how many minutes of silence we've sat in. I only now realize it's dead quiet. Without taking my eyes off the freeway, I hand her my phone. "You wanna play some music?"

"Yeah," she says really, *really* quietly.

Yeah, I hear her. I've always been able to hear her.

I try not to wince.

I don't look at her, but I can feel her studying me before she scrolls through my Spotify.

I exhale a short breath, run my fingers through my hair, clench the wheel. "Been thinking I might need therapy for therapy. Is that normal?" I say it lightly, but it's not such a joke.

She knows it. "What part did you not like? Because I thought it went pretty well."

My muscles are too tight, and I adjust my posture in the seat, not able to get comfortable. *It's not you, car. Promise.* "I dunno."

I do know. I just don't know how to talk about it.

Luna goes silent in contemplation. She wants me to discuss this—no, I think she *needs* me to. She's faster to speak and asks, "Did you hate every part?"

"No...I like that she seemed supportive of you learning more about past events if that's what you want to do."

Silence falls again, not the type that's easy to share.

Paparazzi aren't tailing us, but Frog and Quinn are. I switch lanes. They mimic my moves in their security vehicle. I hit the cruise control.

Luna still hasn't found a song. Probably because she'd rather talk.

I rub my mouth a couple times, then grip the wheel again. "I didn't like what she said after she realized I could hear you," I tell her, my voice nearly hollowed out. Why is this so hard for me to discuss? I feel like it gives it permanence, and I just want it to fade away.

Luna wracks her brain. "That part?" She's surprised. "Why?"

"She was sitting there analyzing my breathing, the way I was sitting, and how I responded to you—and the *second* I heard you whispering, she had something to say about it?" I shake my head a couple times. My voice isn't rising. It's nose-diving, and now I'm trying not to whisper. "I could hear you and understand you because you were sitting right next to me. There wasn't some deeper meaning to it, and I didn't like that she was trying to pull one out."

Luna rotates more towards me. "Can I hold your hand?"

I glance from the road to her, seeing she's exceptionally calm, and maybe I'm not tanking this moment. So I slide my right hand into hers and drive with my left.

She touches her fingertips to my fingertips. "I know you might think you're not unique, but you do catch what I say better than most people. There've been plenty of times just in the past couple of months that I thought there's no way you could hear me, but you did."

I run my tongue over my molars, fighting the burn in my eyes.

"I don't want to upset you—"

"It's alright. It's alright," I breathe, swallowing hard. "Normally, I would love it. I'd love knowing I won't miss a thing you're saying. I'd love knowing I can hear you better than anyone else can. But what she said back there—she ruined it. 'Cause now when I hear your whispered words—I just hear *her*. Saying the only reason I hear you is because of *my* childhood trauma. What'd she call it?"

"Hyper-independence. That you likely grew up in a state of extreme self-reliance and your unstable environment caused you to be on alert for threats…which is why you have super bionic ears."

It bothers me about a hundred times less when Luna says it. She's not that put off or acting like I'm now fissured down the middle, and I take a deeper breath. "Yeah…" I exhale another breath and clasp her hand.

It's hard to deny that I'm hyper-independent. Especially when Farrow has mentioned our extreme independence being a detriment before.

I sigh out, "Let's just forget she said it. Pretend I can only hear you this well 'cause I have a superpower."

"Is it so bad?" she whispers.

I hear her really clearly. "Is what?"

"Knowing the origin of how you can hear me so well." She tries to turn more toward me but the seatbelt yanks at her body. "Lots of superheroes have powers from their environment, from trauma, from catastrophes. Spider-Man getting bit by a radioactive arachnid wasn't exactly a *sweet* moment. It was painful, and it's sad that it happened but it doesn't make his powers any less amazing. Good came out of bad. Light out of dark."

I'm choked up for a solid minute, and fuck, I wanna pull over and look at her, touch more of her than just her hand. It feels like she's reaching straight into my heart and cradling it with force—like she sees it's in one piece and won't bleed out. I glance from the road, to her, the road, her, road, Luna. "Girl, you keep doing this to me," I say in one breath.

"What?"

"Making me fall in love with you." I'm still choked. Don't know how I managed to say it at all, but I clear the ball out of my throat. "Don't stop."

Very softly, she says, "I never will."

33

PAUL DONNELLY

I never will.

She's said that to me before. It's a common phrase, I know, but the first time she said it, we were in New York, too. Sometimes I feel like her memories are right there. Simmering. Slowly seeping out.

Might just be hopeful thinking on my part 'cause I know how badly she wants to remember everything. And yeah, I want that for her just as bad.

While Luna stays back at the Cobalt brothers' bachelor pad, discussing the Fizzle CEO race with Eliot, I hit the gym with Beckett. Only, we take an excruciatingly awkward elevator ride to the rec level on the fifteenth floor. I'd like to say I'm not the one making this shit uncomfy.

But it's me.

And O'Malley.

That's right—Beckett's bodyguard has joined us. Dark-haired, pale Irish complexion, the lightest soul-sucking blue eyes, and the most punchable face you can imagine—that's Chris O'Malley. That's the shithead who told Luna he knows her better than I do.

I hate that he's the same age as me.

I hate that he's from a do-gooder, well-loved Irish-American family in South Philly.

I hate that the Catholic church adores the O'Malleys but spit on my parents.

I hate that on paper, he's the inverse of me.

I hate that I hate everything about him. 'Cause he shouldn't be worth the amount of *raging* blood coursing through my veins.

At least he's not here to lift weights as Beckett's friend. He's on-duty. The gym at the apartment complex is accessible to anyone with a key. *He better be standing outside the gym and not in it.* I really will walk out like a petty asshole if I have to curl a dumbbell and stare at his snide face.

I level my eyes on the descending numbers.

Beckett is between us, wearing joggers and a loose-fitted black muscle shirt. The two of us are holding water bottles, but we're all sharing the suffocating tension. I sense Beckett glancing from O'Malley to me before he asks, "What's the story here?"

"There is no story," O'Malley says plainly.

I would agree and say, *Yep*, if not for the fact that *he* broke the silent bodyguard oath first. The one that says to leave clients out of our bullshit—so they'll be unaware of any bad blood between body-guards and they'll always trust the security that's protecting them.

He fucked me over in front of Luna at the bowling alley.

Can't forget it.

Then we threw fists and ended up brawling on a bowling lane. All in view of the famous families. So acting like we're cool, like there is no beef between us, isn't going to work. Beckett will remember the fight.

"There is a fucked-up story. You want that one?" I ask Beckett, not able to look away from the digital floor numbers.

O'Malley jumps in, "It's not anything you should be concerned about, Beck." *Beck.* He calls him by his nickname. Since when? I have to remember the one time O'Malley was *nice* to me was because we both genuinely love Beckett.

"I'd like to know," Beckett says, sounding cautious. Like he's not purposefully trying to instigate a world war.

We're closing in on the fifteenth floor.

And then the elevator screeches to a halt. We're between floors.

"You've got to be shitting me," O'Malley mutters, pounding the number 15 button. He seems almost more irritated being stuck in the confined space with me than I am.

Beckett checks his phone. "No signal."

I open the emergency box and take out the corded phone. Operator comes online, and I report the outage and chat for a second, then hang up. "They're working on having it up and running in five minutes. They don't think they'll need to send anyone out, but they'll keep us posted."

"Well," Beckett says, tensed. "My mom would call this fate." He turns to the two of us. "Here's an opportunity to work it out."

"It can't be worked out, Beck," I say to him.

Beckett's yellow-green eyes stay calm but carry slight sadness as he asks, "Do you believe in second chances?"

I think he's asking about himself. This is really the first thing we've done together since our big falling out. And it's being derailed by a busted elevator and O'McFugly.

"He's not looking for a second chance," I tell Beckett. "He thinks he's done *nothing* wrong."

O'Malley lets out an aggravated noise. "Fucking *Omega*. You all are the same." He shoves his phone in his gray slacks. "You have zero morals. Zero ethics to stand on. And when Epsilon calls you out on them, you play the victim. I'm not the fucking villain, Donnelly."

My nose flares. "Take another look in the mirror."

"Why don't you?" he snaps.

"Been looking and I see enough flaws to know I'm not anything that you'd think is respectable, but what about you? Get off your fucking high horse, man. You're no better than me."

"Again, I'm not *fucking* a client."

"Whoa," Beckett cuts in, protective over his family. That includes Luna, thank God, and he knows me well enough that he's not trying to protect her from me.

O'Malley threads his fingers against the back of his neck, instant regret hitting his eyes. Yeah, he popped off in front of Beckett and now he's glaring at me like I provoked him there.

Come *on*. "Not everything is my fault. Not everything is on me," I say with heat.

O'Malley works his jaw, then turns to Beckett. "I know your family *loves* SFO because, obviously, they're *family* now. But in our profession, what they've done is out of bounds. What Donnelly is doing with Luna—when she has *amnesia* and can't even remember him—that's the fucked-up story."

I see red, and I have to intake a sharp breath to cool off.

"Luna is emotionally attached to him," Beckett explains like it's not that strange. "She chose Donnelly."

O'McFugly is staring me down. "Why do you think that is?"

I cut in, "I didn't fill her head with *bullshit* to get her to trust me, Chris. I'd never do that to anyone."

"No one can confirm that, Paul."

"Believe what you wanna believe then," I say. "Believe the absolute *worst* about me. You already have since the day I met you. Why stop now?"

Beckett has a hand against the side of his face like this is real deep shit he didn't realize we were wading in. It stinks. It's rotten. And we all want out, but swimming for an escape feels *impossible*.

"I tried to like you," O'Malley admits in a tight breath. "But you make it really fucking hard."

"And you don't? Why would I ever wanna be friends with a guy who constantly rags on me and my family?"

"Your family is fucking awful," O'Malley spits back.

"You don't think I don't know that?" I sneer between gritted teeth. "You don't think I wished they were different?"

"Not really—you defend them every chance you fucking get."

"From people like you!" I shout. "Who see my parents as 2-D caricatures. You think they sit there, get high, and plot heinous crimes like they're fucking Dr. Evil. You don't even know how many months they've spent trying to get clean. How hard it was for them every *single* time."

"They made their bed every *single* time," O'Malley forces. "But why are you so fucking intent on rolling around in those dirty sheets, man? It's *disgusting*. Get out."

Get out.

Like it's so easy.

Like I haven't tried.

I taste acid, and I swear he's the *only* one that digs this deep under my skin. I try to breathe out a hot breath, to calm down. "You don't get it."

"I don't get that you're so fucked up in the head, you're *still* sympathizing with the people who kidnapped Luna. Your so-called girlfriend."

"Sympathizing?" My face twists. "I coulda killed them *myself*. You weren't in that house. You have no..." I swallow the words, glaring at the elevator buttons.

"Your parents—"

"They weren't even involved," I interject. "Leave 'em out of this."

He's quiet for a beat, taking a second to respond—which he rarely does. But then he says, "The Donnellys are all the same. You drag each other down. Your dad will drag you down too." His blue eyes bore into mine like a jackhammer, and I wonder if there's a warning in them.

Get out.

Even if I could, staying in contact with my dad is still a necessity for security at this point. They need me to be in communication with him, and there's a part of me that wants to throw it back in O'Malley's face. To prove to him he's wrong. That my parents *are* better. They *have* changed.

"O'Malley," Beckett says gently.

"I'm done," O'Malley mutters, rotating away from me.

I inhale and exhale, trying not to seethe, and the elevator jerks back to life. *Appreciation, elevator gods.* The second the doors slide open, I'm out. My stride is hot and quick to the gym. Luckily, Beckett asks O'Malley if he can stay posted outside.

I can escape that oxygen-sucking black hole, at least.

The sleek gym houses state-of-the-art machines, a water bottle refilling station, several racks of free weights and medicine balls, and televisions that air GBA News. It always smells like bleach and lemon, a familiar scent. Can't even count all the times I've worked out here with Beckett back when I was his bodyguard.

Now I'm here as something else to him. Not sure what. Feels more like we're in a friend limbo.

The gym is empty, outside of an older man crushing a workout on an elliptical. He's wearing earbuds and too in the zone to pay attention to us.

"Weights or treadmill first?" I ask Beckett, knowing his routine flipflops between the two.

"Whichever you'd like." He pops the cap of his water and takes a swig.

I throw up a loose finger-horns, then nod to the treadmill.

After a quick stretch, we choose two machines side-by-side, and I fuck with the settings on mine—debating whether I wanna go my absolute hardest or do a light jog.

The only time I ever workout on a treadmill is with Beckett. Back when Loren asked me if I run, I feel like I blocked this whole thing out. I pushed Beckett *so far* out of my brain. The thought of reaching there was too painful, and it's strange that I'm here now.

And there is no ache. Not even the slightest burn from a cut. It feels easy, as easy as this used to be with him. Maybe it's 'cause he's not butchering me to open up about O'Malley or my parents. He's leaving that conversation outside the doors.

It's the type of friendship I love.

It never asks too much of me. It never rips me open.

It just sews me back together.

Beckett catches my eyes and says, "Race you?"

Like old times.

The corner of my mouth curves upward. "Alright. Let's see if you can keep a three-minute sprint without huffing and puffing."

"Funny," he smiles over at me. "You probably haven't run in two years. You've packed on—what, ten pounds of muscle?"

I grin. "Thanks for noticing, man." I press two fingers to my lips and blow him a kiss with them.

He grins back. "One-minute intervals?"

"Yeah. Start at three miles-per-hour." We walk at level three.

A minute passes, and at the same time, we both increase the speed to four. Then five, six. Our walk morphs into an easy jog.

We're facing floor-to-ceiling windows. On the fifteenth level of a high-rise, it's almost as if we're running through the skyline. We see New York in all its glamorous, rugged beauty. Like Philly, this one has its charm and its destruction.

Think that's what makes it so beautiful. It's not perfect. Nothing real is.

Ten mph, and we're at a sprint, our stride lengthy. Sweat has built on our brows, and we keep casting glances over at each other. To see who's gonna bail first.

He gives me a thumbs-up—not to tell me he's doing well, but that it's time to increase the speed. Eleven mph, and my blood is hot. I breathe deep measured breaths. My tendons shriek at the fierce stretch, but it's a good burn. I'm flying through New York.

Right alongside my old friend.

I check on him.

Beckett is agile, lithe, even as we're encroaching an all-out pace. His stride is grace. His footfalls come much softer than mine. I'm pounding the track. As he intakes each lungful of air with precision, I see a difference in him.

He's older.

He'll be twenty-four this year. But it's not really his age. It's his demeanor—like he's jumped more hurdles, ran more miles, traveled through bumpier terrain, and this, running at a controlled and deliberate speed, comes easier.

Twelve mph. He's looking over.

I'm grinning. I've got way more in me, but my breaths are heavier.

Thirteen, fourteen, fifteen hits, and we're only watching each other now. Beckett grins back—and we'd both be cursing if we could speak. Then we're laughing at sixteen, at the run-for-your-fucking-life pace that's busting both of our asses, and nearly at the same time, we pull the plug.

I laugh and gasp for air, hunching over the handlebar. "Fuck me."

Beckett laughs, "Not too bad." He catches his breath faster. "I thought you were going to trip at twelve."

"Nah, no treadmill's gonna take me out." I hop off the machines and stretch my tight hamstrings. Then we take a water break. Sharing the seat of a weight bench, we stare out at the city skyline.

Beckett towels off the sweat dripping down his temples.

I suck on the nozzle of my water bottle. Breathing so much easier. It's almost hard to believe I just had a serious conflict in the elevator.

Water rushes down my throat, and something about what Luna said in the car races back to me. I wanted to pretend the origin of who I am didn't exist. There are too many twisted memories I'd rather forget, but for some reason, it felt better when she acknowledged my past with my present.

I could sit here and never bring up the past with Beckett again. Run forward. Don't look back. Never look back. But I dunno— I'm not sure that'll create anything lasting. I'm not sure I ever built *anything* that could last with him. He gave me so much of his life, and I never let him see all of mine.

I couldn't.

I ran away from it. But it was always there. It was there when he got into cocaine. It was there when I wished I told him to stop. It was there when I never said a word.

It was there when he chose drugs over me.

Last we brought up the past, we let unsaid things hang in the air like a dead, unburied body. I want to put it to rest.

"You remember that one night on the way to Pink Noir?" I

say lightly. "You had a rough performance. Your hamstring was bothering you, I think?"

"Yeah, I remember." He gazes out the window. "Hans was driving." He names his personal driver. "I took a line in the backseat. It was the first time I did it openly in front of you."

"It wasn't so you could perform better, Beck. That night, you did it just to keep moving, and I should've told you not to."

Beckett blinks a few times, pain cinching his reddened eyes. "I wouldn't have listened." His voice shakes, but he clears his throat. "And I'm sorry. I'm sorry I thought you didn't care what I did, when you're someone who cares about people—more than I think humanly possible, sometimes. I'm sorry I didn't care about you as much as you did me—"

"That's not…" I trail off.

"It is true. I knew your parents were addicts, and I didn't stop to think maybe it would've bothered you."

"You're not a mind-reader."

Beckett smiles a little, staring out at New York. "You don't even know how good you are." His eyes, full of emotion, meet mine again. "I was lucky to have you as a friend. Every day. And I took it for granted. Because when I lost it, it felt like my world went dark."

I scrape a hand through my damp hair. "I tried to forget it all. My time in New York with you. It still hurt, man." I don't think it every really stopped hurting.

Until maybe right now.

"It's all I could remember," Beckett breathes. "I tried telling myself a thousand *fucking* times that I got you transferred off my detail to protect you. That it was about me *caring* about you. But really, it was just so I could keep using and feel okay about it—but after that, I never felt okay." He rubs at his wet eyes. "Charlie hated me—not like *literal* hate."

"I was about to say." Towards Beckett, Charlie could never.

"I frustrated him more than anything. There were some days, I think he couldn't even bear to see what was inside of me anymore."

Beckett expels a slow, heavy breath. "I never thought I was hurting myself, but when I could feel how I was hurting him…it was the end. I couldn't take it, then Scotland made it harder but also easier to quit. There've been times where I thought about it, but I haven't used since."

I nod a few times. "I'm proud of you." I feel it in my chest. Pride for my friend.

He tries to smile. "I don't think I deserve it."

"You know, for a dancer, you're pretty fucking terrible at giving yourself grace."

Beckett laughs, the sound deeper, and I grin at him, laughing a little too. And I nod to him. "Don't be so hard on yourself. You're too limber to wear shackles, you know. No one should be chained down like that." I can't help but glance at the door. Where I left my ball and chain.

"Epsilon and Omega hate each other," Beckett states.

"That obvious?"

"Since Scotland, yeah." Beckett zeroes in on the door. "But I didn't realize how deep it was between you and O'Malley. I thought it was a group hatred, not anything that personal."

"He's just a fucking prick." I take a hotter gulp of water.

"I can ask for a new bodyguard—"

"No. Don't. You move him 'cause of me, he'll throw a fit and I'll have the rest of SFE breathing down my neck."

He nods.

I ask, "Do you like him?"

"O'Malley?"

"Yeah."

Beckett folds his towel. "He's not anything like you, but he's made time move faster when it was going too slow some nights. He was fun. Until…"

"Until he got jumped protecting you." I feel responsible. "I'm sorry—"

"You weren't the one with the bat," Beckett murmurs, then

pauses. "I do like him, Donnelly, but I hate what he said in the elevator. I don't think he really even knows you."

"Why do you say that?"

"Because if he did, he'd never question how you'd treat Luna. Or your motives behind getting with her." He lets out a laugh in thought. "I can name over a dozen situations where girls, too drunk to consent, tried getting in your pants. You gave them water. You tried calling them a cab. Sometimes they were so relentless, you were struggling to even stay at the bar without being groped, and you just took it."

"Nah, you usually got us out of there." Beckett did care about me. Maybe he's right. Maybe it wasn't to the same degree, but he noticed me. He saw, and he had the power to leave, since I only had the power to follow as his bodyguard.

He left for me.

Time and time again. He made sure I was good. I made sure he was good. It was Beckett and Donnelly Take New York. Bright, happy days. They're not gone anymore. I can remember them.

I smile softly over at him. "So...what do you think of me and Luna? You still pissy about it?"

Beckett grins at the floor, then shakes his head. "I was *so* angry."

I'm glad we can both smile about it now. "I know. You stormed out of the suit fitting like I ate all your McDonald's french fries."

He laughs. "Yeah, well, it felt like you moved on completely, and I'd never...have this again." He'd never get our friendship back. "I wish I'd known earlier about you liking her."

"I didn't tell anyone for the longest time. It took me a while to process it, honestly. Think it was supposed to happen slowly."

"Still," he says, "I doubt there's a more perfect match, for either of you. It makes so much sense in hindsight, Charlie was shocked we didn't see it sooner."

I forgot being close to Beckett means I get all the fun nuggets about Charlie. I grin. Yeah, knowing Charlie has likely read about the first time I fucked Luna—having the inside scoop into some of his thoughts makes me feel like a kid with a million-bucks in a candy store. I'm back on an equal playing field with the most unpredictable Cobalt.

And I'm now on stable ground with my favorite one.

When we stand up to start gathering weight plates, I hug him. Glad to have him back. I know he feels the same.

34

PAUL DONNELLY

I finish a set of chest presses. Then switch with Beckett so I can spot him during his reps, but as he slides a weight plate off the barbell, he says, "You should come to the ballet. Not as security. Just as..."

"Your hottest friend," I smirk.

"Eliot would fight you on that."

"I'd let him have it. We'd know the truth though." I watch him put the heavier weight away on the rack.

He straddles the weight bench. Not lying back yet. "Really, I meant as Luna's boyfriend. You should take her on a date to the ballet. I can get you free tickets."

I nod in thought. "You think she'd like it?" I haven't ever asked if she enjoys the ballet. I love the music, some pieces more than others, and I miss seeing Beckett perform.

"Yeah, I do." He sounds assured. "We've never been too close, but Charlie has always had a decent read on her. He says she has a fascination with people. It's probably easy to watch us perform and try to imagine what the fuck is going on behind the curtain."

I grin. "Can imagine it," I nod, knowing plenty of the dancers from being granted access to his world. "You, giving Leo a back massage."

"I'd rather cut off my hands." He lies back on the bench. "He'd probably give me the saw."

"Match made," I tease.

"In hell." He wraps his hands around the barbell, about to lift it, but the door opens. Our heads swing over to Joana Oliveira. She's fitting in AirPods, but as soon as she sees Beckett, she moves slower to put them in her ears.

She's my best friend's sister. Twenty-one, like Luna. Jo has been crashing at SFO's studio apartment where Oscar stays from time-to-time. It's down the hall from the Cobalt brothers, so I'm not surprised she's using the building's gym.

Beckett lets go of the bar. Sitting up, he fixates on her face. "What the fuck happened to you?"

Jo has two black eyes. A nastier bruise blemishes the golden-brown skin of her cheek, and her lip is split. I'm less concerned than Beckett 'cause I've seen her look worse.

"I got my ass handed to me," she retorts, coming closer. "You want to watch it? It's all over YouTube." She's a pro-boxer. Her bigger fights are televised. "Go get off on another girl knocking my lights out."

"I'm not a sadist." His voice isn't biting.

She takes out her phone. "Must've mixed you up with Charlie."

"Also not a sadist." Beckett looks her over. "I wouldn't take pleasure in watching a woman get punched in the face."

She's approaching me for some reason. "I would've thought that'd be the highlight of your year. Joana's face meets the floor."

"I'd enjoy throwing you on a bed more."

It falters her stride.

"Or I'd push you against the wall—I think you'd like the wall," Beckett says, his voice so sensual and smooth, if I were blindfolded I'd believe he was fucking her out in the open.

Jo has lost her bearings. Their eyes are locked.

My guy has a way with the ladies. Seen it time and time again. But this one is supposed to be off-limits. Oscar's sister and all.

Still, I'd ship it. Mostly since I've been sensing how much he likes her.

Jo recovers fast. "Or maybe the only thing I'd enjoy," she says slowly, "is my knee in your groin."

"So you're the sadist then."

"*No.*"

"No?"

"How's that mattress on your back? Still heavy?"

Beckett gives me a brief look like, *see, she's a borderline brat.* Then says to her, "Why? You want to test it out."

"That lumpy overused thing?"

I try not to laugh.

A smile pulls at his lips. "If that's what you have to tell yourself."

Ignoring him, she spins to me. Phone still cupped in her hand. "Do you know someone named Zale Dubicki?"

My brows catapult. "Tricky Dicky?"

Beckett makes a *what the fuck* face. "Who?"

"Tattoo artist from Old City." *From the first place I apprenticed.* Same place where Scooter works. "What are you doing with Tricky Dicky?"

"Frog is setting me up with him. Technically the guy she's talking to, Scooter or whoever, is setting me up with his friend. It's a double date. She said you might know Zale, so I could pick your brain about him."

Fuck.

I scrunch my brows, eyes tightened 'cause I'm witnessing the start of a five-car pileup. "Your brother know about this?"

She glowers. "Do *not* involve Quinn or Oscar, *please.* You're supposed to be the cool one."

Oscar is gonna lose his shit and not in a funny ha-ha way. He thought Frog could benefit from getting to know another girl around her age, especially since she lost Luna, so he gave her Joana's number. Well, now Frog has roped Jo into her Scoot situation.

I stand in a casual lunge and grip the racked barbell from behind the weight bench. Best thing I can do is have Jo trust me. "Been the cool one. Still the cool one," I assure her.

Beckett rises off the bench and rotates to me. "What's wrong with Tricky Dicky?"

Jo snaps, "Why does there have to be anything wrong with him?"

"With a name like *Tricky Dicky*?"

"You're literally called *the bad boy of ballet*. I wouldn't touch you with a fifty-foot pole."

Oof.

He makes a face like her math isn't mathing. "But Tricky Dicky is in reach?"

"Yeah." She shrugs. "He's probably great in bed."

I cut in, "You okay with him being thirty-five?"

"Thirty-five?" Jo's face falls. "No, he looks like...twenty-five, tops." She shows me his photo. He has two tattoo sleeves, dark shaggy hair, and a septum piercing. He's clean-shaven and thin, which makes him appear younger.

"He's just skinny," I tell her.

Joana reexamines the pic. "No way."

"I'm telling you, he's in his mid-thirties. He's older than Scooter."

I'm not gonna judge the age-gap. I have a decent-sized one with Luna, even more so if I count the years she's mentally missing. Sometimes, I do feel it—just in the fact that I've already experienced things she's currently grappling with, and that extends beyond sex.

I don't mind it though. But if I had a crystal ball at eighteen, I would've thought it'd say I'd be with an older woman. Definitely not anyone this much younger.

Now, I can't even imagine being with anyone but Luna. It feels like we were made only for each other.

Joana is considering. "He's older than Oscar." I don't think that's appealing to her.

"You're gonna cancel then?" I ask.

She's quick to say, "No, because Frog will still go. I don't think she cares about Scooter's age, and I'm not leaving her with both these guys. But you should come." She's speaking to me, not Beckett. "Bring Luna. It could be another triple date."

Except the last triple date included Farrow and Oscar, my best friends. Scooter and Tricky Dicky are worse than knockoff versions 'cause I don't know 'em that well. I haven't talked to those guys in over a decade. It sounds like a bad time, for more than just myself.

"You are dating Luna, right?" Jo asks. "My brothers said you were official after I asked about the rumors."

"Yeah, we're together." *But she doesn't remember you.* Joana has no clue Luna has amnesia. She's not completely a part of the trusted inner-circle, and I also don't want to put my girlfriend in a position where she's gotta pretend to know Jo for a few hours.

Beckett is looking at me like I should go. Oscar will be doing the exact same, and all of SFO will be breathing down my neck. No one trusts Scooter. And Jo is basically asking me to go to look out for Frog, too.

I ask, "You sure you don't just wanna kick these guys to the curb?"

"I doubt she will. I don't know Frog that well yet—but she kept saying how this guy is *so* in touch with his emotions. That he's sensitive. That he gets her. Either he's her soul mate or he's playing her and she's buying it. So if you think he's a creep, then we should be there for her."

I nod. "I'll ask Luna." I need her to be okay with going first. If she's not into it, I figure I can go solo still. Never been one to feel weird about dropping in on a double date.

FEBRUARY

"You think your body only cares for one thing. Anger. Rage. Beating the crap out of something. Anything. You think that makes us different than humans. You think that makes us *evolved*. It doesn't. We're all pulled under anger and either drowning or fighting to reach brighter emotions. Joy. Hope. *Love*. Can you imagine it? Being beneath a sentiment as strong as love?"

– *Beneath a Strong Sentiment*

FANATICON FORUM

We Are Calloway

Posted by @donnelly_we_stan

Luna x Donnelly ARE in a serious relationship. Here's why...

The latest pics in Celeb Crush. Those are proof enough. No one goes to paint pottery with an FWB. They're not f*ck buddies, guys. They painted cereal bowls together!!! And yeah, they got paint on each other too, but it was cute. I get the ppl who don't want them together bc of his family, but they LOOK happy and in love. Let those of us who love them, love them.

@Charlie4President: they're making out in 90% of the pics. Then she's straddling his lap. The PDA is ott. It's just sex. You're reaching.

@Core6Supremecy: They would've announced their relationship by now like Marrow did. This is prob a fling.

@PhillyNative: I saw them on the street around Superheroes & Scones the other day, and his arm was over her shoulder. Seemed more than just friendly, so if they're not a couple, then they're for sure sleeping together.

@XanderOnlyXander: Anytime a couple has been legitimate, Lily has verified. We've heard absolutely nothing from her either.

@hehecallowayxx: What if this is just a security ploy to throw the scent off the real couple? LunaQuinn. #LunaQuinnRise!!

@Eliot'sWife2019: LunaQuinn isn't a thing.

@WAC77Lover: Idk. @hehecallowayxx might be right. There's a few pics where Quinn seems pissed at Donnelly.

@Season4_WACgold: Isn't Quinn with that girl on Twitter? Nessa-something??? He's not single y'all. She's been posting Lives about this. He even appeared in one.

@MindfulMadness12: ~~You think them painting each other was cute? It was weird af. They were in public.~~ *Deleted by mod-bot for breaking forum rules.*

@NorthernStars: Their ship name should be *dirty duo* lol

@StaleBread89: Dirty duo who? I only see a Lunnelly.

@KitsullettiNewsReport: Dirty duo fits them. Especially since this isn't a legit relationship. It prob won't go on for much longer.

@RoseKnowsMyName_1: Don't forget to vote on the recent poll! (Link: How long do you think Luna x Donnelly will last?)

@Crepes34: They won't make it to March. She'll be kissing another guy by then.

DONNELLY'S DAILY PLANNER
Sunday, Feb 10th

Today's Focus: mingle with the famous fams as Luna's boyfriend + survive the Super Bowl with all limbs intact. (Not sure who wants to sever my dick. Hope it's not Lily. Money's on Rose 'cause she's the dick-severing queen. Avoid her?)

To Do:

- Drive to Hale House for Super Bowl party. (Birds vs. Bills. Gonna be a bloodbath.)

- Blend. Like my favorite smoothie. Just blend right into the fam dynamics.

- Show Luna why the Eagles are #1 in my heart (and they should be in hers too imo)

- Don't forget the chips and salsa.

Notes: First big gathering with her parents, aunts, uncles, and whole family since the holidays. Survived those, can easily survive this. Think they see me more as her bf, not as a bodyguard? Hope so.

Not fucking Luna is getting harder and

harder (pun intended). The time hasn't felt right to go all the way. That'll change. Soon?

Also! went on that triple date with Luna. Never seen her that quiet. She said she was okay tho. Can't blame her for not chitchatting much. Tricky Dicky and Scooter are f-ing losers. Never been more sober in my life. Froggy got wasted, and Scooter wanted to spend the night with her. I said *no* and this mf-er got in my face. It ended with Quinn decking him. Frog crying. Luna and Jo consoling Frog. A shitshow. Best part was dancing with Luna under the blue lights. For a sec there, it felt like the whole world was ours.

Other news: my elf is a Procrastination King. Guy has been learning ASL for fun instead of working on his Fizzle presentation.

Not good news: accidentally scared a student at Dalton so badly she pissed her skirt. Granted, I said nothing. Just made brief eye contact. Felt like shit all day. Until Luna made me a PB&M sandwich. Peanut butter marshmallow. Tasted a lot like love.

Meals: waiting until the party to partake. Gonna go down on a burger.

Water. GF's Pussy. Hydrate: Hydrating on the tears of the Buffalo fans instead. (will thirst after gf's pussy later.)

Question of the Day: ~~what position is the best position for a pseudo-virgin?~~ will Luna be able to handle me taking her multiple times ~~in a row? How aggressive can I really be?~~ where in the world is charlie keating cobalt's clothing iron?

35

PAUL DONNELLY

The Hale House is alive. Appetizers, dips, and chips are spread out on every flat surface. Rose keeps frisbeeing coasters as soon as a drink touches wood. Best Coaster Police in town. It seems to be occupying her attention, which I'm all for since I thought I'd be on her shit list. Just by proxy of being on her sister Lily's.

Surprisingly enough, I haven't been on her radar. It's made me less on edge, and I'm wondering if there's nothing to survive here.

Except the potential loss of the Super Bowl.

Not that everyone cares about the outcome. Rose is less than enthused about football, just like her husband and children. I'll love the Cobalts till the day I die, but they're not without faults and this right here is their biggest one.

My guy Beckett is the worst Eagles fan. He's seated on the window nook and chatting with his brothers. He lets out a half-hearted cheer when a major play goes down.

I'd say the Hales are attentive. Most with bowls of chips and eyes locked on screens—not always the TV, sometimes their phones. But nothing compares to the Morettis and Meadows, who are all on their feet.

"Fuck you, ref!" Sulli screams at the television.

Banks collapses on a chair, burying his face in his hands. Akara pats his back.

Thatcher lets out a long, agonized groan. "Come on!"

"You fucking fuck," Ryke growls at the TV. "What fucking was that?!"

I heard how Ryke had four tickets to the Super Bowl. He planned to take Daisy, Loren, and Lily, but Lily wasn't ready to venture into a crowded stadium. So he sold the tickets. It's been easier to bond with Ryke during the first quarter of this game than it has every single interaction with Lo.

Don't know why that is.

Ryke stands several feet from the mounted TV above the fireplace. Unable to sit with all the adrenaline pumping.

"Ref's gotta be working for the Bills," I say to Ryke from the couch. Luna has chosen a seat on my lap. Her legs are draped sideways, her Eagles jersey so big that it hangs below her kneecaps. But she's wearing black leggings underneath. My hand has traveled underneath her jersey more than once.

We thought we were doing a public service taking less space on the couch, but I can tell we're being "observed" like we're a new species. We've never tried to tone it down, but I know the PDA has increased since the holidays. As we've fallen deeper into this relationship, we're just doing what's natural and we're *naturally* more physical with each other.

I don't mind the stares, and Luna's too busy wrestling with an Eagles headband to notice. She made it from scratch. Glued on the poms and everything. But one of the green poms fell off on the way here, and she's been trying to superglue it back together.

The ref upholds the call after the challenge, and I glare at the TV.

We were almost at first down. Now we're punting. Still 0-0. Anyone's game. But I don't like going into the second quarter without points. Makes me all nervous and shit.

Last night, Luna asked me why I love football so much. I told her it's not football. It's the Eagles. 'Cause at one o'clock on a Sunday when I barely had enough for a carton of eggs, the bar down the block would let just about any underage soul in as long as they were wearing

Philly merch. I'd cheer with them during touchdowns. I'd scream with them during interceptions. It was a shared experience that I wasn't receiving at home. And then one day, it just felt like my church. Like every Sunday, I could count on the Eagles. Thick or thin—they'd be playing and they were good enough to have a shot to win.

I never really had a shot.

And I dunno, there's something about the city I love being good enough. It felt like no matter how many people thought *I* wasn't good enough—they'd always be mine. I'd be theirs. I told Luna all this, and then I said, "Maybe it sounds silly 'cause I don't know anyone else who loves a city as much as I do." I ran a hand through my hair. "I'm busier now than when I grew up, so I don't catch every game. But I check the scores."

She shook her head. "It doesn't sound silly. Your love of Philly is one of the things I love about you."

That surprised me. "Ah, so you don't think the Eagles tattoo is a bit much?" It's on the back of my calf. I don't even see it half the time but all the assholes walking behind me sure do.

She smiled wide. "I admit, I like the shrimp smoking on a cigarette a little more." That one is right next to my Eagles tat.

I laughed. "Girl, you already have my heart. Stop trying to steal it again."

It makes me feel better that I opened up to Luna last night. I'm trying my best to keep being that open book—but I'm worried she's going to ask something that's harder to answer. My love of the Eagles—easy. My mom's last name—complicated.

It's so complicated that I've been glad she never brought it up again since she broached the topic in December. Maybe she forgot or I'm just biding my sweet time to get my head screwed straight.

Luna grumbles something under breath as she tries for a second time to attach the pom. "The glue must not be working," she mutters to herself. She shifts around on my lap, and I focus on the sweaty QB on screen to stop myself from getting hard.

She's too cute.

Her little grunts in frustration shouldn't be turning me on. No, sir. No, Bob. (Don't know who Bob is, but I'm picturing a wrinkled geriatric to keep me soft.)

Another grunt. My dick stirs. Okay, we have to find a different tactic.

"I can help," I tell her and just as Luna squeezes the tube of superglue, it squirts out and lands on the top of her hand—right when I grab *that* hand.

Our eyes latch as we realize what just happened.

My thumb. Superglued. To the top of her hand.

"First down, let's go!" Winona hollers and bounces around her mom, until Daisy links arms with her daughter and they bounce in a circle together.

Clapping envelops the living room. I would join the applause. Thumb is out of commission though. Luna tries tugging her hand away, but there's little give.

"Kitchen," I tell her, about to pick her up, but she springs to her feet first while holding my hand.

There are too many people and sets of eyeballs to know who's watching. I don't really care if they think we're taking a snack break or a make-out break or a break for a quickie. We're gonna be ourselves regardless. We haven't been fixating on outside opinions...except, probably, her mom's.

That's pretty much how I feel about the media too. Luna and I don't feel a need to announce our relationship. It'll only put more paparazzi on our ass. And we have nothing to prove to anyone.

I just wish they'd call us Lunnelly.

We're at the sink, the only ones in the kitchen. The door is shut, muffling the TV and the groans in the living room.

"I'm sorry," Luna says quietly. "I didn't know it'd projectile out of the tube. I wouldn't have done it that close." Warm water rushes over our skin. She rubs at the glued spot with soap.

"Why are you apologizing?" I ask. "I'd let you superglue me to you any day of the week."

"Any body part?" Her smile touches her eyes.

I can't look away from her. "Only the best body parts. Dick included."

"I'd rather it be inside me." Her voice is so soft, I almost miss it. But yeah, I heard. Bionic ears and all, and I recognize the origin alright. It's not crumbling me.

I'd rather it be inside me. I repeat her words in my head, and blood rushes straight down to my cock. Fuck. I hold Luna's gaze more than I check out her body. Her desire is fisting me. "One day," I breathe, voice huskier with arousal.

Flush ascends her neck, and her knees knock together, her ankles crossing.

I grin. Yeah, I speak Luna's sex language, that's for fucking sure. I think she speaks mine too. I'm trying to force myself not to pick her up. Not to put her on the kitchen counter. *Not in the Hale House. Not again.* Respect—I'm trying to be better about it.

"Soon?" she whispers. I can see she's eager. She's been eager. I'm the one pumping the brakes—and part of me thinks I shouldn't. Part of me thinks I should keep stalling.

I'm torn. "I dunno, maybe."

"What if the Eagles win?" she wonders. "Would you want celebratory sex?"

I start to smile again. "If I wasn't your pseudo-first, I'd say *yes.*"

"Losing my pseudo-virginity after the Eagles win the Super Bowl sounds like the best pseudo-first time though."

"Not denying that." Our eyes fasten for a hot beat like we're both considering it. Then her attention swings to the kitchen's breakfast table, and blood drains right from her face.

The table is circular and farmhouse style.

It's also brand new.

We saw it when we arrived, but now that we're alone in the kitchen, it's erected a new wave of tension.

"We have to pay for the table," Luna declares, just as the pull on our skin gives under the warm, soapy water. Now detached, I take a couple strained steps back.

"I'll pay," I offer. "It was my idea." I'd do just about anything to absolve Luna's guilt.

She shakes her head and wipes her wet hands on a dish rag. "I didn't say *no* that night. It's not all on you. My mom should be around here..." Her parents weren't in the living room earlier, but they aren't in the kitchen either. "We can do this together."

I nod, down for the idea. "Only one problem."

"What?"

"Your mom hasn't been able to look me in the eye since December."

Her shoulders slacken. "Then maybe it's time to confront her."

"You sure?" My chest tightens as I visualize Lily shoving me out of the house again. Don't know if I can take that happening twice.

Luna nods repeatedly. "I don't want you to feel like you're on pins and needles around my mom. She probably doesn't want that either. This could all be one big miscommunication."

"Yeah, alright." I dry my hands on a dishtowel. Cheering ignites from the living room, and the pressure on my chest heavies tenfold.

I instinctively stare at the door, towards the source of the noise. Luna follows my gaze, and I can't be sure if I look distraught. I just don't know the next time the Eagles will be at the Super Bowl.

She pokes me in the shoulder, which captures my attention in a snap, and I'm smiling. I almost ask her to poke me again.

"You go watch the game," she says sternly, like an order. "It's a necessity."

"Nah, me making you come is a necessity." I grin more off her rosy cheeks. "We both need it and want it. This, though—it's just a want, space babe."

"But—"

"I'm coming with you. The game is..." Can't say unimportant. Can't say I won't miss it. "It's only the second quarter."

"We'll have you back in a jiffy. Promise." She raises her pinky.

I hook her pinky with mine, then with the other hand, I clasp her cheek and go in for a promise on her planet. She's already smiling as we touch the tips of our tongues. My love for her explodes in me, detonating the pressure on my chest.

I ease the promise into a hotter kiss, causing her back to thump into the kitchen cabinets. I bear my weight against her, our tongues wrestling and lips melding. Her body trembles against my flexed muscles like she's on the verge of a climax. *Fuck, Luna.* I clasp the back of her skull, and I have to stop.

Stop.

I break apart, both of us out of breath.

I'm hard as a rock and adjust myself in my jeans.

She lifts her gaze off my crotch to say, "A promise on your planet and mine."

I start smiling. "Double the promise, double the fun." I throw up an *I love you* sign and swallow the arousal out of my throat. "Where to?"

She scans the empty kitchen and half-eaten bowls of salsa and French onion dip. "Uh, I think my mom might be in the garage. We store extra pantry items out there." Yeah, I've seen the shelves with cases of Fizz Life and mounds of toilet paper. Comes with raising four kids and hosting parties.

I follow to the door that leads to the garage. She twists the knob. "That's weird," she mutters. "I think it's stuck." She rams her shoulder against the door while turning, but it doesn't budge.

"Let me try."

She lets me pass. I give it a good turn with half my brute strength, and the entire brass knob breaks off the door as it swings open.

I'm about to congratulate myself.

But I freeze. Oh fuck.

Her parents are going at it.

Luna whirls around, her forehead to my chest, but she's also shielding her eyes with her palms. I hug her against me, about to draw her back into the kitchen.

"OhmygodLo!" Lily shrieks on the hood of the parked Bugatti.

Loren Hale has his hand down the front of Lily's leggings. He peers over his shoulder, curses, and then tries to catch Lily, but she bolts for the shelf of paper towels. Ducking out of sight.

I'm pulling Luna out of the garage, and we return to the empty kitchen together. Luna is hiding in her Eagles jersey.

She only hides in her shirt when she's extremely upset, and my stomach knots. "Where'd my sad alien go?"

"To the land of shame."

"Fuck that," I curse and toss the broken knob on the counter. Swiftly, I pick her up, and her legs wrap around my waist. I join Luna under her jersey. It's dark, and her nipples poke at her thin, lacey white bra. I can feel the heat radiating between her legs. But I don't focus on it.

Glitter sparkles the corners of her eyes. She holds the back of my neck. "This feels a lot like karma."

Could be. I try to read her face. "You alright?" She looks swallowed by remorse, and all we did was try to open a door.

"I feel really guilty," Luna murmurs. "Like I'm setting my mom back in recovery for her sex addiction and I *keep* setting her back."

"Have you talked to her about it?"

"No, but…" Her face contorts in several anguished emotions.

"Luna, *Luna*." I slide my hand off her lower back and up to her cheek. "Why are you beating yourself up about this?"

"Because I don't want to hurt her."

"You've gotta talk to her 'cause I don't think she'd want you to feel like this either."

Luna fights back tears, then nods repeatedly. "Okayokay."

I kiss her lightly on the lips, then pull my head out of her jersey. She slides down my chest, her feet thudding to the floorboards. Someone walks into the kitchen, and we're no longer alone.

Her parents have arrived. Lily is beet-red and half-hidden behind Lo's back.

Her dad's glare is deadly. "The door was locked, Paul."

I point to the broken knob. "We thought it was stuck."

"*I* thought it was stuck," Luna clarifies, her voice shaky. My concern flares, but she steps out toward Lily. "Mom, I'm really, *really* sorry."

"It's okay." Lily sounds out of breath like she ran a marathon. "*It's okay.* Luna?"

Luna wipes at the sudden tears streaming down her face.

It's crushing me. Seeing her cry.

"No, don't cry," Lily rushes out to her daughter, and they immediately embrace in a tight hug. "It's not your fault. It'snotyourfault."

Lo's glower softens on them. "We didn't know you were dating the goddamn Hulk."

"Me neither." Luna sniffs, rubbing at her eyes. Her voice sounds a little brighter. "I'll still love him when he turns green."

I smile, but honestly, I hope I'm never consumed with that much rage. I've already been struggling to rid this bubbling hatred toward my family. It's been surfacing since she got kidnapped.

Lo doesn't like what she said. His glare returns tenfold. Attention back on me. "You," he says. "Come with me."

"Knew we'd make it to third base at some point." It's supposed to lighten the air.

Her dad sucks at scavenger hunts because he can't find the humor in this one. He's locked his glare on me like I'm the target of NASA's ballistic missiles. "Paul—"

Luna jumps in, "We were going to talk to Mom together. That's why we went in the garage."

"Let them talk," Lo tells me. "You're going to help me with the burgers." It's not a question. No room to put up a fight.

Not when I just caught him fingering his wife.

36

PAUL DONNELLY

Luna's dad takes out burgers from the fridge and a jacket off a chair. I avoid the stares from the living room as we head to the backyard. My neck strains from trying to see the score on our way out.

I think I saw a 7. Maybe an 8.

Can't even worry about the game when Lo looks ready to throw me on the grill with the beef. He puts on a red fleece jacket while my nipples perk from the cold. Didn't think to bring a coat. Knew this would be an indoor shindig and whatnot.

Lo and I are the only two souls on the back patio. Steam rises off the heated pool, the water glowing blue, and the trees and fence are coated in an icy layer of snow.

Just as Lo lights the grill, the backdoor swings open. Ryke steps out, slipping a green Columbia jacket on. "I thought I was grilling," he tells his brother.

"We've got it," Lo says with a curt raise of the spatula. "Thanks, but no thanks."

Ryke's hardened gaze bounces between me and Lo. Then he gives him a look I can't decipher.

"Jesus, I'm not going to murder him," Lo says. "He's fine." He nods towards the house. "Go back to the game. Wave a foam middle finger. Flirt with your wife."

"I'm not worried about you murdering him," Ryke retorts.

Lo glares. "I know that. We know that. Can you go?" He rattles the spatula. "Seriously. Go be a craisin. Jump off the roof with your better half. Stop..." He bites back the phrase, but I fill in the blanks. *Stop worrying about me.*

"Fucking fine," Ryke mutters. He opens a storage cabinet on the shingled wall. Not for outdoor pool storage, I realize. It's housing a TV. Before he leaves, he draws the TV out and powers-on the game with a remote. Then he sheds his jacket, handing it to me.

The brothers share a glare-off.

I'm wondering if I should take the jacket or not.

Is that like siding with the Meadows? I only wanna be on Team Hale.

I shake my head at Ryke. "Nah, I like the cold. Keeps my brain all frosty and my dick limp."

Lo waves the spatula at me like I've made my point.

Ryke shoves the jacket in my chest. "Just fucking have it." As he leaves, I feel bad I didn't thank him.

Could've really kissed his toes for putting on the game out here. I don't think Lo would've confessed to having an outdoor TV.

I glance at the screen.

The score is 7-7.

Fuuuck.

Luna's dad tosses burgers on the grill, then mutes the game with the remote. But he leaves the closed captions on. So there is a God.

"My brother thinks you're too big of a stressor for me," Lo admits. "What do you think?"

Feels like a trick question. Then again, most conversations I've had with Luna's dad have felt like I'm one breath away from being hurled on the street. Thought things were getting better. During the holidays, he'd been appreciative when he realized I bought Luna a new phone so she didn't have to deal with harassing texts or calls. Even more so when I looped him in on the whole situation. Told him about Keagan Bell and his friends from New York, how they were behind the messages.

I learned Loren Hale had, in fact, gotten them blacklisted from popular clubs Luna frequented.

For a second there, we were working together again. But it was to protect his daughter. Our common ground has always been about protecting Luna. It's the one thing we can both stand on together.

But walking in on him and Lily probably threw me into Monopoly jail. No passing Go.

Mulling over his question, I splay Ryke's jacket over a patio chair. *My brother thinks you're too big of a stressor for me. What do you think?*

"I think there's probably enough reasons why you *could* be stressed out around me. I mean, I'm still talking to my dad and wearing a wire. It's not something you wanna be reminded of. I get it."

I am that night.

The Night to Forget.

The night Luna's dad and I shared, and even now, my eyes burn reimagining the distress in Luna's voice and Lily's voice over the phone. Coming up on the busted-out windows of the rental car. Unsure of what we'd even find. It's a lot.

It's been a lot.

His brows crinkle. "What about you?"

"What about me?"

He's frustrated for a second and shuts the lid on the grill. "Luna said you went to therapy with her. How'd that go?"

"It went fine. As much as I don't get along with her, I think Dr. Raven is good for Luna."

"How'd it go for *you*?" he clarifies, almost pissy about it.

I start to smile. "Why so interested in me, Luna's dad?"

"You're dating my daughter, *Paul*. Sue me for asking. Or don't. Because I'd bankrupt you." He flashes a half-smile.

I laugh. "You can have my pennies. I'm rich without 'em."

Lo smiles a bit softer at this, like he understands what real wealth is, too. "Was that your first time in therapy?" He reopens the grill lid, checking the burgers.

"I've been before. Never liked it. I still don't."

"It took me a while to get into it," he admits. "Once you get over the *sharing* part, it's easier."

"That's the whole part."

"Exactly." He gives me another dry smile.

"It's just not for me. I don't like sitting there knowing someone's analyzing me. Puts me on the defensive, and anyway, I'm doing fine without it." I speak faster, hoping to change topics. Wind picks up, and I shove my hands in my jeans pockets. Goosebumps are tiny mountains on my arms. "About earlier in the kitchen—"

"We don't need to bring it up," Lo cuts in, his voice a blade again.

I tuck my arms against my ribs. "I thought…maybe…"

"Maybe what? That we're even?"

"Well, yeah." My breath smokes the frigid air. "Lily walked in on us. Luna and I walked in on—"

"I'll stop you there." Lo spins back to me, his gaze darkening. "This is my house. I'll do whatever I want behind a locked door. What you and my daughter did—not equivalent."

I'm struck into silence. 'Cause he's not wrong.

His jawline sharpens in the next breath. "Put the jacket on."

Why? I frown at him like he's jumped chapters in the strange book we've been writing together. "I thought you didn't want me to have the jacket?"

"I also don't want to murder you, Paul." He points the spatula at my face. "Your lips are blue."

I make a confused face at him, then thread my arms through the Columbia jacket. My skin doesn't instantly warm. "Thanks for caring about my lips, Luna's dad."

His face twists through too many emotions to count. "Is that hard for you to believe?"

"Is what?"

"That I'd care about you?"

"Fuck no!! Where's our D?!" Ryke's thunderous voice can be heard inside, and my stomach takes a nosedive into the ground. I barely glance at the screen to see the Bills got a touchdown.

I'm cold—when maybe his words should make me feel warm, but it's just weird. I run a hand against the back of my neck.

Lo grimaces at himself. "I never want you to see me and group me in with your dad—I never want to do *anything* to you that'd warrant that. But maybe I already have."

I shake my head and smile. "Nothing about you two is similar. Don't worry." I zip up the jacket. "You're a good dad to Luna, to Xander, to all your kids. One of the greats." I touch my temple and point to him. "I'm mentally alright. You didn't fuck me up. I'm not a child you raised. I'm the adult who's dating your daughter."

Lo stares harder at me, his brows cinching again. "Do you ever think about that night?"

A rock ascends in my throat.

That night.

The car.

Driving towards Lily and Luna. I blink. Lo and I are heightened in an *annihilating* helplessness. We can do nothing but listen to the call. We drive. We stop. We drive. We run. I blink back to the patio. The grill. The cold.

"Yeah, I think about it."

"Have you talked to anyone?" he asks.

"I can't unload that on Luna." She doesn't remember that night. I'll never paint that horrific picture for her. I don't want to.

"Farrow?" he asks.

"I dunno, briefly." I stuff my hands in the jacket. My cheeks take the brunt of the biting wind. "Have you told Ryke about it?"

"Yeah, everything."

My brows spring. "Everything? The car ride there?"

Lo flips over the burgers. "Yep. I threw up afterwards, too." He shuts the grill lid. "My brother is pushy, but he's been the best thing that's ever happened to me. Time and time again. Most days, I don't feel like I deserve him, but that's my own shit I have to work through." He puts the spatula on a tray, then rotates back to me. "You don't want to talk about it with anyone?"

"I don't need to," I tell him. "I appreciate that you care about me, I do, but I don't need it." I see that's why he brought me out here. I'm not a Lost Boy that needs a Peter Pan. I barely even had time to be a child. "I've been doing alright all the years without that."

Lo's stare is intrusive like he's trying to excavate my soul. "I don't get you."

I shift on my heels. "Not the first time you mentioned that."

"No, I really don't," he says with a deep sincerity. "I'm trying to understand if I'm *cataclysmically* weaker than you or you're just better at hiding it. Because how—*how* do you go through what we did and just shrug it off?"

I blink. My eyes scratch from the dry cold. I could make a joke. Tell him I'm just better than him, but that lie sinks heavy in my stomach like a thirty-ton weight. Dig deep enough, I know I'm not any stronger than Lo. I'm just used to running away from my demons.

Lo meets most of his like they have tee times every Monday. Whereas I try not to shake hands with any of mine.

I open my mouth. Close it. That thirty-ton weight has shoved into my throat.

Lo keeps staring. Keeps excavating. Then he says, "I care about you."

Those four words plunge inside me, and I shake my head, on automatic.

"It bothers you that fucking much," he says sharply. "To have someone *care* about you?"

I scrape a hand through my hair. Unable to swallow the lump.

"I was there, Paul," he reminds me. "I. Was. There." I see his breath. "You don't have to tell me what you felt or what you went through. I was there."

"I wish you weren't," I whisper, my voice low.

"Why?" Lo is earnest, a genuine need to get to know me. But not just what kind of socks I like or how I take my eggs in the morning. He wants to know how I'm feeling. How I'm coping. How I'm going to wake up tomorrow and be okay.

He cares about me.

I've never really had that from…from…

Sucking in a sharp breath, I run my arm across my nose. But my snot dries when it hits the air. "I'm just not used to this," I say.

He nods like he understands all of a sudden. "I know I haven't been easy—"

"No, it's not *you*," I say. "I'm not used to this from…from…"

His gaze sinks into mine, and a realization slackens his shoulders. "From a parent?"

My jaw sets, trying not to cry. My eyes sear as I restrain emotion. Even nodding will admit what I don't want to. That my parents don't care about me—not really. Maybe they never did.

But maybe they could.

Maybe they're starting to.

I end up choking out, "I've never needed it. Maybe at one point, when I was a kid, but…that time is long gone, you know?"

"No, I don't know," he shakes his head. "Because at twenty-nine, I still hoped my dad cared about me. I needed that from him up until the day he died."

What Farrow once told me comes surging back, and I mutter, "It's something I learned to live without then."

Lo brushes a hand through his windswept hair, then reroutes the conversation. "When's the last time you talked to your dad?"

"WOOOOOOO!" Cheering from inside cuts into our talk, and a quick glimpse of the TV, I see the Eagles scored but so did the Bills at some point. 14-17. I should be happy the Eagles are closing the lead, but Lo's question occupies my focus.

"We talked this morning," I tell him. "He asked me where I was gonna watch the game. I think he was planning on inviting me somewhere, but he didn't when I said I'd be here."

Lo adds slices of cheddar to the burgers. "Have you seen him?"

I nod. "Heaven's Hoagies. Last week for lunch. I wore a wire for the cops." They've been happy with my cooperation, and they're still hoping to discover the motive behind the kidnapping. Not sure if I'll ever uncover that sort of information from my dad. He's too careful with his words, and he says he's been told shit from uncles and cousins.

Sometimes I believe him.

Other times, I wonder if he'd even share more than I need to know.

Lo plates the burgers. "Hold that thought." He's quick to take the food inside, and when he returns, he's carrying a few packs of hotdogs. I help toss them on the grill.

"Luna," he starts. "She told me something about him."

That sounds foreboding. "About my dad?"

Lo moves the hot dogs around the grate with a pair of tongs. He's choosing his words carefully. "She overheard your dad talking to you on the phone. She wouldn't tell me what exactly was said. Except that he'd like to meet me—"

"That's not happening," I cut in. "You're not meeting him."

He glares. "Let's table it."

"Nah, let's burn it."

"I'm not planning to lash out at him for what happened. I won't push him to relapse."

That's not what I'm afraid of. I hadn't even thought about that. I'm more so worried my dad will disappoint me and prove he's just trying to gain a foothold into the wealth of the Hales.

I'm quiet.

Lo sighs, "That's not what I wanted to bring up. Luna—she mentioned there was something else your dad said. She told me to ask you about it. So I'm asking you."

Fuck.

Yeah, I know which conversation he's referring to. It's the only time Luna has overheard a phone call with my dad. We were in the car outside Thirsty Goose. Same night Greg Calloway died.

I narrow my eyes at the halftime show on the TV. "What he said was wrong," I tell Lo. "It's not who I am."

"I had a dad who said some stuff that I'd never want reflected on me. Not in a million years. If you think I'll judge you for who your father is, you're wrong."

"You're still gonna be worried about your daughter being associated with me—"

"I'm not worried about that anymore, Paul. Look at where we are."

"Out in the cold," I say, still seeing my breath. "Freezing our asses off for some wieners."

He makes an unamused face. "You're so funny, I think I heard the dead bodies I buried laughing back here."

I grin. "Good ears. Been told I have better ones though, and your dead friends aren't chuckling hard enough."

"I don't have friends to bury."

"How'd you know I want to be cremated?"

Lo smiles at that. "You think we're friends?"

"Getting there." My grin softens, remembering my goal. Be best friends with Loren Hale. It's so close, I can taste it. That juicy scent of a burning hot dog.

"Okay, *friend.* What'd your dad say?" He's asking genuinely. He looks me over and there's a sudden calmness in his amber eyes. I could make another joke.

The door is open to run away from this conversation. Run out. It's so easy to take those doors. But Lo, Luna, the Hales—they're the last people I wanna be running from.

"The hot dogs are burning," I tell him.

"I don't care about the hot dogs."

Right. "My dad was giving me shitty advice. That's what Luna overheard."

He frowns but looks on patiently. He's not begging for more. Not pushing.

It's easy to hold his gaze. Even as sharp-edged as his features are, there is no malice in Lo towards me. No hatred. No anger or fury.

I run my fingers through my hair a couple times. "You're gonna tell me not to trust him."

"Then maybe you shouldn't."

I wince, stopping myself short of defending Sean Donnelly. I smear a hand down my face, rotating away from Luna's dad. Then I come back to say, "He told me to put a hole in the condom."

Lo is all ice. He doesn't even blink. "He what?"

"I would never—"

"No, no, *no*." He raises a hand for me to shut up. "This isn't about you. This is about your dad wanting you to get my daughter pregnant, for what? A cash-grab?"

"He knows I'd be set for life. It was advice for *my* well-being. I don't think it was about what he could get out of a potential Hale grandbaby." I'm hoping. "And anyway, it doesn't even matter."

He scrunches his face. "It will matter. Unless you don't plan on having kids."

"You want me to have kids with your daughter?" I ask like he's flown to some planet I've never heard of or even read about in Luna's fics.

"I want whatever my daughter wants."

She wants kids. This is confirmation, but I've known how much she loves babies, so it's not a surprise. My stomach churns. "Makes sense."

Lo lets the hot dogs blacken to a crisp. "Do you think about your future with Luna?"

Do I think about our future?

"No," I tell him. "I don't need to think about it. She is my future." It's so clear. It's so bright. "It's all I know."

I don't care if there's a white picket fence. I don't care if there's a four-poster bed. I don't even care if we only have a hundred bucks to our name.

She's all I really need.

But I'm not completely sure what she needs from me. I'm scared I won't be able to give it to her.

These talks of our future haven't come up much. She's likely not thinking too far ahead anyway. She's been concentrated on finding her footing in the present, and I'm just glad we have now, today, with each other. Anything more feels like we're stealing sand from an hourglass.

Lo considers this, but he must be recalling what I initially confessed. He's glaring at the pool. "I hate your father."

"I wanna say *ditto*," I tell him. "But there are times I think maybe I still love him. And it's a fucked-up kind of love 'cause I thought about murder when he told me that shit."

Lo comes unglued, his shoulders relaxing. "You can love him," he says. "Just don't let that love give him the power to influence you." He says it like he's speaking from experience.

"He doesn't have that kind of hold on me."

Lo stares at me, uncertain. Only other person who's looked at me similarly, where it concerns my dad, is Farrow. I shake it off and think about the fact that Luna let me share this information with her dad myself. "Luna's a good cookie, you know," I say. "We're both doing this whole relationship thing for the first time together. I'd say she's excelling."

"You make it easy for her," Lo says, and it sounds like genuine praise.

My lips lift. "Thanks for the compliment. Should I be expecting the fruit basket soon?"

"What'd you say you like? Dried prunes?"

Is he trying to give me the runs? "Granny smiths and green grapes, but I could down some prunes. They've never done me dirty." Using a spatula, I scoop the hot dogs off the grill and onto a tray. They're edible, at least.

He scrapes the grill plate with a brush. "If you ever change your mind and need to talk about that night, I'm here." He motions to the tray. "Can you take those inside?"

I figure he'll come in right behind me. After dropping off the hot dogs in the kitchen, I peek out the window. Luna's dad is sitting on a wrought-iron patio chair, camped out in front of the TV like he plans to finish the game by the pool. Alone.

Without thinking, I grab two PuraFons water bottles from the fridge and head back outside. I pull a chair next to Luna's dad and take a seat.

Confusion bunches his brows. "The big screen is inside," he says like I'm delusional. "Along with *heat*."

I unscrew the water and take a swig, clearing a knot in my throat. I recap it slowly, and I manage to say, "You asked me...if you're weaker than me or if I'm just better at hiding it." I glance over at him. "I'm just better at running from it, I think."

"Running from it, huh?" Lo says in thought. "That sounds exhausting."

"I'm not tired." I bow forward, my elbows on my knees. I rip the edges of the plastic label with my short fingernail. "I think I could run until I die. I think I would've. Then I had to stop and go back..."

"For security."

"For Luna," I say. *It was always about Luna.* "I've talked to Farrow about it a bit. That night—I let it catch me. It rooted itself in me. It's *anger* like I've never felt before. I'm not an angry person," I tell him. "Never really have been. But sometimes I'm just so full of fucking rage about what happened." I wipe at the wet creases of my eyes. "I've never hated parts of myself until now. But how the hell do you stop being angry at how much pain the girl you love was put through?"

I'm scared. Terrified. That he's going to kick me out of his house. Tell me I'm not worthy of his daughter. That I can't be around her if I'm feeling this way.

"She's okay," Lo breathes.

I cut my gaze to him, my nose flaring as my eyes well up again.

"She's not in pain. She's okay," Lo nods to me a few times. "Luna survived with you that night. It might not feel like it because of her memories, but she got out. You got her out, Donnelly." His eyes redden as emotion barrels into him too. "She's not in pain. She's the happiest I've seen her in a long time."

I rub at my eyes with my fist, his words nearly opening me at the core. I've never wanted to hurt her. The mere fucking thought has woken me up in the middle of the night.

Lo leans closer and puts a hand on my shoulder like I've seen fathers do to sons in movies. "It's okay."

I shut my eyes, silent tears falling against my cupped palm around my eyes.

"It's okay," he breathes. "It really is."

I exhale a long breath. "It doesn't feel like it. I should be better for Luna." I unzip my jacket and use the bottom of my shirt to wipe my face. "She deserves more."

"She doesn't expect more from you." His brows furrow. "Why are you expecting so damn much from yourself?"

I've never wanted to put anyone out. I've never been a shackle or a burden, and the weight of whatever I'm carrying is *heavy*. A load that my girlfriend doesn't need.

I can't say any of it though. I can't get it out.

Her dad squeezes my shoulder. "You're doing your best. It's enough."

I take a deeper breath, letting that sink in. *It's enough. She's not in pain. She's okay.* I got her out. She survived with me.

She's happy.

I think she's doing even better than I am, really. With a stronger breath, I swig my water, then pass him the second PuraFons bottle. We both glance at the TV.

"Dammit," I mutter.

The score isn't looking too good.

We spend the next minutes talking over the game, which is fine by me since the Bills are leading 17-20. Our defense looks like Jell-O.

Lo tells me about the time Connor and Rose dressed as Batman and Catwoman for Comic-Con. I tell him the story of how I got the shrimp tattoo. Snuck into a concert festival and did it on a dare. Lo shares about the time he forced Garrison Abbey to a Halloween horror maze only for Ryke to punch a clown and get kicked out in the end.

I laugh at that one. The air isn't so thick.

He's asking about the cover-up tattoo on my other calf. I inked over the names of all the clients I've had. Xander's included.

"I finished it the other day," I tell him. It'd been a geometric mess. Didn't have time until recently to fix it. I managed to reconfigure the lines into an otherworldly planet. Bluish and purple, how I imagine Thebula looks from the stars.

"You've really read all her stories?" Lo asks, and that's how we start talking about Thebula. How good of a writer Luna is. How she never gives herself the credit she deserves.

Two seconds left in the game now.

The Bills have the ball. Neither have scored since the last field goal. Still 17-20, and I'm losing all hope the Eagles will pull this one out. Chances are too slim. I feel hollowed open by more than just this loss, and strangely a bright moment tonight has been talking to Lo. So I tell him about the bachelorette party in New Haven where I ended up getting paid after a threesome.

He's not judgy about it. Just asks, "Did you know they would pay you?"

I shake my head. "Nah," I say. "I don't know if I would've done it if I did. But, not gonna lie, it was the easiest cash I'd ever earned."

"And you were eighteen." He hangs on to this part of the story.

"Looked older," I admit. "I'd been to the gym a ton."

"You were still a kid."

I wince. "Nah, eighteen is a legal adult. But I left home when I was just a kid."

"Don't remind me," Lo says sharply. "Because it does make me want to commit murder."

"My grandmom is already dead, so you're gonna have to find a time machine."

"She's probably not worth the jail time," Lo says casually.

"She isn't. She wasn't," I agree.

He knows she was my neglectful guardian when my parents were in prison. And a part of me hurts because I should be talking about all this with Luna rather than her dad, but it's easier talking to him 'cause I'm not dating him.

I can't break his heart. He can't really break mine.

And it feels good sharing with him. Maybe 'cause talking to her dad absolves me of the guilt of not telling her yet.

"If you need—" Lo's voice is cut short as we both shoot to our feet.

No…no fucking way.

Our defense (never said a bad word about 'em) just grabbed the ball after a fumble. Ten seconds left on the clock.

He runs.

He runs farther.

And farther.

He makes it to the endzone.

A pick 6.

A pick fucking 6!

Lo cheers, and we're somehow hugging. I'm screaming so hard my lungs hurt. I can't believe it.

The Eagles win the Super Bowl.

37

LUNA HALE

I can't sleep. The colorful swirls on my ceiling don't ease my mind like they usually do, so I lean over to my nightstand and smack a hand on the galaxy projector. It shuts off instantly, and the room darkens.

My brain does not shut off with the lights.

I keep thinking about him.

Donnelly.

The Super Bowl.

We came back to the penthouse after the game, and I pumped myself up for some epic, earth-shattering sex. I thought there was *at least* an eighty-five percent chance we'd cross the finish line this time. But I am not Jane Cobalt because my math was waaaaaay off.

Donnelly and I kissed and felt each other up for point-five seconds before he got a call from SFE. They wanted to "strategize" about the Fizzle mock panel, so he had to leave, and he didn't return to the penthouse until one in the morning.

Yes, I was still awake when he came home.

No, he didn't come to my bedroom like a sex god ready to claim my pussy in front of the imperial elite on my home planet.

He didn't come to my bedroom at all.

Which is strange.

We've slept in the same bed nearly every night since Christmas

Eve. Whether it's his room or my room, we'll crawl beneath the sheets, and he'll hold me against his chest. I'll curl up in the warmth of his strong arms and the sweet, sexy embrace. Spooning while falling asleep *is* dangerous territory, which might be why it's my favorite.

He gets me off just about every night, and I've grown to crave him in my mouth and to see him come.

I was staring up at my makeshift galaxy in anticipation, but it's slowly morphed into utter disappointment. And I shouldn't feel *disappointed* that Donnelly didn't bang on my door at 1 a.m. He probably thought I was in a deep hibernating sleep, especially since I have class with Professor Rochester tomorrow.

I groan just thinking about *that* stressor. No. I really don't want to trade in thoughts about Donnelly for thoughts about Wyatt Rochester.

So I replay the exact moment when Donnelly received the Epsilon phone call. He grinded forward into a deeper kiss, his hand kneading my breast, and I gripped the back of his head. My fingers threaded the soft strands of his hair. I melted under the weight of his body and how his muscles flexed with each tiny shift of our legs, each sultry kiss.

Then the phone rang. Little wrinkles creased his brow as he patted around the comforter for his cell. I couldn't read his facial expressions during the call. But his six-three build began to tense, and his usual light gaze went heavy.

"I've gotta go to an SFE meeting." He kissed me one more time, then climbed off the bed, scrounging around for his pants. "See you later?"

"Yeah," I replied. "See ya." The dumbest reply of the century! I should have asked, "What do you mean by later? Later tonight? Or later tomorrow?" Or I should have said, "Paul Donnelly, please define the definition of 'later' for someone not of your species."

You know what—I think Epsilon called him away on purpose just to fuck with him. Why else would they have a meeting the night the Eagles win the Super Bowl? The mock panel is two weeks away!

Ugh, I hate those cockblockers.

I roll on my side to see the clock.

1 a.m.

Orion lets out doggy snores at the foot of my bed, and I try to think of something good. A decent memory of tonight: My mom never blamed Donnelly and me for walking in on her and my dad.

To escape the noise of the Super Bowl party, my mom and I talked in my childhood bedroom. We sat on squishy Pizza Planet beanbags, and I scanned the relic of a room. It was mostly how I remembered it. OG Luna left most of our superhero collectibles there. I'd been wondering why my ceramic Spider-Man mug was cracked into pieces and how come the Anakin Skywalker figurine was decapitated. But I didn't ask about it.

My mom seemed nervous, tentative. Probably because involuntary tears left my eyes in the kitchen, and she knew I was blaming myself.

I held my pom headband, braving glances at her.

She had been off her crutches. Just a boot on her foot. All her bruises had vanished, and she had a cute temporary Eagles tattoo on her cheek.

"I'm sorry," I started.

"No, it's not your fault," Mom reiterated again. "Your dad and I—we shouldn't have been doing anything during the game. It was our mistake. My mistake." She paused, her face reddening. "You didn't see too much, did you?"

"Not really," I told her honestly. "You were smooshed together so I turned around superfast on instinct."

She smiled but her cheeks were still a deep-red. "You have better instincts than me." I watched her pick up an old Hufflepuff plushie.

"I wouldn't say that," I whispered, the guilt surging like an incoming tsunami. "Mom, if I-I've been making it harder on you…"

Her face fell. "What do you mean?"

"Your addiction. If I've been causing you to regress, I-I'm sorry. Really sorry—"

"Nonono," she said quickly, then tossed the plushie aside to scoot closer and clasp my hands. "Please, *please* don't blame yourself."

I swallowed a knot. "But...but I know you catching Donnelly and me in the kitchen, that probably affected you, and it-it's probably why you've been avoiding him."

She squeezed my hands, and her eyes carried an emotion I didn't expect. *Guilt.* It was like looking in the mirror. *How could she feel guilty?* She innocently walked in on us, and it was *her* kitchen. "I'm working through it...and I don't want you...I need you to know..." She huffed out a breath, struggling for the words. "I can overthink and spiral, and it'd be hard for me to walk in on *any* of my kids in that kind of position." She spoke fast. "Not just you. Okay?"

"But it was me," I muttered.

Mom thought this through. "When your brother was little, he'd forget to knock on the door before coming in the bedroom. Maximoff," she clarified. "Your dad wanted to ground him because he kept making the same mistake, and one day, he almost walked in on us having sex."

Oh. "I didn't know this."

"It was...a long time ago." She smiled a little at the memory. "It was hard for me to even *think* Moffy did something wrong, when it felt like my addiction was why he needed to be grounded. That if I weren't a sex addict, there wouldn't be a problem, and I was causing the issue."

"You feel the same way now?"

She nodded. "But it's more complicated...which is why I've been taking some time to figure it out." She gave herself another resolute nod, then said, "Oh and I really thought maybe you'd want the event to pass...to cool off. I didn't want *this*"—she motioned between us—"to feel like an ambush."

She had been giving me time too.

I started, "But the table—"

"I didn't want to get a new one because I thought it'd make you feel ashamed. And sex is *nothing* to be ashamed of. But every time I

349 KRISTA & BECCA RITCHIE

saw the old table, it's all I could think of." Her cheeks were the shade of a firetruck at this point.

"I understand why you got it," I told her. "And I'm not ashamed, Mom. Maybe I'm a real weirdo because I'm not even that embarrassed." It's been a fleeting feeling.

Her eyes softened. "That is a superpower."

"Sometimes it feels like the opposite," I told her.

She shook her head strongly like I was so, so wrong. Suddenly, her brows pinched in confusion. "Then what's wrong with the table. Is it ugly?"

I shook my head. "No, I love it, but it's just..." She saw the same emotion crash into me.

"You feel guilty?"

I nodded. "You only bought the table because of us, so we'd like to pay for it. Donnelly and me."

"No."

"*Please.*" It took a little more begging before she relented. And I asked the scariest question because I wasn't sure I was ready to hear the answer. "Do you still like him?"

"Donnelly?"

"Yeah...do you like him? Do you like us together?"

She replied with the colloquial *mom* response. *As long as he makes you happy. As long as he's good to you.* It sunk my stomach, but she tried to reassure me. "I think you're meant to be."

"Okay," I breathed.

"I mean it." She made me look up. "See these." She pointed at her narrowed green eyes with two fingers. "They have witnessed and predicted many romances, and they know love. I see yours, Luna. And my beautiful, radiant daughter once told me, 'There are people in the universe who make you feel at home.' And Donnelly made you feel like your galaxy is the *happiest*, most exhilarating place to be. That is love."

It must've been how I felt then, but it's also exactly how I feel now with him.

I started crying. "I told you this about him?"

She smiled through a sheen of tears too. "You did."

I had shared my feelings about Donnelly with my mom—when I didn't think I had opened up to anyone. I'd told her. We hugged, and I used the plushie to dry my face.

All was well.

Though, she said she would talk to Donnelly on her own, too. It sounded like a conversation she's preparing for, and maybe it'll be a little harder than the one with me.

Orion lets out a teeny *woof* in his sleep, and the noise pulls me out of the recent memory. I smile and struggle not to attack-hug him, so I reach for my phone. Worst decision ever. A calendar notification pops up. Reminding me about the Fizzle presentations.

Greaaaat. Trying to come up with a new Fizzle product or a marketing strategy is like trying to catch air. And this is supposed to be one of the most important parts of the competition. It's not something I want to wing at the last minute. But I have no ideas— not even bad ones.

Inspiration is a ruthless hoe. That's what Eliot always says at least. If I could guzzle a jug of inspiration, I would right now.

Wait…I sit up swiftly and turn my galaxy projector back on. The most brilliant plan just light-bulbed inside my head.

I need to get high.

Some of my *best* ideas have been formed while stoned.

Jumping out of bed, I'm careful not to disturb my Newfie, but my footsteps stop near the bathroom door. With Donnelly on the other side of the bathroom, there is a great and terrible urge to use the perks of the Jack-and-Jill.

To go see him.

Why didn't he knock on my door when he came home? Because he didn't want to wake me from a deep-sleep. It's the same revolving answer I've smacked into. But what if it has nothing to do with protecting my sleep? He could just be pumping the brakes on sex.

He wants slow. I'm craving fast.

We are at a roadblock. If I knock on the bathroom door, will he think I'm knocking for sex? Will he ignore me?

My gut drops just at the mere image of being ignored by Donnelly. I can think of nothing more soul-shattering. So new plan. I'm not going to knock on his bathroom door. I'm going to exit my room and enter the hall, then knock on his *front* door. Thinking of knocking on his doors is kinda dirty, but that's where I'm at. Sex sizzling the brain.

If he ignores this knock, then I can blame it on a variety of things. He might be fast asleep. He might be thinking I'm Thatcher. Or he could think I'm a Sleep Goblin. There are just so many more factors that don't include "I'm purposefully ignoring Luna Hale because I don't want to have sex with her right now."

Which is valid. He can deny me sex, if he so wishes. I'm not trying to be pushy! *I'm really not.* But rejection—I do not want to meet right now.

And little does he know, this isn't about sex.

This is about marijuana.

In the hall, at his front door, I raise my fist and then reconsider knocking. What if he doesn't want to get high with me? I pull at the hem of my oversized Kansas T-shirt. It stops just above my knees, and since I only have panties on underneath, I shouldn't loiter in the hallway too long.

Is it normal to fear rejection from my boyfriend?

It's the last question in my brain before I knock.

A solid, agonizing ten seconds pass before the door cracks. When he sees it's me, he swings it open even wider. Relief washes over me, and then I'm suddenly bathed in heat. Holy...*wow.*

My gaze drops.

My lips part.

Donnelly is naked. Like buck-naked.

Only a pillow covers his crotch.

38

 **LUNA HALE**

Donnelly holds the pillow with a firm hand like he's hiding a boner. Sexy thick veins protrude from the top of his palm—*stop looking at his hand, Luna.* Because it totally appears like I'm staring at his dick. But that's unreasonable because his dick is behind the pillow. Fully covered. He's technically not even naked! He's wearing that pillow. Ha!

I nod inwardly like this makes so much sense.

Taking in his face, I see his hair is all askew. Cheeks slightly flushed.

"Am I interrupting something?" I wonder.

"Not gonna lie to you, Hale," he tells me. "You were."

Ohhhhh. My cheeks bake. And he's staring at me with heavy-lidded eyes like I'd been the main character in his imagination.

"I…you didn't want to, with me?" Did that make sense? I jab a finger towards the door. I think he follows.

"Thought you were asleep," he says with a scorching glance down my body.

"I would've let you still…" *have sex with me, touch me.* It's the unsaid thing, and I prop a hip on the door frame. He's so near, I can feel the heat radiating off his naked body.

"While you were asleep?" he asks with a spark of worry flaring his eyes.

"I mean...yeah?" Why am I suddenly sweaty and nervous? Oh, maybe because he seems freaked out. Okay, not *freaked* out. Concerned, really. "I give you permission. If you're feeling in the mood next time..."

"I gotta wake you up first. I can't just stick it in you while you're asleep." Him talking about sticking his dick in me is making me throb between my legs, but I'm listening to what he's saying.

"Even if I consent?"

"You sleep way too hard for it to feel consensual for me," he explains. Okay, I get it, and I'm nodding. His lips begin to lift, and he says, "You can pretend to be asleep though."

I smile and blush because that is one of my highest sexual fantasies lately. I often imagine him discovering my body on a foreign planet and trying to awaken me with hot and heavy thrusting.

Our eyes are hooked, and I can't stop nodding. "Cool cool," I say.

He's smiling, and he shifts the pillow but keeps his erection concealed.

"So you were just...?" I ask.

"Jerking off, yeah." He grins at my cheeks that've likely gone bright red. "What's up?"

"Your dick," I tell him, unable to stop myself.

He laughs. "Facts."

His humor really settles the restless energy coursing through me. I tell him, "I'm about to go make some weed brownies and then have a Fizzle brainstorm session. Wanna join?"

He barely thinks on it. "Count me in."

"Cool," I say but I realize I don't know whether he's "in" for the brainstorming session or the edibles or both. I guess I'll find out.

"Cool," Donnelly nods in agreement. And then we both just... stare at each other. Should I leave? Should I go into his room? No, definitely not. I wasn't invited. *Please invite me.*

I'd really like to watch him come.

We could come together.

He could even take my pseudo-virginity. Like he can read my

brain—or possibly, he's envisioning the same carnal thing—his muscles contract. His fingers dig into the pillow like his cock is aching behind the barrier.

Leaning my temple on the door frame, I grip the wood with my fingers. My pussy clenches as arousal slams more forcefully into me.

Donnelly drinks in my reaction and the tiny breath hitched in my throat. My heart starts quickening, like it's on the precipice of being tossed overseas.

I want sex.

He wants sex, right?

I want it so bad I could jump on him right fucking *now*. I'm clenching my legs together so tightly, I probably resemble one of those life-sized Nutcrackers. The pressure feels nice on my pussy, but I'm dreaming of something deeper. A fullness. In me.

Him.

"Donnelly," I whisper, his name a near-*whimper* on my lips.

"Fuck," he groans like my sole presence is tempting every last cell of his body. Then he glances at his bed behind him. *Yes, yes, yes.* His eyes are back on mine, more conflicted, and my stomach sinks.

Nooooo.

He's shifting the pillow, incredibly pent-up, but there is no invite.

Before the actual rejection comes and stings any worse, I say. "Godspeed." Whirling around to leave, I feel him grab my wrist.

"Wait."

"Hmm?" is all I'm able to muster, but I turn back.

"Come here." He draws me against his firm chest, but he drops my wrist to clutch the back of my skull. We're a head-on collision, our lips crashing together in a hungered, aching second. His tongue slips inside my mouth and—he pulls away. Just his lips. But we're pressed so close together still. His forehead touches mine. His knuckles dig into my belly from the hand that's bracing the pillow over his cock.

"We can't," he says, eyes pinched closed. "I can't stop myself right now if we keep kissing."

"You still think it's too soon?" I murmur.

He's quiet before he says, "Yeah. I can't tonight."

"Philly won the Super Bowl—"

"It's not that. It's just the talk with your dad. Seeing your parents going at it—lovingly, but still. A lot happened tonight. We should give it some distance, you know?"

I can't tell if it's for me or for him. But maybe it's both. "Okay, yeah." I try to sock away any lingering bits of disappointment, but I'm less disheartened and more so overly aroused.

Tension continues to swirl around us. It feels too taut. The longer I'm welded to his chest, the more likely I might rub against him. And I want to respect his pace. I don't want him to regret having sex with me.

So I back away.

Our eyes latch. He clears his throat, but his voice is still hoarse from arousal. "If you ever want to recreate the scene between Kilgore and Emmalina down the line, I'd be open to that."

Kilgore and Emmalina. They're the main characters from *Armagedd It On* which was a campy erotic apocalyptic story I wrote but never finished. It quite literally only has two chapters. The characters never actually have sex together, despite what the title suggests. They do mutually masturbate in front of each other though.

My cheeks heat. He read *Armagedd It On*. I shouldn't be shocked by this when he admitted to reading most everything I've written.

Still.

"I would be open to that too," I say, and I almost ask what *down the line* entails. Five days? Five months? Five years?! But I can see his body flexing even more, and I don't want to cause him more stress. Plus, I would really love to pop the brownies in the oven, head back to my room, and touch myself.

He nods, and I walk backwards through the doorway. I don't know how to end this.

He's struggling too.

So I just kinda…walk away. It's the best I have.

And then I whip up the quickest brownie batter I've ever made.

Brownies are done and somewhat eaten.

They feel like a weak batch. I've only ever assisted in making them one time. I was seventeen and at Tom's bandmate's house. Warner's dad was a major stoner, and he didn't mind us using the kitchen for such activities.

Leftover brownies are now sitting on my dresser. I also ran out of time to touch myself before Donnelly knocked on my door—so I feel a little like a live wire. Pent-up, *yes*. Trying to concentrate on the task at hand, *also yes*. High, *not yet*. At least I don't think so. It's only been ten minutes, and edibles usually take longer to hit me.

"What hasn't Fizzle already done?" I ask more to myself than the other living souls in my bedroom (including Orion and Moondragon). I pace, throwing up a soft spiky glow-in-the-dark ball and catching it back in my hand. Donnelly lounges on my bed, careful not to disturb the sleepy Orion at the foot.

My boyfriend watches me from the corner of his eyes as he sketches in a notebook. He also wears wire-framed reading glasses, and his lips lift every second or so in the start of a sexy smile.

Paul Donnelly just had an orgasm.

I was not a witness to it, but I know of its existence. It's almost like the knowledge and mental visual has stimulated me even more than seeing the event.

And he's so casual on my bed, as if he's sat there a million-and-one times, which I know can't be statistically possible. So his casualness comes from somewhere deeper within.

I pace.

The lava lamp casts purple shadows on the wall, but most of my lights are on, so it's not that dim-lit in here. I toss my spiky ball higher and it sticks to the ceiling. While I wait for it to slowly unstick, I say, "Fizzle has dark soda, diet soda, clear soda, aspartame-free soda, orange soda, cherry soda, all the sodas. They make PuraFons bottled water, energy drinks, teas, and sports drinks. What's left?" The ball releases from the ceiling and drops into my palm. "More bubbles? Less troubles."

"My type of motto," Donnelly says, his smile mirroring mine. "Girl, hit me with the bubbles."

I wish I had a bubble machine in this moment so I could manifest them for him. Instead, I pretend to be a blowfish and puff out my cheeks.

He grins wider. "Your invisible bubbles are by far the cutest."

I blow out a breath, releasing my cheeks. "Yeah, but invisible bubbles won't win over Uncle Stokes." I wince. "Not that I even have a shot. Pretty sure having a traumatic brain injury isn't going to roll well with the board."

"Do they know?" Donnelly wonders.

I shrug. "No clue. But I think I'd have to disclose it." I sink down on the white globe chair and rotate three-sixty.

"I don't know your Uncle Stokes that well. But he's the big boss man of Fizzle, right? So why would he go through the trouble of including you if it'd just disqualify you in the end?"

"Because he's *nice*." I brake using my feet, just to face Donnelly. "My dad jokes how Uncle Stokes was the embodiment of Captain America. Moral and just and a good guy. There's a hundred percent chance this is a pity thing to make me feel better about being included."

Donnelly grimaces. "If he's putting you through all this when he already plans on saying *no*, then he's the opposite of nice. He's a dick. But you think he's not—so only reasonable conclusion is that he thinks you have a shot."

I narrow my eyes at him. "Did we really just go through mental gymnastics to get here?"

"I'll do mental backflips for you anytime, babe."

Babe.

I try and stop myself from floating to him like he's lassoing me into his chest. *No. I need to concentrate.*

"So I have a shot," I say, taking in this newfound confidence with the deepest of breaths. "More bubbles. Less troubles." The motto is working its way into me. "The only thing I can think that's bubblier than soda is maybe…champagne? But I think my grandfather never went that route for a reason."

"Your mom?" Donnelly wonders, a ballpoint pen between his fingers. My mom's sex addiction could've been a factor. Especially since she's married to a recovering alcoholic.

"Maybe," I breathe. "Or maybe the soda market is too family-friendly to introduce alcohol in the mix. I don't know." I kick the desk and rotate in my chair again. The room blurs, then slowly comes into focus as I decelerate.

I'm simultaneously getting somewhere but also hitting a wall.

Donnelly flips a page in his spiral sketchbook, and his pen flies in hurried lines and arches. His concentration attracts me just as much as his shirtless chest. Tattoos scatter his white skin in random but aesthetically pleasing patterns. A longer strand of hair brushes his forehead, and he pushes it back without looking up from the drawing. I listen to the scratch of his pen on paper, and I wonder if this is weird—how much I could just watch him sketch. How attracted I am to his very essence on my bed.

It's hot how he brings up his knee, just to give his elbow a rest. His biceps are cut without him needing to flex, and I have the sudden urge to trace the line of the muscle. With my finger and my tongue.

Squeezing my thighs together creates an artificial pressure, which helps the current build-up of arousal.

"What are you working on?" I wonder.

"Bubble Queen." His eyes lift to mine, his lip quirking.

I smile, then leave the globe chair. Headed his way. "Is she cute?"

"Cutest of her galaxy."

Sinking next to my boyfriend on the bed, I peer over at the sketch. He angles the notebook so I can see. Black ink flows in beautiful lines. Presiding on a tower of coral is a queen—but not just any typical fantasy monarch. Bubbles billow from her flowy hair, and soap suds hide her toes. Her Oscar-worthy dress is haute-bubble-couture, and she blows a tinier bubble with her delicate hand.

"She looks so fragile," I say quietly. "Like no one can touch her or she'd just pop."

His eyes sink into me for a beat. Then he sketches a man at her side. Donnelly draws smoky whisps around him. All soft lines. Almost invisible. Deep longing seeps from the penned irises like he's hopelessly in love with the Bubble Queen. My heart capsizes from Donnelly's talent. I knew he could design tattoos and sketch faces, but this is something different entirely.

He's drawing a story.

"Lucky for her," Donnelly tells me, "she has the Shadow King by her side."

"And no one can touch him," I say. "Because he slips right through their fingers if they try." I narrow my eyes at the page. "What if they're not a couple? They're actually on warring kingdoms, feuding with each other for centuries."

His brows rise. "You'd turn a romance into a tragedy?" He's genuinely shocked I'd be rooting for the demise of our fictional couple.

"Not a tragedy. But their love story is not so easy. They have a centuries-old feud to wade through. They have the trauma of not being able to be touched by anyone. But through all of that, they're destined to be together. They just don't know it yet—they can't know."

Donnelly's pen stills on the page. He takes his glasses off and searches my features. "I thought you'd want Bubble Queen and Shadow King to have an easier time is all."

"Some epic romances aren't born from easy times," I say softly. "They're born from strife and conflict and sometimes horrible shitty things happening."

He knows I'm not referring to our fictional couple anymore. His fingertips brush the top of my kneecap, the featherlight touch unearthing my teeming desires. I go still. I don't even breathe. Like one little movement will send Donnelly fleeing to his bedroom.

"Luna." The way he says my name makes me press my thighs together again. Donnelly slips the pen behind his ear and gently closes the notebook. His eyes travel over my movements, watching me intently. Then he says, "I don't want you to believe we wouldn't have made it if we didn't go through something terrible together."

Trauma-bound.

The idea that we're only a match-made because of our shared traumatic experience. If this were true, then I would've never fallen for him the first time. And I was instantaneously attracted to Donnelly the moment I woke up in the hospital—before I even knew what horrible things had happened.

"I don't think it," I whisper. "I think we're..." A brain itch, one I can't quite scratch, and I frown and shake the strange feeling away.

With Donnelly this close beside me, I inhale the scent of him. Minty and musky, a heady mixture I could bathe in. His forearm is braced on his kneecap. Angled towards me, he looks me over once more. It's a lustful but caring caress, and my heart thumps a little harder.

Uhhh, I just want him to touch me. His jaw looks stubbled and rough, and I imagine running my fingers down the masculine planes of his face and his shoulders. I'm afraid if I even try, I'll end up straddling him, and I'm attempting his speed. *Slow.*

You can go slow.

I wriggle and tug the hem of my black Kansas tee down. I nearly expose my neon-green panties, and now that my hand is so close to my heat, I consider touching myself. I try to lock my knees together.

He sweeps me again. "What do you need from me?" he asks.

"Huh?" I frown.

"What do you want me to do to you?"

My clit throbs in response. "Huh." I say it less like a question and more like a stupefied girlfriend.

His lips quirk into the hottest smile I've ever seen. "Anything but my cock inside you. What do you want, space babe?"

39

LUNA HALE

I roast from pure desire. "Did you ask OG Luna that question?"

"Not in that way," he admits. He settles his hand on my knee. It's electrifying. My thighs quiver, and I try to control myself. Why is this so intense—being touched by him?

I fixate on how turned-on he seems from my body's uninhibited responses. "My imagination runs deep, you know. We could go to some interesting places."

He grins, and I wonder if he's thinking about earlier, how I proposed that he fuck me in my sleep and how he's game to pretend sleep-fuck me. "Oh, I know."

The room swelters. Am I high? Am I dreaming this? I don't really care either way. I just want to stay right here.

Donnelly slides the pen out of his ear and into the spirals of his notebook. Though, he keeps the pages open on his lap. With bed pillows behind our backs, we're both propped against the headboard, and his gaze stays on mine with an intimacy that makes me blush again. "What do you want me to do to you?" he asks.

"Whatever you want to do to me." I'm a breath from throwing myself at him and saying, *I'm yours!*

A smile teases the corners of his lips. "I wanna do too many things to you."

"Yes," I nod.

He laughs.

I don't think. "Could you put your fingers in me," I say on impulse. "I just want to feel them in me."

My heart hammers as he presses on my kneecaps, and my legs lower flat to the bed. I watch his left hand, the one closest to me, dive underneath my black baggy shirt. He hooks a finger around my neon-green panties and slides them down my thighs. Farther. Until the fabric slips off my ankles.

I love this mysterious voyage.

"You breathing?" he asks, the huskiness of his voice another caress, and I nod a lot. His smile glimmers his blue eyes, and it's hard to look away, even as he draws my shirt up to my hipbones, then higher and higher. Exposing my breasts. Donnelly leaves the shirt on me, the fabric bunched near my collarbone and tangled with my kyber crystal necklace.

The rest of my body is bare. Naked. Wanting. *Needy.*

Without angling towards me, he's just relaxed like we're watching TV together. Only, the TV isn't on, and he's become more enrapt with my vulnerable form. He traces the shooting star tattoo at my hipbone, and then he brings those same fingers to his mouth, sucking two of them. The image is orgasm-worthy, and I'm surprised I hold it together.

"I'm already wet," I whisper, thinking he's worried I'm dry.

Donnelly smiles like I'm cute or adorable, but I also just want to be so *sexy* that he can't help himself and must destroy every *inch* of my being. He slides them out of his mouth. "Didn't want to put them in you cold."

He was warming his fingers for me.

He's going to finger me.

Confetti cannons are blasting from my ceiling. The invisible spectators are throwing a parade around the mattress.

I'm so eager, so excited, that I miss the part where his hand descends between my legs. He slips one finger inside me, and my knees instinctively knock back together. I cage his finger by squeezing tight. Ah, the fullness. It feels so blissfully good.

"Deeper," I say into a tiny moan, staring at his hand against my pussy. My well-lit room is giving me an epic view of this exploration, and I'm all for it.

He's knuckle-deep in me. "You gonna stop clenching?"

"Maybe...not."

He grins, but his breath shallows in pleasure. "You're too fucking tight and swollen. Unclench and I'll go deeper."

"I'm not that tight," I argue in a carnal haze.

"Give me your finger." He reaches over my body with his right hand and clasps my index finger. He squeezes it with a good amount of force. "That's what your pussy feels like. Only warmer. And wetter." Can he always describe sexual acts to me?

I just nod. *Keep going, please.*

He's grinning. "That turn you on?"

"Uh-huh."

He releases my hand, but I almost grab for him to stay. He leans back against the pillows. His left hand is still cupped against my pussy. It's the sexual leisure of it all that does me in.

Then he moves his finger. A *come hither* motion? Whatever he does, it instantly arches my hips and pricks my nerve-endings. "Fuckfuck," I cry, inhaling sharply.

He pauses, letting me catch my breath.

Holy shit...I never want this to stop. I want his hand to live right there. "Three fingers," I pant.

"Let's start with two."

I let out a puff of air. "Why?" I frown. "Your cock is bigger than three, and I've taken that before."

"It's been a while. We're gonna start with two," he rasps, voice husky, and I'm captivated at his insistence to safeguard every piece of me. It's doubly attractive and causes me to buck my hips into his *one* finger.

He smiles back at me. "Let me put in another one before you start thrusting."

"I'm not going to thrust."

"Your hips are lying to you then."

I laugh under my breath and those laughs morph into a moan when I feel finger number two. Oh wow, oh my God. I snap my eyes closed.

"This hurt?" he asks.

"No," I whisper under a heavy breath. "It feels amazing. I want more, but I also want it to last forever."

"Know that feeling well."

Without looking—because if I have the sexy visual, I might come and this'll all be over—I reach between my legs and grab hold of Donnelly's wrist. The heel of his palm is flush up against my clit. I try to push his hand harder, wanting more.

Please.

"I'm already as deep as I can go, babe," he tells me, and then he starts pumping his fingers.

I tremble. "Waitwait," I breathe out and open my eyes.

He immediately stops. His muscles contract, but I make a concerted effort not to take a glimpse at his fingers inside of me.

"Can you...?" I lose sight of the words, uncertain about them. "I love this, and...can you...?"

"Just tell me what you want, Luna," he says, sweeping my face. "I'm not gonna judge you." He hasn't so far. Even the one tiny hiccup where I learned he won't have sex with me while I'm dead-asleep, he didn't look weirded out, just *concerned.* Everyone has likes and dislikes, and I really love discovering more of his, too.

"Can you sketch?" I ask. "But while your fingers are inside me?"

With a rising smile, he kisses the edge of my eyelid, then bends his leg. He props the notebook on his thigh, and using his right hand, he draws while his left hand pleasures me. His fingers pump inside. Long, delirious strokes. *OhmyGod.*

OhmyGod.

His fingers understand my pussy, what I like already, but I'm watching his face more than his hand.

He zones into the sketch, and it's right now that I discover that Paul Donnelly is a fantastic multi-tasker. He sketches beauty with one hand and makes art out of the other. I feel like a masterpiece under his touch.

His thumb circles my clit, and I cry out. He does that more than once.

And his eyes hit mine, and he takes in how I'm watching him. It is *him*. All of him. That drives me to an edge. His abs flex, and he grips his pen a little tighter, like he's forcing himself not to roll on top of me.

Donnelly returns to the sketch, but his fingers create hotter friction in me. He's teasing a sensitive spot inside me—it's mind-blowing. *OhmyGodOhmyGod.* My toes curl.

"I'mgoingtocome." It rushes together. I dizzy. All the pooled arousal that'd been amassing from earlier tonight has catapulted to a treacherous peak. I pretend this is what we do together. Every leisure day. In the living room of our own little house.

I sit on the couch beside Donnelly, and he fingers me while he sketches. He turns the everyday mundane into fireworks and explosions between my legs.

I'm so wet, his fingers make a loud squishing noise. He doesn't make fun of it. One more caress in me, and my hips buck into his hand. "*Donnelly.*" I pulsate around him. Moaning, I turn my face into the pillow.

"There we go," he breathes out, but I can't tell if he's talking about the art or me. He's locked-in on the ink and paper.

My vision is blurry, and I snap my eyes shut as I tumble farther off the cliff. That climax is a full-body release, and I quake under the soft extra strokes Donnelly gives me.

When I open my eyes, he's still sketching. Not even watching me.

Why is that so fucking hot?

"Want me to keep them in you?" he asks, referring to his fingers.

"No," I say, worried I might full-on ride them if he does. "You can have them back."

Gently, he slips them out, and I put my hand to my forehead in a salute.

He grins. "You saluting my fingers?

"Yes."

He looks at me like I'm all the stars in his sky, and it leaves me breathless for a moment. Then I shift my thighs a little and tense up. He frowns, "You alright?"

"Just…wet," I say. "Like really wet. It's kind of…a lot."

"I'll eat you out in a second. I'm almost done with this." He casually returns to the sketch, and it's hard not to notice the erection against his sweatpants.

"I can blow you."

"Nah," he says. "You're supposed to be brainstorming. You can't do that with my cock in your mouth. Here—" He hands me the sketchbook. "Just give me a sec." He pushes himself off the bed, and before I know it, he's out the door.

Orion *woofs* in his sleep. Yes, we've been doing naughty things beside my dog, but he's more like a fluffy mound of fur when he's snoozing. Hardly aware.

I try not to freak out about Donnelly's sudden disappearance, and I glance at the sketch. Wow…my lips part in disbelief. He drew *me*. The me right now. Here. On this bed. The long lines of my legs, my perked nipples, the Kansas tee bunched up at my collar, the galaxy tattoo on my thigh.

My O-face.

I look undeniably *sexy*. Sultry. Like a woman he imagines fucking. Or making love to.

My heart swells.

Donnelly is back in a jiffy. He has a red Wawa plastic cup and takes a swig. He comes closer, and I see it's just water.

He's hydrating.

A smart bean.

He offers me the cup, and I take a sip before passing it back. Setting it on the nightstand, he says, "Give me your best Fizzle ideas." He climbs back on the bed. This time, he's between my legs, and his eyes meet mine. As if to remind me about Fizzle.

"More bubbles," I say in a raspy breath, and that same breath catches as he kisses my pussy. And not a peck. It's a masterful, deep kiss. I shudder and moan, fisting the sheets on either side of me. He's licking and sucking me into oblivion. I'm not sure how this is supposed to make me *less* wet—but I'm not complaining.

He looks up at me. "So more bubbles?"

"More bubbles," I nod, being carried into another orgasm. "More bubbly. More bubbly bubbles. Fizzing fizz."

Donnelly eases back to say, "I like where this is going."

"Fizzing and jizzing," I say. Okay, I might actually be high now.

Donnelly laughs against my pussy. "Grandfather Calloway woulda loved that one."

"Hopefully he can't hear me from his grave…or see me. You don't think that saying his name is like calling upon his ghost, do you?"

"He's not Beetlejuice," Donnelly says, his voice muffled against me. Thoughts float away as he devours me. And my thighs tremble beside his face. *Fuckfuck.* I crave his cock, and this, *this* is torture. The best, best kind. After a beat, I hear him say, "Luna, keep going."

No, I can't. He is eating me out like I'm his first and last meal, and I'm already so sensitive and swollen. "*DonnellyDonnelly.*" I come, crying into my bicep.

He reaches up and pulls my arm away. Then rises to kiss me on the lips. I taste myself, and it's a sweet taste. And all I can think is, *I love him.* I really, really love him.

His elbow is beside my head. On my comedown, I whisper, "Maybe we should do a séance."

"Yeah?"

"Uh-huh. Get the Ghost of Grandfather Calloway's advice. I'm sure Kinney would love that—though I don't think she wants Xander or me to be CEO. She said it should be Charlie." I think *everyone* thinks it should be Charlie.

I squirm my thighs a little.

Donnelly clutches my bunched-up tee. "Is this a special shirt?"

NOBODY LIKE US **367**

"Not really."

"Can I take it?"

I frown. "Is this for brainstorming?"

"It's for your pussy."

I smile. "Yeah, take it."

He pulls off my baggy tee, and I help yank the fabric off my arms. I'm completely naked now. He presses the fabric against my pussy for a minute, wiping me up, and then throws the shirt to the ground. "Better?"

Oddly. Yes.

I'm still wet. But it's not as uncomfortable.

I nod, and he returns to his spot next to me, leaning against the headboard. "Pop goes the fizz," I tell him in a giggle. My head feels light like it's made of cotton candy.

"A Fizzle for your thoughts," Donnelly replies, which makes me giggle harder. Maybe it's the way he's saying it? Or I am most definitely high.

"I'm going to give you the benefit of the fizz."

Donnelly grins. "Only kind of benefit I want."

I'm about to butcher another idiom when his phone rings on the nightstand. I frown. He frowns. There's such a small list of people who'd call him at three in the morning *without* an emergency.

He reaches for his phone, and his face darkens when he sees the caller ID. I watch him answer it. "Ian?"

My stomach drops.

Why is Tom's bodyguard calling Donnelly?

40

PAUL DONNELLY

Ian and Vance Wreath throwing up the bat signal at me is a rare sight. I'm struggling to make sense of it as I ride in the backseat of their coveted Range Rover.

The famous ones were in Philly for the Super Bowl party, so Tom and Eliot are crashing at the Cobalt Estate tonight. The Wreath brothers also spent the night in Philly—but at Epsilon's house, the one located in the gated neighborhood.

"You said they snuck out?" I ask again, trying to gather the facts. Luna texted her best friends before I left the penthouse and jumped in the Range Rover. She hasn't received a response from either of them.

I can still taste Luna—that's how fast I flew out the door. I smell her heady floral scent all over me. Don't want them to smell her. I feel like a fucking feral animal right now who was interrupted during mating season. Like I will rip into anyone who goes for my girl.

Main thing calming me down is my mental fortitude. Hyper-vigilance skyrocketing. Just wanna make sure Tom and Eliot are alright. I've thrown the hot interaction with Luna into the back of my brain. I'm not even stoned. Sober and limp, I fixate on this search party.

"Whatever you want to call it," Ian, the newly-minted SFE *lead* says from the passenger seat.

I couldn't believe Price gave him the promotion.

Mainly 'cause he's not the first I'd think of as a leader. Then again, he's only ever been a bodyguard to the Cobalts, and all the Epsilon bodyguards who protect the Cobalt Empire follow in line with him like he's a seven-time Super Bowl champ.

Greer would've been a better fit. He's the most senior Epsilon bodyguard. He's the copper-bearded Navy vet who's typical military. Strict with the rules. Can be a dick but he's loyal. He turned it down though. Think he likes the simplicity of protecting Winona Meadows and not the headache of corralling a bunch of men in addition to it.

Jon Sinclair—the vulgar and sometimes hilarious Navy vet—got transferred to Alpha. Lily has two full-time bodyguards now. It's why the SFE lead position freed up in the first place.

So…technically…Ian Wreath is above me in security's hierarchy. He can order me around if he so pleases.

"It's not like they're kids anymore," Ian continues. "They don't have to sneak out of their parents' house."

"But they didn't contact you two first?"

Vance is behind the wheel. He casts a cagey glance at his older brother. He keeps doing that. It's putting me on edge, and I'm in the narrow middle seat in the back so I can catch their side profiles.

"No," Ian says, typing on his phone. "They didn't shoot us any texts, but we have orders from Rose and Connor to have security on them, regardless of what they want." Heightened security has been in place since the kidnapping. High-threat levels all around.

"I'm surprised you didn't call O'Malley for backup," I say, watching Vance rotate the wheel.

"You think you're our first choice?" Ian retorts.

"Nah, didn't think that. Wouldn't think that. 'Cause you all would choose the basket without the darts."

Ian makes sure I see his glare. "Like you're the only one who can hit a target, right?"

"Yeah, of those of us here, I'm the only one who can call Tom and Eliot at three a.m. and risk waking 'em up and it not be classified as *unprofessional.*"

"It is unprofessional."

"Maybe if you did it," I say. "Maybe if you were still *buddy*guards, you'd be tiptoeing that line, but I'm not even on that line, man." I'm trying to get them to understand that. "I'm dating their best friend. I can call them as a concerned friend or even on behalf of Luna. Which is what I'm about to do—"

"Do *not* call them," Ian says like an order. "I'm serious, Donnelly."

This is fucking frustrating. "You're really gonna let your feelings about me affect the safety of your clients?"

Vance casts another sharp look to his brother.

I tense.

Something's not adding up.

We're whizzing past Reading Terminal Market. Still in Center City. I look back at Ian. "Did you not hear what Price said at the last meeting? The whole point of me joining SFE is so you have deeper access into the family. To *protect* them. So fucking use me."

"Bet you're used to that," Vance mutters.

Being used.

Yeah.

I'm the informant, the rat, being used by private security and the cops. But he could be referring to me turning tricks. What used to be a wishy-washy rumor in security about me getting paid for sex is now a full-blown fact thanks to my dad. Bodyguards overheard it while I was wearing a wire, and Oscar told me that it's spread throughout the whole team.

"Bet you're used to coming in last place," I say with less heat. "Don't know how that feels. Wanna describe it for me?"

I hit a nerve with Vance. His hands tighten on the wheel. Someone doesn't like being called a loser. If you can't take it, don't dish it to me.

"Do you ever shut up?" Vance retorts.

"Nah, it's a disease. I can give it to you. Maybe you can share something insightful." I stare out the window. Where the hell are we going? I snap my eyes back to him. "I thought we were headed to Fishtown." We're now going towards Villanova, a rich neighborhood where the Crow lives.

They say nothing.

What the fuck...

I go absolutely still, only shifting my gaze. "Not going to Fishtown then," I mutter. "You wanna tell me what's going on?" I ask Ian.

"They're not in Fishtown. We decided to take a detour."

A detour.

He's the one who said Eliot would most likely be in that area of Philly because of Frankford Hall, a German beer garden he loves. But it's not open this late, so I already had my doubts.

"You get a tip or what?" I ask him.

"Just sit back," Ian says with a side-eye. "*Relax*. You're along for the ride. We'll tell you what you need to know."

Fuck you, too.

I glance out the window. It might be late but Philly is still alive. Poles are greased. Celebratory chants echo through the old high-rises, and green confetti litters the sidewalks.

Even amid everything, I start to smile.

I love this city.

I will always love this city.

It'll always be mine.

Ian and Vance start checking on me with short glances. Like they're expecting me to play Tetras on my phone or watch replays of the game. Instead, I'm keeping track of where the fuck we're going, and let me just say, it's nowhere I'd put money on Tom and Eliot being.

We're now out of Philly.

We're not even in Villanova.

"Turn here," Ian whispers to Vance.

We do three loops. We're making circles. I try not to laugh.

They're mad. "Shut the fuck up, Donnelly," Vance snaps.

"Said nothing." I raise a hand in defense. "You like circles. No shame in the circle game."

Ian tells his brother, "Ignore him. Just drive."

I flip my phone in my hand. There's a five-percent chance Vance is actually lost. I'm not a dummy. They're trying to get *me* lost.

But I keep my eyes on them and the highway signs flying by.

"How'd your family's watch-party go?" I ask them. "Must've been hard with your little brother playing for the enemy." James Wreath is the Bill's best kicker.

All three Wreath brothers look like classic American-bread football stars. Clean-cut, coifed brown hair, brawny. But only one of them made it to the big leagues.

"I didn't think you knew shit about that," Ian says with another glance back at me.

"About your little brother?"

"About our family. That there even was a watch-party."

I heard about the party on comms. They mentioned it more than once. What'd they think, I had them muted?

"I pay attention," I say.

"Sure," Vance mutters.

I stare out the window, watching the landscape change from city to pastoral. "Vance Harrison Wreath. Twenty-seven. You were a prized soccer player in high school, then started as a kicker for Penn State's football team, graduated with a Bio degree that's gone unused. Think your mom didn't like that. But you gotta do you, and with zero military or MMA experience, you followed your big brother into security. Do I have that right?"

Vance says nothing.

I'm gonna take that as a *yes*.

"Ian Rohan Wreath. Love the middle name by the way. Thirty-four. *Legendary* tight end of Penn State but got robbed of the NFL. Competitive year and all. You trained in MMA before joining private security, where you've been for almost eight years." He's the bulkiest of the three brothers.

Ian is in quiet contemplation.

What the hell, I keep going. "Your dad went to Annapolis. Prestigious stuff. So did your grandfather. Instead of following their footsteps into the military, you were able to use their connections to get into private security."

Ian nods a few times, then says, "Paul Donnelly. Twenty-nine. High school dropout. Son of two meth addicts. You followed your more talented friend to Yale and all the way back to Philly. He gets with a Hale, and you think, *yeah, I'm going to do that too.* And so you seduce the girl you think is easy-pickings. Luna, the most sexual—"

"No," I force out, my eyes flaming. "Is that seriously how you see me? You think I'd just look at the lineup of girls like they're…." I can't even finish the fucking statement—I'm burning alive. "Fuck you, man." I heat in place. "You wanna call me a dropout, a slut, a methhead, a loser—I don't care, but I'm *not* someone who'd intentionally prey on Luna. The fact that you think I did, just to what? Be a part of the families? It's more fucked-up than I actually am, so *fuck you* again." I adjust in my seat, lit on fire and I contemplate rolling the window down.

I feel Ian checking on me a few times, but I'm glaring out the window. Unable to even look him in the eyes right now. 'Cause I just wanna pry them out of his skull.

Everything he said courses back through my brain, and I end up snapping back, "And don't ever fucking talk about her like that again." I know what he was implying.

I think Ian is going to be quiet, but he ends up saying, "I was going to say Luna is the most sexualized in the media. Doesn't mean I believe that."

I work my jaw, trying to calm myself but I feel like there's too much dirt already piled on top of me.

The car ride is five-times as strained.

Vance whispers to Ian, who just shakes his head a few times, and the handful of moments he tries to meet my gaze, I cut it to the window. Away from him.

I swallow a fiery pit in my throat. "I left for a reason, you know," I tell the car window more than them. "You think I'm *just* like my family, but I left 'cause I was nothing like 'em." I lick my dry lips. "And Farrow—yeah, I followed him. Just like you followed your brother. But I didn't think...I didn't *plan* this. I'm not with Luna because of her family. Or because of Farrow. Or because the world thinks she's fucking *easy*. I'm with her 'cause we see in each other what few people see in ourselves. The heart of her is so beautiful it hurts to talk about it at times." I take a sharp breath. "My whole life, I've been running towards a light at the end of the tunnel, and you can think it's fame or money or whatever sick thing you wanna believe about me—but that's not the heart of me. It'll never be. 'Cause the light is her. It's the feeling I have when I'm with her. When I see her. When I'm afraid she's gone. It's Luna." My voice breaks, and I rub a hand down my face, my body tensed up.

I try to ease back in the seat and focus on the drive.

Ian and Vance say nothing. I don't want them to. I'm hoping they remain absolutely fucking quiet.

My phone buzzes.

I check the text.

I heard back from Tom. They never left the Cobalt Estate.
They're still there. — Luna

Yeah.

I'm not even surprised at this point, but I am relieved they're not in harm's way. They're safely tucked in those silky blue Cobalt sheets. Best news of the night. But it's sitting alongside the worst news: This whole search party is a sham. A setup.

41

PAUL DONNELLY

Biggest question of the night: Where the hell are Ian and Vance taking me?

Luna messages again.

> Do the other bodyguards already know Tom and Eliot are at The Cobalt Estate?? Why'd they ask for your help??
> — Luna

Pulling my eyes off the car window, I send back: Explain later. I'm good tho. Don't wait up for me. I add another quick text beneath it: Love you, space babe 👾 💀

I can't concentrate on my phone. So I don't check her reply right away. Vance has turned down several roads. Missed them all. We bump along the roughly paved street, and I see…more farmland?

It's dark. The moon is gone. I can't see shit—other than what looks like a barren grassy field.

Once they pull up next to two parked SUVs, I know we're not alone. This was a group effort.

"Get out," Ian orders, but I'm already jumping out and walking into the beam of the headlights. It's where the rest of Epsilon waits.

Cruz Jr. and Greer are smoking cigarettes. Others are on their phones, but they put them away as soon as I come into view. Exhaust plumes from the ass of the cars. They left them running.

My blood is so hot, I can't even feel the cold wind against my face. "We breaking bread or breaking bones?" I quip.

"You tell him?" Greer asks Ian as both Wreath brothers join the fold.

"Not yet." Ian stuffs his hands in his bomber jacket.

"Tell me what?" I ask lightly.

I think they'd rather have me on edge 'cause the first thing O'Malley says is, "How's Luna?"

She's safe. The glare I give him could scorch the earth. Any joke I could make just explodes in my head. I'm already amped from the car ride. "Why do you care?" I ask.

"You went home with her."

"We live together," I retort, aware of the audience around us. They stay quiet like this is my contentious shit with O'Malley, and they're keeping their hands clean of it. At least this isn't an eight-on-one dogpile. "You have a problem with that?"

"You know I do," O'Malley says, rubbing his hands in the cold. "And for the sake of being *honest* tonight, I *honestly* think you're the worst *fucking* bodyguard who coulda ever gotten with her." His South Philly lilt breaks through. I dunno why it irritates me.

"Tell me how you really feel," I say lightly, but I'm smoldering inside. "Go ahead."

"That's not why we're here," Ian cuts in, and I see a weird softness in his posture and eyes. Fuck him. I don't want his pity.

"You're a low life," O'Malley tells me. "Just like your dad. You only crept into security 'cause you're attached to Farrow Redford Keene."

"Hale," I correct.

"What?"

"He's Farrow Redford Keene *Hale* now, but keep going. What else you got?"

"You're fucking insufferable."

"I'm glad I'm making you suffer. And?"

"Luna just got *kidnapped*. By your own family. You don't even care how much media attention you stir up. You make out with her in broad daylight. Are you going to fuck her in public too? Invite your cousins to join—"

I storm forward, and Greer jumps between us, hands outstretched on our chests.

"What the fuck, O'Malley?" Greer whisper-hisses.

O'Malley and I are impaling each other with caustic glares. Rage and adrenaline course through me at rapid speed, and I spin out of Greer's hold.

Just to walk several feet away from them.

Towards the overgrown blades of grass. Rolling fields in the distance. An endless night sky. I set my hands on the back of my neck and try to breathe.

Calm down.

I squat, my pulse pitched. I hear them talking behind me.

"We should call this off," Cruz Jr. says. "I don't feel good about it."

"Why?" O'Malley rebuts. "He doesn't give a shit about you or any of us. He purposefully fucked with our cars."

Car.

One car.

Glitter on the seats, and yeah, I've known they've been pissy about it. So what—they bring me out to a deserted field to haze me?

Whatever they have planned—it's nothing.

What O'Malley just said—I hate that it feels like everything.

"Donnelly," Ian calls out.

With another deep breath, I stand and go back to the firing line. Eight men. Security Force Epsilon.

Ian Wreath (Tom's bodyguard)

Vance Wreath (Eliot's bodyguard)

Chris O'Malley (Beckett's bodyguard)

Chris Novak (Ben's bodyguard)

Greer Bell (Winona's bodyguard)

Ryan Cruz Jr. (Kinney's bodyguard)

And two young rookies: Vlad Kosko (Audrey's bodyguard) and Hart McKenna (the floater)

Come to think of it, with Sinclair off the Epsilon roster, the oldest bodyguard on SFE is Greer at thirty-seven. They've always acted like they're filled with the most valuable experience and some *ancient* wisdom. Unlike the "young hot shit" that is Omega. But, really, both security forces could be reflections of the other.

There's not much difference.

We're all from Philly. We're all a mix of military and martial arts. We've all been through the security ringer.

Threats. Stalkers. Rabid paparazzi. Aftermath of a car crash in the pouring rain. Being snowed-in in Scotland. Searching for the girl squad in Italy. The Olympics. The Summer Fest shooting. Assaults. A kidnapping.

They know how cruel and demanding this job can be.

But I just don't feel like I'm one of 'em. I am Omega. It's not even that SFO is known in the media and SFE are more invisible. It's something deeper.

The divide is monstrous between us, and I have no clue why Price and Akara thought it'd be smart to put me with them.

I'm not surprised they're waiting for Ian to talk. He's the lead.

Ian nods to me, "You're new here."

My brows shoot to the sky. "I'm new here?" I point at my chest. "Been here almost seven years. How long has Kosko been here? Four months?"

"You left Triple Shield," Ian reminds me. "You're back working for Triple Shield. You're new again."

"Right." I look at them. "So what—you wanna do some trust falls? Team building exercises? You know, we coulda gone paintballing. You didn't have to bring me all the way out to fucking Okehocking."

McKenna, a lanky redhead, gapes at the team. "He knows where he is?"

"I thought you threw him off?" Novak asks Vance.

Greer and Cruz Jr. are smiling. I wonder if they'd give me a cigarette.

The bodyguards to the Cobalts have a bigger bone to pick with me. I know it's partly because my family tried to jump Beckett, which sent O'Malley to the hospital. It's been personal for these pricks.

"A pancake breakfast," Ian suddenly says, and my stomach clenches. "That's the initiation you first had into security. A pancake fucking breakfast."

I try not to grimace.

That was up to the Tri-Force back then. Two of which are now Omega: Akara and Thatcher. So I don't mention it.

I also don't mention how I never asked for the breakfast. While I was told to eat, I knew Farrow was being dropped in the Poconos and told to run in the dark. I hated every second of it.

The Tri-Force knew I would. But I think they just wanted to ensure I wouldn't follow my friend. That I would do as told.

And I did.

Everyone else had it harder than me. Novak still complains about how he had to walk a maze-like route in Center City for eight hours.

"No pancake breakfast this time. Got it," I nod. "What do you want from me?" I look to each of them. I've given so much of myself to security. I've got nothing left to prove to myself, but they might see me as a liability still—'cause I'm tied to the people who hurt the Hales.

I always will be by blood.

By name.

They probably think it'd just be easier for everyone if I quit—but I'm not quitting. And they're going to struggle getting me to a place where I would.

"Take your clothes off," Ian orders.

I see the doorway of the row house. My cousins standing inside. I blink. Then I shrug off my jacket. Brought one this time and now I'm tossing it to Ian. I'm that frosty Disney princess though. The cold never bothered me anyway. I smile a little to myself, and SFE starts arguing back and forth.

"It's below-forty now," Greer says. "Let him keep his shirt and pants."

"This isn't supposed to be *easy*," Novak refutes.

"Dude, he won't die without a shirt," McKenna pipes in. My eyes ping back and forth as each guy speaks. Senses heightened and humming. I barely move a muscle.

Ian motions to me. "Keep the rest on, Donnelly." Feels odd how nice he's being. Not sure if I like it.

"How the hell is this pushing his limits, Ian?" Novak retorts.

"Stop listening to fucking Greer," O'Malley adds.

While they all bicker amongst themselves, I just grip the back of my long-sleeve shirt and pull it over my head. I'm stripping my belt. I unholster my gun. I pry the earpiece out of my ear and unhook my radio, and they go quiet when I step out of my pants.

"You want my underwear too?" I wonder.

"No," Ian snaps like I'm insane for even voluntarily stripping this far.

It's freezing, and I tuck my arms close to my body but I don't complain. I'm clenching my teeth so they won't rattle.

"Didn't his family make him strip?" Vance whispers to someone. Don't see who.

"Put your clothes back on," Ian orders.

"Nah, I'm good." I can see Novak, O'Malley, and the rookies won't be satisfied unless this is difficult, so let's make it difficult.

Ian curses under his breath. I read his lips though. He said, *Fucking Donnelly.*

"He passed his psych eval, right?" Not sure who muttered that. I tense.

"Yeah, he did."

I'm focused on them. "What now?"

"We're leaving you here," Ian says with a heavy sigh. His brother collects my clothes, boots, gun, and radio off the ground. I'm left in socks and boxer-briefs. "Find your way back home."

Figured.

"Your phone." Greer comes forward to take the only thing I'm holding.

This is where I hesitate. *Luna.* That's my lifeline to Luna. It also contains personal texts. Photos. Of her and me. "I'd rather not."

Ian pulls away from the other bodyguards too. Closer, he whispers to me, "Personal bullshit aside, you need to trust us like we're trusting you."

Trust them.

I could ask, *how can I trust you when you lied tonight?* But if this is my initiation into Epsilon again, then the point is to blindly follow. To not ask too many questions. To listen to your lead. It's basic Intro to Bodyguard shit that they don't think I've passed.

"We won't fuck with your phone," Ian assures.

"Maybe you won't. I don't know the rookies. And you think O'Malley trusts me? You think he won't go through my messages with my girlfriend?"

Greer and Ian exchange a glance. Then after a quiet deliberation that I'm excluded from, I expect them to relent and let me keep my phone.

They don't.

Instead, Ian says the worst thing he could say, "O'Malley. You're staying behind too."

"What?" O'Malley snaps, his breath frosting the air.

"No," I tell Ian. "I'm fine doing this on my own."

"You're doing this shit together," Ian decrees and holds out a hand. But not to me this time. "Your phone, O'Malley. And your clothes."

"Have you lost your fucking mind?" O'Malley says to Ian.

"Hey," Greer glares. "He's not your best buddy right now. He's your lead. You wanna talk to him like that, go join Omega."

Can't even defend my SFO brethren. I'm too pissed off about being stranded outside Philly with someone I wanna rip to shreds. I'd call him the spawn of Satan but I figure the devil's sperm is prettier and more fun to be around.

Angrily, O'Malley strips to his boxer-briefs like me, and we both hand our phones to Ian. I make sure to lock mine. Password isn't so easy to crack, unless they know the year my Lord and Savior Jon Bon Jovi released the album *Slippery When Wet*.

We're given one flashlight and an AirTag. The tracker is in the event they don't hear from us by eight a.m.

"Don't kill each other," Ian says before they all climb into their vehicles. Tires kick up dirt as they peel out onto the main road. Headlights swerve away, and I'm left in the pitch-black, freezing cold with Chris O'Malley.

He switches on the flashlight, and I'm assuming the contempt across his face matches the same look on mine.

And then I chuck the AirTag as far as I can throw it. It goes flying over the tall weeds of the field.

"What the...what's wrong with you?!" O'Malley gapes.

"I don't wanna be found," I say heatedly. "Fuck you and fuck the other Chris." Novak is his best friend on the team. "And fuck the rest of Epsilon."

He has to chase after me as I set the hot, furious pace. My lengthy stride warms my body, but the second I see O'Malley beside me, I only think about pushing him in the ditch.

"You think we're happy you're here?" O'Malley snaps back.

"Why would I ever think that?" I retort. "You've all made it more than clear you think I'm a garbage bodyguard and a garbage human—when I've never made *any* mistake in security to warrant that." I walk faster, hoping he'll slow down.

He doesn't.

O'Malley stays at my side and illuminates the deserted road ahead of us. Farmland on the right and left. "You're *famous*. People know who you are, and that's only gonna escalate the longer you and Luna are together. It makes this job more complicated, so yeah, we don't want you here. Omega is the one in the news and on magazine covers. It makes no fucking sense for you to be Epsilon."

"Something we agree on," I mutter. I wish I asked Cruz Jr. for a smoke before he left.

We walk on the dirt. Hurts less than the loose gravel.

Silence falls for about five blissful minutes, and we focus on staying warm. I blow in my cupped hands. He's shivering and muttering curses. I'm hoping the nearest gas station isn't more than four miles out, but who knows. With my luck, it's probably a hundred miles to sanctuary.

"That must've been some car ride with the Wreath brothers," O'Malley says. Can't see his face all too well in the dark, but I assume he's glaring. "What'd you do, blow them?"

"Yeah," I say tightly. "I gave them world-class BJs."

"You did get paid doing it."

"You have a funny way of asking for a fist in your face." I try to see his expression, but the light is only hitting the road, not our features. His obsession with me and sex is just odd at this point. He always finds a way to bring up my past turning tricks, and there've been a couple times that I've thought he's into me.

Like sexually.

Is this just a hate-the-person-you-wanna-fuck situation? I dunno.

I try to outpace him. He won't let me. I sigh out an aggressive breath, "I'm not quitting. Whatever you and SFE throw at me, it won't get me to quit."

O'Malley lets out a pained laugh. "Yeah, *we know.* There is nothing we could do to you, outside of killing you, and none of us hate you enough to go to prison."

"Aw thanks," I murmur.

O'Malley sighs now. "Really, what'd you tell Ian? Because before tonight, he was supposed to—"

"Be a prick? Haze me further? What'd you have? Silly string? Honey? You want the bears to eat me?"

"Jesus Christ," O'Malley groans. "You're like a fucking jack-in-the-box."

"I dunno, you look like the bigger clown to me."

He sighs again. I wish he'd stop sighing. Everything he does is nails scraping down a chalkboard right now. "He was supposed to make it harder for you."

"Trust me, he did." I can't think of anything worse than being stuck with O'Malley in this situation.

In the next ten minutes of silence, he glances over at me more than once.

"You wanna say something?" I finally snap. "Or are you just checking me out? 'Cause we've been over this, I'm straight—"

"But you've blown how many guys before?" O'Malley slings back.

I glare. "Why so interested? You asking for one?"

His laugh sounds more brittle, and I see his cloud of breath in the dark. "I'm *not* hitting on you, Paul. I would never hit on you, trust me."

We've both said that phrase.

Trust me.

Seems impossible.

"Alright, Chris." I stare back at the never-ending road. "If you're not secretly in love with me—"

"Insane—"

"—then you must be jealous."

He laughs for real now, like that's ridiculous. "Jealous? Of you?"

"I never thought it till recently," I admit. Why would he ever want to put himself in my shoes? He has the better parents. The better family. The better life. Right? Except now maybe I have something he does want.

It sears every muscle in my body, but I say it, "You wanna be with Luna."

"Yeah, *no*," O'Malley forces. "Do I think she's cute? Yeah."

I suck in a boiling breath and try to calm down.

"But I wouldn't date a girl eight years younger than me, and I definitely wouldn't go for someone like her."

"What's that supposed to mean?"

He shakes his head a few times, searching for the words. "I'd never trust her."

Fuck me, I'm burning alive again. If snow were falling, it'd melt as soon as it kisses my skin. "Sleeping around while you're single doesn't make you a cheating whore."

"Just a whore, right? You would know."

I rub my face with both hands. Beyond aggravated. We haven't broken our stride. "So you're not in love with me. You don't want to fuck me. You're not jealous." I drop my hands and shake my head now. "What'd I do to you?" I glare at him. "The way you act around me, it's like I fucked your girlfriend."

O'Malley staggers. He falls a couple steps short, and I spin around on him, my pulse shooting to my throat.

"Wait...did I...?" I breathe.

The flashlight hurts my eyes as the beam hits me, but he fists the neck of the handle, letting the light shoot to the sky. We're illuminated enough that I see visible pain sharpening his cheekbones.

"Who? When?" I question, trying to rack my brain for a name or a face. "How?"

42

PAUL DONNELLY

"Forget about it," O'Malley mumbles, about to continue hiking down the road, but I catch his elbow. He jerks out of my grip. "It was forever ago."

"Yeah, and you still haven't let it go."

He laughs. "How can I? It was the *worst* year of my fucking life, and to top it off, she cheated on me with *you*."

My head is spinning. "Who?"

"Mikaela Fleet."

I shake my head slowly. It's not ringing any bells.

"Five foot two. Brunette. Neck and arm tattoos."

My brows jump. "You were dating a girl with neck tats?" That doesn't seem like his type of classy. It's mine, yeah. Not his.

"Never again," O'Malley says coldly. He shivers as we stand in place but neither of us restarts the trek to a gas station. "The whole two years with her was toxic, but that year…" He stops himself, like the words are excruciating to unearth. I'm getting the sense he rarely talks about her.

"What about it?"

"She drove every knife into me you could think of. She would break up with me, then get back together, then break up again. Over and over. Like she had a sick fascination with seeing me *agonized* over losing her, and I was young and too in love to see what she was doing." His face twists at the memories. "Then she pays to have sex with *you*. While we're still together. A guy she knew I didn't like. And she tells her friends about it. It was humiliating."

My stomach clenches. I guess that's why he's never brought it up. He's even shaded with embarrassment now, and he avoids my eyes.

As sad as his heartbreak is, something…isn't calculating here. "You sure I slept with her?"

"She had *pictures*. Not of your face. But how many guys have a scorpion tattoo above their dick?"

"True." I rub my arms a couple times, warming myself. I did let some people take pics of my body. That's 'cause I turned tricks *before* I got a job in security, and I wasn't too cautious about what anyone could post on the internet. I didn't care.

I wonder if she wasn't someone who paid. Did I just meet her at a bar? She's not the type I would've went for though. I'd hit on sorority girls, law students in pencil skirts, pre-med perfectionists wanting to let loose—not saying they can't also have neck tats, but that combo is harder to find.

Just thinking about all of this is making my stomach overturn too. Feels like I'm mentally betraying Luna, and I hate digging that far back. In my mind now, she's my first and last pussy.

"You're positive she paid me to sleep with her?" I ask him.

O'Malley glowers. "She told me she did. Who the hell would lie about that?"

I shrug. "I stopped turning tricks when I was twenty-three."

"It was before that." He shivers. "I was twenty, so you must've been twenty."

Twenty.

I stare up at the beam of light. His worst year was one of the darkest years of my life. My parents were released from prison. I'm back in Philly more often that year. I'm happy to see them. They start off sober. The summer is blistering hot, and my mom asks me to come over one night for dinner.

She's high.

She shows me to her friend. Who pulls out cash. He asks me to get on my knees.

My pulse races, and I blink and blink.

"Donnelly?"

"Hmm?" I look at him. "Twenty?"

"Yeah...?" His concern is so rare, I almost believe a UFO flew by and we've been abducted.

I shake my head again. "Nah, I didn't know you when we were twenty. We met in security, and I would've been twenty-three."

"Yeah." He nods, but a red tint ascends his neck. "I didn't know you."

"But you said Mikaela slept with a guy you didn't like. You can't dislike someone you don't know."

O'Malley stops shivering, as if blanketed with the heat of his slip. He covers a hand to his face, and I go eerily still.

"No," I say, my heart pumping on overtime. "No." I shake my head more fiercely. There is one single way he could've known about me back then, but it's so unbelievable to me. When maybe it shouldn't be. Still, I'm shaking my head so fucking much, I think my neck might snap. "You can't be...you're not..."

"Related to you?" O'Malley grits out with the tensest breath, like he's caged this truth inside his soul for a lifetime.

Yeah.

He has.

I'm so angry, I see blood-red in front of my eyes. "There are a thousand O'Malleys in South Philly. My mom's not a part of your family."

She's Bridget O'Malley, but I always assumed that her branch of the family did not touch any part of Chris's tree. 'Cause he would've said something. He would've, at the very least, told Triple Shield when I was sitting on a hot seat being grilled about the Donnellys' ancestry.

"She's basically *dead* to my family," O'Malley states.

I feel sick. "I don't believe you."

"She has nine brothers. Blake O'Malley is one of them. My father." He bangs a hand on the flashlight as the beam flickers. "*Stay away from the Donnellys.* That's what I heard growing up. You all were like an urban legend when I was a kid." He stares out at the field. "But nothing was worse than the cautionary tale of Bridget O'Malley. Sean Donnelly got her pregnant. At *fourteen*. With you."

Yeah.

With me.

I say nothing. I can't speak.

"Our family is *religious*. Sex out of wedlock is bad, but sex at fourteen? Pregnant at fourteen?"

Please stop saying fourteen.

I'm unblinking.

"Yeah, they wanted nothing to do with her. Which, looking back now, I hate them for. Because how can you throw out a child...?" His eyes redden, and he's still avoiding my gaze. "But then, I was just a kid eating what they were feeding me, and I hated the Donnellys. I still do. I got robbed at the fucking Quickie-Mart by one of *your* cousins when I was fifteen."

I try to speak again, but I literally can't even open my mouth.

"I knew all about you." He looks at me now. "My family kept up with news about Bridget, even though they wouldn't contact her—it was just validation for them. That she was a lost soul. It sounded like it."

I bet.

"You were born. She got into heroine. Then meth. She fell deeper into the fucking cesspool of the Donnelly family and there was no out. There's never an out." He holds my gaze. "So when I finally met you, face-to-face, at Studio 9, you weren't an urban legend to me anymore. You had dropped out of high school. You had done meth with your parents. You'd gotten paid to fuck my girlfriend. Everything I knew about you was irredeemable to me."

I nod a few times, my chest concaving. Like a seven-ton Mack Truck is running over me. "You know the funny thing?" I choke out.

"I would've given *anything* to grow up next to you. I woulda instantly loved you." I watch his face fall. "Now you're just another cousin I wish were dead."

I rotate away from him.

"Donnelly."

I run.

"Donnelly!"

I don't look back.

I can't outrun him.

It's not that he's faster. It's that I pull my hamstring. And I slow down and limp a little. Glaring at him as he rolls up next to me.

"A gas station should be close," he says, like he didn't just drop the *biggest* bomb on me. He keeps smacking the flashlight. Maybe as something to do 'cause the light is working fine. "I never told anyone...you know. Not even Price."

It's clear he would've taken this to his grave if he could've. "Why?"

"I didn't want to be known as your cousin. And it'd surface...a lot that I don't like talking to anyone about."

"Ditto," I mutter, squinting as a tiny ember of light shines in the distance. "Land ho."

It's still tense.

I'm not looking at him.

He's making brief eye contact with me. "Did you think a lot about your mom's side of the family when you were growing up?"

"Yeah." I nod. "I thought about how awful they were to her. How they gave up on her and *left her* in a piss-poor situation that they could've saved her from. Saved *me* from." I side-eye him, then glare ahead. "But that's about the same time I realized no one was gonna come save me." I take a breath. "I never dreamed about the O'Malleys swooping in and taking me to a cozy bed and handing me a warm meal. 'Cause if they were good people, I would've already been living with 'em. So I thought she must've come from dirt. Not from your good *ole* O'Malley family."

He's quiet.

I'm quiet.

We don't talk until we reach a tiny gas station. Two pumps. One car outside, a silver Volkswagen. Craving warmth, we jog up to the entrance—fuck, I really tweaked my hamstring—and the bell dings as we slip inside.

Only in our underwear, I doubt this is the weirdest thing going down on Super Bowl Sunday. Technically, it's Monday now. Four a.m.? I search for a clock, wandering down the candy aisle. Mostly to get away from O'Malley.

I need space.

He's taking charge and approaching the cashier. A fortysomething blonde scrolls on her phone and drinks a canned Fizz. She startles seeing his half-naked self. "Sir, you can't be in here without clothes." She sounds scared.

O'Malley raises a calming hand. "I'm really sorry. Can I borrow your phone? I need to call a ride."

"Y-you should go." She's the only one working here. She sees my form dipping in the back but hasn't caught sight of my face. I worry about crowding and making her feel threatened or intimidated. But I can't say skulking in the back is doing any better.

O'Malley tries a few other tactics, and she a hundred percent thinks he's gonna steal her phone if she passes it over.

So I go to his side. "Ma'am, I'm—"

She gasps, her eyes lighting up in recognition. "OhmyGod." She puts her hands to her mouth and shoots up from her seat. "You're Paul Donnelly."

At first, I'm afraid she's about to back up like the Boogeyman of Dalton Academy has sprung out. But when she drops her hands, she's smiling.

"I can't believe it's you," she says in disbelief. "Oh my God. Liv is never going to believe this."

I grin. Mostly 'cause O'Malley looks highly annoyed. This has quickly turned in my favor. "I can leave Liv a voice memo," I say, and I explain our situation. A dare for security. She introduces herself as Kera. After a voice memo and quick pic of me and Kera, O'Malley is shooting me a look to *hurry up*. She's doing us a favor. Least we can do is be nice about it.

"You're on Epsilon, right?" She's blushing. "I...um, follow *We Are Calloway* on Reddit and Fanaticon."

"Fanaticon's dope," I say and nod. "And yeah, I'm on SFE now." I don't point out O'Malley since he prefers to be incognito. I'm not blowing up his spot, and she's not taking pictures of him to post on the internet. "You mind if we use your phone? Gotta call someone for a ride."

"Yes, please. Here." Kera passes over her cell phone. "Are you calling someone on SFO or maybe Luna?" Her eyes brighten at this. "I think you're so sweet together."

I smile. "Me too." Whoever we call, they're gonna meet Kera. Lucky for me, those near the top of my call list won't mind that.

Instead of hogging the phone, I let O'Malley use it first. I figure we'll ride separately.

He dials a number from memory. No one answers. Then another number. That rings out too. His frustration mounts, and he shakes his head. "It's after four a.m. No one's awake."

I take the phone, and the first number that pops in my brain is Luna Hale's. I shouldn't call her. I would've never even considered it way back when. I probably would've just tried to hitchhike home or wait for the bus in the cold. Even if I have friends that'd come pick me up too. Farrow. Oscar. All of SFO.

But she once told me to call her if I needed a ride.

So I'm gonna call my girlfriend.

She answers on the first ring. "Who is this?"

"Donnelly. Your planet partner."

I thought it'd cheer her up hearing that, but her stress-level piques. "Are you okay?"

"I'm alright," I whisper. "You haven't gone to bed?" I'm slightly turned away from Kera and the checkout counter. On instinct, O'Malley blocks Kera's view of me. He pretends to be interested in a *Celebrity Crush* magazine, so she can't secretly snap photos of me. Like *I'm* the famous one in need of protection.

"I tried, but I felt like something was wrong. Whose phone are you calling me on? Why is this a random number?"

I hate that she stayed up worried about me, but I try to push that feeling away. She loves me, and this is a side effect of love I need to get used to. Still, I'm wondering if I could've reassured her more. Left better texts. Or maybe it's okay that she's concerned. Maybe it's not such a bad thing.

I walk a few feet into the chip aisle. "Don't freak out."

"Okay." Her voice pitches.

"I got dropped off in Okehocking Preserve—"

"Dropped off? Eliot and Tom's bodyguards left you there? In the middle of the night? Did they take your phone?"

"It's an initiation sorta thing."

"Uh-huh." I hear her feet hit the floor. "I'm coming to get you."

"Luna, *Luna*," I whisper fast. "I'm not there anymore. I'm at the nearest gas station. Don't go anywhere alone. Wake up Quinn or Frog. If they're drunk, call another bodyguard."

"You're okay?" she asks again.

"Yeah, just cold. They took most of my clothes, but I'm fine. O'Malley is sharing in my misery, so that's a plus."

"O'Malley is with you?"

"Yep."

The line goes quiet. "You still there, space babe?"

"Are you *sure* you're okay?" she asks. "Because nothing good ever happens when the Reverse-Flash is alone with the Flash."

I smile. One night while rewatching episodes of *Beneath a Strong Sentiment*, I ended up telling her more about my dislike towards O'Malley, and she concluded that he sounded like the inverse of me.

She called him the Reverse-Paul.

"I promise I'm fine," I whisper, but I can't lie and say this night with Reverse-Paul has been *really good*. It's been...eye-opening. Painful, almost. "I'm gonna get off the phone with you so you can call a bodyguard, alright?"

"I love you," she says really fast.

It fills my lungs. "I love you too." *Keep it together.* I rub my burning eyes. "Watch out for UFOs. Remind your extraterrestrial friends not to beam you up without me."

"They'd be the enemy if they did that."

"Yeah, I'd fight 'em."

"Me too." Her worry hasn't vanished. I hear it in her unsteady voice. With one last, *see ya soon*, we hang up, and I immediately delete the number off Kera's recent calls. After I pass the phone back to her, O'Malley and I keep our distance from each other. Except for the one time he flashes me a page from *Celebrity Crush*.

Surprisingly, it's not a photo of Sulli's baby belly, which has graced nearly every headline with those paternity speculations.

It's a pic of me kissing Luna outside of Superheroes & Scones. My hand is up the back of her purple sweater.

I come closer and swipe the magazine out of his clutch. The Hales, Meadows, and Cobalts—they're like us! They read books. They love movies. They go shopping!

A text bubble on the pic reads, *They kiss!!*

The title of the headline: **SEXY LIKE US**

"Slutty was right there," I joke. "Wasted opportunity, if you ask me." I shove the magazine back in his chest.

"It'll only get worse," he warns.

"Yeah, I don't care," I say and brush a hand through my hair. "Life is worse without her." I go back to the checkout and ask Kera if I can use the bathroom. She hands me a key. O'Malley is doing this thing where he's scoping me out from head-to-toe and I don't like it.

I'm getting the feeling he wants to ask me about Bridget or maybe even his ex-girlfriend who I can't remember. I'm very close to a max threshold of sharing, and I gotta get out. So I spend about fifteen minutes in the bathroom, just perusing the graffitied walls and rewashing my hands.

Someone named Bob was here in 1992.

Jodie and Evelyn are *together 4 ever.*

I exit the bathroom to a mop of dark hair and piercing blue eyes. "You need to shit?" I ask him and toss him the keys.

"Just making sure you weren't doing anything stupid," he mutters.

"Like what? Getting high?" I glare. "With *what*?" I motion to our naked selves. "I didn't shove anything up my ass. But you—maybe you put a fucking soul up yours. Why don't you go dig deep and try to pry it out."

He stares at the keys with a look I don't understand, honestly.

I swallow a rising knot. "What?"

He slowly lifts his eyes to mine, and I must be high. I must've hit my head in the field. This must be all a simulation or I'm in a coma. 'Cause the look he's giving me can't exist. And very quietly, he says, "I'm sorry."

I just start shaking my head.

His eyes flit up and down me. "I never…"

"Never what?" I breathe.

"I never thought you'd want to be saved from that." It's the rawest thing he's ever said to me, and I stare right at him into the great abyss of discomfort. He whispers, "I thought you were just one of them."

He thought I was born a lost soul. I was born an addict. I was born to corruption and darkness. Why would someone like me ever crawl towards a light?

I nod a few times, and the only thing I manage to say is, "I don't need saving." I stop short of saying, *fuck you,* so I think I'm handling my anger alright.

Walking away, I peruse an aisle of jerky and Fruit Roll-Ups, thinking about Luna, and O'Malley keeps his distance, thankfully. Kera makes short conversation to pass the time, and I can't say how many minutes pass before the bell dings and my superhero arrives.

Literally.

I grin as Spider-Man bounds inside. Her backpack is slung on a shoulder, and Luna's spandex outfit conforms every inch of her body. Her round, delicate face is hidden behind the mask.

I take it back about not needing saving. I could be saved by Luna Hale every day. Just for this moment to exist.

Luna practically leaps into my arms, and I hug her lanky frame and twirl her in a circle and sing the short Spider-Man theme song. She presses her forehead to mine, and then I whisper in her ear, "Come to rescue me, Spider-Man?"

She nods. "I'm at your girl-friendly service."

"Best there is." And then I quickly set her down, seeing the bodyguard she brought with her, as he storms down the candy aisle.

Farrow. He's hawk-eyed on O'Malley like a target, like he drove me outside Philly and stripped me naked and left me in the freezing cold. Which…he partially did, but I stripped myself and he's also suffering with me.

"You motherfucker," Farrow says between gritted teeth, and O'Malley walks backward into a fridge of beer. He's always been scared of Farrow, but I've never seen him shrink back like this.

I sprint around these waist-high convivence store shelves and ignore my shrieking hamstring. "Farrow!" I call out, catching up to him. I step in front of O'Malley and put a hand on Farrow's chest. "It's fine. I'm fine. They didn't touch me, alright. It wasn't like that."

His narrowed gaze is drilling into the guy behind me, but he sees that O'Malley is also only wearing underwear and socks too.

Farrow cools off a bit and steps back.

I glance behind me at Chris. He's breathing funny. "You alright, man?"

He glares at me.

So I'm gonna say that's a *yes.*

He was jumped on Halloween though. It wasn't that long ago, and I'm not shocked he's a little shaken. Farrow has put larger guys on the ground.

My best friend follows me back towards the checkout where Luna waits. With Thatcher? "What's he doing here?" I ask Farrow.

"Man, I didn't come alone."

It's good Luna has two bodyguards. Extra security on the street at this hour is smart, even if Thatcher is still suspended. He must be on "unofficial" duty. He's busy speaking with Kera and passes her an electronic tablet. He's having her sign an NDA.

"You have a smoke?" I ask Farrow while Luna unzips her backpack.

He's digging in his pocket, his eyes flashing hot towards O'Malley. Then back to me, he asks, "Initiation? Into what?"

"It's a team building exercise," I say lightly. "We're working together." I think O'Malley must hear me because he comes a little closer.

"Some team."

"Well, you wouldn't understand since you're allergic to cliques."

Farrow cracks a shadow of a smile. He hands me a pack of cigarettes and the lighter. "Don't let them treat you like shit."

"I'm not," I assure, slipping a cigarette behind my ear.

He nods, believing in me.

I throw my arm over his shoulder, bringing Farrow closer to whisper, "She's okay?" She's rummaging in her backpack still, but he knows I'm not referring to this one moment but rather this whole thing. The drive here. He's been with her.

He'd know.

Farrow nods, smiling like he's enjoying me being in a relationship. "Yeah. She's just worried about you."

Luna speaks through her mask. "I didn't have time to go through your closet, so I grabbed something from mine that I thought would fit you." She hands me Princess Leia's long draped skirt and a Carraways black band tee, which looks like it'd be big on Luna but tight on me. Her head swerves to O'Malley. "Sorry, I didn't bring anything for Reverse-Paul."

"Reverse-Paul?" He looks at me like *I* made the nickname. I know my superheroes pretty well now, but that is too much of a Hale thing to do. Last time I checked, I'm still a Donnelly.

"You're the uglier version of me," I tell him.

He rolls his eyes. "Yeah? In what universe?"

"Mine." Luna raises her hand.

I grin. "My favorite one." I look to O'Malley. "You want the shirt?"

"No, I'm good." His voice is quieter. It's clear he wishes someone he liked, and who liked him, picked up the phone. He's uncomfortable, and it makes me feel like shit. Maybe it shouldn't, but he's outnumbered now. Four to one, and I'd rather not shun him.

I toss the shirt to Chris.

"I said—"

"Your abs are scaring the potato chips." I step into the skirt and focus on Luna. "Where's the keys?"

"Oh, Spider-Man always drives." Luna nods like this is a rule I should know.

"Not tonight when Princess Leia is around," I tell her.

Luna relinquishes the keys in my palm without a fight, but Farrow steals them from me. "I can drive back. I drove here."

"Spider-Man always drives, huh?" I tease her.

"I did drive," she says.

I frown, confused, and I look over at Farrow. "You take two cars?"

"Yeah," he answers.

Why?

Thatcher joins us, and I realize the guys threw shirts over pajama bottoms. They ran out of the penthouse.

It's not making sense. Not until I tell Kera *thanks* again, then walk out into the cold with my arm slung around my girlfriend. I stop short beside the ice chest. Luna's Volvo, a security SUV, and Mazda are parked near the two pumps. Leaned up against the cars are Akara and Banks…then Quinn, Gabe, and Frog.

And Oscar. His arms are crossed tightly over his chest. He's against the door of the Mazda. He must've taken his husband's car.

And I realize, they aren't here for Luna.

They came here for me.

I love my family. It crashes against me, and I look down at the pavement, trying not to fucking cry. When I get it together, I look up and I nod to them in *thanks*, unable to speak. They don't need to say anything to me. Words don't feel as good as what they just did.

Being present.

Being there.

I inhale a strong breath.

"You called the cavalry?" O'Malley asks me.

"Nah. They just came." I can tell Gabe is drunk. He's bearing too much of his weight on Quinn and fighting to keep his heavy-lidded eyes open.

I laugh, and I tell everyone, "I'm alright." This time, I really believe it.

Akara nods to me, and he's one of the last to pile into the cars. As though ensuring I really am good.

Oscar tosses his keys to Thatcher, then says to O'Malley, "You can ride with Moretti."

"Great," O'Malley mutters. No one's ragging on Chris. Despite whatever he thinks of SFO, none of us would kick a guy while he's down. He pulls on the Carraways tee and disappears into the Mazda.

I have my arm around Luna in the back of the Volvo. With Oscar in the passenger seat, Farrow peels out onto the street. Blowers expel hot air, and Luna pulls off her mask. Her hair is all matted and frizzed, and her eyes sink into mine.

I kiss her.

We make out, really.

For maybe five or six minutes. Could be longer, but who's counting? I feel more than put back together. Each kiss is possessive and passionate and exultant. Like I'm exploding into joy. Anger and pain are so far gone now, and I hang on to these simple moments. And this unmatched feeling. I smile against her lips. She clings tighter to me.

When we come up for air, Oscar has had enough.

"Answers, bro. Literally give me anything. You can suck her face later."

Luna blushes just a little, but she's smiling too. I laugh, and I could tell him how much I hate Epsilon. How they're still the pricks they've been.

But it's not really what comes to mind.

"You won't believe it," I say to Luna, to my friends. Farrow's eyes flicker to the rearview, and Oscar has turned fully to meet my gaze in the back. And I tell them, "I'm related to O'Malley."

"Ha-ha," Oscar says. "Seriously. Give me something real."

"It's real. Deadass. Chris O'Malley is my cousin."

He might've taken it to his grave, but I'm not taking it to mine.

FANATICON FORUM

We Are Calloway

Posted by @super-sleuth2015

Why I think Donnelly is no longer on SFO...
We've all seen the big leak on Celebrity Crush by now.
That apparently Donnelly does NOT get along with
Epsilon and they don't even like him. No one is asking
the real question. Why would he even be taken off SFO
in the first place? I think it's bc the families don't want
him to be famous. They're protecting Luna from all the
attention, and it's also why Luna x Donnelly haven't
announced their relationship.

@SFOpride9: This is def plausible. But we don't even
know if the leak is real or even credible. Celebrity Crush
just said it was an "inside source" which could be anyone.

@wander_lust: Does he get along with anyone? First
it's with Loren Hale, now half the security team? I still
can't believe they didn't fire him.

@XanderOnlyXander: If this theory is true, I think we
can safely verify at some point that their relationship is
not only real but might be more serious than a lot of the
people on here want to believe.

@suckmypotatoes: Have you seen that vid of the way he grabs her face when he kisses her? I'd make him my boyfriend too. It's so f-ing hot.

@HalesAreMyEverything: Omg I know. That one gif of him picking her up onto the hood of her car is the hottest thing I've seen on here. I still can't believe they did that in the parking lot at Penn.

@LeeLoo5: I wish I went to Penn. Can you imagine running into Ben Cobalt? I would DIE.

@CobaltTwinsStanAccount: Why are ppl thirsting over Donnelly all of a sudden? Did we forget his family KIDNAPPED Luna???

EMAIL FROM THE TRI-FORCE

FROM: pricekepler@tripleshield.com, akarakitsuwonksecurities.com, jonsinclair@tripleshield.com, thatchermoretti@ksecurities.com, ianwreath@tripleshield.com
TO: *all triple shield bodyguards, all kitsuwon securities bodyguards*

As you should've already heard, the Tri-Force has been reestablished as an authority overseeing all security firms. It will contain *all* leads and owners of both Triple Shield and Kitsuwon Securities. No matter which firm you are employed under, the two are working cohesively together, and we're maintaining this cohesion throughout the new year and moving forward.

We expect complete compliance.

Now, we've seen the recent leak regarding Security Force Epsilon, and we're looking into how *Celebrity Crush* could know about in-fighting in SFE. In case you need reminding, ALL private information must stay with you. Not just about these families but about the security forces you work for. If you've shared any private info about your job with your family, your friends, your significant other, etc. and they've run to a tabloid, you will be terminated.

If we find you are the one in communication with a tabloid, you will be terminated immediately.

On a better note, an H.M.C. Philanthropies event has been scheduled for May. It'll be the biggest of the year. Some of you may be participating. Volunteer list will be sent out later. We'll begin security prep for the event next month.

It's a Fight Night in Vegas.

Best Regards,

Price Kepler, owner of Triple Shield Services
Akara Kitsuwon, owner of Kitsuwon Securities Inc.
Jon Sinclair, Alpha Lead
Thatcher Moretti, Omega Lead
Ian Wreath, Epsilon Lead

DONNELLY'S DAILY PLANNER
Sunday, Feb 17th

Today's Focus: be careful with your gf but not too careful. Ride that dangerous line to the moon.

To Do:

- Pick up X at Hale House.

- Mock Panel with the Fizzle Five (gf will be there — don't mix bodyguard duties up with bf duties).

- Show Luna the promised land (wawa. Not sex *yet*).

- Take her pseudo-virginity.

Notes: Today's gonna be the day. Gonna go the distance with Luna. Physically. Think we've been making big strides everywhere else. Just need to take her to wawa first. Feels right check-marking that box beforehand. Been a long-time coming.

Good news: Thatch is *almost* officially back on-duty. March 1 is the day. Heard the good news during a penthouse fam dinner (mac + cheese with chicken, courtesy of yours truly and my space babe). Also heard SFO's "group therapy" sesh ended with Frog feeling ganged up on. She walked out. Akara consoled her? Idk. Feeling like Froggy needs me. Just don't know how.

Might call in sick when Epsilon has their therapy sesh.

Also! The Procrastination King has been chitchatting with Spencer during study period. She's always busy with academics tho. Think he likes that about her. Spencer = happy distraction. Easton = painful distraction. Xander's bff isn't doing so hot.

ALSO!!! who the fuck is leaking shit about me + Epsilon to tabloids???? No fans should know about that. Still think it's an inside job. wondering if SFE is trying to make me look bad so I get fired.

Fuck them.

Meals: wawa with the gf. Then going to town on the gf's pussy. Eating good today.

~~Water:~~ **GF's Pussy:** Refer to "meals" and also,

gonna fuck her tonight. Thirst will be quenched.

Question of the Day: ~~why does Cherry Fizz taste like blackberries?~~ would Eliot kill charlie for the Fizzle throne? ~~Would Ben?~~ would Xander?

43

PAUL DONNELLY

"Salem, here girl." *I shake doggie treat*s at the bottom of the Hale's staircase. Salem is perched on the third step and eyes the treats with a good dose of skepticism. Like I'm planning to feed her arsenic.

Poison isn't what I had in mind. Even if she looks like she'd rather bite me.

Still love her.

She's a picky pooch though. With one whiff, Orion would sprint after these bacon bits. Yesterday, I offered Salem chicken treats. Week before that, beef.

She must be a vegetarian.

Every weekday when I pick up Xander to take him to Dalton, Salem comes running. Just to growl at me. There's been a constant rift, and nothing I do seems to mend it.

I continue my stare-off with the Newfie. After a beat, Salem barks twice, then races up the stairs. Away from me.

"No bacon. Got it," I mutter and shove the bag of treats in my back pocket. Easier blaming the treats than myself. Don't want to think too hard on what it means for that dog to dislike me so much. Especially when she belongs to Kinney.

"Donnelly?"

I flinch.

Lily's voice catches me off guard, even more so when she rounds the corner. She's holding a steaming cup of coffee between two hands, and she's dressed in X-Men pajama bottoms and Black Widow slippers.

A week has passed since the Super Bowl, and she's avoided me every time I drop by. I didn't think today would be the day. Feel unprepared is all. My jeans are ripped.

I rub a hand through my hair. "Hi," I say like I'm meeting my girlfriend's mom for the first time.

"Hi." She steps forward and takes a deep, readying breath.

"Jesus, Dad! He's not doing okay there! Why can't you see that?!" Xander yells from the second floor. Lily and I both look up at the staircase as he shouts, "It's not about me being stressed!"

"You're my first priority—"

"I'm fine, I'm fine, I'm *fine*. You know who's not okay?"

Easton.

I know this has to be about Xander's best friend. Easton was so shaken in the parking lot on Wednesday, he wouldn't get out of his car and go into school. Xander sat with him and missed his AP History exam. Easton's dad wasn't happy about his slipping grades. He decided a good punishment was to strip his son's bedroom of everything except box springs and a lamp.

Xander told him, "Just finish the school year at my house."

"Live with you?" Easton asked.

"Yeah," Xander nodded. "Live with me."

They talked about whether Easton's parents would even allow it and decided they would. But only if the famous Loren Hale asked them.

"My mom has a borderline obsessive crush on your dad," Easton said. "It's disturbing considering she's married. But who can blame her when her husband is the second coming of Nosferatu."

I assume Xander broached the subject to his dad. And he's not meeting the outcome he'd imagined.

I can hear Lo's response to his son. "They might say no, bub.

Even if I ask them for permission to let Easton stay here—it might not go how you want. *That* disappointment on top of your senior year and Fizzle and college admissions is a lot—"

"I'm not going to kill myself!!" Xander shouts at the top of his lungs. It punches me right in the gut, and I glance at his mom beside me.

Lily's eyes widen, and she cages her breath.

"So you aren't stressed?" Lo fires back.

"Of course, I'm fucking stressed!" Xander screams.

"Backtrack. Take a breath, you and me. Let's talk about this at an indoor decibel..." Lo's voice tapers off, and they must be walking farther away from the staircase.

Lily clears a ball in her throat. "We should go somewhere else." She takes a quick peek back up the stairs, maybe thinking Xander might start shouting again. "I want to talk to you."

Lily wants to talk to me. Her big readying breath makes more sense. I follow her into the living room, then to the kitchen. I'm trying to ready myself for this conversation too. But I keep thinking of all the reasons why she'd hate me.

I'm attached to the monstruous family that attacked her.

I hooked up with Luna in her kitchen.

She might even believe I'm too old for her daughter.

I've got strong defense mechanisms, and my guards are rising. Being vulnerable in front of Lily might be the path forward, but I can't figure out how to lower those draw bridges right now.

I just follow.

Her eyes dart around the kitchen. "Uh...this way." She leads me to the laundry room and switches on the light. As soon as I enter, she shakes her head. "No, let's try somewhere else."

On autopilot, she leaves the laundry room and goes for another door. It's the garage. Knob is fixed, and as soon as she touches it, she drops her hand.

Have I desecrated that many places in the Hale House? My muscles strain.

Panic shoots in her eyes, one that looks a lot like anxiety. So I just say, "Backyard has a nice atmosphere."

Her gaze swings to the window, and she frowns. "It looks cold."

"I like the cold."

Lily considers this, then shakes her head. "No, we can talk inside." My chest untightens a bit. 'Cause she's letting me stay inside these sacred four walls. I didn't think she'd want that, but maybe this is just to avoid frostbite.

Luna's mom brings me to the home office.

"You can sit," she says, gesturing to a rolling chair.

So I take a seat while she stays standing. She's still cupping the coffee mug, and I try to sit straight. The more I look at Lily, the more tension builds.

I thought this divide would only exist with Lo, but since the Super Bowl, I've felt the closest to Luna's dad—and now I feel the furthest away from her mom.

"Donnelly," she says. "I…there's…" She lets out a frustrated breath. "I've actually said this speech ten times. Printed it out too. Read it to Lo."

I try to smile, but I hate that she's been worrying over what to say to me. "How'd that go?" I ask.

"He thought I was too nice."

"You can be mean, not that you need my permission to lay into me. But it's deserved, so…" I wish my pulse would slow the fuck down.

"You think it's deserved?" Her green eyes crawl over me. It's making me feel exposed, and I lean back in the chair.

"I dunno, maybe. Yeah." I nod. "I'm sorry—for not respecting you and Lo and your home like I should've. I'm sorry for…for what happened. To you and to Luna—"

"That's not your fault."

I can't look at her now, and I hear the feet of a footstool scraping against the floorboards. When I glance back, she's sitting across from me. Her coffee mug is on the desk.

"I'm happy for Luna," Lily professes. "I'm happy my daughter found someone so completely and utterly compatible for her. Even before her amnesia, the way she talked about you was...magical."

I'm feeling a *but* coming on.

But you're disgusting, Donnelly.

But you're toxic.

But you're bad for her.

But I can't have you in my house.

She sucks in a breath before continuing. "But I'm also so fucking *mad*," she says through gritted teeth like she's holding back angry tears. "I'm a sex addict, and for you to do a sexual act in my house in a public space. That's *not* okay. Walking in on one of my kids having sex has been a nightmare and fear of mine since Maximoff hit puberty."

"I didn't know that," I say, almost choked. I'm hit viscerally by her words. She's not yelling. Not raising her voice. That's somehow even worse. "I'm sorry—"

"I know," she interjects fast. "I'm not trying to twist a knife any deeper. I just need you to know why it's hard for me and why I'm upset. I don't want to look at you and picture you naked or doing *that*." Flush reddens her cheeks. "It's what I've been picturing, if I'm being super honest, and it's not right as Luna's *mom*. I wish I could scrub my brain of that moment, but I can't." She intakes a bigger breath. "It's made me feel guilty, like a terrible mom, like I'm screwing up, and I just need you to *please* keep this all in mind when you're with Luna."

I start to nod, but I ask, "Just for clarification and all, you're saying no PDA in front of you, right?"

"No, no." Her eyes pop out. "I'm not barring you two from kissing. I wouldn't do that! Kiss all you want. Just *don't* have sex in a place where I can walk in on you. *Please.*"

"Got it," I nod. "Won't happen again. Promise."

Lily exhales, then stares off in thought. "Actually..."

I brace myself again.

"...I think we should talk about your intentions with Luna."
She sits straighter too. "Because she *loves* you. Like head-over-heels
smitten, would do absolutely *anything* for you in love."

My lips rise. "Likewise."

Lily doesn't smile back. "But she doesn't remember the past three
years. She doesn't remember what she's done and experienced, and I
hope you're keeping that in mind. Because if you're not..." She jabs
a threatening finger at me, but it's not that intimidating coming from
Lily who's all soft edges. I force back another smile so I don't look
like a jackass. "You're not someone I'd *ever* want for her."

That phrase drills right into me.

My inward smile is gone. "I've thought about it more than you
know."

"Good." She's still scrutinizing me. "I had my worries, honestly,
after I walked in on you two. You're stronger than her. You're older
than her. And she's *very* taken by you."

"This isn't just about sex to me," I try to explain. "What's between
us—I'm not with Luna just to sleep with her. And I'd never misuse
her trust in me. It'd kill me if anyone did that to her."

Lily eases more. "Okay. Good. This is good." She exhales again.
"And I don't want you to think I don't trust you. It's just that I'm
more protective..." Her chin quakes a little, but she lifts it. "I want
to make sure she's okay. After what she went through...it's important
to me."

A gnarled feeling wrestles in my chest. "I feel the same way,
you know." I glance at the wall, my eyes burning. "Thought I was
protective of Luna before, but after what happened, it's pretty much
multiplied by some unquantifiable number—and I wouldn't...I
won't *ever* let anything like that happen to her again. It'd..."

It'd break me.

It already broke me once, but it would do damage that could
never be undone. Those words, I can't release. They're knotted in
my throat. Instead, I manage to say, "I love her more than life itself.
I've never loved anyone like that. Just Luna." I take a breath and

somehow meet Lily's eyes. "I could tell you my intentions are to keep loving her like she deserves to be loved. But I'm not aiming to love Luna. It's never been a goal to love her. Our love existed before I even knew it could. It's there. It'll always be there. For better or for better—'cause life is only worse without her."

Lily sniffs loudly. Her tears well. "Thank you."

I almost start crying. "No, I should be—"

She shakes her head vigorously and stands up. I follow suit, and she's telling me, "You don't need to give me anything…else. Nothing else." Her compassionate gaze says, *you've given enough.* It slams into me, and I try to exhale the ball in my throat.

"All I ask," Lily says, "is that you *always* treat Luna like she's your moon, your stars, your entire galaxy, like she's every fragile and mighty thing."

It's the easiest thing anyone could ask of me.

"I will," I breathe.

"Now…" She picks up her coffee mug and takes a tiny sip. "What's your ship name? Because I keep seeing 'dirty duo' and that doesn't sound magical enough for a 'Luna and Donnelly' pairing."

I laugh into a grin. "Been thinking the same thing."

After patching things up with Lily, I drive Xander into Center City for the mock panel. I would've driven Luna too, but she had to run over to campus this morning. Wyatt Rochester doesn't accept any essays by email. It has to be turned in by hand.

He's a real dick.

But she's powering through the semester. Can't wait for it to be over so I can stop imagining the Roach's hate hard-on for her.

Xander is rifling through his backpack. He's not in his normal graphic tees and hoodies. He threw on the blood-red suit he wore to Homecoming. Dressing to impress. Complimented the get-up as soon as I saw him, and he asked, "You don't think it's too much?"

"Nah. You look sharp as hell. Like a contender."

He smiled at that.

In the passenger seat, he's digging out a ballpoint pen. "I get my dad wants to prioritize me over my friend, but I don't see how Easton living with me will make me *more* stressed?"

"It sounds like it's more about Easton not being allowed to live with you and how that news would affect you."

"It'd suck," Xander concludes. "But he can't be afraid of me meeting a low. I told him that."

"Communication," I grin. "Looks like we were both nailing it." One hand off the wheel I give him a *rock on* gesture, then pick up my energy drink and take a swig.

Xander smiles back. "The talk with my mom went well then?"

"She's not shipping your sister with anyone else, so I'd say so." I set the can back in the cupholder without taking my eyes off the road.

"Yeah, I never thought she would. My mom's smart, wise one. She knows real love when she sees it." He pulls out a binder. "I just wish my dad would stop asking if I need you at my door during the nights again."

Lo must be sensing Xander's heightened stress if he's been pestering him about nighttime security. It's hard to forget about Xander taking my straight razor at the Fanaticon Convention. It was only two months ago, so I have a healthy amount of concern too.

"It's alright if you need it," I say.

"I don't." Xander shoves his bookbag between his feet. "You don't have anything to worry about either."

I frown. "What would I be worried about?"

"My sister—I'm sure you'd rather spend your night with her doing…" He cringes at me.

"Don't think about it," I start to smile.

"Too late."

I laugh.

He *almost* smiles, but instead, sighs out, "Look, you don't need to be stuck watching me sleep. I'm stressed out but I'm fine."

I rotate the wheel with one hand. "One of my favorite past times is protecting you from your sleep demons."

He snorts, but he's smiling now.

"I also don't have a brother like the Morettis," I remind him. "There's only one of me. So I'd only do nights half the time like before. If you're worried who the other bodyguard would be—"

"It's not that," Xander cuts in. "I really don't want *anyone* at night."

"Then what do you want?"

"New anti-anxiety meds. I'm almost positive the ones I'm on stopped working three months ago. But the idea of having to go through a bunch of different prescriptions and all the side effects just to find another one that works makes me want to kill myself."

"Let's not do that," I say easily. And I'm wondering where this newfound casual talk of suicide is coming from.

Xander mutters, "Sorry."

"You can be snarky," I tell him. "Been thinking you were supposed to be a Gemini." I take another sip of energy drink. "You have two sides. You're snarky, then you're soft and sweet."

Xander stares out the windshield, and slowly, his lips upturn. "I think that's just a Sour Patch Kid."

"People do act like they've got a sugar-rush around you."

He laughs, the sound so bright in its rarity. It instantly makes me grin. Even though paparazzi are riding our ass and we're headed towards one of his big stressors, the air is light and his eyes shine with happiness. He plays AC/DC on shuffle. Soon, we're singing to "Thunderstruck" together and pounding the wheel and dashboard respectively. He's rolling down the windows, letting the breeze enter the car. Unworried in this second.

This moment.

The power of eighties rock, I'd say, but I also know it might be the power of me.

44

LUNA HALE

Uncle Stokes apparently loves Panera **Bread.** This is something I never knew until today, when he shut down the entire Panera café in Center City just for the Mock Q&A Panel—five other Fizzle board members in attendance. It's such a strange fun fact about him that it makes me question how well I actually know my uncle.

Xander clutches a binder under his arm like it's a football, and I shuffle through a stack of index cards. We're seated at a booth together, a strong fresh-baked bread scent in the air. None of the other Cobalts have arrived yet, and in ten minutes they'll be verging on *late*.

My eighteen-year-old brother hawk-eyes the front doors. Worry creases his brows. "You don't think they'll just throw this competition?"

I shake my head. "We all agreed not to. None of them would go back on that promise." I peek over at the double doors too. "They're probably just stuck in traffic." I'd ask Donnelly since he has a direct communication line to the Cobalt bodyguards, but he's still securing the café with Frog and Quinn. Apparently, there's a backdoor that doesn't lock properly.

"Wouldn't this have been easier at Fizzle Headquarters?" He pops the tab of a Lightning Bolt! energy drink.

"Maybe the board doesn't want other employees bothering the five of us," I tell him and slurp an iced coffee. Frog brought me one this morning before we left for Penn. She's a thoughtful bean.

I make a mental note to knit her a scarf before the weather changes. Knitting is strangely easier than I remember it being. OG Luna must've practiced more, and the fact that I've subconsciously retained this skill is a super-duper plus.

It makes me wonder if I've retained other skills. Will having sex come back naturally to me? Or will I be all floppy and fumbly the first time?

Morning thoughts. I want to say they're random, but sex has been circulating my brain at all hours. Every time I look over at Donnelly and a sexy grin draws his lips upward, I bake in heat. It's a yearning, aching need. I want to fling myself on him, and I want him to twirl me.

Like last week, at the gas station the night of the Super Bowl. I'd never been so worried about him (that I can remember). But as soon as he saw me and his grin appeared—it no longer felt like a crash-landing. All felt right in the galaxy.

And I finally learned about his mom's last name. *O'Malley.* He didn't even know she was related to the bodyguard O'Malley until that night. I understand how complicated it might've been to share that info—because I did have a million questions afterward. Like why he never imagined they'd be related in the first place.

He had a lot of reasons. A top one being there are tons of O'Malleys in South Philly.

I stare off in thought. If I think longer about Donnelly, *twirling* is the most chaste act I want him to do to me. Now I'm back to remembering how it feels when his body bears against mine. The sensation of him *rocking...*

"Don't they have private board rooms with doors and locks for that reason?" Xander asks, snapping me back to the here and now. Panera Bread and Fizzle. Potential sexcapades, be gone! I focus as he adds, "So employees won't bother board members during their business meetings?"

"Yeah, but there hasn't been a press release about the race for a successor," I say softly, "so I'm guessing it'd be kinda suspicious if we were all at Fizzle together."

"Because Panera is so much *less* suspicious." He takes a nervous swig of energy drink. His amber eyes dart around the café, and he's not so interested in the loafs of wheat in the bakery. He's zeroing in on the entrance where extra security already stands guard.

I straighten my index cards, but I can't study when Xander seems paranoid. "Are you okay?"

He slumps, then catches his bad posture and sits up. "Fine. Just not looking forward to seeing Ben."

"I don't understand how you two still have so much friction."

He tosses his binder on the table. "It's not one big thing. It's little things." He leaves it at that, then eyes my index cards. "What'd you write down?"

"The names of the board members."

Xander catches a glimpse of the five board members and our uncle in corporate attire. They're seated at a wooden table in the middle of the empty café. He drops his voice to ask, "You know their names?"

"Yeah, those five are Krisha Kapoor, Javier Meléndez, Chett Wagner, Gunther Ackermann, and Adaline Dupont."

It's public knowledge, all accessible on the Fizzle website. They're all over-forty with Chett Wagner being the oldest at sixty-seven. He was the closest to our grandfather of the board members at Panera.

I tell Xander, "I did a deep-dive and stalked them on social media. Most are only on LinkedIn, but I still got some of their interests down. Adaline doesn't like…dark chocolate…" My voice trails off as Xander's chest collapses. "It's dumb though. I probably won't need them." I shove the index cards in my crossbody bag. "What's in the binder?"

He blinks. "Nothing. It's a prop."

Oh. "You look the part," I tell him. "Better than I do." My chunky dark-blue sweater says *Weirdo* in green lettering, a Christmas gift from Tom and Eliot. They have matching ones. I'm wearing it over a silky black spaghetti strap dress that sort of resembles my nightgown.

I wonder if it looks like I rolled out of bed.

I didn't think about that...

Xander runs two hands through his hair. "Why didn't I figure out their names?"

"You know them now," I say. "Here." I give my index cards to Xander.

He exhales a long, arduous breath. "Thanks, sis." He shares half the stack so I can keep studying. His leg is jostling under the table.

"No one would blame you if you dropped out," I remind him.

"I can't quit," Xander mutters, flipping over the index card to read Javier's hobbies. *Pickleball, backgammon...* "I have to be able to do this or else Dad, Mom, and everyone else will look at me like I can't handle everything."

"I believe you can handle everything."

Xander lifts his gaze to mine, his chest rising, and I smile at him. Truly, I believe he has it in him to finish the race. I just...really, *really* don't want him to win. That secret isn't so secret. He knows I'm trying to beat him.

Doubt flickers across his face for a half-second. "You won't say that after you remember the last three years."

I frown deeply, not knowing what he's referring to. From my vantage, he's so much different than the Xander of three years ago, who would've rejected the very notion of public speaking. But he's here right now. Ready to do this mock panel even if it gives him a truckload of anxiety.

Maybe he can't see what I see.

"That's super optimistic of you," I tell him, "that you think I'll remember the last three years."

"You will," he says strongly. "And the next time Kinney calls me glass half-empty, I expect you to vouch for me."

I make the Vulcan salute. "On my honor."

A half-smile quirks his lips. Then the front door swings open. All three Cobalts have arrived with their bodyguards in tow.

With one minute to spare.

45

LUNA HALE

The five of us are seated at a long table in front of the business-clad board, who occupy another table. A common Q&A setup except there are no microphones since Uncle Stokes and the board sit so close. They're sipping on French onion soup out of bread bowls and crunching on salads.

I wonder if they've squeezed this in during a lunch break. Will that be one of us someday? Having so little time that we work on our breaks? Life being all-consumed by Fizzle? It's a bleak outlook. One I don't want for any of my cousins, but especially not my brother.

Uncle Stokes says, "This won't take long. We know some of you have places to be."

They all look to Ben.

I don't have my cousin's Google calendar, so I don't know what pressing appointment he has. But the entire board seems to be in the know.

Xander lets out an irritated breath and leans into my shoulder. "It's probably something stupid like hockey practice."

So Xander doesn't know either. It at least makes me feel better that I'm not the only one out of the loop. Our uncle types on his phone, then says, "Each of you have a set of questions to answer. You're to pretend that you're at a press conference and you're here representing Fizzle."

Nerves ambush me. The kind that tightens my stomach, and my index cards slip from my fingers. *Shit shit.* No one look at me! I scoot my chair back and lean down to pick them up. Eliot, sitting next to me, helps. People are definitely looking.

Mr. Wagner, as he introduced himself, with his salt-and-pepper hair and his I-wake-up-at-four-a.m.-just-to-hit-the-gym body beneath a tailored suit is intimidating enough. Now he has judgy eyes.

The silence is so loud.

After I've gathered the cards, I face them down on the table and scoot my chair back in. The legs make the brashest *screech*.

"Luna, you good?" Uncle Stokes asks.

My heart is about to make a prison break out of my chest, other than that—yeah.

Except, *no*.

My uncle is too worried about me. I might as well have Amnesia Girl written on my forehead. I'd rather be meeting six sets of judgy eyes than one pair of worried. Because how do I convince someone I'm healthy enough for this position?

"I'm good," I manage to say. "Proceed." Proceed?! I just told my uncle who is CEO of one of the richest companies in the world to *proceed*.

I'm tomato red.

Uncle Stokes doesn't seem to care as he focuses on Charlie. Maybe my uncle's ego is the size of a grain of salt. Despite Captain America being moral and just—he does have at least a walnut-size ego. Still, I think it's sacrilege to consider my uncle as *the* Captain America like my dad does. In my life, that's always been my older brother. Moffy even found his very own Bucky Barnes in Farrow.

The happy thought eases me.

I take a giant breath.

"Charlie," Uncle Stokes begins. "Stand up, please."

Charlie rolls his eyes—well, a partial eye roll. It seemed to stop midway. He stands from the table.

"Out in front," Mr. Wagner requests.

"Right," Charlie says dryly. He rounds the table so the board can get a good look at him. "Appraise the cattle."

Xander nearly chokes on a sip of Lightning Bolt!

Eliot is grinning beside me and says under his breath, "Dig that grave, brother."

Ben seems to be chatting quietly with Krisha Kapoor at either end of their respective tables. As if he knows her already, but that'd be strange. It's more likely they just met.

"The commentary is unnecessary," Mr. Wagner reprimands.

Charlie bites his tongue and forces a smile.

The board scribble on the notepads and type on tablets. Charlie's golden-brown hair is askew like he'd been tugging at the strands, and his wrinkled white button-down is half untucked from his black slacks. His loafers are shiny, and I wonder if they're jotting these meticulous notes or if they're just writing, *bedraggled, not CEO worthy*.

"You can sit," Mr. Meléndez says without looking up. He's very direct, it seems. Most of them are. Like they have very little time to waste. Our uncle is clearly the warmest of the bunch, and that's probably because he's related to us.

Charlie returns to his seat.

"You went to Prague yesterday," Uncle Stokes says. "Will your travel decrease once you become CEO of Fizzle?"

Charlie doesn't even blink. "No."

Whispers ignite from the board members. Ms. Kapoor and Mr. Ackermann are the most peeved by his response. They use their hands to shield their lips, like we can read them. Mr. Wagner quiets everyone.

Those of us on the panel all lean forward to look at Charlie. We agreed *not* to throw this, but it's hard to say if he's tossing in the towel. He's not putting on a façade. In a way, he's delivering *himself* to them, and it's admirable.

Yet, alarming.

What if he's not chosen?

Uncle Stokes glances warily from the board, then back to his nephew. "How will you handle the workload while also keeping up your travels?" he questions.

"Remotely," Charlie deadpans.

The board continues their grumbling softly. Even Adaline Dupont is stabbing her salad aggressively with her fork.

Uncle Stokes scoots forward. "Your relationship with Maximoff Hale has been divisive in the media. Not only is he a shareholder, but he plays a significant role within the company, as he helms a charity that Fizzle is actively involved in. Would you be opposed to working alongside him as future events arise?"

Charlie looks mildly irritated. "If you love him so much, then make him CEO."

"We would," Mr. Ackermann states flat-out. "But he's not in contention. You five are."

"Would you work amicably with him, Charlie?" Mr. Wagner questions.

It takes Charlie a tense minute, but he grinds out the word, "Yes."

"Do you like Maximoff Hale?" Ms. Kapoor asks. "Press will prod you on this."

"What's not to like?" Charlie says dryly.

Mr. Ackermann turns to the board. "It sounds like he can't stand him."

"I *like* him," Charlie emphasizes. "I trust Moffy with my life. With the lives of my brothers and sisters. With the lives of my cousins. If the world were ending, he's who I'd want at my side...third."

"Who are the first two?" Adaline asks with the tap of her manicured nails on the desk. She's now very interested in Charlie. Salad abandoned. She's bowing forward.

"Wouldn't you like to know?" Charlie snaps.

Adaline smiles suggestively. Uh, I don't think that was a come-on from Charlie, but who knows, I guess.

"We can move on," Mr. Meléndez says.

"Eliot," Uncle Stokes gestures my best friend forward. "Out in front, please."

And so Eliot lets the board inspect his confident, dapper poise, as though he stepped right out of *Mad Men*. He's selling the dark-blue suit that perfectly frames his six-foot-four build, the shiny gold cufflinks on his wrists, the polished mahogany-brown loafers—and even his shampoo, his hair styled like he ran his fingers casually through the strands instead of *tugging* haphazardly at them.

I can even smell his spritz of sandalwood and leather cologne. Wealth doesn't wear him. His aura so naturally fits inside the regality of his legacy, it's simply understood that Eliot Alice is the son of Rose and Connor Cobalt.

The board seems satisfied.

"You can sit," Mr. Meléndez says while typing.

"Eliot." Uncle Stokes speaks once my best friend is back in his chair. "If a theatre company were to offer you a job, would you quit your position in Fizzle to take it?"

"No," Eliot answers clearly, concisely. Zero hesitation.

Xander mutters a "shit" under his breath.

Eliot exudes CEO energy. It's obvious.

"Why not?" Uncle Stokes asks.

"Because I keep my commitments."

The entire board loves this answer. Straight-forward. To the point. Nods of approval down the line. I take mental notes.

Charlie seems annoyed and rocks back on his chair legs to try and steal Eliot's gaze. But Eliot is zoned in on the board and ignores his brother.

"Eliot," Adaline, who prefers being addressed by her first name, points her pen at him. "Unlike Charlie, whose romantic affairs are largely a mystery to the public, you've been seen kissing a variety of women. Leading some tabloids to call you a modern-day rake. What do you have to say to that?"

"A modern-day rake," Eliot muses with a rising grin. "Seventeenth-century Restoration comedy is among my favorites. *The Rover* by Aphra Behn, you've heard of it?"

"I can't say I have," Adaline says, looking him over like she's the Bachelorette on TV and he's one of her potential suitors.

"I love it. And I've played a many-a-rake on stage. It's also a wide range. If we're talking charming, witty scoundrel, then possibly it's apt. Sexist pig, that's hardly me."

Mr. Wagner jumps in, "If we asked you to keep your personal affairs more discreet, would you?"

I twitch at this question, but Eliot hardly bats an eye. "Yes, of course."

Charlie lets out an audible sigh. "He's lying."

"Don't listen to my brother," Eliot says without breaking his gaze from the board. "He doesn't know what I'd be willing to do."

"Why do you think he's lying?" Mr. Wagner asks.

Eliot stiffens, only slightly, beside me.

Charlie gestures a hand to him. "He's a fucking *actor*."

"Language, Charlie," Uncle Stokes says.

"I'm being honest," Eliot tells the board, but I have my doubts. Because he is very convincing, and I could also see him agreeing to all stipulations just to take the crown from Charlie.

"Let's move on, if you're ready," Mr. Meléndez asks Uncle Stokes, who nods.

"Luna." My uncle zaps me to attention, and he motions me to round the table like Charlie and Eliot had done.

Okay, I've got this.

With a deep breath, I take a quick glance at Donnelly. He's grinning while leisurely perched against the entrance beside Frog and Quinn, and he gives me an *a-okay* kinda hand gesture. Then he sticks his finger in the hole and winks at me, and my smile mushrooms at the dirty signal.

I calm, not so anxious anymore, and I present myself fully to the board.

"Hi." I wave in a rainbow pattern. *This is me.* I sense the ladies noting my hair. It's a half-up hairdo. Glittery purple and pink ribbon are tied around two buns.

The men seem more concentrated on the *Weirdo* lettering on my sweater.

"Take that off, please," Mr. Wagner requests.

"My sweater?"

"Yes."

I hesitate. "Um…" Alarm bells go off.

I'm not wearing a bra!

It's silk. It's low-cut and revealing. Do I just do it? Do I avoid or will that dock more points off my name? Maybe if I was more versed in competing for things, I wouldn't be as indecisive.

I panic and glance at Donnelly.

His lips have lowered into a concerned frown. His eyes dart back to the board, as if they're exposing themselves as enemy droids.

"Is it important?" I ask Mr. Wagner. "It's kinda cold."

"Do you think the role of CEO is important?" Mr. Wagner shoots back.

Okaaaay… "Yes."

"Then yes."

Uncle Stokes gives him a half-warning look, but it's feeble. My dad's would be lethal.

I grip the bottom of my sweater but stop myself. "This is more appropriate than what's beneath."

"The sweater," he snaps.

"She's trying to tell you *no* while being polite about it," Ben cuts in, and my head swings backward, surprised that he was the first to say something. He's visibly pissed. "What's worse is you know that, and you don't even care."

Mr. Wagner glares.

"What's the point of taking her sweater?" Eliot asks Mr. Wagner too. "You didn't ask for my suit jacket."

"He must be a perv," Charlie says with the cock of his head.

Mr. Wagner glowers. "Excuse me?"

"Charlie," Uncle Stokes chastises. "Chett Wagner has been a prominent board member before you were born. He was a close confidant to your grandfather, and he's been your number one advocate for this position. You'll show him some respect."

"What reason would he have to see under her sweater?" Charlie retorts with less fire than Ben and Eliot. "Give me one."

I hear one of them mutter "nepo brat" under their breath. It might've been Gunther.

Xander is swinging his head back and forth like this is a tennis match, and he's losing sight of the ball. Whereas my boyfriend is taking these deep controlled breaths like he's forcing himself not to rush out to me. When we lock eyes, Donnelly shakes his head at me like *don't*.

Don't take off my sweater.

He can see the mere thought is making me uncomfortable.

I won't do it.

I keep my arms at my side.

Mr. Wagner swallows a hot gulp of water from his glass, then with fiery narrowed eyes, he addresses Charlie, not me. "We're at a mock press conference. A publicist would ask Luna to take off her sweater before she confronted a single camera. She can't wear anything with *that* word on it."

Weirdo?

"Being a weirdo isn't a bad thing," I end up saying.

Ms. Kapoor smiles, and yes, it's a pity smile, but at least I'm winning *someone* over.

"*Mock* press conference," Charlie emphasizes. "It's pretend. Don't tell me in a real scenario someone wouldn't have a jacket on hand for her. And in that *real* scenario, you wouldn't see under her sweater."

"You've made your point," Mr. Wagner glares.

To shut down this topic, I jump in, "I'm keeping my sweater on, thank you."

Scribbles and typing.

I'm told to sit, and when I return to my seat, Xander leans a shoulder into me. "You okay?"

"Uh-huh," I whisper and give him a thumbs-up.

He tries to breathe.

"Luna." My uncle's voice jolts me again. "Your fiction has caused a stir in the media." So we're going there. I'd been preparing like this was speed-dating with the board members, not a damage control Q&A. "As CEO of Fizzle, you won't be able to write publicly anymore. Will this be a problem?"

Yes.

"No." The word bursts from my mouth.

The room is quiet, and I avoid staring directly at the board this time. I don't want to overanalyze their reactions.

I can't even say if my answer is a lie. Would I truly quit writing to be CEO? I have no earthly clue. But I'd do just about anything to keep my brother from becoming a zombie in a business suit. Xander currently death-grips his energy drink next to me.

"Would you be willing to tell the world that the published fiction is not yours?" Uncle Stokes asks.

I shift in my chair. "That would be a lie." I make a mistake by glancing at Gunther Ackermann. He's typing profusely on his tablet. That can't be good.

"But," I say quickly. "I would be open to lying if it was a better lie. It's just that my stories can easily be traced back to me, so it's a lie that I would be caught in."

Mr. Ackermann glances up, his eyes catching mine. He doesn't give anything away—but he's stopped typing. That feels like a better sign.

"Her public persona," Mr. Meléndez whispers to the board.

Adaline chimes in, "There are rumors you're currently dating that bodyguard." She stabs her pen in Donnelly's direction. And all eyes train on my boyfriend.

He's relatively blank-faced. Giving nothing away. He is a sneaky one.

"Yep," I say to Adaline. "I've heard those."

"Would you publicly confirm the rumors, if asked?" she questions.

"Yes, but I'd rather do that in my own time and more systematically."

"What do you mean?" Mr. Ackermann questions.

"I mean, there's a better and more opportune time to tell the world I'm dating Donnelly. There's no point in doing it now. If it could benefit Fizzle to wait, shouldn't I wait?"

They all glance amongst each other, and I wonder if they're surprised that I'd even want to slam on the brakes to announcing my relationship. But it's not super important to me or to Donnelly to even confirm it at all. The public could guess forever, and it wouldn't change our feelings for each other or how we interact.

"Would you deny the rumors?" Mr. Wagner asks me.

Adaline pipes in, "She shouldn't. It's better in the long run if she's in a committed relationship like her mother." They don't want me to appear promiscuous, I'm realizing.

"Even if it's to him?" Now Mr. Wagner is pointing at Donnelly like he's the number one suspect in a police lineup.

I wish they would stop doing that.

"Yes," Adaline replies. "It can be spun." *Spun.* In a good light, she means, and funny enough, the reality of Donnelly *is* the best light.

"That's all, Luna. Thank you," Uncle Stokes says, and I lean back, thinking I didn't totally fuck up. I'm proud of myself, even.

I smile over at Donnelly, and his grin reappears. He makes a hand gesture that means *I love you*, and I return the gesture by making a heart with my hands. Yes, the board sees. No, I don't really care that they do.

"Ben," Uncle Stokes calls him up.

Ben slides out of the chair and towers at six-five. He's not hunched. He carries himself like a collegiate jock and even wears a Penn sweatshirt and jeans.

As they appraise him, his muscles seem to tighten, his stance hotter. He looks like he could kick over the board table and shove the food, notebooks, and electronics off the surface. It's simmering aggravation.

It's palpable to me, but maybe not to them.

He's told to take a seat.

He returns to the end of the table. Ms. Kapoor gives him a friendly smile, and he produces one back. Then he asks the board, "What questions do you have for me?"

Uncle Stokes says, "Fizzle has partnerships with different companies, events, and venues, such as ballparks, music festivals, and sports leagues. How would you feel if we did campaigns that involved beef or meat?"

Ben opens his hands and shrugs. "I'm vegan. While I'd love if the entire world would be vegan, I know it's not *realistic*." He shoots this at Charlie, and I know Charlie often calls his youngest brother an *idealist*. "I don't prescribe this belief onto anyone else. I'm aware of the ties this company has, and I'm still here."

"Why are you here?" Mr. Wagner questions. "Do you really want this job?"

Charlie makes a show of turning his chair toward Ben at this one.

Ben glares at him, then tells Mr. Wagner, "If it's what's expected of me, I'll honor it."

"Will you?" Charlie asks mockingly.

"Shut up, Charlie," Ben snaps. "I could say the same about *you*."

"I'll do as I'm told like an *obedient* son, but you?" He drums the table, staring Ben down. "Your soul is so fragile and *delicate*. You think it'll even survive a week in a corporate blender?"

Ben addresses the board, "What Charlie is implying is that he's soulless."

"I have no soul to take," Charlie agrees. "Perfect for corporate bargaining." He spins back to the board and spreads his arms like *choose me*.

"That's not who you want representing Fizzle," Ben says to them.

"He's too sensitive," Charlie says to the board. "You hire him— you're hiring a ticking bomb that will go off *repeatedly*."

Ben winces. "Are we sure you aren't the bomb?"

"You think you'd be good for this company?" Charlie says directly to his brother, the air tensing. "You'll either destroy it or it'll destroy you. You're. Too. *Soft.*"

"Brothers," Eliot interjects fast. "Cease and desist."

Ben is grinding his teeth, unable to respond.

Xander's eyes have widened like we just watched a slow-moving car crash. "Holy shit," he mutters to me.

Yeah, that was bad.

I'm thinking Charlie and Ben just knocked each other out of contention.

Ms. Kapoor speaks to the rest of the board. "My daughter-in-law Layla knows Ben quite well from Fizzle events, and she's always said how personable he is. I truly think this interaction is not a good reflection of what he can bring to the position."

They whisper to one another before Mr. Wagner asks Ben, "How will you answer questions related to Charlie?"

"Not kindly," Ben answers honestly.

Charlie says nothing.

Eliot puts a hand over his own mouth, trying to be quiet—or maybe he's hiding how distraught he actually feels. All Eliot has ever wanted is for his brothers and sisters to be as thick-as-thieves, but Ben is the outlier. The odd peg that doesn't always fit into the Cobalt Empire mold.

The black sheep among lions.

"Ben, how is your relationship with Xander?" Adaline asks. "There are rumors you two don't get along."

"We're okay," Ben says, taking a quick peek at Xander. "We're just not as close as we used to be." The strain is also now palpable. "I'd never say anything bad about him."

"But me," Charlie holds out a hand.

Ben speaks in French, and I instinctively lean into Eliot for a translation. His face has tightened, and he looks...sad.

But he whispers to me what Ben said, and my heart plummets.

You hated me long before I hated you.

Charlie, again, says nothing.

"Thank you," Uncle Stokes tells Ben.

The last of the Fizzle Five takes center stage.

"Xander," Uncle Stokes motions him forward.

My brother inhales measured breaths while he's being assessed out in the open. I wouldn't say the blood-red suit is wearing him, but he's more unsure than Eliot. Less heated than Ben. Less unfriendly than Charlie.

Maybe more composed than me?

Once he's back in his chair, Uncle Stokes says, "Xander, you're the face of a generation. Would you be comfortable being in ads and campaigns for Fizzle?"

Xander nods.

He doesn't even speak. He's a little ashen. I wonder if he might puke.

All the Cobalts watch him intently, and their intensity might be more nerve-wracking for Xander than solely facing the board. I'm way more used to the Cobalt brothers than he is.

"Would you be willing to declare a business major in college?" Uncle Stokes asks.

Xander blinks. He applied to colleges as "undeclared" and told me he was going to figure it out Freshman year.

He nods.

For some reason, his silent answers are enough for the board. I have a sudden, sinking feeling in my gut that this is all for show. Do they already have a winner picked out?

No. *No.*

They wouldn't waste their time with a mock panel, let alone four other planned engagements, if they did.

"That's it," Uncle Stokes tells us. "The board and I will discuss, and then I'll send you all an email with your rankings."

"Rankings?" I blurt out. We're getting ranked?!

"It's so you can see where you fall before the final presentations and you can make adjustments to improve. It'll also be a good motivator to try harder, if this is something you really want." At this, the board all resume their lunch and chitchat.

I scrape my chair back at the same time as Eliot. He's already calling out for Ben, but Ben shrugs him off and leaves quickly.

"Did you have to go in on him *that* hard?" Eliot glares at Charlie.

Charlie pushes in his chair. "What do you think it'll be like with men twice his age, Eliot? They don't play nice in Fortune-500s. They'll toy with him like he's a mouse they're trying to catch for shits and giggles."

"He'll be the CEO," Eliot reasons. "He'll have power."

"Power is only valuable if you know how to wield it," Charlie says. "Ben lets too much crawl under his skin."

"Including you," I mention like a factoid.

Charlie lowers his gaze on me. "Including me," he agrees.

Bang!

I jump, and Charlie and Eliot push me and Xander behind them. Paparazzi are pressed up against the glass. Donnelly is speaking in comms. I think a camera lens must've made impact with the window. A few posters are also visible.

I LOVE YOU, XANDER HALE!!

XANDER! IT'S MY B-DAY! WILL YOU HUG ME??

My brother's location leaked.

He must've been spotted getting out of the SUV. It's the only real possibility. Xander slings his backpack on his shoulder, and he gives me a half-hearted smile. "This is what happens when the elusive cryptid makes a rare appearance."

It kind of hurts my heart that he's calling himself a cryptid. Like he belongs among the likes of Bigfoot, Grey alien, and Loch Ness Monster.

"Time to go," Donnelly slips between the Cobalt brothers to reach me and my brother. "The backdoor isn't secure."

I feel Frog's hand in mine, and I notice how the Epsilon bodyguards are hustling the Cobalts out of Panera in a flash. Frog gets me safely in the passenger seat of Donnelly's security vehicle. "We're right behind you," she tells me before shutting the door.

Xander lies down in the backseat, his headphones on. Pretty sure he's just trying to avoid being seen by paparazzi. The camera flashes hurt my eyes, but Donnelly's able to maneuver us onto the street with ease.

"So we drop off Xander and go to Wawa?" I ask Donnelly about our plans.

"Can we raincheck the Wawa?" he asks, eyes flitting to me, then the road.

I try not to be disappointed, but my stomach nosedives. "Okay, yeah." I frown. "Is there a reason why?"

"Just feeling more like ramen to-go. That good with you?"

I smile over at him. "Yeah, I could do ramen."

He relaxes, like he'd been worried I'd be too dejected. It does suck that our Wawa outing is put on hold, considering I've *really* wanted to go with how much Donnelly brings it up. But I promised I'd wait and go with him, and it'll be more fun if he's invested in the moment.

Plus, there's no harm in waiting for a hoagie. Waiting for him to sleep with me—now *that* has been a true test of my patience.

46

PAUL DONNELLY

Postponing Wawa, which meant postponing having sex with Luna, made the most sense in my head. 'Cause I haven't been able to shake what Lily said to me—the part about taking Luna's amnesia into account. It's fucked me up all day, really.

Goal: don't hurt Luna.

Seems easy enough, but I'm her *first* this time around. She's inexperienced, and I'm thinking it's just better if we wait a bit longer.

There's no harm in prolonging this.

After the mock panel, ramen at the penthouse, and a marathon of a cancelled sci-fi show called *Raised by Wolves*, I jump in the shower... with Luna. It's not the first time we've showered together in our Jack-and-Jill bathroom, but the more I slam on the brakes to fuck her, the more it feels like I'm edging myself with no release.

Pent-up is a weak word for what I am, but I've got it under control.

Standing behind Luna, I shampoo her light brown hair, she melts into the moment and sinks against my chest. Her ass almost brushes up against my cock. We're talking about *Fizzle* though, which is about as attractive as a concrete block.

"What's your *unbiased* opinion?" she asks again, since I told her she was the mock panel winner in my eyes.

I dip my head to whisper against her ear. "I'm always gonna be partial towards you, babe."

Her breath hitches, and I harden at that tiny, aroused noise she makes. My blood runs hot. Vapor encases us, and the glass of the shower is already fogged.

I inch back so she can't feel my erection rub up against her. She tries to look, but I start talking, hearing the huskiness of my voice. "But I'd bet a ham hoagie that Charlie and Ben are at the bottom."

"Uh-huh," she agrees. Her eyes are closed while I skate my fingers through her hair in a melodic motion. "I think they did the worst too. But I still might be at the bottom."

"You didn't blow it," I tell her. Genuinely, I believe Luna held her own. She would've gotten my vote, and yeah, I might be biased.

I see her and I just see beauty and triumph. Even if the world believes Hales are the most likely to fail, Luna has proven to be the most likely to persevere.

To me, that means more.

"I did make an enemy out of Chett Wagner," Luna says. "I don't know if giving him my sweater would even win me points."

Remembering the sweater ordeal is reigniting an inferno in my lungs. It took too much willpower to keep my feet rooted to the ground and my mouth shut when Chett Prickner wanted Luna to strip. Don't know why he thought it was a reasonable request when she was *clearly* uncomfortable.

I'm glad she has the Cobalts to defend her, but I don't love that she's in these positions with older, more powerful men to begin with. Chett Prickner should know better, and I was a little ticked off her uncle just sat there. He's the CEO. He has the authority to shut down *anyone* on the board.

I'm just a lowly bodyguard and her boyfriend. I'm supposed to shut up and act like wallpaper, or else I might get reprimanded by the Tri-Force and get suspended. I want to be there for Luna while also being there for her younger brother, especially during this stressful period of Xander's life.

It feels like a tightrope. Think I'm nimble enough to walk it.

I tell her, "Whether you took it off or left it on, that prick was gonna try to be up your ass about it no matter what. *Try* being the key word 'cause I won't let him in your ass."

She peeks over her shoulder at me. Her smile rises. "It's a very sacred place."

"Only the worthiest allowed to enter." I give her a once-over, and one of my hands leaves her hair to touch the softness of her ass.

"You," she says, her breath caged in arousal. "You are the worthiest one, Donnelly."

My cock twitches, and as she instinctively arches her ass into me, I clutch her waist and spin her around to face me. "Let me wash the shampoo outta your hair." I clear my throat a little.

She nods and crosses her ankles. Her thighs are glued together, and I'm staring at her beautiful naked form and perked nipples while she leans her head back and closes her eyes. Water cascades into her hair and trickles down her soft skin. I wash out the soap suds, sliding my fingers through her light brown strands.

"Do you know if I've ever had anal sex?" Luna asks quietly, and I hear her over the water gurgling into the drain.

"No, I don't know," I say, my muscles flexed. I'm hot and bothered talking about her ass and sex, but I want in her pussy more than anything. "You didn't with me."

Her cheeks are flushed, and her eyes open onto me. "I don't plan to ask Charlie about it."

I smile down at her, finding her arousal cute. "Why not?"

"I doubt he'll have the answer since the diary mostly revolves around my time wishing I could be with you."

I didn't expect that response. My chest rises in a deeper breath. I cup her cheek and kiss her. Not thinking about how it'll be harder to pull away. Not thinking about anything other than *the need*. The need to be as physically attached to Luna Hale as I am emotionally strung to this girl, and I deepen the sensual kiss and push her up against the wall.

She moans against my lips. "*Donnelly.* I need…"

"I know," I breathe, my forehead against hers while her hands glide down my waist. Warm water pelts us and rolls down our bodies.

Her palms descend to my cock, and to distract myself from lifting her legs around me, I ask, "What'd you drink exactly?"

"Elderflower. It's poisonous to my species," she whispers. We've been roleplaying most of the night, and she said she drank something to where she needs human touch for 24-hours to survive. Skin-to-skin contact. If I stop touching her, she dies.

It's why we're showering together.

I'm attracted to Luna alone, but add in these weird scenarios, and she might as well be smothered in pheromones that I can't escape. I'm *starving* for her.

"You're so hard," she whimpers, squirming against the wall. She's staring at my cock and flexed muscles, and as she squeezes me with too light of force, I hold her head to the tile.

And I whisper against her ear, "I'm the only one who can keep you alive, yeah?"

She moans out an *uh-huh.*

"You're dreaming about my cock, aren't you?"

Luna struggles to jerk me off, hypnotized by my words, by the way I thread my leg between her thighs and break them apart.

"You want me buried inside you?" I cling to her pleasured gaze, and those eyes—her eyes—might as well be fisting me with hotter friction than what her hand is creating. "You want to feel every inch of me in your tight, *wet* pussy so you can survive the night?" My lips brush her ear. "You want me to fuck you like you've never been fucked before?"

"Without restraint," she murmurs. "Fuck me without restraint."

I want that too. But lately, all I am is *restrained.* I kiss the nape of her neck, then dip my hand between her thighs. She's so easily aroused, just like before her amnesia. Luna is already soaked. The instant I thumb her clit, she arches her hips into me and cries out my name.

I keep talking to her. "You want me to come inside you? Make you mine?" She's nodding into another moan. "You want me to rock so deep and hard and *rough?* That no one but me will ever feel your pussy again?"

"*Please*," she begs.

I put one finger inside Luna, and she pulsates around it. Her orgasm ripples out of her, and pre-cum coats the tip of my dick.

"*Please, please.*" She's still begging.

Fuck. Me.

I can't. I can't. My body says *fuck yes, fuck her.* Big brain is still not there. I just kiss her, hoping this is enough for both of us. Our passionate make-out morphs into Luna dropping to her knees.

Not the first time this has happened. We've been going down on each other in the steam when we find ourselves in the shower together. Been having fun. Tonight is different though. It feels like a limit.

Her mouth is around my cock and with the heat and the water and my pent-up need—it's taking every cell inside me not to grab underneath her arms, hoist her up, hook her legs around my hips, and drive my erection inside of her.

I need to come. *I need to come now.* Holding the back of her head, I flex forward, my cock sliding between her lips, and her eyes flit up to mine while she touches herself—that does me in. I release in her mouth, and she hits a second climax.

Jesus.

I think she could go again, honestly, and I want to exhaust her with my cock. I really fucking do, but this is too much for me. Will I regret taking her pseudo-virginity like this? I dunno, and that uncertainty scares the shit outta me enough to stop.

After we wash off, I shut off the shower and keep our pinkies hooked. Stepping out, I say, "Maybe we should pump the brakes on taking showers together? If it's alright with you, we'll just wait until we have sex to do it again?"

Luna nods slowly. "Yeah, okay."

I look her over. She seems at ease with this plan and more relaxed after coming. The air is light between us while we mosey around the bathroom without breaking physical contact.

A black towel is slung low around my waist, and we're scrounging for our toothbrushes and paste.

She's telling me about her hunt for a new therapist. With no prodding from me, Luna decided to let go of Dr. Raven. I didn't want to be the reason she kicked her to the curb, but I am the sole reason. Apparently, Dr. Raven still thinks I'm not good for Luna and that she's obsessing too much over me. Even after the joint session. Which has just obliterated Luna's trust in her. She thought the joint session would change Dr. Raven's opinion of me, but it didn't do much.

I've been talking more with Lo, and he said it's a good thing she's finding a new therapist. That it's not my fault this one isn't panning out. It made me feel less like a bad influence.

"I really, really like Dr. Frisk," Luna says. "We spent fifteen minutes just talking about our tattoos. She has an aardvark with a bifocal on her arm."

It's good hearing she's already connected to someone new. I tell her that.

Then I ask how her college courses are going, since I'm not around for those. She's acing Astronomy (knew she would), scraping by in Economics, and holding on for dear life in Television and New Media.

She spits some Colgate into the sink basin beside mine. "He's just a know-it-all. But not like the know-it-alls who can back their shit up. He's the one who chose *We Are Calloway* and he doesn't even know about the Fanaticon forums. How do you teach a class about *new media* without talking about the social medias that cover television?" She leans a hip against the counter, turning to me as I continue brushing my pearly whites. She has a palm on the counter, and my hand covers hers.

I'm learning new things about Luna.

Like how she doesn't always use a towel after a shower. She put on a thick bathrobe. Neon green, the hood is an alien head with floppy antennas that bob around when she talks. Looks like something from Urban Outfitters. Water still drips down her legs, her footsteps creating shallow pools. She doesn't mind. Neither do I.

"In conclusion to this essay," she says. "Professor Roach is a dick."

I spit in the sink and toss the toothbrush in a cup. "I volunteer to kick his dick."

"You're way behind," she tells me. "Eliot already volunteered. About forty times." She hops up on the sink counter, careful to keep her hand beneath mine.

I rub a fist against the fogged mirror. "With that much enthusiasm, I'm shocked Eliot hasn't made a surprise appearance in your class."

"I don't think he trusts himself." Her eyes dance around me as she watches me uncap the deodorant with my teeth. "Um…" She clears her throat. "You sure about what you said earlier?"

"One hundred percent, I'll never fuck in a Wawa. Holy grounds and all."

She smiles. "No, the other thing." She scoots farther back on the counter, her shoulders hitting the mirror. "About the shower…and waiting."

I try to read her expression, but it's a little difficult. If she's been mulling this over more, then maybe she's not as okay with waiting to shower together until we have sex.

I take a second to collect my thoughts. Stepping closer to Luna, I touch her bare knee with my other hand and skate my fingers to her calf. Squatting down, I grab eye drops from the depths of the cupboard.

"I'm sure," I tell her. "But if we need to talk about it, we can." While I rise back to my feet, I track my hand up her body, planting it firmly on her knee that peeks out of the bathrobe.

She's all heavy breaths. "I don't need to talk about it. I know you want to go slow, and it's not time yet. I was just making sure you're sure."

"I'm sure that the next time I'm naked in a shower with you, I will fuck you in there, Luna," I tell her. "Very sure about that."

Her lips part. "Glad we nailed that down."

"Jesus wasn't the only carpenter," I say.

Her smile hits her amber eyes. "You're a carpenter with magical hands," she tells me. "Keeping me alive is so very thoughtful of you."

"Would never let you die." I squeeze her kneecap, then tilt my head back and squirt drops in my dry eyes.

I feel her watching me. "Even though we're not having sex, we can still talk about what you'd do to me, right?"

She loves being teased to near-torture. It's been a massive turn on for me too. "What I'm gonna do to you *every night*, you mean?" I slip her a grin.

"And morning," she smiles back. "You can't forget the mornings."

"Morning fuckings are a must for my space babe." I add another drop to my left eye, then rub the excess liquid out of the crease with my wrist. "It's no joke either. Once I break the seal, I'll be honoring every sexual thing I've ever said to you."

She releases the sexiest breath, like I just entered her. She clutches the bathrobe at her thighs, and I harden again. Especially as she says, "If I need it, we'll have to do it immediately and in weird public places."

Fucking in weird public places—that has my name written all over it. Hers, not so much. She's *famous*, but I think I can manage this without anyone seeing.

"Public bathrooms, private planes, the back of a car, then we'll get weirder," I say. "I've got your needs covered, girl."

She's flushed and keeps her knees fastened together. If I see her pussy right now, I will drop to my knees and eat her out. Temptation is real.

"Handcuffs?" Luna asks with shallow breath. I grin, until she says, "You can handcuff me to the bed."

My whole stomach plunges out of my body. All I see is her handcuffed to *that* bed in *that* rowhouse on *that* night. I'm rigid, and I think I nod. Can't be sure.

She's tensed. "Donnelly?"

I keep my hand on top of hers, but I take the other off her knee. Just to run my fingers through my wet hair. "That's…" I literally can't fucking speak. Can't say anything else. My nose flares, and I'm staring at the wall.

"Can you…can you look at me? What's wrong?"

I look at Luna. I hold her worried gaze, and I manage to say, "I don't think I can do that—handcuff you to the bed."

She frowns. "Why…?"

I'm shaking my head. "Please don't…" *Don't ask me.* I can't tell her. I don't want her to know why. My chest is on fire. My ribs are contracting around my lungs, making each breath more strenuous.

"Okayokay," she says fast. "It's okay, Donnelly."

I rub at my eyes. "Maybe I can do it—"

"No, I don't need it. I don't even want it if it's something you don't want."

Alright.

Alright.

I exhale a long, measured breath, releasing the tightness off my chest. "You sure?" I look at her again.

She hooks our pinkies. "Yes, with a good earthly promise attached."

I toy with one of her bathrobe's alien antenna and start to smile. "I love you, you know that?"

"Yes." Her eyes well. "I love you too, do you know…that?" She blinks, her gaze drifting beyond me, as though she's thinking hard about something. Her brows pleat, and her lips fall farther open.

My face drops. "Luna?"

Her breathing becomes erratic and ragged. She's not staring at anything. It's like she's zoned out in her head. "Luna, *Luna,*" I say, rattled suddenly. I wave a hand in front of her face. She's not responding.

I touch her wrist, and her pulse thumps hard and frenzied against my two fingers.

"LunaLunaLuna." I take my hands off her completely, done with our game. Is she having a panic attack? I pull down the hood of her bathrobe and clutch at her cheeks. "Hey, look at me. *Luna.*" I tap her cheek repeatedly. "Babe, come on." She's breathing even harder. Come on. Come on. "*Luna!*"

47

LUNA HALE

Memories.

It's strange how some are so vivid, so vibrant that you can almost *smell* the very room you're in, while others are fogged hazy pictures. Snapshots with burnt edges and discolored film.

This memory transports me.

I smell the room: musty mold, cigarettes, and a sourness that roils my stomach.

I hear the voices downstairs. Mutterings and curses from men I don't know. Voices jumbling together in mix of "we fucked up" and "where is she?"

I see him.

Coming into the bedroom. Fear, concern, and sheer rage latched to his eyes.

I see my mom in the driver's seat. I feel arms around my waist, pulling me away from her.

I hear her screams. Her cries. Her pleas. "DON'T HURT HER, PLEASE! PLEASE!"

The entire night rushes through me like firecrackers, popping in quick succession. It's not all chronological, and I struggle to piece it together, so I focus harder like if I stop trying to remember it'll all slip away forever.

"STAY IN THE CAR!—*Luna!*"

I startle and blink from the harsh bathroom lights. Donnelly's hands cup my cheeks. "Luna," he says, searching my eyes like he's trying to find me.

"Donnelly?!" Farrow calls.

"She's in here!" Donnelly yells.

Huh. I'm still sitting on the bathroom counter. Alien bathrobe on. I must have zoned out in my head. Farrow rushes in and says to someone behind him, "Just stay back there."

"If she's decent, I'm coming in." *My brother.*

Farrow must make an executive decision because he shuts the door behind him and keeps Moffy out. I slip my gaze to the floor, trying to go back to the memory. "Wait," I tell them. "I want…to remember." *Please don't let it fade.*

"Luna," Donnelly says, lifting my chin. His gaze meets mine in panicked urgency. "I know you want to remember. But whatever this memory is, it's giving you a panic attack."

Farrow's wrapping a blood pressure cuff around my arm.

I just now realize how heavily I'm breathing. Deep labored breaths like I can't seem to fill my lungs with air. Blinking a couple times, I tell Donnelly between breaths, "You…told me…to stay… in the…car."

He blows back. His eyes become haunted, and he's shaking his head over and over. And I know, I know this is the last thing he wanted me to remember. He wanted to shield me from it. Protect me. But he could never protect me from what's inside my head.

The night I was attacked.

I remember it.

All of it.

EMAIL FROM SAM STOKES

FROM: samstokes@fizzle.com

TO: dontemailme1882@yahoo.com, eliotalice@gmail.com, benpirripcobalt@upenn.edu, aragorn1225@gmail.com, queenofthebula@gmail.com

After the mock panel, the rankings are as follows:

1. Charlie Keating Cobalt
2. Xander Hale
3. Eliot Alice Cobalt
4. Ben Pirrip Cobalt
5. Luna Hale

48

 **LUNA HALE**

I don't go back to sleep after the memory
surge. For a while, Donnelly just holds me, but I'm jolted into an alert state with my thoughts and emotions on a turntable. And we decide to get some fresh nightly 3 a.m. air. Bundled up in jackets and beanies, Donnelly and I take Orion for a leisurely walk in Center City.

Snow dusts the city sidewalks. Barely any living soul out right now. I feel guilty for waking Frog and Quinn at first, but Donnelly has assured me they're used to the strange hours. They'd be happier being woken up to protect me than being left asleep.

They follow behind us, rather than out in front, and it feels like it's just me and my boyfriend on a nighttime stroll after an intense moment together. I wouldn't say our spaceship has experienced turbulence. More like, emergency lights are flashing, and we're both not totally certain how to shut them off.

Donnelly seems too awake to want to return to the penthouse anytime soon. He mumbles with a cigarette between his lips, "Uncle Stokes doesn't know how to count. 'Cause five should be one and one should be five." He's reading the Fizzle rankings on my phone, then passes it to me and blows smoke upward.

I vape. "I just wish he gave us more information on our placements. I can't improve if I don't know why I'm last."

"You could ask him," Donnelly suggests.

"I will," I sing-song and nod, thinking I'll try to get some feedback. Orion sniffs around a grate.

"That fire hydrant has your name written all over it," Donnelly tells the burly Newfie, and Orion hikes a leg to pee on said fire hydrant. He listens more to Donnelly than he does to me, and I like that Orion sees the goodness that I see in Donnelly.

"Good boy, Orion," I say, and he wags his tail and barks in excitement. He tugs at the leash in Donnelly's hand, and we continue our trek. Finding ourselves in Logan Square, a city park where benches circle a giant fountain.

Donnelly wraps Orion's leash around the foot of a park bench, and after brushing snow off the seat, we sit together and stare out at a stone turtle, which typically squirts water out of its mouth. It's frozen tonight.

Donnelly glances at the burning cigarette between his fingers. "You're positive you don't wanna call your neuro-doctors?"

"I will when the sun comes up," I assure him. Farrow okayed me to go for a walk once my heartrate and blood pressure were normal. Donnelly has been sweeping my features for signs of breakage, as though the memories of that night would surely pulverize every last piece of me, but I'm not shattered.

The pain of that night—it hurts—but it's also accompanied by so much *clarity*. The empty spaces are beginning to fill.

He eases each time he sees my lips tic upward in a smile—each time, he realizes I'm not a puddle he needs to scoop up off the floor. I think he'd do that, too, if he had to. I think he already has, and my love for him swells inside me again.

After Donnelly takes a drag, he asks, "You remember everything?"

"Yeah," I whisper.

He taps ash onto the ground. "Did they…they didn't…?" He fights for the words. "You told me they didn't try anything with you that night, and I just wanna be sure—"

"They didn't," I say fast. "They just left me upstairs." *Handcuffed to the bed.* Where Donnelly ultimately found me.

Donnelly leans back, a long breath leaving him. His powerful relief washes over me, and I breathe deeper too. And then he snuffs the cigarette under his boot. Just to grab my hand and lead me to the fountain.

"The turtle is calling," he says. "Guy looks lonely."

I smile at the reappearance of light in his eyes. "How many earthlings can speak to turtles?"

"Just this one." He helps me onto the fountain's snowy ledge where he stands.

I balance with him, and he presses his hands to my neon orange beanie. Our smiles inch upward while we look deeper into each other. Despite the return of a bad memory, it's a pretty night after a light snowfall. Stars twinkle above us, and the emergency lights in our spacecraft aren't strobing as harshly.

I tell him about it. "There aren't any alarms. It's quiet and peaceful in our spacecraft, and the lights—they're shades of purple."

"And pink," Donnelly says. "You're bathed in pink."

"And green," I smile with him. "They're the kind of colors you'd see at a club on Thebula."

Donnelly grins into a laugh. "Turning an emergency into a dance floor. I love us."

Us. There is an official *us* now. A Donnelly and a Luna bound together. It's not a sad *us*. It's a vibrant, grinning, buoyant *us*, ascending higher and higher. I haven't thought much about where we'll land. Staying on this voyage with Donnelly matters more to me.

"I love us too," I tell him, just as our phones ping.

We check the texts from my bodyguard. Frog has sent a few photos of us on the fountain. Where we're smiling at each other. Where Donnelly has his hands on my head and stares affectionately into my eyes. Snowy Philadelphia, the stars, and fountain are perfectly framed in the background.

It looks like a Philly love story. It's beyond beautiful.

"Sorry!" Frog calls out. "I'm preserving the moment! Not trying to ruin it! *Shit*," she curses to Quinn. Then shouts to us, "Continue as you were! Make out! Kiss. Do the deed. We'll look away."

"*Frog*," Quinn groans.

"What? No one's around. Let them get it on."

"Thanks, Froggy!" Donnelly calls out, then smiles down at me, but a sudden, jarring thought kicks me in the chest. The wind is nearly knocked out of me. He holds my arm. "Luna?"

"Xander…"

Donnelly takes out his phone again. "What about him?" He's scrolling through his messages, but I doubt my brother has recently texted.

I blink a few times, then focus on my boyfriend. "That night… they kept saying, *Where's Xander?* They kept mentioning he wasn't in the car with me and my mom. Did you know that?"

Donnelly shakes his head, his body tensing. "We knew the plan wasn't to kidnap you though."

"What'd they want with Xander?" I ask him quietly.

"No clue," he breathes, "but I'll ask my dad. See if he knows anything."

49

PAUL DONNELLY

"*You didn't wanna bring your girlfriend* around?" my dad asks, shelving new bottles of Hendrick's and Jameson behind the bar counter. The Rhino hasn't opened yet. It'd be dead quiet in this biker bar, if not for The Cure playing over the speakers.

He put it on for me. Said something like, "You loved them when you were a kid." Couldn't believe he remembered that.

"She's sleeping." I sip the glass of bourbon he poured me.

He gives me a weird look. "It's two p.m.—is she allergic to the sunlight?"

"Long night," I say vaguely and rotate the glass on the sticky wood. I could've gone back to sleep with Luna, but I craved answers more than shuteye. Feels like my duty to find 'em, and I wouldn't be able to sleep with this loose thread bothering me anyway.

"Huh." He looks me over while unpackaging a whiskey bottle. "Girlfriend troubles?" His concern is unusual. Still don't know what to make of it. "From where I'm standing, you have nuthin' to worry about. 'Cause if she's still with you, after what our family did, I doubt there's anything you could do that'd push her away."

The wire is hot against my chest, but I've mostly stopped caring what security would overhear. I even thought about not informing anyone of this interaction. A big part of me wanted to go to my dad as a son first and foremost, but if he says anything important, I need it recorded.

Before I can respond, he's adding, "But what do I know about relationships? Just been with your mother all my life." He smiles like it's some sweet childhood romance and not a horrific one.

"You ever think maybe you should've let her go?" I ask him.

He rests a full bottle of whiskey on the bar and holds on to the neck. "Are you rethinking this thing between you and that Hale girl? I know there might be rough patches, but there are more upsides than downsides—"

"Everything's good between me and Luna," I say lightly. "I'm talking about you and Bridget."

"Your mom," he says with a slow nod. "Sure, I thought about ending things a few times. I'd bet she'd say the same about me. We're both not without faults, but I love her. It's...it would kill me to cut her out. I couldn't. I won't. And she's doing great now. She said you talked to her on Christmas."

"For a bit." I twist the glass of bourbon and smoke a cigarette with my other hand. "She's thinking she'll be let out soon?"

"Soon-ish. We could pick her up together. I know she'd love that." He smiles over at me, and it's not like I haven't picked her up from prison before. *It's different this time.* I can't say exactly why or how, but it just feels so fucking different. Sean's more thoughtful than ever before, and Bridget called me on *Christmas*—and not because she wanted anything.

"Yeah, alright." I take another drag, blowing smoke away from him. "About the Hales—"

"The Hales," he says with a tight, uncertain sigh. "Look, if you're weighing my relationship with your mom against Loren Hale and Lily Calloway—I can't help you there. We didn't grow up *loaded.* Drugs weren't an escape from boredom for us—it was an escape from poverty."

"I wasn't trying to compare you. I know it's not the same."

His jaw tics, but he nods and then asks, "Am I ever meeting any of 'em? Those people—they're important to you, aren't they? Your girlfriend, her dad, her mom? At some point, I wanna meet 'em."

His insistence gives me pause. "Why?"

He's frustrated. "'Cause how else am I gonna be a part of your life if you keep me out of most of it? It's like you don't trust me or something." He gestures from my chest to his.

"I trust you," I assure.

"Doesn't look like it. Looks more like I've done a whole hell of a lot for you, and you've done nothing for me. But it's fine. It's fine." He backs up from the bar, from me, hands in the air to cool off. "I'll stop pushing."

I snuff the cigarette in an ashtray. "Lo does wanna meet you."

"You call him *Lo*?" He's irritated now. Jealous, really. He glares at the grimy, band-stickered wall. "Well, aren't you two best friends."

I laugh hard. "Yeah, he wrote me in his will and everything," I joke. "He's leaving me a single buck. Can you believe that?"

His smile returns. "So 'best friends' is too far then?"

I shrug. "Think Lo would rather befriend a ground mole than me at times." I don't add how I'm growing on Lo—that being friends with him feels less and less like a longshot and more like an in-arm's-reach reality.

"That hard?" he asks.

"Parents don't love me, but I manage to steal a few hearts."

He nods a few times, and I swear there's a flicker of pride in his eyes. "Yeah, you do." He pours himself a glass of whiskey. "Do I need to go through his assistant to set up a date and time or what?"

"I'll just let you know when and where." I'm not in love with the idea of this meeting, but Lo has been as persistent and adamant as my dad. So it's gonna happen. "Really, I wanted to ask you about that night...with the Hales."

"That night," he repeats, his gaze darkening. "The hearing is in April. 'K, no one's gonna talk while they're stuck in jail, let alone waiting to be sentenced."

"Can you just ask around about Xander?"

"Xander Hale?" He's genuinely confused. "The kid you protect?"

"That night, they were asking about Xander. I just wanna

know why. The original plan might've involved him."

He digests this. "Alright, yeah. I'll see what Ollie knows and go from there." He sips his whiskey, and when I go to grab my bourbon, he slides the glass towards his chest. "You look like you've barely slept. Go get some rest, son."

I inhale. "Thanks."

He nods back with an expression I can easily read. It says, *I'm here if you need me.*

As I stand off the barstool, I leave with a strange mixture of guilt and relief. And I only think one thing.

I wish I didn't wear a wire.

My dad doesn't deserve to be used by me.

50

PAUL DONNELLY

We're on the pool table in the penthouse's game room. Sitting on the green felt, I hold her soft leg across my lap with gloved hands, and the familiar hum of the tattoo machine fills the quiet. She's lounged backward on her elbows and slides an 8-ball into a corner pocket.

Every now and again, I look up at her. Never tattooed a girlfriend before. Never had a girlfriend until now, and it's different than when I tattooed Luna as a friend. It's more intimate in a way—even though it's about the *least* intimate spot I've inked on her.

"That hurt?" I ask.

"Nope." She tries to peer at the ink on her calf, her excitement overflowing. We'd been playing *strip* pool together (every shot missed, you gotta take off an article of clothing). I'm down to only black drawstring pants, and Luna's just wearing a lime-green thong and my baggy AC/DC tee. We didn't even finish playing.

'Cause in the spur of the moment, she asked if I could tattoo her.

Got my equipment out of my bedroom, and here we are. It didn't take long for her to decide what she wanted. She's cashing in on her Christmas present: a matching tattoo. I inked the same design on the top of my thigh a few days ago. Just to make sure it's something she wanted to commit to.

I could tell she loved it, so I wasn't shocked she requested it tonight.

Above us, the stained-glass chandelier casts warm light on Luna's fair skin. Been working on this one for the past three hours, and I'm just about done. It's not a hundred-percent American traditional style, my main forte. The lines aren't as bold, but there is a pop of color.

She squirms just a little, and I lift the machine away from her skin. "You sure you're alright?"

Luna can't remember sitting for her leg tat that took multiple sessions. Then again, she can't remember *ever* getting a tattoo. This must feel like the first one.

"Mmm-hmm," she nods. "Sorry if I'm fidgety. My butt is going to sleep."

I grin. "Tell your butt to stop counting sheep."

"It wouldn't help. My butt is a true rebel. But I'll survive. Carry on." She gives me a thumbs-up.

I set her leg on the table, then snap off my gloves and push my glasses up to my head. "Give me a sec." Standing, I step off the pool table like it's not a far drop—I've jumped off much higher. I land on two feet, and in an easy stride to a wet bar, I collect a velvet green pillow off a leather couch.

Her smile expands when I climb back on the pool table.

"Lift your sleepy butt," I tell her.

She arches her hips, and I prop the pillow under her ass.

"Better?" I ask.

"Yes. My butt thanks you."

I give her a *rock on* hand gesture before snapping on new gloves and reclaiming her leg on my lap. Luna touches her cheeks with her hands like she's trying to feel her smile. It's really fucking cute.

Reading glasses back on the bridge of my nose, I return where I left off. Before the needle touches her skin, I check on my girlfriend one more time.

Been doing that a lot. Assessing. Rechecking. My hypervigilance switched to "on" mode and hasn't shut off since she remembered the night of the attack.

That was a week ago.

We're in a good place—me and Luna. But the return of that bad memory from that traumatic night—before she's recalled any good ones—it's put me on edge. I feel like I'm standing right outside a tripwire. If I take one more step, everything around me will explode. I keep thinking what would've happened if she were alone when she relived that memory. If she went into a state of panic with no one around.

Not to mention, I'm pretty fucking positive I triggered that bad memory.

I confessed this to Oscar. It's not like he wrangled it out of me either. He called me while I was on my way to pick up Xander for school.

"We're going to Salt tomorrow," Oscar told me. "I'm not taking no for an answer, bro."

"Reverse yes," I countered.

"I don't even know what that is. You're not getting out of this."

"Never met a restaurant I liked that's named after seasonings. Salt. Pepper. Oregano. Sage. No thank you."

"That's because your ass hasn't lived in New York in forever," he said. "You've forgotten how good Salt is—and besides, they have a new location in Philly now. You have zero excuses. Especially since I'm paying for you and Luna as a thank you for watching over my baby sis on that *ridiculous* triple date with Limp Dicky."

I laughed. "That limp dicky had a stiffy for your sister, man."

He choked on a noise like he short-circuited. "You're really trying your hardest to get out of a free meal."

"Nah, just busting your balls." I stopped at a red light. "I don't need repaid for watching out for your sister. And Jo's tough, you know. She doesn't take shit from anyone."

"Still," Oscar said. "It's been a while." In so few words, I could tell he missed me, and I'd missed hanging out with him. He was right that I did like Salt when I lived in Hell's Kitchen. Maybe I had forgotten.

But I said, "Just not in the mood. Raincheck."

Oscar got all quiet on the phone, and I figured I was doing a poor job of not sounding like a Johnny Raincloud.

Then he asked, "Is this about Luna getting a memory back?"

Farrow might've told him. Or maybe it'd been making its rounds through security since Luna didn't keep it from her family. It was bound to spread.

I coulda said *no*. Instead, I found myself saying, "I triggered it."

"What...? How?"

"She asked me to handcuff her to the bed." I clenched the steering wheel. "I should've said *sure* or *anything* other than what I did."

"What'd you do?"

"Think I made an expression like she shot me in the stomach. It sort of felt like that, at least." I exhaled a heavy sigh. Oscar knew the night she'd been kidnapped I had found her in the rowhouse handcuffed to the bed. He'd read the report. "Out of *everything* I could've done to help her, why the fuck did I trigger *that* bad night and not a good one? We've got so many more good ones, and it's like the universe is telling me I have shit luck and I shouldn't touch her—"

"Stop. Bro, stop." His voice caved. "You can't take on that kind of blame."

I just listened.

He said, "No one knows what triggers her memories or why that one came first. Even Redford doesn't have that answer. So stop thinking you own a crystal ball or that you're a death knell for Luna. You're *not* that. For anyone. Legitimately. You've only ever been a harbinger of life."

"You saying I'm a good omen or what?" I asked quietly.

I thought he'd rib me, but he was serious as he said, "That's exactly what I'm saying. You're the precursor for good things to come, Donnelly. I've known you for over a decade, and you don't bring harm or toxicity to the party." He kept going. "You won't let anything drag you down. Not your family, not a shitty situation, not a drunk fuck at a bar, and not yourself. And don't blame yourself now, bro. I highly doubt Luna would want that."

"She doesn't know," I said.

"Well, she's going to find out. Guilt is like a leaky faucet. At some point it'll be obvious the bathroom is flooded."

I knew he was right.

And I felt better after talking with my friend. Deep-down, I needed someone to reassure me—that my hands, my touch, my entire being aren't causing Luna more pain. That I'm not fucking her up.

I shed my thoughts to focus on the tattoo.

Gotta do it right. Though, it's been literal *years* since I've blown out a line. I still want Luna to have my best art. It takes another fifteen minutes to finish up. After wiping the ink, I appraise my work with a smile.

"Finished," I say, relinquishing her leg.

"Really?" She sits up and tucks her knee to her chest to get a closer look. Her smile is instant when she examines the fresh ink. It's a pinky promise between a feminine alien and a masculine human— just their hands. One is shaded a vibrant lilac purple, and the other is grayscale. I framed their hands with stars, a comet, and a ringed planet.

It's identical to the tattoo on my thigh.

Her eyes glass, and I see the words overwhelm her features before she says them. "It's beautiful, Donnelly." She wipes at her watery gaze. "I love it."

It burrows so deep into me, and I can't look away from Luna for a second. Not gonna lie, I'd tattoo every inch of her just to see that reaction again.

"Need your leg back," I say, and she extends it over my lap. Heat ramps up as our eyes flicker to one another and meet with sparks of desire. Don't know what else to call it. The intensity of our attraction is a visceral heartbeat. It's pulsing between us. *Alive.* The headiness is fucking insane. Feels like I could get high off her.

But I need to focus. Cleaning and bandaging the tattoo, I tell her, "There's more in your future if you want 'em. Girlfriend privileges and all."

She bites the corner of her smile and nods. "Perks of dating a tattoo artist." She tosses up a Vulcan salute, and my cock twitches like it has suddenly become a sci-fi fan. Really, it's just her number one fan.

While I'm sitting on the pool table with Luna, my legs are spread around her. She watches me use a medical-grade, waterproof bandage to protect the ink on her calf, and her fingers brush the top of my foot. She's tracing the bold lines of an American traditional tattoo—a daggered red heart with a ribbon that says *Love Me*.

Her eyes flash up to mine again. "What should my next tattoo be?"

"You wanna pick out the design first or the spot on your body?" I snap off my gloves and pack away the machine and ink.

"Uh, the spot, I think." She gives me a more assured nod. "Definitely the spot."

I skim the length of her body while she falls back onto the palms of her hands. Luna is *hot*. Like out-of-this-world, I could take her in point-two seconds if I don't control myself *hot*. The hem of her shirt rises on her thighs, and her bare skin teases my dick. Our eyes latch again, and I tell her, "I've got some ideas."

The suggestion is clear. I'm not hiding how much I want to fuck her.

She swings her knees, left and right. "I could use a professional tattoo assessment." Before I blink, Luna pulls the AC/DC tee over her head. No bra underneath, her nipples are already perked mounds. And the band of her lime-green thong rides high on her hips. She spreads her legs open, and every feral button is pushed inside me, sending me on overdrive. I want to mount her and attack her with pleasure—she's looking at me like she's *pleading* for it.

My brain is shouting something else at me. And it's not to stop us.

I jump off the pool table again. This time, I head to the door and flip the lock.

Don't need anyone walking in. I'd like to thank Lily Calloway for this inner growth.

51

LUNA HALE

I can't catch my breath and he hasn't even done anything sexual to me yet. Is this finally happening tonight? Is Donnelly about to abandon all reservations and completely, undeniably take me?

Pleasepleaseplease, I beg.

Multi-colored lights flash on the silent pinball machines behind Donnelly as he treks back to the pool table. He clears the surface of his tattoo equipment, and my heart thrashes in needy anticipation.

Touch me. Touch me.

Mental persuasion powers are working! He's on the table with me, and his hand skates up my knee as he comes closer, and I watch his hungered gaze fixate on my pussy. Barely hidden behind the see-through mesh of my thong.

I fall off my palms and lie back against the green felt. "Assess me." I extend my arms in a T-shape and set my feet flat on the wooden edges of the table.

He's not shielding his hard-on. His erection is molded against the black fabric of his cotton pants. *He's so big.* Eagerness overwhelms me. I want to touch him. I want him to do way too much to me. My head is whirling at high speeds.

And then Donnelly places a hand on the surface beside my face. He's hovering over me, and I'm aching beneath him. His lips tic upward, the grin sparkling his blue eyes, and his husky, masculine voice tortures my resolve as he says, "Before we start, I need to remind the specimen that this professional tattoo artist *only* performs these naked assessments on otherworldly creatures."

"You haven't given one to a human?"

He shakes his head. "And since you're the only alien I know, these assessments are reserved for you."

I swallow, entrapped by Donnelly. His ability to make me feel extraordinarily beautiful and irreplaceable and supremely powerful is a natural-born gift I'm lucky to meet.

I'm so, *so* aroused. His large hand encases my cheek like he's examining a tattoo placement beneath my eyes. I force my arms to stay in the T-position, but I feel like I need to hold on to him. Like we're about to reach zero gravity in our space pod, and I'll float off the table if I don't brace my body against his body.

His knee digs into the table, not bearing his weight on me. I want him. I want him. *I want him.* The chant grows louder in my head.

His fingers trail lower...to the hollow of my collar. I shiver at the featherlight caress, and his abs flex. "Throat is a painful spot," he breathes.

I manage to get out, "We can table that one." I watch him study the length of my arm, his fingers drawing agonizing lines across my thin bicep and to my knuckles.

"Not there," I pant. "Lower."

His grin is shadowed by his own arousal, like he's struggling to resist too. "Not here?" He's lacing his fingers with mine, and he stretches my right arm above my head and pins our clasped hands to the table. OhmyGod.

"*Donnelly,*" I cry and try to buck up into him.

He's careful to lean his pelvis away, but he's still close. His sexy voice warms my ear. "Calm down," he murmurs, and I know he's telling me—but I wonder if he's also telling himself too. "I've got more of your body to examine, space babe."

Yes. Yes, he does. I nod rapidly. "Continue your voyage."

Donnelly drinks in my naked, vulnerable form. "Here?" He circles a finger around my heart, then takes my breast in his hand.

My lips break apart as he kneads and then toys with my nipple. *Oh…fuck.*

I squirm against the table. My legs kicking up gently.

"Looks like these might be too sensitive," he whispers.

"Uh-huh," I swallow an aroused knot.

He's placing electric kisses against my neck, my jaw, my collarbone, and I shudder as each one pricks my nerve-endings. I pulse between my legs. *Donnelly, Donnelly, Donnelly.* His name is trapped in my throat.

My free hand flies to his waist. Holding on. *I'm holding on. I'm ready.*

And then he tells me, "I'm flipping you over."

Right. He has to check out my back and ass for potential tattoo placements. Or is he going to enter me from behind? Can both be possible?

I'm on my belly now, and I stretch my arms upward like I'm sunbathing in the nude. A few billiard balls knock into my legs, the sensation cold unlike the heat of his hands. I crane my neck, doing my best to look at Donnelly.

He's knelt on the pool table. To avoid a head-on collision with the chandelier, he bends towards my body.

"Zero tattoos on this side," he says, sliding his hands down my shoulder blades. "Blank canvas." I strain my neck just to watch him assess my body. He seems entranced by every inch of my slender back, which curves toward my tailbone, then rises into the slope of my bare ass. Exposed in my thong.

"What about getting one on my spine?" I ask, loving the idea of a large back tattoo. "But big."

"You want big?" His brows hoist, a carnal look in his eye. It's a dangerous look that I covet and crave.

"Mmm-hmm," I nearly moan, and Donnelly sinks down on me. I feel the firm muscles of his chest and abs against my back, and I dizzy as I face forward. His strong arms glide over mine, sheathing me with his body like we're in a solar storm together and I can't be exposed to the elements. It'd make a hot fic.

I mentally jot this down for a short story later.

His lips brush my cheek, then ear. "I'll give you big." He grinds forward, letting me feel his hardness against my ass. *Fuckfuck.* He pushes again.

"Yes," I cry. "*Please.*"

He moves one arm off mine, just to hook a finger in the band of my thong. I think he's about to yank them down, but he draws my panties higher up my hip. The fabric teases against my swollen pussy.

I moan into the table. "*Donnelly.*" My pulse is out of control now, the anticipation rattling me. "On my ass," I rasp. "One on my ass." I hope I'm making sense.

"You want a tattoo here?" *He gets me.* Donnelly slaps the side of my ass, and I mumble out pleasured *yeses.* He grabs the flesh, soothing the sting, and I dig my ass back into him.

A choked groan escapes his mouth, and he mutters my name into my ear. With his two hands, he cups my hands together above my head, and he flexes his hips, rocking forward. It would be deep, penetrative sex...if he actually penetrated me.

I arch back into him. *Pleaseplease.* He grinds forward, forcing my hips flat on the table. Oh...God. I throb and clench. The pillow from our tattoo session got knocked on the floor, but I don't think I'd even need it propped under me. I'd rather Donnelly take hold of my waist and angle me himself.

...I wonder if he has done this to me?

Brain itch. I can't see *any* piece of this memory though. A new kind of frustration mounts.

While he simulates sex from behind, I writhe beneath him. The friction is torturing me in the best-worst way. I sense his muscles contracting, and it's clear we're both losing it. His kisses are more ravenous against my neck, and he has a handful of my hair. I'm reaching back and trying to yank down his pants.

I want him inside of me.

I expose his ass.

I feel him reach down between our bodies. I hope he's adjusting himself so he can push inside me. Instead, he rubs my clit.

I twitch and moan out his name. "I need...*please*." It's killing me.

He's whispering against my ear again, telling me to breathe this time. Am I breathing? My hips lift. I grip the wooden edge of the pool table. Take me, take me, *take me*.

I'm on birth control.

He already knows I take a pill every night. So this wouldn't stop him from just slipping in, but he's not pushing inside of me. I don't feel that abrupt fullness.

As I cast a quick glance back, I see a flicker of resistance in his eyes. *Nonono.* It's suddenly clear he's not about to fuck me for the first time (that I can remember).

Before disappointment surges, I shut my eyes and listen to the pulsating, needy ache between my legs. I don't want to only come by his fingers. I need more.

"Can you put the pool cue in me?" I ask so quietly, but I no longer question whether he can hear me. I know he can.

I open my eyes, but I'm faced forward. I can't see him behind me. "I just...I want to feel...it's dumb."

"It's not dumb," he says gently. "Can you turn to look at me?"

I roll onto my back. He's knelt off my body again, his waistband riding low on his hips. The V-line of his muscles are sexy, but I'm less turned-on by the fact because a new tension hangs between us—and it's not the sexual kind anymore.

My face burns in a multitude of emotions. It's not that I think he's questioning my freak-level. I'm pretty confident he's more attracted to my oddity than my normality at this point.

He's trying to catch my runaway gaze. "It's not dumb, Luna. You wanna feel full, and you know I wanna go slow. So you asked for something else."

I intake a deep breath. "So will you?"

He contemplates, glancing over at the stick against the wall. Then back to me, he says, "No offense to the pool cue, but it's not going in you before me."

I deflate. "When will that be?"

His brows pinch in thought, and he tries to give me a reassuring smile—but something seems to be wrestling inside Donnelly that I can't see or understand.

It's making this whole thing more painful.

"I'm trying to be patient," I whisper to him, "but I'm starting to feel like…" My eyes sear as tears threaten to surge. *Never mind.* I hop off the table and find the baggy AC/DC tee.

"Luna." He catapults off the pool table much faster, and he catches up to me as I pull the shirt on. "Can you talk to me?" His distress mirrors mine.

"I don't want to pressure you. I'm not trying to pressure you." I scrounge around the feet of the table for my sweatpants, finding them in a heap. I step into them while he's skating both hands through his hair, leaving them on his head like he's winded.

"Luna…" He drops his hands.

"It's fine." My voice shakes.

"It's not fine. This isn't fine." He's sweeping me for cracks. "I just don't fucking understand." He's confused and alarmed.

I'm frustrated and hurt. "I know you said…you said you're not waiting for my memories to come back, but it feels like you are." Tears prick my eyes, and I wipe at them to stop the waterworks, but it wets my hands. "You're waiting for when I'm whole and okay and for when you know you won't hurt me because *this* version of me is too broken—"

"No, Luna—" He's cut off as the doorknob jostles, then there's a knock and muffled voices outside.

Our roommates.

"They must be in here," Thatcher or Banks says. Their voices are too alike for me to differentiate.

"Luna!" Jane calls out. "We have a marvelous plan to play poker! There may or may not be amendments to the rules! You and Donnelly should join!"

"Losers have to wash dishes the whole fucking week!" Sulli chimes in. "It'll be fun!!"

My throat is too swollen to respond.

Donnelly hasn't looked away from me. "Game room's occupied!"

"They're fucking," a Moretti brother concludes, loud enough for us to hear.

We aren't. It's an added layer of angst into an angsty, messy situation.

"Donnelly would've led with that," Akara says from outside the door.

"Not if Luna wouldn't want us to know," Jane notes.

"What if they're not doing okay?" Sulli asks. "When's the last time you've seen them?"

A fist pounds harder. "Hey, open up!" Akara shouts, concerned.

Donnelly strides over to the door, unlatches the lock, and cracks it open, but before he can even articulate a truth, Thatcher, Banks, and Akara spill into the game room with a couple six-packs of beer. The cute part, which almost distracts me, is Baby Maeve in a Valentine's heart swaddle. She's content in Thatcher's burly arms.

My cousins are in tow, but I avoid Jane and Sulli and try to make an invisible exit.

"Luna?" Jane must see my hurt in my mad dash.

I've tried to be better—to be more open with the people I love this time around—but I can't be this ripped apart in front of my roommates. I don't like this feeling, and there's only one person I really want around me right now.

I aim for the door.

"Is everything okay?" Akara asks Donnelly. "…is she?"

Donnelly is only watching me.

Air. I need air.

"Luna," Donnelly calls softly as I squeeze between him and the exit. He doesn't grab me. He doesn't stop me.

And thank God, he doesn't let me go alone.

52

PAUL DONNELLY

I don't know if she needs space, but I'm too afraid to give it to her right now—like if I don't fix this in this *second*, I might cause more damage.

We're on the penthouse rooftop. Steam rises off the pool, but she's made her way to the brick ledge that faces Philly in all her nighttime beauty. A thin orange haze paints the skyline, like the sun just dropped behind the world moments ago.

It should be freezing, but my blood is hot like I've been jogging around a crash site, uncertain about what to do with the wreckage.

I snatched a fuzzy white blanket for Luna though. She's clutching her elbows, and goosebumps pimple her skin. I come up behind her. "I know your species has already perfected temperature control and all. But thought you could use this."

She rotates away from the city and sees the blanket. "We haven't... perfected it either." She shrugs. "We're no better than humans."

"I don't believe that," I say in a near-whisper, my throat drying out. The cold isn't helping.

Luna lets me tuck the blanket over her shoulders, so I'm thinking this hole I gotta climb out of might not be as deep as I feared.

And then she says, "You want in?" She opens her arms to welcome me into the warmth of her blanketed embrace.

It crashes into me. Her love.

Yeah...

I want in, and without listening to anything but my body, I walk into her arms. She's gentle and sweet and everything I could've ever dreamed of having from a girlfriend during an intense...situation?

I definitely wouldn't call it a fight. It's a missed signal. She's speaking Thebulan, and I can't get the translation back fast enough, not any more than she's been able to receive mine.

I wrap my arms around her shoulders out of the blanket, liking the cold. "I don't see you as broken," I tell her. "I promise it's not that you don't have all of your memories of me."

Confusion crinkles her brows.

I try to read more of her expression. "Luna..."

She's holding on to my waistband. "You said you don't understand, but *I* don't understand either." Her eyes drift past me, filling with tears again.

I hate seeing her cry. Think a baby lamb dies every time Luna sheds a tear. It's a million times worse knowing *I'm* making her cry. I'm slaughtering lambs. I'm making it hard for little kids to count 'em to go to sleep. A generation of insomniacs—my doing.

"It's starting to feel like rejection," Luna whispers. "And I don't want it to. I don't want you to have sex with me because you feel sorry for me either. Or you're only trying to fulfill my needs. I want you to want me—"

"You don't think I want you?" My brows jump, my stomach in knots hearing that. "Most *hours*, having sex with you is all I can think about. I want inside you so badly, I'd rip through space and time just to get to you." I cup the back of her head. "I had you lying on the pool table with your ass against me, and from my head to my toes, I wanted to fuck you *tonight*, Luna. I could barely stop—"

"Why are you trying to stop?" she cries, tears falling down her cheeks. I'm about to wipe them, but she brushes at her face before I can.

"I can't bear the thought of..." *hurting you.* I cut myself off from saying it. 'Cause I am hurting her. I thought prolonging sex would *help* her in the long run, not cause her pain. If I keep pulling away when she thinks I'm getting closer, I'm gonna keep hurting Luna. And myself too. Her hurt is my agony.

That much is clear.

"Donnelly?" Her chin trembles.

"I'm afraid," I choke out, my eyes scalding and wet. "I've been afraid of hurting you—that if I make one wrong move too fast, it'll inflict pain that you won't be able to come back from."

Luna ponders this. "Can you forget I'm kind of a virgin?"

"No," I say strongly. "No, I can't. I won't. And I'm not waiting for you to remember what sex feels like to sleep with you."

"Then why do you think you'll hurt me?"

I start to shake my head. "I had sex with you and then you were kidnapped, Luna. I broke a promise to your dad doing it, and it's felt like the one thing in my control is to wait this time around. 'Cause if I waited, then nothing bad could happen to you." I let out a pained sound. "I think I hurt you tonight though." It's eating at me.

"I'm okay," she says with a nod. Her tears have dried.

I take a deeper breath, trying to ease.

"You won't hurt me if we sleep together," she assures. "I was right when I wrote that you are the best of humankind. Because being close to you has only brought me the best that humankind can offer. It's made me feel strong and whole and loved. The *very* inverse of what you're afraid of."

I rake the heel of my palm against my wet cheek now. "Think you have a new talent. The banishment of fears."

Her smile lights up my whole world. "They better be afraid of me. Because I'll come after them again and again, and my bite is deadly. They'll *never* win."

I laugh into a grin. "You hear that? It's the sound of my fears scurrying away from your poisonous teeth."

She chomps them, and fuck me, I'm in love. Drop everything, I'll die for her kind of love. She's the last name I'll whisper on my death bed kind of love. The universe makes no sense without her kind of love. It will be just her and me until the end of time kind of love.

So I tell her, "I love you, Luna Hale." I look deeper into her. "You've made me feel more loved than I ever have been, and I'm sorry it's taken me this long to figure things out."

"Don't be," she whispers. "You were always with me. You never left me alone in our spacecraft, and I know what you went through that night to find me. I can remember, and..." She draws closer into my chest. "You needed time. If you still need it—"

"I don't need it," I say. "I've got enough clarity." I look her over. "Having sex with you won't cause a world war, but it might rock your whole universe. Your planet ready for that?"

Her smile mushrooms. "Beyond ready."

I nod a couple times, my lips rising. The clouds have parted. I realize whatever darkness leeched onto me from that night, it's nourished itself through my fears. It can't grow any stronger if I don't let it.

I touch the blue kyber crystal around my neck. I haven't taken it off in a while. It's still there. It's been there.

I won't ever be a reason we're suffering. We've withstood enough, and I only ever want to embrace the light with Luna. It's right in front of me now.

I'm staring straight into the moon. Her eyes shimmer radiant amber hues. We share an emerging smile.

"I wanna take you somewhere tonight," I tell her.

She searches my eyes, her eagerness returning. "Where?"

I grin. "The best place on earth."

53

LUNA HALE

The best place on earth is not his bed.

It's Wawa.

Donnelly took me to Wawa, which is weirdly enough my favorite part of tonight. I might as well be entering a sacred place with how much Donnelly has talked about it—how much he loves and cherishes it.

Yet, there's no one in this Wawa. I don't know why I find that the most surprising thing as we enter the convenience store.

"Is it usually this…dead?" I whisper to Donnelly like I'm in a library.

Donnelly makes a pray motion with his hands. "Place is just holy. Some people aren't worthy to step inside."

I smile as we walk down an aisle of juices. "I'm not sure what I did to become worthy."

Lately, my increased sex drive has felt more like a notch in a bad category. I mean, I just asked Donnelly to fuck me with a pool cue—and while I kinda still think the idea sounds hot, I'd rather have him inside me. We are on the same page there.

I never want my needy-self to pressure Donnelly too much. But it's nice knowing for a fact that his sex drive *is* as high as mine, and he hasn't been icked out by Variant Luna or solely trying to appease me. Pity sex sounds soul-crushing, and I'm relieved he'd never do that to me.

My insecurities went poof in the night, and I really hope I calmed some of his too.

He curves an arm around my shoulder and kisses the side of my head, making me smile. "You didn't have to do anything to be worthy. You just are." That hits me extra hard—and I turn my gaze to a bottle of green veggie juice, trying to stop myself from sudden waterworks. I can't cry in Wawa! It's a hallowed space.

Donnelly tugs me farther into the store near paper coffee cups. Wawa's red eagle logo is on every single one. Frog and Quinn must've stayed posted at the entrance because I don't feel them following us.

My boyfriend places two hands on my shoulders. "What'd I say?" Concern inflects his voice, and I realize he thinks he upset me.

It's the opposite though. "You said I'm worthy by just being me," I confess. "Some days I feel that too. Other days, I'm sitting in Television and New Media, and everyone reminds me I'm a Hale in a way that makes me feel like I'll never stop having to prove myself. Even my uncle's feedback kinda confirmed this. He said there's no reason why I'm last other than everyone just outperformed me, and it's like in order to win, I need the Cobalts to fail. Because who I am isn't enough." I lift a shoulder and swallow the growing lump in my throat. "But you make me feel like I don't have anything to prove at all. I am worthy. I think I just needed to hear that today."

Donnelly wraps his arms around me and draws me into a hug. One that's bone deep. Everything feels luminous in his arms. Not just this moment in Wawa but the road ahead of us.

He places a kiss on the top of my head. "It's an age-old story, you know. Never let other people dictate your worth. If I let 'em, I'm pretty sure I'd be a wet noodle."

"I'd scoop you up," I nod.

"Put me in a bowl?"

"Yep. I'd twirl you with my fork and slurp you in my mouth."

Donnelly *oofs* like he's both turned on and envious. "That's it, you're not allowed to suck off Wet Noodle Donnelly while I'm still alive and kicking. He's off-limits." I laugh, and he's woven his arms around me from behind like he's claiming me from any multiverse variants. He's walking me to a kiosk.

I clutch his arms around me. "I do know a little something about being a jealous variant."

"You should write a self-help book about it. Assist all our variants," he says. "I'd read the fuck outta it too."

I think he's the only one who'd truly understand it, but I don't mention that. The bell dings to the entrance, but the older man who dips into Wawa hardly pays attention to us. He beats us to a kiosk, and I watch him hurriedly select his coffee order from a digital menu.

This isn't a normal "order at the counter" establishment. So I'm genuinely happy to have Donnelly as my Wawa guide.

"What's the best part of this place?" I ask him as we reach the kiosk.

"Wawa can turn any day around and right side up."

I didn't expect that answer. He's scrolling through the menu, not realizing my smile is so big that it hurts my cheeks.

"Has it been officially tested?" I ask.

"Over and over. By the world's second-best test subject. Me." He slips me a grin. "Which is also why I brought you here. Can't give it the stamp of approval until the world's first-best test subject tells me what's up."

I like how he calls us both test subjects. We both love trying new things—it's something I've known, but it slams into me more profoundly today.

We haven't eaten dinner yet, so he's scrolling through food options. I'm deeply aware this isn't some random outing. It's a date.

He called it a date on our way here.

Nervous jitters invade, and I rock on my feet. "But what if I give Wawa a low score?" I ask.

"Wait to make your judgments until *after* you've had the Italian hoagie. Toasted."

"What happens if I don't get it toasted?"

"We can no longer be friends. I'm sorry, space babe. It's just the rules."

He kids, but I do know it'd hurt him if I didn't love Wawa. The problem is I've been so hyped for this that I doubt anything could make me hate it.

I bite my lip. "We could no longer be friends but there's no rule about not being lovers, right? So we could still sleep together."

His finger stops on the screen near a roast beef hoagie. He stares down at me in a way that makes me blush. Donnelly is both much older than me and much more experienced in earthly things. What attracts me most isn't his age or how he can lead me if I'm lost—it's that he's as comfortable in his skin as a person can be.

I'm drawn to his essence, even now. When we're just talking about *hoagies*.

Very un-seriously but still seriously, he says, "If you get your Italian hoagie un-toasted, we won't be anything to each other, Hale."

I'm grinning now. "It would turn you off that much?"

"Complete turn off."

"What if I crawled into your bed naked? You still wouldn't sleep with me?"

He's shaking his head. "Nope."

I can't stop smiling. "What if we're the last two people in the *entire* galaxy? The survival of our respective species would depend on it."

He makes a face. "Nah." He's struggling not to grin now. "I can't fuck a Toasted Hoagie Hater."

"Your turn-offs are mighty specific."

"Give me yours." He checks me out, and I can't even say whether more people have entered Wawa or whether anyone has recognized us, outside of the camera-flashes against the windows. Donnelly seems to register those, but it never changes how he acts around me.

"Guys who hate glitter," I nod. "It might be messy but it's shiny."

"That's a good one," he nods back at me. We're nodding together, and our lips tease with these affectionate smiles, as though we're

NOBODY LIKE US **479**

acknowledging the powerful force of our attraction. We've been dating for two months, so this isn't a first date on that account—but something about *this* date feels magical and easy.

Like…we're just meant to be.

It's a welcoming feeling after some of the tougher moments we've weeded through, and I think, right here and now, Wawa is special.

It can turn everything around.

"Guys who are embarrassed by me," I add.

"You mean my enemies?"

I laugh, flushing more, and he tries to focus on the menu but we're stealing glances at one another. As he taps the screen, he says, "Some of my favorite nights are the ones that start off shaky. It just reminds me that a bad night can always turn good."

"Hope," I sing-song. "You've made it very infectious. I think I've caught a case of it."

"That's 'cause I've been smothering you with it for a while." He tilts his head back at me. "Full confession: you asked me to infect you, so it's been a consensual smothering."

I smile even harder. "I did?"

"You did."

"Maybe I knew…" I shake my head to myself. Memories are on the verge. Maybe they have been this whole time, and instead of being frustrated this one isn't coming out, I'm choosing to believe it is there.

It's always been there.

It never really left me.

He weaves a casual, loving arm around my waist and uses one hand to tap in an order.

"We should ask Frog and Quinn if they want anything," I say, pulling out my phone. Donnelly's hand dips beneath my puffer jacket and AC/DC tee, his fingers skimming the bareness of the small of my back.

My cheeks heat, and a pulse returns to the spot between my legs.

Sex. Donnelly. Sex. Donnelly. The need beats stronger, but I try not to expect it. Because there is a *slight* chance he could still slam on the brakes. He could get in his head about it in the moment, and I'd rather just relish in the present.

But I can't deny, I am extremely horny.

Like, my skin feels radioactive, and his touch is making me too wet. My panties were already soaked before we left.

Our eyes catch, and he must read an odd look on my face because he asks me if this is *okay.* Him touching me. I reaffirm that *yes,* I want him to publicly grope me.

"A lot, a lot," I add.

He grins and kisses my temple, then right outside of my lips, then my lips. I swear I hear the *click, click, click* of camera flashes. But when I check, paparazzi aren't inside Wawa, and they stay camped behind the window.

I'm still hot all over when I text Frog for her hoagie order.

Donnelly waits for it.

"Frog wants Italian on ciabatta. Not toasted."

He makes a noise of disgust. "Buffalo doesn't know what she's talking about. She's getting it toasted." He types it into the kiosk. It's also the first time I've ever heard him call Frog *Buffalo.* She's from Buffalo, New York, and I'm guessing the nickname doesn't happen often because he said it like a pseudo-insult. I prickle in defense like she's my...friend.

She is wearing the emerald green and bright pink striped scarf I knitted her.

My phone buzzes in my palm. "Quinn wants a veggie with parm, lettuce, onion, and tomato. Toasted."

"My man, Quinnie," Donnelly grins, punching in the order.

I watch his fingers—and I remember how good it feels when they're inside of me. I hate that in this sacred place I have sex-brain. It really didn't help coming here right after the pool table. I should've changed my panties too. They're wet and a reminder that I am indeed in need of a release.

His fingers crawl higher up my spine, tingling every inch of me.

I'm ready.

I've never been so ready in my life.

I just want to be railed by him! Is that too much to ask?

Donnelly glances to me, then the kiosk, then back to me, his desire pooling in his blue eyes and dripping slowly down my body. "You gotta stop looking at me like that."

"Why?" I whisper.

"'Cause it's making me want to fuck you against the condiments, and we can't desecrate Wawa at this holy hour."

I flush into another smile. "Look away from me then," I say quietly.

"No can do, Hale. My eyes have chosen you."

"Your eyeballs chose well."

"Yeah, they did." He stares right into my core, reaching into the very depth of me, and my smile softens on him.

I slip my fingers in his beltloop. "Will you order for me?"

"I've got you." He's typing on the screen, and I think it's safe to say that this night has become one of my favorites. One beautiful enough to be recorded for eternity.

I piece every detail together, every fragment of affection, all the simple and shining things, and I hope this tapestry always keeps me warm. I wonder how many more I had with him, and it's not a sad fact anymore. It's not a dark feeling of loss. It's a bright one of discovery.

54

LUNA HALE

We eat our hoagies in my Volvo. Donnelly parks near the Schuylkill River, and we must've lost the paparazzi tail because no cameramen hop out of their vehicles and try to attack our windows. It's warm in the safety of the car, and the moonlight sparkles the dark water.

"Try this too." He splits his toasted Italian with me. And so I give him half of the toasted ham hoagie he ordered for me.

I smile into my first bite of the Italian. It's an explosion of meaty flavor. It melts in my mouth—the bread a perfect softness. I make a satisfied noise, and his grin expands. He passes me a soft drink, and I wash down the bite.

He unwraps his hoagie. "Verdict?"

"Let me try the other one first."

"Girl, you know how to draw out the suspense." He looks out at the river, like he's ensuring no one has snuck up on us. It makes me a little nervous, thinking maybe we're in a dangerous area, until he slips me a smile.

After a bite of the ham, I make an *mmhmm* noise with a nod.

"You like the ham better?"

I give him a thumbs-up, still chewing. It's hard not to take another bite and keep eating, but I must rave first. "Earth's best hoagie right here." I raise my hoagie-half like it's being abducted into my spaceship. "Away it goes. It's boarding the S.S. Thebulan Starcruiser."

"The royal guard gonna eat it?"

"Nope. It'll be displayed in a museum. Full of Earth's greatest artifacts. I'll be sure to reference you as the donor."

"*Ham hoagie*, donated graciously by Paul Donnelly, kickass human and the queen's boyfriend." He nods. "I dig it."

I smile at his words and scoop fallen lettuce back between the bread. "Does that make you the king?" I ask him quietly.

"I hadn't really considered it." He's swishing the fountain soda, trying to shift the ice for more of the drink. "I'd say you're more so my queen."

I think this over. "But if we're together, then that would make you…"

"Queen's boyfriend," he says. "To be king, we'd have to be…"

Oh. *Oh.* Why did this hit me so slowly?! We'd have to be *married.* My eyes pop a little bit.

He's quick to add, "I'm not looking to be a king. I don't want anyone kneeling at my feet, especially because I'm gonna be kneeling at yours. Gotta worship my queen."

It fills me with warm fuzzies. The panic of accidentally surfacing the talk of marriage dissipates. Our relationship hasn't even met the three-month mark, and I know I'm twenty-one—but with my amnesia, I feel eighteen too.

Marriage isn't anything I've thought about for myself before. I've written a wedding or two in my fics, but those weren't about me and my life. Last I remembered when I woke up, I was looking forward to graduating high school and being on my own.

In my long list of things I'd like to experience, I can confidently say that *marriage* lies close to the bottom. It feels extraneous right now. It's not an artery to the heart. It's not the blood rushing inside. It's like an appendix. It can be removed, and the body functions more or less the same.

But what if marriage is something Donnelly wants sooner rather than later? What if our visions of the future aren't even similar?

I don't want to find out. Not right now, at least. Hypotheticals of the future feel disruptive to this perfect date.

I sink my teeth back into my hoagie. Devouring most of it. I'm only able to leave the butt of the bread for the museum. "You think it's special enough?" I ask him. "The bread butt of the hoagie?"

"We can add an engraving: *three-fourths eaten by the queen*. Your alien-kind will probably worship the ham hoagie butt, not you."

"I only really care about one person worshiping me anyway."

He smiles over at me. "Who is he? I gotta kill him."

I laugh. "You're not allowed to hurt yourself. I forbid it."

He kisses my knuckles like I am celestial royalty. My heart swells—then catapults at sudden movement out of the car. I intake a sharp breath.

"It's just a bird," he says, squeezing my hand in comfort.

I'm abnormally jumpy. "Can we go back home?" I ask so quietly. "I love Philly, but I'm anticipating a paparazzi attack at any second… and it's…" I shrug, unable to find the words.

"We weren't gonna be out here much longer anyway," he says easily, like it's not such a big deal. I ease, and when he reverses and we're on the street, his hand slides into mine.

My heart hasn't slowed, and I realize why. "This isn't over just because we're going home, is it?"

"The date?" he asks.

"Yeah."

His grin lights up the road ahead of us. "It's not over yet. Not until we go to sleep."

We've been lounging on the floor of my room. Not sure why we end up on the ground and not the bed, other than it's fun to lie on mounds of blankets and against pillows, and Orion can't take up half the floor like he can the mattress.

My lava lamp casts purple shapes along the walls, and twinkle lights sparkle around my bed behind us. Donnelly and I have been reading the comic book series *Saga* by Brian K. Vaughn together. It's an epic space opera, one we've both individually consumed before.

Apparently, I suggested it to him years ago, and I've learned he was quick to read anything I recommended.

As we study each panel, I love hearing Donnelly's thoughts about the art. I planned to gift him a digital drawing tablet for his birthday, but I might not wait until August. I think he'd like messing around with it.

About two hours in, our conversation skids away from *Saga* and veers into steamier territory. "You don't have a porn preference?"

"That shock you?" Donnelly grins into a sip of Lightning Bolt!

I'm also partaking in an energy drink, not wanting to sleep anytime soon. He's leaning a bicep on a fuzzy white pillow, relaxed into it. I face him with crossed legs. "Kinda. I would've thought you'd gravitate towards a specific category."

He shakes his head once. "I never watched much porn, to be honest."

My brows spring.

He laughs into a swig. "Now I really got you."

"It doesn't turn you on?" I wonder.

"Nah, it's not that." His eyes flit over me, then away for a brief second. "Where was I gonna watch it? I didn't grow up with a lot of privacy, and I'm not talking about your lack of privacy—the American royal kind. Mine was just a buncha people in and out of a cramped apartment. My room was barely *mine* to begin with. My parents didn't pay for internet either. The cell phone I bought myself in high school—it was cheap and archaic and only made calls." He combs a hand casually through his hair. "I'd do a lot of weird shit, but I wouldn't pull up porn at a public library or a café with free Wi-Fi."

"That's probably wise," I nod.

His lips lift. "Your brother does call me *wise one*."

"He's not wrong," I sing-song and sip the energy drink, unable to really look away from him. I love learning more about Donnelly, even the tougher, sadder parts of his childhood. All these pieces make up who he is.

He skims me. "You watch any porn?"

"Yep. But not so, so often. I knew my mom was addicted to it at one point, so I always tried to limit how much I watched. But still..." I shrug. "I clicked into a lot of sites, and I like NSFW gifs. They help with writing new positions for steamy chapters."

Donnelly bends a knee, resting his elbow on it. I like how he moves his body. Is that strange? "You've got a favorite porn category?"

"Yep." My face bakes in heat, but more so with how Donnelly is undressing me with his eyes. Like he's imagining slipping off the baggy black AC/DC tee I'm wearing and stripping me of my sweatpants. I take a bigger gulp of Lightning Bolt! "You'll never guess it."

"Hentai."

"Nope."

"Bondage."

"Uh-uh." I shake my head, and I like how his guesses aren't questions. He says each one with certainty.

"Feet."

I smile. "Wrong again."

"I'll never guess it, huh?" He takes out his phone. "Maybe 'cause I don't know the categories off the top of my head." He's looking them up now. "Cumshot."

"Very good guess. I like that one."

"Funny, so do I." He's scrolling. "But in real life."

My clit throbs at the molten hot look he gives me, and I dig the heel of my foot into the spot between my legs.

"What else do you like in real life?" I sound very eager because I'm dying to know more about his preferences.

Problem is, he's more interested in figuring out mine. "I gotta solve this mystery first. Scooby Doo wouldn't be happy with me." He stares at his phone. "Big Dick."

"Nope again."

"I feel like Cosplay and Role Play are too obvious." He squints at me like I'm an intriguing creature. "Toys?" It's the first one posed as a question.

"You don't sound confident."

"Toys," he says with certainty while locked on my gaze, and I can't deny how hot it is. So hot that I wish my favorite category were toys. His South Philly lilt is also entrapping me, his mere voice flirting with my desires.

"Not toys."

"Alright, you're gonna have to tell me. There are a million categories, and I must be far off."

"Quite a ways off." I try not to be nervous about confessing this, but a wave of anxiety rushes as I rip the Band-Aid and say, "Gang bang."

"Gang bang," he repeats with a slow-rising grin into a sip of his energy drink. "Why gang bang?" He's not freaked or jumping to conclusions, which is why my anxiety washes out like the roll of a wave.

"It's not that I ever wanted a threesome or anything. I never really desired to be gang banged in real life," I preface. "Most especially not now. I mean…it makes me physically sick thinking about anyone else touching me but you." I flip the aluminum tab back and forth on the slender can.

"What turned you on about it?" he wonders.

"How sex seemed to have no pause. She'd come and then she'd be full again. I just liked the idea of being taken over and over and over." I glance up at him.

His muscles have flexed, his cock clearly hardening against his black cotton pants, and he mutters a sexy, "Fuck." He scrapes another hand through his hair, then downs a larger swig. He's stripping me with his gaze again.

I fidget a little, starting to *really* ache for him. "What's your favorite sex position?"

ACTUAL

"Asking me a question you can't answer back, I see."

"I never told you my favorite?"

"Nah, it never came up." He taps the can, thinking. "For the most part, I like giving, so I get off seeing what does you in."

"There's nothing that feels better for you?" I ask.

"Think I'd have a harder time finding a position I didn't like. But if we're talking about what I picture doing to you, then yeah, I have favorites. It changes with my mood." He's eye-fucking me.

I desert my energy drink and lean back on my palms. Hoping he can see that I'm ready. He can have me.

I'm right here.

"I think I have a new fantasy," I say with shallow breath.

"Yeah?" Smoldering temptations thicken the air.

"Yeah," I whisper. "It's for you to do whatever you want to me."

Donnelly picks himself off the floor. Six-foot-three. He towers—and he's on the prowl. Being hunted by him is an instant stoke of arousal; the embers burst inside of me. He uncrosses my legs and scoops me up underneath the thighs—hoisting me against his chest.

An aching whimper leaves my parted lips. I clutch the back of his neck. He's holding me with effortlessness beneath my knees like I'm light as a feather. Even though I'm fully clothed, I'm angled at a perfect position—my heat up against his erection, and I wonder...

"You like this position?"

"Not for your first time." He throws me on the bed.

I land on my soft comforter. Breathless. Holy...fuck. *My first time.* Is he...is he really going to go all the way with me? Is this happening tonight? I'm not sure if I can handle another psyche out, but I'd understand it if he has a mental block. *Don't expect sex.* That's the best course of action.

Donnelly pulls his tee off his head, chucking it aside. Orion *woofs* at him from the floor, like he very much approves of his mom and dad taking these sizzling strides towards each other.

I'm just as enthralled with him as he is with me, our eyes canvassing one another with ferocity. Anticipation is at an all-time high *again*. Twice in one night.

Standing at the foot of the bed, Donnelly is shedding his own pants. He's fully naked and extremely hard. His erection is a mouth-watering tease, and I have the urge to take him between my lips. I *love* blowing Donnelly. It always gets me off. But I also crave for him to pilot this spaceship.

Uncharted territory, headed for a brand-new galaxy, *here we go*.

"Do you...?" I pant, considering what most guys would probably desire next. "Do you want me on your lap?"

"I want you on your back." He captures my ankle, yanking me down towards the edge of the bed. My breath ejects. "To start."

To start!

Yes, *yes*. Please let this last *forever*. He's sliding my sweatpants down my hips and thighs with a more aggressive sensualness than usual. His movements have always been seductive, but he's not at an agonizingly unhurried speed.

He's untamed. His possessive, starved hands tear the fabric off my ankles. He immediately goes for my lime-green thong, and I tremble as my need mounts.

"Donnelly," I moan as his lips track down my abdomen while he rips the thong off my legs and feet. *OhmyGod*. He's kissing the inside of my thigh. He's kissing right outside my pussy. I'm unbelievably aroused from the torment of the pool table session and now *this*.

He licks between my slit, and my legs jerk in pleasure. I cry out when he sucks my clit, then he rises off me. He rests a knee on the edge of the mattress and pulls the AC/DC tee off my body—then he plunges his tongue in my mouth. He's a world-renowned kisser. I bestow him every accolade Thebula can offer.

I love how fiercely he clutches my face when he kisses me. He guides my tongue with his into a sweltering dance, and I would twirl around with him forever, if I could.

Breaking apart, I catch my breath.

"I'm not gonna wear a condom unless you want me to," he tells me.

This is *really* happening!!!

"No condom," I rasp.

He grins, but the haze of his arousal overtakes it. I'm lying on my back, completely bare. I watch him soak up the lines of my feminine form, my perked nipples and my hipbones.

Both of his knees are on the bed now. He's kneeling. His muscles so contracted, I wonder if he's resisting or if he's just so turned-on that he needs to flex to keep from coming.

He grips his erect shaft. "You ready for your first nightly fucking?" he asks, voice husky.

I can't even respond in actual words. A whimpering noise leaves my body. *Yes, please. Don't slow down.* He does *slightly* drop speed. To torment me.

Donnelly lifts my hips and positions his long cock on top of my abdomen, showing me what's about to happen. "You're gonna have to take all of that."

I pulsate. "Please, *please.*" He seems so much bigger than my thin frame, and the idea of his cock disappearing inside me and extending to my belly button is driving me over the edge.

Donnelly hooks an arm under one of my knees, and while his mouth meets mine, he bends my leg towards my chest. Opening me wider.

His tantalizing kisses dizzy me, and I grip his biceps for support. His forehead presses against mine, and he whispers, "I'm not stopping unless you tell me to. You can't handle anything, you say something."

I nod eagerly.

He holds my face again, as though knowing I'm going to squirm and writhe, and he's planning to keep me steady beneath him. *He's been with me before. He understands my body.* It's a calming fact before the giant plunge.

"Take a deep breath." He stares into me. "'Cause I'm about to run your tight, little pussy so hard."

When he grinds forward, it's not a simulation anymore. I gasp at the sheer fullness when he enters me. My mouth is agape, and breath has evacuated my lungs, especially as he begins thrusting at a hypnotic pace.

I clench around him. Unable to even buck my hips upward. He's pounding at a rate that disorients me, and I'm consumed by every mind-blowing second.

Sex—sex is both too tremendous and not nearly enough. I. Want. *Everything.* I cry against the large palm of his hand, his love an undercurrent that swells a greater need inside me.

I want everything...but only with him.

"*DonnellyDonnelly.*" My hands fall off his biceps, unable to even hold on.

A groan scratches against his throat, and he changes his pace to slow, then aggressively fast. My eyes flutter at the blissful torment. I can feel him checking on me while he rocks—but these sensations throttle my body into another dimension.

I moan at the intensity, the friction. The way my body jostles under him with each thrust. I come without warning, seeing stars.

"*Fuck,*" Donnelly groans under his breath, his arousal inside of me. He's still hard. He's still moving, and I'm being built back to a peak.

He changes positions, just slightly. Sitting up, he's kneeling between my legs. Both of his hands are under my kneecaps, and he stretches my thighs open even wider while he fucks me, easily hoisting my hips to meet his length. It's one of the hottest sights I've ever seen. From this angle, I have a total view of his tattooed body and his pierced cock pumping into me.

I prop up on my forearms to see every inch of him disappearing in me. "OhmyGodOhmyGod," I mumble.

"You clench around me again, I'm gonna *come* all over you." It's a carnal threat. "*Luna.*" It's a warning.

"*Yesyesyes,*" I gasp.

"You've gotta take me for longer than this, babe."

I fall off my arms, a puddle of lust and love.

And then Orion jumps on the bed. "Down, boy," Donnelly says while thrusting. For some reason, Orion isn't listening to the one person he always obeys. His tag wags excitedly, and he licks my cheek.

Donnelly pulls out of me.

"No," I whine, way too needy.

"I'm not going anywhere." He corrals Orion off the bed and leads him to the door. Quickly, he locks our dog outside the room, and I'm hooked on his hot, naked stride back to the bed.

We pick up where we left off.

He's knelt between my legs. He flexes back in.

I mutter *yeses* into a high-pitched noise. His heavy, pleasured breaths light me on fire. Sweat has beaded on our skin. In the next beats of our fusion together, he lightly touches my clit and pounds deeper in me. I lose it.

My back arches into a cry, and Donnelly curses, in his own head-rush—but he drags his cock out of me fast. He fists himself with two pumps, spraying my breasts with his cum.

I stick out my tongue to catch it.

His grin appears with a grunt, and I watch his cock twitch into another erection. Oh. *That* turned him on, big time.

Correction—*I* turned him on. Like Donnelly, all I did was what I wanted. We are very, very sexually compatible. It is proven.

I wipe his cum off my cheek and lick my finger.

Donnelly's chest rises and falls heavier.

"I need the taste of your seed," I say into a smile. "It's imperative."

"Yeah?" He's pulling me higher up the bed, my head meeting a pillow. His mouth brushes against my ear. "You can keep tasting it 'cause I'm not done fucking you."

I love him. I love him so much, my heart is hammering at high glorious speeds. We're on our sides. He pulls me back against his chest. Spooning. He has my leg drawn up to my chest again. The deeper, the more intense, and I'm so happy he loves giving me thigh-quakingly *deep*.

But this position is new, and as he slips inside me, I feel *fuller* somehow. He moves for barely a minute before I cry out, "I'mgoingtocome." The orgasm rattles my entire body, but he holds me still against his chest. The force of his arms is sending me. When I intake some oxygen, I murmur in the pillow, "Again."

He's stopped thrusting.

"Please."

He's still hard. He's still in me. What's the hold up?

"*Please.*"

He's slow this time. His lips skim my sweaty neck, then hit my ear as he whispers, "I can barely fucking move in you, you're so swollen. You feel that?"

I try to nod.

"You feel how deep I am in you?"

Yes.

"You feel me *buried* inside you?" Another thrust.

Fuckfuckfuck. I moan, "Don'tstop*don'tstop.*"

"I can't stop," he whispers sexily against my ear. "Our worlds depend on me penetrating you over and over and over again."

Holy...my eyes start to roll. He is a giver, and seeing me unravel ignites him. His pace is vigorous. I cry his name into the pillow.

He murmurs against my ear, "My little fucking weirdo." He nips my lobe with affection.

Black dots flash in my vision—I've heard him call me that before. I don't know where or why, but I feel those words pool in my soul. Like that's where they've been.

That's where they belong.

This climax is body-trembling. He releases inside me, and I feel his cock unloading. I black-out for a second, and I'm a hot, sticky mess in his arms. Still, I like his sweat and the dampness of the tangled comforter and sheets. There's something sultry about the aftermath of what we just did, the tangible remnants of our sex.

I don't want to clean off.

I want to make a bigger mess. "Again," I rasp.

"Let's take a break." He pushes a calm hand through his hair, the come-down oozing his muscles. "You're too sensitive."

"No, I'm good if you are." I'm about to straddle him, but he pushes me back gently, then his fingers skim my clit. I flinch into a gasp. Like he electrocuted me. *Whoa.*

He's searching my eyes. "That hurt?"

I shrug. "We could just try…?"

"It won't feel as good for you again," he tells me. "We can wait. This isn't…" He trails off, his gaze drifting far away.

"What?" I catch my breath.

"This isn't the last time," he says with a single nod to me, and I can't make sense of his expression. But I just nod back and accept that we'll be able to do this again and again. Later.

Donnelly leaves the bed to open a window. Letting cold air rush through the room. Purple shapes from the lava lamp bathe his skin in an iridescent hue.

"You okay?" I ask as he comes back with a pack of cigarettes.

"Just déjà vu," he mutters, his arm slipping around my shoulders. "I'm alright." He smiles down at me. "You want a towel?"

"Not yet."

He nods, his lips still rising. "How'd it feel?"

"To lose my pseudo-virginity," I smile, "it felt like the greatest take-off of my life, but only because it was with you."

He kisses the top of my head. "You sore?"

"Not in a bad way. It kinda feels like you're still inside me."

He peels a sweaty strand of hair off my cheek, tucking it behind my ear. I try not to yawn. I'm slumped more into his chest, and I tilt my chin up. Just to observe him. He lights a cigarette between his lips. He seems very content and happy.

My smile softens. "Was sex super different with me this time? Than before I got amnesia?"

He blows smoke away from me, his brows furrowing. "You wanna know?"

I've been afraid these details would make me insecure, but now,

I'm just more intrigued. "Yeah, I do. Am I needier?"

He grins. "Not by much." He puts the cigarette back to his lips.

"Really?"

"Yeah, you've always been eager, but it is different this time."

"How so?"

He's thinking. "It's more intense." He reaches for an empty energy drink can on the nightstand, and he taps ash into it. "Your reactions are heightened. Your body used to always tremble, but now it's like you're going through a fucking exorcism when you orgasm, and it's…" He's grinning into a drag of the cigarette. "It's hot. Really hot."

I flush. "Why do you think that is?"

"Probably 'cause you had bad experiences with other guys before I came around. Your sex drive wasn't even as high as it is now."

"I didn't know that."

"Yeah…sorry, maybe I should've told you earlier, so you could tell your doctors."

"It's okay."

He passes the cigarette to me. "This is usually my favorite part."

"Of sex?"

"Yeah." He smiles at me. "Everything is just peaceful. Body, mind, the space babe I made come four times."

"Mmm-hmm," I blow a line of smoke. "You're really good at it."

He pinches the cigarette out of my fingers. "Fucking you comes naturally."

"I feel the same way for it being my first time, but I have a feeling if I did this with someone else, it would've been sloppy." I battle a yawn. "I know you're the only one I ever remember sleeping with, but I think you're a pro."

"A sex pro?"

"Uh-huh."

His muscles tense beneath me, and I watch him take a much longer drag. I'm about to ask if he's okay, but he tells me, "I've always enjoyed sex, but I never knew it could be like this until I got with you."

"Like what?" I ask him.

He holds my gaze tenderly. "Loving."

It floods my lungs with helium. I float to his lips, kissing him. He cups my cheek, and when I pull back and sink against him, I blink a ton to stay focused on my boyfriend. Observation cannot cease! Must continue…exploration…of human.

My human.

Vision blurring, I see the outline of his jaw and his hoop earring. I think his lips rise. "Sleep, Luna."

I fight exhaustion. It tugs at my eyelids. "I don't want this to end," I whisper.

"I'll be here when you wake up. I promise." He seals it with our pinkies. Another earthly promise made, I sink against his calm heartbeat and fall fast, fast asleep.

MARCH

"Love is the one thing we're capable of
perceiving that transcends dimensions of
time and space. Maybe we should trust
that, even if we can't understand it."

– *Interstellar*

CHARLIE & LUNA'S TEXT THREAD

March 6th

10:32 a.m.

Charlie: Are you sick of screaming newborns yet?

Luna: Yes and no. It's kinda cute when Maeve and Cassidy cry together. I pretend they're in their own screamo metal band as duo singers. Cry Baby Cry. Or Pacifier Letdown. Band name might need workshopped. Ideas?

Charlie: Move to New York.

Luna: Who will make Pacifier Letdown merch?

Charlie: Their other adoring fans. Our nieces have plenty.

Luna: True. They're both already Instagram royalty after the pic Jane posted where they're sleeping and hugging. Did you see it?

Charlie: Yes.

Luna: Did you think it was cute?

Charlie: Not enough for 10 million likes.

Luna: Fair.

Luna: I love Philly, you know. More now than I ever have. It's more than a place to Donnelly. It's a part of him. I can't see myself ever leaving.

55

 **LUNA HALE**

I pocket my phone after texting with Charlie.
It's a Wednesday.

Which means I'm split apart from my boyfriend for most of the morning and afternoon. While he protects my brother at Dalton, I'm whisked away to an Ivy League by my bodyguard chauffeurs.

Except, Quinn Oliveira is noticeably MIA from the driver's seat—unless he's transformed into the beefy blonde Gabe Montgomery (highly unlikely).

I've seen Gabe protect just about everyone lately, including my nephew Ripley. Donnelly calls Gabe the "SFO floater" so I guess he's floated to my detail today.

"Where's Quinn?" I ask from the backseat. We're ten minutes out from Penn's campus.

Frog swipes sparkly pink gloss on her lips. Not using a mirror, she's scanning the streets while Gabe drives. "We think he has the flu," she tells me. "He's been hacking up a lung all morning."

Donnelly told me he used to live with Gabe, Frog, and Quinn three floors below the penthouse, but I still can't wrap my head around it. In my mind, he's always meant to be right on the other side of our bathroom.

Gabe fixes his comms earpiece, one hand on the wheel. "Could just be a 24-hour bug. We don't know what he has until he sees the doc."

Frog stabs the wand of gloss in the tube. "Good thing Farrow is bringing him a flu test then." She twists the cap and lets out a huff. "I need to get this off my chest. I swear Nessa gave him the flu. She's been sneezing all weekend and calling it seasonal allergies."

I've met Nessa.

Not in the sense that we've been introduced. But I've observed her from a distance.

Many times, after Quinn gets off my detail, a short, excitable brunette will be waiting for him in the apartment complex's lobby.

She's trendy and fashionable like Frog, but Nessa rarely wore the same outfit twice. Her wrists and neck sparkled with delicate layers of silver jewelry and cute heart pendants. I wasn't shocked when Quinn told me she's a beauty influencer with her own social media channel. She looks like she's stepped out of an Instagram post with 1 million likes.

Other occasions, Nessa has appeared on Penn's campus while Quinn was *on*-duty. She's waited for him outside of my Astronomy class before.

Quinn usually tries to steer her away and remind her he's working. She'll steal the moment to kiss him in front of Frog, and she'll always have pastries and thoughtful gifts for him, like a handcrafted bracelet or a beanie he'd forgotten in the cold. It seems to touch Quinn's heart.

Frog calls it love-bombing.

"It's suspicious," she's said to me before. "No one, not even my own *mom*, has given me a gift every single day. It's like she's saying sorry for something."

"Maybe she knows it's wrong to distract him from his work, so it's like a preempt apology," I theorized. "Or maybe she's doing it because she knows it gets under your skin. I don't think Nessa likes you very much."

"Well, I don't like her," Frog mumbled. "It sucks that Joana is Quinn's sister because she's *amazing*, and I'd rather run into her a million times over than that..." She growled out and slurped her iced coffee, stopping herself from calling Nessa a bitch.

This sunny Wednesday, she has no iced coffee. Just the lip gloss and a stylish fanny pack and a grumpy look on her face.

"Is Nessa over your apartment a lot?" I wonder.

"Yes," Frog says at the same time Gabe says, "Not really."

Frog balks. "*Not really?* Gabe, she keeps her shampoo and conditioner in the bathroom. Last week, I found her extra razor supply under the sink."

"Which shampoo is hers?"

"The one in *French* that costs over a hundred bucks," Frog says in disbelief that he hasn't noticed. "Also the same one that I was told *do not touch* by Her Royal Highness."

"Sharing is caring," I sing-song.

"Exactly," Frog says. "Like, I don't care she has high-end shampoo taste, but don't put it in my shower and tell me I can't even smell the thing." She slumps down in her seat and glances my way. "I did take a whiff."

I smile. "What'd it smell like?"

"Rose petals and happiness." She sighs heavily. "No wonder Quinn's obsessed with her. It has to be her shampoo." She says it like she can't find any other rational reason he'd be dating Nessa. If her redeeming qualities begin and end at her shampoo taste, then I wonder why Quinn would stay with her for this long too. Donnelly says they've been together for a year now.

We chitchat some more about Quinn, talking like friends. These car rides to and from college are some of my favorites. I imagine this is the easygoing friendship Frog might've had with me before I lost my memories.

Unlike the friendships I can barely piece together, I find comfort in this one I'm rebuilding with her.

"Are you still seeing Scooter?" I ask her.

Gabe goes rigid.

"Sometimes we meet up for coffee to *talk*," she emphasizes to Gabe.

I'm not a thorn to Frog like her two roommates. Donnelly told me he's trying not to hound her about Scooter too. We're both afraid pushing Frog away will just push her into a flapping red flag, but the alternative isn't any better since she's still communicating with him.

"I said nothing," Gabe defends.

"I know what you're thinking." Frog sighs. "We're not dating, okay. That date was awful. I recognize that and accept it, but he's still my friend."

Scooter was super touchy-feely with Frog, especially when she slipped into a drunker state. She could barely stand, and he was territorial, not letting Donnelly or me or Joana help her. At one point Joana threatened to knock him out, but Donnelly was masterful in the art of deflection. He got Scooter to let her go by doing shots with him and Tricky Dicky. Then I scooped an arm under Frog and guided her to the girl's bathroom.

Frog continues, "He was just looking out for me that night. His intentions were in the right place, and he apologized for being rude to Donnelly—and you know, I don't have to keep explaining this to you or to Quinn. It's exhausting." She rotates to me. "Quinn *loathes* him now. He won't even let him in the apartment."

"He smells," Gabe defends his roommate with two words.

Frog glares. "That's his cologne."

"Cheddar cheese isn't a cologne."

Frog groans, then turns to me. "Do you see what I'm dealing with?"

I do see that her response to my question was just bringing up Quinn again. I sense romantic inklings. If Quinn were single and asked Frog out, I wonder if she'd dump Scooter to the curb in a heartbeat.

"You have very protective roommates," I tell her. "It's not such a bad thing."

Frog thinks this over. "Yeah, that's true." She adjusts the mic clipped to her Penn Cheer tee. "Thanks for being there...I know I've said it like seven times now, but I mean it." She slips me a smile before surveying the road again. "Especially since I can't remember a lot of it."

She blacked out. That's the scary part, and as someone who also can't recall events, it's a frightening situation. I don't even know if I have similar black-out wasted experiences. Maybe I do. Maybe when I was nineteen like Frog, I found myself in the same place.

And I'd hope that people I trusted were there to keep an eye on me.

"It's what friends do," I say simply.

"Good friends," Gabe mumbles under his breath.

Frog snaps him an irritated look.

"You hear that?" Gabe pretends like he said nothing.

I almost laugh.

"The sound of my sense of humor decaying—it's very loud," Frog mutters and glares out the window.

I wish I had iced coffee to cheer her up. I dig in my backpack for anything helpful, but my spiral binder of Economics notes will only induce boredom.

Gabe's phone rings, and Frog picks it up for him. "It's Millie Kay." *His girlfriend.* She's also the surrogate who birthed Cassidy, my baby niece.

"Tell MK I'll call her back," Gabe says, focused on driving. "And that she looked cute yesterday in that red dress, and to have a good day, and I'll catch up with her at dinner, and to decide between steak or pizza—"

"Would you like to hire a receptionist?" Frog asks before answering. "Hi, MK. Gabe says he'll call you back." Frog repeats *everything* Gabe instructed and then some. She's on the phone with Millie Kay for another three minutes, hyping up Gabe's cooking skills. "Go for the steak. It really has no business being that good."

Once she's off the phone, Frog speaks quietly in comms. Then her attention returns to me. "How are you and Wonder Bread?"

Instantly, I picture myself intertwined with Donnelly in sweaty sheets from this morning. It's been over a week since he took my pseudo-virginity, and he's been inside me every night and morning since then. Sex has been a natural, blissful piece of our relationship, like it's the ingredient that makes bread rise or the secret that makes cherries grow plentifully from a tree.

I smile wide and say, "Fruitful."

She gasps. "You're pregnant."

Gabe's neck snaps but he's careful to maintain eye-contact on the road.

"No wait," Frog crinkles her nose. "That doesn't make sense. You two are taking things slow." I did mention that Donnelly and I were in a slo-mo zone together since my amnesia.

I could be vague, but I'm still trying to share more. "We had sex, actually," I say into a giant grin.

Frog lets out a louder gasp while Gabe puts *both* hands on the wheel like my news might flip the vehicle over.

"You *are* pregnant."

"Nope. We've just had an abundance of extraordinary sex."

She lets out a soft squeal. "I knew this would eventually happen. But it's still shocking. Like knowing the ending of Titanic but crying anyway. Only this happens to be a happy shock and not a grab-a-box-of-tissues shocker."

I don't tell her how Donnelly and I cried beforehand. How we went on a magical date to Wawa afterward. How the night became one for the storybooks of our love.

This—I could share this, I want to share this with my friend, but how do I verbally express the sheer depth of those soulful moments that are living and breathing inside my heart? It's not as easy to speak about love, as it is to write it.

Once we're parked and walking across campus, Frog mentions her virginity status and asks me if I think it's worth it to wait for the right one.

She's not making eye contact; her vigilance is on college students locking their bikes and others powerwalking to the library. So I take a second to respond.

Is it worth it to wait?

Even though I did lose my virginity the first time around to someone else, I can't remember it. I'm glad that Donnelly feels like my first now. And maybe that won't last forever. I might get memories back of the other sexual encounters before him, and I'll have to be okay with that.

But OG Luna is *me*. Those three years paved the way for me to be where I am today. Had I not been with other guys first, would I even have had the courage to be with Donnelly at all? Would I have even woken up in that hospital and had this connection with him now?

I'll never really know.

But I believe every timeline matters. The one I forgot and the one I remember. And the merging of the two. They all make up who I am.

So I tell Frog, "The right one will be with you whether you're a virgin or not. And if he's the *right* one—I'd like to believe he'll make it feel like there was no one ever before him."

Gabe stands outside the door of Television

and New Media. He doesn't want the presence of a new "student" to be a distraction. So only Frog and I are seated at the U-style conference table.

I do what I do every Monday, Wednesday, Friday. Open my laptop and ignore the hell out of the three girls sitting across from me. Stassi, Beverly, and Jeffra combined have morphed into some Bermuda Triangle that vanishes your self-esteem if you make direct eye contact. Frog calls them hobgoblins. She also covered her Stanley in Studio 9 stickers the day after Stassi complimented it.

I'm popping up my notes app when Frog stiffens beside me. Uh-oh. My mind shoots to the Bermuda Triangle. What are they doing? I don't hear any hissing—a good sign.

Frog's brows knot. Her shoulder bumps mine. "Luna," she whispers, leaning in. "I'm just learning this now, so don't be upset—" She touches her earpiece.

I try not to freak out. Frog is listening intently to comms. Making the most dramatic pause ever.

"Apparently..." she whispers. "Ben is coming here."

I short-circuit. "Ben?"

She nods.

"My cousin? That Ben?" I whisper back. It makes zero sense, even if he's a student here. It's a *big* college. We rarely run into each other on campus. Why would he track me down? He could've just texted.

I can't inquire further.

The empty seat beside me, usually reserved for Quinn, is filled by a six-foot-five collegiate jock. My cousin. He does not go unnoticed.

Several girls intake sharp breaths like a son of Zeus just dropped from the sky. However, the guys seem less than impressed.

Carson crosses his arms and cocks back in the office chair. "Drop/add period ended a while back, man. How'd you pull strings to get in here?"

"Does he need to pull any strings?" Stassi asks, lowering the screen of her MacBook. She tries to capture Ben's gaze, but he's busy rifling through his gym bag. "His dad is Penn legacy."

Jeffra chokes on disbelief. "No, Wyatt's class is the Fort Knox of classes. He wouldn't have let a *Cobalt* slither their way in." She says *Cobalt* like it's a disease.

"Are you broken?" Stassi whisper-hisses to her. "The Cobalts are—"

"I grew up in the same neighborhood as them, Stas. They're nothing special. *Especially* that one. He's a knockoff of a knockoff."

I blister. Great, now Jeffra is throwing stones at my family.

Ben has a thousand-yard stare, pausing briefly in his hunt for...a water bottle. It's decaled in environmental stickers, some puns like *I be-leaf in you.* That one might be more Winona's doing. Though I heard they're not as close since Ben went to college.

He shoves the gym bag at his feet. "It's not some elaborate scheme," he tells the class. "I've been enrolled in the course since the beginning of the semester. I just haven't been able to attend in person." He acknowledges me next to him with a smile and the lift of his fingers in greeting and tells me, "I had to get some practice times rescheduled with my coach."

I smile back, but I'm still orbiting a mysterious planet. *Why are you here?*

"How are you not failing?" Carson asks, dumbfounded.

Ben doesn't answer that.

Jeffra grinds her jaw. "If Wyatt is letting you turn in assignments by email, that's blatantly *unfair*."

I wish one of them would ask the important question.

Why is he here????

Since when does Ben even care about Television and New Media? Last I heard, he hadn't declared a major, but I doubt he'd choose communications. Then again, I can't be so sure. What if he struck a friendship with a *We Are Calloway* producer and became interested in TV?

He could have a secret desire. He's always been social and friendly, but that doesn't equate to being an open book. I've run into plenty of students on campus who'd swear they're good friends with Ben, but if I quizzed them on his favorite things, I wonder if they could even accurately list five without scouring the internet for answers.

Maybe Ben has a knack for letting others skim the surface of him and they believe they've reached the core—but they're not even two-inches deep.

Ben doesn't give Jeffra Yankton the time of day. It irks her, which only makes me smile, and Ben shares it with me. He's sweet. That's what most in our family say about Ben.

He's sweet and daring and outgoing.

Of what I've witnessed from the mock panel and overheard from Winona and Vada and been told by Xander, my Spidey-senses are saying that is not the entirety of my cousin. Maybe not even one-half of him.

Which makes me wonder…who's even seen the entire iceberg of Ben Cobalt?

He's more of a mystery to me than Charlie these days.

He runs his fingers through the wet strands of his hair. Did he just finish hockey practice? Did he take a shower afterwards? More questions.

I'm about to ask one when Wyatt Rochester saunters to the podium, a Starbucks coffee in one hand and a paper bag in the other. "Someone parked in my spot this morning. The bakery ran out of the last pain au chocolat—so I was forced to go to Starbucks. If one of you would like to ruin my day further, you can head out now because I'm not dealing with it." He scans the length of the class, and his brows jump when he stops on Ben. "Look who's finally decided to grace us with their *magnanimous* presence." He pauses. "Mr. Cobalt." It's a cold greeting. "And here I thought you were trying to flunk out on purpose."

Ohhhhh. So he is failing this class. Why didn't he drop it when he had the chance during drop/add?

"Sorry about that," Ben says with a polite hand raise. "Coach wouldn't let me out of practice, and you don't take sports exemptions—but I reworked it. Everything should be fine now."

"You'll have to ace every exam and turn in all your assignments to even *pass*. But if you think that's *fine*…" He frees his hands to applaud. "Way to lower the Cobalt standards."

Jeffra has a snide grin.

Carson mutters, "Damn."

Stassi still checks Ben out like she's plotting ways to speak to him after class.

Ben scoots forward. "Maybe you shouldn't throw stones at glass houses, Professor—"

"Wyatt or Rochester," he cuts him off. "You'd know to call me either if you showed up the first day."

"Rochester," Ben concludes.

"Say what you mean, Mr. Cobalt. We're all open here." He uncaps a dry erase marker.

"I mean your family owns *tabloids* that print lies and whose entire goal is to profit off peoples' suffering. So how can you talk about *standards* when the Rochesters have none?"

I brace myself for blowback.

The class is collectively caging breath.

"You don't think your family profits off tabloids?" Wyatt tips his head. "Consumers drive what's printed, and as long as they're interested in the Calloway sisters and their children, there will be tabloids and lies spread about your family. And your family will use that attention to sell carbonated corn syrup and a second-rate Powerade. Am I wrong?" He's asking me?!

All eyes have descended upon my roasted cheeks.

"Uh," I sit up straighter. Of course our families profit off being newsworthy. It's social currency. Any successful business would take advantage of press, whether negative or positive, to sell their products.

The thought of giving the Roach kudos or even a thumbs up makes my skin crawl. "You are wrong," I say. "Ziff Ascend tastes way better than Powerade."

"Idiot," Jeffra snickers under her breath and shares a snide smile with Beverly.

Ben tells Wyatt, "So what if my family uses that attention? Just *stop*. Stop printing lies. Stop printing clickbait."

"So then we print a boring lede. Our tabloids go under, someone else will rise from the ashes and become *us*. The only way to get rid of what you hate is to change consumers' interests, and your family has rooted itself in the cultural foundation of the world for decades. You're not going anywhere. Someone will *always* profit off you. You will *always* profit off them. Welcome to the symbiotic relationship between you and your viewer and the press." He faces the whiteboard. "Let's take a critical look at the cultural zeitgeist surrounding the cult hit reality show we've been discussing all semester."

He writes out, *Princesses of Philly.*

Ben sighs and heaves backward in the chair like it's disheartening. He eyes me and whispers, "All semester?"

"Yeah, sadly."

The Roach scrawls on the board, *Get inside the Calloway sisters this February.* "This was the tagline for the show."

We discuss how the show was intentionally marketed to hook viewers into the sex angle since my mom's sex addiction was *the* current event at the time.

Sex sells. It's not such a new concept.

"What made this show different from any other reality show?" The Roach points to a student. "Ross."

"All the sisters lived together?"

"*The Real World* did it first. Come on, do better than that." He calls on *Jeffra.*

I sink down.

She lifts her chin. "It was what happened afterward. The show ended abruptly with the leak of Rose and Connor's sex tapes."

"Ben's parents," the Roach says with a cruelness.

"Unconsented," Ben snaps back. "They didn't *plan* to release those tapes at that time. They didn't even know they were being filmed."

"This isn't a course on ethics."

"Ethics *should* be involved when it comes to media."

"But they aren't always." He speaks in German, as if Ben would understand the language purely by being a Cobalt. I've seen many strike conversations in different languages with Eliot, who knows a little of everything but a lot of German and French.

Ben, however, just stews quietly and never responds.

"The importance of POVs with the timing of a cultural phenomenon," the Roach says and spins back to the whiteboard.

It's the only chance I have. I lean into Ben's shoulder. "Did you learn German in the past three years? And why are you here?"

"No," he whispers. "And Eliot said Jeffra was in your class, and you needed backup." He takes in my complete and utter shock.

"Was he wrong?" Ben frowns.

No...I just...this is *Ben*. He should be off chilling with his hockey friends. Flirting with all the girls like Stassi that admire his status as Cobalt royalty. He shouldn't be here, subjected to dealing with Jeffra.

Eliot's the one who I would've suspected to pull strings and audit this class with me. Why did he enlist Ben's help instead? Is it just because Ben's the one already enrolled at Penn?

I shake my head. "Jeffra is Jeffra." I want to say I can handle her on my own, but that was never the case in high school. I'm not sure if things have changed for me now, and I don't reject Ben's help. Not when he's flunking a class *for* me.

Still, I want to give him an out. "I appreciate it, but you don't have to be here, Ben."

"I kind of do." He's evasive, trying to focus on the board.

I frown. "Because of Eliot?"

"Because of me. I had to tip the scales." He swigs from his water bottle, then recaps it. "I've done some shitty things, and I needed to do something good."

If it makes him feel better being here, then I'm happy to experience the pits of a Jeffra Roachy hell with him.

I see the Bermuda Triangle slyly using their phones while the Roach's back is turned. They're likely alerting their troops that *the* Ben Pirrip Cobalt is in their class.

It's like catching a lightning bug in a bottle.

My focus zones somewhere else, away from the whiteboard. Away from the class. Little lightning bugs—no, tiny *lights* dot my vision. Prick my memory. Blood rushes out of my head. Woozy, I lean back.

Dr. Frisk told me to take deep breaths when I felt myself zoning out. Deep breaths. *Don't panic*, she said. *Just relax into the memory.*

So I do, and I remember an umbrella with tentacles. *My* umbrella. I remember it's mine. I remember the jittery feelings of being near

Donnelly but not *with* Donnelly. I remember the tiny fairy lights sparkling around his grin.

I remember the winter wonderland decorations in the gymnasium.

I remember being swept into his radiance. I remember falling in love with him.

A happy memory.

This is the first big *happy* memory I've felt in its entirety so far.

Homecoming.

I remember all of it.

"Luna," Ben's voice draws me out of my head.

I blink my eyes open, not realizing I shut them. Lights are out, and a clip from *We Are Calloway* projects on the whiteboard.

In the dark, Ben's concern is an overflowing volcano. "You don't look well. You're clammy." He's speaking to Frog. "She might need electrolytes. I have some in my bag." He's digging in his gym bag, risking the Roach's wrath.

Frog puts a water bottle in my hand. "Drink this."

"I'm okay," I whisper to them, but I'm overwhelmed and near tears. They don't realize they're *happy* tears. The memory is so vivid. I can hear The Cure playing. I can feel Donnelly's soft touch grazing my elbow, then my lower back. Electric.

His touch has *always* tingled every inch of my body.

It's difficult to walk away from the memory when I want to drown inside it, but I take a few breaths and search the room, thinking I've become the center of unwanted attention. Most concentrate on the video clip.

Except Jeffra. She arches a brow at me like she's about to claim I had an orgasm in the dark. After watching *The OA* video, I wouldn't put it past her to do it. But strangely, her mouth stays shut.

I'm not sure if it's Ben's presence or the Roach's self-proclaimed bad mood today. She probably just doesn't want to rock the boat, and I don't want to waste any more of my brain space on her.

No, I need to keep my brain as empty as possible.

I smile. I'm ready for my memories to fill it.

CHARLIE & LUNA'S TEXT THREAD

March 11th

8:08 a.m.

Luna: Are you looking forward to the tour bus?

6:49 p.m.

Charlie: No.

FANATICON FORUM

We Are Calloway

Posted by @lorensfavtaco616 #wac-mod

Cobalt Brothers Runway Photos Megathread
Discuss the photos from the Calloway Couture promotional campaign for their Spring line. Charlie Keating Cobalt, Beckett Joyce Cobalt, Eliot Alice Cobalt, Tom Carraway Cobalt, and Ben Pirrip Cobalt all walk the runway and give a sneak peek behind-the-scenes of getting ready. Photos are posted exclusively on Vogue. (Article is linked.) Please be respectful of each other and the families, or you will be banned from the WAC forum.

@EliotCanHaveMyBbs: Whoa. Guys, these are incredible! Eliot is a natural model. Anyone else thinking that?

@CallowayCouture91: I can't believe they took photos in the dressing room!!!

@VampireRodrig0: Chill. They didn't take any pics getting dressed. Just doing makeup and hair. So...not that revolutionary.

@RCCAlwaysForever: Can we talk about how well the brothers are all getting along? Like ZERO drama came out of this runway.

@WACC77Lover: It's because they're friends! The media just likes to pit them against each other, I swear.

@Charlie_Does_Me: Back to the important topic people! Charlie Fucking Keating. He is stunning!!! If Calloway Couture doesn't pick him up to be the face of future campaigns after this, I AM SUING!

@WhatUpButtercup: Xander would have hit this out of the park. He should have been invited.

@hehecallowayxx: God, Charlie is HOT.

@Doitforthegram: Why is this even a thread? They're a bunch of spoiled nepo babies. Deleted by mod-bot for breaking forum rules.

@CobaltTwinsStanAccount: We need a thread just dissecting their suits. I know everyone is talking about The Eliot, but The Beckett is *by far* the most stunning. The black on black? And it's slim and fits his body soooo perfectly.

@BitchBossXOXO: And a thread about who has the best walk!! My ranking: Beckett, Eliot, Tom, Charlie, Ben.

@MoreKeatingPlease: Charlie should be wayyyy higher. He killed it. #OslieForever

@CobaltsNeverDie: I love how the Cobalt brothers are all besties. Warms my heart.

56

PAUL DONNELLY

"*I have a bright idea. Let's focus on why we* love each other," Eliot says, his arms outstretched between Ben and Charlie's chests. He's only in sweatpants since he flew out of his bunk to separate his brothers.

"What did you expect?!" Charlie shouts back in annoyance at Ben. Their voices have been escalating for the past five minutes. "It's a competition. We're *competing*."

"You're *cheating*." Ben balls an old, faded baseball cap angrily in his hands. "And only to bury *me*."

Eliot says, "I suppose I might be asking for the world."

The tour bus lurches over a pothole, and I grip the table in the front section of the bus to steady myself. Ben catches onto a storage compartment above Xander's head, careful not to fall into him. My elf is seated and reading some romantasy novel Audrey Cobalt lent him. He's blocking out the explosive fight with noise-cancelling headphones.

Eliot stabilizes Charlie against the cupboards. They're near the locked bathroom (Luna is still in there).

Safe to say the mini-marketing campaign for Fizzle is off to a bumpy start. The Fizzle Five have various meet-and-greets and photo ops scheduled this week, and board members have been dropping in to judge 'em.

Tensions have been bubbling since everyone boarded the tour bus 72-hours ago in Los Angeles, and they boiled over after the stop in Nevada.

"Anyone want a bagel?" I try to defuse the ticking bomb.

"Sure," Charlie says flatly.

"Look, progress," Eliot sighs. "Perhaps I won't have to call Beckett."

Ben is still staking Charlie with a glare. Might need a hundred bagels to stuff in the crater between the two of them. One package isn't gonna do the job.

Cream cheese might help. Moving around the bus, I search for a knife and package of plain bagels. Nothing like breakfast at nine p.m.

Reminds me of Farrow, really. Last time I was on a bus like this, all of SFO were traveling together for the FanCon tour. Great times.

Now it's just Oscar, Epsilon, and me. Weird mix, especially since SFE aren't being the shitheads that I know 'em to be. They've been… different since the hazing initiation with O'Malley.

Can't put my finger on how exactly, other than they're less prickish.

Makes me feel funny inside. Not sure I like it.

Right now, I'm the sole bodyguard survivor on this bus—outside of Ian Wreath, the SFE lead. But he doesn't count 'cause he's steering the wheel.

Security's bus tails the one I'm on. It was added for redundancy— since during the FanCon, the bus broke down in the middle of nowheresville. Two buses are better than one. I'm not "exactly" riding with the famous ones out of special treatment for being Luna's boyfriend.

Xander requested me here.

No one asked him *why*. It's not unusual for him to want his bodyguard closer, but I know it's not purely because he needs my protection. He knows if I'm on the bus, I can spend more time with Luna.

So it is because I'm dating her.

Can't deny that I've slept better being in the same bed as my girlfriend. She's woken me when I started thrashing a few times, but I haven't sleepwalked since the holidays.

"You set me up—just admit it," Ben says to Charlie.

I spread cream cheese on a bagel half and cast a quick glance at the bathroom. Luna has been in there a while.

"I'm not denying it." Charlie has a cranky expression. Seems like Ben truly irritates the shit outta him. "You're gullible and naïve. *Perfect* traits for the future CEO of Fizzle."

Ben works his tensed jaw. "That's our *dear* brother." He's talking to Eliot. "I believed Charlie. I trusted him for one moment, and what does he do?"

"Again, we're *competing*," Charlie defends. "If I thought Eliot would've fallen for the same asinine ploy, I would've used it on him. But he's not—"

"Naïve, yeah, I know what you think of me," Ben says tightly.

"You just proved today it's what you *are*."

Eliot has a hand on his forehead, unsure of how to resolve this.

Cobalt peacemaker—he is not. This isn't the first blowup either. The lion cubs have been tearing at each other's throats every night on the bus. Blood is being spilled, and gotta say, I hate it. Feels like fratricide.

Xander suddenly leaves for the narrow aisle of bunks. Quickly, I follow and check on him. He's lying down on a bottom bunk, adjusting a pillow behind his head and flipping off the reading light. Bathed in darkness.

"Everything good with you?" I ask him.

"Just *exhausted*, after everything today, and that's not helping." He means the fighting. He rubs at his tired eyes, and I nod a couple times. He's unquestionably the most popular during these mini meet-and-greets. Fizzle's coordinators only allow a hundred ticketed guests inside the venues, but the fans all rush for Xander first.

He's been more overwhelmed on this tour than any day at school.

Which is saying something because his senior year has been riding him hard.

"Your new meds alright?"

He teeter-tots his hand like *meh*. "Too soon to tell, I guess."

"Want a bagel?" I hold out the one I just slathered in cream cheese.

"I'm good, thanks. I'm just gonna FaceTime Easton. See if he's fed Erebor." His best friend has been living with him since the beginning of March.

I'm happy this one thing went right for those two. They needed that. Xander's dad came through big time.

"Tell him to give the Lonely Mountain a pat on the head and a *good girl* from me," I say, mentioning his Newfie by her nickname. It reminds me that Farrow and Maximoff are dog-sitting Orion while Luna and I are gone.

"Will do, wise one." He gets comfortable on the pillow. "You mind shutting the curtain?"

"Don't do anything I wouldn't in there," I grin. "The list is short."

His smile appears before I swipe the black privacy curtain to his bunk. He's okay. We've established a close enough bond that I'm positive he'd tell me if he needed something more.

Cobalts are now arguing in snappy French. I scour the front section for Luna. Booth seating is empty. Ian is alone and busy concentrating on the dark road of the Nevada desert as we head into Arizona.

I frown at the bathroom. *She hasn't come out yet?* Without alerting the Cobalts, I knock lightly on the door and whisper, "Luna?"

I hear…nothing.

My pulse pitches. "Luna? You good?"

She moans a little.

I jiggle the knob. *Locked.* My stomach is in knots. "Can you let me in, babe?"

Eliot, Charlie, and Ben go quiet as I try to break into the bathroom. She's not responding anymore. I throw the bagel on the counter and slam my shoulder against the wood.

"Luna!" Eliot calls. She says nothing. Hurriedly, he's whipping open drawers.

"She's been in there for over fifteen minutes," Charlie says, eyes darkening on me.

My pulse is a jackhammer. "Luna, can you hear me?" I twist the knob and use my body weight again.

Eliot is asking something to Charlie in French. I can't think of anything except, *Get in the bathroom. Get to her.* All three Cobalts are searching for a tool to pick the lock, but I hear movement.

"Luna," I breathe.

Then she cracks the door open. She's sheet white and clammy and woozy. I put my knuckles to her forehead, but she tears away to go hug the toilet. Puking.

Concern obliterates and propels me to my girlfriend. Crouching behind her, I gather her sweaty hair in my hand while she mostly spits into the toilet.

"Tell Ian we need to reroute to the nearest hospital," Charlie says to Eliot.

"Forward thinking, brother. How very Maximoff of you."

Charlie rolls his eyes. "Forget it."

"Too late. It's already in the history books."

I reach back for the sink and find a washcloth in the cabinet. I wipe Luna's lips. Her eyes are shut, and her cheek is pressed exhaustedly to the toilet seat.

"No hospital," Luna croaks, then hoists a shaky thumbs-up. "Just nauseous from the bus ride and..." She dry heaves again.

"Is she...with child?" Eliot asks.

It's a record-scratch in my brain. "She's not pregnant," I say lightly and rub her back. My stomach is churning. Could she be though? Only if her birth control didn't hold up against my sperm. "She'll be alright. Can you get a water for her?"

After Eliot brings a bottle of PuraFons, I shut them out to give her some privacy. Luna leans weakly against the sink cabinet, and I sit beside her.

"Try to drink this." I unscrew the cap and put the water to her lips.

She takes tiny sips. Her eyes still shut. "It's coming in waves…"

"Nausea?"

"Memories," she murmurs. "Blips and pieces all swirling together…nothing *complete*. Just a lot of…fragments."

"It's dizzying you?"

She tries to nod. "It's…disorienting." She presses her soft cheek to my arm, and I curve an arm around her, kissing the top of her head. *She's okay. I have her in my arms.*

"Anything good?" I ask in her hair.

Her lips rise, eyes closed like she's dreaming pleasant things. "I remember your favorite color."

I grin. "And what is it, Hale?"

"Violet."

I kiss her again, my eyes burning, and *fuck me*, I dunno why this hits me so hard. It's minuscule. It's not even a full-blown memory like her experiencing Homecoming. "Important stuff," I say seriously, a little choked. I clear my throat. "Favorite colors and all."

"What's mine?" she quizzes, her breathing measured but deeper. Color flushes her cheeks again.

"Neon green, and you were very clear it needed to be *neon*. 'Cause plain ole green reminded you of a forest, and you love the color of glow-in-the-dark stars."

Tears well beneath her lashes. "I love you," she murmurs.

I thumb away the wet streaks. "I love you too, Luna."

"No, I *love* you." She's adamant, her eyes finally opening on me. "Like I don't know if I can live without you kind of love."

It balls up in my throat. "My life would be…" I choke up, my nose flaring. "My life would be so dark without you."

Disbelief touches her. "You're so full of light without me."

"I've lived to find you," I breathe. "You are my light side, Luna Hale."

Her chin quivers, and she holds me around the waist.

Our future. We're not spelling it out. She's not asking where I see myself in five to ten years. But I'd have an answer.

I'd say, *with her.*

With Luna.

It's simple, I know. But for me, drawing Luna has never been some basic, plain picture. It's so alive. I can almost smell and taste the composition of her. It's a billion cosmic scents captivating me.

Luna has hopped up on the sink counter.

Feeling better, she's nibbling the bagel I made. I only left the bathroom to grab it. The Cobalt brothers have reignited the same argument in the tour bus's lounge.

"Eliot can't put it to rest," Luna whispers to me. "He's most used to stoking the flames, not extinguishing them."

"Charlie could end it. Just apologize for sending Ben on a wild goose chase."

"I think he's hoping Ben will be so annoyed with him, he'll just drop out."

"That's not a very nice brotherly thing to do." I tiptoe around calling him *shitty* because A.) he's Beckett's twin. And B.) he's become a friend to Luna, strangely.

I value friendships, and I'm not gonna knock hers.

"Maybe it's his way of trying to protect Fizzle," Luna shrugs.

Still, what Charlie did would irk me too. Ten-minutes before the photo shoot, he told Ben that Chett Prickner needed him to pick up his dry cleaning. Ben missed the photo op since Chett never sent his laundry there, and he never even gave Charlie those instructions to begin with.

It was a lie to derail Ben.

He succeeded. Ben looked like a flake to the board.

Worst part is, Ben trusted his older brother, and Charlie shot a hole through that trust.

"You shouldn't have believed me!" Charlie yells, and our heads swing to the shut door. The fight on the other side. "Why would Chett ever ask you to pick up his laundry? He has a personal *assistant* for that, Ben. You're competing to be the CEO, not a fucking errand boy. What if Gunther asked you to take coffee orders for mid-level employees? Would you do that too? Would you get down on your knees if Adaline insisted?"

"Moffy would've done the same thing!"

Luna slides off the counter, hearing her brother's name. She opens the door, and we look out at Eliot standing cautiously between both brothers.

"Precious Moffy," Charlie mocks.

Luna has bristled, her nose crinkling.

Charlie sees her, then my disappointment. Guy doesn't deserve a bagel for the Maximoff slander. That's my best friend's husband. My girlfriend's older brother.

He exhales a tight breath. "Moffy is nice and so far from *naïve*," he tells Ben. "You've never seen him in the corporate world. He's forceful and persuasive. He's not the wrecking ball. *You are.*"

I feel around my neck for my mic cord and earpiece hanging over my shoulder. Took it out when I was in the bathroom. I'm so close to radioing Oscar in the other bus.

Ben lunges for Charlie.

"Whoa!" Eliot yells, pushing him back. "Brothers!"

"Let's breathe together," I suggest. "Heard meditating makes your dick grow an extra inch." It's a joke that falls extremely flat.

Tough crowd.

I lift Luna's wrist and bite into the bagel in her hand. She smiles over at me, but it vanishes as Ben groans out, "You're not even giving me the chance!"

"You don't even want it," Charlie sneers.

"You don't know that!"

"Drop out!!"

"Why don't you?!" He tries to bulldoze Eliot to reach Charlie, but Eliot is strong enough to physically corral his brother.

Charlie shoots back, "If you can't hear this shit from me, how are you going to hear it from anyone else?" He didn't just hit a nerve, he hacked at it.

"Ow," Luna winces.

Ben's face breaks, anger doubling, tripling. "Did it *ever* fucking occur to you that I'd rather hear it from anyone else?!" he screams. "Did it?! Maybe I don't want to hear it from my own brother!"

Eliot speaks urgently to Ben in French.

"Relax?" Ben growls. "Why am I always being told to relax?! Why is no one ever telling *him* to shut the fuck up?"

"I'll make this easy for you," Charlie says. "Since you seem to want tricycle wheels." He beelines for the front of the bus and speaks to Ian behind the wheel.

Comms sound off in my ear. "SFE lead to Oscar, Charlie's requesting to stop the bus. I'm pulling over."

"Everything okay?" Oscar asks.

Ian doesn't reply since he's dealing with hauling this massive vehicle to the side of the road. I do the proper thing and alert my friend.

I click the mic and whisper, "Ben and Charlie fight."

"Fists?" Oscar asks.

"Nah. Harsh words though." Luna peers out of the window. Nevada's desert provides a beautiful but desolate landscape. The bus's headlights illuminate dirt as we pull onto the side of the road.

We're at a full stop, and Charlie wastes no time to exit into the warm night.

Outside, Oscar runs to catch up to his client as Charlie takes off on a desert stroll.

"He's trying to unnerve you," Eliot reminds Ben. "You're playing right into his hand, brother."

"It's okay that he's provoking me? Because it's a competition, right?" Ben fits on his baseball cap, like he can't even stand to look at Eliot either.

"It's just Charlie being Charlie. He's an ass, but aren't we all?"

"You've never been cruel," Ben mutters, avoiding him. "I'm going to bed." He rotates towards the hallway of bunks, but Xander has appeared.

Xander's hands are on the red headphones at his neck. "Charlie is the last person we need to be pissing off," he says to everyone. "Do we really want him to quit this thing?"

They all exchange hesitant glances.

No one's actually thrilled at being named CEO.

"I am trying to win," Eliot tells them.

"Only to beat Charlie," Luna pipes in. "If he drops out, it's like him handing you the position rather than you battling for it."

Eliot cringes. "That can't happen."

Oscar's voice floods my ear. "I'm heading back to the bus with Charlie, and I'm going to be riding with him for the duration of the tour."

O'Malley asks, "Why?"

"It was either that or he's flying to Prague."

57

PAUL DONNELLY

Four days into the mini-marketing campaign tour. Only three left, and it's been relatively stable since the Cobalt meltdown last night where Charlie stormed off the bus. No fistfights. No screaming matches.

At the Phoenix stop, Luna gave fans handcrafted *Fizz is the Future* alien buttons. She'd brought the supplies on tour and had received permission from her uncle to use the trademarked Fizz logo. I've been helping her cut the art out of photopaper and assemble the buttons during the long bus rides.

Fans ate 'em up. Knew they would.

I proudly wore about four on my *Security* shirt too. O'Malley looked like a surly sour-puss when fans were eager to take pics with me, but I was more shocked when Ian approved it. I asked why later, and the SFE lead said, "You were taking heat off Xander."

I knew the distraction had been helping him too. Just didn't think Epsilon valued my bits of notoriety is all.

They do *not* love that Oscar is now on the "talent bus" with me. Their ill-feelings might have something to do with their perception of Omega always getting special treatment. It's not like I'm on Omega anymore, but since all my friends are, I'm Omega-adjacent.

O'Malley decided in the name of Fairness and Equality that *all* the full-time bodyguards would ride on the talent bus too. Leaving only temps on the security bus. Tonight is the first night on a crammed bus with people I don't necessarily like, and I wish they'd go back.

Also, O'Malley shouldn't even be on this tour. Beckett (his client) is a thousand miles away in New York. My unfortunate luck is all thanks to the one and only Rookie Flu. Quinn spread it to his roomies recently. With Gabe and Frog out for the count, it left security in a pickle for this tour.

No one wanted to put a temp on Luna, and Omega's already been stretched thin with Sulli's highly publicized pregnancy. Girl's about to pop any minute—and leaving the house is like performing an Ocean's Eleven-level heist.

So Omega and Epsilon came together and agreed to shift Ian Wreath (Tom's bodyguard) and O'Malley to Luna just for the tour. Pretty positive the bosses don't care about my beef with O'Malley, or if they do, this is a stupendous way to test me and my dedication to Xander.

Been thinking everything is a test these days.

Can't sleep. I'm wired from the constant noises inside this packed bus. I hear voices from the front and footsteps padding across the bunk aisle to reach the rear lounge. Muffled, indistinguishable chatter. I'm not straining my ears to catch the words.

I've got better things to do.

Luna is leaning against my bare chest, my legs spread. We're on the bottom bunk together. The privacy curtain drawn shut to enclose us. With enough room for me to prop my back on a pillow, I have my arms woven around her body, and I'm drawing on a digital art tablet while she's holding it. The screen glows in her hands.

She bought it for me. "Just because," she said. "And I want to see your art. It's a selfish purchase in that way, I guess."

It's one of the least selfish things anyone has ever done for me.

I could never justify spending money on one. Not when it made more sense to buy ink and tattoo supplies. Tattooing is a cost-benefit since I can charge people. Drawing is just a pleasure.

I thought there'd be a big learning curve to transitioning from paper to a digital screen, but I picked it up fast.

"Is that what you're going for?" I ask her as I add wispier white strands to Queen Solana's hair with a stylus pen. Her skin is a lilac purple, and her round, delicate face resembles Luna. I even drew the curves of her body with Luna in mind.

"She's perfect. Can you slide over to him?" She points to the tall, shirtless fellow beside the queen. Guy is smoking hot. Queen chose well. He's a carbon copy of me and my good looks, after all.

It's character art Luna requested.

I track over to him, and she says, "He's missing an earring and your *win some lose some* tattoo on your wrist."

"You like his smirk though?"

"Smirk is on point."

I grin down at her. "Think so too." She can't see me. She's a thousand percent concentrated on the tablet in her hands, and my grin widens while I zoom in on his wrist.

When I've executed those final details, she raises the tablet and appraises the two characters side by side. Alien royalty and a human bodyguard.

I can't see her expression. Not as she asks, "Would you want to create a whole story with me?"

"What do you mean?"

"I've been thinking about using elements of the Thebulan saga to create an allegory of my life…of your life, of our past and present together."

It crashes into me like a ten-foot wave, and I'm almost swept under. "You wanna write our love story."

"And I want you to draw it."

I'm stunned to silence. Did not expect that to come out of her.

Luna rotates around to face me, kneeling between my legs. "You can say *no*. I plan to write it anyway as a comic storyboard. It might help me process the pools of memory. But it'd be a big endeavor to draw each panel."

"You're kidding yourself if you don't think I'll draw the whole fucking thing."

She blows back, overwhelmed tears springing. "Really?"

"Really," I nod. "I've got all the time in the world for you, for us, for *this*. Especially if it'll help your recovery." It'll be better if she can visualize her words, and I'd love to add that element for Luna. "It's just for us?"

"Yeah. Just for us." Her smile flushes her cheeks. "I'll have to alter some of the Thebulan lore. Solana will need to be a princess since my mom will be the queen of the Thebulan royal family."

"I can work on a rough sketch of Homecoming."

We brainstorm a storyline of how Princess Solana attends her brother's dance at a galactic, more *Thebulan* version of Dalton Academy. We'll workshop the name. There, Solana sees the human guard her family hired to protect him.

"Does this princess have a jellyfish umbrella?" I ask.

"Yep, but it's a real glowing jellyfish."

"That's dope," I grin and sweep her soft features, then the length of her. My love for Luna slams into a visceral need to kiss her. To press her against me. To fuck her.

Her breath shallows.

Our gazes latch in desire, but we do our best to talk about the comic. The sexual tension strains her voice at a certain point. I'm so fucking hard.

That's it. I tuck away the tablet in a wall pocket inside the bunk.

Footsteps patter down the aisle. More muffled noises around the bathroom, I'm assuming, but Luna barely pays attention to the jumbled cacophony. She's crawling on my lap. Her black silky nightgown pools at her thighs as she straddles me.

I skate my fingers over her collar, slipping off her spaghetti strap. Blood pumps south, my cock tensing against my drawstring pants. Her lips ache over mine while she whispers, "I need you. Ineedyou." She's grinding on me.

I'm torched. Dying for Luna. I hold her face and murmur in her ear, "Be very quiet."

She's nodding repeatedly.

We've had sex every night in our bunk. Been nearly silent each time, but too many people are awake and on this bus now. I don't like her on top when anyone can fling open the curtain and see her.

We go under the gray comforter. We're on our sides, making out like it's our destiny to be lip-locked. Heat ramps up to the thousandth degree. We're a furnace together, blazing hot.

She shudders, gripping my neck like she's struggling not to release a moan. Sweat builds on my flexed muscles, and I kiss her deeper, our legs threading.

"Off," she rasps, tugging at my pants.

With a couple maneuvers, I free myself of my pants and boxer-briefs. Then I flip Luna and drag her back to my chest. An aching, soft noise ejects from her parted lips, and I breathe against her ear, "Quiet, or I can't fuck you how you need to be fucked."

She digs her ass into my cock.

Fuck. I trail kisses up her neck.

Sheets are sticking to our damp bodies, and I draw them down to my waist. If anyone opens the curtain, they'd just have a real good view of my tattooed back. Luna is facing the wall. The window curtain is flung open. Nighttime in Arizona. The view is a blur as the bus moves at about fifty-five. Not too fast, not too slow. Exactly how I wanna take Luna.

I look under the covers while I lift her nightgown up her ass. My cock twitches like it knows it needs to be inside her pussy.

"I'll be quiet," she murmurs and cranes her neck to peer back at me. "I'm asleep. I won't make any noise." We're spooning like when we go to bed. She waits for me to agree to her fantasy.

I grin. "Turn back around. Aren't you supposed to be asleep?" I catch sight of her smile, then she's facing the wall again and pretends to be still.

She'd have to be a fucking Academy Award winner to pull off being dead asleep while I feel her up. Girl has the most reactionary body I've ever and will ever touch.

One stroke up her thigh right now, and she trembles, then tenses to force herself motionless. I hear her shallow panting, and the noise is fisting me. I need inside her. Bunching the silk fabric at her hips, I tear her panties down her legs. She doesn't stir.

And I flex slowly into Luna, watching her lips part and her fingers dig into the sheets.

Her eyes stay shut though.

God, she feels so fucking swollen and wet. I clasp her hip and rock against her with deep thrusts, and her legs wrestle beneath the sheets. *That's right, Luna. Wake up.* I slow and pull farther out, then ease all the way in. Doing it three times until her breath catches.

I tug her nightgown down and expose her breasts to the wall. *You should feel so lucky, wall and bunk window.* I thumb her hard nipple while fucking her pussy, and the friction is pummeling my senses. I do everything to focus on her needs and not my lit nerve-endings.

'Cause I'm not coming yet.

She is though. Luna orgasms when I suck on her neck and thrust, and my hand flies to her mouth to stifle her sudden moan. Her whole body shakes against me, and I take deep, cavernous breaths so I won't climax with her. *Calm, calm.*

My heart rate slows.

I don't drag my cock out of her.

I'm too hard, and I stay nestled in her warmth as she pulsates around me. She's a lot. It's like being electrocuted, lit on fire, and drowned all at once. Most especially since I love all of her, every vibration, every moan, every overcome look she flashes at me— every cute, weird thing she does.

If I were eighteen, I think it'd be hard not to instantly come inside her. But I've got enough skill to last for hours.

I quicken my pace and hike her knee upward for deeper entry. My hand still envelops her mouth since she's whimpering in pleasure. Not sure if anyone but me can hear, but I don't take the risk. Deep, hard poundings inside Luna, I sense her on the verge in *seconds* again.

Wake all the way up, I think as I slam into her.

Her eyes flutter open, love and pleasure pooled in those amber orbs. I grin as I whisper against her ear, "Look who's awake for their nightly fucking." She moans against my palm, her ass grinding back into me.

Jesus *Christ*.

I hold her hip still and remove my hand off her mouth to kiss her. Leaning down, I angle her head and my lips press to hers before our tongues tangle. She tries to devour me, but she's losing it. Melting in the haze of our sex. 'Cause I don't stop thrusting.

I break away so I can breathe too.

"*Donnelly*," she cries softly.

"Shh, shh."

Fuck, *fuck*. Her pussy is clenching. This feels...I grip my hair and force myself not to shoot a load. *Fuck her deeper. Fuck her harder.* The animalistic need swallows me whole, and I hug her tighter against my chest.

Luna reaches out. Her hand smacks the window, fogged from the heat we're emitting, and her palm streaks down it.

"Donnelly," O'Malley suddenly whisper-hisses right outside my bunk. "Wake up. There's a security meeting."

You've gotta be kidding me.

I stay inside her.

Luna doesn't even notice him. She's on the edge and basically fucking me at this point, grinding back into my cock.

I clear the rasp out of my throat. "Be there in a sec," I whisper back.

"No, *now*."

Like I know him so well—even though I really don't—I reach behind me (my shoulder threatens to pop out) and snatch the curtain, expecting him to try and whip it open.

He does attempt it, but the curtain jerks against my tight grip. Not budging.

"You wanna see me buck-ass naked, Chris?" I launch back.

"Just come out here." He's annoyed.

I'm pissed. I don't wanna fuck Luna with anger. *Ever.*

"Just give me a second, *please*," I force.

He exhales. "Hurry."

I kiss her cheek and pump once, twice, three times inside her with deep strokes—she comes silently but forcefully. I let myself release in Luna. Anyway, I don't think there's a choice with how tight she's pulsating around me. I swallow a groan, my muscles on fire, and I watch her eyes roll back.

Her body slackens.

My pulse spikes. "Luna." I pull out of her quickly. "*Luna*." I lean over her, tapping her cheek. She's unconscious. I wipe her sweaty hair out of her face and throw the hot comforter off her body. She's cognizant less than thirty seconds later.

It's not the first time she's blacked out from sex. Her neuro-doctors say it's fine. Nothing related to her amnesia.

She gives me a weak thumbs-up and gathers oxygen inside her lungs.

Quickly, I cover her breasts with her nightgown. "I'm gonna get you something to drink." I kiss her cheek, then move fast out of the bunk. Careful not to open the curtain too much. And yeah, I'm naked.

O'Malley is waiting in the aisle. "Jesus...fuck, there are *clients* around," he whisper-hisses, seeing me in my birthday suit.

"Or are they asleep?" I fling back, not slowing my hot stride to the front section. It's empty, besides Novak behind the wheel. I'm guessing Epsilon's meeting is happening in the rear lounge.

"What are you doing?" O'Malley has followed me.

"Searching for your funny bone."

"Your dick isn't funny," he says flatly.

I find strawberry Pop-Tarts in a cabinet, then snag a PuraFons water bottle. "Don't really care about making you laugh, to be honest." I ignore him on my route back to Luna. Squatting at the bottom bunk, I hand her a Pop-Tart and uncap the water for her. Every fiber of my being is screaming at me to stay. I hate leaving her when she just blacked out from sex.

She's gulping the water. "It's okay."

"What's okay?"

"If you have to go." Luna places a quick kiss on my cheek, then my nose. "You'll be back." She's certain.

Her belief makes me feel good. My heart is so deep within this girl, and I never want it back. "Yeah, I will be."

Her eyes veer past me. "Whose legs are those?"

O'Malley is standing behind me.

"No one's," I say lightly. "I won't be long." I grab my pants before I shut the curtain. Stepping in them, I face O'Malley's irritation. I've been waiting for him to bring up Luna. It wouldn't take a brainiac to see that I just had sex with her.

He's quiet, and I can't understand his expression. Barely even one-fourth of it.

"What?" I ask him, straightening up as I pull the band of my pants to my waist.

"I'm no one," he states. "Just never thought I'd hear you say that about me."

I hold his gaze. "'Cause I'm the nobody. The waste of space. Waste of a life."

He opens his mouth, then shuts it. Taking a beat to say, "I don't think that."

"But you did."

"Yeah," he admits, swallowing hard. "Yeah, I did."

I don't know what I'm feeling. My stomach overturns like a waffle-iron being flipped in succession with no stop. I'd rather endure this Epsilon meeting than stand here and try to process my emotions. So I say, "Let's do the thing."

58

PAUL DONNELLY

Group therapy.

That's what I've walked into. Would've acted like I had black lung or a sinus infection if I knew beforehand. Maybe that's why no one told me.

The circular booth is crammed with the Wreath brothers, O'Malley, me, and Oscar. The latter of which shouldn't be a part of the Epsilon meeting, but they're being "inclusive" they said. If this strange union between Epsilon and Omega means I can spend more time with my best friend, then I'm not throwing a stink about it.

Chris Novak is exempt from this get-together since he's keeping all our souls alive by driving the bus. Never have I wished I passed a driving test more, but I flubbed it before coming on tour. Failed it back before the FanCon too. I can't even be mad at myself that I'm not qualified to drive this beast. It is what it is.

But I have no "get me out of this group therapy" card to play at the current moment.

Somehow, I ended up wedged between O'Malley and Oscar. I actually like when O'Malley tells me, "You smell disgusting."

'Cause I have a full right to say, "You look disgusting."

Oscar stiffens like I'm not being myself.

Granted, if I liked O'Malley a smidge more, I would come in less hostile and just say, "If the scent of an angel disgusts you, you're gonna have a serious problem in heaven, man."

I don't love being a big jar of salt. It's bad for my cholesterol. But I still don't like him. I don't even care that he's my cousin. I might *never* like him. He might never like me.

"I'd rather look it than smell it," O'Malley says under his breath. Which I can hear. "Well, I think you're full of shit," I mutter.

Oscar offers me his snack-sized bag of Lays. There aren't enough chips to share, so I know he's worried about me.

"I'm good." I exhale the heat in my chest.

"Rise above," he whispers.

"Don't know what you're looking at, but I'm a flotation device."

"I'd believe it more if you didn't let him put holes in your water wings, bro."

He's not wrong.

I laugh into a smirk. "You come for my rubber duckie next, and we're gonna throw fists."

Oscar grins into a crunch of potato chip and laughs. Epsilon guys are being just as gossipy, shifting more towards one another, whispering. Ian and Vance are twisting their mic cords around radios. Done with comms for the night. O'Malley is chatting with them while flipping a notebook like he's about to start a college lecture.

I lean into Oscar to whisper, "Let's ditch."

"Pass." He shakes the chip bag. "I think this'll be good for us."

I squint. "Dicking down is good for us. Getting dicked down by Epsilon, not so much."

"Bro, you are Epsilon." Oscar lowers his voice another notch. "Trust, we've tried to claim you as one of ours, and they play tug-of-war with us like you're their new special toy."

I make a face. "Why? They don't even like me."

"They like something about you. They act like you're theirs. It's been aggravating the ever-loving fuck out of me and Redford."

"They're trying to make you jealous," I realize.

"I don't think it's that," Oscar says. "They're not pretending to care about you."

No time to contemplate that—all three Epsilon bodyguards turn their attention to us. I'm thankful I never grabbed a shirt 'cause I'm burning from the inside out.

"Let's start with discussing the last tour stop in Phoenix," Ian presides over the so-called meeting. "Donnelly?"

Me, start? I nod to O'Malley. "What's with the notebook?"

"I'm logging hours for our meetings." He clicks a pen.

My brows rise. "Didn't know you became a secretary."

"I volunteered," O'Malley says. "It's called stepping up."

"We'll never get through this if we don't cut the bullshit," Ian pipes in quickly, speaking to the two of us. "Price *asked* for detailed notes. If Akara asked you all for the same thing, you'd give it to him, wouldn't you?" He's eye-balling Oscar.

"Of course we would," Oscar replies.

"Great," Ian sighs out and motions his energy drink at me. "The Phoenix stop. How'd it go for you?"

"Fine," I say lightly, but I feel like I'm on a hot seat. "No security mistakes. Smooth sailing. Clients were safe and happy. Nothing to complain about."

"You were okay with fans taking photos with you?" Ian ensures.

"Yeah, that's alright by me if it helps Xander and causes less of a mess." I grip my kneecap underneath the table, just so my leg isn't rattling with impatience.

"Frog and Quinn weren't here this time to protect Luna," Ian puts out there.

What's he getting at? "Missed them, but it's better than catching the flu."

Vance tosses a stress ball from hand to hand. "Anyone think it'd do us all a favor to axe the rookie girl? She's a hundred pounds soaking wet. What happens when a guy goes for Luna?"

Guy goes for Luna. My breath shortens, and I stare off for a boiling second. "No one's going for her."

"No one thought she'd be kidnapped either," O'Malley jumps in.

I shift forward. "Frog weighs more than a hundred pounds.

Come on. She's not a garden hose," I gesture to Vance.

"Whatever, you know she's small," he shrugs.

Oscar crinkles his emptied chip bag with a serious look. "She's trained in defensive maneuvers. She's not supposed to tackle a three-hundred-pound threat, and Akara has already rectified any issues by putting my baby bro with her."

Ian nods a few times. "That's good enough for me." He rakes his hand back and forth through his pretty boy haircut, then eyes me. "With Frog and Quinn gone, did you worry about Luna at all?"

"No," I say with heat. "I wasn't distracted. I knew you were protecting her."

"Then why do you sound like that?"

Defensive? I sound defensive. I slam back into the seat and let out a weighted sigh. No one is really coming at me. No one is trying to rip her away from me. They've knowingly let me sleep in the same bunk as Luna. O'Malley even knew we were having sex tonight, and he said *nothing*.

"How much do you trust us?" Ian asks me.

"I trust you'll protect her," I tell him. "I never doubted that." Do I trust they'll look out for me? Not really, but I have Omega. Coming forward again, I rest my forearms on the table. "But it'd be easier to trust you on a personal level if there wasn't a nark in SFE." I glance between them. "Who's running to tabloids about me?"

"You think it's us?" O'Malley's jaw unhinges like I'm smoking crack. "We *hate* the media."

"It's someone in Epsilon, man. It has to be. 'Cause everything that's leaked has pertained to SFE." I'm prepared for them to say I've gossiped to Omega. That there's a plausible explanation for SFO to be the root of the problem.

"I think it's one of our temps," Ian says.

"That new guy with the mustache. Bernard?" Vance throws out there. "I don't like him."

"Me either," O'Malley agrees. "Novak caught him obsessing over Luna's social media account."

I wonder if a house has landed on me and I'm in Oz. "Why did no one tell me about this Bernard fucker?" Did Oscar know?

He's sifting through the empty chip bag.

Suspicious.

"Because Luna's not your client. She's your *girlfriend*," O'Malley emphasizes.

"She's not really your client either," I say pointedly.

"Guys," Ian shakes his head, giving O'Malley an annoyed look.

O'Malley throws up his hands like, *What did I do?*

I stare at my friend. "Oscar? You know about this?"

He turns to me. "We all thought it wouldn't be good for your mental health to hear that one of the temps is jerking off to her picture."

"Now he's jerking off?"

"Metaphorically, bro."

I rub my face with two hands. "Who's *we*?"

"Epsilon and Omega...and Alpha."

Oh, the *whole* fucking team.

"Redford wanted to tell you. He was pissed. So don't be angry at him."

I'm not angry they're trying to protect my sanity. Just upset that they think it needs protecting at all. "I can handle that sort of information. And why isn't Bernard kicked off the temp roster?"

"Price wants to gather enough evidence against him, in the event the temp tries to file a wrongful termination suit," Ian says. "He probably won't be around for another week."

Alright.

I ease back and try to calm down.

Trust goes two ways. I'm positive they trust me to protect Xander. Maybe they think I'd leave them out to dry just as much as I believe they'd throw me to the wolves as an afternoon snack.

Giving into this open forum, I end up saying, "I appreciate you all looking out for Luna."

"We care about you too," Ian says, validating what Oscar told me earlier. *They're not pretending to care about me.*

I can't wrap my head around it. "I get her. But me?" I give them all a soured look.

Vance squeezes his stress ball and turns to his brother. To which Ian admits, "I don't think we really knew you. Back when you had to infiltrate your family—we thought it'd be easy for you."

My eyes sear. I can't speak.

Oscar pats me on the back like this is good. It's progress.

It's not. Not for me. What's worse than feeling like they hate me—is feeling like they *pity* me. Frustrations bubble. "I don't need you feeling sorry for me. Everything you ever hated about me—it's true. My family are meth-heads. I'm a slut. Don't even have a GED. So whatever you think has changed, it hasn't." I go to stand, but Oscar tugs me back down.

I can't even play dumb to take the spotlight off me.

"Just give it a few more minutes, Donnelly," Oscar encourages.

Ian says, "Look, knowing more about you, I doubt any of us could even do what you did."

"What you're doing," O'Malley adds under his breath, but it's with more concern than I can process.

Omega caring about me—I love. We've had each other's backs. I would die for them. They'd go through hell for me. Epsilon caring about me—odd, *peculiar.* I don't trust it. Probably because I don't fully trust them.

I buck forward to peer out the door, expecting Oscar's husband to come barreling in with his production crew. Saying, *Gotcha!* It's all for show.

But Jack Highland-Oliveira is nowhere to be seen.

My phone suddenly vibrates on the table, slicing through the thick silence.

"Can you silence your calls for the meeting?" Ian asks me.

The number is unknown.

"Nah, gotta take this one." My tone is light, and I'm quick on my feet. Standing on the booth, I climb over Oscar's thighs and hop on the floor. Holding on to storage compartments overhead, I move toward the front of the wobbly bus and answer with the cell to my ear. "Who's this?"

"It's so good hearing your voice, honey. It's been too long."

My legs buckle under me, and I sink into the booth at the front of the bus. "Vanessa?" My mom's best friend. "How'd you get this number?"

"Your mom gave it to me."

What *the fuck*. Why would she do that? She knows I'd rather chop off an ear than listen to Vanessa for two minutes.

My dad said Vanessa was the reason my mom broke her parole the last time. But I couldn't stand her long before that. She'd give me freezer-burnt ice cream, and I thought she was a saint. You coulda told me she was Mother Teresa, and my little uncorrupted brain would've believed you. I ignored the fact that she'd talk shit about her friends behind their backs. Ignored how often she did meth with my mom.

'Cause she'd ask Bridget if I had dinner. 'Cause she'd remember I was in the room more than my own mom ever did.

Then she'd crouch to my height and ask me if I knew how to pickpocket. If I could go steal ten bucks for them. And I started wishing she'd forget I existed.

Very few things felt worse than that as a kid—than believing someone *cared* when all they were doing was using you.

What's she want now?

I press the heel of my palm to my forehead. "I'm working. Don't have time for chitchat."

"Aw, come on. You could give me five minutes to catch up. I heard you're on that tour bus anyway. You probably have lots of down time." She's been tracking the publicized tour stops. Not good. *Not good.*

My chest is tight. "What'd you want?" As I ask it, O'Malley, Vance, Oscar, and Ian crowd the kitchenette, and I dodge their intrusive, overly concerned stares.

"I heard you're not actually dating that Hale girl. That it's one big scam. There's a lot of opportunities in that, you know."

I'm supposed to play along. "Yeah?"

"I'll be in Salt Lake tomorrow. We should talk then."

"Can't. Like I said, I'm working." I rotate away from the audience and stare out at the blurry Arizona landscape as the bus treks along. "But I'll call you back tomorrow. We can talk about it then."

"Looking forward to it. Take care, honey."

I hang up and lower my phone. It hasn't fully sunk in yet—what just happened. I'm processing at a snail's pace.

"Who was that?" O'Malley asks me.

"The Easter bunny," I mutter. "Says he prefers parsnips over carrots."

No one's laughing, partly because I can't hide my emotions from my face.

Oscar's silence is the most biting. Normally he'd be the one to volley a joke back. Instead, he's shaking his head. "Really, bro. Who was that?"

I wipe a hand over my mouth. "My mom's friend Vanessa. She's been tracking the tour. She wants to meet up in Salt Lake for something. She's been fed the same lie the rest of my family has—that I'm fake-dating Luna, using her, and…" I trail off at a jarring thought, unblinking.

"What is it?" Ian has an authoritative presence. He's taking this whole "I have seniority" thing to heart. Only problem is that Oscar technically is the most senior here. But I'm guessing that doesn't count when Oscar is Omega.

These extraneous details are strangely calming me. I take a few breaths. "My dad cautioned me that there'd be a time where the family would need proof that I'm using Luna. I don't know what she'll ask me to do, but I said I'd call her back tomorrow to stall and figure out a plan."

"How well do you know her?" O'Malley asks me.

I shake my head. "I haven't talked to her in years."

"But she's a threat?" Ian asks to ensure.

"I don't think she's well-liked by most of the Donnellys. I don't even know if she has that many friends who'd be considered threats. I think she'd like to get in through me, though."

"We should nip this here," Ian says to Oscar.

They all throw out strategies, the main one being to cancel the Salt Lake City tour stop. It gains traction, and they're talking around me while I begin to accept what's going on.

My nose flares, and I grind back an onslaught of emotion. This should be over. I sent the rotten apples to jail. There shouldn't be this dangly little thread hanging loose, but my mom—why would my mom send *Vanessa* to me like that?

My head is pounding in my hands.

"He shouldn't be in contact with anyone *but* Sean and Bridget," Oscar says. "He's not supposed to be roped in further."

"He shouldn't even be talking to Sean *or* Bridget," O'Malley refutes. "If it weren't for them, this woman wouldn't be crawling towards him. They will keep *pulling* Paul back in."

My dad had nothing to do with this. It's getting harder to defend them. I hate that they might be proving O'Malley right.

It's a slow-sinking blade in the gut. Raw emotion starts to cloud my vision. On automatic, I rise from the table. "I need some air," I tell them and shove my feet in my shoes. I head to the driver.

Novak is blissfully unaware of the shit going on. So when I request to stop on the side of the road, he's all confused wrinkles.

He still does it.

I get the fuck off the bus.

The dry Arizona air is brittle to intake. A million stars speckle the clearest night sky I've ever seen, not a single cloud. No haze. Milky blue and stunning violet shades flow cohesively together up above. Lit brighter by a waxing gibbous. Luna told me the moon phase for March 15th.

One day shy of a full moon.

Cacti jut up from the reddish desert, and rock formations carve out their own towering homes among the vast scenery. There isn't a single soul on the deserted road. My blood won't cool. The pain in my chest won't let up. *How far can I run?*

I walk fifty paces into the desert sand. Far enough away that I can't be heard by anyone but the snakes and the coyotes and the kangaroo rats.

And I scream.

59

 **LUNA HALE**

Headphones on, I listen to a joint playlist that
Donnelly created for us, and I wait for him to return to the bunk
after his security meeting ends. "Dreams" by The Cranberries makes
me smile. I flip over my arm and run my fingers along ink. Lyrics in
Farrow's handwriting.

Being on a tour bus hasn't sparked major memories of the
FanCon from the past. Not many bits or pieces either. Sometimes it
feels like a make-believe world where Donnelly and I had so much
time together that I've forgotten. But then I have these physical
reminders in indelible ink.

I hug my arm to my chest and stare out the tiny bunk window.
We've been stopped for a few minutes, and the landscape isn't such
a blur anymore. Stars twinkle against the moonlit sky, and I press my
fingers to the glass and connect a constellation.

And then I tunnel into the luminescence. I go completely still.
A memory so jarring—I choke on breath, tears crease the edges of
my eyes, and emotions feel more like anchored weights in my belly.
My fingers slip off the glass, and I double over from the power of
it.

Donnelly…

Ripping my headphones off, I spring out of the bunk in my thin
nightgown. I'm half-running into the main area of the bus. All the

bodyguards whisper quietly among themselves—but I don't see Donnelly or Oscar.

O'Malley and the Wreath brothers send me confused looks.

"Donnelly?" I ask.

"He took a walk," Ian says.

Took a walk? I frown and then remember…we're parked.

I make a dash to the very front of the bus. No one stops me, which I think is odd until I climb down the steep stairs and see Oscar outside. He's propped against the hood. He's staring off in the distance, but his attention veers to me when my bare feet touch the warm pavement.

"Hale," he greets.

"Where's—?" I start.

Oscar points towards the sandy flatland, and that's when I see Donnelly a hundred feet away. The only human among cacti and pricker bushes. And beneath a clear desert sky.

Without thinking, I race towards him.

60

PAUL DONNELLY

My throat is raw, and I'm just looking up.
Searching for a better feeling that'll rid the one in my body. It's
beautiful out here. No place to mope. I wonder if we're in UFO
territory. If I'll encounter a little green guy, or purple. Hell, aliens
might be the color of a tropical Fruit Roll-Up.

Think Luna would like that.

"Donnelly!" Her voice floods my ears.

I twist around and see her running after me. The brightest light
in my world is coming towards *me*. I'm entranced, engulfed into her
orb. Her bare feet sink into the desert—her breath rushed, heavy.
She pulls up a fallen spaghetti strap of her nightgown when she rolls
to a stop in front of me.

"Luna…"

She skims my eyes, which must be bloodshot, and she says very,
very quietly, "What are you doing out here?"

I can't take my gaze off her. "I think I was waiting for an
extraterrestrial. Five-foot-five. Light brown hair. *Gorgeous* amber eyes
that I never wanna stop looking into."

"I'm sorry I took so long."

"Nah, don't be." I clear my throat, but a glassy film is over my
eyes. "I'd wait an eternity for you."

She reaches out and hooks her fingers with mine. "I know what we are…"

I ease. "And what are we, space babe?" I draw her closer, and my hands settle on her hips.

"It's been written in the stars," she says with all the love of every timeline, of the past and present and our future. "And this—it can never be unwritten."

I'm almost knocked back. How could she know…? "You…?"

"I remember."

A dam ruptures inside me. I fall to my knees. She drops down with me, and she's holding my face while our tears leak out. I hug her to me. *She remembers.* I'm crying.

I never imagined she'd remember me on the Hale's rooftop under a night sky, where I told her we're written in the stars. I never imagined she'd repeat it back to me.

It's not heartache that's tearing through me. It's the immensity of my love for Luna. Of the hope I've been cradling as it explodes into blistering light.

I've never experienced anything this powerful in my life.

I cup her cheeks. "You remember," I choke out, pure elation, joy, love rushing at full-speed into me.

"I remember." She presses her forehead to mine, her cheeks wet. "I've realized…that I could never truly forget."

I do the only thing that makes sense. I kiss the moon.

61

LUNA HALE

We collide like a comet impacting a planet. We are the Big Bang, destroying and creating all at once. His hands are on my cheeks. My hands grip his hair. Our lips search and seek and we're teeming with life and energy and discovery.

Not everything is lost.

Not everything is found.

But I am no longer floating. I've landed on solid ground, and in the aftermath of my arrival, I've been taken into loving arms.

We're home.

EMAIL FROM SAM STOKES

FROM: samstokes@fizzle.com
TO: dontemailme1882@yahoo.com, eliotalice@gmail.com, benpirripcobalt@upenn.edu, aragorn1225@gmail.com, queenofthebula@gmail.com

After the mini-marketing campaign tour, the rankings are as follows:

1. Charlie Keating Cobalt
2. Eliot Alice Cobalt
3. Xander Hale
4. Luna Hale
5. Ben Pirrip Cobalt

Luna has requested feedback, so I'll be adding short notes from here on out.

Xander: You clearly are a favorite among your peers, but you showed a lack of initiative to engage. Even with the photographers. The board would like you to be more personable and try to put yourself out there. (-1 spot in the ranking)

Eliot: Great people skills. The board is overall very impressed with how you captivated the audience during the meet-and-greet portion. (+1 spot in the ranking)

Charlie: Our focus group loved the "intense" and "sophisticated" photos of you that were taken by our photographers. The board is satisfied. (- neutral, no shift)

Luna: Job well done all around. I loved your spunk and outside-the-box thinking regarding the buttons. Thank you for being present. (+1 spot in the ranking)

Ben: The board was disappointed with your no-show appearance, and they fear your feud with your brother will hinder marketability. Charlie has more vocal fans than you. Please keep this in mind. (-1 spot in the ranking)

62

LUNA HALE

"What's your working theory?" I ask my older brother in the penthouse kitchen. We've been pouring Chex Mix and M&Ms into serving bowls, but we paused when my phone pinged with the latest email from Uncle Stokes.

Now we're leaning against the stove, and Moffy rereads from the screen in my hand while feeding his daughter a bottle. Piercingly loud chatter and heavy footsteps resonate from outside the kitchen. It sounds like a circus has blown through the penthouse, but none of the chaotic noises disturbs my brother's train of thought.

"They're planning on picking Charlie," he deduces. "He'll be their first option unless he pisses off the wrong shareholder or board member."

"That's what I thought too," I mutter. "But I *still* don't get why they'd go through this whole competition if they already plan to pick him."

"To find a backup to Charlie." Moffy lifts his gaze off the phone and onto me. "He's not reliable, and they'd need assurance that if he said *no* at the end, they'd have another viable option."

"So we're actually fighting for second."

"Unless Charlie implodes on someone." He tilts the bottle so Cassidy can suck the last drops of milk. "But dear world, do *not* let that doomsday happen. Sincerely, one grateful human."

I smile. "You want him to win then?"

He licks his lips, thinking. "I want whoever *wants it* to take it, and I know that's not Charlie. He'll admit it's not him." He eyes me, but in such a Moffy way. He's not stuck on the purple star-shaped stickers on my cheeks or the swipes of glitter. He's trying to read my innermost thoughts.

"Are your Professor X mind-reading powers kicking in yet?" I ask him.

His mouth pulls in a smile. "They might've jumped me. I think they're most strong with you."

I touch my temples like Professor X. "You're thinking *Luna Hale is the most badass of the Fizzle Five.*"

Moffy feigns shock. "Right out of my brain. She's a genius." He says that last part with such deep sincerity, and I see how much my brother values my intellect. It swells deep inside my heart. He nods to me, "Do you want it? To be CEO?"

I shrug. "It's not really me either." I wiggle Cassidy's teeny-tiny toe, and she smiles against the bottle. "I had fun during the marketing tour, but that's not what being a CEO really entails. And I'm not sure I'm ready for my future to be so defined. I like that there's some ambiguity, new paths to uncover and explore." I crinkle my nose at Cassidy and her big brown eyes widen with curiosity at me.

Moffy seems lost in thought. I wonder where he went, but I don't need to ask. His forest-green eyes focus on me. "Have you and Donnelly talked about your future at all?"

"Like…?"

"Marriage?"

"No." My cheeks roast. "Has he…has he talked to you about it?"

"No, *no.*"

"I'm…not that ready to bring up topics like marriage and babies," I confess to my brother and slump more against the stove. "I'm afraid our visions of the future aren't similar, and then what? We breakup? That feels…*excruciating.*" My eyes well just contemplating a fictional breakup. I can't even imagine how gutting it'd be in real life.

"I get it," he tells me. "I was *not* ready to talk about marriage for a long time. It freaked me out."

"Really?"

"Yeah, I wanted to just be in a relationship with Farrow since he was my first one. Anything more felt like too much too fast."

"What changed?"

"I almost died in a car crash." He puts the empty bottle on the counter behind us. "And the *too much* felt like *not enough*. I couldn't picture my life without him. But it's a colossal, life-changing decision and commitment. So if you're not ready or if it's not what you want, don't feel pressured into it."

I frown a little. I also can't visualize my life without Donnelly. And I feel *supremely* committed to him already. Like I'd donate a kidney and eyeball if he needed it. I just can't see how tying the knot would intensify these feelings when *everything* we've been through is a greater declaration of undying love to me.

Moffy burps Cassidy against his shoulder. Soft pats on her back. "Before anyone comes in here, I wanted to talk to you about what you told Farrow in December, I think it was?"

I instantly smile. Ah, I've been awaiting Moffy to broach this topic. Which means my little seedling I planted inside Farrow actually sprouted! "About me donating my eggs?"

"Yeah. That was...that *is* a really big, generous thing, sis."

"Are you crying?" *Oh my heart.* "Captain America doesn't cry." I've never seen Moffy tear up like this—or actually, I *have*. I've been remembering chunks of the day he married one of my favorite people on planet Earth, and Maximoff Hale definitely shed happy tears, even if the rain slipped them away.

"There must be an onion around here." He sniffs.

"Onion-cutting bandits at play," I nod, my eyes glassing too. I'm choked up.

"We love you so damn much," he expresses. "Farrow *really* wants to see my resemblance in a kid, but I'd rather our next child have Farrow as the biological dad like Cassidy. It just makes more sense if..." He looks deeper at me. "If the Hale part comes from you."

My chin quivers. It's one of the most validating feelings in the world. To be the chosen DNA for their future baby because they love me. Because I am a Hale. Because there should be more Hales thriving in this universe and the next.

I hug my brother so tight, careful of Cassidy in his arms.

He squeezes me back with the brotherly toughness of our youth, and when we pull apart, I ask, "How many kids do you want? Because I'm willing to donate as many eggs for the Marrow lineage."

Moffy laughs and rubs circles on Cassidy's back. She's a smiley baby. "We're happy if we just have one more, but I think we'll try to have four total. It wasn't so bad, was it?"

I smile brighter at him. Being a child of four? "I can't imagine a life without them." Without Kinney and Xander. And like I've summoned our younger siblings, they barrel into the penthouse kitchen with our massive, furry dogs in tow.

The entire Newfie litter has been together tonight, and Orion has pounced on Erebor, Salem, and Arkham like he hasn't said hello to them in forever. When he *lives* with Arkham and sees him every single day. All their tails wag, and I'm just happy my siblings' dogs seem to accept and love Orion's hyper behavior.

"Did you see it?" Kinney waves Xander's phone at us.

He slides on a leather barstool and grabs a bowl of pizza bites I microwaved ten minutes ago. "Tell Kinney I don't care what a bunch of Fizzle employees think about me being anti-social."

"It's bullshit," Kinney curses. "Xander 'showed a lack of initiative'—he was *there*. On a smelly, man-musky, stenchy bus crammed with the *one* person in the family he doesn't get along with."

"You did well, Summers," Moffy says with love.

Xander almost smiles. "Yeah, but not for third place. My goal isn't to be ranked high or low. I'm just trying to finish the thing without quitting."

Kinney huffs beside me. Crossing her arms, she tells me, "You should be higher too."

I smile big, and I swear her lips rise. "Thanks, Kinney."

She leans a little into me, and my heart mushrooms beyond human comprehension. Which must mean I'm in a celestial plane. I've felt a revived relationship with my little sister this year. She's called me a few times a week to chat about an astronomy club she joined at school and the basketball games she's sat through to support her JV cheerleader best friend Audrey.

And I haven't closed off to her. She knows all about the comic book Donnelly and I are creating for fun. The one we *just* conceptualized a week ago on the bus. Kinney insisted the character based off her should be named Princess Amethyst.

Nowhere can I remember feeling this close to my sister, so maybe it isn't revived exactly. More like, it's born for the first time.

"What I don't get," Kinney says to me, hoisting the email between us, "is why Uncle Stokes used the first person 'I' when giving you feedback and no one else."

Huuuh? I peer closer, surprised I missed that. He wrote, *I loved your spunk and outside-the-box thinking regarding the buttons.* "He didn't say the board loved them," I realize.

"Getting Uncle Stokes in your corner is still big," Moffy tells me. "He's the CEO. He has some sway."

"He just feels sorry for me," I mumble.

"Kill them," Kinney says coldly. "Kill them all." She's quoting X-Men.

"Who's gonna tell Mom and Dad that Kinney murdered our uncle?" Xander banters.

"Not I." I raise my hand.

"It will be stealth murder, you troll."

He acts like he's about to chuck a pizza bite at her face, and she points his phone at him. "I will smash this into tiny little pieces, don't you dare."

Xander has a huge smile and lightly tosses the pizza bite into Moffy's mouth instead. I join in, sticking my tongue out, and we're both trying to catch the pizza bites Xander launches at us. Laughing when our dogs gobble up the fallen ones.

Kinney shakes her head, her lips curving upward. "Juveniles."

Our dogs suddenly skedaddle away from us, and I look over to see Farrow and Donnelly leaning casually in the entryway, watching all of us with rising, affectionate grins.

I inhale a deep breath. Will I wake up abruptly and find myself in the hospital? Will I realize every moment after my head trauma was all in my imagination? It'd be a sci-fi twist of epic, gut-wrenching proportions. And I hate that when I'm so overwhelmingly happy, when things go *right*, I can't fully accept it's my reality.

Amazing things can happen to me. Life isn't all trips and falls and failures. It can be easy and hopeful and so, *so* loving. I believe this is real.

"Your happiness is showing, wolf scout," Farrow says, his smile stretching.

I'm not the only one cherishing the moment too.

"Good," Moffy says strongly.

Our Newfies greet Donnelly and Farrow with licks and head-butts into their palms. Then a growl rumbles out of Salem. My stomach drops. She's fixated on Donnelly.

"Doggie!" Baby Ripley gasps at Salem. The little boy is in Farrow's arms. He tells his dad, "She's bad."

"She's good," Kinney defends quickly. "She likes him."

"She likes me?" Donnelly's brows jump.

"Duh." Kinney blushes a little. "She's giving you extra attention. She doesn't do that for people she hates." She glances around at all of us, nervous. "What?"

"I believe it," I sing-song.

Kinney relaxes, more so when Donnelly tries to feed Salem a pizza bite and her dog approaches with less tentativeness.

"So you love *pizza*," Donnelly muses as Salem eats out of his palm. "Girl after my own heart." He smiles up at me, like I am the true girl with his true heart.

Smiling, I make a heart with my hands.

"When's this thing supposed to start anyway?" Kinney asks, handing Xander his phone back.

I check the microwave clock. "T-minus ten-ish minutes." Thunderous laughter resounds in the living room.

The party is out there, and I collect a couple serving bowls of various munchies to deliver to the rest of our family. No parents are at this penthouse gathering. It's a siblings and cousins get-together. With significant others included.

Jane and Moffy invited everyone, and not a single person said *no*. Even Beckett had tonight off ballet and decided to spend it here, of all places. It's nice to know that no matter who's fighting with who, Jane and Moffy will always be the glue that brings us all back together.

I think our parents would be over-the-moon to know it.

"Whose idea was this?" Xander asks as we head into the brick-walled, industrial living room. Omega bodyguards have already summoned Donnelly like he's needed to complete their beer-drinking cluster. They're reminiscing about hunting for the girl squad in Italy.

The teenage girls hear and all shout about how they were *fine*, and they didn't need rescuing. The bodyguards just sip beers with grins and *Sure, Jan* expressions.

"Whose idea was it to…? Throw a party?" I ask Xander.

"To hire a *psychic*," he clarifies. "You know Eliot has been calling it the Psychic Penthouse Party all night? PPP."

"Catchy." I pop a Frito in my mouth.

Xander steals a handful out of the bowl. "Catchy and fun until the psychic says you have one year to live."

I crunch slower on a Frito. My eyes widen. It dawns on me. We're all about to hear our futures *out loud*—and I've yet to discuss mine with Donnelly.

63

LUNA HALE

Among a packed penthouse living room, I have trouble not picking out and zoning in on Donnelly. He's miming the shape of an apple or butt while talking to SFO, and they're laughing at his story. My superpower might be one of detection. To be able to spot the man I love in a crowd of five million. Not that there are five million bodies stuffed in here.

More like twenty or so.

Donnelly must feel the power of my gaze. He slips me a quick grin and sticks his tongue between two fingers.

My smile expands. Lighthearted feelings teem in the air, despite the impending "future doom" a psychic might bring.

Donnelly is safe. That's all that really matters. It's not a worry I had this strongly...not until I heard about the phone call with Vanessa. His mom's friend. It's why we skipped the Salt Lake tour stop. It's why he looked so distraught all alone in the desert.

My heart ached when Donnelly struggled to explain how he didn't trust Vanessa, but more than that, he was afraid he couldn't trust his mom anymore. *Again.* Because it wouldn't be the first time.

"Of what I could fucking hear," Sulli says, returning to the loveseat where I'm perched on the armrest, "they're discussing a 'perfect peach' poll online that Thatcher won." She plops on the cushion, very pregnant and in threat of giving birth any day now.

"Recon Queen," I praise.

We fist-bump with grins. It's only been this month where our friendship has peeked out of the rubble. And *not* because I could remember all of our past together, but because our banter naturally returned bit by bit during roommate dinners. It's largely due to her effort. Sulli would sit beside me and not create a clique with her husbands.

I started feeling more like *we* were a friendship pair the way Moffy and Jane often grouped off, but Jane isn't with my brother now.

"Oui," Jane smiles brightly beside Sulli and strokes Ophelia, a white cuddly cat on her lap. "Five gold stars for our Sulli."

Of all Jane's fur babies, Ophelia has been the most jealous of Baby Maeve's arrival. Sulli says she's a stage-five clinger. To which, I would agree, but I wondered if they thought *I'm* a stage-five clinger to Donnelly. The "you're obsessed" and "trauma attachment" comments from my old therapist have stuck with me. I am usually with my boyfriend when I'm not at college and he's not working.

Very quickly, they both professed, *no*. Well, Sulli said, "Fuck no." And Jane said, "Absolutely not." But it was this month I realized I needed to spend more time with my roomies and less time stuck in my room. Especially before Sulli gives birth and is in the joys and throes of caring for a newborn.

It's why I'm actively separated from Donnelly at this party. We can be apart. Space isn't a *bad* thing. He's not so far away.

I should probably stop ogling him though.

"...I hope they keep posting pics of the three of us giving them the bird," Sulli says about the paparazzi, who swarm the happy triad every time they step out of the penthouse. "They're so fucking aggravating. Like, we get it—who's the baby daddy? No one knows. Not even *me*, so stop fucking *asking*." She huffs.

Jane gives her a comforting back rub.

"And on top of me freaking out about delivering a human being, it's terrifying thinking I won't make it to the hospital in enough time and I'll have those creeps filming me." Tears spring out of her eyes, and she grimaces. "What the fuck? Why am I crying?" She's often said her least fav part of being pregnant is her hormones going haywire.

"I only see tears of joy," I note with a nod.

Sulli starts to laugh, wiping the creases.

I smile, and ask the two of them, "Whose idea was the psychic anyway?" I wasn't present during the party planning.

Jane drums her lips. "It was a collective thought, I'm fairly certain."

Sulli gapes. "No, it was *your* idea." She explains to me, "We were at a production meeting with Jack for *We Are Calloway*." They've been filming the docuseries, which I decided to bail on this year. "And Jack asked which events we'd consent to be filmed, and we got off on a tangent thinking about parties we could throw. *Jane* then mentioned how it'd be fun to invite a psychic to the penthouse."

"You seconded me," Jane grins, her chin resting on her knuckles.

Sulli grins back. "Yeah, but only because I want to know *your* future, not mine. Remember the fortuneteller we met when the tour bus broke down?"

Jane clues me in, "It was during the FanCon tour. You'd flown back home by this time."

Good to know I'm not actively missing this memory. I wasn't a part of it to begin with.

Sulli twists her water bottle cap. "Fontina predicted my future. She said I'd fall in love with two men."

Jane looks unconvinced. "I believe she said you'd *fall*."

"The rest was implied," Sulli reasons. "What if this psychic says *I sense grief in your days to come*—then I'm going to panic and think this baby won't make it…"

I pat her shoulder.

"It's not real," Jane says consolingly. "It's a parlor trick. They analyze your body language and any information you happen to give them. It's a cold reading, not a precognitive power."

"Tell that to Kits. *And* Banks. *And* your husband!" They're all very superstitious.

Jane informs me, "Thatcher was a vote against the psychic."

"Not everyone has to participate, right?" I ask them.

"She might read the room," Jane warns.

I straddle the fence of wanting to hear a possible future outcome and sitting this one out. Sulli says she'll be on the sidelines with Akara and Banks. For how stoic and stringent Thatcher is, he's a softie for Jane, and he's agreed to do a reading with her.

There are no camera crews here, so I figure this party was never on the table as a "filmed" event. It'd definitely limit who'd accept the invite, and I bet they hoped everyone would come.

We end up chatting about Jane's wedding planning business since Faye and Hudson are getting married soon. They're the story supervisor and boom operator on Jack's production unit that Donnelly told me about a while back.

"Will you open your services to the public?" I ask her.

"No, friends and family only," Jane says, Ophelia purring in content on her lap. "I'd be swamped with requests otherwise, and it wouldn't be because I'm good at my job but because they'd just want to meet me." She muses, "I think I'd also struggle to pick out just one candidate."

I think she would too. Jane has a big heart, and she'd want to be there for too many people at once.

"I love being a mom," Jane says to me with a glowing look. "*But if the right opportunity were to present itself, I'm open to new terribly exciting paths.*"

"Except Fizzle CEO," Sulli puts out there.

"Except that," Jane says.

The fact that *Jane* of all people rejected the career path I'm in the running for is a wee bit anxiety-inducing. She's been a CFO. She's a math wizard. She has a bubbly, effervescent presence. She's a *Cobalt*. On paper, she'd be a perfect selection for successor. Much better than Charlie, even.

Weirdly enough, I'm glad she's not competing.

I'm glad she's not someone I need to beat.

I wonder if I've grown a competitive bone in my elbow or my toes. Welp, time to get X-rayed. I kinda wish Donnelly were beside me, so I could tell him I need a full body X-ray. He'd get it the most.

But he's not gone. He's in reach.

No glass wall separates him from me. Whenever I want, I can step into his arms. And he'll hold me. He'll kiss me. And dance with me.

I smile and sip a berry seltzer.

A timer buzzes on Jane's phone, and Ophelia catapults off her lap. "Merde," Jane springs from the loveseat. "Their cakes—I forgot to put them in the oven."

Ben and Winona's birthdays are close together, and we all wanted to celebrate them a couple days early since we're all here. Jane, Sulli, and I whipped up vegan cakes for them, and our other roomies made Funfetti cupcakes for everyone else.

The vegan cakes needed to chill in the fridge overnight.

I rise off the armrest to help Jane.

"I have this. You two stay," Jane says and squints in slight threat, as if she'll plot our undoing if we move our butts. She weaves through Beckett and Charlie who call after her in French, but she ropes them into following her into the kitchen.

Sulli watches her go. "She's either babying me while I'm about to burst—or she's still trying to salvage our friendship for us."

"The latter, I'd guess," I tell her. Jane has tried to intervene in reconnecting me and Sulli by leaving us alone together, and it has left us in awkward silence before. Jane tends to fill those pauses. But after a while, it's made us laugh. So I guess Jane's attempts have helped, after all. "She knows you like being on your feet and moving around, even if your back hurts." Sulli is a tough bean.

She touches her belly, hidden in an oversized Studio 9 sweatshirt that might belong to Banks. "I know things will change after this little champ comes, but I want you to know...I'll always be here for anything you need, Luna. *Anything*. Even if it's just a Monday morning talk while we eat Cheerios. And I might need it too because you're one of my best friends, and I'd miss you." She's crying again, and tears build in my eyes.

I slide down into the cushion beside her. We hug, and I say, "I'd *love* that." I realize how much I feel loved by Sulli and how much I love her—because aching strands of grief tug at my heart even thinking I could lose her.

Perks of being roommates, I'll still run into Sulli all the time. We'll dish about Thatcher's updated *penthouse rules* he sticks to the fridge while I give her extra marshmallows from my Lucky Charms. Last time we read his rules, we were attempting to cook blueberry pancakes for the house (Jane left us together), and we saw a new rule about "no sex in the game room" which we both think is a dumb one meant to be broken.

After we pull apart and wipe our faces, we snag new drinks at a refreshment table Moffy set up for the party. Sulli rests her shoulders on the brick wall and unscrews her water. "I'm still shocked Ben came."

"Me too." I pop the tab of another seltzer and see Ben alone. He's sitting on the twisty iron stairs that lead to the rooftop pool. He briefly checks his phone before scanning the noisy party.

Sulli and I have great powers of deflection because he never looks over here. Also, he's more interested in watching Easton and Xander drink beers and chat. Easton props a shoulder leisurely against an expansive window—a breathtaking sunset view of Philly thirty-three floors above ground. My brother motions around with his hand, in deep convo.

They don't notice Ben.

"What happened to them?" I ask Sulli. "Ben and Winona?" Because at this point, Winona would bee-bop over to Ben and possibly slide down the twisting banister for fun. It'd be his idea first, and she'd likely follow after he did it.

Instead, Winona is skidding across the hardwood in her socks with Vada and trying not to spill their Solo cups of beer. Our parents gave the high schoolers permission to drink if they spend the night. So that's pretty much why the alcohol is flowing.

I figure Sulli would know what's up with Winona since that's her little sister. "I'm used to seeing Ben give Winona noogies," I tell her. "It's kinda sad seeing them on opposite sides of a room."

"Yeah, it's still fucking strange." Sulli watches her sister stop herself from a full-body collision with Eliot. She falls on her butt, in a fit of laughter with Vada. "Nona says it's different now that he's in college and she's still in high school."

Ben sees the girls tearing up from laughter on the floor. He smiles a little, but he seems sad. Sometimes in Television and New Media, as the lights dim to play video clips, he stares off with a morose expression. I've asked him if he's okay, and he'll just nod.

"They grew apart?" I wonder.

"Maybe, but that's not what I think," Sulli says. "My theory is that Ben knows my sister is dreading every year she gets older—how she's scared to turn eighteen and have these fucking media vultures obsessed with her. They're already printing bikini photos and she's still a *minor*. Same thing happened to our mom."

Aunt Daisy was a high fashion model, but the press sexualized her a lot, just because she was deemed "the hottest Calloway sister." I don't have to dig deep in Fanaticon Forums to find posts about Winona's beauty and how she's a Daisy Calloway lookalike.

"Ben's now surrounded by college guys," Sulli explains. "And I think he doesn't want them around her. He knows it's better if Winona stays in high school, so he's distanced himself a lot."

That theory sounds likely to me, and it means that Ben is sacrificing his friendship with Winona to ultimately protect her.

Sulli takes a pee break, and I moon-walk over to Tom and Eliot who sit on the frame of the blue couch. They swing around when I approach from the back. Tom tastes my berry seltzer and gags. "Dude, that's foul." He checks the expiration date.

"Give me." Eliot tries it and makes a confused face at Tom. "And what exactly do you think it tastes like?"

"Straight cough syrup."

"I like it," I shrug. Tom lets me try his mixed drink. First sip, my eyes bug out and I cough a little. "*Whoa.*"

Eliot snatches the Solo cup and tastes the drink too. He barely flinches. "Straight vodka." He cocks his head. "Trying to get drunk without me, brother?"

"It's a sipper," Tom says, "and I'm celebrating."

"By yourself?" Eliot questions. "Without your two *very* best friends?"

"Very best," I chime in with a nod.

Tom clinks his Solo cup against my seltzer can and then Eliot's water bottle. It's a little shocking Eliot isn't drinking at a party, but he said he needs to be sober to soak in the inevitable drama. We take sips in unison, and Tom announces what we're celebrating. "The Carraways officially have a new drummer." By his surly expression, this decision might not have been his. "Alfie Busby."

"Who?" Eliot and I say together.

"I know next to nothing about him," Tom explains. "I heard his demo and he's *okay*. The label either said to choose him or they'd drop the band. It was tempting, but we're too close to finishing the first full album, and they're talking about sending us on tour. But I swear if they make us open for Nothing Personal, I will jump off a bridge."

"And survive," I note.

"Gloriously," Eliot finishes.

We all cheers with our drinks again and overhear Audrey tell Kinney, "I would let him take me, but not *sweetly*. A full-face grab, hair pull—he can even throw me over his lap." Tom chokes on his vodka, and I pat his back while Eliot stands off the couch and zeroes in on their sixteen-year-old sister.

"Audrey," Eliot says with a devious smile. "Who needs to die tonight?"

"Oh, you there." Audrey looks at us while Kinney pets Salem at her side.

"You knew we were here," Tom rasps, trying to clear his throat. Eliot passes him the water.

"Did I?" She plays innocent, but Cobalt mischief is in her eye.

"He's likely fictional," Eliot says. "Let me guess. Damon Salvatore." He's the bad boy vampire from *The Vampire Dairies.*

"Wrong and wrong."

"Not fictional, great," Tom coughs out. "Another topic for my weekly therapy session."

Kinney and I share a secret smile, like this kind of banter is familiar. My sister and I know what it's like to be friends with Cobalts. This might be the first we've truly bonded over that.

Eliot squints at his sister. "If he's real, give me his phone number."

Audrey blushes. "I don't have it. *Yet.* He's much older than me anyway, and it'd be wrong to pursue him—but the *minute* I'm eighteen, it's game over." At this, Audrey glides away with my sister.

Eliot shakes his head and sips some of Tom's vodka. "I might go to jail for murder that day."

"Leave that to Charlie," Tom tells him. "He'll eviscerate anyone five feet from her."

"I'm not leaving *murder* up to Charlie to protect our sister. It'll be too clean."

"Yeah, and he won't go to jail. Because he knows not to write his name on it."

I muse out loud, "Audrey can't wait to be eighteen while Winona wants to stay young forever."

"Oh the tragedy," Eliot mutters into another sip of vodka, which Tom steals back, just as Jane shushes everyone and says the psychic is at the door.

While Jane welcomes a short silver-haired lady, no taller than five-foot, into the penthouse, the party quiets down. She has a radiant smile on my cousin and she even cups Jane's one hand around her two palms. It's a benevolent, warm greeting.

"She seems fake," Eliot whispers to us.

"Yeah, not angry enough," Tom whispers back.

"Based off what?" I ask under my breath.

"The fortuneteller in *Princesses of Philly* looked mad," Tom explains. "She's the one that told our mom she'd likely have twins. And lookie there." He motions his cup to Charlie and Beckett. The Cobalt twins are side by side near the kitchen entryway, watching their older sister direct the older lady farther into the living room.

She's telling Jane to place two chairs in front of the TV. In a matter of minutes, there's a perfect setup for public readings.

Nerves swarm my stomach, but Eliot calms me when he whispers, "It was a lucky guess. Twins run in many families. Case in point." He nods towards Thatcher and Banks.

"Hello all," the lady announces with a jubilant glow. "I'm Cordelia. It's my pleasure to meet all of you tonight."

Many of us return the sentiment. I give her a silent Vulcan salute.

"Now, I'll be reading energies and palms. It's most helpful if you keep the space as quiet as you can, but if you feel inclined to talk— which I hope you'd want to, since these can be quite revealing—I just ask you do so at a whisper. Thank you, now I'll be taking a little walk around the room."

She strolls past the coffee table and peers past most of us, not making direct eye contact. I wonder if she's a medium too. When she reaches the cluster of bodyguards, my dog rushes up to her, and Donnelly is super quick to catch Orion at the torso.

"Sorry," Donnelly says. "Don't know if you're a dog person. He's friendly though."

Cordelia scratches his furry head. "How could I not love this beautiful creature?"

I beam, and Eliot whispers, "We've lost Luna."

"She's suckered in," Tom agrees.

She loves my dog. Of course that'd earn her brownie points. I'd give her the entire brownie tray for looking past Orion's defiant nature and seeing his kind heart instead.

Cordelia smiles up at Donnelly. Okay, *now* she's making super intense eye contact, and I try not to panic. Especially as Donnelly's eyes flit briefly to me across the room, then back to her.

No one murmurs.

Not as she says, "You are why everyone is together."

Uhhh, that's wrong, right? Jane and Moffy are why we're all here. Eliot mouths to me, *phony*. I mouth back, *not nice*.

He mimes stabbing his heart with a sword.

Donnelly nods a couple times and grins, "Good on me then."

"Yes," Cordelia smiles joyfully. "Very well done. I'll see you again in a moment." She crosses the room and eyes the ceiling with a big breath. "There is a great deal of love here. Some of you have had many firsts within this space." She waves around absentmindedly while appearing deep in thought too. "You all will have *lasts* as well."

Bodies shift. Whispers. Jane has an analytical expression, like she's processing how Cordelia came to this logical conclusion.

Eliot whispers to me, "It will be my last sip of Tom's drink." He takes one more sip. "Regretful."

Tom laughs under his breath.

I try to smile, but Cordelia lets out a sorrowful sigh. A bittersweet sentiment touches her pale blue eyes. "Time is so precious, isn't it? Wherever you all may go, they will always remember you and they will call you back." She gestures a lithe hand to my brother.

Maximoff.

And then to Jane.

My throat swells. I've felt the importance of remembrance more than most, I guess. *Don't cry. Don't cry.* Everyone has gone quiet again, as it hits deeper with some.

Charlie isn't amused. He probably believes it's a parlor trick like his older sister. I wonder if he's thinking Cordelia did a Wiki deep-dive and figured out Maximoff and Jane are the ties that bind. But then why would she even say that thing about Donnelly?

She tilts her head. "Many will divide, it seems. As time pulls some in a new direction...sooner than you think."

Charlie rolls his eyes, then catches me staring and cocks a brow.

I shrug.

He mouths, *vague*.

She's being vague. *True*. Except she says, "In this room, only *six* will remain where they are." She spins on her heels. "You." She points at Kinney, who flinches. "You." She points at Audrey, who gasps, but Kinney relaxes knowing her best friend has the same fate.

Cordelia sweeps past Winona and Vada, and my sister is back to looking horror-stricken.

"They're in two different grades," Eliot whispers. "A split is imminent." Winona and Vada will graduate first.

"You and you." Cordelia rotates so fast to Tom and Eliot that I jump. Neither are taken off guard, but I realize she veers past me. "You and you." She points out Charlie and Beckett.

Those four Cobalt brothers live in Hell's Kitchen together. Also an easily searchable fact online.

"Those six, but you two…" Cordelia stops in front of Oscar, whose arm is around Jack's waist. "My two exceptions, since you will remain but you're always on the move, aren't you?" She asks if they're okay with touch, and they say *yes*. Then she asks if they'd let her read their palms.

Oscar looks to Jack. "What do you say, Long Beach?"

He smiles a loving, mega-watt smile. "Ride the wave."

Together, they splay their hands out, and Cordelia traces their lines. "Beautiful." She smiles up at them. "A beautiful love. A beautiful life." She touches Jack's cheek. "Do not stress." Then to Oscar, "You will be there for him, always. It's your heart's true destiny. One day, you'll even have a son." She clasps their hands together.

Jack smiles politely, but he's stunned.

"Breathe, meu raio de sol," Oscar says.

"You too, Os," Jack says since Oscar is a deer-in-the-headlights, and they laugh, then kiss.

I smile but take a nervous sip of seltzer.

Cordelia meanders around, connecting with different energies, I guess. Her dangly silver earrings sparkle in the dim lamp light of the room. "So that is six who are motionless, and only two exceptions."

"You didn't name anyone who lives in the penthouse," Sulli says loudly and eerily.

Cordelia simply cocks her head, as if she didn't know.

My heartbeat hammers.

"It's a theory," Jane says, easing the strain in the room. "But a very good one." She mimes the tip of a top hat to Cordelia.

"My pleasure, dear," Cordelia smiles, then addresses us all, "The rest will shift. That includes you all." She gestures to the cluster of bodyguards. Akara, Banks, Thatcher, Farrow, Oscar, Donnelly, Quinn, Frog, and Gabe. All of Omega, plus Donnelly who's technically Epsilon.

Cordelia expresses to them, "Many faces outshine yours, but you aren't forgotten here." Her smile softens lovingly. "Thank you."

Her immense gratitude towards them takes me aback and floods my lungs. It's as though she's thanking them for their acts of service. For keeping the rest of us safe and alive. They protect us without thanks needed, and I've never really heard it given from a stranger this strongly.

My tears surge, and Sulli cries quietly next to Beckett. "Fuck," she mutters, wiping her eyes. Beckett puts his arm around her.

SFO are the reason I was found.

I look at Donnelly. *Thankyouthankyou.* I'll tell him again tonight.

Rubbing at my eyes with my fishnet sleeve, I restrain more waterworks, and Cordelia is wandering again. "Now, now, now..." She says, searching for something. "There is a strong presence among you...so strong. I feel...the energy like a..." She molds the air with her hands. "A beacon...she calls to more than one."

Must be Sulli attached to Akara and Banks.

And then my stomach plummets. Because she comes to a complete stop.

Right in front of me.

64

LUNA HALE

I freeze. Cordelia isn't staring past me. She makes direct eye contact. "You…" Say I'm not the beacon! If I am one, then I'm only calling to Donnelly.

I open my mouth. Fear staggers my breath, and Donnelly pushes out from Omega, maybe to reach me, to calm me down. *I won't cheat on you. I'd never cheat.*

Then I relax when she says, "You're the deepest emotional tether…because you're tethered to the one who's brought everyone together." *Donnelly.* "And the one who will call you back." *Moffy.* "And more…yes, you call to more people here. You've called to them quietly and possibly without you really knowing." Why is Kinney crying? Xander tries to console her with Salem.

There are more wet eyes that surprise me. Like Winona's.

"The beacon." Cordelia smiles, but it teeters in and out like she's overwhelmed. "Will you take a seat?" She motions to the chairs blocking the TV. Where everyone can stare.

"Uh…" Will she predict my future like Oscar and Jack's? "I…"

"Take your time. I'll return," Cordelia says kindly, then holds out a hand to Eliot. "You'd like to go in her place." It's not a question.

"She knows me so well," Eliot teases with an alluring smile. "To the stage?"

"If you wouldn't mind."

"I'd love nothing more." Eliot walks backwards to give me two thumbs up like it's easy peasy. Not so hard.

I exhale and check on Donnelly.

He's whispering with Farrow and patting Orion. I ease more knowing he's not worried about me or alarmed about her energy reads.

As Cordelia takes Eliot's hand and examines the lines in silence, quiet conversations escalate throughout the room. Tom watches his brother intently, but I sip my seltzer and do a quick people-watch sweep. Ben has left the iron staircase. He's much closer to where I stand because I catch him whispering to Vada.

"Are you with Easton?" he whispers.

What?! It nearly snaps my neck in their direction.

"That's not what I wanted to talk about." Vada sounds frustrated.

"His hand touched your thigh weirdly."

"Mine touched his too. Probably weirdly by your definition, but whatever. Look, before Winona kills me for asking—what'd you do to get the T-Bags to stop messing with her?"

"Why?"

"I just want to know, Ben," Vada whisper-hisses. "*Please.*"

"Nothing, I did nothing."

I strain my ears, but their conversation has ended. Quick peek over, and I realize Ben has moved away from Vada and sunk back on the iron staircase. He's on his phone now.

"There, there," Cordelia runs her fingers down Eliot's palms, then intakes a deep breath and stares upward at the ceiling. "'These violent delights have violent ends, And in their triumph die like fire and powder, Which as they kiss consume.'"

Tom leans into me to whisper, "Romeo and Juliet. She must know Eliot is a thespian."

Eliot grins and applauds. "Perfect oration."

Cordelia smiles sadly at him. "You will help the voiceless find a voice, but it won't be without consequence."

"Ominous," Eliot widens his eyes with a smile. "What else?"

She pats the top of his hand. "Continue to love with your whole heart. It's why they all love you with theirs."

I brighten and whisper to Tom, "That's really sweet."

"Yeah, and she got you again."

It's not so bad to intake the hopeful, loving messages and disregard the sad ones. Even if they aren't real future predictions— we can still believe in the good. At this, she releases Eliot from the spotlight, and she whirls around.

Her attention lands on me. "Ready now?" Her voice is so soft and gentle, I find myself nodding.

Eliot's reading was more ambiguous than I thought it'd be. I can do ambiguous. So I walk forward and plop into the creaky kitchen chair. Eyes are hot on me, but I concentrate more on the frayed strings of my jean shorts.

"Wonderful. Now…" Cordelia says soothingly. "You, again." She's picked out Donnelly from the crowd. "The moment has come. Would you join her, please?"

I open my mouth to relinquish him of this obligation. He might not want his future read, but he's already at my side, taking the seat. When our eyes meet, a grin spreads across his mouth, and it really is like we're two astronauts piloting a spacecraft together.

Destination: *Unknown.*

Is Cordelia our map?

Or maybe it's what Jane said. She's reading our body language. Our gazes that clutch tightly and caress softer—his hand that naturally slips on top of mine while my fingers dig into the seat. It's reassurance and caring and love.

I breathe easier.

He grins wider.

"How long you've traveled to be where you are," Cordelia begins, a sentimental look in her eyes, and she takes our palms. One in each of her hands.

My pulse flies away from my body as she inspects my small, soft hand to Donnelly's much larger. His is scarred and callused in comparison. No one is murmuring or muttering like when Eliot was here. They're transfixed silently on us, and I see Donnelly rethinking this.

Maybe we should end it early. Get up? Leave?

"You have matching lifelines." She peers from one palm to the other. "They are so very, *very* long." *Don't cry. Don't cry.* My eyes glass. I hear a few gasps and *thank Gods* mumbled.

Donnelly grins over at me, and I murmur so quietly that only he could possibly hear, "Everlasting, we are."

He leans in—his gaze straight ahead while his lips brush my ear. "I knew it from the start."

I turn my head a fraction, our lips nearly skimming. "I believe it," I whisper. Because Donnelly has always believed in me. He's always believed in himself. Then when there was an *us*, he believed in that too.

He's punctured my cynical heart and filled it to the brim.

Cordelia muses, "Two souls inextricably intertwined...there were many paths, but all would always lead you to each other. There is only life together."

Destined. The overlapping timelines of our love has already made me believe that we're meant to be. I didn't really need a stranger to confirm what I feel for me to take stock in it.

"Now..." She exhales, her smile on him, then me. "You will have—"

"Sorry to interrupt," Donnelly says quietly to her. "Love this and all, but if you're about to say anything about kids, could you just write it down and not show us?"

Good idea. I'd rather this not be known right now. What if it's a disappointing prediction? What if she says we'll *never* have a baby— not even in the faraway, distant future?

Cordelia tips her head in a sweet nod. She procures planetary stationary from her worn satchel. She scribbles on the purple paper, then folds it into threes. Handing it gingerly to Donnelly, Cordelia says, "You will never fail her. She will always be with you."

Tears try to sting my eyes.

Donnelly is choked up a bit, not such a skeptic. He nods in thanks and clutches the prediction. And then Cordelia sweeps us all with the same fond smile when she entered the room.

Her gaze slows on the Moretti brothers, and she says, "Be happy."

Thatcher rotates fully away, shielding his overwhelmed face, and Jane speaks rapidly and quietly to him, her eyes flared in concern.

To everyone, she says, "All of you. Simple joys are the sweetest. Aren't they? Now…" She takes a calming breath.

Orion barks and his paws scratch across the floorboards while he races to Donnelly for comfort. What'd he run away from?

"You alright, boy?" Donnelly ruffles his furry head with two hands. Orion pants at me like he's ensuring I'm here too, and I bop his nose with love. He licks my fingers. Cats suddenly spring out from the hall like we're in Jumanji and animals are escaping certain doom.

"What the hell?" Xander mutters, lifting up his feet. "Moffy…? The ground is *wet*."

A slow trickle of water slips towards us. A loud *bang* jars me, and noises pierce my ears as people run towards the danger. Directions are yelled from bodyguard to bodyguard, from sibling to sibling—I can't keep track. My pulse goes haywire.

I stare at the water pooling in from the wide hall. "Are we sinking?" I ask like we've somehow boarded the Titanic. Is this all a simulation? Did I drown and never wake up? Fear tries to transport me, but Donnelly clutches my cheek and I'm on my feet with him.

"Are you okay?" I ask him.

"Yeah, you?"

"Uh-huh," I say, right as the sprinkler system switches on. Water sprays everyone in the packed living room. Audrey shrieks.

"Two pipes have burst!" Thatcher calls out from the hallway. "Banks, I need you! The valve is bent to fuck, and the water won't cut off!"

"Roger that." He races to the source of the problem. "Nine!"

Banks locates Akara before he disappears. "There should be a master water shut off valve in the building."

"I'm calling maintenance now."

An inch of water already soaks the hardwood.

The penthouse is flooding.

65

LUNA HALE

"There are zero nanny cams in Luna's bedroom," my mom reiterates for the literal fourth time as Donnelly throws a duffel on my bed. "Please keep all private matters to your private bedroom."

I'm grinning, just happy my mom is allowing Donnelly to stay in my childhood room. Even if it is because Easton is occupying the guest room down the hall. She could've made Donnelly blow up an air mattress and camp out in the home office.

I feel like the two of us have leveled up in a way.

"Thanks, Mom," I say, on my knees as I dry off Orion with a Power Rangers bath towel. Donnelly and I are still soaked from the sprinklers.

It took maintenance three chaotic hours to finally shut off the master water valve. Something Jane called *questionable competence.* Within the first twenty minutes, we had already loaded the cars with animals, babies, and important personal items. It was clear no one would be spending the night there. Anyone who was sober became DDs and drove to our parents' houses.

Mom has a hand on the doorknob, and her eyes swim with warmth. "I know I should be very upset that your apartment flooded, but it's nice having all of you back under one roof."

"Might be longer than you think," Donnelly warns her. "Building manager said it'd take seven days to evaluate the damage." He digs in a duffel pocket. "If we need to get a hotel—"

"What? No, no, no." Mom raises her hands like she's stopping traffic. "Stay a week, a month, a year, the door is *always* open."

I smile more at Donnelly. His chest rises. He seems beyond touched, and he nods into a slow-rising grin. "Thanks, Luna's mom."

"Lily," my mom says. "You can always call me Lily."

"Thanks, Lily."

At this, she leaves us, gently shutting the door behind her, and Donnelly returns to the duffel pocket. "I love your mom. She's one of the greats."

"Yeah," I murmur, trying not to think about *his* mom and how she hasn't been that for him…ever. It crushes my heart. The penthouse flooding might be a less distressing topic. "Do you think Cordelia tampered with the pipes?" It's a running theory in my family group chat.

"The little old lady? Nah," Donnelly says lightly, leaving behind the duffel. I didn't see what he took out. "That was her first time inside the building. Plus, I got a good look at her when the first pipe burst, and she was as shocked as the rest of us."

Jane found the psychic through her sweet mother-in-law Nicola, who knew about Cordelia's precognitive abilities through another friend. Those channels are innocent enough. I'd question Cordelia's intentions more if she knew Grandmother Calloway, but she's far removed from that ugly social circle.

But Jane did fess up to telling Cordelia to stay positive. No negative or sad or grief-stricken readings. Which made more sense. Moffy and Jane would never want a psychic to tell any of us we're going to die soon, and to nip that possibility, Jane ensured Cordelia would spread good news and happy vibes.

Security doesn't believe there's foul play. Not when there's zero evidence.

Donnelly feeds Moondragon fish flakes. Then he wanders to my off-kilter bookshelves and studies them. He tells me, "All I know is that she either has some special power or she's just good at reading people." He doesn't mention the broken Spider-Man mug. Just spins around and examines my childhood room like he's archiving the fauna of a new planet.

"See anything you like?" I ask.

He swings his head. "Looking at her."

My heart soars, and after sufficiently drying Orion, I glide over to my boyfriend. He hooks his arms over my shoulders and we kinda sway in the middle of my room. "Thanks for letting me into your life, Hale."

"Thanks for letting me into yours, Donnelly."

He blinks for a second. Faint worry creases the corners of his blue eyes. He staggers on a word, but then breathes out, "You want me to grab the tub from the car?"

My printed stories were safely preserved in a plastic tub, which Donnelly ensured made it into the Volvo before we left the penthouse. Likewise, his digital tablet had been stored in a drawer. It dawned on me on our ride here that outside of Moondragon and Orion, our most prized possessions were my writing and his art.

"It'll be okay in the car," I say quietly. Is he…is he not telling me something? I've sensed this before, but I've never pushed. I still worry about prodding and detonating our relationship. Everything feels so *right*. Why would I change that?

Maybe it's too naïve. Maybe it's not how real, lasting relationships work.

So I ask, "What'd you take out of your duffel?"

"I was just making sure it was dry in there." Going to his duffel, he pulls out a slip of purple paper, the corners wet. He hands it to me.

Cordelia's prediction of our future. Of whether we'd have kids. Maybe she wrote exactly how many.

"You wanna read it?" Donnelly wonders, combing a hand through his damp hair. "'Cause I could wait, if you wanna wait."

I stare at the folded paper. "I could wait," I say softly. "It's not anytime soon, anyway. I mean, we're not even…we haven't even…"

Engaged. Wedding. Marriage.

"Yeah," Donnelly bobs his head a few times, but now he's trying to feverishly read *my* expression. Are we on opposite sides of these big deal-breakers?

He rubs a hand over his mouth, our eyes locked with a knowingness that neither of us verbally acknowledges. We're not ready to implode *us*.

I'm not even sure I'd want to survive that implosion.

66

PAUL DONNELLY

Static clings to the laundry as Farrow and I pull clothes out of the dryer. He tears his black sock off my Scorpions shirt and tosses the tee to me. "You're so lucky you threw your shit in with my load and not Lo's."

"He'd enjoy it. Everyone loves my loads," I joke.

Farrow squats, digging deeper into the dryer. "See, this is a pet peeve for about ninety-five percent of the population." He throws baby burp rags at me, which I fold for him. Farrow is part of the five percent who don't have a problem with sharing a wash and dry cycle. That's only if he likes you though.

"It's what I always say." I stack the burp cloths. "Nothing wrong with a frugal bitch."

He sifts through mixed up pairs of boxer-briefs. "You can be a frugal bitch all you want, but saving ten bucks on the water bill isn't going to register with your girlfriend's rich dad. What is going to register is having to touch your underwear." He chucks my black pair at me. "You're also so fucking lucky you don't wear the same brand as Maximoff."

I grin. "Don't want me sharing undies with your husband?" I tease.

While reaching into the dryer, he flips me off with his visible hand. We're both smiling.

Farrow pulls out a handful of jumbled clothes. Tearing off a lime-green thong from his Third Eye Blind shirt, he gives me an *only with you* look.

I laugh. "You forget I'm straight?"

"You forget I'm gay?"

"Nah, it's my twenty-eighth favorite thing I know about you."

Farrow chucks Luna's thong at me. "That high?"

"The other twenty-seven things are just your music preferences."

His laugh fills the laundry room, and he flips me off again. I catch another pair of panties he tosses at me.

Farrow peels off a mesh neon pink thong from a sock. "Did these get mixed in or are you doing her laundry for her?"

"I asked if she had anything dirty she needed washed." I set the folded laundry on the marble counter behind me. "It's not a big deal."

He flings the mesh thong at me. "You ever think we'd be with siblings?"

I snatch it out of the air and shake my head. "Odds seemed pretty low."

"I've dated guys who had sisters," Farrow reminds me. "It wasn't that low."

I keep shaking my head. "It'd make everything more complicated if I did that. Whoever you were with—they wouldn't want me around if I hooked up with their sister."

I didn't care about falling in love as much as I cared about keeping Farrow in my life. When I was seventeen, he was the *best* thing that ever happened to me, and I don't even know if he fully understood it.

'Cause I never made a big thing out of it either. I preferred it that way. But this year, we've been talking about it more than we usually do.

Farrow sweeps me in thought. "That's why I knew you really liked Luna." He separates Maximoff's gym clothes into a basket. "You never jeopardized our friendship over anything. Not until her."

Yeah. But he never put up a stink about it. "You always liked me and her together," I realize.

He nods with a smile. "You're good for each other."

I grin back. "Or you hoped I'd marry into the Hales so I could be your brother for life. You wanted me stuck on you."

He rolls his eyes. "You don't need to marry my husband's sister for that to be true." He raises and lowers his brows at me like it's a simple fact. We're family. I'm not exiting his life stage right.

It's not so simple to me. Seeing as how I'm getting the feeling I might never get married. "That's good since I don't think Luna wants to marry me."

His face just falls. "She said that?"

I lift my shoulders stiffly. "I could see it in her eyes."

"Okay, but if she didn't *say* it, then you don't know what she's actually thinking. You need to have a full-blown conversation with her."

"I know she doesn't wanna talk about it, and I can't blame her when I haven't even told her a major part of my past that I'd like to burn up, honestly." Guilt festers. "It feels like I should've said something a long time ago, especially the more we have sex."

Farrow frowns. "You never told her you turned tricks?"

"Nope." I lean back on the counter. "Now it feels worse that I kept it from her. Like oh yeah, Luna, by the way, I've been paid to fuck girls and blow dudes before…" I trail off as the laundry door opens.

Luna's dad enters.

Farrow and I instantly go quiet.

Lo's attention descends to his daughter's thong in my hand. And I don't say a word about it. He grabs a bottle of Tylenol out of the medicine cabinet. "For the headache you're giving me."

"Don't forget the tissues," I tell him and point to the Kleenex on the third shelf. "For the tears you'll shed when I'm gone."

"Of joy." He flashes a half-smile, then says to both of us, "Breakfast is done, son-in-law and whoever you are."

I grin. "Dementia's already setting in?"

Farrow laughs into a wider smile.

Lo goes to the door. "You wish you could reach my age."

My smile softens. "Yeah, I do."

"You will," is all he says before leaving.

I look to Farrow. "Think I'm warming up to him."

"You're definitely becoming his favorite." He says it seriously.

"We're getting there," I laugh. "Anything is possible, kids. Just gotta put a little heart into it." I twirl her panties on my finger, then clutch them in thought. "Have you ever fucked Maximoff to help him fall asleep?"

His brows lift. "That came out of fucking left field."

"Nah, been thinking about it."

"About me fucking my husband?"

"About how it was four a.m. and Luna was still wide-awake and she specifically wanted to have sex so she could fall asleep."

Farrow slows his movements, shutting the dryer door. "She was having trouble falling asleep again?"

I nod. "Now that she has her memories back from that night, they keep her up sometimes." I'm glad she was honest and open about it with me. "I get wanting to have sex to relax, but I'd already made her come four times around midnight."

Farrow considers this. "Maximoff has never asked me to fuck him to sleep, but that's also because he's paranoid about being a sex addict. He'd stop himself more than I'd need to stop him from being compulsive in bed."

I love that Luna doesn't descend too deep inside her head while we're fucking. It's so *visceral* having her that uncontrolled, that untamed. "She'd go until she passed out every night if I didn't stop her."

"Damn."

"Best lay in the fucking world though. Baptize her with my cum seven times a week."

"Okay," Farrow cringes. "That's where you lose me."

I grin. "She makes a cute cinnamon roll when I—"

"Oh my God," he interjects like his ears are bleeding.

I laugh hard.

When the sound fades, Farrow rests against the dryer and says, "I'm not specialized in sex addiction, but I just wouldn't make it a routine." He clarifies, "Having sex to sleep."

"Yeah," I agree. "Wasn't planning on it." Since Luna has given Farrow consent to discuss her medical care with me, we talk more about my girlfriend's health and mine too.

Insomnia. PTSD. Night terrors. Sleepwalking.

"One day I might do it," I say about the sleep study he's always recommending. "But right now, I feel like I could sprint down Broad and sing *Don't Stop Believin'* at the top of my lungs, so think I'm doing alright."

Farrow looks me over, his lips upturning. Like he sees it too. Then my phone goes off, and he picks up the hamper.

I groan seeing the text from the big boss man.

"What's wrong?" Farrow comes closer.

"You know how Price heard I slept in Luna's bunk on the tour?"

"Yeah?"

"Well, now he wants to ensure Luna isn't a distraction while I'm on-duty. So he's putting me on Ben's detail today while she's at Penn."

At least Thatcher will be protecting Xander. That's what Price texted. We've been one holly jolly security team lately, so it's not surprising he's poached one of Akara's men for the day.

Farrow makes a winced face. "Who the fuck ratted you out to the boss in the first place?"

"Don't know. O'Malley swears up and down it wasn't him. None of Epsilon even acted like they had a problem with me bunking up with Luna. And if they did, I wish they would've just told me to my face rather than run to *Price*."

"Oscar said something about Epsilon's rookie floater," Farrow says in thought.

"Hart McKenna? Was it that he looks like your asshole ex? 'Cause Oscar and I have already talked about that."

He rolls his eyes into a glare now. "Can you let *Rowin* die in your brain and conversation?"

"Not when McKenna could be his twin. Look at me, got a cousin out of nowhere."

"It wasn't out of nowhere, and he's not his twin. And *no*, Oliveira didn't bring that up. Just that...McKenna seemed off. I'd keep an eye on him when he's around."

I appreciate the heads up, and I'm about to tell him thanks when our phones buzz at the same time. Farrow drops the hamper to check his cell.

It's official. We bought the apartment space above Studio 9. Signed the papers this morning. Sry, guys. We couldn't wait any longer for the repairs to be done. The baby might come any day. We'll miss living with everyone, but this is a permanent move for the three of us. We aren't coming back. – Akara

Farrow and I share a shocked look. Akara, Banks, and Sulli are leaving the penthouse for good. They're moving out.

"Did not expect that," Farrow says.

"They've always been the spur-of-the-moment ones. Makes sense they'd just run out and buy a new place since they ran out and got married."

"Yeah," Farrow sighs. "Shit."

"Shit," I stare out, realizing Luna's gonna be sad Sulli won't be around anymore. Just when she'd been reconnecting with her.

We've been living at the Hale House for a full week already. The structural damage to the penthouse is so extensive, the original seven-day repair timeline has been extended. It might be a month or two.

"What'd that psychic say about *lasts*?" I ask Farrow. "We'd all have a *last* there? Could be the last time any of us step foot in the penthouse."

"She was just guessing and seeing what stuck," Farrow says, lifting the hamper.

This one might've stuck.

'Cause I'm starting to believe no one's going back.

67

PAUL DONNELLY

Being on Ben's detail feels more like I'm a fly on the wall rather than the Boogeyman scaring away teenagers at Dalton. Didn't think I'd miss the latter, but here I am.

Spent most of the morning chilling in the hockey rink stands and watching Ben practice. He's the fastest on the ice.

Of his whole team.

Always been that way. I've seen him play hockey in high school—when Beckett attended his little brother's games—and he'd sweep past his rivals with the puck. No one could catch him.

But today, at practice, Coach Dorsey benched him. A ton.

"Your coach might need glasses," I said when we left the rink.

"He hasn't let me start most of the season," Ben told me. "He thinks I haven't earned it. That I just made the team because I'm the son of two celebrities. I doubt there's anything I could do to change his mind, outside of altering my DNA and having full facial plastic surgery."

"So you're saying he needs worse eyesight," I nodded. "We gotta steal his contacts."

Ben laughed. Made my day hearing it, especially since it's his 19th birthday today.

Brightest side of the afternoon is when we end up at Television and New Media. Per Epsilon's request, I'm not to go *into* the classroom. The consensus is that my presence will be a distraction since it's rumored Luna and I are dating.

Don't disagree.

And I'm not trying to flunk my own giant test from Price. I can protect Ben while being in arm's reach of Luna. Did it during the mini-marketing tour just fine—I protected Xander while Luna was there. But apparently it appears like I just slept with her the whole time.

The door is shut, and I lean on a Film Club poster in the hall. Quickly, I type out a text to my girlfriend. Her class has a "no texting" policy, but she said the Roach is never early. And class starts in five minutes.

We're only one wall away, space babe. Make a wish. I press send.

Seconds later, she responds.

Finally in the same multiversal dimension. I shall wish for your long fruitful life and the same for your offspring.
– Luna

My stomach tenses at *offspring*.

"So they sent the *alleged* boyfriend." The masculine voice breaks me away from my phone. The thirtysomething is gripping a Starbucks coffee in one hand and a half-wrapped honey bun in the other. Don't know how long it's been since I saw someone under fifty wearing a sweater vest—so there's that.

"You're the prof?" I ask—but I know exactly who he is. Who his family is. I'll never forgive him for The Royal Leaks, even though that's all been settled privately among hotshot lawyers.

"Wyatt Rochester," he clarifies. "Please tell me you're not going inside. I don't need my class to turn into a *Celebrity Crush* article." He takes a bite from the honey bun.

"Thought your family is trying to buy *Celebrity Crush*."

He swallows his food. "Doesn't mean I like reading the trash."

He tilts his head. "So?"

"Not going in, Little Debbie."

He glances at his honey bun, bristles, then says, "Good call." He leaves for the classroom, and irritation rides me hard. Don't love being on the same page as him. Only saving grace is he's not failing Luna. She's pulling a solid B. (Deserves an A, if you ask me.) So even though his family has booked themselves a spot in hell, he'd be more villainous if he graded her unfairly.

While I wait for the class to end, I receive a new text.

I'm not going to prom. Neither is Easton. — Xander

I'd have to conduct a security meeting with a couple more guys from Epsilon if he decided to go. Xander has been on the fence, so I'm not too shocked he swung this way.

Just thought maybe he'd want to ask the girl from his study period. I type and send: Not even with Spencer?

He's fast to reply.

It's not her thing. Too many ppl she doesn't know. I don't blame her. Homecoming was ok. Best part was going to Lucky's afterward. — Xander

No one really knows of Spencer Sadler at Dalton Academy. She might as well be a ghost. I've kept my ears peeled, and the few times Xander has mentioned her in class, a student will reply, "Who?" And the only guy who seemed to recognize her had this ugly revelation, "Who's even friends with Spencer? She barely talks to anyone. All she does is set the curve like a bitch."

Glaring at a teenager—not my finest moment. Still don't regret it though.

Xander has been careful not to talk Spencer up. She's trying to keep her head down and graduate, and if anyone sees that *the* Xander

Hale has a new acquaintance that he converses with one period a day, they'd be all over Spencer in the halls. Wanting to know details about him, prodding about what shampoo he uses.

Easton gets flagged down daily. Guy is bullet-proof to any questions about Xander. It's like he's the real undead. Told Luna all about Xander's friends while we were in bed one night. She wanted to know more about Easton since he lives down the hall. I ended up talking about Spencer too.

Luna smiled, "My brother would befriend a vampire and a ghost."

New Media ends, and students rush out

the double doors. Ben towers over everyone, and he's only third out—storming ahead like someone pulled a fire alarm. I'm quick to catch up to his side.

"Sorry," he says, adjusting his slipping gym bag.

"Why are you apologizing?" I wonder, looking ahead and easily keeping his lengthy pace.

"I know you would've liked to say hi to Luna, but my next class is on the other side of campus. If I don't catch the bus, I have to sprint. Half the time there's not room on the bus—*shit*." He almost runs into a garbage can in the building, but narrowly avoids it. 'Cause I tug him to the left.

"Alright, Quicksilver." I redirect him to a rear exit. Less people. Easier to navigate. "Let's go this way."

He follows. "Moffy's Quicksilver. Not me." He says it like a fact. Which I guess it is one. Maximoff's namesake is Pietro Maximoff—aka Quicksilver.

"That's true," I say. "Doesn't mean you aren't fast." No one's bombarding him—which is why I picked this route. Though, I'm thinking this path would've been a good choice for Xander. Maybe it doesn't matter to Ben whether he's pushing through crowds.

We're outside. Tulips bloom in the flower beds. Spring is close but not quite here.

"Hey, Ben!"

Ben spins around on his heels. Walking backwards. "Cole! Hey, can't talk. Trying to make the bus!" He whirls back around. Three more steps, and a girl with French braids cuts off his path.

"Ben, hey, you going to the St. Elmo party this weekend?"

"Maybe. Text me the details, Leah." He moves around her like he's being picked up with the breeze. Long strides that take me one-and-a-half steps to catch up to. He's not graceful like Beckett. He's not water.

More like, he's tornadic. His peers are sucked into his sphere and get off on the static discharge, until he blows away.

"Katie!" Ben calls out on the way to the bus stop. "Nice job on the Spanish pres." He speaks to her in the language.

She beams. "Gracias, Ben!"

He walks and talks and pulls out a blue Ziff sports drink from his gym bag, leaving the duffel half open. I think about Xander. How he triple-checks his zipper before going into the hall—stressed someone will try to steal his belongings.

Ben smiles at a tall athletic brunette. "Happy Birthday, Chantal. It's today, right?"

"Yeah." Her smile is huge. "Thanks, Ben." I wait for her to wish him one back, but she doesn't register it's also his birthday.

Come to think of it, none of his friends from Penn have said a thing about his birthday today. Odd, really, considering it's on the Cobalt Wiki page. I'd look that shit up. But I also love this fandom. So…

"What up, bro?" A jock clasps hands with Ben at the bus stop.

"No, I know, man." Ben talks. "We choked last night." He never pauses long enough for a full conversation. "Take care, Miles!" He's on the bus, not searching for a seat. We stay near the doors and grip the handles above us as the bus bumps along the street.

I wanna ask him how many people he knows by name at this Ivy League. Home to over nine thousand undergrads. How can he even keep them all straight? But those are questions for a later date. Tab them into: The Mysteries of the Cobalt Empire. Right under what the hell happens on Wednesday nights.

We've jumped off the bus.

He's power walking into a science building, and I easily mimic his pace now. Ben takes a swig of his Ziff. Inside, he tells me which classroom he needs to be in. We near an emptier hall.

Turning a corner, he stops abruptly and even backtracks to the ajar door of a science lab. He swings his head to me like *did you see that?*

I peer in the lab. Among beakers and vials and empty black tables, I recognize the short blonde who's in a full-death glare at the professor. Harriet Fisher—she was Luna's lab partner last semester.

Feels uncomfortable, even from out here. Harriet and the professor are strangely the only two in the lab, and they're speaking with heat of a personal conflict, not strife over a failed grade or broken test tube.

Ben's not moving anymore. He twists his head back for some reason. I follow his gaze. No one's in the hall. The whole building is starting to quiet as doors slam shut.

I check my watch. "You're gonna miss the start of class."

"Yeah, I know." He nudges the door to the lab further open. He's moving toward Harriet—then the professor grabs her elbow.

Ben shoots forward like a bullet. "Hey!" He drops his gym bag, and alarm slams me forward too.

The professor jolts from Harriet like an electric fence zaps him. Hurriedly, he whisper-sneers something to the girl, then tries to make a quick exit.

"Whoa," I glare and reach out to stop him.

He raises his hands high like I'm infected waste he's stepping around. "Mind your own business and I'll mind mine."

"Don't be a sleezy professor and maybe I will!" I shout after him. He's gone. Fuck that guy. Boils my blood thinking he might make passes at other students, and I speak hushed in my mic about the professor to my boss.

Ben studies Harriet while she breathes hard. He's not moving, so I stay put and grab his gym bag off the floor.

Her nose flares, knotted brows not relaxing. She rights her book-bag on her shoulder and sets a glower on Ben. Combine that with a leather jacket swallowing her frame, combat boots, and ripped plaid pants, she looks ready to curse him out. But then she says, "Thanks."

Ben frowns and glances at where the professor left. "What was that?"

"Professor Turner. He teaches Molecular Biology of Life. Luna and I took him last semester."

Ben gestures his blue sports drink at her. "No, I meant *what* was that. Why was he grabbing your arm like that?"

She blows out a breath so hard it rustles her blonde bangs. "He's a fuckwad, that's why." Her eyes flit to me, just recognizing I'm standing by. "Hey. How's Luna?"

"Sparkly," I say. "As always." Luna still doesn't remember Harriet, but I don't mention that since Harriet's unaware about Luna's amnesia.

Ben runs a hand through his hair. "Can we rewind? Why is he a fuckwad? What'd he do?"

"What are you Scooby Doo?" Harriet frowns so deep her scowl darkens.

He shrugs. "I don't know. Is this a mystery that needs solved, Harriet Fisher?"

She lifts her chin higher to meet his gaze. "No mystery here, sorry to break your heart. Turner just got the wrong impression after we made an agreement." Harriet crosses her arms. "And you do realize your brother Tom hates me—?"

"You've already told me that."

"Just jogging your memory," she says. "Pretty sure you'll be disinvited to the next Cobalt soiree."

"That's actually impossible," Ben says. "I could piss off every sibling, and they'd still invite me and try to hold some elaborate family intervention."

"Ruthless love," she muses. "But from where I'm standing, Cobalts don't like strangers or interlopers or *me*."

"I can be friends with who I want."

I observe the exit and not them. Feeling more like a fly again. Trying not to buzz too loud.

"Since when are we friends?" Harriet asks. "I've run into you *twice*. I've said less than a hundred words to you. You do realize that's a low bar for friendship, right?"

"Is this your way of telling me to raise my standards?"

I glance back at them.

She's looking at Ben like he's out of his mind. "*Yes*."

He tips his head in thought. "Alright, then let's start over. You're officially my only friend."

She glares. "That's not what I meant." And then she groans into a heavy sigh. "Look, it's not a big deal, dude. I gave Turner a blow job in exchange for a favor, and now he wants more than one blowie, so I'm fending off an ugly hammerhead shark."

I rub my hand across my mouth. *You're a fly. Do not buzz. No flapping.* My stomach is clenching.

Ben blinks, looking her over.

Harriet raises her brows. "Say something, Friend."

"What favor is worth blowing a hammerhead shark?" Ben asks, glaring back towards the door like he'd wish the professor would materialize. His hands twitch at his sides, like he's restraining from curling his fingers into fists.

Harriet casts a glance at...me?

What do I have to do with giving blowies to professors?

Ben connects the dots. "This is about Luna?" He's asking her.

My girlfriend took the same class as Harriet. With the same creepy, crusty professor. Acid drips in the back of my throat. All my muscles have tensed.

"Can you not tell Luna? Please?" Harriet pleads to me. "She didn't ask me to make the deal. I did this on my own accord because I felt bad she had to miss labs. And after everything that happened with the kidnapping—I thought Turner was being a cruel piece of shit by not allowing her to finish the course off-campus."

My gut sinks, and I skate a hand through my hair. My palm stays on my head. "You did that for Luna?" *Fuck.* Even I don't feel good about it.

"I don't know," she mumbles and winces. "Again, not a big deal. It meant nothing, and I've given blow jobs for less." *Trust me, so have I.* "It's not like I got naked for the guy."

"Small blessings," I say lightly.

She relaxes.

Ben's jaw steels, but he has a sympathetic look on Harriet. "He should be reported."

"Do whatever you want. Just leave my name out of it. I have too much to lose. Maybe you don't understand that…"

Ben nods, twisting and untwisting the cap of the sports drink. "I won't mention your name. But if he's still a problem—"

"He won't be when the semester ends," Harriet interjects. "I'm out of this place in May. I've been accepted into the honors program at Manhattan Valley University. It's the hardest program to get into on the East Coast because they offer full rides. Too good to pass up."

"Over Ivy?"

"Yeah, MVU has a great pre-med program, among other things." She sizes him up and down. "I'm honestly shocked you chose Penn over it."

"Why?"

"Philly. You're the only Cobalt boy here."

Ben goes rigid. "I'd never go to college in New York." 'Cause he's got good taste. Knows the Tastykakes are fresher in the boxes from the Acme. Knows the Wawa coffee comes piping hot from Center City. Knows how beautiful the orange sunset sky looks behind City Hall.

Knows how Philly will always be there for you, no matter what, no matter when.

Yeah.

I know it. Not really sure what this city means to Ben.

Harriet nods slowly. "Gotcha. Well…have fun here, Friend." She slaps his shoulder like he's one of her pals, and she's heading briskly out of the lab.

"Wait!" Ben calls, sprinting after her in the deserted hall.

I'm a foot behind him.

She spins on her heels, and he jogs back to her side. "Take my number. In case you need security. It's a package deal with me. So if you're feeling uncomfortable on campus, I can come to you with my bodyguard…at least until May."

"How would that work? They're hired to protect you, not me." She glances at me.

I chime in, "If some crusty professor is laying hands on you, we'll step in." I tell Ben, "I'll let Novak know." He's his 24/7 bodyguard, and it's the least I can do for what Harriet did for Luna.

Harriet takes out her phone. "You know what…fuck it, I'm not prideful enough to turn away backup."

Ben smiles down at her, which starts to pull one out of Harriet. She smooths her lips like it's a weird feeling.

They quickly exchange numbers. "See you around, Fisher."

"See you, Birthday Boy."

It takes him aback. Shit, it takes *me* by surprise after today's lack of b-day wishes.

She walks backwards, moving slowly away from him. "I didn't stalk you exactly. I was doing my homework on Tom a while back. For the drummer audition. Your page was pretty small." She squeezes her fingers together. "Where's all the accolades?"

He smiles. "Siblings took them all."

She mimes tears with her fists, her smile rising. Think her own smile surprises her. She startles into a frown, then gives him a stiffer wave.

They depart like they've known each other for four years and not four minutes.

Don't know if this is something Ben does with everyone. If he's just that good at collecting friends or if he honestly wants to start over with just Harriet.

I do know he's missed half of his Bio class.

I also know my dad just texted me.

Meeting up with Loren Hale not this Saturday but the next. We've been texting back and forth, him and me. But he wants to make sure you're good with that date. — Dad

I pocket my phone in the empty hallway, standing outside Ben's biology class. And I mutter to myself, "I'm gonna have to be."

APRIL

"The enemy only knows darkness.
I know what the enemy does not...I know
the light."

– Tales of the Jedi: Dark Lords of the Sith #3

68

PAUL DONNELLY

It's D-Day. Day of the Dads. I'm antsy for 8 p.m. to hit, and it's only noon. Blowing out a long breath, I do my fortieth visual scan of Superheroes & Scones. It's a ghost town. Not much to see here.

Floors are swept. No one's browsing the aisles of comics and graphic novels. The geeky merch dangling on wall hooks remains untouched. Vinyl red booths are vacant. No employees smile behind the squeaky-clean countertops or work the espresso machines.

The blinds are even drawn shut.

The beloved comic book coffee shop isn't closed for good, but it's definitely shut down. Been that way since it was used for WAC production crew's nuptials. It won't reopen for another couple days.

The meeting between my dad and Luna's dad is *not* happening here. I'm on-duty, posted outside the *employees only* breakroom. Counting down to when Xander finishes (bad use of a word) so I can clock off and hold my breath for a solid hour.

Or maybe this meet-and-greet will last ten minutes.

Maybe Lo will murder my dad. Or vice versa. Jail might be on the docket for tonight. Who knows?

Being this deep in my head is never a good idea while on-duty, but if I listen at all, I hear the soft sounds of feminine moaning.

All in a day's work, you know—just guarding the door while my girlfriend's younger brother has sex. I wish I could wear earbuds and give them more privacy. I am wearing a radio earpiece.

Problem is, comms are dead quiet right now. I've started liking when Epsilon rags on Omega over the channels. Like when Quinnie received baskets of muffins from an admirer and SFE couldn't shut up about it.

It gave me the chance to say, "Young Stud Muffin coming in hot." And Epsilon laughed *with* Omega.

It's boring when they're not talking shit. Greer will drone on about fly fishing. Not knocking whoever loves wading in the water and flicking a rod. But I now know more about the little squirmy guys in the river than I ever thought I would.

Which is why I've already tuned into Omega's frequency and said *hello* to my old favorites. I haven't gotten chastised for it yet, so maybe it's not a rule I'm breaking.

At this specific moment, there are tumbleweeds rolling through comms.

I hear panting breaths from the breakroom, and I rub the side of my face.

On a car ride home from Dalton, Xander told me, "I don't know how much you heard during study period." *Not a lot.* I'd been on comms. "But we were serious about checking it off together."

"Checking what off?" I asked.

"Sex. Our virginity or whatever." He shrugged. "Spencer is going to Yale in the fall. We're just friends, or…I don't even know if she considers us that. She seemed surprised when I used the word." He adjusted in his seat, nervous even recounting it. "But it makes sense. We're both eighteen, and we both don't want to go into college virgins."

I frowned, one hand on the wheel. "Nothing wrong with being a virgin."

Xander slumped back. "Yeah, there is, Donnelly. At least for *me*, there is. I don't want the anxiety of *who's going to be my first* all the way throughout college when there've already been rumors I've had sex.

I'd rather just have it. And Spencer's the same way. She doesn't want to worry about this dumb life milestone when other college students talk about sex." He explained how she said, *You play truth or dare once, and someone asks your favorite position—then you either become* a liar *or* the virgin.

I told him, "Anyone who'd make fun of a virgin isn't worth being around."

"I know, wise one," Xander said under his breath. "I know, but… maybe she just doesn't want to be made fun of at all." He shrugged tenser that time. "It's happening, man, and I'd prefer if you were the one on my detail that day."

"It'll be me," I assured, and he calmed down with a giant breath. Less as his bodyguard and more as his sister's boyfriend, I wanted to ensure he'd be safe about this. "You got condoms yet?"

"Yeah, I already asked Moffy what brand I should get like a year ago. Not that I really thought I'd be using them then…"

Xander didn't want to lose his virginity at his house. That'd mean he'd have to bring a girl home. His dad would bombard Spencer with questions, and Lo would likely tell them to leave the bedroom door open.

Normal teens don't have a problem venturing to a random basement to screw—or maneuvering around the backseat of a car. That was my first-time experience.

But if Spencer was caught in public with Xander, it'd be sensationalized online. Xander weighed the media firestorm: *Who's house did Xander Hale come out of? Is that a girl he's with? What's her name? Her date of birth? Her zodiac sign? Are they even compatible?*

He figured Superheroes & Scones was the perfect place. It's somewhere press and fans wouldn't question his presence. Plus, he's spent so much time here, it's practically one of his second homes. Firmly in his comfort zone.

When Spencer arrived at the store, I let her inside. If anyone spotted Xander, Superheroes & Scones would become a security nightmare. So we'd already done an impeccable job of slipping inside unseen.

Xander was trying to limit the number of people who knew he was here to me, myself, and I. *So far, so good.* I've kept this from literally everyone…except for Luna.

We share our locations. I told her I'd be stopping by the store with Xander on this rainy Saturday afternoon, but thankfully she didn't ask *why*. I doubt she'd be able to guess what's happening anyway.

When Spencer stepped into Superheroes & Scones, she closed her black umbrella and shook out the wet droplets. I locked the door behind her. She wore the same Dalton school uniform, her brown auburn-tinted hair half-up with tiny, braided strands. Besides the umbrella, she looked exactly the same as she did every single day in the library.

Are we sure she isn't a real ghost? Luna would've whispered to me.

It made me miss my girlfriend. And we'd been apart for only four hours.

Spencer was quiet.

"He's in the back," I said and led her towards the breakroom.

Xander slipped out into the main storefront. He wore his black *House Stark* shirt and acid-washed jeans, his hair styled out of his face. He smiled. "Hey."

"Hi." Spencer stopped a foot away, like there'd been a forcefield around him. She stumbled on his clothes, then looked down at her plaid skirt. "I came from school…"

"On a Saturday?" He smiled a little more.

"Chess club meets every other Saturday morning. I didn't have time to change."

"You need to wai—?"

"No," she said fast. "I still want to do this." She unzipped her backpack, then peered up. "Do you?"

"I want to do this," he confirmed strongly. I kept my distance while he checked her out. "You look great, Spence. Seriously."

She blushed, maybe more so at the nickname. "Thanks. You do too." Then she took out a handful of condoms. "I brought these in case you forgot."

KRISTA & BECCA RITCHIE

Appreciation lightened his eyes. "Very prepared."

"Always," she exhaled.

"Follow me into the abyss," he said and held the breakroom door open for her. The longer they made eye contact, the more deep breaths each of them took, and they relaxed in each other's presence. That was what I'd tried to describe to Luna when she'd asked me more about Spencer.

How Xander and this girl could say nothing for a whole hour during study period, and every time their eyes met, the air would untense.

My phone pings. *Luna,* I hope. I'm grateful for the distraction from any sex noises I'm blocking out of both ears.

Except, it's not Luna. My stomach nosedives when I read the text.

> I'm in the area. Know it's not 8 yet but Carl saw you going into that comic book store. I'm three blocks away. I found out about that thing. Want to tell you face to face. — Dad

My pulse accelerates so fast, I'm lightheaded. *The thing.* I'm assuming that means he's figured out why our family kept mentioning Xander the night of the kidnapping. *Carl.* First time I'm hearing of a Carl—but I guess he must be one of my dad's friends.

I dunno. I don't like that Carl saw me enter this store when I thought I had *zero* tail.

I don't like that my dad is three blocks from here. I can't have *anyone*—let alone my dad—inside this store while Xander Hale is having sex in the breakroom. He trusts me. He piled all his faith in me like I'm Frodo carrying the fucking ring, and I can't fail him.

Think.

Think.

I send my dad a text: I'm working. I'll see you tonight. We can talk then.

I'll just be a minute. — Dad

My heart hammers in my chest, and I swallow a sharp breath as the breakroom door suddenly cracks open. Xander squeezes out in only boxer-briefs, careful to shield the dimly lit room and sofa behind him. I'm not trying to catch a glimpse of anything. Doing my best to divert my gaze from even Xander, but with the way he's breathing and the dampness of his hair and skin, I'm guessing the deed is done.

He signs back to her, then whispers to me, "I need to grab something. Then I think we're gonna watch a movie. If that's okay? I just want to hang out with her for a while."

"You don't need my permission," I whisper back.

"Yeah but Luna isn't around, and I'm keeping you from—"

"You aren't keeping me from her," I interject fast, wondering if he can see I'm slightly on edge. He might think my impatience has to do with his sister. "Don't worry about me and her. We're good. We've been good. And I love my job. I wanna be here. Alright?" After he nods, I ask, "You want me to grab it for you—whatever *it* is?"

"Nah, I got it." He shuts the door fully and searches behind the café counter. I force myself not to text my dad. I don't want Xander to jump to conclusions about me missing Luna or freak out thinking it's not safe here. *Stay calm.* I'm calm.

I'm calm.

Xander returns with a clean dish towel. I say nothing about it, but he must feel a certain way 'cause he whispers, "She said it didn't hurt, but she's squeamish by blood. There's not that much."

"It happens," I reassure him. "What movie you two watching?" I ask not because I'm super interested in their post-fuck flick. I need a rough estimation of how long they're gonna be in there.

"*Far from the Madding Crowd.*" He rotates the doorknob. "It's one of her favorites, apparently. You seen it?"

"Nah. Let me know how it is."

Xander disappears back into the breakroom. Once the door is

shut, I Google the movie. Two hours. *If* they watch the whole thing.

My dad is headed here. There is no stopping that speeding train.

Option 1: I meet him out on the sidewalk. It leaves this room unprotected. It'd be rolling a dice with Xander's safety, and I'm not willing to play that game.

Option 2: I call for backup. But that'd mean exposing Xander's location to another bodyguard, and I'd be breaking my word to him.

Broken bones or a broken promise. It's an easy choice when I put it like that.

Instead of using comms, I dial a number on my phone. Muscles constricted. I wait for Ian to pick up.

"Donnelly?" His confusion is palpable.

"I have a problem."

"You're calling me?" Ian says in disbelief.

"You're the SFE lead, aren't you? This is the chain of command." I grip my phone tighter. Could throw in a joke, but I'm in hurry and my humor has been washed out. "I can't use comms. I don't want this over the whole line."

"What do you need?"

"Who's closest to Superheroes & Scones?" I ask. "I need two or three guys over here to watch the entrances and exits while I deal with my dad."

"Wait, wait, wait," Ian says. "Slow down. Why are you at Super-heroes & Scones? I thought you were at the Hale House."

"Xander didn't want anyone to know he's here, including the entire security team. He's with a girl. So can we keep this between me, you, and whoever shows up? I'm trusting you here." *And if you break this, I will never fucking trust you again.* It's unspoken. Unsaid.

"Yeah, of course. I'm not in the area or I'd come down. I can make some calls, and I think I can get Vlad, McKenna—"

"Not the rookies, please. Don't tell them anything."

Tension strains the line. "Who do you trust?"

"Anyone else on SFE. Just not them."

"I think I can get Greer and Cruz Jr. over to you in ten minutes."

I eye the front door, expecting a knock at any second. "I don't think that'll be fast enough. My dad's a couple blocks away, if that."

"Don't answer the door."

My stomach unsettles, and I'm quiet.

"Donnelly—"

"Yeah, good advice." I want to tell him to phone Omega, but Ian doesn't offer them as an option for the same reason I don't. Sulli had contractions this morning, and doctors said she might go into labor today or tomorrow. Paparazzi have already descended upon Philly General like a cloud of locusts, so Sulli is staying at the hospital until she gives birth. Akara and Banks called all available Omega bodyguards over there.

"Hey," Ian says. "You did good by calling me."

Yeah, let's hope it wasn't for nothing. We both hang up.

Quickly, I call my dad. "Can't meet you at Superheroes & Scones. Pick a place nearby. I'll be there in fifteen."

"I'm not even twenty feet from the door."

"I'm taking a shit, and I can't let you in. Just go grab a beer. It's on me."

"Fine. I'll meet you at Paddy's."

"See ya." As soon as the call drops, my phone buzzes with a text from Ian. He sent me the radio frequency I'll be using to communicate with only Greer and Cruz Jr. I switch the channel and adjust my earpiece.

"Donnelly to SFE, you read me?" I stride over to a backpack I threw on the vinyl booth, moving farther away from the breakroom.

Comms crackle.

"Loud and clear," Greer answers. "Where do you want us to come in? Back door or front?"

"Back." I unearth a black box and click the mic at my collar. "My dad's at the front. Once you're inside, I need someone to post outside of the breakroom while I talk to him. It might be an hour. If you could not alert Xander of your presence, that'd be great. I don't want to freak him out."

"Copy that."

With Xander secured, my headspace reroutes to my dad. I pop the black box and fish out a new mic. Hands shaking, I hook the mic under my shirt to my bare chest. I use voice command to call one person on my phone.

"Paul?" Luna's dad says.

"Dad's in the area," I say fast. "Wondering how you feel about moving up the meeting to...like now. At Paddy's Pub?"

"Take a breath."

"I'm breathing." *I'm shaking.* I can't get the wire to adhere to my sweaty skin. I mutter a curse, which Luna's dad hears.

"You can't postpone?"

"Nah, I can't. I have to meet him right now even if you don't come."

"I'll be there." I hear the slam of a car door. "Tell him I'm on the way. And Paul?"

"Yeah?"

"*Breathe.*"

69

PAUL DONNELLY

Paddy's is having a slow afternoon. I ushered my dad to a secluded back corner. Choosing a four-seater pub table—we're not in view of the street windows or even the bar. A few TVs play reruns of last night's Phillies game. Feels private enough.

"Loren Hale's coming now?" my dad repeats with arched brows, like I'm pulling his leg.

"He'd been in the area too." I suck on a cigarette, trying to relax.

"'K, let's get this out before he shows up." My dad takes a large gulp from his pint of Guinness and then bows forward. "I told you no one would talk before the hearing. Well, you heard they took the plea deal?"

They were facing three first-degree felony charges. Kidnapping, assault, meth. Racked up to a total of fifty years without parole. It's a max sentencing for some of the charges, but if they stood trial, they were looking at doing more time. So they took the plea, and now they're in prison till Luna's seventy-one. Hell, some of them will die in there.

Which is justice to me.

"Yeah, I heard." I blow smoke to the side.

"I got Roark to talk. He has nothing really to lose at this point." He taps ash from his cigarette onto a ceramic tray, cupping the pint with his other hand. "He said the original plan had involved Xander Hale—they thought he'd be in that car going to that putt-putt place or whatever that article said. They knew the Hales' whereabouts from the media, is what I'm saying."

"Why Xander?" I ask him.

"He's the most famous Hale kid, right? Outside of the oldest one who married your friend. Teens lose their shit over Xander Hale. Can't scroll two damn pages on social media without seeing a promoted 'news' article about what he's wearing or caught doing. That goes for most of those families though. He's just the one the shady journalist wanted pictures of. Well, him and Lily Calloway."

I grimace.

He sweeps me, almost compassionately. "You sure you don't want a pint?"

I'm on-duty. "Just wanna smoke." I take another drag. "Did this journalist ask for a certain kind of picture or did they just get creative and decide to beat the shit outta a woman?" Venom seeps into my bloodstream.

He wipes the condensation off the pint glass. "They're pieces of shit. No denying that. And…from what Roark could tell me, the journalist prompted them to *make it good.* Specifically, they wanted photos of him nearly naked."

My stomach roils. "Nearly naked?"

"That's what Roark said." He raises his hands. "They were gonna strip Xander down to his underwear, take some pics, and leave him on the side of the road."

I stiffen. "Why didn't they do that to Luna? Why kidnap her instead?"

"The plan was to leave all the other Hales in the car alone, untouched. The journalist wasn't gonna pay shit for their photos. They were clear about that. Just Xander. Just Lily." He lowers his voice to a whisper. "They fuckin' panicked. They didn't wanna leave her there, so they just took her. They had no plan when it came to your girlfriend—you saw it that night. They were *fucking* idiots." He brings his cigarette to his mouth. "Now look at 'em. *Fifty* years."

I lean back more, chair creaking underneath me. I try to picture that alternate timeline. It's different but the same. Just adding someone else into a boatload of trauma my family inflicts on the people I love.

But this was it.

This was the information I've been tasked to obtain from my dad. There should be confetti cannons and celebratory applause in my head—but it's just quiet. Too quiet.

"They should've dragged the journalist down with 'em."

"No kidding." He blows smoke upward, thinking. "Guy never gave his real name. Roark said he only accepted physical photos at a drop off. Nothing over the internet or text. As far as they know, they were contacting him through a burner phone. He's untraceable, but he paid up so they didn't give a shit."

"There's nothing else known about him? Not even a description?"

"Nah, nothing." He picks up his pint. "Donnellys are at the bottom of the food chain, son. Whoever that guy was, he's more in the middle. He had connections to that big media firm...Rochester Industries. He's not gonna go down."

Rochester Industries. I let out a sigh. Shoulda known the Roaches have their hands somewhere in this moldy cookie jar. It's not completely unexpected either. The first news stations to broadcast photos of Lily that night—they're owned by Rochester Industries.

"Looks like he's here," my dad says, and I snap my gaze behind me. Twisting fully around, I stand as Loren Hale strides into the secluded corner with a wet umbrella. He lifts black Ray Bans to the top of his head, his narrowed gaze could cut glass. But that's also a normal expression for Lo.

He's dressed down in jeans and a plain red T-shirt, and my dad is on his feet, already extending a hand to greet him.

"Sean Donnelly," he says lightly.

Lo's eyes briefly flicker to me, as though checking to see if I'm in one piece. I'm smoking. I'm waiting for a basket of hand-cut chips my dad ordered for the table. Just need this to hurry up. I have about forty-five minutes before Xander might notice I'm gone.

I'm picturing him opening the door and seeing Greer. He's gonna be confused and hurt and all the trust he has in me will obliterate before I can even explain myself.

I can't let that happen.

Lo shakes his hand and forces a dry smile. "You get stuck in the rain?"

"Me? Nah, I just walked here." He returns to his seat, glancing over at Lo's bodyguard from Security Force Alpha. Bruno Bandoni stays posted about ten feet away. His back to us. Eyes on the pub. "You know that guy?" He's asking me.

"Sure do," I say. "Even know he's allergic to shellfish and will put down a whole bottle of warm sake."

Bruno turns his head slightly, and I see his smile.

"Huh," my dad says in thought.

We're all sitting now, and my dad has trained his attention on Lo, who's cutting through him with an intrusive stare.

But my dad's not cowering or shrinking back. "You want a beer?" He's about to flag down the server.

"I'm an alcoholic," Lo states dryly.

"Ah, so you put 'em back better than the rest?" He smiles at the joke.

I rub at the back of my stiff neck.

Lo threads his arms. "More like, I put them back *worse* than everyone else."

"Matter of perception." My dad sizes him up. "No beer then." He tips his head towards me. "You must be rubbing off on my son. 'Cause I haven't seen him turn down a pint in I don't know how long." He acts like this is something we do every Saturday together. Bond over a beer and the Phillies.

We don't.

We never did.

Lo wafts smoke out of his face. He's being dramatic. The air is barely hazy. "I'm not rubbing off on him enough—or else he would've flushed those down the toilet." He's glaring at the cigarette between my fingers and the pack on the table.

"And flush twenty bucks?" I chime in.

"My bad, I forgot you'd rather just flush your lungs."

I start to grin. "You want me to use your toilet? I can clog your pipes as a parting gift."

"Gee, thanks. I'll pay someone to gift-wrap your diseased, toilet-water lungs and then give them to my daughter. She would just *love* that."

He got me there. "Yeah, don't do that."

"Then quit smoking."

"In time," I say lightly, but I don't take another drag.

My dad's watching me and Lo like a ping-pong match. He takes a smaller sip of Guinness, then asks Lo, "You don't smoke, don't drink—what, do you hate tattoos too?"

I laugh hard.

Lo begins to smile down at the table.

"What?" my dad asks me, confusion in his brows.

"Yeah, he hates 'em," I say. "He'd probably try to take a Brillo pad to my body if he could."

"Not a Brillo pad," Lo says. "I've thought about throwing him in a car wash."

"Spending the big bucks on me," I grin. "Just make sure you do the wax cycle. It's my favorite."

Lo just smiles—a fonder and softer one that I've never seen from him. A server brings out the chips and some waters. My dad has gone quiet, but Lo picks up the deadened air and asks him, "You're planning on staying clean?"

"Yeah, that's the plan," my dad says, more tensely. "But it's not always easy. I don't have a staff of sober coaches or anything."

I stiffen again.

Lo seems understanding. "My oldest son created a program called One More Day. It provides aid to those who need addiction rehab. I can get you in—"

"I don't want your charity," my dad cuts in. It shocks me, even more so when he says, "That's not what this is about."

"That is what this is about," Lo says more heatedly. "I have four kids. I can't be the father they need me to be when I'm drinking. You have a son. You can't be the father he needs you to be when you're using. And before you say it's easy for me, it's not. Every goddamn day, I think about it. Every day, I fight it." His eyes flash to the Guinness, then away. "If it's pride—"

"I'm not too proud. I know what I am. I know what you think of me." He cups his pint, the air thicker and strained. "I just don't want my son to think I'm using him for connections."

I frown. "This is the one connection I'd want you to use."

It washes over his face. Like it's such a surprise how badly I'd want him to stay clean. That I'd be willing to draw him into the Hales' sphere for it.

He nods in acceptance. "Alright." He takes a short drag. "What about your mom? Can we get her in too? When she gets out?"

My throat is dry. "Yeah, sure." I look to Lo. I dunno why. His sharp cheekbones and cutting glare should be the least comforting place to rest my eyes, but I ease every single time I remember he's there.

"There's a spot for her too," Lo assures. "But we need to talk about Vanessa."

"Vanessa?" My dad rocks back. "You know who Vanessa is?"

Lo splays a hand at me like *tell him*.

I exhale a short breath. "She called me."

"She called you?" His face darkens. "Like hell she did." His eyes dart to Lo, like he's still surprised I shared this fun fact with Luna's dad. "How'd she get your number?"

"Bridget."

"Your mom?" His voice pitches unnaturally, like I just sunk a knife in his chest. "She's not talking to Vanessa. She said—"

"I just talked to her yesterday," I say. "She admitted to giving her my number, and she gave me every excuse as to why. *Vanessa's clean. Vanessa's only looking out for me and you. Vanessa is gonna help me when I get outta here. You'll see.* It's the same shit, same story."

"I'll talk to her," he nods. My face falls. He adds deeply, "*I'll talk to her.*" He's distraught. "I'm not giving up on your mom."

"I'm not trying to either—"

"You're not giving her a chance!" he shouts, then balls up his fists and leans back again. "She's your *mother.*"

It drives into a place inside myself I can't even see. "I don't even know what that means," I choke out, and I look away from both Lo and Sean. *A mother.* "No, I do." I turn back and stare right at my dad. "It means counting down to being let out of a hospital and hobbling on crutches just so you can physically hug and wish your kid a happy birthday. It means sending over leftover meatloaf because your kid skipped dinner, but you still don't want 'em to go hungry. It means giving them a roof over their head when theirs is gone, for however long they need it." I tell him, "No matter how much I wanted her to be one, Bridget was never a mother to me. Could she become one? I dunno, maybe. But as long as she's talking to Vanessa, I want nothing to do with her."

He's nodding repeatedly, his eyes bloodshot. It's sinking in, I think. "Alright, alright." He wipes his mouth with a shaky hand. "She'll stop talking to her. I promise. I promise. I'll get her to stop."

I'm not holding my breath.

Rain has let up when I jog back to Superheroes & Scones. We weren't at the pub for much longer. Seemed like my dad was in a hurry to track down Vanessa and wring her neck. I texted Lo to listen to the recording from the wire I wore.

At least I don't have to rehash that conversation. But next time I see my dad, I won't be mic'd up. This was the end of me being an informant. It's done.

It's over.

I breathe out the deepest breath when I enter the store. Greer sees me exhaling, but he has no idea how much weight just lifted off my body. Seeing him posted outside the breakroom eases tension off me too. *He kept Xander safe.*

Everything's gonna be okay, as the saying goes.

Greer whispers, "You good?"

"Yeah." I reach under my shirt and tug off the wire. "It's taken care of."

He motions to the door. "He never came out. Sounds like he's still watching the movie." He pats my shoulder before swapping out with me. I thank him before he goes.

Xander messages me from inside the breakroom, asking if I can spare a bodyguard for Spencer. To take her home. He didn't realize she took public transit, and he wants to make sure she gets home okay. But they don't want to be seen in a car together.

"I've got Cruz Jr. on the back door," I tell Xander when he's in the main storefront. "He can take her home, unless you want me to drive her." I explain how I had to call extra bodyguards for the entrance and exits. He seems cool with it, especially now that it's helping Spencer.

"I'll go with Cruz Jr. You can drive her." Xander knows me better than CJ, so he trusts me more to take her home.

I'm able to coordinate with Epsilon to get Xander safely in his car while I take another security vehicle to drive Spencer to her parents' house. After dropping her off, I'm back to the gated neighborhood and radioing in my location. Calling it a day.

I park outside of Epsilon's mansion. Gonna walk back to the Hale House. I shut off the ignition and climb out of the SUV.

"Greer to Donnelly." My radio crackles in my ear. "Bravo Zulu."

Banks once told me that guys in the Navy only give out a Bravo Zulu (job well done) as highest praise. Didn't expect to ever hear it from anyone, let alone the most senior guy on Epsilon.

Definitely didn't expect to hear it today.

Bravo Zulu.

With more pep in my step, I smile and go home to Luna.

DONNELLY'S DAILY PLANNER
Sunday, April 21st

Today's Focus: date the girl, love the girl, you know what to do.

To Do:

- Regular Sunday afternoon protecting X.

- Date night! Ballet in NYC with your gf.

- Celebrate Tom's 21st b-day afterward. clubbing??

- Let the good times roll.

- + tell gf about my past with sex. Time has come.

Notes: Another Fizzle event in the books. MLB x Fizzle collab got off on a weird foot with the bat boy being handsy towards Luna. Xander told me to step in. (Best wingman. Facts.) Also, it confirmed I wasn't hallucinating. I swooped in so fast, I coulda been the Eagles mascot. Flirted hard-core with my girlfriend on home plate. Kissed her. Twirled her around. Nothing could top it.

Not even rubbing elbows with a few baseball legends.

Fav event so far.

Before the MLB collab, a Kitsulletti baby graced the earth. Seven Kitsuwon Meadows. Dope ass name imo. Born on the 7th of April. Healthy baby, healthy mom, two happy dads. Media is rabid for newborn pics. Triad are holing up in their new apartment above Studio 9. Don't blame 'em.

Penthouse = uninhabitable. They're demoing four walls? Idk.

Still living at the Hale House. Still waiting to move back in.

Also! wtf is happening to The Independent? Heard the building management is jacking up the rent on the whole block. Trying to run out all the Philly staples to put in a chipotle prob.

Meals: Eat an Eggo at the Hale House. Tom's b-day dinner at a NYC French joint.

~~Water:~~ GF's Pussy: Satisfied and gratified. Already fucked her good. Gonna eat her out tonight *pray hands*

Question of the Day: How hard is it to forge adoption papers? (Brb gonna ask Beckett to adopt me for a Wednesday Night Dinner.)

EMAIL FROM SAM STOKES

FROM: samstokes@fizzle.com

TO: dontemailme1882@yahoo.com, eliotalice@gmail.com, benpirripcobalt@upenn.edu, aragorn1225@gmail.com, queenofthebula@gmail.com

After the MLB x Fizzle Collab, the rankings are as follows:

1. Charlie Keating Cobalt
2. Eliot Alice Cobalt
3. Ben Pirrip Cobalt
4. Luna Hale
5. Xander Hale

Your feedback:

Xander: Again, please put yourself out there. Spending most of the time in the dugout reading a book will not earn you any points. (-2 spots in the ranking)

Ben: Way to bounce back. The board loved your involvement with the camera crew and your athleticism. You showed you were willing to do whatever was asked. (+2 spots in the ranking)

Luna: The board thought you were a little awkward trying to hit the ball for the shoot. If there are any situations that you feel unsuited for, remember you can say no. However, I appreciate the initiative, and your demographic from our test group had strong reactions to the photos of you and Donnelly on home plate. We'll talk later about possibly using them for marketing. (- neutral, no shift)

Eliot: Overall, a favorite. You have the tenacity, engagement, charm, and fervor to serve as a successor. Keep it up. (- neutral, no shift)

Charlie: The board would like to see a little more tenacity like Eliot. How much do you want this? Show them. (- neutral, no shift)

70

LUNA HALE

Date nights with Donnelly are hallmarks to my life now. I love them, I love them, I love him. We were eating out of the same Wendy's french fry container in the Volvo, driving to New York for the ballet, and I looked over at him while he was passionately describing a new panel for our comic book—and I thought, this is the best part of our date.

And then we sat side by side as the lights dimmed at the ballet. Butterflies fluttered in my stomach, and romantic music to Swan Lake filled the theatre. Beckett leapt with such effortlessness and grace. While our eyes were on the stage, Donnelly's fingers brushed along my neck and down the length of my shoulder in absentminded, affectionate strokes. Like he was painting a picture in the dark. And I thought, *this is the best part.*

Then at a French-inspired bistro for dinner, we celebrated Tom's birthday and shared mussels. He made sure I got enough to eat, and I thought, *this is it. This is the best part for me.*

It's now one a.m., and we've been club-hopping for the past hour. And as the cool night air kisses my skin, and Donnelly warms my body by folding his arms over mine, I know the best part is everything. It's all of him. Every moment, every second. Our date nights could be us doing nothing, and I will never stop loving them.

I will never stop loving him.

These declarations swell inside me, but they teeter uneasily at invasive thoughts of the future. Where are we going from here? What's next for us?

Can't this moment just last forever?

I'm clinging to the present. Maybe because I still see how fleeting a moment can be. Sulli is gone. Not *gone* gone, but I thought…I thought I had so much more time being her roommate. She was going to eat Cheerios with me and laugh about the penthouse rules. It wasn't supposed to end yet. Then the rug got ripped out from under my feet.

She left. She…moved on. Everyone is going to move on, eventually. I'm not ready. *I'm not ready.* I want to preserve where we all are.

Bottle the essence and never cast it out to sea.

So that's what I'm doing. Inhaling the electric essence of tonight. Bottling it deep. In case this is the last one I'll ever have like this.

At Pink Noir, a favorite club among Beckett's ballet friends (they've joined us on this endless celebratory birthday night), I'm sweaty and sticky from dancing with Donnelly, and we take a breather at the bar. He whispers in my ear, "I need to talk to you later."

"Okay." Not sure what about, but he's relaxed and carefree, so I'm guessing it's not such a critical talk.

After ordering waters, our fingers stay hooked, but we're turned away from one another and speaking to different groups of people.

My ears catch his convo with Oscar. "It's going to close down, bro. It's been around since the eighties. The owner is like a hundred," Oscar says to Donnelly. "Even if he could afford to keep the bar open, he'd probably cash out and retire. Legitimately, it's sad, but security will find a new hangout bar. It's time to move on."

"It's *The Independent*," Donnelly says passionately. "There is no moving on, man. It's supposed to outlive us all!"

Okay, I feel a bit better knowing I'm not the only one wanting to Medusa people and places so they turn to stone and stay right where they are.

Forever.

And ever.

Please?

"...and then she left happy," Beckett finishes a short story to Charlie about a one-night stand. They both angle their bodies to include me, even if I haven't said much. "It was fine, if not uneventful."

"She was too nice," Charlie deduces. They both nurse glasses of chilled tequila.

Beckett lifts the glass to his lips. "There's nothing wrong with nice."

"There is for you," Charlie says, elbows on the bar. "You like a hate-fuck."

Beckett sees me watching too carefully, and I wonder if my invisibility cloak is glitching. "He's exaggerating," he tells me like we're discussing something *mundane*. Not, you know, his sex life. Except, maybe he does think his sex life is mundane! Bingo! I've solved this quadratic equation.

I shimmy my shoulders, drink some water, and ask, "By how much?"

"By nothing," Charlie says the same time Beckett replies, "A lot." To which Beckett says in a sip of tequila, "Let's talk about something else."

"What's a Bad Anne?" I ask.

Charlie and Beckett swing their heads in unison to me. It's one of the few twin-like mannerisms I've caught them doing tonight.

"Where'd you hear that?" Beckett wonders.

"Backstage at the ballet tonight. I overheard the staff, I think. They looked like instructors or directors of the company. They kept referencing a Bad Anne. Like a bad apple?"

Beckett winces like that's not quite right.

Charlie is glaring. "You all call her *Bad Anne*?"

"Not us," Beckett says with a sigh. "The staff knows she's not up to par, Charlie." Beckett explains to me, "There's Beth Anne and Roxanne. Every dancer I know calls them by name, but our staff has taken to referring to them as the Good Anne and the Bad

Anne. Partly because they're close friends, but mostly because Roxy has been trailing behind NYBC's standards." He's staring into his brother. "*Stop*."

"I said nothing." He downs a swig of tequila. I grimace at how that would've burned, but Charlie has the same irritated expression.

"You don't even know her," Beckett tells him.

He replies in French—with a phrase that I'm fairly certain means, *I'm aware.*

I sense tension. "Is it bad if he does?"

Charlie and Beckett say nothing, as if gauging how to respond. But Beckett ends up warning his brother, "She's soft." I know they're still talking about the Bad Anne.

Charlie downs the rest of his tequila.

"Beck!" Donnelly calls on the other side of me. "What's the name of that one hotel near Central Park? Where they put mints on your pillows?"

Beckett rounds my body and joins the other conversation behind me. Leaving me with Charlie, who's flagging down the bartender and ordering more tequila. "Want anything?"

"Uh-uh. I'm hydrating."

Charlie comes right out and tells me, "I promised Beckett I'd never be involved with anyone in his company."

"But you like her?"

"I can't like someone I don't even know." He spins his empty glass, then hears Eliot and Tom singing a French song loudly together while in pursuit of us. Charlie side-eyes me. "Your best friends."

"Your brothers," I tell him.

His lips nearly rise, then he pushes away from the bar, just as Eliot and Tom encroach.

"Going so soon?" Eliot tries to sling an arm over Charlie's shoulder, who slips out of the embrace. "We're running him off, Tom."

"On my birthday?!" Tom scoffs in mock offense. "Charlie Keating? How could you?"

"How could I not?" Charlie says, moving in the direction of the bathroom, not the exit. Oscar is quick to detach himself from the other convo to follow his client.

"No pissing on Tom's birthday!" Eliot shouts after him.

"Yeah, dude, you must pee your pants!" Tom yells.

I laugh, and they settle on one side of me since Donnelly is still holding my hand. Friendship trio intact. Eliot and Tom did not, in fact, rope Donnelly into it. Instead, every time I've hung out with my best friends, Donnelly has just spent more time with Beckett. Rebuilding the bond they used to have. But it's different this time around, Donnelly said. He feels closer to him. Because he's not his bodyguard.

He's just his friend.

"What was that about?" Eliot asks me, referring to Charlie. "Spill."

"Hate-fucking," I shrug, then tilt my head. "I've never had a hate-fuck that I can remember."

"That she can remember," Eliot notes and mimes to the bartender more waters. Then he pushes the tequila that Charlie ordered at the birthday boy.

Tom sways, verging from tipsy to drunk. He holds on to the bar. "That's depressing."

I nod in agreement. "I don't like thinking about BD."

"Big dicks?"

"Before Donnelly," I say.

"Dark times indeed," Eliot props an elbow on the bar. We turn slightly to face the club. Pink strobe lights sweep bodies swaying rhythmically on the dance floor. I wonder how many professional dancers frequent this club.

Just as I think it, one of the ballet dancers from Beckett's company thrusts out of the sweaty throngs and jogs up to the bar so abruptly, I have to break my clutch from Donnelly. He physically barrels through our chained hands like we're playing Red Rover.

"Sorry," he barely apologizes, bowed halfway over the bar. He yells out, "Kevin!"

"One sec, LV!" Kevin calls back, sounding friendly. He's pouring espresso martinis for a gaggle of girls at the other end.

This dancer is too familiar—his dirty-blond hair nearly brown with the sweat. He greets me with a blinding smile for point-two seconds, as if feeling the heat of my stare. "Leo Valavanis. Your cousin so rudely forgot to introduce me." He snaps a wiseass look at Beckett, who's very, very close. Right on the other side of Donnelly.

Beckett narrows his yellow-green eyes. "Purposefully."

"Which was rude," Leo says. "But it's okay, you have a laundry list of flaws, and you do like to keep it *clean.*"

My eyes pop out.

Eliot and Tom are too far away and can't hear this over the music, or else I think they would've shot forward.

Donnelly has the faintest grin, and he shakes his head subtly to me, like saying, *it's okay.* Weird. But Donnelly knows the ballet dancers better than most. When we were backstage, they all shouted, "Hey, Don! Hey, Don!" and "Welcome back, Don!" like one big inside joke.

I often forget he spent years inside Beckett's daily New York routine.

Beckett's jaw twitches. "Why are you still here?"

"I ask the same thing about you every day, Cobalt," Leo says. "Why is he still around? You're all technique. No passion. And then I realize…" Leo grips the bar casually. "You are nothing without me, and I'm nothing without you." They share this deep, fiery look—like an aggravation is burning a hole through both of them from their unceasing rivalry, stoked by their ballet company.

"LV!" Kevin motions him down the bar.

"Bye, Don," Leo says to my boyfriend. To me, "The cousin." Then to Eliot and Tom, "The brother and the brother." He winks at Tom.

Beckett bristles and stares him down, and Leo grins wider at Beckett. "What? You love it, Cobalt. Do you hear that? It's the water *roaring.*"

Beckett is often referred to as being calm like idle *water* among the Cobalt Empire.

Donnelly laughs only when Leo has gone. "That was clever. Just sayin'."

"He's infuriating," Beckett refutes and glares down at the end of the bar where Leo is speaking to Kevin. I sense a spark of hate, but it's not like me hating Jeffra. Or Donnelly hating O'Malley. It's a lingering hate, a gripping hate...an attraction.

Which makes sense why Donnelly knew Beckett wouldn't be offended by Leo's insult. Not if he's kinda into it.

What throws me off though—I always thought Beckett was straight.

In the next minute, Beckett asks Donnelly if he wants to step outside for a smoke. Donnelly kisses my cheek, saying he'll be back in a few minutes. Frog and Quinn have been hanging ten or so feet away, pretending to dance, but they're mostly watching me at the bar.

Likewise, Eliot and Tom's bodyguards hover close, and I notice O'Malley trailing after Beckett, protecting my cousin during this nighttime extravaganza.

"The archrival," Eliot muses while Leo carries his mixed drink back onto the dance floor.

"He winked at me. You see that?" Tom slurs a little, sipping more tequila.

"I saw his eye twitch funny," Eliot insults.

Tom clears a lump in his throat and watches Leo rotate his head to the music like the melody is coursing through him. "He's...sort of hot."

What? My eyes widen again.

Eliot goes still. "Come again?"

Tom mumbles out something, then sips his tequila.

Eliot snaps his gaze to me. "Did he just say, *I'd let him fuck me?*"

I nod. "I think I heard a garbled version of that, yep."

"I have *vies*," Tom slurs. "Okay, I can *see*." He gestures dramatically at the crowds. "And you know what...I know it's wrong. Because

Beckett Joyce wouldn't want *him*"—he flings an arm backwards, then points to his chest—"with me."

I nod robustly, nervous for this messy scenario. Since I have a hunch Beckett is kinda into Leo. "Yep."

"But I've got *vies*." He puts a palm to his chest.

I stroke the back of his head, and Tom relaxes at the touch. And I say, "He has *vies*, Eliot."

"If he likes his *vies*, he'd keep them off our brother's adversary."

"But he's so hot," Tom groans like it's a struggle. "And he *winked* at me."

"Eye twitch," Eliot shoots me a look to say the same.

"Coulda been a dust particle itch." I sing-song, "Possibilities."

"You know…" Tom stares sadly at the tequila. "He's my secret… the crush." *His secret crush.*

My mouth falls. "Holy…wow, Batman." This is getting worse.

Eliot shuts his eyes like he'd prefer to apparate out of the club. "Wake me up when this nightmare ends."

"Eliot, dude, seriously," Tom turns to his brother. "I think I really like him. Like he…winked—"

"Tomorrow, *tomorrow*, brother. You will feel differently when the hangover and treason set in."

"Yeah…you're probably right."

"Hydrate," I say, and we all swig waters together. Bathroom break time. We let Tom use the toilet first, and Eliot and I stand in the black-painted hall lined with film noir posters. *Double Indemnity. The Maltese Falcon.* And neo-noir films. *Brick. Blade Runner.*

Charlie is nowhere to be seen, so maybe he slipped out of this quiet alcove already.

"…I'm their favorite, yet I'm not number one," Eliot says, reading the email from Uncle Stokes for the first time. It was sent earlier tonight. "Where's the lie?"

"We're fighting for second," I remind him.

"I'll dethrone my brother," Eliot assures me, his eyes gleaming on the phone. "One way or another." I'm not sure he's completely accepted the consequence of beating Charlie. It means he'll be stuck in a corporate job for *life*.

"You're the closest to it," I tell him.

"You're not so far behind." Eliot pockets his phone.

"The test group had *strong reactions* to the pics of me and Donnelly messing around on home plate." I tug at my mesh sparkly blue top, seeing a liquor spill seeping into my visible bra underneath. "Uncle Stokes didn't say *positive*. So they could be strong *negative* reactions."

Eliot points out, "They liked those flirty photos enough to want to use them for advertisements."

That's true. And for marketing, having a strong reaction of any kind is better than having an indifferent one. I'm just not sure they'll ever see me as a viable candidate. Maybe I'm more useful as a tool to promote Fizzle, but not run it.

"I don't even know why I care so much," I mutter to myself. The thought of losing this opportunity—that feels so far out of reach anyway—has been flipping my stomach.

Eliot doesn't hear. He drinks the last of his water and chucks the plastic into the trash bin beneath the *Blade Runner* poster. It's quiet here. Mostly due to our bodyguards barricading other clubbers from entering by announcing the bathrooms are occupied.

Which they are.

One is out of order. The other, Tom is taking his sweet time in. Eliot knocks on the door, checking to see if he's good. When he gets the *okay*, Eliot spins back to me with a more serious expression. "You haven't remembered anything about what I told you yet?"

His secret. The one I forgot. "No, I...I don't remember." I see his jaw tense and face pinch. "You were hoping I would?"

Eliot scrapes a hand through his wavy hair. "It's the worst thing I've ever done. It killed me..." He exhales. "I never wanted to tell you the first time, but I couldn't keep it in. Now it's *festering* in me, and..." He grimaces, his blue eyes veering to a gold-framed mirror between the bathroom doors. He drops his gaze abruptly, like he can't even stare at his own torment.

It hurts. "I don't have to know."

"You deserve to," Eliot murmurs. "It involves you."

My pulse skips. "Me?" I didn't think his secret had *anything* to do with me.

"I was just trying to protect you." His eyes redden. "From Jeffra."

Jeffra. I open my mouth, but no sound escapes. *Jeffra.* I know what he's trying to say. Brain itch. It's scraping at the surface, but I can't *see*. Frustration heavies my breathing. "You did something...?"

"After she bullied you in Penn's dining hall—"

"The YouTube video," I interject in realization. "You spoke to Jeffra when I left the dining hall." I totally forgot to ask Eliot about that video clip. "She whispered something to you."

Eliot drops his voice a fraction. "I wanted to know what it'd take to get her to *stop*. To stop making your life a hell. And she said..." The words sound thick in his throat. "*Sleep with me.*"

It crashes against my lungs. I rock back, winded. "Eliot—"

"She's *twisted*. She knew it'd kill me to betray you, and it'd pain you to know it."

"Or she has a thing for you."

Eliot cringes, "Yeah. Or that. Which could be for my benefit."

I wince. "Eliot, *no*. You didn't have to do that—"

"I didn't have sex with her," he cuts me off fast. "I fully intended to follow through. I even thought I had a leg up on Jeffra because I'd tell you the truth. I'd *never* keep it a secret for her to use against me or you. So I met her at her dorm one night, and once I was there, I started thinking about how easily she could go back on this deal. We'd have sex, and she'd keep harassing you. So I made her a different offer."

Okay, *okay*. My heartbeat tries to slow. "What kinda offer?"

"We could exchange nudes. She'd have dirt on me, and I'd have dirt on her."

"She agreed to that?"

"I think she gets off on humiliation. Which isn't my kink, but she seemed fairly annoyed when I had no issue letting her see me naked. I'm in theatre. Or *was* in theatre. Quick-changes backstage were routine, but..." His expression turns grave again.

"But what?"

"She played me." He grinds his molars. "I didn't want to see her naked—I didn't want to give her that sort of satisfaction. So when she took her photos, I turned my back and gave her privacy."

"Eliot..."

"I know. *I know.* I sent her mine, and she sent me a fully clothed selfie blowing me a kiss. To mock me."

"But she hasn't leaked your nudes?"

"No, but I'm betting she's showed half her friends. I don't care. *I don't care,*" he repeats seeing my face twist in guilt. "It's not your fault, Luna. This was *my* choice. I'd do anything for our family, you know that." He eases as I nod back. "The worst part is knowing Charlie wouldn't have been duped. He would've eviscerated her... but why...why the fuck couldn't I?" His gaze falls. "I go too far, but still, it's never enough."

I fling my arms around his muscled body in a sudden hug.

Eliot squeezes me back, and I tell him, "Thank you for loving me enough to try." I feel his chest collapse as he releases a breath.

He whispers, "Always."

I'm glad he's not Charlie. There's never any question of how much Eliot loves me and how many times he would die for me. It's unwavering loyalty with no obligation to return it, but I hope I can always give it back. There is no one who deserves as much devotion from our family than him.

Tom tries to clink his heels like a Broadway star on his bathroom exit, and he stumbles and trips into Eliot's arms. We're all laughing, especially as Tom throws a drunken, triumphant fist in the air.

"Duke's on 10th?" Eliot suggests an all-hours diner in Hell's Kitchen.

Time to sober up the birthday boy.

The caravan of party people shortens as Beckett's ballet friends hip-hop over to another club and Charlie bails to who knows where. Oscar has to follow him, so Donnelly is down a friend from Omega.

Bulbed marquee lighting frames the humongous Duke's on 10th sign. The retro American diner looks straight from the 1950s. Teal vinyl booths, Elvis Presley booming through a jukebox, and the clink-clank sound of spatulas flipping burgers on a griddle. It smells like ketchup, fries, and greasy onion rings.

Outside of two women with dark mascara and drunken giggles, slurping milkshakes at the bar, the diner isn't busy.

Donnelly carries me piggyback to a vacant booth, and we're singing happy birthday to Tom with Beckett and our bodyguards while Eliot pretends to orchestrate the off-key melodies. I don't want this night to end. My heart pangs. *Bottle, bottle, bottle. Preserve, preserve, preserve,* I chant to my brain.

Don't forget.

Never forget.

"Will you remind me?" I whisper against Donnelly's ear. "If I ever forget this?"

Donnelly slowly lowers me to my feet and spins around to face me. All the while, my family spills into a vacant booth behind him. He holds my cheek with such love. I melt into his palm, especially as he says, "You won't forget, Luna," he whispers. "It's like you said, you never really could. And if you ever need reminding, we're creating something bigger than a diary."

Our life together. Visually depicted in a comic book.

The comic book has been helping both of us process the past. Donnelly with his childhood and me with my memories. I haven't considered how it could be a map in case I ever lose them again.

What overwhelms me the most...Donnelly is the one drawing the map. His love is bled into the pages.

He breathes, "We can add this night to it."

I slip my fingers in his beltloops. "It'll go down as a best-best night for Princess Solana. But she has *many* of those with Vaughn."

His eyes sparkle. "Ditto." We're about to kiss when my phone beeps in my butt pocket. Donnelly drops his hand off my face as I retrieve it.

I check the text, and my face plummets with my stomach. "Luna?"

"I don't...understand." My breathing shortens.

> You have any pics you wanna send me of tonight, space
> babe? ;) — 215-555-9000

I look up at Donnelly. "I think someone's trying to impersonate you."

71

PAUL DONNELLY

What the fuck is going on? Luna lets me take her phone, and I tell her I'll handle this while she orders us burgers. She slips in the booth beside Beckett. While she's perusing the menu and trying to keep a happy face, I'm hoping to squash this threat like...now.

No random asshole should have her new number.

This shouldn't be happening.

Luna and her cousins are blissfully unaware that someone has been leaking our location all fucking night. It's the strangest thing. 'Cause no one is tailing us. We've had temps scout the whole block for a car or a person who's tracking our footsteps from one club to the next.

Nothing.

There isn't even *paparazzi* here. They're all busy flocking Philly and the new Kitsulletti baby. We've had the occasional Charlie stan show up, but besides that, none of us can figure out why there's a live-feed update called "Tom Cobalt's birthday night out" with our whereabouts. It's all being posted on a tabloid's social media.

People keep commenting, *pics or it didn't happen.* There aren't photos, so this Donnelly-impersonator asking my girlfriend to send pics—it smells like spoiled Chicken of the Sea.

"What about that one guy?" Quinn asks me, watching me type on her phone.

I've already caught up Quinn, Frog, the Wreath brothers, and O'Malley—the only bodyguards at Duke's on 10th—on the text-spam Luna just received. I'm off-duty, and none of 'em care that I've popped a squat at their circular table. We're near the windows and entrance. Out of earshot from Luna and the Cobalts but they're still visible.

"What guy?" Ian asks with scrunched brows.

"Think he's referring to Keagan Bell," I say. "The guy who'd been harassing Luna with texts. It can't be him though. He doesn't have her new number."

"He could've found it," O'Malley rationalizes. "It wouldn't be that hard." They've all stopped flipping through the menus, their attention rooted on this potential threat.

"He never tried to impersonate me." I send a message off Luna's cell: Who is this?

He's quick.

Your boyfriend, silly. — 215-555-9000

I frown. "This has to be a prank."

"And a bad one," Quinn makes a face. "Don't they know you're with her right now?"

"I dunno…" My head is pounding.

Frog picks up her phone. "Don't we have a list of numbers Luna saved as *unknown* in her contacts? We can see if there's a match to this one."

Who even has Luna's new number? Her family. And security…

The rat in Epsilon. That Bernard temp already got canned. Maybe he wasn't the one spilling private intel to the tabloids. I peer around at each of them. Are they among me? It's hard for me to believe. O'Malley, Ian, and Vance wouldn't risk the safety of these families for a tabloid cash-grab.

I read out the 215 number, then I ask, "Did anyone say anything over comms about me splitting up from Luna tonight?"

NOBODY LIKE US *641*

"I did," O'Malley raises a finger. "I said you went out for a smoke with Beckett."

"I said Luna went to the bathroom with Tom and Eliot," Frog remembers.

Ian goes rigid. "You think this is coming from inside, Donnelly?"

"It makes the most sense."

O'Malley nods, "Whoever is in comms range can listen to our frequency and figure out where we're going without physically having eyes on us."

"Fuck," Vance groans.

"What if it's Novak?" Frog wonders. *Ben's bodyguard.* I've never gotten along with Chris Novak, but he's been a bodyguard for too long to pull this fireable offense now. His *dad* was in security too.

"That's not his number," O'Malley says defensively.

Frog reasons, "He stands outside the door of TV and New Media every day and has opportunities to talk to Wyatt Rochester—of Rochester Industries. Who has *connections* to tabloids."

"Froggy has a point," I say. "When I subbed in for Ben, Wyatt talked to me alone."

O'Malley shakes his head repeatedly. "No. *No.* We all know Novak. He'd *never* put any of them in harm's way for a quick buck. And his dad was around when the Cobalts were *toddlers.* He'd kill his son if he sold-out the whole team, and Novak fucking loves his dad."

Ian tells me, "It can't be Novak."

"I don't think it is either," I mutter.

Luna's phone pings.

Just wanna look at some pics of you from tonight.
— 215-555-9000

I grab my phone off the table and type in the 215 number in my personal contacts. I blow back at what pops up.

"What?" Quinn asks.

"Type in the number. You've all got it saved."

"Fucking *rat*," O'Malley sneers. "I'm going to strangle him. I'm going to twist his *fucking* neck for this shit."

"Right behind you," Ian heats.

Vance sighs out into a growl and gives Quinn and Frog an apologetic look. The rat is on SFE. It's a rookie. The one Oscar had a bad feeling about.

Hart McKenna.

I realize, "He's the floater. Has he floated to Ben's detail before?" I ask Quinn and Frog. "During the New Media class?"

"Oh yeah," Quinn glares.

"It's definitely him," Ian confirms. "The number is the smoking gun. I'm calling Price." He rises from the table, phone to his ear.

Epsilon is pissed, but I couldn't be happier. We've finally trapped the squirrely little mouse. I pocket Luna's phone with mine.

"Gotta celebrate with my girlfriend." I stand. "Caught the last rodent—outside of whatever's on O'Malley's head."

His mop of dark brown hair stares back at me. O'Malley flips me off. "Go choke on a cheeseburger."

"*No.* 'Cause I don't trust you'd give me the Heimlich, and I love my life, thank you and goodnight…" My voice tapers off as I lock eyes with a woman outside the diner's window. It can't be…?

Is that…?

Fire alarms set off inside my body, telling me to evacuate. *Run.* I peer back at Luna. She's waving a french fry at Tom and smiles a little. *She's safe. She's safe.*

She's okay.

"Donnelly?" Frog says uneasily. "Are you—?"

"Yeah, I'm fine." I intake a short breath. "Duke's on 10th—did that get leaked yet?"

Quinn checks social media. "Yeah, ten minutes ago."

She knew I'd be here.

I can't let her inside. So I round the table, about to leave, and O'Malley twists in his chair, seeing the woman through the window. Her eyes haven't come unglued from mine, not even as she brings a cigarette to her thin lips. "Who is that?" O'Malley asks, tensed. "Donnelly?"

"I'm getting rid of her."

The bell *dings* on the door as I exit into the foggy night, the air a little chilly for April, but I welcome the cold, as usual. The marquee bulbs of Duke's on 10ᵗʰ light up the sidewalk, and I check left and right and see she's alone.

Thin brown hair pulled into a pony, her white cheeks sunken and pock-marked from the meth. She's all bones, and she picks at the reddened flesh on her elbow—a tic.

You can't be here. What are you doing here? Why come at all? Questions die in my head the moment her lips curve in a familiar, endearing smile.

Vanessa.

"It's been so long. Look at you." She puffs out smoke and motions to my body with the cigarette in hand. "You look good. God, when was the last time I saw you? You must've been twenty-one, twenty-two?"

"About there." My voice sounds choked. I'm not wearing a radio. No gun. Tonight, I haven't been a bodyguard. And I know I'm trying to protect more than Luna and her family now. I need out. "You gotta leave."

Her smile falters. "Now that's no way to treat an old friend of your mom's. She really misses you, you know?" Vanessa unzips a crocodile-skinned purse. "I found this digging through some old boxes, and I thought you'd want it. I figured you might not have too many photos of you and her together." She hands over a creased photograph.

I'm not thinking. I just take it. Haven't seen my mom in years. Not even a picture. But I never forgot her hair. Vibrant red. Like it'd been set on fire. Never forgot her shadowy, lost smile or the emptiness of her eyes.

We're side by side on a couch. I'm forcing an unsure smile up at her. She's staring at nothing. No one. She's already gone.

"You were around seven there. Remember that?" Vanessa asks.

"Your mom was twenty-one." She takes a longer drag, then blows into the air. "Same age as your fake girlfriend."

My stomach churns. "Real girlfriend."

"It's me, Paul. You don't need to pretend. I know the truth—"

"I fell in love with her. It's real now."

Vanessa grimaces and itches harder at her elbow. "It can't be real love, baby. She must be playing you…"

I step closer and hold out the photo. "I don't want it."

Her face fractures. "Just take a breath. We're all in this together… yeah?" Her eyes pinch in confusion. "I've got some people lined up for you. It's *nothing* like before—so hear me out. They're fans of yours. They just want you to show up. You give them a peck on the cheek, make them feel good for a few hours, and they'll pay you upfront—more than you can even believe."

"No—"

"No?" Her face contorts.

It hits me in the gut. That I might've never said *no* to her or Bridget. Not like this, not in my whole life. "I'm not doing that—"

"It's *nothing*," she nearly spits. "A peck? A handshake? For Christ's sake, you don't even need to hug them. What's the big deal?"

"I've got a girlfri—"

"Honey, that won't last. That family will kick you out of their home when they figure out what you've done, and you'll be *wishing* you had this money waiting for you. And what about your mom, huh? She's gonna need help when she gets out. I'm *just* trying to make sure you're all on two feet. The people I love. I'm not even asking for anything. Not one buck."

"Then you won't care that I'm not doing it."

Disgust twists her face. "You wanna be like your piece of shit father? Is that it?" She steps towards me. I step back. She slams the heel of her palm against my chest. "Is it?!"

I'm unblinking. I see my mom smacking the shit outta my dad until he's cowered into a ball, shielding his head with his hands. I intervene, and my dad pushes me against the fridge.

NOBODY LIKE US **645**

"Is it?!" Vanessa slaps me across the face—cigarette still between her fingers, it burns my cheek, and the honking New York traffic suddenly amplifies to a million.

People explode out of the diner. O'Malley is the fastest to reach her, and he thrusts himself between me and Vanessa.

"Don't push me!" Vanessa yells.

I squat down, gasping for breath in a constricted airway, and I press my white Blondie band tee to my face.

"Donnelly?" Luna kneels to me. "Donnelly?"

Luna. Fear envelops me, and on instinct, I let go of my shirt, and I pick her up around the waist, pressing her chest to mine.

"Donnelly, wait." She grips my shoulders. Her legs dangle like I'll put her down any second, but I won't.

I distance us from Vanessa and try to hail a cab from the curb. "We're getting out of here."

Frog and Quinn jog to reach us.

Then Vanessa yells out at Luna, "You don't wanna be with him!" It's vindictive, soulless shit I'm trying to escape. "You know what he's done?!"

I stiffen, but I don't drop Luna. I keep her in my arms, and she's holding tighter to me. Her legs wrap around my waist. *Come on, cab. Come on. Please.* It flies past us.

Frog steps into the street to hail one.

O'Malley barricades Vanessa from storming over here. His arms are outstretched. She spits in his face, and he wipes it off as she yells at him, "You're gonna hit a woman, tough guy?!"

He shoves her *hard.*

She lands on her ass.

A cab has stopped, and Frog opens the door. I set Luna on her feet, and she crawls into the back. I glance one last time at the sidewalk. Where the photo of me and my mom lies on the cement.

I watch O'Malley crouch down to Vanessa. "You *scum* of the fucking earth—you ever lay a hand on my cousin again, and you'll find yourself behind bars with your friends. So you better run.

You better fucking *run* until your feet bleed and you never think of coming back."

Vanessa is shaken, wide-eyed. It's the last of her I see, then I climb in the cab beside Luna and shut the door. After I give the name of the hotel we're spending the night at, I can't speak. Not one word. I lift my shirt back up to my eyes, and she touches my thigh and leans her weight on me.

Feeling Luna—it's the only thing helping me breathe.

72

PAUL DONNELLY

"I was gonna tell you tonight about it.
It's why I wanted to talk to you," I whisper—I dunno why I'm
whispering. We're alone. We've been alone in this four-star hotel for
an hour. Luna's apologized a few times since it's not the Ritz, but
it's her hotel of choice when she stays in Hell's Kitchen. Because it's
closest to Eliot and Tom's apartment.

It's nicer than she realizes.

I wouldn't even care if we were in a cardboard box under an
overpass right now. I'm glad we're not though. This is a thousand
times better.

We shoved the shower curtain to the side and filled the bathtub.
Luna squirted lavender body wash in the water. Smells good. And
we've shed our clothes and sunk down in the warmth, our legs
threaded.

I take deep breaths. Partly, I'm scared to touch her. Like she
might not wanna touch me after this. "That was Vanessa—and she
was right when she said you don't know what I've done." I pinch my
eyes with the soapy water, and it just burns more. When I drop my
hand, I swallow hard and stare into Luna.

She bows closer, which nearly crushes me. 'Cause she should be
pulling farther away, shouldn't she? Her fingers touch my temples,

her forehead pressing to mine. It's impossible to abandon her eyes. I murmur, "You might not love me after this."

"No," she says adamantly.

"No?" I choke on a wheezing laugh. I haven't told her anything yet. "You're so sure, babe?"

"I know the secret of our universe," she whispers. "I'm sure."

"You gonna tell me?" I cup her cheek with a wet hand and search her eyes. "Don't leave a human hanging. Might dangle...I dunno what the fuck." I break down, losing my train of thought. Tears prick me, my face tightening, and I pinch my eyes again, pulling my head away from her.

She stays intimately close. And so softly, she whispers, "I've loved you at your weakest, at your strongest, at your most broken. And you've loved me at mine."

I hold her cheek again, drawing back while I cry.

"There will never be a day where I won't," she says shakily, her tears cascading. "You don't need to be afraid to lose me, Donnelly. I'll always love all of you exactly as you've loved all of me—that's the secret of our universe."

I shut my eyes, letting those words flow over me.

Gently, I open them. Gently, I kiss her. As our eyes cradle each other, I brush my fingers into her hair. Water sloshes around us as her knees shift against mine. She's edging closer to my body. Luna burrows her face into the crook of my neck, and I weave my arms around her back, skating my fingers down her spine.

She's nestled so deep in my emotions, in my soul—extracting her has seemed fatal for a while. Now, I'd rather die before anyone attempts it. I'll never love anyone as much as I love Luna. She's it.

She's everything. She's been *everything* I could ever hope for and dream of.

If this might change how she sees me, then so be it. I can't keep this part of my past from her anymore.

"I sort of fell into it at first," I whisper. "I was eighteen." I tell her what I told Lo. How a bachelorette party asked me to basically strip, but it spiraled into paying me for sex. "But I made a mistake," I breathe. Her eyes are back on mine.

"What do you mean?" She dabs at my cheek with a washcloth. It stings, so I know the cigarette burn is bad, but I don't recoil.

"I told my parents about it, about how the girls paid me to have sex. It opened a door I couldn't close for a long time. They'd put me in positions I didn't know how to get out of."

"Weren't they in prison?"

"In and out," I whisper. "They needed money, so I felt obligated to help them. Like if I could send 'em something more, they'd stay clean. So I did what I could. It was easy money. Too easy sometimes."

Luna contemplates this. "Did you like it?"

"Being paid to have sex?"

"Yeah?" Her brows crinkle in thought. "Was it something you hated doing, I guess I'm asking?"

This is harder to answer. "I love sex. If I didn't love it, I wouldn't be having it with you as much as we do." I trace a tiny freckle on her shoulder, then lift my eyes to hers. "There were times I was alright with it. I could chalk it up to a fun night. Others, I regret with my whole life inside me. Like if I could turn back the clock, I'd kick my ass so hard it'd bruise, and I'd say, *get out.*"

Her arms tighten around me.

I comb a wet hand through my hair, dampening the strands as I push them back. Curling longer, grown-out pieces behind my ears. Then I rest that palm on her neck. "Most of the situations I hated were ones I didn't set up. Things I didn't plan for or even wanna go through with." A ball ascends my throat, and I clear it. "I wasn't a little kid, you know. I made my own choices, but I didn't appreciate being baited. Felt like my mom would do that a lot. I'd go visit her, and she'd...she'd leave me with people who were looking to pay for a quickie or a blow job. Men, sometimes."

Luna flinches, her eyes saucers.

I gauge her shocked reaction. "I shoulda told you earlier—"

"It's okay—"

"It's not though," I whisper. "You shoulda known."

Luna shrugs. "I didn't ask for your sexual history, and I can't even tell you exactly who I've slept with or what I've done because I've lost so many memories. My body count could be higher than yours, you know, and I bet it wouldn't make a difference to you."

"No, it wouldn't," I murmur.

We're both untensing.

"How'd that go?" she wonders. "You with a guy?"

I tilt my head in thought. "I thought it'd be a good experience to see what I like. Then I realized I'm definitely straight. Never had anal with a dude. But I've sucked some dicks for cash, and I didn't feel a thing, really. Just wanted the money."

I tell her about one of the worst times. Got a black eye 'cause the guy tried to pin me down, and I was having none of it. I fled the room, and when I exited into the kitchen, my mom apologized to her friend—said not one word to me.

I hated her for a second there.

Then I let it go. I always let it go, and later, I thought I loved her again.

"I don't think you should be around her," Luna concludes very gently.

"I know," I say, feeling the same lately. "I've wanted things to change, for her to get out and get clean and *stay* clean, but it's always been better when the door is shut between us."

Luna runs the washcloth over my kneecap. "Does Farrow know?"

"Yeah," I whisper. "Oscar and Farrow are the only ones who know almost everything. They were in my life when my parents popped in and out of prison—when I started turning tricks." I stare off, my nose flaring at a sudden thought. "Farrow called me one night...asking where I was. I'd never had someone *search* for me. Like I...like I was someone worth finding. But I was afraid to be found."

"Why?" she breathes.

"I didn't wanna put him out. I didn't even wanna carry my own baggage, and I was trying to drop it, not fling it on someone else." I run my hand over my mouth, my eyes glassing. "He'd already done so much for me. Without wanting *anything*. Not even a thank you." I tell her how I didn't let him find me that night, but he saw the black eye the next morning.

It'd been the same night I regretted to my core. I didn't lie to Farrow about it. I knew him well enough by then that he wouldn't act like I was a broken bird. After I told him what happened, he said, *Whatever makes you feel good, keep running towards that. Anything else, it's not worth it.*

"Back then, I think we needed each other in a way," I tell Luna. "Farrow was never trying to fix me like something was wrong. I already loved myself, and I didn't wanna be around anyone who'd put me down. I just needed someone to care, and he needed someone to love who he was. 'Cause his dad never really got the whole picture of Farrow. He loved what his son could do for him through medicine. Same way my parents loved what I could give them."

I dive a hand under the water, feeling the small of her back. Luna looks deeply into me, and I keep talking.

I tell her how I stopped doing it at some point during my time at Yale. My parents got sent back to prison, and I let Farrow take calls from my dad. I had made connections through that initial bachelorette party, other college girls wanting to pay, and I never accepted those kinds of offers again.

I talk about how there'd been a rumor on the security team of me being an escort. It started around the same time O'Malley was hired. "I've had sex in Philly for money, not just in New Haven, and I figured a bodyguard knew someone who I fucked. Now I know it was probably O'Malley."

I tell her about his girlfriend—what I learned about the night of the Super Bowl.

"You can't remember her?" Luna asks.

"Not really, no." I shake my head. "I don't know if I blocked it out or if it was just unmemorable or what."

Luna nods, understanding. She's contemplative though. Gears

seem to click rapidly in her brain, and I take the washcloth from her hand.

"You can ask me anything," I say.

She sweeps my face like the answers are there, but they're not on the surface. She's gonna have to ask, and I need her to because I don't want anything wedged between us from this.

Luna clutches my leg beneath the water. "Did getting paid for sex feel differently than doing it for free?"

"There were a lotta times I wish they didn't give me money afterwards. I woulda fucked for free. Woulda felt better about it. I think the transaction was what bothered me, more than anything. The act of sex—I liked."

She stares at the filmy layer of soap on the water. She's in her head about something.

I whisper, "What's going on, Luna?".

"When I have sex with you, I can kinda get lost in the moment."

My lips rise. "Yeah, I know." I catch her gaze that shifts uncertainly, and I tell her, "It's hot."

She starts to smile too. But she's nervous. "I'm starting to worry I haven't paid enough attention to your needs like you do mine. I don't want you to feel like you're only pleasing me, like I'm a paying customer—"

"I've never felt that," I interject. I've never wanted her to reevaluate all the times we've had sex, but it's natural she would. It's one of the reasons why sharing this part of my life was so hard.

"When you offered to show me what good head felt like, why'd you want to?" Luna asks, bringing up the one-time experiment she recently remembered.

It'd been our first sexual encounter, and Jane walked in on us.

I think back. "When you said it was just *okay* for you, I thought you must've had some mediocre experiences, and I wanted you to feel good." I grin off the flush on her cheeks. "I was confident in my ability to eat a girl out—just didn't realize eating out an alien was gonna do me in for life."

She beams. "You're the only one who survived the deadly act."

"Hunger Games Pussy Victor," I joke. "Paul Donnelly."

She grins now, but it softens. "It didn't feel like a transaction, did it?"

"No," I say strongly. "You didn't pay me to go down on you. I volunteered. And I enjoyed it more than I think you're realizing. I *love* sex. It was for your benefit, but also, I wanted to taste you." I'm not sure how much blunter I need to be, outside of describing in vivid detail how I was getting off on it.

Luna sinks back against the tub, away from me. Except, she clasps my biceps and pulls me with her. I root a hand on the ledge to keep some of my weight off her frame.

She breaks her legs apart around my waist, and it takes an ungodly amount of energy not to unplug the drain, let the soapy water escape, and slip inside her.

Luna clasps my neck with two hands, an uncertainty still in her.

"Tell me," I prod.

"What about how we've joked that you've been at my earthly *service?*"

"I am at your earthly service, space babe. Not for money—but out of love. I'm gonna be at your service for as long as I'm alive. You know that?"

Her eyes well, and she nods.

Good.

"I'm going to be at your otherworldly service for as long as I'm alive," she says so softly. "You know that?"

I nod back. "Yeah, I do."

Marry me.

Feels like we just did. Still, I don't surface it right now. We kiss—aching, plunging, soulful kisses that grind my body into hers. I do unplug the drain, and I make deep, sensual love to Luna in the tub. We fuck until her breath is too ragged, and my heart won't slow down.

We shower. I wrap her hair in a towel when we come out, and with one slung low on my hips, we're brushing our teeth. Only, my toothbrush is in the corner of my mouth. I have her foot in my hand. "Does it make calls out of the Milky Way?" I mumble.

"Uh-huh," she says, mouth full of toothpaste suds. "But best reception is to Wawa."

"Girl, say no more." I put her foot to my ear, stretching her leg higher. She's very flexible, and she's laughing while brushing. I speak to her phone-foot. "I'd like to place an order."

"Ham hoagie!"

"One ham hoagie for my…"

Her joy steals my breath, and I want every day with her. No less than that. With her foot up to my ear like a phone and a toothbrush in my mouth, I say, "I wanna marry you."

Luna goes wide-eyed. She slows brushing her molars. "That's… not on the Wawa menu," she mumbles before spitting in the sink.

I relinquish her leg, my pulse pounding harder. And I spit out toothpaste too. We rinse and turn back to each other.

Casting a quick glance at the mirror, I see the reddened burn-streak across my cheekbone. Don't think it'll scar, so there's that shiny positive. It's easier to confront a cigarette burn than the possibility of being rejected right now.

But we've gotta do this. I screw the cap on the toothpaste and look her over. She has on a hotel bathrobe and stares at the pools of water at her feet.

"You don't wanna marry me," I say.

Her eyes snap up to me. "What?"

"You don't wanna marry me," I repeat, the pain like a dagger sunk in my heart. Funny enough, I've got that image tattooed on my foot.

Her face breaks. "Why do you have to say it like that?"

"I dunno how else to say it, Luna."

She holds on to the counter. "It's not that I don't want to."

I frown. "What is it like?" I shake the excess water off my toothbrush and slip it back into my Dopp kit.

She watches me. "I've felt like we've flown so far beyond marriage in commitment and love. Like if we tied the knot, it wouldn't even encapsulate a third of my feelings for you."

I didn't expect that. "Being my wife is too basic," I tease with a slow-edging grin. "Too earthly. Needs to be weirder."

She's contemplative. "Can you say that again?"

"Weirder?"

"No, before that."

I know. "My wife."

Her eyes glass, and she shrugs, then buries her face in her palms so I can't see her expression crack again. I pull Luna in my arms, holding her against my chest. "I'm not trying to pressure you—I don't wanna pressure you." I rub tears off her cheeks while she wipes the splotchy patches with her bathrobe sleeve. "You're only twenty-one, and I'm not gonna propose anytime soon. Or at all, if it's not what you want."

"I want it," she croaks.

It takes me aback. "Luna—"

"It doesn't sound too earthly." She wipes her nose with her sleeve. "I'm already yours. It's like it's branded inside, and I haven't needed anything outside. But I want it. One day. Not now. Not tomorrow. I want to get excited about our future together. To finally look beyond and see what waits and never question its existence. And if time is short for us and we die too soon—"

"We won't—"

"—then oh well. Because we're kinda already married on my planet."

I grin. "What's kinda married?"

She laughs tearfully. "I didn't want to scare you, but we are wedded for all-time, without end."

"When did that happen?"

"In the bathtub," she sniffs, her silent tears still falling. I thumb them away, and she says, "Your intergalactic vows were very beautiful."

My love for her burrows deeper. "So were yours, sad alien."

"Not sad. *Very* happy."

I let her go to find a box of tissues under the sink. Handing them to Luna, I express, "I'm not in a rush, but down the road, I do wanna marry you the earthly way. And I never thought I'd marry anyone, but I never imagined I'd love someone as much as I love you. I like that it'll be something to look forward to, but..."

"But?" Luna freezes.

I'm bracing myself. She can see I'm preparing for an impact. "But...before we got married on your planet, I probably shoulda told you that I don't want kids."

Her gaze drops.

She didn't expect that.

"Luna...?"

"No kids? Like *zero*?"

"Zero," I confirm.

Luna moves slowly into the dimly lit room. *Fuck me.* I scrape a hand against the back of my head, and I follow while she plops on the edge of the hotel bed. The curtains are wide open. Glittering New York on the other side of the window.

I lean against the dresser and give her a minute or two.

Turns out she needs five before she speaks. "You don't think you'll change your mind?"

I exhale a strained breath. "A baby is forever, Luna. You can't send it back."

"So it's the commitment of one?"

I shake my head, confused. With anyone else, I wouldn't wanna commit to raising a child with them, but with Luna...

I wouldn't call myself a commitment-phobe.

She even mentions, "You've practically adopted Orion."

"Yeah. He's my big fluffy son."

Luna opens her hands. "See. We already have a child."

"He's not a *human* baby," I say gently.

"Our baby will be part-alien." She's grappling with how to make this work.

I lick my dried lips, my throat burning. And to tell the complete truth, she's making me smile right now. "Are the alien genes dominant or recessive?"

"Dominant."

"Yeah, that's probably for the best..." I trail off and shake my head. "Luna."

"I don't want kids *anytime* soon. It could be many, many years from now."

Many, many years. I rest my elbows back on the dresser. "You're fertile for a window of time. It can't happen after a certain period."

"Unless we hop into a cryopod. We could be frozen in our thirties for a few decades and pop back out." She's smiling off mine. "Science has come a long way."

"How much *hope* are you huffing?"

"Maybe you shouldn't have infected me with it."

"Nah, I'm not regretting that." I soften a loving look on her. "I can't even picture you not having a baby." It hurts my heart just imagining. "You'd be a great mom."

"You'd be a great dad."

"Maybe," I say. "It's responsibility that I've never wanted 'cause there hasn't been a point in my life where I've been totally stable. I've been looking out for myself, and when I felt like I had that under control, I started looking out for your family."

"You don't think you'll reach a stable point in the future? To where you'd want one then?"

I dunno. "It's felt like a dream," I admit.

"A baby?"

"Stability enough to have one." I let out a breath. "Where I feel like I can touch something that innocent, and I won't harm it." I lock eyes with her. "My past has been breathing down my neck, and it's bad enough what happened to you because of it. I *never* want our kid to feel that kind of pain."

"Our kid?"

I rock my head back. "We're not having a baby."

"Part-alien baby," she corrects.

"*Luna,*" I say with a smile.

She sighs, then nods. "I know what you're saying. I get why you'd feel that way. But…"

"But?"

"But hypothetically, if your dream were to come true and everything felt stable enough for a baby, *then* would you maybe consider one?"

I stare off, unable to even visualize that. Before I answer, I ask, "Would you still be with me knowing we will not, under any circumstance, have a baby together?"

Her body sinks. "This is a deal-breaker, isn't it?"

"I don't even know how to let you go," I admit.

She shrugs. "I might not even be fertile."

Why does that roil my stomach? I brush two hands through my hair.

"Which would be bad…" She winces, staring out at New York. "I forgot to tell you…"

"Tell me what?"

And then she explains how she offered her eggs to Farrow and Maximoff. The most crushing thought is knowing Luna would have to see a baby with her features and never have one herself.

I smear a hand down my face.

"I can take it back—"

"No, you can't," I say. "I'm not doing that to my best friend."

Luna scoots back on the bed. "The answer is *yes.*"

I drop my hand. "Yes what?"

"Yes, I'd still be with you if we never have kids. I'd only want to be the mom to your baby, and the key part here is *you.* You are what I really want first and last."

I exhale a long breath and nod. "Maybe I'd consider it."

"Maybe?" She brightens.

"It's a really big maybe, Luna."

She nods a lot. "Very big. It's overtaken all of New York. I see it right there." She points to the window.

I grin over at her. *We're okay.* We're going to have a future together. "You wanna open Cordelia's prediction?" I didn't have it in me to trash it. A part of me has wanted to know what the future holds with Luna. To have one at all with her is what matters to me.

"Not now." She rests against the pillows. "I kinda just want you to hold me."

I'm about to push away from the dresser when my phone lights up.

It's Xander.

I read the text with cinched brows, so I'm not surprised she's asking, "Who is that?"

"Your brother. He accepted an offer from a college." He's been in between a few universities, and wherever he goes, I need to go. And I tell Luna, "I know where I'll be living."

And it's not in Philly.

MAY

"Luminous beings we are, not this crude matter."

– Star Wars: Episode V – The Empire Strikes Back

FANATICON FORUM

We Are Calloway

Posted by @wampa4president

Underrated couple of the fams = Luna x Donnelly

I will not accept any haters who keep saying they're *not* together. It's been FIVE months. They're a couple. Dirty duo is an awful name. The one Lily suggested is 10x better. Now can we please have more posts discussing how freaking cute they are?

@CharliesBebe: None of the pics at the Fizz Gala show them doing their normal PDA thing tho. Sry but they might've broken up.

@cinnaroll33: Donnelly is a bodyguard. He was at the gala to protect Xander. It's not that weird he'd be doing his job and not humping Luna.

@HolyHalesSpiderman: THANK YOU FOR THE LUNA DONNELLY LOVE! Finally!! I'm so sick of the posts that keep speculating their legitimacy. As I've said from the very beginning, they're a real couple.

@XanderOnlyXander: I agree that there is too much evidence now to suggest this is a hoax or a short-term fling. Especially since Lily replied to someone's IG comment what their ship name is. (#Lunnelly) That should be enough proof.

@WWRCD_1989: Lily has been known to throw off the public via social media. It's been posted like five billion times in here already. Remember when she kept tweeting pics of Tahiti as the fam vacation? They ended up going to Greece.

@WAC77Lover: Ugh, we can't have this derailing a million ways, guys. Either Lily is a verified source or she's not.

@wampa4president: This post was supposed to spark love for Luna x Donnelly. Not more speculations, please. #Lunnelly

@HotDoggie_21: Does anyone look at Donnelly and think, god he must smell like an ashtray?

@StaleBread89: Bet he smells like almonds and joy.

@SFOorBust: I think they're cute. Have you seen their TikTok video together? Where they're dancing to a viral song? It's clear they love each other. Anyone who says differently just doesn't want to see Luna end up with him.

73

LUNA HALE

I never considered Donnelly could be ejected from our spaceship, just for him to board another one going in the opposite direction. I thought flying debris would explode our vessel first.

But he's not coming back to the penthouse.

He's moving. Without me. Just when we bonded over the possibilities of our future—instead of being torn apart by them—this tailspin happens.

He's still here. Xander hasn't graduated high school *yet.* Donnelly currently splays printed pages of our love story on the mattress of my childhood bedroom. I'm sitting on the surface of my wooden desk. It's covered in Marvel stickers, reflecting my mildly obsessive childhood love of Star-Lord and Gamora. I'm trying to concentrate while jotting notes on flashcards, but all I can think about is Xander.

College.

Donnelly.

Moving.

Contractors are putting new flooring in back at the penthouse. Plus, a fresh coat of paint. The reno is nearly finished, but I'm about as excited to go home as a kid receiving coal on Christmas morning.

It won't be the same without my boyfriend one bathroom away.

"This distracting you?" he asks me, motioning to the colorful, ethereal pages on the bed, some spilling onto the floor in organized chaos. We've pored hours into the story, messing with the chronology to better reflect my amnesia, and Donnelly played with contrast and vibrant pigments in the art to illustrate his feelings from childhood to present.

It's beautiful. Stunning, even.

It normally would be a distraction from prepping for the Fizzle final presentation. Which is in two weeks. But it's not what's derailing me.

Long distance relationship.

LDR.

It's hard to believe that's going to be our label soon. "No," I mutter. "I don't think I'm going to go to the Fight Night in Vegas." It's a quiet thought spoken under my breath, but he hears. For once, I'm wishing his ears weren't bionic.

Donnelly backs away from the comic pages. "No?" He senses something is *very* wrong and comes over to me. I'm trying not to mope. I have *him*. His love is all I really want. And I know, no matter how physically far away, we have technology to keep us close, always.

My legs dangle off my desk, and I love how he edges up to me, his hand sliding up my thigh as he stands between my knees. *He won't be able to do that soon.*

He sees the blank notecard in my hand. Yes, I've written nothing. "Luna—"

"Finals are next week, right before the Fight Night," I explain, my neck hot. "The last exam for New Media is supposed to be impossible, and I'm gonna cram for it." I set aside the notecards and pop the tab of a Lightning Bolt! can. As I feel his gaze roam over me, nervousness flutters inside my stomach. "It kinda sounds exhausting to go on a long flight to Vegas afterwards. And I know we planned it as a date thing since Xander isn't going, but you should still go. I know you want to support your friends."

The charity Fight Night has a star-studded line-up of celebrities, professional fighters, and famous bodyguards trained in either MMA, boxing, or Muay Thai. Donnelly tried to sign up, but the

Tri-Force shut him down and said if he wanted to fight, he'd have to pass another psych eval and a sleep study in order to be thrown in the ring.

Both security firms are looking out for Donnelly these days. It's clear to me they treat him like an asset, but they also care about his well-being like family.

And he'll want to be in Vegas to cheer on that family. Oscar, Quinn, and Joana are all fighting, along with Thatcher, Banks, Akara, O'Malley, Farrow, and others.

"You don't wanna support Maximoff?" he asks, confused.

The charity Fight Night is run through H.M.C. Philanthropies. My brother is the CEO, so naturally he'll be there. He's on the card as a celebrity—but even though he's fighting, it's not the main event match.

Most of our family will be in attendance, including my parents, aunts, uncles. The only one who's really vocalized staying at home is Xander.

"I think he'll understand I'm prioritizing college." I shrug. "He'll have a lot of people rooting for him, and maybe it's a good thing you'll be in Vegas while I'm here. It'll be a test run." My face is roasting.

Realizations jump his brows. "A test run for when we're—"

"Long distance. Uh-huh." I nod a lot. Too much. Anxiety sucks. I gulp the pineapple-flavored energy drink.

Donnelly rubs my thighs in comfort. *He won't be able to do that anymore.* "Been getting this strange feeling this isn't about Vegas but another city."

I flick the aluminum tab back and forth on the can. "New York." A city that I've had no bad feelings towards is suddenly shadowed with Dark Side energy. Worst part: I'm projecting said negative energy, and that makes me want to fling myself on my bed and wallow like an un-flipped pancake. "What are the positives again?" I ask him.

"There are lots," Donnelly says. "For one, Xander chose it. That's a good thing."

He was between Penn and Manhattan Valley University. My

brother had been worried about an Ivy League course load, especially seeing how much I study, but when Easton asked Xander to be his roommate at MVU, the decision was easier for him.

He wanted to go to New York to do college with his best friend.

Guilt sets in because I still wish Xander chose Philly. Even if Donnelly and I urged Xander to not consider us in the decision. He'd been torn for a while because of us. Donnelly said he shouldn't be my brother's bodyguard if he's willing to alter his life for him—that Xander has done it enough trying to give him more time with me.

And my brother—he *needs* Donnelly in his life. Donnelly's a calming force. I know that because he's calming me right now.

"What else?" I ask.

Donnelly steals the energy drink, taking a swig. "You'll be killing it at Penn. Getting a shiny Ivy League degree."

That's been the plan. I've already signed up for a couple summer courses, and I'm considering a double major. Business and Marketing. Despite the Roach's surly ways and the targeted course material on my family, I've loved learning about marketing strategies and the TV business.

"Anything else?" I wonder.

"New York is barely an hour away," he reminds me.

"It's more than an hour." *More like almost two hours.*

"Barely."

I try to nod.

"We can FaceTime," he says. "Every morning, every night. It's like I'll be right next to you, space babe."

"I'm just greedy for your presence, your touch. I think it's always been that way." I melt into his hand that slides across my cheek, and I ask, "How are you so okay with this?"

"'Cause I know we'll survive it. After everything…this is nothing, Luna." His thumb strokes the glitter beneath my eye. "My little cynic. Back in action." His grin coaxes a smile out of me. "She's cute though. Extra sparkly."

I smile more, but a weird feeling wrestles inside my stomach. We can survive anything together—I don't doubt it. Not one bit. But a part of me is sad knowing this next chapter will be something we're trying to endure.

Don't think about it.

The better distraction *is* our love story spread on the bed, and I hop off the desk to help Donnelly lay out the rest of the pages.

"You sure you don't need to prep?" He's asking me about Fizzle.

I haven't received the email from Uncle Stokes about the Fizzle Gala yet, so I'm not sure how I fared. I could tell Gunther and Chett found me awkward, even though I had a decent time chatting with a shareholder about my grandfather. I liked hearing more about him from a new perspective. It filled in more pieces of who he was, and from what I gathered, he was very much cherished by his employees and his colleagues as a kind-hearted, benevolent man.

It makes sense why my mom really loved him.

"I still have time," I tell Donnelly. He's already helped me with a vital portion of my presentation after I asked for his artistic assistance. He's a *great* boyfriend. The best in all galaxies. "I'd rather do this with you."

I hug him from behind like I'm his barnacle. I sense his grin, and he lifts me up in a piggyback like that's where I belong. Superglued to him.

"That one." I point to a page on the pillow. "That's the climax."

"We love a climax."

"In zero gravity," I add.

"Floating and moaning."

I smile so big, my cheeks hurt. He can't see, but I kiss his neck and slip down his body to collect a fallen page. It's slipped partially under the bed frame. Kneeling, I slide it out and overturn the page. My breath hitches as emotion surges.

Comics aren't always just blocks of square panels telling a linear story. They can be circles and triangles—whacky, weird shapes. Panels can bleed into the next. Characters can even escape the frames of them.

I stare at these broken panels shaped like a shattered kyber crystal. Inside each one is a piece of our history together.

Donnelly carries me down the stairs of a grimy rowhouse, where I'd been taken.

We're on our knees under a desert night sky, holding each other.

We kiss beneath a disco ball, mirrors refracting light all around us.

He makes love to me for what feels like the first time.

More little moments. Some, I can't remember fully yet. Some, I can. And beneath the kyber crystal panels is a human man with his arms outstretched. Like he's carrying the fragmented memories so they don't tumble away and disappear.

Tears flood my eyes, and I wipe them fast before I wet the paper.

Not again.

I sniff.

"Something wrong with that one?" Donnelly comes over to see the page.

"Nothing's wrong." I clutch it tenderly, carefully, treasuring every line of ink. My love for him swells so mightily inside of me. "Everyone should know who you are."

He opens his mouth, but nothing comes out.

I pick myself off the floor, still protecting the art with a soft grip. "'When the world has decayed and all I've ever known has disappeared in time you should know the very best of humankind is him,'" I recite my Unearthly Reader passage I wrote. "'I hope he's immortalized in this text. Please, keep him alive'—it's *you*, Donnelly. You're worth knowing, and this..." I stare around at the scattered pages. "It shouldn't just be for us."

"This story isn't just mine," Donnelly says. "It's *ours*, Luna. If you're sayin' what I think you are—"

"Let's publish it."

He intakes a breath. "That's what I thought..." He tilts his head, searching me. "It's not a small jump. Even with the sci-fi elements, it's pretty obvious this is an allegory of what happened that night."

The night of the kidnapping. The one we haven't shared with the public. This comic book isn't a direct translation. It's a sci-fi love story—where he's a part of my galactic world before I literally crash-land on Earth. There are plots where we're in a space pod in zero gravity. Everything we've felt, we've translated through the genre we love.

But he's right, it's easy to see the reality beneath the fiction. "I want the world to know," I tell him. "This is the way. This is how they find out."

Donnelly grips my gaze like he's ensuring this is real. "They'll know you lost your memories."

I nod.

"They'll know about my childhood."

I can't read his expression fast enough. "If you're not ready—"

"No, I'm ready." He takes the page from me. "Think this has helped me become ready for people to know. You were wrong though." His eyes lift to mine. "It's our love that's worth sharing. It's so big it's spilling around us, and this…" He holds the page up. "Is the best damn thing I've ever read. And I say that with my whole chest and a hundred-buck wager."

I smile bigger, excitement bubbling. "We're doing this? We can send a submission to my dad, see if Halway Comics would want it first."

He wavers suddenly.

I frown. "The sexy parts aren't too graphic," I say, thinking this is the hang-up. Donnelly didn't draw NC-17 level smut, but sex is most definitely implied. "I think it'll be fine if my dad reads it—"

"It's not that." He points to the alien princess on the page. "We used pieces from your Thebulan saga."

"So?"

"You won't be able to publish it as a novel, Luna."

"I'm publishing it *now*, as a comic book. Volume one of maybe many." I add quickly, "And I know it's not the Thebulan saga. It's very different and I only took tiny parts, but in a way, maybe that's what

NOBODY LIKE US *671*

my childhood writing was always supposed to be. A steppingstone to here and now. Every piece of who I am has led me to this place with you."

Donnelly looks overwhelmed.

Every memory with him, every strand of his life and mine are threads woven together, and this tapestry of us is infinite. Because it won't be buried in a wall. This won't be left for only me to find. It will never be lost. It will always, *always* live on through you.

"I don't ever want to be invisible." I take his hand. "I always want to be seen with you." Sudden nerves join the thrill, or maybe thrilling things are naturally nerve-wracking. "I just hope people don't one-star bomb it."

He laughs and pulls me closer to his chest. "If they do, they don't have our great taste. We've got the palates of angels."

"Divine," I nod.

"Unearthly."

"Humans will know us," I let this sink in.

"As they should." He clutches my cheek, a radiant grin in his eyes. "Who wouldn't love a Lunnelly?"

EMAIL FROM SAM STOKES

FROM: samstokes@fizzle.com
TO: dontemailme1882@yahoo.com, eliotalice@gmail.com, benpirripcobalt@upenn.edu, aragorn1225@gmail.com, queenofthebula@gmail.com

After the Fizz Gala, the rankings are as follows:

1. Charlie Keating Cobalt
2. Eliot Alice Cobalt
3. Luna Hale
4. Xander Hale
5. Ben Pirrip Cobalt

Your feedback:

Ben: You were on the phone for half the gala. It's unacceptable. The board expected far more from you. (-2 spots in the ranking)

Xander: You made minimal effort to socialize. But thank you for sticking it out. (+1 spot in the ranking)

Luna: The highest you've ranked thus far. Well done. (+1 spot in the ranking)

Eliot: A true gentleman throughout the evening. No mayhem, no pranks, no drama. The board only questions whether it's all an act, as Charlie continues to remind them. (- neutral, no shift)

Charlie: Be more cognizant of how you talk to shareholders. The board expects this to change if you are selected. (- neutral, no shift)

This is the last email you'll receive regarding rankings. The final presentations will conclude this evaluation period. Please come prepared and on time. A successor will be chosen after a private closed-door deliberation, and we'll follow up via phone call. Thank you all for your participation. We truly believe the future of this company will be in good hands.

74

This is the last email you'll receive regarding rankings. The final presentations will conclude this evaluation period. Please come prepared on time. Each of you will be chosen after a private closed-door deliberation. We will follow up via phone call. Thank you all for your participation. We truly believe the future of the company will be in good hands.

PAUL DONNELLY

Beep.

The *buckle your seatbelt* icon illuminates above my head. Turbulence rumbles the commercial airplane, and the interior lights dim for the red-eye. Flight attendants brew coffee and whisper in the galley alcove.

Hitching a ride on commercial feels foreign. I've been flying on private jets for so long. It's not even the top five strangest things about tonight.

I'm in first-class. Aisle seat. And Ben Pirrip Cobalt is my passenger buddy. He hasn't spoken since we boarded. He's stretched out his long legs. With AirPods in his ears, he gazes out of the circular window as the bright Vegas lights fade in the distance.

We're flying away from Sin City. Lasted a total eight hours there.

Now I'm making my way back to my girlfriend and my elf. After one *long* layover in Atlanta, I'll be in Philly tomorrow night. This was the only flight available at the last minute, and Ben always flies commercial when he's alone.

"Sir, would you like anything to drink?" the flight attendant whispers to me, since most passengers have already whipped out their neck pillows and put on sleeping masks.

I need to stay awake. "A coffee, thanks."

She smiles at my accent on *cóffee.* "Boston?"

"Philly."

Her eyes flash to Ben, who shuts the visor over the window and faces forward. Recognition slowly washes over her—knowing he's Connor and Rose's son—but she keeps a polite smile like this isn't the first famous face she's seen on a plane.

She captures his attention. "Sir, anything to drink?"

Ben pulls out an AirPod. "No. I'm good. Thank you." He manages to smile back, but as soon as she's gone, his lips flatline, and he works his jaw like emotion is barreling back into him.

"You wanna talk about it?" I ask quietly.

He shakes his head a few times, heated, and shoves the AirPod in his ear. I'm curious if he's engaged in a meditation app to find his calm, happy place. His phone is slanted towards me, and I peek over. He's listening to Led Zeppelin.

I watch the flight tracker on my screen. Less than four hours till landing in ATL. Not too bad. *Not too bad.* Except, in the quiet— alone with my thoughts—I can't stop thinking about Vegas.

Fight Night. Televised for all the at-home viewers.

They got a good show.

I watched the live event in the third row next to Frog. She seemed antsy. Like me, she'd taken the trip in support of security. Not there as a bodyguard on-duty. Her cousin Akara would be fighting, and she also wanted to be a friend to Sulli, who brought Seven along. The first big outing for the popular newborn.

With the core six in attendance too, the Masquerade Hotel & Casino could've rivaled the White House with the amount of private security floating around. So I didn't think Frog was fretting about anyone's safety.

I'd been wrong though, in a strange way.

Moretti vs. Moretti. Thatcher and Banks were squared off in the ring, but unbeknownst to the audience, the boxing match had been choreographed in advance. By Banks. They weren't a match-up at first. The plan had been for Thatcher to duke it out with Oscar, but Banks didn't want anyone to injure his twin. Thatch's recovery from his surgery, after the Summer Fest shooting, had been slower than I bet most of us realized.

He's one of the stubborn ones. So he wasn't gonna drop out of the fight. Second best thing was to make him fight Banks.

I still thought I should've been up there, but I accepted my place. Cheerleader. I didn't half-ass it either. I shouted so much my voice started going hoarse, but during the clash of the Morettis—that's when I really worried about Froggy.

She kept intaking sharp breaths and swaying from side to side. She'd check her phone like she was obsessing over the time. She'd smooth her clammy palms on her velvet emerald-green dress and fiddle with her dangly silver earrings.

Scooter was on the other side of her. It'd been one reason why I stayed so close. Couldn't believe she invited the guy, but after she had rehashed how that came to be, I'd realized that he'd invited himself.

He tried passing her a vodka cocktail. "Here. It'll take the edge off."

She pushed it back, too anxious to drink.

"Can I talk to you?" I asked Frog over the commotion.

She nodded vigorously. "Yeah, *yeah*, I need to talk to you too." She practically yanked *me* out of the venue and onto the carpeted casino floor.

We ended up sitting at two Flaming 7 slot machines, and I lit a cigarette while she clutched her knees. Facing each other. "It's Quinn." She purged out his name like it'd been festering inside. "It's not good, Donnelly. He shouldn't be on the title card—let alone the *main event* match. Not while…" Her face was torn up.

"Frog," I consoled and immediately snuffed out the cigarette on a plastic ash tray. "While what?"

"*Nessa*. She…" I saw the gutted look in her eyes, and my stomach started eating itself.

I shook my head. I'd abandoned the idea that Quinn's girlfriend could be abusive. *Nessa*. *Vanessa*. I'd convinced myself lately that it was all fucked-up in my brain. That I didn't trust girls with that name. That's all. He was fine. There was *no reason* to go to Oscar. No reason to pry deeper into Quinn's personal life.

No reason to be a better friend. The one he needed. It hurt knowing I failed him somewhere along the way.

"I think she hurts him," Frog said. "He has this *massive* bruise on his back, and when I asked him about it, he got so defensive of her before I even mentioned her name. And I know the Oliveira brothers were pro-boxers, but if he's being physically...if she's hurting him like that...I don't think he should be in that ring."

"We'll stop him," I said.

She exhaled, releasing her grip on her knees. "You believe me?"

"I had a hunch too. I just didn't want it to be true." My voice sounded hoarse again. I couldn't even chalk it up to being a kickass cheerleader.

Then I saw Scooter in the distance. Lingering near a blackjack table, he scanned the casino for Frog, and I kept her at the slots for one more second.

"Don't go yet," I said.

"Quinn—"

"*You*," I emphasized and cocked my head toward Scooter. She could see him. He hadn't found her yet. Before she defended him, I said fast, "You're so quick to see red flags in others. You see what Quinn is going through, but why can't you see what's happening to you?"

Her eyes reddened. "I...it's not the same."

"Yeah, it is." I hadn't wanted to be too late for Quinn, but like hell was I gonna be too late for her. "He's manipulative. He preys on your emotions. He's not good people, and you've got good people around you. And when this is all said and done, it's gonna be you, me, and Quinn." Tears started running down her cheeks. "You're gonna protect Luna for a *long*, long time, and I'm going to be with her forever. You won't ever lose her or me. I'll always be here for you—and not just 'cause you're her Number One Protector. You're my friend. My friends are family, and you've gotta release this guy from your life. I know what it's like to have friends who don't want anything good for you, and it's soul-sucking. Don't let anyone dim your light."

She nodded, hugged me, and wiped her face with the back of her hand. I wished I had tissues to give her. Best thing I could find was a cocktail napkin on our way out. She told off Scooter right there, and I didn't give him much chance to grovel to Frog.

We were in a hurry to find Quinn.

The main event had already begun.

Oscar vs. Quinn. The Pro vs. the Young Stud. Brother vs. Brother. Round one.

Bruises marred Quinn's chest and ribs, which seemed to be confusing Oscar at the start. Days leading up to the match, Oscar kept telling me, "Get ready to see my baby bro knock my lights out."

Quinn had always been the better boxer.

He let Oscar nail him in the face. He dropped his arms. He barely swung back.

I ran over to Farrow, pushing through venue security who asked to see my badge. I reached him at the base of the ring and ignored the whip of the cameras. "We gotta get Quinnie out," I said hurriedly. "I don't think he's gonna fight him."

But Oscar felt it too. He stopped, and Quinn buckled into Oscar, burying his face in his chest like a little boy to his older brother. Oscar held the back of Quinn's head protectively, and Farrow and I climbed onto the ring, slipping under the ropes, and got them off the main stage.

No one needed to see it on TV.

"Coffee." The flight attendant hands me the paper cup, partially waking me from my thoughts, but when she retreats, I blow on the steaming liquid and think back to Quinn.

We'd been backstage in a *get ready* room. Quinn sat on a flimsy fold-out chair, leg jostling while he tried to drink water with electrolytes. Oscar was pacing and trying not to strangle the figment of his brother's abusive girlfriend.

Nessa wasn't in the room with us. Just me, Farrow, and Frog.

"It's not her fault," Quinn said.

Farrow and I exchanged a pained look.

"It *is* her fault," Oscar snapped. "That thing on your back? That's from a *fist*, so don't you dare tell me you fell into a fucking doorknob."

Quinn stared up at Frog. She sat across from him on another flimsy chair. "Where's Scooter?" he asked.

"We're not talking about *Scoot* right now," Oscar fumed. "We're talking about what's happening to you, bro."

"Quinn?!" Nessa called from outside.

Quinn recoiled.

Farrow, Oscar, and I turned.

Frog stood.

But Quinn whispered back, "No, Frog. Don't…" He had his hand out like he wanted her closer to him, so she dragged her chair beside his instead of leaving.

Farrow and I confronted Nessa. Oscar couldn't do it. I think he would've said something he'd personally regret.

We stepped outside the room. Backstage hallway full of sound equipment and crew walking by.

"I know he's in there," she said. Her cheeks were beet-red. Not because of me. Farrow was looking straight through her, like her ugly insides were unzipped and exposed. She scrambled for words. "Please, I just want to see if he's okay. I *love* him."

"Think it's probably better if you never talk to him again," I told her.

"What?" she squeaked. "Quinn!"

"Look at me," Farrow said pointedly.

She did.

"We know."

Her chin quivered. "I-I don't know what—"

"You've been abusing him," Farrow said flat-out. "You don't hurt people you love, so you can fuck off."

She burst into tears. "QUINN!"

Farrow called security to get her out.

Back in the room, Oscar nodded to us in appreciation, but Quinn had his face in his hands. He was bent out of shape hearing her.

Even more so when Joana called Oscar on the phone, asking why we kicked Nessa out of the room like two big bad wolves. Apparently, she went crying to Joana and painted us out like monsters.

"Don't tell our sister," Quinn said to Oscar.

He held his hand over the receiver. "Jo will find out sooner or later, and if she does months from now, she's going to be *furious* you let her defend that bat shit crazy—"

"I can't do this," Quinn gasped out.

"Take a deep breath," Farrow said in his doctor voice. Though, he'd tell you he doesn't have one.

"We can take that breath together," Frog posed to Quinn, his bloodshot eyes lifting to her. "Me and you. Right now."

Together, they inhaled big, exhaled bigger. Quinn held Frog's gaze in a calmer second and said, "You end things with him, and I'll end it with her."

She said strongly, "Deal."

"That fast?"

"I wish I'd been faster."

He choked out, "Me too."

Oscar, Farrow, and I glanced at each other, and we seemed to silently acknowledge how we were once there—grappling with relationships and messing up, trying to make sense of our mistakes. Righting ourselves and walking forward any way we could. It's never-forgotten youth.

And even though Oscar's married, Farrow's married, and I'm in a committed relationship now, we might still find ourselves tripping once in a while—but that's the thing about being surrounded by good people.

You never really fall too far.

The airplane rattles and dips, and out of instinct, I clutch the middle armrest. Ben pops his AirPod out as the pilot comes on over the intercom. "We're heading into a rough patch of weather up ahead, so we'll be turning the seatbelt sign on for the next hour or so and suspending beverage service for the time being. Thank you."

Ben sees me release my grip. "Nervous flyer?"

"Something like that," I mutter. Really, I was reaching out for him...to protect him. I'd volunteered to accompany Ben to Philly as his bodyguard, and if we both go down in this plane, at least I died trying to keep him safe. I'd say I think I can live with that, but I'd be dead, so...

"I'm sorry you drew the short stick," Ben says genuinely. He's still radiating heat, but it's never been at me.

"I pulled the long stick, actually," I tell him. "I wanted to be here. Sort of had to strong-arm Novak for it. You're well-loved in Epsilon, you know. No one dislikes following you around."

He slowly puts the AirPods in a case. "Would you consider yourself Epsilon or Omega?"

It's the first time anyone has asked me this. It never felt like I lost SFO. I never could lose them. But I never thought I'd feel like I was a part of Epsilon. I didn't. Not until I was off-duty at Duke's on 10th and O'Malley was there when I needed someone to look out for me.

He could've let me suffer. Hell, he could've let Quinn or Frog intervene. Instead, it was him trying to give me the metaphorical Heimlich while I was choking.

I smile in thought. "Both," I answer. "I'm both."

Ben rubs at his wrists, restless. I don't think tornados love sitting too still. He uncaps his water bottle. "You want to go back to Luna?" he asks.

"Yeah," I say. "I miss her. Being at that club tonight—it's just not the same without her." If this was a long distance relationship test, then I failed it. 'Cause first opportunity to be with her, I didn't just take it—I wrenched it out of another guy's hands.

Novak might be happy in the end. I could've just saved him from dying in a plane crash.

"The club," Ben exhales a hot breath, unblinking at the blank screen in front of him. After the Fight Night, most of us were at an 18+ club called Verona in the casino. Even the girl squad squeaked their way in.

I saw Ben.

Beneath strobe lights in a back corner, he'd been chatting rapidly with Winona. His concern visceral from halfway across the club. She looked distraught, and I didn't understand it.

I wasn't sure anyone else saw it, honestly. Everyone was paired off, and I'd been people-watching and checking my phone.

Then I read his lips. It looked like he shouted, "HE DID WHAT?!"

I saw him find Vada. I saw him leave her with Winona, and then he ran out of the club like his feet were on fire. I left Oscar and Jack, and I ran after him. He slipped out from under Novak's sight, and so I texted Epsilon that Ben was on the move. He jumped in a cab before they could've even put a bodyguard on him. But I was there, and I climbed in beside Ben.

He didn't say a word about it. He's used to security. Novak wanted to trade spots at the airport, which would've been the polite thing to do. But again, I wanted to go home to Luna, and it took a thirty-minute phone call to get him to concede.

It was easy to go back on-duty. I've had my radio on me. *Just in case.* And I texted Oscar to collect my shit from the hotel room. To make sure it comes back to Philly. He called, asking about Ben. Everyone's worried about him. I'm betting his phone has been blowing up.

So here we are. In first class. No luggage. Barely any personal items. And I have no clue why he's trying to get to Philly.

"The club," I repeat the two words he said. "You know it's not healthy letting things eat away at you."

"It's not eating." Ben is still unblinking. "It's devouring...slowly." His face twitches in pain. "Winona thinks she was drugged."

I stiffen. "When?"

"At school." Ben stares at the seat pocket in front of him. "You weren't there." My stomach tries to unclench. In those halls—

all those teenagers feel like my responsibility. He adds, "Xander had been at the MLB collab that day, so he wasn't at school. No bodyguard was inside Dalton, she said."

"She thinks she was drugged?"

He scratches at his neck. "She's going to tell her mom and dad tonight. Security will probably know about it soon."

The plane quakes again, and passengers reach out for the chair in front of them. When we settle, I whisper, "We might crash though. Might as well tell me now."

Ben rests his head back. "It was Tate."

"She's sure?"

"Nona said he *snickered* when she drank out of her Hydroflask at lunch. Later, she ended up stumbling into the bathroom, feeling like she might pass out. She called Vada, who called Easton...and when they found her, Tate had been in the hall, *waiting*."

"You don't know what for," I say, trying to cool him off.

"I do know what for. I know *exactly* what for," Ben says, pulling out the safety pamphlet in the back of the seat as something to do. It's better than him scratching a hole in his arm. "He's told me what he'd like to do to Winona and Vada and my own *sister* in graphic detail—to piss me off, to get under my skin. He's not the only one in Dalton who'd say this stomach-turning shit to me, and I tried to befriend them so they'd stop. But that...that was..." He looks sick.

Luna told me Ben did something to stop the T-Bags. To stop *Tate* from harassing Winona. She wasn't sure what exactly.

Instead of prodding, I might break the seatbelt rules and go grab him a water from a flight attendant.

Then he says, "I couldn't be their friends. So I made a deal with him."

I let go of the seatbelt buckle.

Ben closes the safety pamphlet. "I knew he wanted Adderall. So I lied to my therapist, got a prescription, and supplied Tate with it throughout my senior year. I did the *one* thing I stopped talking to Xander for." He swallows hard. "And Xander—he was giving antidepressants to someone who needed them. What I did—was so much worse."

"Intentions were good," I mention.

Ben lets out a pained sound. "Yeah. Tell that to Rose and Connor. My parents would be mortified to know their hypocrite of a son dealt drugs in prep school." He picks at the peeling corner of the pamphlet. "I'm the worst Cobalt, and it's by a landslide." He says it like a fact.

"Nah, you're not that bad," I say lightly. "I think Charlie actively fights for that title." It's a risk bringing up Charlie with Ben, but he drops his gaze, thinking.

He slips the pamphlet back in the seat pocket. "I stopped," he says. "After graduation, I was done, and I figured that *I* was the reason the girls were being harassed in the first place. It was all to provoke me." His nose flares, his eyes welling. "But it wasn't." He bows forward, his face in his hands.

I put a palm on his back.

"Sir," the flight attendant whispers. She mouths to me, *Everything okay?*

"Can I get a water?"

"Of course." When she returns with one, I twist the cap and hand it to Ben. Sitting up, he takes a few swigs and tries to calm down. Hopefully talking about it helped some. I tell him he shouldn't blame himself for something so far out of his control.

He mutters something about *cause* and *effect.* I dunno.

My worry shrinks when his breathing steadies.

"Why'd you bolt to the airport?" I ask him when we're both relaxed back against the seats. He's taking out his AirPods again.

"I just need to get home."

Yeah. I nod.

I know the feeling.

Turbulence rattles us for a long extended five minutes, and I stare up at the ceiling. *Please, plane, don't let me die. I just wanna see her one more time.*

75

PAUL DONNELLY

Luna is dead asleep when I'm finally back in PA. Don't want to wake her. I could probably stomp around like Fred Flintstone, and she still wouldn't stir. She's cute, hugging a pillow to her body, and I imagine she's wishing it were me.

My smile fades. Yeah, that hurts. We won't be sleeping in the same bed when I move to New York. Hugging a pillow will be her new normal.

And my new normal.

Sharing a bed with Luna brings me comfort too. But to stay in Philly with her—it means I'd have to ask for a transfer off Xander's detail or I'd need to end my career in security. *I can't.* This time in Xander's life—I feel called to be there for him.

I can't quit on her brother. I'd regret it, and who knows, maybe this long-distance thing won't be so terrible. We'll make it work.

Orion is whining at me, so I take him for a nighttime stroll out in the gated neighborhood. I'm wearing the same gray Moody Blues tee from Vegas and the airport. Haven't showered yet, but I bought a stick of deodorant during the layover. I don't stink. I smell like a bouquet of honeysuckle. Like Luna. I've still got her scent all over me, and I hope long-distance won't ever wash her off.

It's a warm May. Crickets echo in the motionless quiet. I'm

scrolling on my phone for websites that sell body pillows with printable photos. Orion sniffs the curb, then trots ahead.

We pass the Cobalt Estate. I dropped Ben off there for the night. I'd rented a car so we wouldn't have to take a rideshare. One of his aunts or uncles would've picked us up at the airport, but the whole brood is in Vegas.

Did what I could. Got him home safely. *Five gold stars to Donnelly.*

I smile, and farther down the street, Orion pisses on a lamp post. "Let it all out," I encourage. "You think she'd like my whole body printed on a pillow or just my face?"

He pants up at me.

"Whole body. Agreed."

I tap on my phone with one hand, then go still.

A *crunching* noise lifts my gaze. Orion's ears twitch. Then I hear violent, shattering sounds. Alarm tries to thrust me forward. "I'll be back in a sec, I promise you." Hurriedly, I wind the leash around the lamp post. "Don't talk to strangers."

He woofs.

Then I bolt. I run toward the crunching, shattering, *cracks.* Adrenaline courses through my veins, and I cut down the next street. Taking a sharp right. My breath blazes in my chest, and the blue crystal necklace thwacks against my sternum.

Tate. Tate lives in this neighborhood. Ben never told me to take him to his dorm. He told me to drop him off *here.*

"I just need to get home," he said on the plane.

Only solace beating through me is knowing Ben considers the Cobalt Estate *home.* I lengthen my stride, and my tendons and quads scream. I sprint in the dead of night to Tate's stone mansion. I know the place. I've seen it. Security has had our eyes on it before.

Horseshoe driveway. Fancy carport. Lantern wall sconces lit with fire, flames flickering on either side of the door.

I spot the mansion down the road.

And there's Ben. He has on a blue zippered jacket, the hood fallen off as he smashes a baseball bat into a parked Porsche.

I don't shout and wake the whole street.

I run harder. My fucked-up hamstring flames in my leg. I don't stop. Side windows are already busted out of the Porsche. Windshield cracked. He slams the bat onto the hood—so forcefully, with so much raw strength and rage, the metal concaves into a massive dent, and the impact rocks the whole vehicle.

His pain explodes into each swing, and porch lights switch on.

"Ben!" I yell now, coming up to the mailbox.

He sees me, then he sees Tate exiting onto the front lawn.

"What the fuck, man?" Tate sneers. "You're going to fucking pay for that!" He marches toward Ben, and Ben says nothing, he just drives the end of the baseball bat into Tate's gut.

Once he's on the ground, Ben straddles him and lays a fist in his face. He coldcocks him. He's *out*. Ben lands another blow in his jaw before I pry him off Tate.

Ben tries to charge forward, but I put him in a lock.

"You gotta stop," I whisper. "Breathe."

He fights to take a breath—but also to storm forward. I draw him onto the road and rotate him away from Tate, so he can't see him anymore. Anger. Hate. Pain. I know how easily it feeds on the pieces of yourself you love. And I don't want that for Ben. I wouldn't want it for anyone.

Life rushes through me. Running away from my name. Racing toward those who filled my lungs with air. Meeting Farrow in a tattoo shop. Smiling as we got chased out of a house party. Laughing at Yale with my friends as we strolled leisurely down those college streets. Joking with Omega everywhere, every place. Strutting the catwalk on a tour bus during the holidays.

Watching the sun set in Greece. Dancing in a pub with the one-and-only. Falling in love slowly and abruptly.

I know what I've been for myself. I know what people have been for me. I know what I hope I'll always be for others.

Ben gasps for oxygen, rattling. He screams out. Then Tate's parents rush onto the lawn. By the guttural wail of the mom, you'd think her son was dead. He just got the shit knocked out of him.

"Call 9-1-1, Henry!" she screeches.

"The Porsche!" the dad wheezes.

I release my arms off Ben. "Go home before they call the cops." They'll press charges. I can see it in their eyes. Battle of the fists will be battle of the lawyers.

Ben staggers back, his face broken. "I don't care what happens to me."

"I care," I tell him. "Your family cares, and I've got a dog tied to a lamp post, so if you care about him, you'll go untie him and bring him to Luna for me. Please."

He moves backward, then nods once, twice, and heads for the street before disappearing out of sight.

76

LUNA HALE

I thumb through my notecards with sweaty palms. Final presentations are held in Fizzle's boardroom. With Uncle Stokes at the head of the long intimidating conference table, I imagine he's a variant Captain America (my brother is the tried and true) and he's searching for the newest recruit in the Avengers.

I wait inside the boardroom for my turn. I wonder why they've allowed us to observe each other's presentations. To shake our self-confidence? To cause a nervous perspiration? They shall not succeed! I rub my clammy hand on my white trousers.

I even sport a matching blazer, but underneath, I wear Donnelly's black AC/DC tee. It's tucked into my waistband. He warned me the shirt might be unlucky, but I only sense good fortune having a piece of him here with me. Plus, it smells like his musky and minty scent. That alone eases some nerves.

I'm not even sure if I'm more anxious about Fizzle or the meeting that Donnelly and I set up at Halway Comics, where we'll be facing my dad on a business-level.

If all goes horribly wrong here, at least I have that. I can't bomb two times in a row, right?

You won't bomb at all.

I give myself one self-encouraging breath and nod.

Right.

We're sitting in a line of chairs pressed to frosted glass walls of the boardroom. Well, Charlie *slouches*. Xander taps his foot nervously. Eliot is stoic, confident, *poised*.

And Ben—Ben is nowhere to be seen.

He officially dropped out of contention.

When Ben brought Orion back home that night, I stayed with him while Donnelly called security to sort through the police situation.

Luckily enough, Donnelly knew the cops who showed up to take statements. They were the same ones he'd been working with as an informant. So they came in subdued and weren't looking to throw the gauntlet at Ben. It's all hush-hush through our family's lawyers now, but I heard mutterings that assault and vandalism charges weren't being pressed.

And not because the Cobalts paid anyone off. Rumor is our family threatened a criminal charge against Tate for harassing Winona, but without much evidence, I doubt it would've stuck. Still, the fear was enough for his parents to wave a white flag and even put their house up for sale.

After Ben had talked with the police on the front stoop of my parents' house, I got Uncle Connor on the phone. He was already on a private plane back to Philly with Aunt Rose.

We hung up, and Ben wavered, looking down the road. The Cobalt Estate would be dark, empty rooms and echoing marble floors.

"You can spend the night," I offered. Xander and Easton were already asleep, but the house felt more alive with our dogs and the knowledge that people were present. "Moffy won't mind if you crash in his bed. I can change the sheets."

"That's okay." He sunk down on the couch and stared at the black screen of his phone.

I sat beside him. "What about the couch?"

Just as I asked, his phone lit up with a FaceTime call.

From Beckett.

He almost hit the red button, but then he accepted it. Beckett was walking a mile a minute in an airport. I imagined he had a phone in one hand, luggage in the other.

"I'm fine," Ben said, his voice taut and constricted. "Luna's with me." He flashed the phone to me, and I gave a Vulcan salute. Then back on himself, he said, "I'm spending the night here on the couch." He paused. "I had to deal with something. It couldn't wait."

"Neither can this," Beckett said. "Move to New York. Live here, please."

"Charlie—"

"For me, for yourself, move to New York," Beckett pled, and then he angled the FaceTime. Charlie was at the airport with him. They were already in Philadelphia. Apparently, they had left Vegas not long after Ben did.

To find their brother.

Move to New York.

Ben didn't give Beckett an answer that night, but before I entered the boardroom today, I heard the news from Eliot.

The youngest Cobalt brother dropped out of Penn, and he's transferring to the same college Xander is attending in the fall. Ben's going to New York.

"There's always room for more," Eliot tried to pitch me for the umpteenth time.

I'm at a crossroads in life. I know it. Whatever I decide in the next couple of weeks, it could change the course of my entire universe.

First things first, *ace* this presentation.

"Eliot," our uncle calls upon my best friend to take center stage. He flashes me a coy, wicked grin, then the mischief washes away as he strides to the front and commands the boardroom with pure confidence. He is the true Loki, I realize.

It's not Charlie. Eliot is the one pretending to be someone he's not, all for shits and giggles.

No one sees through it. They're smiling and jotting notes as he describes a new product called *Levitator*. It's another energy drink like Lightning Bolt! He proposes a wild marketing plan with hot air balloons decked out in Levitator logos all around the country.

By the end, I'm pretty sold.

Awesome, okay.

They love him.

"Nailed it," he whispers to me, back in his seat.

Xander is next, and he takes about five minutes to describe a commercial and rebrand for Fizzle's Sprite knockoff. It's a pre-existing drink that needs revived. None of them are writing notes. Most seem worried as Xander trips up on his words and stammers. He glances nervously to me, and I flash two thumbs up.

He breathes. And when he's back on my other side, he exhales, "I did it."

"You did it." We bump knuckles.

His smile appears, then he leans forward like he just got off a rollercoaster. "Don't ever let me do that again. I think I'm gonna hurl."

It's safe to say public speaking is not for him.

"Luna."

My turn.

I put away my notecards and go front and center.

"I have a PowerPoint," I remind Uncle Stokes. He slides the remote to me, and before I click into the main slide, I address the board. "My grandfather loved this company. I've always called it his brainchild, but it wasn't really a baby to him, I've realized. It was the embodiment of his love for my mom and my aunts. So the success of Fizzle is important to me—because its foundation was built on love and family. And I want it to always embody those things."

No one is speaking.

No one is scribbling notes.

Okay, that might be bad. As I angle towards the screen against the wall, I remember how much I love my proposal. How much *I* believe in my product and pitch. And how much Donnelly believes in me too.

I light up the boardroom with visuals of the future. "Fizz O'Naut." The tallboy aluminum can has wrap-around tattoo-styled art. American traditional, thanks to Donnelly. A purple astronaut holds the same can and floats in a bubble.

The tagline: *fizz me up*

The board leans in for a closer inspection.

"Is it beer?" Chett Wagner asks.

"No," I smile. "It's water, but it's cool to drink water." I click, and the slide shows a blue version of the astronaut. "Sparkling water." Another slide. Green with a lime in the astronaut's hand. "Flavored water. It could be supplied at breweries, festivals, sporting events, for anyone who wants the feeling of drinking a beer but would rather hydrate. *And* it's more environmentally friendly than plastic."

I go into demographics and numbers, and they ask a few more questions before I'm done. My smile hasn't shrunk.

"That was awesome," Xander whispers with the biggest smile. It magnifies mine even more.

Eliot grins in pride. "Well played."

Yep, I'm on cloud nine. I've soared to a beautiful height, and I love it here. Whatever happens, at least I put in maximum effort. I gave it everything I could. Still, I'm crossing my fingers, toes, eyelashes and any invisible limbs—all in hopes that Charlie bows out of the race.

And that's when I finally accept how much I really, *really* want to win.

"Charlie," Uncle Stokes calls.

Quit.

Drop out.

I'm manifesting my destiny, okay.

It doesn't work.

Charlie stands among the board, and he doesn't give a resignation speech. Instead, he says, "I present to you *nothing*."

Mr. Wagner flusters. "Nothing?"

"This has to be a joke," Ms. Kapoor mutters.

"No joke," Charlie says. "If you choose me, I will do nothing. I will not destroy the company, but I won't better it either. I will simply ensure that none of you run Fizzle into the ground—and if you think it's for some hackneyed reason like *love* and *family*..." Ouch, direct hit at me. "It's worse. It's because I know where my money comes from. And I do *love* to travel." He sports an irritated smile. "So choose me, and this is what you get. *Thank you.* The pleasure was never mine." He exits without a single word.

Eliot claps and tries so hard not to laugh. "Standing O, brother!" I wonder if anyone can hear him through the wall.

Eliot is the only one on his feet.

The board sees, and now they seem unsettled by Eliot. The real mischief-maker is showing. But as we pack up our things, I still hear the board advocating for Charlie.

We were always fighting for second.

Second.

It's a better placement than I think anyone would expect for a Hale. Can I have that at least?

Halway Comics.

Future number two. An opportunity not yet given or taken.

My dad has spoken very little behind his desk. We delivered the draft of the comic book (volume one) to him not too long ago, and he's given no indication he's even finished it yet. He asked to meet us. Hence, Donnelly and I standing side by side, too much anticipation to even sit. We're waiting for any reception or feedback.

Dad flips open the draft and slips on reading glasses.

"It's a space opera," I say, nervous. We should've come in with an actual pitch, but I figured we've talked about this comic at the dinner table with him. He didn't need a formal presentation.

Big mistake.

He probably wants *professional.* To see how much we're really invested in this project, and it's a whole lot. So I start saying, "The story mirrors our lives, but it's sci-fi with an alien princess and a human and a little bit of time travel."

"It's soft sci-fi," Donnelly adds, studying my dad too.

"Uh-huh," I nod. "The mainstream market should be able to digest it still. It's not that bizarre."

"Just a lotta weird," Donnelly grins.

I smile too, but mine flickers in and out. And Donnelly's lips gradually drop into a frown as my dad combs through a few more pages.

"We can take out the sex," Donnelly mentions. "If that's the problem—"

"That's not the problem, Paul." Dad removes his glasses—to pinch his eyes. Because he's crying. Or at least, he's trying to restrain the sudden onslaught of tears. He shuts the comic and raises the front of the manuscript to us. The title visible in all its glory.

Human Him, Cosmic Her

Written by Luna Hale

Illustrated by Paul Donnelly

"If you don't let me publish this," Dad says, clearing his choked voice, "that would be the problem. Because this, what you two created—your love, your lives, through space and time—it's the best goddamn submission I've had in decades."

My chin quivers. *Don't cry. You're a professional.* "You have to say that."

"No, I don't," Dad says sharply, searching in the desk drawers. For tissues, I think. "I could've said the art is trash and the panels don't make sense."

"Art's not trash," Donnelly starts to smile. "Panels make all the sense to us. It's a winner. We know it."

"Does she?" Dad places his proud eyes on me. "Do you, Luna?"

Yes.

"It will resonate," I say deeply. "It's known."

"It is known," Dad agrees, holding my gaze with even more pride. It swells triumphantly inside me, and I wipe my cheeks quickly with my blazer sleeve. He extends the tissue box, and I take one as he says, "And your mom would be very upset if I rejected it. She's already read it front to back three times."

Wow.

Dad stands. "I read it four."

Donnelly grins. "Wanna go for five?"

He smiles back, no sarcasm attached. "Thank you for sharing your story with me, Donnelly."

"You can call me Paul." His voice is raspy, choked. He clears it too. "Thanks for helping me love my name again."

It's not something he's running from anymore.

Dad comes around the desk, and he hugs me first—his love so mighty and resilient. And he shakes Donnelly's hand and brings him into a hug too.

Weirdly and beautifully enough, I'm not expecting an asteroid to crash down and crack open our universe just to swallow us into a black hole.

I believe our future is very, very bright.

77

PAUL DONNELLY

_Lo_ passes around a bowl of mashed potatoes. Meatloaf already sliced and dug into. A homecooked meal spread across the dining table. This isn't my first family dinner. Been eating with the Hales since the penthouse flooded, but this night hits different.

I'm not preparing for a quick sprint out the door. I know for a fact I won't have to be light on my feet. I'm comfortable and laughing with everyone when Ripley says _oopsie doopsie_ after Maximoff accidentally splatters ketchup on his shirt.

"Careful, wolf scout," Farrow laughs harder.

"Want this?" Maximoff tosses him the ketchup. "It's defective."

Farrow shakes the plastic bottle with a stretching, self-satisfied grin on Maximoff. My best friend knows how to undo his husband at almost every meal. Maximoff tries hard to stay aggravated, but he's smiling at Farrow now too.

He squirts the ketchup without a mess. "You were saying?"

"I fixed it for you," Maximoff gestures to the Heinz bottle. "You're welcome."

"I never said thank you."

He groans, and we all laugh. Xander reaches across the table for the pepper, bumping a water glass, and Easton catches it from being knocked over.

"Shit," Xander curses. "Thanks, East." He offers him the shaker. "Pepper?"

"Yeah, I'll take it," Easton says. He's been using a fork and knife with cotillion-esque etiquette to cut his meatloaf. Feels like a Cobalt is at the table, but he never seems out of place. Everyone makes sure of it. Maximoff has already asked him about chess club, and Lily's told him how she picked up his cap and gown for graduation next week.

Kinney offers me a basket of garlic bread. I take a piece, and as the conversation morphs into a discussion about the best overall ending in the MCU, I lean back and rest my arm around my girlfriend's chair.

"*Guardians of the Galaxy Vol. 3* has to be in the top two at least," Luna defends her favorite.

"I mean, we all agree nothing will beat *Infinity War*, right?" Xander says.

"God-tier," I pipe in with a *rock on* gesture.

"Meh," Lo says, just to disagree with me.

"Meh?" Luna, Kinney, and Xander respond together like he's had a brain transplant in the past two-seconds.

"The last Thor movie ranks higher."

Kinney has a face like she smelled a fart, which is killing me and Farrow, but we're doing our best to not double-over laughing. She deadpans, "What happened to Dad?"

"Body-snatchers at play?" Luna asks me.

I touch my chest. "Still Donnelly." I put a hand on her head. "You feel like my space babe." I'm about to kiss her at the table for a taste-test.

"*Kidding*, kidding," Lo cuts in and sends me a look like PDA is disgusting, don't do it—but he's already given his wife a wet willy at the table. So the threat feels less like a threat. More like a suggestion.

I kiss my girlfriend *politely* on the temple. Nothing risqué or pearl-clutching.

"*Spider-Man: No Way Home*," Lo mentions, and they all talk animatedly about how that *is* a viable contender to *Guardians*. But not *Infinity War*.

This is the night. It's the one where I completely, *fully* understand that I'm not going anywhere. That this is it.

This is permanence.

It's been building inside me—this feeling of acceptance from a family who had every right to never accept me. They brought me into the fold, and now I just know they're not gonna let me go so easily. For once, it's not me clinging tooth and fingernail to the better path. It's holding on to me.

My lips curve higher, and I take it all in more strongly.

How Lily asks Xander and Easton if they have enough yams—previously frozen and microwaved to perfection. They're a Hale favorite. How Kinney sneaks chunks of meatloaf to Salem beneath the table. How Lo sees and pretends to be in on the secret with his daughter. How Maximoff checks on his own daughter from the baby monitor, and in those moments, Farrow stares lovingly at him.

How Luna tips her head on my shoulder, like she's a little tired, but she'd rather stay here with everyone than disappear to her room.

It's warm and happy and soulful, and I'm not just sitting inside it. I'm a piece of it. *Yeah.* There's not much better than this.

If there is, I know I'll feel it one day. Sky isn't even the limit. I'm always gonna shoot for the moon.

But the one next to me—it can't be beat. I smile down at Luna.

And then a phone rings. The whole table goes quiet. Sam Stokes said he'd be calling the remaining Fizzle Four tonight—to give three rejections and one humongous offer. Xander and Luna have had their phones face-up on the table, waiting for their uncle.

Luna's screen is blank.

"It's not my phone," Xander tells everyone.

And then I realize, it's my phone. I dig it out of my pocket, and my stomach flips. It's my dad. "I'll be a sec." I slide out from the table, standing. Off Lo's sharp concern, I say lightly, "It's God. You want me to put in a good word with the big guy upstairs for you?"

"Yeah. Tell Him you're not funny."

"I could, but I don't think He'd believe me."

Luna laughs.

On my way out the door, I grin at Lo. "Your daughter still thinks I'm funny."

He flashes a dry smile. "Thank *God* for that."

"You bet I will." I lift the phone to my ear.

Humor fades with my grin as soon as I leave them behind. As soon as I'm on the living room couch and I'm wondering if my dad just wants to chat, if he's looking to meet-up for a beer or what.

"You busy?" he asks me.

"Just eating dinner." I unearth Baby Ripley's pirate parrot stuffed animal from between the cushions.

"With who?" His voice is quiet, almost timid. Not how he usually sounds, that's for sure.

I frown. "My girlfriend's family."

"Right," he murmurs.

I sink back slowly. Was he expecting an invite? It's not my place to open those doors to him, and I don't really want him around Luna yet. "You working tonight?" I ask casually.

"Nah, I've got the night off." His voice cracks a little, and he coughs out a strange sound. "There's somethin' I wanna talk to you about."

I tense. "Alright."

"This is gonna be the last time I call you."

Confusion balls up like white noise in my ears. "What?"

"This, right here, it's the last time we talk."

My hand goes to my mouth, my stomach in knots. "You're using—"

"No. I'm clean. Been clean, and I'm gonna join that program the Hales run. I'm gonna get your mom in it too when she gets out. But this...this is goodbye."

I don't understand. *I don't understand.* My eyes start burning. "What do you mean?"

"After the whole Vanessa *shit*...her tracking you down, I can't promise you that Bridget won't trust that woman again, and I can't leave your mom. I won't leave her." His voice shakes. "I talked to

Bridget and she's also not gonna be in contact with you anymore. You can think we're choosing each other over you, but that's not it for me. Not exactly."

A rock ascends my throat. Elbow is perched on my rigid thigh. I have a palm to my forehead like my skull has gone heavy, and I tighten the phone to my ear. "What is it then?"

"I'm letting you go."

It slams deep into me, and raw emotion builds so rapidly, I start crying into my hand. It's relief and guilt for feeling relieved and something else...something more...

"I'm letting you go, son," he repeats, his voice breaking again. "You're a good man, and it wasn't 'cause of me or her. It was despite us. I can see that. And the best thing for you now is If I let you go."

It's love.

What I'm feeling. It's the first time I've ever truly loved my dad. 'Cause what he's doing is out of love for me. It's a selfless act, and I woulda never imagined he'd release me from his life and let me live the one I built without him.

I wipe at my face and manage to say, "If you're sober a decade fro—"

"Nah, let's not get into that," he cuts in quietly. "Maybe it'll happen, maybe it won't. I might kick the bucket before then. Haven't really taken care of the ole body here." He sniffs hard. "Important thing is you aren't involved in any of this. You don't need to be." He takes a staggered breath. "This is goodbye. You get it now?"

"Yeah," I murmur. "I get it."

"That's good." He pauses, the line straining.

I rub my wet eyes and sit up more. "Take care of yourself, Dad."

"I'm gonna." He's crying. I can hear it. "Live long."

I plan on it. Last thing I say to him is, "You too." We hang up, and I stare in a daze at my phone, emotions knotted in my throat. Laughter bellows from the dining room, and I follow it, knowing exactly where I want to be.

Meatloaf devoured, all that remains are

soupy bowls of chocolate chip ice cream. We wait at the table for Sam Stokes's call. I whispered to Luna that I'd tell her about my dad later—that it's nothing bad. Maybe they can all see I'm riding on some weird mixture of happiness. Heartache and pain have been left in the dust behind me, even if there's still a sting of guilt for feeling happy my dad chose to let me go.

"Daddy, lookie," Baby Ripley says to Maximoff while Farrow wipes berry puree from his cheeks. The two-year-old is still in his highchair between his dads. "It's a birdie." He's showing Maximoff the artwork he drew on his arm.

Luna smiles over at me. Before dinner, we were playing with Ripley, and he decided to color on himself instead of the paper. He wanted tattoos like his papa.

"You drew that bird?" Maximoff says, sounding impressed.

"Yep." Ripley brightens.

It's a blue blob, really.

"Boy has talent," I say seriously. "A regular Picasso."

Kinney loves babies like Luna. She's unable to hide a smile. "Are those markers safe for a baby's skin?" she asks.

"Yeah, they are," Farrow says lightly, near laughter as Ripley points out a caterpillar and a dog among the scribbled mess. "Hold still, little man. Your face is dirty."

He stops wiggling and lets Farrow clean off his mouth.

Lily and Lo excuse themselves for a moment.

Xander pops open a Sprite and checks his phone. "What's the over-under that Uncle Stokes is screwing with us and he's *not* calling tonight?"

Luna sends a text. "Eliot said he hasn't heard anything yet either." She's more anxious, double-checking her friend's message. In all honesty, I think she wants to be chosen.

She hasn't verbally said it, but I see her.

She's put so much heart into every challenge the board threw her way, and she's enjoyed rising to the occasion with her own ideas and beliefs.

I smile more at Luna. She can't see. She's still texting Eliot, but I keep my arm around her. Proud of her, no matter which way the wind blows.

Lo slips back in the dining room and props the door open with his foot. "Guess who decided to drop by in the flesh?"

Sam Stokes walks in. Guy has a great poker-face. I'm getting absolutely nothing, other than he has dark circles under his eyes like he hasn't slept much. His snazzy black suit says he came from work.

"Let's talk in the living room," he suggests.

Luna is clutching the life out of my hand. I'd let her have it. Arm and all.

78

LUNA HALE

"I won't be long," Uncle Stokes says, but he makes himself comfortable in a chair beside the fireplace.

Xander and I are the only two on the hot seat. The old couch squeaks as I shift a little. Nervous jitters.

Orion sniffs my uncle's loafers like an intruder has entered the house—which is fair. Uncle Stokes has only met my dog a handful of times. Which begs the question, *why* the house visit? Is he afraid to deliver crushing news over the phone?

"Orion," I call over and pat my lap. "Come here, boy."

His tail wags, and he gives Uncle Stokes an expectant look. He wants pets, and I'm about to call him again when Uncle Stokes starts scratching Orion with *two* welcoming hands.

I perk up and smile.

Then Uncle Stokes zeroes in on my face, and I can't decipher his thoughts fast enough. My smile falters. Soooo I did *not* prepare for this physical encounter.

Even if I did, I wouldn't have stopped Ripley from drawing green swirls on my cheeks. I think they're pretty. Donnelly let my nephew color on him too. Blue squiggles on his face.

He's standing near the staircase with everyone, even my parents. I take a quick peek behind me, and he sends me an encouraging smile.

I breathe deeper.

NOBODY LIKE US **705**

"Let's start with Xander." Uncle Stokes gives Orion one more pat before cupping his hands together. He just now notices the Sprite in my brother's clutch. "Of course you're drinking Sprite," he sighs out. "I think we can both agree you aren't going to be the CEO."

"Yep." Xander raises his Sprite to that, smiling.

Uncle Stokes smiles too. "Good job sticking with it. I'm proud of you. So are they." He motions to everyone behind us.

Xander gazes back at our family and his best friend, and I want to say my younger brother looks happy. But more than happiness lightens his amber eyes. It's immense love that he has for himself tonight.

I breathe in a slow breath, starting to realize Uncle Stokes likely stopped by to hand out consolation prizes. A soft, gentle job-well-done.

"Luna." Uncle Stokes sets his total attention on me. "I'm going to be as frank as possible because you deserve to know what happened behind-the-scenes."

"Okay…"

"The board was not receptive towards you. Initially, they felt as if you were too…quirky?" His eyes flash above me, and I assume my dad is drilling a death-glare into him.

"You mean *weird*," I say outright. "You said you'd be frank."

"Weird," he shrugs, as if that's not it entirely either. "Your leaked fiction had tentacle…scenes in it, and most of them just couldn't look past it. They didn't think you'd represent the brand well, but I've found you to be engaging, intuitive, creative, *innovative*, from the very start. It actually reminded me of my time as CMO."

I forgot he used to be the Chief Marketing Officer of Fizzle.

"Anyway," Uncle Stokes continues. "The board had been very set on Charlie up until the Fizz Gala. He'd angered a few shareholders, and after that point, most started to lean towards Eliot."

"So who did they choose, Eliot or Charlie?"

"Post-presentations, they felt they couldn't trust Eliot."

"So Charlie," I nod. "Charlie is the successor."

Uncle Stokes shakes his head. "No, Luna. It's not Charlie. It's not

Eliot. And I want to make this *very* clear when I offer you this...you are being chosen because you were the best. I've believed that, even before they could see it."

Do not cry. You are a professional.

And you might just be a CEO one day.

I blow out a measured breath as emotion wells.

Uncle Stokes leans towards me. "Your presentation was exactly what the board was hoping for. Your reputation was the only real knock against you, and there've been plenty of people who've been tarnished in the media and risen out of it. Some have even led entire franchises to success." His smile is one of complete faith in me. "I want you to be my Iron Man. Help me make this company *better* than it's ever been."

I'm stunned. Speechless.

I won.

They're choosing me. But it means more...because Uncle Stokes *wants* me. I'm not a default winner. He believes in what I have to say.

"I'm..." I'm still lost for words. My family is quiet. Xander is gauging my feelings. Most are uncertain of whether this is good or bad news for me.

None of the Fizzle Five have expressed a clear desire to work in the corporate world.

I want this.

I've been sensing how much recently, and now that it's here, I could crawl out of my skin in elation. I peer behind me.

Donnelly is grinning from ear to ear. He looks like he's restraining himself from hurdling the couch and tackling me in a bear-hug. He blows me a kiss, and overwhelmed tears start to surge.

He knew.

He could tell I wanted it.

I really love him. *I really, really do.* Turning back to Uncle Stokes, I wipe my eyes with the heel of my palm.

"I don't expect you to accept this tonight," he says. "You'll want your lawyer to look over the contract first. I'll email it to you first thing when I leave. But I wanted to open the floor to you, to see if you have any concerns."

"Sammy," my dad calls out. "That *big* thing you promised you'd tell her. *Tell her.*"

Uncle Stokes sighs, eyes on me.

I frown back at my parents. "Did you know?"

Mom gives me an excited smile. "We did not *not* know."

"Your uncle knew I'd feed him to our pet *iguana* if he didn't tell us first," Dad says.

"What pet iguana?" Uncle Stokes asks.

"The one I'd buy just to eat you." He flashes a dry smile.

Uncle Stokes sighs. He does that a lot. Heavy sighs. Then he expresses to me, "Your parents love you very much, and it goes without saying, they don't want you to accept this position if you don't want it. I feel the same, but I really need you. Greg's will was clear. We have to pick a successor from your generation, and I don't want anyone else. So please, *please* consider this."

I am.

More than he knows, maybe.

"What's the big thing you need to tell me?" I ask.

Uncle Stokes shoots another tight look at my dad. Clearly, he didn't want to divulge this, but he must've promised him. "My health—the reason I'll one day need to step down as CEO, which won't be anytime soon. I'll hopefully be training you for years. A full decade, at least. But my health has taken a toll due to the stress and demands of this job."

"The *stress*," Dad emphasizes behind me. "The *demands.*"

"I hear him," I mutter, thinking. It's not the stress that's worrisome. It's something else entirely. "I plan to publish a comic book—"

"With your boyfriend," Uncle Stokes says. "*Human Him, Cosmic Her.*"

"You know?"

"Your dad has already informed me, and I've already had multiple meetings with the board. If what you said was true about confirming your relationship to benefit Fizzle, they would like to leverage the comic book in Fizzle's favor. We can cross promote. And all in all, they believe whatever you create with Donnelly will only help your public image, and I have to agree after your dad sent me a draft."

He's read the comic book?!

I'm a shocked Pikachu.

And I check to see if my boyfriend is okay with this. "It's up to you too."

"Boss babe, you tell me."

I smile wider. "You wanna cross promote with me?"

"I'll crisscross applesauce anything with you."

I laugh with him, and we're nodding to each other. *Okay.* Okay. This is starting to feel real.

Uncle Stokes seems a little more relieved, but he's still caging some breath. That can't be good for his health. Maybe he should take up meditation. Or get a fish.

"So," Uncle Stokes says gently, "you can continue writing for Halway Comics. Your dad has helmed two companies at once, and I think he'll be able to guide you on how to manage it."

"*Only* if you want to work for Fizzle," Dad says sharply.

Multiple paths.

It's twice the workload, but it's also twice the opportunities. It sounds way more exhilarating to have both rather than only having one clear-cut defined line.

I'm a messy timeline. I guess it's only fitting if the multiversal *me* has multi-roads to take. Plus, I'll have a long time to really understand the role and responsibilities of a CEO. I'm not being thrown into the position at twenty-one.

Until then, I can learn.

I like learning. Which brings me to... "What about college?" I ask.

"You'll need to graduate. Your majors—Business and Marketing—are absolutely perfect. The board might want you to go for an MBA, but I can talk them out of it if it's not in your plans."

My plans. Little does he know, they've been morphing from a blob-of-a-person to full-blown Power Ranger right now. Taking shape. Taking flight, hopefully.

I scoot forward on the couch. Anxious sweat building at the next question, but I need to pose it now. "And what if I don't graduate from Penn?"

I choose to only focus on Uncle Stokes, but his eyes flicker behind me. I can see he's reading the confusion in the room.

Because I've never brought this up to anyone.

Not even Donnelly.

"What college are you considering then?"

"Somewhere in New York."

"Wait, really?" Xander twists to me, on the cusp of a smile. Like he's trying not to get his hopes up.

Uncle Stokes winces. "Fizzle headquarters are in Philadelphia, Luna. It's easier if you're here."

A knot tightens in my throat. "I know…" *But Donnelly.* I want to be with him *physically.* Every night when I go to bed. Every morning when I wake up.

"You should stay where you are," Uncle Stokes says. "Stay the course. Graduate from Penn." He asks if I have any other questions, but this last one has swollen my esophagus. I'll email him anything else I can think of, and he shakes my hand more like I'm his protégé, less like I'm his niece.

I'm liking the idea of being the Iron Man to variant Captain America.

But right now, I really need to talk to Donnelly.

"He never said I couldn't go to school in New York," I tell my boyfriend on the front porch stoop. Nighttime crickets chirp in the dark, and lightning bugs flicker across the lawn. I'm sitting on the railing, and he has a hand on my thigh.

He brings his other hand to his lips, smoking a cigarette. "He said it'd be easier if you were here though." He blows smoke upward. "And it's *Philly*. You're meant to be in this city."

I stare so deeply into him. "You are Philly to me. You are where I'm meant to be. You're the real destination, Donnelly. You always have been."

He looks overwhelmed. And he places an affectionate hand on my head. It slips down to my back, until he draws me closer to his chest. I hug him around the waist. His heart beats hard against me.

"We can make long distance work, Luna," he says.

"I know that," I whisper. "*I know that.*"

He pulls back to see my face. "Then why not try it out? If it's easier on you—"

"It won't be easier for me to be away from you," I say quietly. "What would be easier is if I went to New York and didn't go to an Ivy. The course load would be manageable on top of everything else."

He considers this. Embers eat the paper of his cigarette. "You really wanna live in New York, babe?"

"I really want to live with you," I profess. "I want to stay in the same spaceship and make the landing together."

"Well, when you say it like that," he says, a grin edging across his mouth. "Which planet you think we'll be touching down on? Yours or mine?"

It's the clearest answer in the sky. Maybe it's always been there. Already written in the stars.

"Ours," I smile up at him. "This time, it'll be ours."

79

PAUL DONNELLY

Oscar and Farrow carry handfuls of beer bottles at the neck, bringing them over to a wooden high-top table near me. I'm unpacking my tattoo machine and ink on a lower round table that I already sprayed with disinfectant.

The Philly billiards bar is closed until July. We got special permission from the owner to use the space for security today. "Anything you need from us," Oscar asks me.

"Keep this area free of pussycats, please and thank you." I count the individually wrapped pre-sterilized needles I brought for this special occasion.

Oscar shoos a stray tabby out from under the table. "This can't be sanitary."

"Brewery cats are a thing," Farrow says, his arm relaxed on the high-top.

"Yeah, they chase the rats away," I slip on thin-framed reading glasses. "Don't see McKenna anywhere."

"Good riddance." Oscar tips his beer to his lips at that major firing. We heard Akara and Price made McKenna cry on his way out the proverbial door. He's being sued for breaking his contract, and they'll be squeezing a pretty penny out of him. I hope it deters any newbies from running their mouths for an easy buck.

I snap on gloves, careful about the order of operations here.

Cleanliness is the most important thing to me when I tattoo. Art always comes second.

"Look at that," Oscar nods to the bar.

I cast a grin in that direction. Where a six-foot-seven Moretti draws the bartender over the counter mid-conversation and kisses the hell outta her.

"Thatch, already hitting on the owner," I say loudly enough everyone can hear.

Jane smiles brightly against the kiss and laughs, which causes Thatcher to pull back and shoot me a strict, reprimanding look for breaking his make-out time with his wife.

"What?" I smirk. "You don't like facts now? Thought they're your favorite thing."

Thatcher starts to smile and returns his attention to Jane.

We're not at just any billiards bar. We're at *the* billiards bar in Center City—the one that stinks of fried tater tots and Marlboros. The one where security has spent late nights unwinding and chalking cue sticks and sipping watery tap beer. The one that stays open past closing if you're having a bad night. The one where many have tried to run us out for being "from L.A." when we're all born and bred in this great state of PA.

It's The Independent.

Jane Eleanor Cobalt saved it from becoming a Taco Bell, a Chipotle, some fast-foodery chain with no heart or history inside Philly. And she's expressed her wishes to keep it exactly how it's always been.

With the addition of any lost cat.

Today, she's just a temporary bartender until the official reopening, but Luna said she could see Jane filling in wherever necessary when the bar is short-staffed. That it's just in her nature to do many things and help when needed.

"So what's the deal with New York?" Oscar asks me.

"Besides your favorite person moving back there?"

"*Jack* Arizona Highland-Oliveira. You mean that favorite?"

"Nah, meant myself, but I can make some room for this Jack guy." I've missed spending time in New York with Oscar. Those days protecting Beckett feel like a lifetime ago now. I really didn't think I'd ever go back—especially while in a serious relationship.

"This Jack guy," Oscar repeats with a shake of the head. "Seriously, bro. Should I be popping a bottle of champagne and toasting to you coming to New York or do I need to include Luna in the toast too?"

"I'm going," I tell him. "That's all we know for sure."

After a lawyer examined Fizzle's contract, Luna made a counteroffer—which included a stipulation that she could complete the remainder of her undergrad education at Manhattan Valley University. Where Xander will be.

To have both the girl I'm in love with and her brother that I'm protecting on the same campus—it's the dream scenario. I just can't see how hard the board will fight to have Luna remain in Philly.

"She's going to New York," Farrow says it like a fact. "It's more or less whether she has to reject Fizzle to do it."

I don't want her to have to make that choice. "Their loss," I mention.

"No shit," Farrow swigs his beer at that. "Oliveira, you ready for your brother to live in New York?"

Quinn and Frog will be moving if Luna does.

"Never been more ready." Oscar rests his back on a structural beam decaled with beer stickers. "He needs to be around me and Jo." His gaze drifts. "Speaking of my baby bro."

In walks Quinn, Gabe, and Frog. All off-duty.

Oscar makes a face at Qunnie. "Still with the tropical buttondowns."

"What?" Quinn opens his arms. "You said it was Pacific Sun Realness."

I chime in, "Because you're the realest motherfucker I've ever seen."

"Don't get too excited by that compliment," Oscar tells Quinn. "This real motherfucker says that to everyone."

"Blue-eyed shameless motherfucker," Farrow amends, his smile expanding.

I grin back. "Hottest guy you've ever seen," I tease.

"Eh, no. That'd be my husband."

"Finally, you admit it, Redford," Oscar exclaims. "Maximoff is hotter than you."

I clap. "Truth always comes out."

Farrow gives him a middle finger, then me, and I laugh. Then everyone shows up and gathers around the table, and by everyone, I mean Security Force Omega.

Change was coming—we all could feel it, probably long before the psychic prophesized a split. Farrow, Thatcher, Akara, and Banks are all fathers. Oscar is married. I'm building a life with Luna. We're each moving in new directions—and even if we quit this job in time, there's one fact that will always remain the same.

We are SFO.

"Order of hierarchy," Oscar suggests, passing around the beers. "Kitsuwon's up first."

Akara pulls his T-shirt over his head and pushes a hand through his black hair. "Donnelly," he smiles. "No blowouts."

"Only clean lines for the best boss," I promise.

It was three days ago when I finally learned why I was really put on Epsilon. Akara asked me to stay back at Studio 9 during a group meeting between all three Forces.

So I grabbed on to a boxing bag, just casually standing on the gym mats. Barefooted. Expecting nothing.

Then Akara said, "I lied to you."

It stung. "What?"

He rubbed his knuckles, his breath shortened. "I lied—I said that Price wanted you because he needed a famous bodyguard in his firm. It's not really why—it's not the whole reason, man. It never was."

"Akara—"

"No, wait." He held out a hand. "We came up with a plan to try and bridge his firm and my firm, to where we could be cohesive and work *peacefully* together. We needed a bodyguard to swap firms and build trust between them. Price asked for Quinn, Frog, and Gabe. And I told him *no.*" His eyes reddened. "I told him there was someone better. I told him to pick you."

I inhaled a sharp breath. "Why...why are you just telling me this now?"

"Because it worked, and we were afraid if you knew, it never would. Because you were the only one who'd likely get close to making Epsilon feel a bond with Omega. You're the heart, Donnelly. Not just of the Yale boys, not just of SFO, but of the entire security team. As much as all of us didn't want to share you, it'd be more selfish to keep you."

Yeah.

That got me choked up.

I really love Akara, and he did more for me than he realizes. All my animosity towards O'Malley and SFE is gone. I hated carrying that hate in my heart. I feel more like myself being free of it.

At The Independent, Akara lies down on the table. He has a chest-plate tattoo piece that extends down his bicep. We've all agreed on the same placement of this ink. It's going on our ribs.

The tattoo machine buzzes, and I'm careful with my linework while everyone chitchats around me. In bold serif lettering, I ink the letters: SFO

Thatcher is next.

Jane wolf-whistles from the bar when he strips down. We all rib him for it, and he couldn't care less. He watches me discard my gloves, the needle, and I disinfect and snap on a new set. I've inked "Cinderella" on his ass before, so this is nothing for Thatch.

I place a stencil on his ribs, then get to work.

Luna once asked me which bodyguards I thought would always and forever stay in security. For a lot of us, this is a purpose, but our purpose can change with time. For others, this is oxygen, and they'll suffocate without it.

So when she asked, the first name I said was Thatcher Moretti. When we all slowly retire our radios and guns, he'll be the last one standing. It's my million-dollar bet.

And that's sayin' something 'cause I don't have a million to bet at the moment. But Halway Comics is giving us a seven-figure advance for our comic. Split in half with Luna—I'm gonna be the flushest I've ever been.

Oscar is third on the table.

"I ran out of stencils," I warn. "Gonna freehand yours."

He glares. "I'm cackling inside, bro. Stencil me or you're dead."

"Might choose death."

"You're not a dumb motherfucker." He lies back, and he's shaking his head. "I can't believe I'm letting you do this."

"Me either." I snap on new gloves. He's always said he'd *never* let me tattoo him. And I do have enough stencils. After it's perfectly placed on his ribs, I ask, "You sure?"

"I'm sure I've lost my ever-loving mind." Then he sighs into a grin, nodding. "Only because I love you."

"Took you this long?"

"Don't make me laugh—not while the needle is going." Haven't touched him yet. "*Redford.*"

Farrow pops a bubblegum bubble. "Man, I'm not holding your hand."

I'm laughing. Once I control myself, I go calm and concentrate. Oscar will be in security for the long haul. Much longer than most of us, but one day, I know he'll pass the radio over too.

He gives me solid praise when I've finished the three letters. It's an easy tattoo, but it doesn't mean less than an intricate one.

Banks is next.

Both Moretti brothers have the most physical scars, and Banks has experienced more chronic pain than anyone I know, so a little tattoo is barely a prick to him.

Luna asked if Banks would follow Thatcher and retire at the end of the line. Not the middle, not the beginning.

For Sulli and Akara, I could see Banks wanting to protect her for the rest of his life. But in addition to that, I think he'd stay in for his brother. To be with him. Till the end.

He pats my back when I finish. "Second-best one." He flashes his ring finger—showing his inked wedding ring. It's number one to him.

As it should be.

Akara appraises Banks' tattoo with a grin. He'll always be the man behind the operation, and someday, maybe even soon, he'll hang up the metaphorical gloves and just run the show.

"Farrow," I call up.

He tugs off his black V-neck. Instead of lying down, he sits on a chair.

Oscar swigs his beer. "Of course his maverick ass isn't getting a rib tattoo."

There's not enough space on Farrow's ribs. The most symmetrical placement is the very back of his neck. So I tattoo him above the large gray sparrow that fills most of his back.

Farrow Redford Keene Hale.

I know him the best. So my best bet is that he'll let go of security one day, but when his old man retires, he'll take over the med team. Maybe some will even be shocked that at the end of it all, he'd choose medicine. But it wouldn't shock me.

"Your turn," Farrow tells me, and I show him my machine. He sanitizes his hands, snaps on a pair of gloves, opens a new needle, and I'm on the table. Getting a tattoo from Farrow. He has the steadiest hands, and the most experience watching me tattoo—so I trust him.

Looks perfect.

"Quinnie." He's next. Then Gabe, then Froggy.

The three rookies have a longer road ahead of 'em. They'll be around for Luna. I believe that. Gabe Montgomery—the resident SFO floater—is moving into MK's apartment this summer. She lives in Center City. Things got serious. Couldn't be happier for the couple.

Frog lifts her shirt up while lying on the table. "How badly will this hurt? Don't lie."

"You won't even know I was here."

She squeezes her eyes shut. I'm glad she's a tattoo virgin or else it would've meant she'd have ink from Scooter. She backed out of the sketch that he'd drawn to memorialize her Auntie Mint, and she asked if I could design something for her instead.

I was honored to.

Frog powers through her first tattoo. We all notice Quinn holding her hand for support. No one says a word out loud about it. They've been adamant they're just friends, and that's probably a good thing, considering they're coming out of bad relationships.

When I'm done, I clean up, and I have a drink with my family. We'll never go far. Akara raises the bottle first, looking around at each of us with reverence, familiarity, nostalgia, and love, and he nods, "To Omega."

We lift our beers. "To Omega."

80

 LUNA HALE

"That's the last thing?" Moffy asks, dropping a cardboard box labeled Luna's Bathroom Stuff onto the wooden floorboards.

"Yeah, that should be it," I mutter, quiet. Not *sad* exactly. New beginnings are hard because they follow an ending. Losing my memories shortened my time with my cousins, with my brother—in ways I hated. In ways I wish I could get back.

And I am reclaiming that time, but not with Moffy anymore. I'm creating a new timeline in New York with a different brother. With different cousins.

Moffy stares around the two-bedroom, unfurnished apartment, taking it all in. No one ever moved back into the penthouse. They sold it after the renovations. For Moffy and Jane, it was time to write a new chapter with their own families.

They really missed the Rittenhouse-Fitler District, especially since it's closer to parks. Moffy and Farrow bought a newer, bigger townhouse than the one that burned down. It has a private courtyard, garage, rooftop terrace, and the latest security tech.

Jane and Thatcher purchased a slightly larger townhouse right across the street. They're all in Philly.

I'm not close by. I'm not even a thirty-minute drive. I can't even walk across the street and say hi.

FaceTime. It's what Sulli and I assured each other when she left. *We'll video chat.* We'll call. We won't forget.

Moffy's forest-green eyes fall onto mine. *This is it.* My lungs swell, and my nose stuffs up.

"I don't want to say goodbye," I whisper.

"You don't have to," Moffy says strongly, but he's fighting emotion too. "I'll always be around. One bat signal away. I come running."

I know it'll be true. "I'll be using it for non-emergencies."

He smiles. "Those are the best calls. By far. In *every* damn universe."

"All of them." I try to sing-song, but my voice cracks.

Moffy bops my head like when we were kids. "I love you, sis." We hug, and tears wet the corners of my eyes.

"I love you too, Moffy."

Donnelly enters with Orion, the leash wound around his hand and a fishbowl tucked protectively under his armpit.

Farrow waits for my brother at the doorway. Moffy heads there and tells Donnelly, "Take care of my sister."

"Impossible not to," Donnelly assures, nodding a few times. "Take care of my brother."

Moffy looks back at Farrow, and with his whole soul, he says, "Every damn day."

Farrow smiles affectionately, and his arm swoops around Moffy as they leave. He brings my brother in for a kiss, and they disappear out the door.

New York.

While Donnelly sets Moondragon on the sleek marble countertop in the kitchen and releases Orion, I yank the cord to the preexisting blinds. Evening sunlight floods the quaint, empty living room, and I stare out at a new yet familiar landscape. Glittering high-rises and heavy foot traffic on the sidewalks below.

The view isn't the best part of stepping out of the spaceship.

The best part is turning around, and he's right here with me.

Donnelly is grinning, leaning on the kitchen counter. "Once upon a galaxy—"

"Somewhere in the cosmos," I add, coming closer.

His hands settle on my hips. "There was a human and an alien princess...who'll one day be queen." His love fills me to the brim.

"The One Day Queen," I murmur.

I'm officially the successor to a multi-billion-dollar soda empire. I had a ton of leverage being the only clear candidate for the position, so Fizzle accepted my terms. My parents were proud that I stood my ground and didn't settle for a path I wasn't one hundred percent on board with. Now I'm transferring to Manhattan Valley University, and I start this fall with Xander. I ended up with mostly A's this semester at Penn, and surprisingly, Wyatt Rochester gave me one. I aced the New Media course.

I'm proud of myself, but I doubt anyone could rival Donnelly's sheer pride in me.

I'm about to soar towards his lips, but I frown and squint behind him. "What is that?"

"What's what?" He twists around.

"On the counter by the stove."

He's confused at first too, and I follow there. It must be a house-warming present. A brown wicker basket overflows with fruit. "Did my brother leave a fruit basket?"

"I think he dropped it off. I don't think it's from him though." Donnelly is smiling at the abundance of Granny Smith apples and green grapes.

"Are those dried prunes?" I pinch one between my fingers. Who'd gift someone prunes? It dawns on me before Donnelly even finds the note.

I read over his shoulder, recognizing the handwriting instantly.

Paul,

For the past, present, and future.

Loren Hale

"We're best friends," Donnelly tells me with the flash of the card.

"I believe it." They even have inside jokes.

His grin softens rereading the card, then he tucks it back in the basket. Seeing the card and being in our home together, I suddenly think of the future.

"Do you still have the prediction?"

"From the psychic?" he asks, and off my nod, he says, "It's in my duffel."

"Would you want to...should we?" Nervous butterflies swarm my stomach, but they're flapping with excitement too.

"I would, if you want to."

"I would."

"Alright." He hesitates. "You're sure?"

"I'm sure."

I give the *okay*. The go-ahead. Ready for takeoff. Donnelly strides out of the living room, veering into a bedroom where he threw his duffel. Anticipation races my heart, and I walk into the empty space. We'll be sleeping on a mattress tonight. No bedframe. But these uncharted steps, soon-to-be taken with Donnelly, only exhilarate me.

We can paint a celestial mural on the wall. Or maybe the ceiling. We've even considered turning the second bedroom into an office where he draws and I write.

And we're not so far from family. My brother didn't want to room on-campus, so he's living in the apartment next to ours with Easton Mulligan. Right across the hall, the security team has rented a separate apartment for my bodyguards Quinn and Frog.

We're in Hell's Kitchen. Same high-rise as the Cobalt brothers. Not the same floor.

Familiar but different.

I'm very used to that.

Donnelly takes a while, and I wonder if he lost it. Orion *woofs* up at me, and I busy myself with finding his kibble and pouring water in a bowl.

Be patient. Be patient.

Patience is not within me. I practically race into our new bedroom. Bare mattress on the floor, no sheets—Donnelly is sitting on the edge and digging out clothes from his duffel, a little distraught.

"I'm gonna find it," he assures and tosses out a pair of jeans.

I sink onto the mattress beside him, crossing my legs under my butt. "It's okay."

"It's in here. I know it's in here."

"Maybe this is…" *meant to be.* I trail off, right as he unearths a crumpled purple slip of paper from the depths of his luggage.

It's in his hand.

We say nothing.

He's breathing heavy from the search, but he scrolls on his phone and taps into a music playlist. Filling the quiet with eighties rock.

Donnelly takes my hand in his. "Whatever it says, it might not come true."

"I know. But it also *might* come true." I stare into his sparkling blue eyes. "We don't have to look."

"I wanna look."

"On the count of three?"

"Yeah." He takes a breath. "One, two…" And he unfurls the paper on three, while I rest my cheek against his arm and peer at the baby prediction.

"Wait…" I breathe, my brows bunching in confusion. Water droplets stained the purple stationary and bled some of the blue ink. "Does it say *one* or *none?*"

He tries to smudge the ink, but it's dried into a partial blobby mess. "I can't tell. It's either one or none."

One or none.

My pulse calms, and I smile at him. "I'd be happy with one or none." I meant it before. I'd be happy with just me and him and our animals.

Donnelly cups my cheek. "Me too, space babe." And then he lifts me and tosses me higher up onto the mattress.

I laugh, especially as he plants his feet on either side of me. It's a wondrous sight to behold, the entirety of my boyfriend. Inside and out.

I never want to stop exploring him and understanding him. Even on the days where we're both confused, I know we'll take the time to listen and figure each other out.

"We've made land," I say, propping myself on my elbows.

"Feels sturdy." He sinks down on his knees. Straddling me.

"Uh-huh. Gravity is good." My heartbeat accelerates with giddiness at his nearness. "Oxygen levels?"

"Deteriorating." He leans forward, his palm rooted to the mattress near my cheek "Rapidly."

"That's not a problem," I whisper.

"No?"

"Nope." Flush warms my body. "We'll just have to perform mouth-to-mouth."

His grin lights up the universe. "Knew I loved our planet." Slowly, gradually, with every bit of anticipation, Donnelly lowers his lips to mine and kisses me.

Soon, we're a sweaty mess of intertwined limbs and roaming hands. His forehead presses to mine while he unleashes my breathless moans. There are unearthly promises of *forever* and *mine*. I feel him discovering and rediscovering all of me. Atmospheric conditions are of bright, unrelenting beauty.

I will go on every voyage with Paul Donnelly. This one, the next one, the last one. It will always, *always* be known.

SUMMER

Epilogue I

PAUL DONNELLY

It's been an uplifting, peaceful summer for most of us. One of the greats. Highlighted with a celebration on the rooftop of Superheroes & Scones. What used to be a makeshift putt-putt course has been cleared out to make way for camping chairs, coolers, and a few fold-out tables. Plus, enough open space to dance.

It's the middle of the day.

Sun is bright. Barely a cloud in the sky.

I lounge on the wide brick ledge, smoking a cigarette as pop music pumps from a nearby rooftop. Mostly it's just family up here. Kinney has her elbows on the brick near me, watching the parade of rainbow and effervescence and love crowding the Philly streets below.

Gotta admit, it's the first big smile I've seen from her all summer. Especially as Winona, Vada, and Audrey gather around her and hand her a confetti cannon. They pop them over the edge and little pieces of colorful paper take flight in the air.

The girl squad are splitting up. Winona and Vada are finishing their senior year at an all-girls school. Their parents withdrew them from Dalton Academy after what happened with Tate, but it'd been Winona's idea to change schools. And Vada wanted to go with her.

Audrey didn't, and Kinney chose to stay with her best friend.

As a fellow ride-or-die, I can definitely understand sticking by your closest friend through the thick of it all.

Now they're hanging on to each other like it's the last summer of their whole youth. I wanna tell 'em it's hardly the end. There'll be more triumphs, more unexpected reunions, more paths crossed and many more paths taken. 'Cause when you really love someone, they're gonna come back. They can never really fade away.

I peel my eyes off the parade and back on the rooftop. Every shade of paint has made its rounds during this daytime party. Luna already ran her rainbow fingers down the left side of my face. I grin, seeing Jack swipe a paintbrush along Oscar's cheek. He's drawing a pink heart.

And Oscar—he's roped into his husband's sunny sphere. He rotates Jack's baseball cap backwards, just to kiss him.

I *love* Pride. It's every month, every year, never-ending—'cause there'll never be a moment I won't celebrate all kinds of love and my closest friends.

Akara, Banks, and Sulli blow soapy bubbles at each other with plastic wands, messing around near the coolers with bright laughter and slugs to the arm. Sullivan has Baby Seven snug to her chest in an olive-green swaddle, and when the newborn wakes, they make faces at him until his smile is so wide, his giggle screeches. Never heard a baby that young giggle *so* much, but Seven is nothing but excited to be alive.

Baby knows what's up. He has a beautiful life ahead of him. I just know it.

Xander, Cobalt boys, and more family sport Rainbow Brigade buttons since Kinney passed 'em around to the allies and those who identify as LGBTQ+. She gave me *four* to wear, so I'm rising on her favorites list, if I do say so.

I blow out smoke into the sky. Thatcher tries to put a sunhat on a squirmy Maeve. The baby wiggles to the beat of the music in Jane's arms. Maeve bounces in a little rainbow tutu, and Jane can't stop laughing. Thatcher has the largest smile I think I've ever witnessed firsthand from him. He's one big smitten kitten.

I laugh to myself and put my cigarette to my lips. Catching sudden sight of the most beautiful girl in the galaxy. Luna—my everything. She brings Cassidy over to Maeve so the babies can bee-bop to the pop music together.

Off to the side, Farrow and Moffy are crouched down to their son, unwrapping a mummified Ripley. He's twisted himself in colorful streamers, and for a brief moment, as he spins out of the strips of yellow and orange, the little boy's blue eyes meet mine.

I only see light and love in them.

Emotion balls up in my throat.

And it's not long before Luna looks back at me. Cheeks streaked with glitter and paint, ribbons in her hair blowing in the cool wind. Her gaze, her whole being, beckons me forward. I snuff the cigarette on the brick, and I follow the light into the dancing crowd.

Living can be as easy as breathing.

I've met many blissful moments in my life. Wouldn't let anyone steal those from me, and here and today and what lies tomorrow— it's more simple, blistering moments of happiness. Beating and singing at my soul.

It's what I live for. These small seconds. The ones that fill your lungs to the brim and pick your feet out from under you.

Music and laughter pull everyone to the middle as we all dance. Raucous, boisterous sorta dancing where we're all singing the lyrics to the song, off-key, and at the top of our lungs. Throwing hands up high to the sky. I'm swept up, and I cup her cheeks, grinning down at Luna as she grins up at me. We're all surrounded by a feeling. One absent of fear and shame.

I love my people. I love they can be who they are. I love myself the same.

Confetti rains down on us, drifting from other rooftop parties. Smiles and embraces of love and belief and joy surround me and Luna. I kiss her as strands of paper cling to our bodies. My fingers thread through her ribbon-tangled hair. When the world ends. When this one chapter to our book closes. I'd like to think that those who know us best will say there was nobody like us. That we left this world how we lived inside of it.

Fully, devotedly, lovingly.

Strange and weird.

SOMETIME FAR,
FAR AWAY

Epilogue II

 LUNA HALE

The clock is counting down to take-off and a wardrobe malfunction is in danger of aborting our current mission. Tucked together in our space pod—okay, in a backstage dressing room—Donnelly wields a needle and thread with expert precision.

He's been the go-to craftsman for a long time now. Fully beating my skills in ironing on patches, hot-gluing dioramas, and sewing hems and torn buttons.

"This is the strangest tear. The whole thing wants to come apart," he mumbles with the needle between his lips.

"A glitch in the matrix," I nod, not sweating such a tiny wrinkle in the timeline of today.

"I gotta have a word with the matrix." He trades the needle for a bag of safety pins. "Tell it to lay its hands off my wife's clothes."

I see my mushrooming smile in a floor-length mirror and Donnelly assessing the damage to the back of my dress. He's behind me, and his blue eyes meet mine in the mirror every so often. Those blue orbs sparkle with more than a grin. They're galaxies of adoration and hope. Full of all the places we've ventured, all the minutes we've shared—these endless, infinite years of *ours*.

He rotates me one-eighty. "Think we might need to fix the front before the back."

I face him and cup the bust of the glittery lilac dress to my chest. It tries to fall off my boobs. Strips of tied fabric are supposed to fasten the front together, but when the seventeen buttons popped along my spine, the front unraveled. He starts knotting the straps across my chest, yanking them tighter.

"I could just throw a T-shirt over it," I say. "I can ask Kinney to grab me one."

"What about your bell sleeves?"

"I'll cut them off."

"Cut off the one part you love the most? Nah, that's not happening."

It's not like he's wearing anything fancy. He has on a Van Halen shirt I gifted him years ago and jeans. My eyes flash to the clock on a makeup vanity.

He grins down at me. "Losing faith already?" He yanks again, and I bump closer to his chest, my breath jettisoning. His knuckles brush along the crevice between my breasts, and electric currents tingle from my arms to my toes.

Donnelly's touch never grows old. I doubt it could.

My cheeks warm. "I have faith in you. Just not so much the dress. It's a slippery beast."

"That's 'cause it wants to slip off you when you're around me."

I smile wider. "Is it a jealous dress?"

He drops his voice. "Or it's helping a human out and knows exactly how I want you."

"In the unearthly flesh."

Donnelly looks enamored with me, and I breathe in deeper. Our eyes veer more than once to a wooden wardrobe in the corner of the room. The doors to it are closed.

Then I crane my head over my shoulder. Looking back at the mirror, the gaping slit exposes my shoulder blades and spine. He's torn off the buttons. "I kinda like the backless look."

"Yeah? I was gonna safety pin it."

"No, don't." I never thought I'd love a tattoo more than the galaxy on my thigh that Donnelly created, but the artwork along my spine always steals my breath when I catch sight of it.

Constellations all woven together, each a different color. Green stars connect to form Sagittarius, then violet lines and starbursts make up Leo. A colorful star system belonging solely in my universe. I could spend hours gazing at the steady, sharp lines and how the stars touch different spots of my back. I love when Donnelly kisses along each one.

I know time is slipping faster, and this is an hourglass we can't turn over. Time has always been a funny thing to me. Overlapping, tangled, blurred lines of now and then.

I can't really know if I was able to remember *everything* I lost, but I felt comfortable enough to finally read my diary myself. Bits and pieces that I wrote seemed foggy and faded, and maybe that was amnesia, or maybe we all forget the little details unless we write them down.

Still, I find myself wanting to steal minutes and seconds, to press *pause* sometimes. To extend a moment into infinity.

I face forward again and watch Donnelly tighten the laces near my belly button. His forearm flexes, and black ink among his spindling veins spells out: *El-Rey*

My stomach somersaults at a thought. "I forgot the metallic markers." I wince. "I must've left them back in Philly on the kitchen counter."

Donnelly is still focused on my dress. "They're in your bag."

"What?" I frown.

"I got 'em, boss babe." He flashes a smile at me, and my lips lift in reply.

Yeah. He keeps me from floating away most days. I'm not CEO of Fizzle *yet*. But after graduating with an MBA, Uncle Stokes named me Chief Marketing Officer. The same position he once filled a long, long time ago. Donnelly has been by my side each step of the way, always reinstilling his belief in me every time my own slips.

Some days are harder than others. But I chose two careers, knowing this path was going to be filled with bumps and potholes. All that matters is that I believe in myself. That I can. That I will.

"And we're done." Donnelly steps back. "Take a twirl, space babe."

I spin on my sneakers, the shimmery fabric fluttering around me. And then I twirl right into his arms, and when he catches me, my grin expands. "No nip slips," I say. "I think we're good to go. We just have to collect our Padawan."

Donnelly slides his hand in mine, and we both venture to the wardrobe. As he reaches for the handle, we can hear a muffled voice.

"And then there's a sea dragon, big and bright—" The voice cuts short when Donnelly opens the door. Beneath hangers of loose fabric and tulle is a six-year-old. She beams a flashlight at the pages of a book that's propped on her kneecaps.

Elara Rey Hale.

She stares up at us with wide blue eyes. Her pink lips form a surprised O like she didn't expect time to move this fast while she's lost in fiction. Her purple alien antennas flop, and she pushes them back up into her chestnut brown hair. "One more chapter, Mommy, Daddy, *please*."

Donnelly and I share a bright look.

She's adorable. Too cute for this earth, and I get giddy every time she demands to cosplay as the Thebulan Princess Solana. Her purple leotard glitters like my dress.

I check the time. "We only have a few minutes."

Elara reads a few more lines, muttering to herself.

"*Please* and thank yous to the little alien who can bookmark her page," Donnelly tells our daughter. "Your mommy is right. We have to go."

She huffs a little but earmarks the passage, and Donnelly scoops her up from the wardrobe so quickly that she drops the paperback. Her fit of giggles is music to my ears. I bend down, careful not to rip the fabric ties of my dress and pick up the book.

Donnelly holds our little alien upside-down. "I can hear the floor!" she tells us. "It's giving me all the secrets."

"Yeah, what's the floor telling you?" Donnelly asks her, his smile shifting to me.

"It loves Mommy's shoes, and it thinks you should have glitter on yours, too."

I nod in agreement. "There's never enough glitter in this world."

"Stamp," Donnelly says in agreement and flips our daughter upright and back on her feet, and he casts another adoring look back at me.

I love him.

Paul Donnelly Hale.

Married on Earth, we were. But nothing was as momentous as the day Donnelly stared into my eyes and said, "Let's make a baby."

"What?" I almost didn't believe him.

"I wanna have a baby with you."

"Now?"

"Now."

Donnelly finally believed he could welcome someone so innocent into his world, and they'd never be harmed. Stability, light, and peace—he found perfect balance and harmony among all living things.

But I always knew the force was in him.

Elara holds his hand and then reaches out for mine. She likes to walk in with us like she's a "big girl" and not on her dad's shoulders like when she was four.

I take her hand. "Ready for take off?" I ask her.

She nods vigorously. Her round face more like mine.

"You strapped in?" Donnelly asks after grabbing the messenger bag off the floor.

She mimes putting on a seatbelt. "Ready."

Together, the three of us walk out of the dressing room and down a narrow hallway. She skips and swings between us, a ball of effervescent joy.

Our one and only. Our little Gemini.

I have her constellation inked below the Leo on my back. In shades of fuchsia.

Security leads us to the main door, and when Donnelly's phone pings, he stops short and drops Elara's hand.

We wait for him to unpocket his phone. He up-nods to a few bodyguards, recognizing them as they pass and join our personal detail for the event.

The day we learned I was pregnant, he retired from security. He's a comic book illustrator. A tattooist. A former bodyguard. But he'd tell you his favorite job on our planet is being Elara's dad.

He frowns at the Caller ID. "It's Farrow," he says, and I nod for him to take it.

"We have a minute," I tell him, but in truth, I think we'd both make a thousand minutes for Farrow. I watch him answer the call, and he's all frown lines before he grins.

"Yeah, okay. I'll tell her." He hangs up, and it's my turn to be confused. His blue eyes hit mine. "Farrow says he'll babysit this weekend."

Elara hears, and her smile reaches her eyes. "Overnight?"

"Yep," I say. "We have to go to New York for a little bit. You'll be okay at Uncle Farrow and Uncle Moffy's for one night?"

She nods rapidly like she cannot wait until she's there. Not that I blame her. Four of her cousins are under that roof. Ripley, Cassidy, Violet, and Walsh. My brother and Farrow wanted me to be the egg donor for V and Walsh. A girl and their youngest boy. I cherish them just as much as my other nieces and nephews. But I'm really happy Moffy and Farrow got to have some Hale genes sprinkled into their brood, and there's not a day that I don't feel honored they chose me for the task.

"Can I stay there three nights?" Elara asks us with a flutter of her eyelashes.

Donnelly and I share a look. She's a negotiator. Donnelly once said, "She gets that from you, boss babe." But I'd like to think she just knows what she wants and she goes for it. Donnelly has that in him just as much as me.

"Nah," Donnelly shakes his head. "One night. Otherwise I'm gonna miss you too much, El-Rey. Who's gonna do the morning crossword with me?"

"True," she says in a serious look. She gasps. "My book."

"Safe and sound." It's under my armpit. "Ready?"

Donnelly opens the door to a cacophony of voices and sudden, abrupt applause. Lights flash in our face as we wave to the packed auditorium and reach a desk. Comics are stacked high. I get Elara situated next to me on the third chair, and Donnelly sets out a pile of stickers in front of her. Metallic stars that she asks if they'd like next to our autographs.

I take a seat beside my husband, and he passes me a shimmery permanent marker.

The line coordinator lets the first fan up to our table. They already hold tight to a comic book.

Human Him, Cosmic Her.

It became a worldwide success, sparking a movie franchise and over three-million copies sold of the first volume. We're still writing it. We're on volume ten.

It never ends.

Our love story. Our family. Our past, present, and future. All encapsulated inside one epic, otherworldly space saga.

Donnelly looks to me, and love floods through his eyes and explodes in technicolor inside my heart. Some days this feels like a dream, to do what I love with the person I love, and I could pinch myself. But I don't have to.

Dreams this beautiful can't really be dreams at all.

I know. I believe.

Acknowledgements

There is nobody quite like all of you. The dear, beautiful, human, unearthly, magical readers of the Like Us series. This series means so much to us—so much more than we will ever be able to adequately express. It has lifted us out of dark times and given us rays of hope and light when we weren't sure there were any to be found.

There are so, so many of you over the course of us creating this series that have truly impacted us and inspired us and made us so happy to be alive. Sometimes it was just one email, one message at the perfect time. We've never forgotten you. We'll always remember how deeply you all loved these characters and these stories, and how much your love was woven into each new book. There was never a day where we didn't feel so immensely grateful for those who connected to these romances and families and bodyguards.

Thank you for reading. Thank you for being here on whichever planet you call home.

Over the past seven years while writing the Like Us series, we've been thankful for many people—*so* many, we could probably fill another chunky novel. We can only name a handful, which is the hardest part for us—but please know we love all of you and we hope that it's always felt beyond this section of the book.

Thank you so much to our mom. She's a behind-the-scenes power-house and the reason why we never had to shut down our signed store. She's a magical little busy bee and ensures readers receive signed books, and we're grateful we can share her with all of you.

Big thanks to our agent, Kimberly, who continues to champion us and our work and has found homes for all thirteen of these books in audio. We can't imagine what the series would be without the incredible audiobooks.

Our immense gratitude goes to the admins of the Fizzle Force— Jenn, Lanie, and Shea—who have been with us for all the highs and the lows. You three will always be the Reverse Bermuda Triangle to us, showering us with the light and love to keep going.

Haley, thank you for the most gorgeous special edition covers and a friendship that we treasure. We will always cherish your art forever. Your love and support have lifted us up sky-high, and to know you are a part of this series means everything to us.

A big, heartfelt thanks to all those that have made such amazing art for this series. Thank you immensely to Margot and Andressa for sharing your talent and for bringing these characters to life in the most beautiful way for so long. We love you two so much, and your friendship has been a bright spot to us since the very start of the series.

And not only would Donnelly be smitten by all the artists, but we are very lucky and so very grateful that our work could inspire others' creativity. It blows us away every damn time.

Thank you to more friends we've made along the way: Alyssa, Juana, Andrea, Laura, Em, Marie, Sarah, and so many more—we love you all to Thebula and back again.

To our patrons, we're going to try not to break down in tears here. But we started Patreon after *Alphas Like Us* because we truly did not think we could continue writing full-time. Starting Patreon was our last swing for the fences. You all are the reason these books exist. There's no sugar-coating that. Without patrons, we would have stopped writing in this world and with these characters years ago. So thank you, from the very bottom of our hearts, *thank you*. Because the universe that doesn't include these books is a universe we don't want to live in.

Patrons are also the reason this book has the best title in the world. You all voted on it, and you chose *Nobody Like Us*. We couldn't have picked a more fitting end title.

And thank you again to you, the reader.

You've read so many of our words, and we are so honored that you stayed with us and the characters you love to reach this bookend.

It's our thirtieth novel.

And thirteen books belong to this series. We write chunky ones. We write multiple books for couples. We write after the HEA. But you show up and you're here to read the next one. And the next. And then finally, you make it to Book 13. And that—that's true magic. It's cosmic. It feels a whole lot like love ;)

Thankyouthankyouthankyou.

It is never, ever goodbye.

Always, until next time.

All the love in *every* universe,
Krista & Becca

Shake Shack & The Space Babe

LUNA HALE

When I'm out and about in the city, I sometimes pretend that I'm an undercover spy on Earth. The hood of my oversized hoodie obscures my face, and I stuff my hands in the little kangaroo pouch. (I don't know what else it's called, but Sulli agreed with me that "kangaroo pouch" is the absolute "best fucking" name.) My shoulders also naturally bow forward when I'm trying not to be noticed.

But the hunching and the hood over my head has a purpose. It's so I can scope out Philly undetected. No one knows that I'm from another planet. Here to examine human life and all that it has to offer.

Including its edible delicacies.

The bell to a Shake Shack in the Rittenhouse area chimes as I enter with my trusted otherworldly companion. Only, he fell from his spacecraft when he arrived on Earth, so he's unknowing of his alien origins.

He thinks he's just my human bodyguard.

I smile at the backstory to a simple food outing. It's more fun this way.

Quinn Oliveira does a silent sweep of the Shake Shack on our way to the counter. He's mastered the furrowed brow "I'm not hear for chitchat" brooding stare. The scar below his eye kinda makes him more menacing too.

He fought an extraterrestrial baddie with razor-sharp nails. The scratch to the eye was *brutal*. I didn't witness it, but he's the talk of our otherworldly workplace. Starbeam Intelligence Corporation. SIC for short.

I really need to write all this down. It'd make for a cool short story to post on Fictitious.

"Are we grabbing and going?" Quinn asks me.

"Uh-uh. I'm gonna eat here." No one is giving us any second glances or even a double-take, so I'm going to milk this anonymity while it lasts. "If I can, I want to take my time eating one of Earth's greatest foods: *the burger*."

He stuffs his hands in his bomber jacket. "Earth's burgers aren't that great."

I glance over at him. "So this isn't your first time on Earth?"

Quinn just smiles like I made a funny comment. His company is nice to share—he's not rolling his eyes, mumbling "oh my gods" or acting like I'm the most embarrassing creature on this planet.

We reach the counter, and I know Quinn is okay to eat here. He's very go-with-the-flow since he's attached to whatever I wanna do.

The Shake Shack employee asks what I'd like.

"A SmokeShack with fries and a vanilla shake." I look to my otherworldly companion. "I got you. What do you want?"

Quinn gives me a short and sweet look. "Thanks, but…"

I know the ending. *Thanks, but you're not supposed to pay for a bodyguard, Luna.* Yeah, yeah.

I could pin this on him falling from his spacecraft, but he's not suddenly acting out of the norm. There's never been an instance where he would let me pay for him like he's Eliot or Tom.

Quinn is twenty-one.

I'm turning nineteen in only twenty days, and with our close ages, I guess I figured he'd be more like a friend to me when he became my 24/7 bodyguard. Sometimes I wonder if he'll change his mind. Like maybe he's decided today that he's a friend of mine.

But the longer he's been on my detail, the more I've realized Quinn Oliveira is like a protective older brother.

"...you know how it is," he finishes.

I nod, understanding. Once I pay and grab the receipt, Quinn orders a vegetarian 'Shroom Burger and a bottled water. He's such a healthy eater that I sometimes wonder if my food choices make him internally gag.

Externally, he's never appeared that repulsed.

Our food doesn't take long to come out, and with our two trays in hand, we choose a table with a booth on one side and two chairs on the other.

"I'll sit here, if that's okay?" Quinn is already sliding into the booth, even as he asks me. His back is to the wall, and he has a direct view of the small dining area. He's been my bodyguard for almost a whole year, so his need to have the best vantage of threats isn't new or that surprising.

"Yeah, that's fine." I pull out my chair, and I take a quick glance at my surroundings that I'm about to turn my back to.

Only a few tables are occupied. At a high-top table near the big windows that look out at the city street, three human teenagers with school backpacks are chatting and only munching on fries. A lone man (also likely human) is reading on his phone and eating a burger at another table. In a booth, a human baby and human mom are together.

The teenagers seem to be half-interested in us, and I sit down quickly before I catch their gazes.

After I slurp my milkshake, I ask Quinn, "The scar under your eye—what happened?" I don't know why I haven't asked before.

In my mind, I've made up a bunch of different scenarios. He fought off Darth Vader on the cold ice plains of Hoth. He battled a cyborg in a post-apocalyptic future and saved a crumbling town. I know none of these things are real, but I always imagined a scrappy, battle-worn Quinn Oliveira with a tested resilience.

And I guess the details are fake, but the spirit might be true.

He swallows a bite of 'Shroom Burger and unscrews his water bottle. "I was boxing—pro-boxing," he clarifies fast. "It was a fight. The guy got me in the eye pretty good."

"Did you like it?" I wonder.

"Boxing?"

"Uh-huh."

"No," he doesn't even hesitate. "I think I hated it." He takes the biggest bite of burger, stuffing his mouth, maybe to avoid answering another question about the subject.

"Were you good at it?" would've been my second question. Because there is sadness in being great at the things you despise. I don't know what's worse. That, or being awful at the things you love.

I could be an awful writer. I chew on my straw before slurping again, hoping to rid the tossing sensation in my stomach. If I suck at writing, it won't make me stop creating stories for myself or Fictitious—because I know I love it too much. If you hate what you're great at, I guess the struggle is to find the will to stop, but once you do, you're free.

"Are you thinking of going to South Philly Brew?" Quinn asks since Sulli asked if I wanted to join her earlier today. I think Moffy and Jane are already there. Sulli has probably made it, too.

I shrug. "Maybe later." I had a Shake Shack craving, and I've thrown off public attention so much today that I wonder if I can extend it for longer. "You want to join them?" SFO will be where my family are.

"I don't care either way," Quinn says, and I believe him. He acts like joining all the other guys isn't too important.

While he takes another bite of mushroom burger, I notice that he hasn't touched his radio much.

I smile into my bite of burger.

He's a wild card among security while he's protecting me, but he's my wild card that can slip away without alerting the bodyguard fleet. But, in the past, he has confessed that he's told SFO things that I've told him. Mostly to do with my ex, Andrew Umbers.

My guess: Quinn is partially a rule-follower. He likes to bend the rules when he can, but he's not a total rebel.

And he's way better than *before Quinn*. BQ is an era of bodyguard protection that *royally* sucked as an American royal. I'd been so burned by bodyguards who'd tell my parents *everything* I'm doing, and it's nice to have the inverse now.

I'm about to scroll on my phone to check Fanaticon forums for *The 100*. I'm on a rewatch binge, and it's fun to reread episode discussions.

But it takes only a second to realize my phone has died.

Damn. I pocket my useless cellphone. "Have you watched *The 100* yet?" I ask him since he said he'd try the show out.

"Uh, just one episode?" He has an apologetic look. "Like ten minutes of it. It was…interesting."

I shrug. "It's not for everyone." I pop the lid off my milkshake and stir. "Have you watched anything lately?"

He thinks. "ESPN?"

It should be noted that my otherworldly companion comes from a different planet in our solar system. Where ESPN is the main form of entertainment. "That'd be cool if there was a new sport with bungees and glow-and-the-dark outfits and they televised it. It'd be called something…like…" I mentally try to brainstorm names and realize I haven't made up enough fictional sports in my stories.

Now I *really* wish I had my laptop on me. There could be a love story involved with the players. Oooh maybe it's forbidden to date your teammate. Or would a rival team love story work better?

Quinn is a lot quieter.

I look up, seeing him trying to avoid the teenagers. He's wadding up his trash and tensing more. He casts a few glances that way.

I take the smallest peek over my shoulder.

One of the girls is not-so-slyly taking a photo of us, her phone beneath the table.

I look back to Quinn. "Covers are blown." I munch on a fry.

"I think they noticed me first," he admits, his face tightening. "Sorry." He's the most popular among the security team in the media. The Casanova of SFO. I've seen that nickname trending on Twitter before. His frustration bunches his brows.

"It wouldn't last forever," I mention, not that upset. We were bound to get noticed at some point.

And I'm happy SFO didn't get fired for gaining some fame. Security thought it'd be a detriment or a distraction to their job, but I'm selfishly glad my bodyguard is experiencing what I'm experiencing. Quinn understands what this feeling is like, and I guess it makes me feel less alone having someone from SFO here.

He bows his head a bit, maybe hoping to allude her camera shots.

Even if we've been caught, I'm not really in a hurry to leave. They're not bothering us for autographs or anything, and there aren't that many people here. So I just finish half my burger in peace.

The bell to the door *dings*, but I don't turn to look at whoever has entered Shake Shack.

Quinn blows back in the booth, his muscles tightening even more. His eyes seem to say, *shit*. Like he's going to be in trouble. Huh...?

I sip my milkshake slowly.

"What are you doing here?" Quinn asks, and before I turn, there's already a response.

"Looking for her."

Donnelly.

His voice is unmistakable, and I try to shelter a burgeoning smile. Is he human or is he alien? I peer over my shoulder just as Donnelly reaches the table. *Origins unknown.*

His chestnut brown hair is ruffled from being outside, and he pushes the strands back with one hand and grabs the vacant chair beside me with the other. "This seat taken?"

"Not by any human life form. I can't speak for any invisible extraterrestrials, though."

He grins. "Guess I gotta take my chances." He does this thing where he rotates his chair to face me, not the table. And I know it's mostly so his back isn't to the teenagers and other earthlings eating burgers—but I pretend it's also because he likes looking at me.

Maybe he does.

Quinn frowns with the shake of his head. "How'd you find her?"

Donnelly rests a forearm on the table and looks over at him. "Photos on some fandom sites caught you two in the area." He motions his head to the teenagers' table without glancing at them. "Then they must've been the ones who tweeted a pic of you two here. 'Cause I saw the Shake Shack logo on her drink."

If Starbeam Intelligence Corporation were interested in new hires, Donnelly would be a perfect candidate. He has top-notch spy skills.

"Busted by the milkshake," I quip.

"Chocolate?" he wonders.

"Vanilla." I offer him a slurp.

He tries it, and my pulse shouldn't pitter-patter. We're only sort of now just friends. The kind of friends who once hooked up for an experiment. *My* experiment.

It wasn't even that long ago. Just last month. But is he here to hang out or...? I don't know why else he'd be here. We haven't exactly hung out one-on-one at all.

Quinn seems more edged, and I wonder if this is about security, more than it's about me. He finally asks, "I thought you'd be at South Philly Brew?"

He passes me the milkshake. "Left early, then grabbed my radio." He has his earpiece dangling on his collar, but he fits it in his ear while looking at me. "Everyone's been wondering where you are."

I take this to mean that everyone was worried about me.

I'm not easily forgotten. It feels good to be remembered by people you care about.

Donnelly remembered me.

"My phone died," I mention.

"You want me to tell them where you're at?"

"Sure," I shrug, not minding.

Quinn grimaces and sinks partially in his seat.

"What's wrong?" I frown, not knowing why this update is bad.

"Quinnie," Donnelly is about to touch his mic, trying not to laugh. His smirk grows as Quinn looks more distressed. "Just let him rip you a new one and move on with it."

"I didn't do anything Farrow wouldn't have done, so why am I going to be chewed out for not answering comms?"

Quinn is going to get in trouble for not telling security where I am?

"Farrow does get slapped on the wrist, man. And he still does it. Consequences and all that be damned."

He sighs out roughly, then nods and motions for Donnelly to use comms.

I watch Donnelly speak to comms. "Donnelly to SFO, I found the space babe." His blue eyes flicker to my eyes, his grin on me.

I feel my smile expand.

He replies to them, "Shake Shack. Her phone is dead." Another pause. "Sure thing, boss." He takes one more beat. "Some fandoms posted pics of her in the area." After that, he looks to Quinn. "Akara says to get on comms."

Quinn straightens up in the booth and unwinds the cord to his radio. He's not muttering about how it's such bullshit. He seems more readied to take the heat.

I appreciate it more than he probably knows. "Thanks," I whisper over to him, but I don't know if he hears me.

Once Quinn has his earpiece in, his brows crinkle. "Wait, slow down. What was that, Thatcher? Cheese fries...? Two orders?"

Quinn focuses on me. "Tom and Eliot are asking for two orders of cheese fries."

I grin now. My best friends must be at South Philly Brew, and they want some food. "Tell them, it's coming up."

He relays my message to Thatcher, who'll tell Tom and Eliot.

"I'll put in a to-go order on our way out," I tell Quinn once he's done talking to Thatcher.

Quinn nods and grips his empty water bottle. "I need to take a leak."

I wonder if that's bodyguard code for *the boss wants to talk to me*. Or if he really does need to pee.

Donnelly is turned towards me. "I got her," he tells Quinn.

He has me.

I know he means protecting me, but I let those three words roll over in my head. Probably for too long. It's been determined that he's not exactly here to hang out.

He came here just to make sure I'm okay.

"You can go piss," Donnelly adds casually.

"Thanks," Quinn says tensely and stands up. He mentions something about how he's on comms if Donnelly needs him. And then he leaves for the bathroom.

I slide my fries over to Donnelly. "Fries are better than the shake."

He tries one. "Oh yeah. These are dope." He eats another one, and I want to ask him about the Scotland trip. He's going as Farrow's friend, not as a bodyguard, and I'll be there too.

Hawaii, I remember the code name for the trip. Just in case someone overhears. But all those questions fall to the wayside when I catch Donnelly glancing towards the teenagers—and then more so out the windows. Out at Philly.

He has this far off look in his eyes, and I wonder what he's thinking about.

"How long are you off-duty for?" I ask him.

"All night. Your brother's schedule isn't that hard so far." He's been assigned to my younger brother's detail. It's a recent development. It hasn't even been two weeks. I thought he'd always be Beckett's bodyguard and living in New York, but now he's in Philly. Around my family.

I don't know if he likes it any better. Or if he's wishing he could go back to Beckett and the Cobalts.

All of that seems too personal to ask. Too much for what we are.

He asks me something next anyway. "I dunno if your brother likes me or not yet."

"I think he'll like you."

"Yeah?"

"Xander has a good heart...and I think he appreciates when people are genuine." I frown in thought. "But sometimes, I'm not sure if he can tell if people are being disingenuous."

"Can you?" Donnelly wonders.

I shrug. "Maybe."

He gives me a soft smile that fades pretty fast. "Hey, you know any Elvish?"

"Yep." And so I teach Donnelly a line of Elvish that I know well.

"Lasto beth nîn, tolo dan nan galad," Donnelly repeats after me. It takes a few tries with his South Philly accent, but he get is quickly. "It means, what?"

"Hear my voice, come back to the light."

Donnelly begins smiling and nodding. "Sick."

"Starbeam Intelligence Corporation. That's my kinda SIC."

"Mine, too. Sign me up," he says while standing. I just realize Quinn is walking back to the table.

I rise with him, about to go order cheese fries. "Are you coming to the pub?"

"Nah, I was just there. I'm going home." He takes out his earpiece and turns off his radio. "I'll catch you later, Luna."

I throw up a Vulcan salute. "Farewell."

He flashes the "rock on" symbol, and when he turns his back, I watch him leave. As Donnelly pushes through the door, he casts a single glance back at me, and the light inside his eyes and his grin illuminates inside of me.

Where is home for you?

I wish I could've asked him. But maybe, again, that's too deep. I like how easy this was between us, and while I wait for cheese fries with Quinn, a smile still on my face, I realize that I love today a thousand times more than I ever thought I could.

Milton Keynes UK
Ingram Content Group UK Ltd.
UKHW040027120324
439300UK00004B/128